# PUSHING ICE

*Ace Books by Alastair Reynolds*

REVELATION SPACE

CHASM CITY

REDEMPTION ARK

ABSOLUTION GAP

DIAMOND DOGS, TURQUOISE DAYS

CENTURY RAIN

PUSHING ICE

# PUSHING ICE

## Alastair Reynolds

ACE BOOKS, NEW YORK

**THE BERKLEY PUBLISHING GROUP**
**Published by the Penguin Group**
**Penguin Group (USA) Inc.**
**375 Hudson Street, New York, New York 10014, USA**
Penguin Group (Canada), 90 Eglinton Avenue East, Suite 700, Toronto, Ontario M4P 2Y3, Canada
(a division of Pearson Penguin Canada Inc.)
Penguin Books Ltd., 80 Strand, London WC2R 0RL, England
Penguin Group Ireland, 25 St. Stephen's Green, Dublin 2, Ireland (a division of Penguin Books Ltd.)
Penguin Group (Australia), 250 Camberwell Road, Camberwell, Victoria 3124, Australia
(a division of Pearson Australia Group Pty. Ltd.)
Penguin Books India Pvt. Ltd., 11 Community Centre, Panchsheel Park, New Delhi—110 017, India
Penguin Group (NZ), Cnr. Airborne and Rosedale Roads, Albany, Auckland 1310, New Zealand
(a division of Pearson New Zealand Ltd.)
Penguin Books (South Africa) (Pty.) Ltd., 24 Sturdee Avenue, Rosebank, Johannesburg 2196, South Africa

Penguin Books Ltd., Registered Offices: 80 Strand, London WC2R 0RL, England



Previously published in Great Britain in 2005 by Gollancz.

ISBN 0-441-01401-1
ISBN 978-0-441-01401-9

PRINTED IN THE UNITED STATES OF AMERICA

*For my wife, with love.*

"Stars have their moment, then they die."

—Nick Cave

# PROLOGUE

Her name was Chromis Pasqueflower Bowerbird and she had travelled a long way to make her case. The faint possibility of failure had always been at the back of her mind, but now that her ship had actually delivered her to the Congressional capital world, now that she had actually frameshifted to New Far Florence across all those dizzying light-years, the faint possibility had sharpened into a stomach-churning conviction that she was about to suffer imminent and chastening defeat. There had always been people eager to tell her that her proposal was doomed, but for the first time it occurred to her that they could be right. What she had in mind was, even by her own admission, a deeply unorthodox suggestion.

'Well, it's certainly a nice day for it,' said Rudd Indigo Mammatus, joining her on the balcony, high above the cloud-girdled tiers and gardens of the Congress building's footslopes.

'Abject humiliation, you mean?'

Rudd shook his head good-naturedly. 'It's the last perfect day of summer. I've checked: tomorrow will be cooler, stormier. Doesn't that strike you as suitably auspicious?'

'I'm worried. I think I'm going to make an idiot of myself in there.'

'We've all made idiots of ourselves at some point. In this line of work it's almost obligatory.'

Chromis and Rudd were politicians, political friends from different constituencies of the Congress of the Lindblad Ring. Chromis spoke for a relatively small grouping of settled worlds: a mere one hundred and thirty planet-class entities, packed into a volume of space only twenty light-years across. Rudd's constituency, located on the edge of the Ring – where it brushed against the fractious outer worlds of the Loop II Imperium – enveloped a much larger volume of space but only a third as many planet-class entities. Politically, they had very little in common, but by the same token they had very little worth squabbling over. Once every five hundred years, when the representatives were summoned to New Far Florence,

Chromis and Rudd would meet to swap world-weary tales of scandal and chicanery from their respective constituencies.

Chromis fingered the ring on her right index finger, tracing the interlocking, hypnotically complex design embossed into its surface. 'Do you think they'll go for it? It's been eighteen thousand years, after all. It's asking a lot of people to think back that far.'

'The whole point of this little exercise is to dream up something to commemorate ten thousand years of our glorious Congress,' Rudd said, with only the slightest trace of irony. 'If the other representatives can't get off their fat backsides and think back another eight thousand years before that, they deserve to have the reeves set on them.'

'Don't joke,' Chromis said darkly. 'I heard they had to send in the reeves on Hemlock only four hundred years ago.'

'Messy business, too: by all accounts there were at least a dozen non-recoverable dead. But I wasn't joking, Chromis: if they don't bite, I'll personally recommend a police action.'

'If only everyone else felt the same way.'

'Then damn well go in there and see to it that they do.' Rudd offered his hand. 'It's time, anyway. The last thing you want to do is keep any of them waiting.'

She took his hand chastely. Rudd was an attractive man, and Chromis had it on good authority that she had many admirers in the Congress, but their friendship was strictly platonic: they both had partners back on their homeworlds, held in stasis cauls until they returned from New Far Florence. Chromis loved her husband, although many days might pass between thoughts of him. Without his help convincing one hundred and thirty worlds that this was something they had to support, the memorial plan would have stalled long ago.

'I'm really worried, Rudd. Worried I'm about to screw up nearly a thousand years of preparation.'

'Keep your nerve and stick to the script,' Rudd said sternly. 'No last-minute clever ideas, all right?'

'Same goes for you. Remember: "intended recipient".'

Rudd smiled reassuringly and led her into the stratospheric vastness of the meeting room. The chamber had been constructed in the early centuries of the Congress, when it had aspirations to expand into territory now occupied by neighbouring polities. Space not being at a premium on New Far Florence, the hundred-odd representatives were scattered across nearly a square kilometre of gently sloping floor space, and the ceiling was ten kilometres above their heads. Slowly rotating in the middle of the room, lacking any material suspension, was the display cube in which their enlarged images would appear when they had the floor. While it waited for the session to begin, the cube projected the ancient emblem of the Congress: a three-dimensional rendering of Leonardo da Vinci's drawing of a naked man encompassed within a square and circle, his limbs drawn twice so that he stood upon, and touched, both shapes.

Chromis and Rudd took their positions on either side of the floor. The last few delegates were arriving by transit caul: black humanoid shells popped into existence in the chamber before dissipating to reveal the occupants within. The femtomachinery of the cauls merged seamlessly with the local machinery of the Congress building. Every artificial object in the Congress of the Lindblad Ring – from the largest frameshift liner to the smallest medical robot – comprised countless copies of the same universal femtomachine element.

Routine business consumed the first hour of the meeting. Chromis sat patiently, shuffling mental permutations, wondering whether she should consider a change of approach. It was difficult to judge the mood of the gathering. But Rudd's advice had been sound. She held her nerve, and when she had the floor she spoke the words she had already committed to memory before leaving home.

'Honoured delegates,' she began, as her magnified image appeared in the display cube, 'we are nearing the ten thousandth year since the founding of our first colony – the beginning of what we now recognise as the Congress of the Lindblad Ring. I believe we are all of a mind in one respect: something must be done to acknowledge this coming milestone, something that will reflect well upon our administration, especially in light of the similar anniversaries that have recently been celebrated in two of our neighbouring polities. There have been many suggestions as to how we might mark this occasion. A civic project, perhaps, such as a well-deserved terraforming or a timely stellar rejuvenation. A Dyson englobement – purely for the hell of it – or the frame-shifting of an entire world from one system to another. Even something as modest as the erection of a ceremonial dome or an ornamental fountain.' Chromis paused and looked pointedly at the delegates who had proposed these latter projects, hoping that they felt suitably abashed at their dismal lack of vision.

'There have been many excellent proposals, and doubtless there will be many more, but I wish to suggest something of an entirely different magnitude. Rather than creating something for ourselves, a monument in our own galactic backyard, I humbly suggest that we consider something altogether more altruistic. I propose an audacious act of cosmic gratitude: the sending of a message, a gift, across space and time. The intended recipient of this gift will be the person – or the descendants of the person – without whom the very fabric of our society would look unrecognisably different.'

Chromis paused again, still unable to judge the mood of the delegates, the blank faces of those close enough to see conveying neither approval nor disapproval. She took a deep breath and pressed on. 'Doubtless we would have achieved some of the same advances eventually – but who is to say that it wouldn't have taken tens of thousands of years rather than the mere handful of millennia it actually took? Instead of a mosaic of polities spread across nearly twelve thousand light-years of the galactic disc, we might very well be confined to a handful of systems, with all the risks that such close confinement would inevitably entail. And let us not forget that the insights that have allowed us to leapfrog centuries of slow development were given to us freely, with no expectation of reward. Our Benefactor sent that data back to Earth because it was the right thing to do.' Here Chromis swallowed, uncomfortably aware that some might be thinking – not without cause – that the very same data had almost wiped out humanity as it struggled to assimilate dangerous new knowledge. But at a remove of eighteen thousand years, such thoughts were surely churlish. Fire had singed more than a few fingers before people learned how to use it.

She heard a few unconvinced grumbles, but no one chose to interrupt her. Chromis steeled herself and continued, 'I know that some of us have forgotten the precise nature of that act of charity. In a moment, I hope to jog our collective memory. But first let me outline exactly what I have in mind.'

She craned her neck to look at the display cube. On cue, her image was replaced by a simulation of the galaxy, as if viewed from far outside: ancient and huge, littered with the humbling relics of the Spicans but empty of life – so far as anyone knew – save for the smudge of human presence spreading out from one spiral arm, like an inkblot.

'The Benefactor and her people are still out there somewhere,' Chromis said, 'almost certainly beyond the Hard Data Frontier – perhaps even outside the galaxy itself. But unless the universe has more tricks up its sleeve than we suspect, they can't be more than eighteen thousand light-years away, even if they're still moving away from us. And perhaps they've already arrived wherever they were headed. Either way, I think it behoves us to try to send them a message. Not a transmission, easy and cheap though that would be, but rather a physical artefact, something that we can stuff with data until we're knocking on Heisenberg's own back door. Of course, there's an obvious problem with sending a physical artefact as opposed to an omnidirectional signal: we have no idea where to send it. But that's easily remedied: we'll just send out a lot of artefacts, as many as we can manufacture. We'll make them by the billions and cast them to the four winds. And hope that one of them, one day, finds its intended recipient.'

That was Rudd's cue to interject. 'That's all very well on paper, Member Chromis, and I don't doubt that we have the industrial capacity to make such a thing happen. But I wonder if you've considered the risks of such an object falling into the wrong hands. Not all of our neighbours are quite as enlightened as we might hope: we already have enough trouble policing the harmful-technologies moratorium as it stands. Stuffing all our worldly wisdom into a bottle and tossing it into the great blue yonder doesn't strike me as the wisest course of action, no matter how well intentioned the gesture.'

'We've thought of that,' Chromis said.

'Oh? Do tell.' Rudd sounded innocently intrigued.

'The artefacts will have the ability to protect their contents from unintended recipients. They won't unlock themselves unless they detect the presence of the Benefactor's mitochondrial DNA. There'll be a margin of error, of course – we won't want to exclude the Benefactor's children, or grandchildren, or even more distant descendants – but nobody else will be able to get at the treasure.'

Again, Rudd played his part expertly. 'Nice idea, Chromis, but I'm still not convinced that you've done the detailed work here. There is no Benefactor DNA on file in any Congress archive. All biological records were lost within a century of her departure.'

'We've got her DNA,' Chromis said.

'Now, that *is* news. Where from, might I ask?'

'We had to go a long way to get it – back to Mars, as it happens – but we're confident that we've retrieved enough of a sample to lock out any unintended recipients.'

'I thought they'd already drawn a blank on Mars.'

'They did. We dug deeper.'

Rudd sat down heavily, as if the wind had been snatched from his sails. 'In which case . . . I must congratulate you on your forward thinking.'

'Thank you,' Chromis said sweetly. 'Any further questions, Member Rudd?'

'None whatsoever.'

There were disgruntled murmurs from some of the delegates, but few of them could begrudge Chromis and Rudd this little piece of theatre. Most of them had participated in similar charades at one time or another.

'Member Rudd is right to draw attention to the technical difficulties associated with this proposal,' Chromis said, 'but let's not allow ourselves to be daunted. If the project were easy, it wouldn't be worth doing. We've had ten thousand years to do the easy stuff. Now let's bite off something big, and show history what we're made of. Let's reach across space and time and give something back to the Benefactor, in return for what she gave us.'

Chromis allowed herself a pause, judging that no one would interrupt her at this crucial moment. When she continued speaking, her tone was measured, conciliatory. 'I don't doubt that some of you will question the wisdom of this proposal, even though it has already been subjected to every conceivable scrutiny by the combined intelligence of one hundred and thirty worlds. The problem is that, for most of us, the Benefactor is no more than a distant historical figure – someone with whom we have no emotional connection. But there is every chance that *she* is still out there somewhere, still living and breathing. She's not a God, not a mythic figure, but a human being, as real as any of us. There was a time when I had trouble thinking of her that way, but not any more. Not since we recovered *this*, and heard her speak.' Chromis nodded gravely in response to her audience's speculative murmurs. 'That's right: we've recovered an intact copy of the transmission that started all of this: the Benefactor's original statement of intent; her promise to give us all that she could. Recovering this transmission was, in its way, as difficult as finding a sample of her DNA. The difference was that the recording was always part of our data heritage: just misplaced, buried, corrupted beyond recognition. It took centuries of forensic skill to piece it together, frame by frame, but it was, I believe, worth the effort.'

Chromis looked to the display cube and sent a subliminal command, causing it to begin replaying the clip. Music welled up and an ancient symbol – a globe and three letters in an alphabet no one had used for nearly fourteen thousand years – spun before them. 'Please adjust your language filters,' Chromis said, 'for English, mid twenty-first century. You are about to hear the voice of the Benefactor.'

Right on cue, she spoke, identical copies of her face projected on each facet of the cube. A delicate-boned woman: looking less like the kind of person who made history than the kind who became a victim of it. She sounded diffident, uncertain of herself, forced into saying something that did not come naturally to her.

'I'm Bella Lind,' she said, 'and you're watching CNN.'

# PART ONE

# 2057+

# CHAPTER 1

Parry Boyce looked up from the rippled red surface of the comet. He cuffed down his helmet binocs, keyed in mid-zoom and waited for the image to stabilise.

Only a breath of thrust held fifty thousand tonnes of ship over his head. The precious mass driver was fully extended now, but still braced alongside *Rockhopper*. A spray of flickering blue lights near the head of the driver showed activity still taking place around the jammed deployment gear. Chrome-yellow robots worked the repair duty, with one tiny, suited figure hovering to the side. He knew it was Svetlana even before his helmet dropped an icon onto her figure.

They hadn't parted well. He'd been on her case about the repairs, but only because Bella was on *his* case. It was getting to them all, sitting out here, doing nothing.

Parry stood on the floodlit edge of the abyss that he had cut into the skin of the comet. The cylindrical shaft was geometrically perfect, an intrusion of order into the otherwise chaotic landscape of the crust. It was a hundred metres deep and fifty metres wide, the curving side already lined with a neat, laser-smooth plaque of hardened blue-grey sprayrock.

He voiced on some music from the Orlan nineteen's files and lost himself in the soaring qawwali of Nusrat Fateh Ali Khan. After what could have been minutes or hours, the floods picked out the moving shadow of another suit lumbering towards him. Whoever it was had just emerged from one of the dome-shaped surface tents set back twenty metres from the rim of the shaft. Beyond the tents sat the angular, splayed-leg form of *Cosmic Avenger*, the heavy lander that had carried them from *Rockhopper*.

Parry tried to read the walker's gait before his head-up ID'd the approaching figure. Feldman and Shimozu moved with the cautious economy of underwater workers – they'd been transferred from DeepShaft's marine division on Earth – but Mike Takahashi was a spacewalker to the marrow. Even wearing a thirty-year-old Russian surplus Orlan nineteen, ballasted with nearly a tonne of depleted uranium, he moved with a loping grace, unafraid to lose contact with the surface for long moments.

The HUD bracketed Takahashi's nineteen and appended his name in pulsing blue letters, accompanied by a Manga-style face icon.

'Nice hole, Chief.'

'Thanks,' Parry said.

'Thing is, it isn't going to get any nicer just because you keep staring at it.'

'I'm thinking it might need another layer,' he said, hands on his hips. 'Maybe just a dab down there?'

Takahashi stood next to him, their bulky shadows spilling into the abyss. The other man favoured glacial Estonian choral music: Parry heard it seeping over the voicelink.

'We need you inside,' Takahashi said.

Parry wondered what was up. Takahashi could have called him inside easily enough without making the trek in person.

'What's the story?' he asked, as they walked back to the tent.

'Don't know. Something's going down, that's all. You checked out the ship lately?'

'A while back.'

'Maybe you should take another look.'

Parry cuffed down the binocs again. *Rockhopper* leapt into view as the Nikons found their focus. Everything looked the same, except that the flicker of repair torches around the head of the driver was absent – nor was there any sign of Svetlana's hovering figure.

'Interesting,' he said.

'Good or bad?'

Parry stowed his binocs. 'Could go either way.' He reached for the tent flap and pulled it wide enough to admit the two men.

The tent was unpressurised: a stiffened dome-shaped shelter, fabric wired with superconducting mesh to afford the bare minimum of protection against charged particles. Gillian Shimozu and Elias Feldman sat either side of a plastic packing crate, playing cards spread across the lid. The cards, some faded and crudely redrawn in magic marker, were printed on thick, texturised plastic, better for handling with spacesuit gloves.

The four suits exchanged protocols with a warble.

'Still time to deal you in,' Shimozu said, looking up as Parry sealed the flap behind them.

'I'll pass.' Behind Shimozu, balanced on a bright-red oxygen pump, a flexy showed a picture of Saturn, with the blue logo of *China Daily* in the top-left corner.

'Spoilsport,' Shimozu said, taking a card from the table.

'Any word from Batista or Fletterick? There are signs we might be in business,' Parry said.

Feldman lowered his hand, revealing a set of aces. 'The driver?'

'Looks like work's been called off. Unless Saul's managed to swing shift changes for his robots, it's got to mean we have a functioning deployment system.'

'Whoop-de-doo,' Shimozu said. She had her antiglare visor tipped down: its near-matte coating blocked any possible reflection from the cards in her hand.

'You could tone down the enthusiasm a smidge,' Parry said. 'I'll ask again: any word?'

Takahashi pointed at the screen. 'Maybe it doesn't have anything to do with the driver at all. They were showing Saturn just now.'

'That why you pulled me in?' Parry asked.

'I thought it was weird. Why show Saturn?'

'Batista and Fletterick,' Parry said patiently. 'Anyone?'

'Maybe there's been an accident,' Takahashi said, wonderingly. The other two had dealt him into the game, but he appeared to be more interested in the screen behind Shimozu. 'Anyone know how to get that feed on my helmet?'

'Use your drop-down menu,' Feldman said testily, as if he'd been over this before. 'Select preferences, then HUD audiovisual display options, then—'

Parry walked past the game to the oxygen pump and picked up the flexy, squeezing it gently so as not to injure the quasi-living thing. The main image was still Saturn, but now a pundit in an overlaid box was talking. Nobody he recognised. Chinese text ticker-taped along the bottom of the screen.

Maybe Takahashi was right. Maybe something was happening around Saturn. But what could be big enough to hold the attention of *China Daily* this long? The major newsfeeds made Bella Lind's fish look like masters of sustained concentration.

That was when his HUD rearranged itself spontaneously, a priority window popping open, filled with Bella's face.

'Parry,' she said. 'Thank goodness. I was beginning to think we'd need to send *Crusader* to pick you up. It appears that the repair squad cut through the power bus to the downlink.'

'Hope you give them hell.'

'Ordinarily I would, but . . . now isn't the time.'

No one said anything. They were waiting for Parry to speak for them. The cards were on the table.

'What's up, Bella?'

'Something big,' she said, 'big enough that I'm going to need you back on the ship, and quickly. But before you leave, I want the driver shaft prepped to accept an FAD.'

'We don't need to chip anything off this one, Bella. She'll fall nice and stable all the way home.'

'I'm not talking about reshaping,' she said. 'I'm talking about blowing it out of the sky.'

Svetlana Barseghian dabbed bright-green disinfectant onto the pressure sores around her groin, then snapped a dosimeter cuff from her wrist and checked that the mission dosage was still on the low side of four hundred millisieverts. She pulled on jogging pants and a black Lockheed-Krunichev Fusion Systems T-shirt, jammed stained grey sneakers on her feet and raked a hand through hair flat and itchy after the spacewalk. She pushed in a pair of pink ear protectors, muting the background noise. Except for the two hours a day when they turned off most of the machines, it was noisier in *Rockhopper* than in the Orlan eighteen.

A warren of interconnecting corridors brought her to the number-two centrifuge. When she reached Bella's office she saw that Craig Schrope was already there. She reminded herself to be on her best behaviour.

Bella invited her in, pushed a cigarette into an ashtray and said something to Svetlana. Her lips were moving but no sound was coming out – Svetlana realised that she still had the ear protectors in. She popped them out and squeezed them back into their little plastic case, then secured it against the Velcro band of her jogging pants.

'Sorry.'

'I was suggesting you might want to take a seat,' Bella said nicely. She waited patiently until Svetlana was settled on a lightweight folding chair.

Bella's soundproofed and carpeted office was the largest private space in the ship; it doubled as her sleeping quarters. The walls were pastel-grey, papered here and there with false-colour seismic survey maps: grainy images of shipwrecks and coral reefs grabbed during scuba expeditions. The only fixture that never changed was Bella's fish tank, all five hundred litres of it.

Schrope hated the fish tank, Svetlana knew. It was a rule-twisting indulgence, exactly the kind of thing he'd made so many enemies stamping out on Big Red. Terrier-boy, they called him back there. Word was DeepShaft had put Schrope aboard *Rockhopper* to get him as far away from Mars as possible.

He sat there now, next to Bella, behind the same desk – the one Jim Chisholm *should* have been sitting behind – twirling a company ballpoint pen and looking pleased with himself.

'Sorry to bring you inside at short notice,' Schrope said, his voice a low, throbbing, catlike purr.

Svetlana shifted on her folding seat, but didn't reply.

'How'd the shift go?' Bella asked. She wore shark's teeth around her neck and a faded red lumberjack shirt, open over a black vest embossed with a gold foil picture: the Titanic Bar and Grill.

'I've had better. Blacking out isn't one of my favourite ways to spend EVA time.'

Bella raised a knowing eyebrow. 'The eighteens again?'

'Same old trimix problem.'

'Don't forget to file the LOC log. Headquarters may make us use that reconditioned shit, but we don't have to like it.'

'Everything's industry standard and space certified,' Schrope said, picking a speck of fluff from his crisp blue DeepShaft zip-up. 'On *Hammerhead* they make do with a lot older than Orlan eighteens without bitching and moaning.'

'That's *Hammerhead*'s problem,' Svetlana said.

'The difference is they don't make an issue of it,' Schrope said evenly. 'But since it's clearly an issue here, I've okayed a consignment of new twenty-twos on the next rotation.'

*Like ticking that one box on a consignment spreadsheet had been the favour of the century . . .* 'Which would be when, Craig?' Svetlana asked, sweetly. 'Before or after Jim gets his ticket home?'

Schrope batted aside her question with a flick of the pen. 'Bella, maybe you should fill Svetlana in on developments. Since this does, obliquely, concern Jim—'

'What developments?' Svetlana interrupted.

'We've had a request to disengage,' Bella said. 'They want us to tag the driver and leave it out here.'

'And the comet?'

'Plenty more where that one came from.'

Svetlana shook her head in disbelief. 'We can't just abandon it, not after all the work we've put in. Driver pit's dug, parasol's already locked in and prepped for spin-up—'

'Could be we've bigger fish to go after. I need some tech input.'

Schrope took over. 'Could we move quickly, if we had to?'

'We're always ready to withdraw to a safe distance,' Svetlana said.

'I mean immediate full power, for an extended cruise?'

Svetlana worked her way through a mental checklist. 'Yes,' she said, cautiously. 'Normally we'd run a few more tests, especially after an extended shutdown like this one—'

'Understood,' Bella said, 'but there's no compelling reason why we can't fire up?'

'No. But Parry and the others—'

'*Avenger*'s on its way back up. They'll be aboard shortly. One more thing, Svieta: specs say we can push the engine to half a gee, if we talk to it nicely . . .' Her voice trailed off; Svetlana knew what she was asking.

'Theoretically.'

Bella narrowed her eyes. 'Yes or no?'

'All right, yes, but it's not something you'd want to do for more than a few hours. You'd be looking at accelerated wear in expensive, non-replaceable components . . . elevated risk of mission-critical failure modes – not to mention the increased structural load on the rest of the ship.'

Bella tapped a finger against a hardcopy of a plaintext e-mail. 'Lockheed-Krunichev tell me the loads are within design lims. If you tell me the engine can hold, I'm a happy bunny.'

The document was upside down from Svetlana's perspective, but she could still make out part of the subject line: something about Janus. Mythical and Roman, she thought. The two-faced god of . . . what?

And the name of one of Saturn's moons.

'It's doable,' she said.

'Good,' Bella said. But Svetlana noticed that she said 'good' with a sigh, as if she had secretly been hoping for a different answer.

# CHAPTER 2

Svetlana pushed her way through the crush of people until she spotted Parry.

At the last rotation there were one hundred and forty-five souls on the ship, most of whom had gathered to hear Bella's announcement. They were plastered around the inside wall of the cylindrical gymnasium, tethered in place with hooks and Velcro and geckoflex and the friction of body on body. The gym – which doubled as a commons and radiation storm shelter – was normally spun to provide centrifugal gravity, but that would have kept Bella from floating into the middle to address the crowd.

'I'm sorry about—' Parry began hesitantly when Svetlana reached him. 'You know . . . that little *thing* earlier. I guess you didn't need *me* giving you a hard time on top of everyone else.'

'No. Not today.'

'It's just that we badly wanted to play with our comet, babe.'

'Boys will be boys, I suppose.' She gave him a quick squeeze, letting him know it was all right.

'All ancient history now, though.'

'So Bella tells me. Any idea what this is all about?'

Parry's concerned expression softened – he knew he was off the hook, for now at least. 'Didn't get a chance to check ShipNet. Was there—?'

'Nothing. No CNN, no Space.com, no nothing. Guess Bella pulled them.'

'That's what I figured. The football fans weren't happy, I can tell you.'

Svetlana tried to look concerned. 'They weren't?'

'Bella pulled the plug on the Kiev game halfway through the shoot-out.'

'The poor darlings.'

Parry scratched his moustache, looking endearingly puzzled. He was a short, stocky man with an open, friendly face, clean-shaven save for the moustache, with a thatch of unruly black hair bursting from underneath his knitted red diver's cap.

'You think something's happened there?' he wondered. 'An accident, something like that?'

'Don't think so. I pulled up a system map – we're on the other side of the Sun from Saturn, so Earth and Jupiter are a *lot* closer. Red could get a ship to Saturn quicker than we could.'

'Clever girl.'

'That's all I've got. I think Bella would have opened up more if Terrier-boy hadn't been there with her.'

'Maybe we should leave the little shit behind on the comet,' Parry said, voice low. 'You know, send him out on an errand, say someone left some paperwork behind. Then forget to pick him up.'

'Unfair to micro-organisms, though. The complex molecules might get upset.'

'Good point, babe. Wouldn't want to offend those poor, unsuspecting pyrimidines, would we?'

'Absolutely not. Even pyrimidines have feelings.'

Parry looked up as a hush fell across the gymnasium. 'Here we go. Guess we're about to find out what's got the little lady in such a tizz.'

Bella coughed. 'Thanks for your attention,' she said. The pumps had been turned off ahead of schedule so that she could be heard without having to shout. 'I'll keep this brief, since we'll have a lot to discuss.'

Floating free at the core of the gymnasium, Bella had her arms folded and one leg tucked behind the other. By accident or design, she had retained a slow residual spin so that she faced everyone in the room once a minute.

'Eleven hours ago,' Bella continued, 'I received a message from headquarters. The message was – to say the very least – startling. Even more startling was the request that followed. I've had half a day to digest this information, and I'm still only starting to get my head around it. I'm afraid the rest of you have even less time.'

Somehow, amongst all the people crammed into the room, Bella managed to spot Svetlana. She made brief eye contact, nodding her head so slightly that the gesture would have been imperceptible to anyone else.

'Once I heard the news,' she went on, 'I took an unprecedented step. As some of you will have already realised, I blocked all outside news from ShipNet. I didn't do this lightly, but please believe it *was* necessary. Shortly after the initial announcement, it became clear the networks were contributing nothing useful to the discussion, and what we need now is clarity – *absolute clarity* – because we have a very difficult decision to make.'

As Bella paused, Svetlana looked around, picking out faces. Tethered near her were Chieko Yamada and Carsten Fleig, from her own flight-operations team, lovers who went everywhere together. A little further around the curve of the gym was Josef Protsenko who, despite looking like a potato farmer, was one of the best mass-driver specialists in the business. There was Reka Bettendorf from EVA ops: one of the three people responsible for checking out suit safety and making sure people didn't black out because of malfs in the air trimix. There was Judy Sugimoto, from the medical section; she'd taken off her glasses and was rubbing away a smear on one lens against the collar of her smock.

There was Thom Crabtree, the taphead, standing alone and isolated, as always.

None of them looked as if they were in on any secrets. Svetlana turned her attention back to Bella, who was speaking again.

'I've talked to my technical team,' Bella was saying, 'and they tell me what we're being asked to do *is* feasible – risky, but feasible. But so is *everything* we do.' Bella closed her eyes, as if she couldn't quite remember the next line in her script, then took a breath and went on. 'Now we get to the difficult part. It concerns Janus, one of Saturn's moons.'

Svetlana allowed herself a small, guilty flicker of pride. She'd figured that much out, at least.

'Or rather,' Bella interrupted Svetlana's thoughts, 'Janus *used* to be one of Saturn's moons. Now we have to redefine it. About thirty hours ago, Janus's orbit began to deviate from its expected trajectory around Saturn.'

People started talking: they couldn't help it.

Bella held up a hand and waited for silence. 'Janus stopped orbiting Saturn,' she said, 'and broke away, following what was initially a very sharp course towards ecliptic south, out of the plane of the planets. That didn't last long, though: after twelve hours, Janus changed direction again, this time turning in the rough direction of Jupiter. The course it's following is strictly non-Keplerian, which means it isn't showing any signs of being influenced by the gravitational fields of the Sun or the other planets. All the same, the specialists say they have a good handle on it mathematically. It will miss Jupiter by slightly less than one AU. Assuming that nothing happens during its Jupiter approach, the moon will cross to the other side of the system. By then it'll be headed out of the ecliptic plane at eleven degrees south, in the direction of the constellation Virgo.'

Bella paused to draw breath, as if even she were having difficulty believing her own words. 'Ladies and gentleman,' she continued, 'Janus is accelerating. It's managing around one quarter of a gee. There was no sign of any encounter with another massive body, nor of any natural outgassing mechanism that could even *begin* to explain such behaviour. The simple fact is that it very much looks as if Janus was never a moon in the first place.'

'A ship,' Svetlana said under her breath, along with about half the room.

Parry's hand tightened around hers. Whatever had happened to sour things between them in the last day was over now, erased into insignificance by this astonishing news.

Bella responded to their murmured speculation. 'Yes,' she said, 'that does appear to be what we're dealing with. It even looks as if the icy surface is starting to peel off in wisps, like camouflage. If that continues we might begin to see what's really underneath.' She smiled at them all. 'There's a problem, though: Janus is getting further and further away, so the view isn't getting any better.'

'Oh, no,' Svetlana said.

'There's only one ship in the system in anything like the right position to intercept and shadow Janus on its way out. No prizes for guessing which ship I'm talking about. The plan is we put the pedal to the metal for three weeks. At half a gee, we can meet Janus and still have enough fuel left to shadow it for five days. Then we turn tail and head back home.'

Bella said nothing for another slow rotation of her body, allowing the commons to erupt into noisy questions before speaking again.

'It's up to us,' she said, raising her voice until the clamour died down. 'No other ship in the system, manned or otherwise, can do this.'

Parry raised his voice. People respected Parry Boyce; they fell silent to let him speak.

'This isn't in our contracts, Bella.'

'Actually, there *is* a clause that covers "additional non-specified activities",' Bella said, 'but that doesn't mean there won't be compensations. Triple our usual danger bonus, from the moment we commit to chasing Janus until the moment we dock back around Mars, with discretionary rewards on top of that, depending on the conditions near Janus.' She waited a beat, before adding, 'That's a shitload of money, people.'

'Triple our usual danger bonus?' Parry repeated.

'That's the deal.'

'I'll buy a nice headstone.'

Bella let them have their laughter. 'Parry's right to mention the danger,' she said, when the room had simmered down. 'That's why this isn't something I'm going to enforce without a clear mandate. I'm giving you all one hour to think this over. In one hour, report individually to your section chiefs. In ninety minutes the section chiefs will report to me. Based on their findings, I'll make my decision.' Bella spread her hands. 'I wish I could give you more information. I can't: there isn't any. I wish I could give you more time, but there isn't any of that, either. The fuel situation is *tight*.' Bella acknowledged Svetlana again: she had timed the remark with her usual care. 'One hour,' she said. 'I'm sorry there's no other way of doing this.'

Bella grabbed a nylon line stretching across the room and began to haul herself towards the wall of the commons. Then she paused and looked back at the gathering. 'Oh, before I forget, since I know some of you are dying to find out. It went to Dynamo Kiev, on penalties.'

Some impulse made Ryan Axford pause on his way to the patient's bedside. He picked up his flexy from his desk and called up the most recent tomograph of Jim Chisholm's skull. He stroked his finger against the false-colour image, rotating it so that the intricate three-dimensional structures became clear. The inside of his patient's skull was now as familiar to Axford as the architecture of his own house, far away on Albemarle Sound. He knew its passages and alcoves, its attic and cellar, its concealed chambers, its cavities, cracks and flaws. He knew its secret monsters.

He had already looked at the scans with a clear, clinical eye, and he knew that he had missed nothing. The disease was already progressing along textbook lines: *diffuse infiltration of contiguous and regional structures of the central nervous system; compression, invasion and destruction of neighbouring brain parenchyma.* It was irrational to expect the images to have changed, yet he could not resist examining them one more time, hoping that he had indeed neglected some detail, a hint of shrinkage.

Axford dimmed the flexy and placed it gently back on his desk. Nothing had changed; nothing *could* have changed.

He caught Gayle Simmons, the duty nurse, leaving Chisholm's curtained-off bedside. She held a blood-filled syringe tipped with a plastic safety cap, a saline bag clutched in her other hand.

'How's our guest?' he asked.

'Comfortable,' she said, her Southern drawl, with its questioning upwards lilt, elongating the word. Simmons was young and keen, transferred into DeepShaft from Northside Hospital, Atlanta. She wore her black hair long and was popular with the other men.

Axford touched her sleeve and lowered his voice. 'Any thoughts about what Bella just told us, Gayle?'

'Whatever's best for the patient, I'm cool with that.'

Axford nodded and peered into her eyes, searching for a clue to her real feelings. She blinked and looked away.

'That's what I was thinking too,' he said.

Chisholm was listening to Charles Mingus playing 'Goodbye Pork Pie Hat'. Axford lowered the music to a murmur as he entered the screened-off area. Chisholm's expression was neutral, neither welcoming nor shunning his visitor – he knew that Axford could be the bearer of the worst kind of news, as well as the best.

'Bella talked to me,' Axford said. 'She wanted to make sure you had all the facts.'

'She didn't talk to me,' Chisholm said.

Axford sat down next to the bed. 'Bella was concerned that you'd feel persuaded against your own judgement if she spoke to you in person.'

Jim Chisholm blinked and squinted upwards, as if taking an interest in something on the ceiling. The light in the room was low, green-tinged and calculatedly soothing. Around the bed, machines ticked and hummed and bleeped in an endless, numbing chorus.

Chisholm reached for a glass of water. 'Did Bella ask you anything?'

'Yes,' Axford said, 'she did. She wanted all the facts at her disposal.'

'What did you tell her?'

'The truth, or at least my understanding of it.'

'Which was?'

Axford chose his words with care. 'You have a progressive condition that, untreated, stands a good chance of killing you within three months.'

'I know this.'

'I still think it's worth spelling things out. I can't cure you, and I can't stop the disease from advancing. I can relieve the intracranial pressure; I can administer anticonvulsants; I can try to stabilise your neurotransmitter and cytokine levels. But the best I can do is slow things down. Short of—' Axford caught himself before he went on, 'Realistically, your only hope of survival is to return to Earth within three months. Sooner would be better, obviously.'

'I know this,' Chisholm said again.

'But I need to *know* that you know it.' Axford leaned closer to him, lowering his voice. 'Here's the deal. When you signed up for this mission, you accepted certain medical risks. We all did. We have to accept that it simply isn't practical to carry a hospital's worth of state-of-the-art surgical equipment, let alone the expertise to use it, on board a ship. That's why we go through such intensive medical screening before they let us aboard. But there is always a statistical risk of something getting past those tests.'

'Where's this heading?'

'If I could have arranged a shuttle to take you home, I would have. Failing that, I have to look at the quickest way to get you back given the options currently on the table.'

'Go on,' Chisholm said.

'Bella's polling the crew. If the answer that comes back is "no", we'll simply resume normal operations. We're due another crew-rotation shuttle in five months. I'm pushing them to send that ship out earlier, but I doubt that they'll be able to shave more than four or six weeks off the schedule.'

Chisholm looked at him, his eyes narrowed. 'Back there you almost said something. "Short of", you began . . . and then you stopped. Short of what, exactly?'

'I shouldn't have said anything. I don't agree with it.'

'Don't agree with what?'

'The company has a contingency plan,' Axford said, reluctantly, 'for cases like yours where the prognosis is poor, and where there is no prospect of an early return to Earth. It's called Frost Angel.'

'Frost Angel? No one's ever mentioned anything anything called Frost Angel to me.'

'It isn't widely discussed outside the medical section. It's something we hoped never to have to put into practice.'

'You have no idea how encouraging that sounds.'

'The contingency is . . .' Axford hesitated, momentarily unable to continue. He had never expected to find himself talking to Jim Chisholm like this. Chisholm was still his effective superior, Bella Lind's second-in-command. What business did the company have in *not* telling Chisholm about something like this through formal channels?

'Ryan,' Chisholm prompted.

Axford steeled himself and said, 'The idea is that we kill you now. It'd be a controlled, painless transition into unconsciousness. Once you're unconscious, there are a couple of options open to me to complete the euthanisation. After inducing cardiac arrest, I'd proceed with a rapid exsanguination, flushing out your blood and replacing it with a cold saline solution. The object is to get as much oxygen out of your body as possible. Oxygen is the engine that causes ischemic damage if your heart stops pumping, so the less of it we leave in you the better. That's one option.'

'I'm just dying to hear the other one,' Chisholm said.

'Instead of the saline flush, we keep the heart running and expose you to an atmosphere containing a high concentration of hydrogen sulphide – around eighty parts per million. After a few minutes, respiration will slow and your core body temperature will plummet. The hydrogen sulphide molecules will start binding to the same cell sites that oxygen normally uses, so – in effect – we lock oxygen out of the loop. It achieves more or less the same result as the saline flush.'

Axford waited for that to sink in. He looked at Chisholm's smooth, untroubled face and read nothing.

'Maybe I'm missing something,' Chisholm said, 'but in either scenario, wouldn't I still be dead at the end of it?'

'Dead, yes, but protected from ischemic damage. That's the point of Frost Angel. The damage doesn't get any worse.'

'And then – when we make it home – they'll bring me back?'

'They'll try their best.'

'How many people have been through this?'

'As part of the official Frost Angel programme? Not as many as I'd like.'

'Meaning none, right, Ryan?'

'I'm not sugaring any pills here. The way things are going, in ten years, fifteen years, they might be able to bring you back. Then again, they might not.'

'I don't get this. You're saying you can shut me down, but you can't operate on my brain?'

'The process isn't complicated. It's – how shall I put this? – within the scope of the services we're set up to provide.'

'You mean you'd be running that saline flush through me no matter what happens?'

'Frost Angel means doing it before the damage becomes extensive.'

Chisholm stared off into the distance for a few uncomfortable moments as Mingus played on. 'You think this is a good idea?'

'I accept the medical logic, given the situation. That doesn't mean I'm jumping for joy at the idea of going ahead with it. It would depend on the severity of the condition, and on the odds of reaching home in time.' Still torn, Axford paused. 'If you wanted it, that doesn't mean I wouldn't oblige. I'd need your consent – otherwise it's murder. I could get into *serious* trouble for that.'

'And we wouldn't want that.'

'But maybe we don't have to freeze you,' Axford said. 'Maybe there's still a way to get you back in time.'

Chisholm nodded shrewdly, like someone who had just got the punch line of a joke. 'Janus, right?'

'My professional recommendation,' Axford said, 'is that you vote for the mission. I've spoken to Bella; when we've completed the Janus rendezvous, we'll return home on the fastest possible trajectory. We may even be able to meet the shuttle halfway. Even if we can't, I still think we can get you home in seven or eight weeks.'

'Is that soon enough?'

'When we get back home,' Axford said, 'everyone will want a piece of us. And when they find out there's a sick man aboard, every nation on the planet will be fighting for the privilege of treating you.'

Chisholm closed his eyes and slumped back against his pillow. Barely audible above the machines, Mingus had moved on to 'Open Letter to Duke'. For a moment the two of them listened to the music, as if somewhere within it there might be an answer neither of them had so far imagined, an option that involved neither freezing nor a risky encounter with something alien.

'They've never brought anyone back, have they?'

'They're getting better all the time. They're up to mammals now. They did a rabbit last year.'

As the car slid along *Rockhopper*'s spine, Bella unzipped her jacket and removed the flexy that had been recharging itself from her body heat. A deft flick of her wrist stiffened the sheet of leathery plastic. The ShipNet menu formed in its iridophores, tinged with a blue-green cast where some of the flexy's living cells were beginning to die.

Bella navigated to her private area and retrieved the latest message from Powell Cagan.

He sat in a living room, its surfaces gleaming with reflected moonlight. Bella heard the faint roar of what she first took to be road traffic, but then realised must be ocean breakers. She thought she recognised the room. One of the framed prints on the wall – a reproduction of one of Cagan's favourite

Nu Metal album covers – looked familiar to her. Across twenty-five years she could almost place the villa and the island.

Cagan never changed much. His white hair was still spiked and gelled in the manner of his youth. He wore a black shirt unbuttoned at the collar, with a pale sweater draped over his shoulders, sleeves tied together across his chest. He was nearing his eightieth birthday, but he could have passed for a retired tennis pro in his late fifties, holding down a good game and a good med programme.

'Hello, Bella,' he said. 'Excuse the interruption, but it appears we'll need to move faster than we expected. The Chinese are further ahead than we thought.' He held up a hardcopy of *China Daily*. The paper cast a pallid glow across his desk. 'They're talking about their own unilateral expedition. They say they've got a crew together and that they're ready for engine start-up. More than likely it'll blow up in their faces, but we have to be ready in case it doesn't. I've spoken to Inga and – although she clearly can't go on the record about this – she agrees with me.'

He said 'Inga' with such affected casualness that it took Bella a moment to realise that he meant Inga de Jong, the Secretary-General of the United Economic Entities.

He shifted in his chair as the roar of surf rose like static. 'A lot of water has passed under our mutual bridges, but I've never doubted your strengths. If – *when* – you have that "yes" vote, you can move on it immediately. There's no need to wait for my confirmation before you begin the chase.' His excellent teeth flashed silver in the moonlit room. 'Good luck, Bella. For old times' sake, all right?'

She smiled at that: not because it pleased her, but because she found it amusing that Cagan still expected her to look back on their affair with something like fondness. The depth of his lack of understanding was awesome, even after twenty-five years.

The image faded. Bella softened the flexy and slipped it back under her zip-up.

The car slowed as it neared the mid-spine machine shop and slid into a reception dock. Bella climbed out and hand-propelled herself through access corridors reeking of lubricant and ozone. In addition to Craig Schrope, there were seven chiefs present. Some of them floated, some had lashed themselves to floor or wall with tie-lines, Velcro or geckoflex, while others lounged on or straddled the outstretched manipulator arms of the deactivated robots.

Bella centred herself, taking time to make careful eye contact with everyone in the room. 'Thank you for getting here on time,' she said.

'Has anything changed in the last ninety minutes?' asked Svetlana.

'Not to my knowledge,' Bella said, 'although it's becoming increasingly difficult to pick out signal from noise where the news is concerned.'

'Janus still doing its thing?'

'Yes.'

'I'd like numbers for its trajectory,' Svetlana said.

'Now?' said Schrope softly.

She looked at him. 'It can wait until we're under way.'

'Well, let's not the jump the gun,' Bella said. 'We may decide we're not going anywhere. Or have you reached a collective decision while you were waiting for me?'

The team chiefs glanced at each other, but no one volunteered to speak for the group. Bella looked at Parry Boyce. His people were the workers who actually had to crawl into comets, taking core samples and figuring out the best way to anchor the unwieldy mass driver if a comet turned out to be worth steering home. They were tough; they formed the largest and most volatile element of the crew.

Beneath his red diver's cap, Parry's open and friendly face gave nothing away.

'Well?' she asked.

'I've a small majority in favour of chasing Janus,' he said, 'split down aquatic and orbital lines, with a narrow win for the orbitals.'

'What do *you* think?'

'I think we should do it. I think it's madness, but I still think we should do it.'

'You had high hopes for this comet,' Bella said.

'There'll be others. There may never be another Janus.' She thought Parry was done, his verdict delivered, but after a moment he spoke again. 'We still want guarantees. We want that triple-bonus agreement in writing. We want it paid even if something prevents us from catching up with Janus.'

'We'll have to be under way before I have any of that confirmed,' Bella said.

'Fine. But if we don't like the terms when they're rubber-stamped, we turn the ship around.'

'Acceptable to me,' Bella said, before Schrope could contradict her.

'That means no company horseshit in the small print.'

'Fine. Anything else?'

'Just a bit.' He handed her his own flexy. Bella stared at the numbers Parry had blocked in: a sliding scale of danger terms, linked to proximity to Janus, far exceeding the bonus she had offered in the gymnasium. 'It's all non-negotiable,' he added.

Wordlessly, Bella passed the flexy to Schrope, who glanced down at it and pulled a sour expression.

'You're talking about terms that will bankrupt the company.'

'It's the company's call,' Parry said easily. 'If they feel Janus is worth our time, they'd better be ready to pay for it.'

'If you bankrupt the company, you won't have jobs to go back to when we get home,' Schrope said.

'The idea is that we won't *need* jobs,' Parry said.

Bella scraped grit from her eyes. 'You should listen to Craig,' she said. 'This isn't only about the company. We just happen to be the one ship with a chance of doing this. The fact that there's a company logo on the side doesn't matter. We're representatives of the entire human species.'

Parry laughed at her. They all laughed at her. She felt like a child in a roomful of adults, coming out with something naive and touching.

'I'm serious,' she said, feeling her cheeks redden.

Parry shrugged. 'So are we. Deadly bloody serious.'

'Parry did the sums,' said Denise Nadis, the head of mass-driver operations. 'In accountancy terms we're still a blip. No one's coming out of this bankrupt.'

Bella sighed, knowing there was no point fighting this one. She looked around at all the other chiefs. 'Let's hear your piece, Denise.'

Nadis leaned forward on the robot arm she had picked for a support. She was thirty-one, a small, intense black woman with long purple fingernails that she somehow managed to keep intact despite being one of the best teleoperators on the ship. She had a nose stud, eyebrow ring and tribal tattoos, worn as a tribute to her late grandmother. 'My people overwhelmingly say no,' she said. 'We push ice. It's what we do, what we came here to do. But if we *have* to accept – if the final result is "yes" – then we'll expect the same terms that Parry's proposing.'

Bella turned to the bald man sitting next to Nadis: Nick Thale, the unassuming head of remote cometary geoscience. Thale's small but dedicated team used remote-sensing techniques – radar, lasers, spectroscopy – to survey comets from a distance of many light-seconds.

'We say go for it,' he said. 'My team would actually kill for the chance to turn their expertise onto something other than another dirty snowball. If you can get us close to Janus, we're confident that we can do some real science for once.'

'Good,' Bella said.

'We do, however, want a modifier to Parry's terms.' Thale glanced at the other man. 'In general we find the terms he's suggesting acceptable. Our quibble is with the clause for surface conditions. As soon as surface operations commence, we demand that everyone is paid at the same rate, irrespective of whether they're in a suit or not.'

'You call that a quibble?' Bella said.

'As Denise pointed out,' Thale said, 'no one's going to lose any money over this.'

'I don't like it,' Parry said, turning to the other man. 'Nick, I know your people are good at their work, but it won't be any of your guys sweating in a fucked-up Orlan nineteen when we reach Janus.'

'Those are the conditions you work under anyway,' Thale said. 'If Janus reacts we'll all have to deal with it.'

'We could use a little less speculation,' Schrope said.

'Right now speculation's the only game in town.' Thale shifted on his perch. 'Here's another thing, too. Whatever happens when we get to Janus, it isn't going to be the usual drill. We won't be running core samples or scouting out locations to attach a driver, so why assume that Parry's people are automatically the ones best suited to go crawling over the thing? The one thing we know about Janus is that it isn't a comet.'

Parry started to interject, but Bella cut him off. 'Parry's people have the most experience at EVA,' she said.

'But there isn't a person on this ship who hasn't been trained in basic suit functions,' Thale said. 'Face it: we'll be dealing with an environment completely unfamiliar to all of us. It seems to me that we'll be making a terrible mistake if we don't make maximum use of our scientists.'

'By putting them in suits, you mean?' Bella asked.

'I'm just saying I don't think it should be a foregone conclusion who gets to wear those suits.'

'It isn't,' Bella said, 'and nor is it a foregone conclusion that there'll even *be* surface operations. Maybe once we get a close look at this thing I'll decide not to send people out at all.'

'What about robots?' asked Saul Regis. 'Do robots count as surface operations?'

'Saul,' Bella said, with a straight face, 'please don't tell me you want danger money for the robots now?'

Regis answered in his usual borderline autistic monotone. 'I mean we should all be on Parry's maximum rate of pay even if we only send robots into the vicinity of Janus. Robots are just as likely to provoke a hostile reaction as people.'

'Robots – and people, for all I know – have crawled over Janus in the past. They didn't provoke any kind of reaction.'

'Janus was hiding then. It isn't now.'

'Maybe we'll all go onto danger money as soon as we look at Janus,' Bella said, tired of arguing. 'Or as soon as we dream about it. Maybe we should be on danger money now, just because we're debating the faint possibility of going there.' There was a chorus of objections, but she shouted them down. 'Svetlana, say your piece.'

'You've already heard it. There's no technical reason why we can't make this trip.'

'And your people?'

'The majority support the Janus operation.'

Bella wasn't surprised. Svetlana's people were engineers, all with an interest in spacecraft design and propulsion. Of course they wanted a close look at Janus.

'And you?'

Bella watched a flicker of uncertainty cross Svetlana's face, as if she *had* made up her mind, but had just been stricken by renewed doubts. 'Yes,' she said, tentatively. 'I think we should go, despite all the risks.'

'And you're still happy about the engine output, and the stress loading?'

'I can't guarantee anything,' Svetlana said. 'All I can give you is probability.'

'Spoken like a true engineer,' Bella said resignedly.

'Thank you. And the balance of probabilities is that the ship will hold together, although they may have to scrap it when we get back home.'

'That's somebody else's problem,' Bella said. 'All right: anything else to add?'

'I'd like to check the numbers on the fuel.'

'Absolutely – I'd insist on it.' Bella turned to face Ash Murray, the head of EVA technical support. He wore a denim shirt open over a yellow T-shirt printed with the ship's drilling-penguin mascot. Murray's team was the smallest on the ship, but one of the most essential.

'You want to go crawling over Janus, we'll supply the fucked-up Orlan nineteens,' Murray said, looking pointedly at Parry Boyce.

Bella nodded, knowing that was as close to a 'yes' as she was going to get.

That left Axford and his medical team. 'Ryan,' she said pleasantly. Axford was a man she liked and trusted. 'We've talked already, and I think I know where you stand. Have you changed your mind?'

'I have a sick man in my care whose best hope of survival is to get back to Earth as quickly as possible,' Axford said. 'Since you can't turn the ship around, and since DeepShaft won't send out an unscheduled shuttle, Janus represents his best hope.'

'Is that what you told him?'

'I didn't pull any punches,' Axford said. 'I don't think he's any happier than I am about nosing around near that thing, but he recognises the lesser of two evils when he sees it.'

'Then you'd vote against the mission if Jim wasn't ill?'

'I'm voting to safeguard my patient's life. You have my word that the people under me feel the same way.'

'I'll see that we don't let Jim down,' she said. 'Or any of your team, for that matter. We have leverage now. It's too late to send out a shuttle, but they can damn well send one to meet us on the way home.'

'You'll guarantee that?'

'Yes,' she said.

'Then you have my consent to take us to Janus.'

That was Axford done: he would shrink back into the scenery now, just the way he had been before she talked to him, listening intently, but with a distracted, faraway look that suggested (quite wrongly, as it happened) extreme inattention.

With Ryan's vote in, it was clear that Janus had won the day, though not by an overwhelming majority. In Bella's estimation some sixty per cent of the crew were in favour of the mission, subject to haggling over bonus pay and working arrangements near the moon. Twenty per cent were unenthusiastic, but would go along with it. The other twenty per cent were strongly opposed, irrespective of the bonus terms.

Bella would have preferred a stronger majority, but at least the ship wasn't split down the middle – and she knew exactly how she felt: Janus was an unprecedented opportunity, not only for her crew, not only for her company, but for humanity as a whole. She'd believed that before she entered the room, and she believed it now.

She held up her flexy, showing the tally of poll results to the assembled chiefs.

'Back to your teams, people,' she said, 'and tell them to start battening down the hatches.'

When *Rockhopper* pulled away from the comet four hours later, a robot had already dropped the fragmentation-assistance device into the shaft that Parry had dug to take the mass driver. The nuclear device was military surplus, recycled from the decommissioned warhead of a forty-year-old NATO surplus Bush III MIRV. It had been dialled to its maximum civilian yield of ten megatonnes.

The comet went up nicely.

That was one piece of ice no one else would be getting their hands on.

# CHAPTER 3

'It's the last good close-up picture we have,' Bella said, 'taken about a year ago, when a cargo slug swung by on a routine slingshot.'

The object displayed on her wall was irregular in shape: two hundred and twenty kilometres across at its widest point; one hundred and sixty at its narrowest. The surface was lightly cratered and gouged, the craters soft-edged and shallow. The ice was a tarnished grey-white, the oily colour of roadside snow.

'What was a slug doing taking pictures?' Svetlana asked.

'University of Arizona paid to piggy-back a cam: some kid finishing off a Ph.D. thesis on dynamic ice chemistry. There are better images on the feeds, and maps that cover the entire thing down to a rez of a few metres, but this is the most recent snapshot in existence.'

'Still looks like a piece of ice to me,' Saul Regis said.

'That must have been the point,' Bella said. 'Janus is about the last place in the system we'd have thought to look for signs of alien intelligence.'

Nick Thale stirred in his seat. 'If they meant to camouflage their activities, why didn't they pick something a bit less weird than a co-orbital moon?'

'I don't know. Hide in plain sight? Pick the one place we wouldn't seriously consider looking?'

The image revealed no hint of wrongness: no suggestion of alien mechanisms lurking just beneath that shell of icy camouflage.

Regis tapped a stylus against the flexy he had spread across his lap. He was a burly man, bald at the crown but with his remaining long black hair worn in a ponytail. His goatee beard tapered to a long braided tail. 'I'm not sure I follow,' he said. 'What was so unique about Janus? Aren't there a bunch of water-ice moons orbiting Saturn?'

'Not exactly,' Thale said, turning to face the robotics specialist. 'Janus was co-orbital with another small moon named Epimetheus. They shared almost the same orbit around Saturn, at about two and half Saturn radii. One of them was a tiny bit closer to Saturn, so it moved just a little bit faster. Once every four years the fast one lapped the slow one, overtaking it from behind. When that happened, the two satellites exchanged orbits: the slower one became the faster one, and vice versa.'

'Freaky,' Regis observed.

'It *is* freaky. Every four years the same thing happens. The moons take turns going fast, like skaters running a relay.'

Bella had read up on it before the meeting. 'It's a pretty unusual set-up. Definitely not the sort of thing you expect to happen by chance, just because two independent moons happened to settle into that—'

She stopped, because they had all felt something shiver through the room. The glass of water on Bella's desk trembled.

She looked at Svetlana. 'Are we okay?'

'We're okay.'

'It's just that I don't remember that sort of thing happening before.'

'It's expected,' Svetlana said. 'We're running the engine in a different operating regime.'

'So it isn't anything I need to worry about?'

'No. Just some mixing eddies in the precombustion tokamak.'

'Fine,' Bella said, but like everyone in the room – with the exception of Svetlana – she had just been forcibly reminded that they were not sitting in some anonymous corporate office building, but were in fact riding fifty thousand tonnes of nuclear-powered spacecraft to the edge of interstellar space, with the pedal to the metal.

They had been under way for three days now, and *Rockhopper* had already picked up thirteen hundred kilometres per second of speed compared to their initial vector around the comet. They were travelling at a shallow angle to the ecliptic, in an almost radial direction away from the Sun. Every second they were crossing the width of the Gulf of Mexico: putting that much extra distance between them and their places of birth. And they were still accelerating.

By the time they reached Janus, they would be thirteen light-hours from home: far enough that a round-trip signal would take more than a day. And they would be moving at *three per cent* of the speed of light, a figure that was enough to put the fear of God into anyone. Three per cent of the speed of light was nine thousand kilometres per second.

With every minute that passed, they'd be falling further from home than the distance between the Earth and its Moon.

A minute or two had passed since the tremor; the ship's ride was now limousine-smooth once more. Everyone was waiting for her to continue speaking, their faces expectant. It was a nice show, but she doubted that any of them were convinced. Their nerves were already stretched paper-thin. For three days the ship had been creaking and groaning like a submarine sinking to crush depth.

'Where was I?'

'Janus,' someone said helpfully.

'Right . . . right. It's just that until four days ago our best guess was that the two moons must once have been part of the same body.'

Craig Schrope had done his homework as well. 'A bigger moon – maybe something Charon-sized. A few billion years ago something must have hit it, smashing it into pieces. The two largest chunks drifted apart from each other on nearly identical orbits.'

'Hence your co-orbital moons,' Bella took up the discussion again. 'But the Janus event shows that it didn't happen like that. It was set up to look that way, but the co-orbital situation was clearly staged: an engineered occurrence designed to look natural.'

'Before any of you ask,' Schrope said, 'there are teams crawling over Epimetheus even as we speak.'

'With kid gloves, I hope,' Nick Thale said.

'I think we can assume that they're exercising all due caution,' Bella said. 'Not that it seems to matter: nothing they've done or observed in any way suggests that Epimetheus is anything but what we always thought it was. Unless the interior mechanisms are spectacularly well camouflaged, it's just a lump of ice.'

'The best guess,' Schrope interjected, 'is that Epimetheus is just an ordinary satellite. The Janus artefact must have been introduced from outside the Saturnian system, and its orbit carefully tuned to produce the co-orbital situation we thought we understood.'

'There are other situations like that, right?' asked Parry.

'No,' Schrope said, 'at least not in our system. Janus and Epimetheus were the only two moons that acted like that.'

'And elsewhere? In other systems?'

'The data isn't good enough for us to tell,' Bella said. 'We have some images of the big Jovians in nearby systems, good enough to pick up major weather systems, ring complexes and Titan-sized moons, but we still can't begin to resolve Janus-sized objects.'

'So in other words this might be unique,' Parry said.

'Or it might be a common enough situation that you can expect to find one or two co-orbital pairs in every system,' Bella said. 'Right now we have no idea.'

'But it could be unusual,' Parry persisted, 'in which case, doesn't it begin to look like maybe that was the point?'

Bella leaned forward, interested. 'A calling card, you mean?'

'I'm just saying we shouldn't rule anything out.'

She nodded sagely. 'Parry's right. We keep open minds and we consider all possibilities, no matter how outlandish. The instant we start making assumptions is the instant we're going to run into trouble.'

'But we're not trained for this,' Svetlana said, looking around the room. 'We're tool-pushers. Bella says we have to keep open minds. I say it isn't our job even to *worry* about that.'

'It isn't that simple,' Bella said, 'although God knows I wish it were. We have just five days at Janus; less if the moon speeds up. That's one hundred and twenty hours, of which every single minute will be precious.'

'The problem is timelag,' Schrope said. He spoke softly, but with a measured ease that suggested a planned statement. 'We'll be too far out to phone home.'

Bella nodded. 'We'll be compressing and transmitting all our data back home, of course, from the moment we're in sensor range, and the experts in near-Earth space will be on it like a pack of hounds, but the earliest we'll hear from them is twenty-six hours after we send back the first images. Once we reach Janus, we won't be able to afford to wait that long for instructions.'

'Still won't make us specialists,' Svetlana said.

'But we're still eighteen days from our objective,' Bella said. 'That's why I've called you here. I want you to start thinking like specialists.'

Parry laughed. 'Just like that?'

'You're all smart cookies,' Bella said. 'If you weren't, you wouldn't have got within a country mile of my ship.'

'None of us knows the first thing about alien life,' Svetlana said.

'Maybe not now,' Bella said, 'but a lot can change in eighteen days. No one's expecting green monsters to come crawling out of that moon when we pull alongside, but we have to be ready to answer if Janus says "hello". We have to be ready with *something*.'

Saul Regis fingered his elaborate beard. He wore a *Cosmic Avenger* sweatshirt showing the fictitious crew standing around the workstations of their sleek thirtieth-century starship. 'How would this work? Us becoming specialists, I mean.'

'As of now,' Bella said, 'I'm putting together a contact working group. I want to keep it small and flexible, which is why I haven't invited all the chiefs to this briefing.' She nodded at Regis. 'I want you to chair it, Saul. I've looked at the background files of everyone on this ship and of all of us you look to be best equipped for the job. You've studied cognitive science and artificial intelligence at research level – and our best guess at the nature of Janus is that it's some kind of robot.'

'I feel overqualified already,' Regis said.

'I'm not expecting blinding insights – just some basic familiarity with the landscape. Does anyone have any objection to Saul chairing this working group?' She waited a heartbeat. 'No? Good; that's settled, then.'

Regis held up his hands in mock surrender. 'I still don't know what you actually want me to *do*, Bella.'

'Start by assembling your team. I think we can take it as a given that the people in this room ought to be on it, if only because we'll be the ones at the sharp end when we start near-Janus operations. I want you to keep the team focused and agile, but you shouldn't discount bringing in anyone else you feel can add something.' Bella flicked her flexy across the table. 'There are some names you may want to look at.'

Regis peeled his own flexy from the wall: it had fluttered there to recharge its batteries, drinking power from the embedded grid. When he touched it, the two devices exchanged secure data via the myoelectric field of his own body, bypassing ShipNet's open channel.

'I still don't know where to begin,' he said.

'Let me show you something,' Bella said. She turned to the year-old image of Janus on the wall. Her hands moved across the keys on her desk. With a flourish of flickering hexels, the image changed abruptly. It was still Janus, but now the image was fuzzy, like a photo of a stone taken through smeared glass.

'This is a synthetic image,' Bella said, 'a visible-light composite assembled using long-baseline optical interferometry, put together from data obtained by six different deep-space telescopes within the orbit of Mars. It's the most recent long-range picture we have of Janus: it was taken less than a day ago.'

The picture showed a different angle from the fly-by snapshot, so the shape of the moon and the distribution of craters looked different, but more than that had changed. There were dark patches in the ice that had not been there before. A second glance showed that the patches were actually wounds: voids where huge scabs of ice, kilometres thick, had come free, or boiled off, or simply ceased to exist. In the dark zones, suggestions of mechanical structures twinkled at the limit of clarity: enormous dark machine parts, curved and coiled, nestling tight as intestines.

'Definitely the money shot,' Parry said.

'The camouflage is breaking away,' Bella said. 'Janus – whatever it is – is starting to show its true form. We already have something to work with: the fact that we really are dealing with an alien artefact, and not some bizarre physical process we just didn't understand.'

'That's not much,' Parry said.

'There's more. I mentioned that Janus is leaving our system at a shallow angle to the ecliptic. Well, now we have a much better handle on the trajectory.' Bella made the image shrink until it was an off-white pinpoint against a star map marked with star names, constellation boundaries and faint lines of right ascension and declination, the astronomical counterparts to latitude and longitude. 'Ladies and gentleman: we have a star, and we have a name.'

'Which is?' Parry asked.

'Alpha Virginis, the brightest star in Virgo.' Bella highlighted the relevant star: it was the nearest one to the small image of Janus. 'Now, I'll admit it's not exactly the kind of sun we'd have expected aliens to come from,' she said. 'Not only is it hot, heavy and blue, but it's also part of a binary system. Maybe they didn't evolve there. But we can't ignore the evidence. That's where Janus is heading. That's the place it now calls home.'

'So the Janus builders,' Svetlana said, 'what do we call them? Virgins? Virginians? Alphans?'

'None of the above,' Bella replied. 'We name them after the classical name of their destination star. Alpha Virginis is Spica.' She pronounced it carefully, 'spiker', lingering over the syllables. 'The Janus builders are the Spicans, and they live two hundred and sixty light-years from Earth.' She beamed at her little gathering. 'There. Don't you feel as if you know them better already?'

'About this mission,' Parry said, 'is it too late to change my mind?'

They all laughed. But not as much as Bella might have hoped.

CNN wanted an interview. Bella took a cam down into the aeroponics lab, attaching it to one of the plant racks with a dab of geckoflex. Aeroponics, with its humid air, mechanical breezes and the soothingly regular chuffing of the aerators, always put her at ease. It was the only place on *Rockhopper* where she could close her eyes and feel, fleetingly, as if she were back on Earth.

'It must be quite a burden, to be leading this mission,' the anchordoll said in her perky, almost cartoon-like voice.

'It's a responsibility, certainly,' Bella said, 'but I have a good crew under me. I couldn't ask for a better team.'

'You must be apprehensive, though.'

'I have a duty to exercise professional concern. Janus may throw some surprises at us, but that's been the case with every comet we've ever steered home. There's never been anything routine about pushing ice.'

'How do you think you'll react if you meet a real-life alien?'

'As opposed to a not real-life alien?' Bella fingered one of the plants on the rack. Patent numbers and copyright symbols were embossed into the glossy green leaf. 'I don't think it'll happen. I think we'll find automated systems, that's all.'

'How do you feel about that?'

Bella shrugged. 'We'll take pictures, run scans, maybe try to extract a physical sample. But I'm not expecting great conversation from a machine.'

The anchordoll huffed. 'Well, we machines may have something to say about that!'

'Yes,' Bella said.

The doll brightened again. 'Captain Lind, you're in charge of a pretty big ship. But it was never designed for this kind of mission, was it?'

'Show me a ship that was.' Bella tried not to sound defensive. 'But we're versatile enough. We're equipped for remote science studies: it's just that we'll be doing a different kind of science from the sort we're normally used to. But we'll cope. We're professionals.' She looked into the cam with what she hoped was the right steely-eyed expression. 'Out here we have a saying: "We push ice. It's what we do."'

'You'll have to run that by me again, Captain Lind!'

'What we mean is this: we get a job to do, and we finish it. My crew are the best. We've got people from the Moon, people from Mars, people from the orbitals, people from marine projects . . . a bunch of underwater guys. Vacuum and water: they're not that different, really.'

The anchordoll's face defaulted to one of its blank states: Bella had lost it again. 'Could you tell us a little bit more about the rest of your crew?'

'Well, they're all good people. I wouldn't want to single any one person out—'

'We've had reports that your second-in-command is going to die!' the doll said cheerily.

'Jim Chisholm has a condition, that's all,' Bella said testily, 'one that needs treatment sooner rather than later.'

'How do you feel about that?'

'I'm not thrilled about it, obviously. Nor's Jim. But we can still get him home in time. In fact – and Jim agrees with me here – Janus is actually our best bet for getting him the medical attention he needs. We'll be home and dry in six, seven weeks.'

'Let's hope so, Captain Lind! Moving on, do you deny reports that you're carrying nuclear weapons?'

'Nothing to deny. We're carrying FADs – Fragmentation Assistance Devices – that's all. If we hook up to a comet that's an odd shape, we might want to chip a few pieces off before we try to push it back home.'

'Some sources say *Rockhopper*'s mission is to plant those devices on Janus and destroy it. Can you comment?'

'I can comment by saying I find that a ludicrous suggestion. Isn't there something more constructive you'd like to ask me?'

'How do you respond to accusations that much of the technology aboard *Rockhopper* that is now being used for commercial purposes was developed with UEE funding specifically ring-fenced for the purposes of averting Earth-grazing asteroids and comets?'

'I can't comment. I just have a job to do.'

'Thank you, Captain Lind. And now to finish, would you like to issue a personal statement to the people back home? Something that encapsulates the way you feel about this mission, your hopes and fears, as you carry the torch of humanity to a place beyond our wildest imaginations?'

Bella stared into the cam. The moment dragged. The anchordoll kept looking at her with a lopsided smile of hopeful expectation. Somewhere in the aeroponics lab the aerator wheezed moisture into the air.

'No,' Bella said. 'Nothing.' She reached for the cam and was about to tear it from the rack when something like surrender washed over her.

'Okay,' she said, knowing that CNN would morph out her hesitation, making her responses appear seamless. 'I'll say this. This is a hard job we've got to do, no question about it. The entire world is depending on us not to make a mistake. We're embarking on one of the most critical expeditions in the history of space travel – maybe in the history of *travel* – and not one of us has been trained for it. Take my word: my crew are the best in the business. But the business is comet mining. We push ice, and we do it pretty well. Exploration of alien artefacts definitely wasn't in the fine print when any of us signed up for this line of work. But we're going to do our best. When we get to Janus, we're not going to sleep until we've squeezed every last bit of data out of the thing. No matter what happens, we're going to keep sending information home. That's our promise to the world.'

Bella caught her breath before continuing. 'I just want to say a word or two about my people. None of us got orders to go to Janus. We received an official request, one that we were free to disregard. I put it to the vote. Some of us wanted to do it, and some of us didn't. It happened that the majority won the day, but since we took that decision, there hasn't been a second when I haven't thought about the others, the good people of my crew who didn't vote for Janus. These are all people who have families and friends back home. And yet I haven't heard one damned whisper of dissent from any of them. From the moment we lit the engine, they put themselves into this endeavour with absolute, unflinching commitment. It's no more than I expected from my team, but that doesn't mean I'm not proud of them. I couldn't ask for a better crew. And we're coming back in one piece. You can quote me on that.'

'Thank you,' the anchordoll said. 'And now would you mind reading out this brief promotional statement?'

Bella poured a nip of Glenmorangie into Svetlana's glass. They were sitting together in Bella's office, as they often did at the end of a busy or stressful day. Bella had dimmed the lights, allowing the fish some rest. She'd also put on some music, a soothing cello piece that Svetlana didn't recognise. It was nice just to have something washing over them quietly. This was one of the few places on the ship where music didn't have to compete with pumps and generators.

Bella tipped up the bottle, coaxing out the last few drops. 'That's the end of our fun. Until the next rotation, at any rate.'

'You get whisky on the resupply?' Svetlana asked, startled. For some reason, it had never occurred to her to question Bella's source for this rare treat.

'Not officially. If there's a resupply tickbox for single malt, I haven't found it yet.' She laughed. 'But I do have my sources.'

'Like who?'

Bella lowered her voice, as if the two of them were sharing confidences in a playground. 'Cargo-shuttle pilots, mostly. Usually guys with at least twenty years' service under their wings, and most of them started on the Earth–Mars run – like Garrison, of course.'

Svetlana found herself glancing at the picture of Garrison Lind on Bella's desk, even though she had seen it a thousand times. He was a startlingly handsome young man in a bright orange spacesuit, his helmet tucked under one arm, grinning broadly, backdropped by an enlarged emblem of one of the old multinational space agencies.

She looked back at Bella. 'I guess they knew Garrison.'

'Knew him, or knew of him. Ever since, of course . . . well, it's not been a problem for me if I need little favours doing. They could get into trouble if they're ever found out, so I do my best not to abuse their kindness.' She shook the bottle one last time and returned it sadly to its shelf, next to another empty one. 'However, it may be time to abuse it again.'

'I'm sure they love doing something for you.'

'They're good guys.'

'They must have had a lot of respect for Garrison.'

'I guess they did.' Svetlana thought that Bella was about to change the subject, the matter concluded, but then she was off again. 'He was popular with most of the people he worked with. Only had to walk into a room and people just clicked with him. I know there are a lot of people like that, but it wears off pretty quickly. But with Garrison, people never stopped liking him.'

They sat in silence for a long while.

Sometimes when Bella spoke of her husband, Svetlana judged that it was only because it was necessary to mention him at a particular point in a story. At other times, Svetlana was less sure. On more than one occasion she had left the room feeling as if Bella had been guardedly hoping they might continue talking about Garrison, but as strong as their friendship was, Svetlana had always backed off. She had never lost the fear that pursuing the subject might hurt Bella more than she realised.

Yet now, more than at any other time, she sensed that Bella was inviting her to talk about Garrison, to voice the unasked questions that always sat between them.

'How long has it been now?' she ventured, knowing that answer without being told. She could count as well as anyone.

'Twenty-one years,' Bella said with a quick smile. 'I can tell you to the number of hours, if you want. I don't know why, exactly, but I've been thinking about him a lot in the last few days.'

'I suspect Janus might have something to do with it.' Svetlana sniffed the amber liquid in her glass, sampling the peaty aroma.

'I suppose so. Garrison would have *loved* to have been part of this. He'd have killed to have made it aboard if he knew what we were going out to do.'

'He'd already have been proud of you.'

'That's what I keep telling myself – as if I haven't already lived up to enough imaginary expectations.' Bella looked carefully at Svetlana, seeming to wait until a lull in the music before continuing. 'I've never told anyone this, okay?'

Svetlana nodded and said nothing, almost holding her breath in expectation.

'Ten or twelve years ago – maybe longer than that – I went through a bad patch.' Bella paused and lit a cigarette. 'Garrison was always the more ambitious one. He was the one with the big ideas, the big dreams. I never saw myself sitting aboard a ship like *Rockhopper*, with a hundred and fifty people under me. Even Garrison would have considered that somewhat optimistic.'

'Times change,' Svetlana murmured. She didn't want to interrupt the story.

'Not as much as all that.' Bella smoked unhurriedly before continuing, 'After Garrison died, I kept on moving. Mostly it was sheer momentum, not looking back, making all the right career moves. Earth to near-Earth ops. Near-Earth to the Moon – I hated it. I can still feel that dust in my eyes.'

Svetlana smiled. 'Everyone hates the dust.'

'So I skipped to Mars. Then skipped Big Red to deep system. And then this *thing* happened. All of a sudden I crashed and burnt. Couldn't function for shit. They cycled me back to Earth and the tender mercies of the company shrinks – depression, they said. Trying to live up to Garrison's lost potential, they said. Like I was trying to have *his* career since he couldn't.'

'Were they right?'

'I think they were half-right. Another part of me thinks they just couldn't deal with me. Little Bella Lind, daring to have a career in space.' She let out a self-deprecating laugh. 'Okay, so I burnt out, but the men around me were burning out as well. You didn't hear the shrinks telling *them* they were trying to live up to someone else's potential.'

'It's still a man's world out here,' Svetlana said. 'Every now and then something happens to remind me of that. Like I'm on some kind of probation. *We'll let you manage this expensive toy for now, but the moment you slip up—*'

'I know you work twice as hard as anyone else in your team.'

'Not because the work's that difficult,' Svetlana said, though she knew there was no need to explain, 'just because they won't tolerate one single mistake.'

'I know. I know exactly how you feel.'

Svetlana sipped at the whisky, determined to make it last. 'I get a bit defensive sometimes. Before this Janus thing happened, I snapped at Parry.

He was on my case about the repairs taking too long.'

'Probably because *I* was on *his* case,' Bella said.

'We were both to blame, Parry for not *knowing* that I was already doing everything possible to get that work finished, and me for not understanding how much pressure he was under to get that driver tapped.'

'You squared things with him?'

'You know how it is with Parry and me. We're pretty tight. Things like that don't last long.'

'You're a good couple,' Bella said. 'Takes some doing, keeping a relationship together out here. Not many places you can sulk on a ship.'

'I guess if we were going to murder each other, we'd have done it by now.'

'That's a good sign.'

'Parry wants to go home. Says he's soaked up enough sieverts for one lifetime. He's talking about putting in for transfer.'

'I heard,' Bella said quietly. 'He's flagged Mike Takahashi as a possible successor. I suppose he wants you to go with him?'

'That's his plan: move back down to Earth, get married, have a kid or two. Parry says he can find work at one of the training centres. Failing that, he says we should open a dive school, dust off those PADI certifications.'

'Sounds pretty idyllic to me.'

Svetlana sighed. 'The trouble is, I worked damned hard to get out here. I'm the chief of flight systems on a fucking nuclear-powered spaceship, Bella. It doesn't get much better than that.'

'Except when someone's squeezing you about repairs.' She smiled and Svetlana grinned back.

'Okay, so that part sucks. But the rest of it's pretty good.'

Bella stubbed out her cigarette and lit another. Svetlana wondered if the cigarettes came up on the cargo shuttle with the Glenmorangie.

'So what's the plan? Rotate or stay?'

'We keep putting off having a proper discussion about it – or rather, Parry does.'

'Maybe putting it off isn't such a bad idea,' Bella said. 'To a certain degree, we're going to be famous when we get back. Not all of us, but certainly the senior crew . . . you're going to need a damned good agent, put it like that. There'll be book and film deals. Chat shows. Lecture circuits. Game development. A lot of possibilities are going to open up.'

'That's what Parry keeps telling me.'

'I'll be sorry to lose him from the team, if it comes to that, but my loss would be your gain.'

'I could do a lot worse than Parry.'

'You making it work gives me hope for the human species.'

After a moment, Svetlana said, 'You could make it work too, if you wanted to.'

Bella smiled tightly. 'I don't think so.'

'Why not? You've got a good few years ahead of you.'

'Let's not go there, all right?'

Svetlana persisted. 'You still turn heads. I know you've had relationships since Garrison died: we've talked about them often enough. What would we do without *in vino veritas*?'

Bella shrugged philosophically. 'Right now there isn't time in my life for anything but this job. *Especially* now.'

'Okay, fair enough, but what about later, when this is all over? Like you just said: a lot's going to change.'

'I worked hard to get here, Svieta, just like you did. I'm not sure I could give all of this up.'

'You've run this ship for four years without a hitch. If there was ever a point that needed making, I think you can consider it adequately made.'

'Time to move on, you mean?'

'Like Parry says, there are only so many sieverts you can soak up in a lifetime.'

Bella gazed at her fish, dark shapes patrolling the unlit gloom of the tank. 'It'll be good to get back home for a while, that's for sure.'

'But sooner or later you'll want to come back out here.'

'I want to see the things Garrison never got to see. Before it's too late.'

'I understand,' Svetlana said. And she knew that whatever emotional ties still bound Bella to her dead husband, whatever matters of the heart remained as yet unresolved, they were too complex, too fraught, to be unknotted in a single conversation. Even between the closest of friends.

Bella's tone lifted. 'Before I forget – I wanted to thank you. You could have made life a lot more difficult for me with that tech input. Instead you came through and gave it to me straight. I appreciated that.'

'I guess we're all in the same cattle boat.'

'All the same – it *was* appreciated.' Bella leaned over to pat the wall of her office, her hand dimpling the soft display surface. 'And – barring the occasional tremor – she seems to be holding together pretty well, doesn't she?'

'She'll hold,' Svetlana said. 'Lockheed-Krunichev build them good.'

Powell Cagan had attached a media file to his latest message: an image of the rival spacecraft, captured during engine start-up tests by the long-range surveillance cameras of the UEE's Replicating Technologies Inspectorate. The new ship looked recognisably Chinese; some lingering influence in its pale blue-green architecture spoke of dynasties and dragons.

'The unofficial word is that they're calling it the *Shenzhou Five*,' Cagan said. 'It means "Sacred Vessel Number Five", apparently, and that name has some historical significance for them.'

From time to time an irregular stutter of hot white light shone from the flared trumpet of the ship's fusion drive. Chemical rockets, stationed around the hull, counteracted the impulse from the fusion motor. The *Shenzhou Five* was still encased in a cradle of support modules, with a mothlike shuttle docked at the largest habitat block. It looked tiny next to the looming new spacecraft.

'The RTI has demanded inspection rights,' Cagan said. 'They've credible evidence that the Chinese have put a forge vat aboard so that they can grow equipment after the ship's left Earth orbit. Beijing's stonewalling, unsurprisingly. Inga will keep up the squeeze to get those inspectors aboard, but even if she fails, it doesn't look like the Chinese will be going anywhere fast.

'Our analysts say their tokamak design's flawed – they'll be lucky if they get that thing out of orbit, let alone onto a Janus intercept. But in the unlikely event that luck turns out to be on their side – and if our political leverage fails – you'll need to be prepared for a more complicated scenario than we originally envisaged. I'm pressing Inga to rubber-stamp an upgrade to your status: if we can rebrand *Rockhopper* as an official UEE expedition, that will give us a lot more room for manoeuvre.'

'How so?' Bella mouthed soundlessly.

'There's still some fine print to be looked at,' Cagan said, 'but our reading of the situation is that UEE expeditionary status would automatically designate an exclusion volume around *Rockhopper*. If they ignore it, you'll be authorised to use reasonable force to prevent commercial claim-jumping. Of course, *Rockhopper* is not *technically* an armed vessel—' Cagan paused. 'I'll speak to you as soon as I have word from Inga.'

He signed off.

Bella sat staring at the blank flexy in a stunned funk. She had not asked for her ship to be reclassified as an instrument of the UEE, nor had she asked for permission to shoot another ship out of the sky if it violated her company's interests.

*Rockhopper* had been under way for a week now. Around the system, a massive coordinated observation programme saw every large civilian telescope trained on the fleeing moon. Even military spysats had been pressed into service, diverted away from the monitoring of hair-trigger frontiers and treaty-violation hotspots to peer into deep space, in the direction of Virgo. Commercial communications networks had been reassigned to cope with the mammoth effort of merging the data from this awesome concentration of surveillance. From near-Earth out to the cold, dark territory of the outer system, space hummed with intense, fevered scrutiny. Every day took Janus further away; but every day also saw more aperture and processing power coming on line, and for a little while the human effort outweighed the moon's increasing distance.

The images had sharpened, revealing the urban intricacy of the Spican machinery under the now broken and incomplete icy mantle. What they were looking at was definitely alien, but at least it stayed still and allowed them to feel as if it obeyed something like logic. The newest images uploaded to *Rockhopper* came with nomenclature: features in the machinery that had been given tentative, resolutely unofficial names. *Junction Box, Radiator Ridge, Big North Spiral, Little South Spiral, Spike Island, Magic Kingdom, Crankshaft Valley*. None of it meant anything, but it was comforting to put some human labels on the alien territory.

Bella thought she could deal with the alien territory – she had signed up for that when she agreed to take *Rockhopper* out to Janus. But no one had warned her that she might also become embroiled in a hair-trigger standoff with Beijing.

*Not technically armed*, Cagan had said, but both of them knew full well what that really meant.

She looked at the fish tank, idly contemplating the mistake everyone made in assuming she'd used part of her mass allowance to make it happen. That wasn't the case. As she'd explained to Svetlana, everything in the tank was already mass-budgeted into the ship, except for the fish. Even the glass was surplus window material, stored here as opposed to somewhere else aboard *Rockhopper*, glued into a temporary watertight box. If refurbishment ever came calling for the glass, they'd have a fight . . . but it *was* theirs, in the small print.

No, the tank hadn't cost her one gram of her mass budget, but she'd had to pull some serious strings to make it happen. It was a perk. So was the big room with the carpeted floor. No one else on the entire ship had a carpet. No one else had decent soundproofing. This, she supposed, was when she started paying for the perks. She had always known it would happen one day.

That didn't mean she had to like it.

'Sorry to dump on a friend,' Bella said when Svetlana arrived in her office, 'especially when you've just got off-shift, but I need your help with something.'

'What are friends for, if not for dumping on?' Svetlana scrunched a finger through her hair, still wet from the shower. She wore jogging pants and a dive-chick T-shirt printed with a mermaid and moving shoals of animated fish. 'What is it now: someone wants another slice of you?'

Bella shook her head grimly. She had already farmed out several interview requests to her senior officers, including Svetlana, and they'd lapped her up: the bright Armenian-American girl with the mind of a nuclear engineer and the body of a one-time champion free diver, one who just happened to be romantically entangled with a space miner with several commendations for bravery during EVA operations. Now even the diffident Parry was getting his fifteen minutes, squirming like something found under a stone.

Too good to be true, they said.

Bella pulled a thick stack of printouts from her desk. 'This is a bit different, I'm afraid. It's delicate – very, very delicate. It can only be entrusted to a safe pair of hands.'

'Suddenly this is beginning to feel like a *major* dump.'

'They don't get much more major.' Bella passed the stack to Svetlana. 'What you've got there are copies of one hundred paintings, selected from over fifty-six thousand individual entries submitted by American school kids between first and third grades. Artistic media range from finger smears to . . . well, something approximating brushwork.'

Svetlana slipped off the rubber band and leafed through the first few sheets. 'Aliens,' she said, in a numbed tone of voice. 'They've got the kids painting aliens.'

'It's educational,' Bella said.

'It's scary.' Svetlana held up one of the pictures: something that resembled the business end of a blue toilet brush, smeared with enthusiastic daubs of green. 'Aren't we supposed to be stopping the kids getting nightmares, not encouraging them?'

'That's for the education system to decide, not us. Our job is to grade the efforts, that's all.'

'Oh, right. So: five minutes' work, right? We just pull a few out at random—'

Bella grimaced. 'There's a bit more to it than that, I'm afraid. They'd like us to comment on the pictures – say something nice and constructive about them. All of them – even the more – *ahem!* – artistically challenged ones.'

'*All* of them?'

Bella nodded sternly. 'All of them. In enough detail that no one's going to get offended . . . no one's going to think we're not approaching this with due diligence.'

'Holy shit, Bella.'

'And we'll be steering clear of expletives, obviously.'

'We.'

'Oh, I've got my own stack of homework to grade, don't you worry. You drew the long straw on this one. I'm the one who'll be up all night reading creative assignments about me and my ship meeting aliens.'

Svetlana slipped the rubber band back around the printouts. 'This can't get any worse, can it? I mean, as if we didn't have enough to be doing as it is.'

'This is nothing. Yesterday I had the *Cosmic Avenger* fan club on my back. They wanted me to comment on which of my crew members best approximated the various fictional characters . . . and how I'd have dealt with scenarios from the show, if they happened to me.'

'I hope you told them where they could shove it.'

Bella feigned horror. 'Oh, no. I just put Saul Regis on the case. Man for the job.'

'Man for the job,' Svetlana agreed, nodding. 'Well, I guess that made him happy.'

'As a pig in shit.'

'Talking of which, I do hope you've lined up something nice and juicy for Craig Schrope. There's a man with way too much time on his hands.'

Bella leaned back in her seat, sensing an opportunity to get something out in the open that had been troubling her lately. 'You and Craig . . . it's not exactly an eye-to-eye thing, is it?'

'We've been over this.'

'I know, I know – he's a suit, you're a hands-on type. But we need suits as well as tool-pushers. Craig's a damn good asset to this company. As bitter a pill as this might be to swallow, he's actually quite good at his job.'

'We're off the record now, aren't we?'

'Absolutely.'

'He rubs me up the wrong way. He's always giving me shitty looks, especially if I venture even so much as an opinion in his presence – as if I wasn't head of flight systems, but some lower-echelon grunt with only a few hours of wet time under my belt.'

'Craig gives everyone shitty looks. I think it's genetic.' Bella paused, wondering how much it was wise to disclose. 'Look, I'll let you in on a secret. He's not had an easy ride out here. DeepShaft tried to keep a lid on it for obvious reasons, but his last assignment on Mars—'

Svetlana looked mildly interested. 'Go on.'

'Head office sent Craig into the Shalbatana bore project. There'd been reports of corner-cutting, dangerous working practices, questionable accounting.' Bella lit a cigarette, taking her time. She always enjoyed spinning out a story. 'Craig uncovered a viper's nest of high-level corruption. At every turn he met with obstruction and hostility, mostly from hands-on types like you and me. Physical violence, death threats, the lot – but Craig sorted that mess out. He turned Shalbatana around. Within six months they were digging faster than any of the other bore sites, *and* they had the best safety record on Big Red.'

'I heard he made a lot of enemies on Mars.'

'Enough that head office decided the only way to keep him on the payroll – and in one piece – was to move him onto another project. Hence *Rockhopper*. But don't give Craig a hard time because he has a grudge against tool-pushers. Good ol' tool-pushers sabotaged his suit, tried to throw him down a service elevator, threatened to get to his family.'

Svetlana looked down. 'I didn't know he had a family.'

'There's a lot we don't know about each other,' Bella said. 'And he's wrong about us, of course – this is as tight and well-run an operation as any in

DeepShaft. But you can't blame him for carrying some suspicion over from his last assignment. It'll just take a bit of time to rub his corners off. Then he'll fit in, I'm sure of it.'

'Okay, I'll try to be patient,' Svetlana said. 'But I still want to see him getting *his* share of homework.'

'Don't worry, that's taken care of. He's got a list of high-school science questions as long as my arm.'

Svetlana patted the stack of printouts on her lap. 'I'm glad we can talk like this . . . I mean openly, without any barriers.'

'And I'm glad I can dump on you, when needs arise.' Bella sucked on the cigarette. 'Like you said: what else are friends for?'

On the eighth day Bella called an emergency meeting of the chiefs. She gathered them in her office and sat impassive, wondering what *they* imagined the problem to be and secretly relishing their squirming discomfort.

'What is it?' Svetlana asked, the first of them to break the silence.

Bella stood up and peeled her flexy from the wall. It came to life in her hands. She held up the brightening panel to her audience.

'This,' she said.

'There's a problem with ShipNet?' Nick Thale asked, looking – like all of them – at the top-level menu.

'There's nothing wrong with ShipNet,' Bella said. 'That's functioning normally. The problem's more obvious than that. It's staring you in the face.'

They looked, and looked. They still couldn't see what she was talking about.

'Do you think the menu structure needs to be reorganised to take account of our new mission profile?' Regis asked.

'Perhaps, but that's not why you're here. *Look.*'

'The flexy needs regenerating?' Parry offered.

'Yes, it does, but that isn't the problem either.' Bella sighed: they weren't going to get it. 'The problem is the mascot. The problem is the penguin.'

'I don't—' Svetlana began. 'Oh, wait a minute. You don't think— Oh, Christ. Why didn't we think of this before?'

Parry looked at Svetlana. 'I still don't get it. What's the problem?'

'You really don't see it?' Bella asked incredulously. 'Don't you see what that mascot actually looks like?'

'It looks like a penguin to me.'

'And what's the nice penguin doing, Parry?'

'It's holding a drill . . . a jackhammer . . . Oh, hang on.'

'Look at it through alien eyes,' Bella said. 'The way that penguin's grinning: don't you think it looks just a tiny bit fierce? It even has *teeth.* Whose funny idea was it to put teeth on it, anyway? And that drill: don't you think there's a danger it might be mistaken for some kind of—'

'Weapon,' Svetlana breathed.

'Holy shit,' Parry said, and started laughing.

'They might think we look like that,' Bella said. 'They might think we're the penguin.'

'And that we're armed,' Svetlana said.

'With flippers?' Parry asked.

'What about the flippers?' Bella returned.

'Don't you think they'll find it rather odd that we've managed to build and fly a spaceship with just flippers? I mean, that would take some doing, wouldn't it?'

'Maybe they'll assume we bio-engineered ourselves to have flippers once we'd achieved a sufficiently advanced technological support society,' Saul Regis said. 'You *could* go back to flippers if you had robots to take care of you. In *Cosmic Avenger*, season two—'

'The issue is not the flippers,' Bella said firmly. 'The issue is the fact that our mascot might give cause for concern to our friends from Spica. It might just make them decide to shoot us out of the sky.'

'Fine,' Nick Thale said, 'so remove the mascot from ShipNet. That can't be difficult, can it? It isn't even as if we'd be giving them access to ShipNet anyway.'

'ShipNet isn't the difficulty,' Bella said patiently. 'The difficulty is the twenty-metre-tall penguin painted on the side of this ship. The difficulty is that someone has to go outside and paint it out.'

'Under thrust?' Svetlana asked incredulously.

'Under thrust,' Bella said. 'And while they're out there, whoever it is can take out some blue paint and slap a large "UEE" where the penguin used to be. As of today, we have official blessing from the United Economic Entities. Everyone on this ship has just been assigned temporary diplomatic status.' She offered them a confiding smile. 'It's time to start taking this seriously, people.'

Parry was in the EVA preparations room, flanked by racks of bright-orange Orlan nineteen hardsuits. He fixed the cam against the wall, then stepped back into its field of view, adjusting his usual red cap. They had asked him to wear a DeepShaft bib cap, but he had to draw a line somewhere.

'You'll get into trouble,' Svetlana warned, sitting cross-legged on a storage pallet. 'Even I had to put the damned uniform on. Took me a day to find it, but I still had to put it on.'

'They can sue me afterwards. There are a ton of DeepShaft logos in the background. Isn't that good enough for them?'

'I doubt it.'

Parry warmed the flexy and started up the anchordoll. 'Okay,' he said, addressing the flexy, 'you can do your thing.'

'Hi,' said the helium-voiced anchordoll. 'You're watching CNN. I'm talking to Parry Boyce, thirty-seven, head of cometary surface operations aboard *Rockhopper* and lucky partner of hot new science pin-up Svetlana Barseghian. How are you feeling, Parry?'

'Okay.'

'That's good to hear. No nerves, no second thoughts?'

'Nope.'

'That's great.' The anchordoll beamed her approval. 'Parry: when you reach Janus, you'll be in charge of any activities that involve humans working in the vicinity of Janus – right?'

'Right.'

'Could you tell us a little more about how that'll happen? I mean, how will you actually get out there?'

'We'll EVA.'

'EVA.' The doll looked thoughtful. 'And for the people at home that means . . .'

'Extra-vehicular activity.'

'That's great. And what does that entail, exactly?'

Parry shrugged. 'Activities . . . outside the vehicle.'

'The vehicle being?'

'*Rockhopper*.'

'That's great. And these activities . . . what would they be, exactly?'

'Janus operations.'

'Meaning activities taking place in the vicinity of Janus, right?'

'That's about it.'

'That's great! And when you talk about activities taking place in the vicinity of Janus—' The anchordoll paused, distracted by Svetlana's sniggering. Parry looked at her.

'What?'

She was creased up on the storage pallet. 'You're a natural, Parry. It's the way you open up . . . the way you give so much of yourself. They're going to love you.'

He reached up and tore the cam from its gobbet of geckoflex. 'If I have to do one more of these, I'll strangle someone. Starting with you.'

Svetlana put on her best innocent look. 'Me? What have I done?'

'You know full well. It's you they're interested in, not me.'

'I can't help that.'

'Well, you could try being a bit less . . . well, clever and attractive, for a start.'

'I'm glad you put them in that order. I'd hate to get the idea that my physical attributes have precedence over my intellectual ones,' Svetlana pouted, drawing her knees up to her chin. She was wearing skin-tight zebraprint skiing pants and a low-cut sleeveless turquoise vest, a combination Parry had always found particularly alluring. 'Or is it because you think my physical attributes are somehow less impressive?'

'Did I say that?'

'Not as such. You could, however, have been taken to imply it.'

'You still look pretty hot to me, Barseghian.'

'Ah, shucks: you're just saying that.'

'No, I'm not.'

She eyed him coquettishly. 'Prove it, then.'

'Here and now? I think there's an EVA party due through in about ten minutes.'

'Oh, right. The dreaded killer penguin.' She sniggered. 'Well, we wouldn't want to take their minds off that vital mission, would we?'

'No, we wouldn't.' He leered suggestively.

'Which only leaves one question: my place or yours?'

'Yours,' he said, after a moment. 'That extra fifty cubic centimetres makes all the difference.'

There was never much privacy on a ship, but Svetlana and Parry made the best of what they had. Her room was little more than a horizontal slot, probably modelled on the most austere and claustrophobic brand of Tokyo capsule hotel. There were one hundred and fifty similar slots, ringed in three tiers around the lower part of the hab, each containing just enough room to sleep, store a few personal effects and, now and then, snatch a few moments of precious seclusion. Svetlana had to climb a ladder to reach her slot, then twist sideways through the gap before sliding shut the long plastic door. It was a squeeze with just one person, and a kind of three-dimensional puzzle with two. But Svetlana and Parry put up with that, and with some ingenuity they had mapped out a range of positions that could just be accommodated without either of them suffering too many bruises.

Making love was the only time when Svetlana welcomed the ship's constant background noise, even though she could never quite disconnect her attention from the rhythms and cadences of that mechanical music. Parry sensed and tolerated her slight absences, while reminding her that it didn't always have to be this way. He meant the two of them returning home, to that sparkling sunlit dream of the dive school.

Parry was a diver at heart. He'd come into space because it was work. He shrugged off the differences between water and vacuum as if they were two mildly different states of the same hostile environment, but Svetlana knew where his heart was. She sometimes missed her diving days, but it didn't gnaw at her like a disease, unlike Parry: dive culture was still thick in his blood. There were two kinds of people in his world: *buddies* and *non-buddies* – people you could trust and people you left on the shore. EVA was wet-time. He talked about Braille dives and incident pits as if they were all still back at sea.

She loved him, but she loved space as well. Now she worried about space getting in the way.

He lay against her now, blissfully calm, only just awake. After they had made love, Svetlana had fallen asleep as well, but now she was prickly and alert, trying not to think about their future. She had glued her flexy to the wall and navigated ShipNet to the news feeds, hoping to blank her concerns. CNN was running Bella's interview on heavy rotation.

Parry watched it over her shoulder.

'I couldn't ask for a better crew,' Bella was saying. 'And we're coming back in one piece. You can quote me on that.' Then the image morphed into Bella saying, 'We push ice. It's what we do.'

'Got to hand it to the little lady,' Parry said, his unshaven chin bristling her neck, 'she sounds like she means it.'

'She does.'

'They're going for it, too. Her picture's everywhere. You'd think she put this ship together with a spanner.'

'She deserves some credit,' Svetlana said, and then regretted the defensive way it had come out.

'She gets all the credit she needs from me, babe.'

'I know.' It was true, too. Some of the men had issues with female authority, but Parry wasn't one of them. 'It's just that I know some people are going to resent her for this, and I can't stand that. They have *no fucking idea* what she's been through to get this far.'

CNN were running a biodoc on Bella, scraped together from video clips taken at various points during her career. Now the flexy showed a young Bella suiting into an ancient, dust-smeared Orlan, somewhere on the Moon. Every now and then they'd break away from the story to cut back to Bella saying, '*We push ice. It's what we do.*'

The words began to drill into Svetlana's skull.

'I think they're beginning to get an idea,' Parry said. 'Good for Bella. High time she got some exposure.'

'Maybe it'll change things for her.'

'Things need changing?'

Svetlana turned down the flexy. 'We had one of our heavy discussions the other night.'

'Nothing you need to tell me about if you don't want to.'

'It's all right. It's not as if Bella expects there to be any secrets between you and me. We talk about you often enough.'

'Only the good stuff, I hope.'

'With you, Boyce, there *is* only good stuff. All we do is sing your praises. Your ears must burn.'

'They do, but that's just the millisieverts kicking in.'

'Ha.' She hated it when he joked about that kind of thing. 'Anyway, we were talking about life stuff, and we got around to Garrison.'

'Not the first time.'

'The first time she really seemed to want to open up about it. Although even then she clammed up pretty quickly as soon as we got serious. It's as if she wants to talk about it a bit, but not too much.'

'So it's still painful for her.'

'It's been twenty-one years, Parry. You've got to get over stuff eventually.'

'Maybe we shouldn't judge. Neither of us has lost a partner the way she did.'

'Okay – but I've known people who have lost loved ones, and they've found a way through it eventually.'

'People are different.'

'I know, but for Bella it's as if she can't move on. She as good as admitted she's having her career for Garrison.' Svetlana rolled over on the bed to face Parry. 'What I keep thinking is it must have something to do with the way he died.'

'No warning, you mean?'

'It can't be the same as losing someone to an illness. They never had a chance to say goodbye to each other. They weren't even together before he set off on that flight. Bella was back on Earth at the time, waiting for Garrison to get a rotation home. Even if they'd had a conversation before he went out, it must have been over the Earth–Mars network. Serious timelag, not exactly conducive to intimacy. And neither of them knew what was about to happen.'

'Unfinished business, you mean?'

'I keep thinking about that tiff we had the other day, Parry – when you were on my case about the repairs, and I bit your head off about it.'

He stroked a finger against her breast. 'I think we kissed and made up about that one.'

'I know – but what if we hadn't ever had that chance? We both went outside the ship after the row. You went down to the comet, I went on EVA to nurse the robots. Anything could have happened to either of us.'

'But it didn't.'

'What if it had? We don't get paid a lot of money because the company likes us. We get paid because it's dangerous out here. I tell you, I'm never stepping into an airlock after a row. Not again. We make up and *then* we go outside.'

He looked at her, marvelling. 'That conversation really got to you, didn't it?'

'I don't want to lose you. I don't want you to lose me. I don't want either of us to go through whatever Bella's been dealing with for the last twenty-one years.'

'Maybe Janus will change things, then. Let her move on. It's going to be a landmark in all our lives.'

'That's what Bella says,' Svetlana said, remembering how they had talked about Parry's desire to go home. Wait until Janus, then think things over.

Wait until Janus.

'I love you, Barseghian,' Parry said, pulling her into a tighter embrace, 'but I wish you'd stop worrying.'

Flexies had been plastered to the wall, their edges staggered like bricks to form a ragged array that showed an object that could only be artificial: fuzzy, glimpsed at the resolution limit of the massive interferometric telescope, but unmistakably a made thing. It was a pipe: round in cross section, ten times as long as it was wide, formed from some kind of lacy framework. It resembled the flutelike skeleton of a tiny, dead marine creature.

'We don't know what it is yet,' Bella said to the small group of people who had assembled in the gymnasium. 'All we know is that we'd have seen it years ago if anyone had thought Spica worthy of a closer look. What we'd have made of it if we'd found it before now is another thing entirely.'

The image being displayed had arrived on the uplink just thirty minutes earlier; it was still embargoed from the media networks, so the news hadn't made it on to the general-access ShipNet channels. Bella had not insisted that everyone attend the meeting; though this was connected to Janus, it wasn't of specific importance for their mission, and she had no wish to increase the burden on an already overworked crew. All the same, most of Saul's working party had taken up her invitation, as had a handful of interested stragglers from other departments.

'You mean this thing was just sitting there all this time?' Parry asked. 'Just waiting for us to notice it?'

Bella smiled. 'It wasn't *that* simple. It took a massive coordinated effort to obtain this image. It's the kind of observation that's made about once a year, when some exosolar planetary alignment is particularly favourable and someone thinks there's a chance of imaging an icecap or a continent. A month ago, if you'd have suggested Spica as the target, you'd have been laughed out of the room.'

'How . . . how big?' asked Regis, hesitantly, as if the question were a kind of heresy that could only be voiced in the most trusted company.

'Big,' Bella said. 'Really, really big. The structure appears to be floating somewhere close to the Lagrange point between the two stars, where their gravity fields cancel each other out. If that's the case then the object is truly enormous: seventeen or eighteen light-seconds wide, and nearly three light-minutes long. If you placed the Earth at one end of that tube, the other end would reach to the orbit of Venus.'

'Agreed on big,' Regis said.

'You'll notice that the long axis of the tube isn't aligned with the vector joining the stars' centres of gravity. Even if that were the case, there'd still be unthinkable tidal stresses working to stretch the tube, but with the tube tilted like that, the two stars are trying to snap it like a dry twig. And yet there isn't a hint of deflection: to the limit of our observational abilities, it appears completely oblivious to the gravitational gradient across it. It's absurdly rigid. It can't possibly be made of any material exploiting ordinary inter-atomic forces.'

'One more question,' Svetlana said, raising her hand, 'and possibly a stupid one: what *is* it?'

'We don't know. We'll probably never know, unless something at Janus gives us a clue. But we can guess. Spica is where Janus is headed. It must be the place it calls home. This is where they live.'

Svetlana looked scornful. 'In that thing? In a piece of scaffolding?'

'Just consider one of those longitudinal spars,' Bella said. 'If we're right about the scale of the object, then the spars are half a light-second thick. Now imagine that those spars are hollow cylinders, with habitable living space on the inner surface. Just one of the spars would have an internal surface area equivalent to fifty thousand Earths. And there are twenty of them. That's a million Earths' worth of living space – and that's if they don't utilise the cross-struts. If they do, you can easily double that figure.' Bella smiled at Svetlana. 'Is that enough room for you, or do you need more?'

Bella had hoped for laughter, but something about the looming Spican structure had touched them all on some disagreeable level. Janus was one thing: it was clearly the product of a culture far in advance of human capabilities. It spoke of a technological gulf that was centuries, even thousands of years wide. But the Spican structure crushed those easy assumptions. This was not the result of a gap that could be measured in the cosy units of historical time.

This was a geological gap, and it required appropriately geological thinking. It spoke of millions of years of disparity.

At the very least.

# CHAPTER 4

The bad thing happened on day eleven. Svetlana was riding a car up the spine from the engine to the hab. She had already passed through the machine shop: it was about a hundred vertical metres beneath her, falling further behind each second as the car climbed higher. She was somewhere else: not exactly daydreaming, because her mind was still on her job, but not remotely focused on her immediate surroundings. A flicker of movement in the corner of her eye was the first hint of wrongness. A brief surge in her own weight was the second.

A moment later she let out an involuntary gasp.

High above, not far from where the spine plunged into the underside of the hab, one of the remaining mass drivers had come loose. It hung at an odd angle to the spine, no longer properly coupled. Horrified, Svetlana saw that it was attached by only a single bracket, and that bracket was buckling like toffee, yawning away from the trusswork of the spine. The mass driver was about to break away completely.

A single thought screamed through her skull: *shut down the engine!* At worst, the mass driver would detach itself and drift slowly away from the spine. They could send out tugs and haul it back, or abandon it to deep space. She had about a second to process those thoughts before she knew there wasn't enough time.

The mass driver fell.

It was a big object, built to bulldoze comets. At half a gee it fell ponderously at first, gaining speed with a certain reluctance. But it fell dead straight and parallel to the spine, as if in some deft illustration of Newtonian law, accelerating all the while until it hit the mass driver suspended below it on the next coupling down.

Three hundred metres above her head, the second mass driver sheered off instantly, its vast mass careening into the spine. Svetlana felt the appalling impact, saw the spine flex unnaturally at the impact point. The car jolted from its guidance rail and ran rough until it came to a juddering halt, only partially attached to the line. Above, the two mass drivers fell in unison, the lower one scraping against the spine as it fell, spitting shards of broken metalwork. There were no further mass drivers beneath the falling pair, at least above Svetlana. She dared to look down and she saw the bulge in the spine that the falling machines were about to slam into: the machine shop.

The two falling mass drivers slid by her stalled car, the wake of their passage slamming her into the seat restraints with bruising force. She felt something crack in her chest, but the car stayed intact and retained its tenuous grasp on the line.

Then the drivers hit the machine shop, and the force of that impact shuddered through her. When she could bring herself to look down again she saw a glittering debris cloud already spuming from the ruins of the shop, sliced clean through on this side of the spine. Yellow robots tumbled out like tiny dried-up spiders. Through the cloud she could just make out the two falling drivers, both tumbling now, but both still intact. The impact with the shop had nudged them away from the spine.

But they were still going to hit the engine.

The crash came quickly: almost as soon as she had registered its inevitability. As the two mass drivers interrupted the ship's smooth acceleration, it juddered in a way it hadn't when they ghosted through the thin fabric of the machine shop. She narrowed her eyes, anticipating the explosion from an uncontained fusion reaction: the explosion that would almost certainly swallow the entire ship up to this part of the spine, in an eyeblink of numbing whiteness.

But the ship was still working. The ride felt smooth, normal. A fusion reaction was a delicate, temperamental thing: it either happened or it didn't. Against all the odds, the engine must have escaped serious damage.

They'd survived.

That was when the adrenalin rush hit her. Her hands were trembling as she reached for the car's communication switch. It hurt to breathe. She flicked the toggle, heard the snap, crackle and pop of cosmic rays.

'This is Svetlana,' she said, hoping someone could hear her. 'We've got a situation here.'

With delicate taps of thrust, Parry brought his suit to a halt above the cathedral-like vastness of the fuel tanks.

Evidence of cautious but urgent human and machine activity was all around him. Suited figures floated around the floodlit engine assembly and moved across it: the plodding, deliberate movement of people using geckoflex pads on their soles and palms. Most of the workers weren't wearing propulsion packs, but no one was tethered. Years of experience had proved that safety lines were more trouble than they were worth. They got in the way, tangling around obstructions and other tethers. Sometimes they themselves were responsible for bizarre, grisly accidents. A swiftly moving tether was a thing of horror.

Parry studied the damage, comparing it against the reports he had read. Things could certainly have been worse. Most of the wreckage the workers were clearing away had come from the machine shop; comparatively little of it had originated from the engine or fuel tanks. In the bright foci where the floodlights were trained, people and machines tugged at debris with exquisite caution, mindful of coolant or fuel lines that might have been pierced just beneath the surface. All the workers had three-dimensional blueprints projected onto their faceplates, but it paid not to put too much faith in them.

'Someone's going to pay for this,' Bella said over the ship-to-suit channel. 'We've tracked down the screw-up to a single incorrect digit in a stress-loading spreadsheet.'

Parry whistled. 'Must be some digit.'

'Someone back home thought we were hauling type-seven mass drivers, whereas we're actually carrying type eights, which happen to weigh quite a bit more.'

Parry tapped the controls and lowered himself towards the fuel tanks. They were arranged like four cylindrical skyscrapers around a narrow central plaza, with the spine of the ship passing between them. The tanks' foundations were mounted on a huge dish-shaped shield assembly which screened most of the radiation from the Lockheed-Krunichev fusion engine; it also served as the anchoring point for the spine.



'Is this a show-stopper?' Parry asked.

'Bob Ungless says we can reinforce the existing driver attachments without too much trouble. We'll have to run at reduced thrust until it's done, but it shouldn't kill us.'

'I take it Svieta isn't up and about yet?'

'I've just spoken to Ryan. She's going to be pretty bruised and battered for a few days.'

'Is she awake?'

'Oh yes. Just try tearing that flexy out of her hands.'

'I might need to speak to her.'

'You've found something outside?'

Parry made an equivocal sound. 'Probably nothing, but I don't think anyone's taken a good look between the tanks yet.' He brought the pack to a halt, disengaged from it and used geckoflex to station himself on the inner wall of the tank.

'We're not expecting damage there,' Bella said.

Parry started descending. 'All the same, we've got a dead cam down there. It happens to be the one that looks up from the shield between the tanks. I'm wondering if something clobbered it.'

There was a crackle of static. 'Okay. Advise you send in a small robot.'

'There aren't any. I'm making my way down on foot.'

'Say again?'

'We lost all the small robots, Bella.' Parry caught his breath, out of practice with flexwalking. 'They were all in the machine shop, so the drivers took them out.'

'It never rains, does it?'

'This is beginning to feel uncomfortably like an incident pit,' Parry muttered.

'Incident pit? Now there's a phrase I haven't heard in a long time.' As Bella well knew, incident pits were underwater situations that turned bad in little increments. Each small step – almost inconsequential in themselves – took one ever deeper into a pit with ever-steepening sides. Near the top, there was still time to reverse the situation and get out. Deeper in, options thinned out fast.

'You know what they say about shit coming in threes, too,' Parry said.

'Something else the guys used to say,' Bella answered, 'anything even *smelled* like this, we'd call it a serious Charlie Foxtrot.'

'Charlie Foxtrot?'

'Clusterfuck, dear boy: CF stands for clusterfuck.'

'I see,' Parry said. He laughed, grimly. 'I suppose you could arrange a clusterfuck in an incident pit, too, if you tried hard enough.'

'I suppose so,' Bella said. She shuddered involuntarily.

'That's something you'd want to keep the hell away from.'

His torch beam glanced against faint, vague shapes some twenty metres below. Parry called up his helmet overlay, superimposing the wire-frame blueprint over his view. The thin red vector lines matched perfectly against the real-time view, highlighting the tanks and the spinal truss. The shield contained a scrawl of complex arterial machinery, delineated in green and blue, difficult to relate to the shapes picked out by the torch.

He pushed himself closer, grunting with each metre of hard-won progress. The tank side was smooth above the scratch in the cladding where the debris had hit: he decided he'd risk drifting his way back to the top, rather than repeating the crawl. Then he would make a point of putting in more time in the gym, rehearsing for exactly this kind of job.

'How's the viz?' Bella asked.

'Not great – it's a Braille dive down here.' Parry tried various combinations of torch, helmet beam and visor filter until he found an uneasy optimum. 'There is *something* down here, though. Actually, lots of somethings.'

'Talk to me, buddy.'

Parry crawled lower, then panned the beam around, whistling at what he found. 'No wonder the cam was dead: there must be about ten tonnes of crap gathered down here, trapped between the tanks.'

'What kind of crap?'

'Highly compacted crap.' Closer now, he was able to identify some of the rubble. Bent, jagged-edged corrugated plates had come from the outer skin of the machine shop. Chunks of red metal had probably broken away from one or both of the mass drivers. Mangled bright-yellow parts were all that remained of several robots, jumbled together like crabs in a bucket. 'It's an unholy mess,' Parry said. 'Are you seeing any of this?'

'I'm getting a very fuzzy feed from your cam,' Bella said, 'enough to see that it isn't good news.'

'Someone's going to have to clear this up.'

'Easier said than done. But you're right – we can't risk any of it shifting and damaging the tanks.'

Parry looked around the bombsite, visualising the clean-up: all of it would have to be carried out by suited workers rather than robots. At least if they worked under weightless conditions they wouldn't have to lift any of the debris free. Once the pieces had been dislodged from the compacted pile, they could be allowed to drift beyond the tanks. Afterwards, when the area had been cleared, they could reinforce any damage to the tanks with sprayrock.

Sprayrock, he thought: now *that* was going to be fun.

'You still there?' Bella asked.

'Yeah. Just wondering why I ever thought space operations would be an astute career move.'

'We all have those days.'

'With me it's fast becoming one of those decades.'

Parry swept the area one more time, making sure his helmet cam obtained good coverage. Then he looked up to where the four tanks framed open space, the hab poised far above, impossibly distant and small, like a child's balloon bobbing on the end of a string. He judged his angle and kicked off.

Svetlana sat on the side of the bed and nervously watched the clearance work. Although drugged to the eyeballs, she retained enough focus to feel genuine anxiety about her beautiful, deadly engine.

'It looks bad,' Parry said, rubbing his forearm; he felt as if he'd pulled a muscle. 'But there's nothing down there they won't be able to clear, given time.'

'I don't want cutting gear near those tanks,' Svetlana said.

'We thought of that. They've taken down powered tools, but nothing that you need worry about. It's just a question of freeing the pieces.'

The workers had formed an efficient clear-up chain. Five of them were down at the base of the tanks, using hammer-drills to break up the compacted mass into manageable chunks. Once loose, they nudged the chunks back towards the open end of the tank assembly. Five more workers were poised on geckoflex halfway up the inner wall, ready to shove the debris back on course if it looked as if it would scrape against the tanks or the spine. Another five waited at the top, three on geckoflex and two hovering in propulsion packs. They caught the arriving chunks and made a quick assessment of their value. The booty they tossed into a sticky web of epoxy-coated fibres; the junk they threw overboard, obeying the old and largely pointless tradition of flinging stuff away from the ecliptic plane.

'The pile's visibly smaller,' Parry said.

Svetlana watched on the cam as the workers at the base attacked a piece of debris. 'Tell them to take care.'

'Just because they're fast doesn't mean they're not good. These are the same people I'd trust with the trickiest jobs on a comet.'

Svetlana forced herself to nod. She could never quite overcome a lingering prejudice against the comet miners. They were too brave, too courageous. Svetlana thought that the only kind of person you wanted anywhere near *any* part of a fusion motor was someone with a strong aversion to risk.

Cowards were exactly the kind of people you wanted around nuclear technology.

'I'm just saying they need to be careful,' she said. 'If there's a leak—'

'Nothing we saw down there suggested a leak. Do me a favour and stop worrying. You need to rest.'

'I've broken ribs before now. They mend.'

'Is there anything I can do for you?'

'Yes,' she said sweetly. 'You can bring me a flexy, please.'

Parry grimaced. 'You're supposed to be relaxing, babe, not working.'

'To me relaxing *is* working. Just do it, okay?'

Parry gave in and returned a minute later with a flexy. 'The little lady won't be thrilled about this,' he said.

'I'll square things with Bella. You just worry about your people.'

Svetlana held the flexy before her face, allowing the device to identify her via a combination of fingerprint analysis, hand movement, breath chemistry, voice, face and retinal recognition.

'Anything in particular you're interested in?' Parry asked.

'Leakage,' she said.

'That doesn't tell me much.'

'If the fuel tanks really were punctured, and if there was a leak into space, it should show up in the pressure readings.'

'Even a tiny leak?'

'There's a limit, obviously – the pressure gauges won't be able to detect a few atoms dribbling into space every second. But it's foolish not to check.'

'Do you think I should tell my people to stop working until you've looked at this?'

'No,' she said, after a moment's reflection. 'It's probably nothing. Just as long as they're careful.'

She navigated to the area of ShipNet concerned with the basic technical functions of the engine. A few more taps of her finger brought up four graphics boxes, each of which contained a plot of pressure versus time for the fuel in each of the tanks, with the time axis along the bottom of each box. She zoomed in on the part of the plot that covered the last twenty-four hours.

'When exactly did the accident happen?'

Parry leaned over and stabbed a finger against the time axis. 'Six hours ago. Round about here.'

She zoomed in on the two hours spanning the accident. 'See that line, Parry?'

'Uh huh.'

'Looks pretty flat to me.'

Parry squinted at it. 'As piss on a plate. Is that a problem?'

'We shut down the engine within ten minutes of the accident,' Svetlana said, thinking aloud. 'Fuel consumption should have flattened out to zero between then and now.'

'Agreed. But you'd have a hard time seeing that kind of change in slope until a *lot* more time has passed.'

'I know. I was just wondering if there'd be any sign of the event in the pressure data.'

'If there's a leak, it's a hell of a slow one,' Parry said.

'Or no leak at all.'

He moved to take the flexy away from her. 'And that's good, isn't it?'

'I suppose so,' Svetlana said. But she held onto the flexy tenaciously. 'I still want to look at these numbers a little more closely.'

'If it keeps you from climbing out of bed,' Parry said. He rubbed his hands against the pockets of his trousers. 'Well, no rest for the wicked.'

'I thought you were done for the day.'

'I just came inside to take a break. Suit needed topping up anyway.'

'You've already been outside too long,' she said. 'Here – let me see that dosimeter.'

He snapped the bracelet from his wrist and passed it to her. She studied the coloured display, with its ominous red-tinged histogram.

'Six hundred and twenty millisieverts, Parry. You keep this up and we'll be able to light the ship with you.' She passed back the dosimeter, her fingers tingling as if the thing itself were a source of radiation. 'Parry, please take some rest.'

'I'll take some rest when you do,' he said, reaching to drag the flexy away from her again. 'How does that sound?'

She tightened her hold on the flexy. 'A lot like blackmail.'

'I'll be back inside in six hours,' Parry said. He kissed her and walked away. She stared at his back as he left the medical area, watching as he paused to talk to one of Ryan Axford's three duty medics. She pushed her head back against the pillow, closed her eyes and allowed the flexy to slip from her hand. She lay like that until the light through her eyelids became darker, as if the sick bay lights had been dimmed.

She waited five minutes, then opened her eyes again.

# CHAPTER 5

Bella visited the sick. She stopped by Jim Chisholm's bed, intending to talk to him about the accident, but found him asleep with headphones on. She moved on to the next partition, where Svetlana was just finishing off a foil-wrapped dinner spread out on a tray.

'On the mend?'

'Miles better,' Svetlana said unconvincingly. In Bella's opinion she looked like someone who had been up all night cramming for an exam.

'I thought you'd like to know that the clean-up work's coming along nicely. We should be under way within six or seven hours.'

'Parry told me they were going to reinforce the tanks.'

'Not a bad idea while we've got people down there – right?'

'Provided we can spare the time.'

Thomas Shen, the duty medic, removed the tray from Svetlana's lap. Beneath it, Bella noticed, was a flexy, its display window crammed with technical diagrams and graphs. Svetlana had scribbled comments and calculations all over the figures.

'Spare the time?' Bella echoed.

'Won't this delay make our rendezvous with Janus even more tricky?'

'Shorter, maybe, but we'd have heard from home if the mission was no longer feasible.'

'If you say so.'

'Something bothering you, Svieta?'

She looked at Bella suspiciously. 'Why? Why do you think something might be bothering me?'

'Browsing through those graphs for fun, were you?' Bella quickly snatched the flexy from Svetlana's lap and held it up to the light, studying the complex read-outs and scribbled annotations. 'These are pressure readings,' she observed.

'I figured there might've been a leak in one or other of the fuel tanks.'

'Was there?'

'Looks like they came through all right.'

'You're still bothered about something. No point trying to hide it, Svieta.' Bella pulled up a chair and lowered herself into it the wrong way around, folding her shirt-sleeved arms across the chair's back. 'I need to know what's on your mind.'

It was a long while before Svetlana spoke. Thomas Shen came back again and fussed with one of the monitoring machines. Bella bit her lip and looked at the other woman, waiting.

'It's the pressure in the tanks,' Svetlana said, when Shen had moved away again.

Bella looked at the displays on the flexy again. 'So there is a leak?'

'No. That's what I was specifically looking for.'

'But something else is bothering you.'

Svetlana looked tormented. 'I don't know.'

'Tell me.'

'When the mass driver hit, it was like a liner hitting an iceberg.'

'We all felt the bump,' Bella agreed.

'Right. But where's the evidence in this data?'

'I don't follow.'

'When the driver hit, the jolt should have made the gas in the tanks slosh around.'

'And it didn't?'

'Not according to these read-outs. It's as if it didn't happen.'

'Wait.' Bella squinted, forcing her eyes to focus. 'Those pressure readings: how are they taken?'

'By pressure meters inside the tanks.'

'How many per tank? I'm guessing more than one, for redundancy?'

'Six,' Svetlana said.

'Located in different places?'

'Yes. Two at the tank poles, four around the mid-section.'

'Well, there's your answer.' Bella tried not to sound too confident or cocksure. 'Each of those pressure curves must be a composite of data from six different gauges. More than likely there's a lot of software crunching those numbers before you see them, suppressing any readings that look anomalous.'

'I thought of that,' Svetlana said, 'but I've dug through the source code and there's nothing that should screen out a major pressure spike. You wouldn't *want* to screen out something like that: it could mean you have serious problems. What if the tank integrity took a hit from all that gas moving around?'

'All right, but I must still be on the right track. Do these curves reflect the true sampling rate in the tanks?'

'I think so, yes.'

'But you're not absolutely sure.'

'No,' she said, with a heavy sigh. 'There's a certain amount of stuff I can check out from this bed, but I can't get at all the code between me and the tanks.'

'Look,' Bella said, her tone conciliatory, 'if it makes you happy, we can ask for a second opinion from home. But we'll have to be moving before they answer.'

'I'd still be happier if I could see the data,' Svetlana said. 'I'd be even happier if I knew why I *wasn't* seeing it.'

'You'll get your answer,' Bella said, pushing herself out of the seat. 'I'll send a message home immediately. If someone gets to work on it fast you should have a response within half a day.'

'And if I don't like the response?' Svetlana said again.

'Then you'll have something to worry about. Now – *please* – get some rest. I'll let you know as soon as we have any news.' Bella hugged the flexy to her chest. 'I'll take this, if you don't mind.'

Svetlana started to say something, but Bella was already on her way out of the room.

No death in a spacesuit is ever good, but Mike Takahashi's was especially bad.

Parry felt it coming. The metal lining of the tank quivered, then quivered again, and again, the vibration becoming stronger each time. Something was coming down to them: some piece of debris they hadn't nailed during the clear-up work.

Three of them – Parry, Frida Wolinksy and Takahashi – were laying down sprayrock. They were standing on the side of one of the tanks, attached to it by the soles of their boots with the crowns of their helmets brushing the spinal truss, their faces aimed towards the shield ten metres below. They were tethered to the work crew at the open end of the tank assembly. *Rockhopper* was under thrust again, accelerating at half a gee. The false gravity assisted the sprayrock application, bedding down the layers of the binary compound before they fused.

Parry's neck twitched as some instinct told him that the danger lay behind him, further up the ship. But his helmet blocked his view, and his tethered position prevented him from twisting around. No more than two seconds had passed since he had first become aware of the wrongness.

His hand moved to shut the trigger of the sprayrock gun. It seemed to take too long. At the same time he intended to speak. He started to say: 'Cut the flow,' but he had barely formed the first consonant when he saw a blur of movement in one of his helmet's HUD windows.

Mike Takahashi was gone.

He had been ripped off the side of the tank. With some spiteful inevitability the debris had caught Takahashi, either bulldozing into him or snagging his tether on the way down. Geckoflex was strong, but its bonds were designed to fail before the seals in a pressure-suit.

Parry's hand finally closed the trigger on the nozzle and the jet of sprayrock halted abruptly. He reluctantly followed its trajectory, down to the base of the tanks. He could see it all now. There was the object that must have taken Takahashi: a lump of unrecognisable equipment the size of a beach ball, half-submerged in hardened sprayrock. And there, next to it, was Mike Takahashi, spread-eagled in the moment of impact. During his fall he had twisted through one hundred and eighty degrees: his face stared up towards Parry and Wolinsky. His head, shoulders and upper chest were free of the sprayrock. The rest of him lay buried under the blue-grey surface, except for part of one knee and the tip of one boot.

Takahashi was still alive, still conscious – Parry could hear him groaning. Neither the initial collision nor the drop onto the bed of sprayrock had killed him. The sprayrock had probably saved his life, cushioning what would otherwise have been a fatal fall against the hard armour of the shield.

Parry dropped the spray nozzle. Everyone else was talking on the common channel. They all knew something had happened, even if they couldn't yet see the fallen man on the cams.

'Quiet, everyone,' Parry said, raising his voice. 'Quiet! *Quiet*, for fuck's sake!' When they finally fell silent, he forced calm into his voice and said softly, 'Hey, Mike – can you hear me, buddy?'

Takahashi drew in a ragged breath. 'Yes.'

'You need to stay still. Keep calm, don't be an airhog, and we'll get you out of there.'

'Okay.'

'How are you feeling down there?'

Takahashi's voice became stronger. 'My leg isn't so good. Hurts pretty bad.'

*Probably broken*, Parry thought: snapped or dislocated when Takahashi was wrenched off the side of the tank, or when he hit the bottom. The articulation of an Orlan nineteen lent itself to that kind of injury.

Again, Parry strove to keep any note of panic from his voice. 'We're going to do something about that pain, Mike, but right now you need to listen to me.'

Takahashi took another ragged breath. 'I'm listening.'

'You're lying in sprayrock. You head, arms and upper body are free. The rest of you is encased.'

'Oh, great.'

'But we're going to get you out of this,' Parry said urgently. 'That's a promise: a cast-iron guarantee. You're going to have to work with me, though.

It's important that you stay calm. That way we'll have all the time we need to dig you out. Copy?'

'Copy,' Takahashi said, with an unmistakable edge of panic in his voice.

'I'm serious.'

'Do something about my leg. Then we can talk.'

'I can't do anything about the leg right now, but I still need you to stay calm. I want you to boot up some music, Mike. Scroll down and find something relaxing.'

'You're kidding me, Parry.'

'I'm not. If you don't choose something yourself, I'll make the selection and pump it through from my helmet. You were never really big on opera, were you?'

'Nice joke, Parry.'

'Who's joking? Make the call, or I'll make it for you.'

'You have got to be—'

'Make the call. And crank it loud so we can all listen in. If you don't comply within twenty seconds, I'll inflict some Puccini on you. *Turandot*, maybe. I know how much you love "Nessun Dorma", Mike.'

'You really are a bastard, Chief.'

'Here it comes. Scrolling down now. Public Enemy . . . Puccini. I hope you're ready for this, buddy. It's going to hurt. It's going to hurt like a *bitch*.'

Takahashi wasn't fast enough, or maybe his suit's audio system was shot. Parry didn't care. He was glad to inflict the Puccini on him. Even if he truly hated the music, it was something else to be thinking about.

Parry called Bella.

'Turn down the racket,' she said. 'I can't hear a thing!'

'Sorry,' he said, raising his voice over Luciano Pavarotti, 'but the racket's part of the plan. I need engine shutdown, Bella. Mike doesn't need any additional pressure on his leg, and we can't risk another piece of debris hitting us down here.'

'You have it,' she said, after the slightest hesitation. Thirty seconds later, Parry felt the tension in the tether line relax as he became weightless again.

'What else?'

'We're going to need more people out here, and someone from medical.'

'I've already paged Ryan.'

Parry twisted around to the left until he could just make out Wolinsky at the edge of his faceplate's field of vision. 'Frida,' he said, 'can you reach my tether lock from there?'

'Think so, if they play out some more slack for me.'

Wolinsky leaned towards him, out of view. He felt a tug as she took hold of his tether.

'Release me,' Parry said, leaning back so that she could undo the snaplock fastener.

For once in his life, Parry would have been happier on a tether, but the lines were nearly at their limit. He felt Wolinsky pat him on the back.

'You're free, big guy. Just be careful down there.'

Parry allowed himself to fall forward towards the surface of the sprayrock. They'd put down a metre and a half when Takahashi fell; most of it would have reached full hardness by now. There might be enough resilience in sprayrock to cushion the impulse from a mass driver, but it wasn't going to help them excavate the injured man.

Parry had both hands on the sprayrock now. The geckoflex did not form a permanent bond with the sprayrock. Reassured, he touched a kneepad against the crust, and then a foot. He removed his other foot from the scarred metal of the tank and planted it on the crust. Now he was able to crawl across to the half-exposed form of the trapped man. He reached Takahashi's upper body and raised himself to a kneeling position, keeping a three-point contact with the crust. Behind the semi-reflective glass of his faceplate, Takahashi's eyes were wide and scared.

'Okay, that's enough Puccini,' he said.

'Luciano and me aren't done yet.' Parry examined him, getting his first good look at the situation. It was worse than he had expected. Takahashi's life-support backpack was completely immersed. There would be no way to top up the suit's consumables unless the rear part of the backpack could be exposed.

But consumables were not the main problem now. Parry cranked down the Puccini a notch. 'I'm with Mike now, Bella.'

'We have you on cam,' Bella said. 'What's your assessment?'

'My assessment is—' But he couldn't be truthful, not while Takahashi was listening in. 'Mike's in one piece. He's conscious and lucid. But we're going to have to stabilise him before we can look at getting him out.'

'Stabilise him?'

'We'll need to expose his backpack.'

'Copy,' Bella said, and he knew from her tone of voice, that slight falling inflection, that she had understood. Smothered in sprayrock, the backpack would not be able to dissipate its own waste heat. The suit would already be getting warm.

Nothing had happened yet, though. Perhaps there was still time, if they moved quickly.

'Bella,' he said, 'how are those reinforcements coming along?'

'I've got three people clearing the number-four lock. They have rescue equipment and cutting gear.'

'What about someone from medical?'

'Ryan's already in five. He'll be outside in a few minutes.'

Parry racked his brain, trying to remember the last time he had even heard of Ryan Axford having to don a suit. Presumably during the last mass

EVA training drill, which had to have been at least eighteen months ago.

'Tell Ryan to take care. I have a feeling that this isn't going to be the last time we need him.'

'Ryan knows the drill, Parry, just like you. How's the patient? Talk to me if you can hear me, Mike.'

'I'm okay,' Takahashi said. 'Head hurts like a bitch.'

*Hypercapnia*, Parry thought. He was breathing too fast, too shallowly, allowing carbon dioxide to build up to dangerous levels.

'Easy, buddy.'

'I could really use something for this leg—'

'Mike,' Bella said, 'you're probably going to have to deal with the pain until we get you inside. If you were wearing a softsuit, we might be able to get morphine into you. But you're not.'

'Bella's right about the painkiller,' Parry said. 'It'll have to wait. But you're a tough sonofabitch and I know you can take it.'

'If you say so, Chief.'

'I also know that a broken leg isn't going to kill you. Look on the bright side: it might even excuse you from any hazardous duties once we get to Janus.'

'But I'll still qualify for that bonus money, right?'

'*And* a medical claim into the bargain. And compensation for psychological trauma resulting from repeated exposure to Italian opera.'

Takahashi managed a grunt of approval. 'Maybe the pain isn't so bad after all.' Then his voice took on an ominous tone. 'Oh, wait a minute.'

'What's up?'

'I'm seeing something here . . . on my HUD.' He fell silent.

'Talk to me,' Parry said.

'Suit says there's a problem. I'm getting a red light on thermal regulation.'

'The backpack's having a bit of trouble dumping excess heat, but we've still got plenty of time before that becomes a problem for you.' Parry sounded so glib he almost believed it himself.

He looked up, alerted by a change in the play of light along the length of the tanks. The rescue party approached, helmet lights bobbing as they completed the last part of their journey using their hands and feet. Bright-yellow emergency equipment festooned their suits.

'Cavalry's here,' Parry said.

The three-person squad reached the hardening sprayrock. Despite Parry's presence, they insisted on testing it cautiously before joining him around Takahashi's half-buried form. Parry's HUD dropped names onto the group: Chanticler, Herrick and Pagis. The first two were aquatics, from his own mining squad, while Pagis was one of Svieta's propulsion engineers. They were all people with a lot of EVA time, used to working under pressure.

They were about to get better at it, Parry thought.

'You see the problem,' he said.

Belinda Pagis was the most technically minded of the three. Through her visor Parry saw her pull a face as she appraised the situation. 'That's not good,' she said, under her breath, but loud enough to carry on the open channel. 'We're going to have—'

'What's not good?' Takahashi cut across her.

'Easy, Mike,' Parry said. 'You just sit back and . . .' He trailed off, lost for words.

'We need to get him out of there,' Pagis said. 'That suit's going to start roasting him alive in about ten—'

'Guys,' Parry said. 'Mike's listening in.'

'Sorry,' Pagis said hastily. 'I thought you were on a different—'

'Well, I'm not,' Takahashi said, 'but you don't have to pussy-foot around the truth. I know *exactly* how much shit I'm in.'

'That's why we're going to get you out of there, and fast,' Parry said, oozing false confidence. 'But you have to help us, too. I want you to keep breathing nice and easy.'

'You're worried about me asphyxiating? Even *I'm* not worried about asphyxiating. I have ten hours of reserve in this suit.'

'Air isn't the problem,' Parry said. 'It's the load on the backpack. The harder you breathe, the more the pumps and scrubbers have to work. That's what we need to think about. That's why you need to keep calm.'

'I have a broken leg here.'

'And you're doing great.' Parry could have strangled Pagis. Until she had opened her mouth, he had really felt that he had the situation under control. He glanced at Chanticler and Herrick, who were busy removing gear from their suits, then back to Takahashi. 'We're going to start digging you out,' he said. 'I know you want to be out of there as fast as possible, but there's only one way we can do this. We have to expose your backpack, which means digging under you.'

Takahashi said nothing. Parry dared to think that he had won the argument. He motioned to Herrick to pass him one of the digging tools, hoping that the diamond-bladed trowel was going to be hard enough to cut through the rapidly setting sprayrock.

Then Takahashi said, with disarming detachment, 'I have another red light on backpack systems. I think a pump's just failed.'

'We're digging,' Parry said, gouging the blade into the blue-grey crust.

'It's getting warm in here,' Takahashi said.

Chanticler and Pagis had begun digging with larger versions of the tool Parry had borrowed, and for a few deceptive minutes they looked to be doing the job. The diamond-tipped blades cut into the top crust to a depth of several centimetres, allowing the sprayrock to be levered away in fist-sized lumps. Parry began to let himself believe that they were going to get out of this without losing a man. They were making slow, steady progress, exposing more and more of the upper part of the backpack. Then the going got harder. They had excavated a square metre of crust to a depth of five centimetres with relative ease when the tools suddenly encountered much harder resistance. It was as if they gone from clay to granite.

It took ten minutes to clear the next centimetre, and by then the tools were beginning to blunt. They were using diamond tools to cut through something that was itself approaching the hardness of diamond.

'Are you nearly done?' Takahashi asked. His voice sounded faint, like a man on the edge of dozing off.

Parry placed his tool down on one of the adhesive patches they had attached to the crust. It was no use. The next centimetre would be even harder. He used his right hand to flip up an armoured panel on the sleeve covering his left arm. Pinching his gloved fingers clumsily together, he tugged out a spool of fibre-optic line and offered the plug-tipped end to Belinda Pagis. She took it with a nod and slipped the line into a compatible socket in her own suit.

'We're not going to get him out in time, are we?' she said.

'The only thing that will get through sprayrock at this hardness is a laser or a torch, but if we damage that backpack before we can free his legs, he's already dead.'

Behind her faceplate, Pagis's eyes darted anxiously left and right. 'We need more time.'

'We haven't *got* any more time.'

'Maybe we could rig up some kind of pressure tent,' she said. 'If we could string a ceiling across him—'

'We'd never be able to make it airtight where it touched the sprayrock,' Parry said.

'Then we use sprayrock itself, form a kind of igloo around him. We seal it at the top, then pump air in.'

'Tricky even if we had gravity, Belinda.'

'We have to do *something*.'

'I'm thinking,' Parry said. Movement caught his eye again. Ryan Axford was gingerly making his way onto the sprayrock carrying a bright-orange medical case. Wolinsky and Herrick helped him keep upright relative to the crust. The medic had put in the basic minimum of suit training, but he lacked the easy agility that came with thousands of hours of EVA time. When Parry unplugged the fibre-optic link to Pagis and switched back onto the general channel, the first thing he heard was Axford's too-heavy breathing.

He sounded worse than Takahashi.

Axford moved in front of the buried man and knelt down, anchoring himself with the patches on his knees. He fixed the case to the ground and thumbed open chunky latches. Inside was a gleaming array of medical equipment, packed tight as a puzzle, and three large tanks of pressurised gas. One metallic blue tank had an angel motif sprayed near the top.

Takahashi's backpack was still largely buried, but his much smaller chestpack was fully exposed. Axford flipped aside the plastic cover that protected the chestpack's diagnostic traces. He raised a hand to his visor, shielding his gaze as he tried to make sense of the trembling histograms and snake-like pulses. With surprising deftness he tapped commands into the little keypad next to the read-out panel, cycling through display options.

After a few moments he paused long enough to look up and make eye contact with Takahashi. Axford nodded once: an acknowledgement that promised no miracles, but that he would do all he could.

Axford then turned to Parry and tapped a finger against his sleeve. Parry spooled out the fibre-optic line and plugged in.

'He doesn't need to hear this,' Axford said, 'but it isn't good. He's already suffering the early stages of heat exhaustion. It's like a hot day in Manila in that suit.'

'It's only going to get hotter,' Parry said.

Axford looked at the abandoned excavation. 'You can't get him out, can you?'

'It's not looking good.'

'Then I may have to euthanise him.'

Parry thought he had misheard. 'I'm sorry?'

'I can put him under quickly if I alter his gas mixture. He's already in pain.'

'Let me get this straight.' Parry strove to keep the edge of hysteria from his voice. 'You're talking about killing him.'

'I'm talking about shutting down central-nervous-system activity. We do it cleanly and quickly, and then we crack open that suit and pump it full of hydrogen sulphide.' Axford touched the metallic-blue gas tank. 'He'll cool quickly. Then we cut him out as fast as we can. Once he's back aboard the ship, I'll run a saline flush to remove the remaining blood oxygen from his system.'

'And then you revive him?'

'No. That's not something I'm capable of doing. That'll have to wait until we get back home.'

'Jesus, Ryan. Is that the best you can offer?'

'If he burns up in that suit and suffers cardiac arrest, ischemic damage will destroy critical brain structure within four to six minutes. I'm giving him a shot at surviving.'

'Some shot.'

'It's a high-risk procedure designed for situations just like this.'

'And you know what to do?'

'It's already in the book. Operation Frost Angel.'

After a horrified silence, Parry said, 'How many of these have you done?'

'This'll be my first.'

'And now you get to test this on Mike?'

'Don't sound so horrified, Boyce. I'm trying to save his life.'

It was the first time he had ever head Axford angry. Parry had the uncomfortable realisation that he had trespassed into the area of another man's professional expertise: just as if Axford had tried to lecture him on the right way to dig a mass-driver pit. 'I'm sorry. It's just—'

'Clinical? Yes, that's rather the point.'

Parry found that he needed to get his own breathing under control before he tripped his own suit's heat overload. 'How much time before you have to do that to him?'

'The sooner the better. It'll take time to put him under . . . I wouldn't want to run the hydrogen sulphide exposure while he's conscious. There's something else, too. This may be the hard part.'

'What?'

'We'll need consent.'

Parry closed his eyes and wished he could be somewhere else. 'I'll issue it, if that's his only way out.'

'Not from you,' Axford said. 'From Mike. He has to know what he's getting himself into.' He reached into the medical case and removed a plastic laminated card the size of a dinner menu. He opened it and passed it to Parry. The card was printed with bold text accompanied by simplified medical diagrams in primary colours. It looked like the kind of thing they put in aircraft, showing how to use the escape slides. The figures in the diagrams had the same look of blank, fatalistic serenity. Attached to the sheet by a nylon line was a magic marker, chunky enough to be gripped in a spacesuit glove.

'Oh, no,' Parry said.

'Oh, yes,' said Axford. 'This is the only way he gets a ticket back home.'

'And when he gets home – what then?'

'We hand him to the Chinese. Or keep him on ice until we can bring him back to life ourselves.'

'There is no other choice, is there?' Parry said heavily after a few moments.

Axford shook his head.

Parry unplugged from the medic. 'Mike . . . Are you still hearing me?'

'I'm here,' Takahashi said faintly. 'Is that Ryan with you?'

'Ryan's here.' *But that's as far as the good news goes*, Parry thought. 'Mike, there's something I need to talk to you about. Ryan says it's too dangerous to get you out with cutting torches. I don't like it, but I think he's right. None of us are good enough to guarantee that we won't touch your backpack or pierce your suit. So we're going to try something different, if you agree to it.'

Takahashi must have heard something in his voice. 'And if I don't agree to it?'

'Then we'll do our best with the torches.'

'Tell me what the other plan is.'

'The other plan is—' In his hands, the laminated sheet trembled uncontrollably.

'Parry, just tell me.'

'There's a contingency for this, a procedure. Ryan will put you under . . . render you unconscious.'

'He needs to know the *facts*,' Axford said firmly. 'We need to be clear that we're not just talking about unconsciousness here.'

Parry held the medical sheet up to Takahashi's faceplate and tapped his finger against the cartoon man whose head was a cross section, revealing roselike whorls of brain and brainstem. Boxed and arrowed flatlines indicated the absence of activity in the CNS.

'Ryan will use your suit controls to euthanise you. It'll be painless . . . like going to sleep.'

'No—' Takahashi began.

'Listen,' Parry insisted, 'there's a good reason for this. When you're out . . . when you're under . . . Ryan can preserve you. You stay like that until we get you back home.'

'I'm dead,' he said numbly.

'You're in stasis,' Axford said, working the Frost Angel tank from the medical case. 'What matters to me is that there'll still be a chance that you can be brought back.'

'What kind of a chance?'

'Better odds than if we try to cut you out of this. That's the one thing I'm certain of.'

'He's right,' Parry said. 'This is the way it has to go down, Mike.'

'There must be something else you can try before we take that route,' Takahashi said desperately.

'There isn't,' Axford said. 'And we're already short on time. You know this, Mike. If our places were reversed, would you trust yourself to cut me out?'

'I'd try.'

'I wouldn't let you,' Parry said. He pushed his faceplate as close to the other man's as he could. It looked warm and wet in there, like the inside of a greenhouse. 'Ryan needs your consent. You have to read this and sign it.'

'No.'

Parry pushed the magic marker into Takahashi's glove and squeezed the fingers until they gripped. 'Just sign the damned thing, Mike.'

Takahashi let the pen go. 'I can't.'

Parry grabbed it and forced it back into Takahashi's glove. 'Sign it, goddamn you. Sign it and live.'

'I can't.'

Red lights were pulsing all across Takahashi's chestpack. The suit was beginning to fail, relinquishing its duty of preservation. Parry closed his own gloved hand around Takahashi's and steered the tip of the pen towards the consent box.

All they needed was a mark . . . an attempt at a signature.

'Mike, do this for me. For all your friends.'

Another red light lit up on the chestpack. Then all the lights flashed once and faded to black. Deep in the suit, some critical circuit had just failed. Parry pushed the pen towards the sheet and started to form the upsweep of an M, and then felt – he hoped – Takahashi's hand move with some intent of its own. The tip slid across the consent box, forming a mark that could almost have been Takahashi's signature.

Almost.

Parry let Takahashi's hand drop the marker and turned back to Axford. 'It's your show now, Ryan.'

Axford waved Parry aside and began to tap commands into the chestpack keypad. The lights flickered back on again, dimmer now. Axford entered some more instructions and then the full significance of what was happening must have dawned on Takahashi, because he tried to push Axford away, out of reach of the chestpack. Axford fell back on his haunches.

'Help me,' he said to Parry. 'Hold his arms.'

Parry looked at his friend, taking in the utter fear he saw behind the steam-smeared faceplate.

'I don't think he wants this to happen any more,' Parry said.

'It doesn't matter what he wants,' Axford answered. 'I've got consent now.'

# CHAPTER 6

It was not the first time that someone had died during *Rockhopper* operations, and Bella doubted it would be the last. But that didn't mean it would be business as usual from now on: although Bella had seen her crew snap back into action only a day or two after a death, sometimes it took much longer. The process of recovery never appeared to have much to do with the popularity of the crewmember involved, or the circumstances in which they had died; it was governed by subtler forces than that, and Bella did not have their measure.

She coped in her own way. Takahashi's medical status might be open to debate, but in her heart, Bella believed it to be permanent and irreversible death, and she treated it as such. She composed letters of condolence, trying to strike the right balance between respectful formality and the personal touch. It was easier than with some of the dead; Mike Takahashi had no close family, so the letters were going to distant relatives and friends.

Sometimes, writing those letters of condolence, Bella found herself wondering who they would find to write to if she were to die. She knew what it was like to be on the receiving end of such a message: she had been expecting a call to tell her when Garrison was being rotated back from Big Red. Instead she heard that his shuttle had smeared itself over half of the Sinai Planum after an aerobrake failure. He'd been returning from Deimos.

Unlucky thirteenth: 13/03/36. The date was burnt into her brain like a brand.

People assumed she didn't miss having a partner, as if the occasional and necessary coldness of her decision-making implied that she was herself frigid. A handful of them understood: Svetlana, Chisholm, Axford, Parry. They did not know everything, nor would she have wished them to. Not even Svetlana knew about the argument Bella and Garrison had had – drawn out by the agonised timelag of an Earth–Mars conversation – just before Garrison left for his final mission. If only they had at least made up before ending the link, before Garrison departed. He'd still have died, but she wouldn't have been left with this twisted feeling of something unresolved, as if that unpleasant conversation was still waiting to be terminated, somewhere in the space between Earth and Mars.

Bella stopped herself before her thoughts fell deeper into that poisonous spiral. Nothing could undo what had happened, but every time she felt as if she had dealt with the matter and was finally ready to safely close the book on Garrison's death, it would return again to haunt her. She had to accept that it probably always would. There were times when she could shut the past out with work and duty, thinking about what might happen rather than what might have been.

But today was not one of those days.

Bella had just finished the letters to Takahashi's distant relatives when she noticed that a communication had arrived from DeepShaft, addressed to her. It concerned Svetlana's technical query about the pressure in the fuel tanks – Mike Takahashi's accident had almost driven Svetlana's questions from her mind. She speed-read the document, then called Svetlana to tell her that the report looked very thorough, and appeared to allay the concerns she had raised.

'My concerns?' Svetlana asked.

'I'm dumping the technical report to your flexy. The executive summary makes the gist of the report adequately clear.'

'Adequately clear,' Svetlana said, pulling a face. 'Well, that's a relief.'

'There's no mystery,' Bella said. 'The way the pressure sensors are rigged combined with the way the software is configured was guaranteed to smooth out a sharp pressure event from the mass-driver impact. The good news is that there's no cause for concern.'

'Really?' Svetlana sounded intrigued. 'No cause at all?'

'The simulations show that the impact wouldn't have led to any structural fatigue in the tanks.'

'There's no impact in the world that wouldn't have caused *some* fatigue.'

'But fatigue we can live with.'

'I'm still not happy, Bella.'

'I'm not *asking* you to be happy: I'm just asking you to stop worrying about this one incident. If anything, we've overestimated the likely effects. Why are you so convinced someone's keeping something from us?'

'Call me cynical, but do you really think DeepShaft's going to be thrilled at the idea of us turning back now?'

'They also want this ship back in one piece.'

'After we reach Janus.'

'Svieta—' Bella began before giving it up with an exasperated glance at the ceiling. 'I should know better by now, shouldn't I?'

'With me? Definitely!' Svetlana said.

*

Svetlana followed Parry through the lock and onto the dizzying tower of the spinal truss. The engine section looked a frighteningly long way below: much further away than it had when the ship was drifting. Parry secured one end of the tether to a truss node and the other to the harness point on Svetlana's suit. She used the ladder that ran parallel to the car line to climb down the truss. At first every step sent a stab of agony into her chest, but after a while she worked out the best way to move to alleviate the pain of the damaged rib.

At one hundred metres Svetlana halted, secured herself to the nearest node and waited for Parry to descend. Then Parry waited in turn while Svetlana moved down another hundred metres. Halfway down the spine a team was working on repairs to the car line amidst robots and flickering cutting tools. Svetlana expected them to show some curiosity as she and Parry passed them by, but they acknowledged their presence with only the briefest of hand gestures before returning to their duties.

Parry and Svetlana continued their descent until they reached the level of the tanks, then the place where Takahashi had died, and then the heavy-duty airlock into the pressurised work environment of the sweatbox.

Once safely inside, the two of them cracked open their helmet seals and lifted their visors. Their breath jetted out in white clouds. No one had visited the sweatbox since the accident with the mass driver, and the environmental system had responded by cooling the room down.

The sweatbox's curved green walls were studded with read-outs, keyboards, telescope-like viewing devices and dark portholes. There were pages of printout, sheathed in plastic and annotated with scribbled corrections in magic marker, stuck to the walls with geckoflex. There were safety notices and bad-taste cartoons, like the one that showed a nervous-looking scientist working on some kind of atomic bomb while his colleague sneaked up behind him, ready to burst a huge paper bag.

Svetlana ripped it from the wall and crumpled it into her pocket. Not the kind of humour she needed right now.

'We can talk here,' she said. 'I've disabled the webcam feed to the rest of the ship.'

'Wasn't that a bit naughty?'

'Not at all. We lost some bandwidth during the accident – the driver severed some of the fibre-optic lines running down the spine. All I'm doing is making sure we use the remaining capacity in the most efficient way.'

'I doubt that the webcam made much difference to the bandwidth,' Parry said. 'Not that I'm going to quibble.'

'Very sensible of you.' Svetlana tugged her flexy from the storage pouch below her chest pack. 'Are you going to wait here, breathing down my neck, or is there something you can do outside for the next half-hour?'

'Such as?'

'I don't know. Listen to some Howling Wolf. Watch the stars go by or something.'

'If it's all right with you, I'll stay and keep an eye on you.'

'I'm not going to get myself into trouble.'

'You're already in trouble,' Parry said. 'So am I if Bella ever finds out I faked Ash's sig on that suit-release form.'

'Ash owes me one,' Svetlana said. 'When he's back on shift I'll remind him that I didn't enter a complaint into the LOC log after that little blackout around the comet. Then we'll see how loud he squeals over one faked sig.'

'You could give scheming lessons to Machiavelli,' Parry said.

'I did. He flunked.'

Svetlana unscrewed her suit gloves and hung them on her belt so that she could work the flexy with her hands. The HUD would alert her if she tried to leave through the airlock without replacing the gloves. She activated the flexy and paged through to the heavily annotated technical read-outs concerning fuel pressure. Then she moved to one of the instrument-crammed walls of the sweatbox and tugged out a fibre-optic line.

'You ready to tell me what this is all about?' Parry asked, his arms folded across his chest. 'Because none of this feels routine.'

Svetlana clipped the fibre-optic line into a port on the underside of the flexy and touched menu buttons to upload new data. 'We tore up the book on routine when we pushed the engine to half a gee,' she said.

'It's to do with the ship, then? You're afraid she'll fall apart?'

'Not that. I just have a suspicion, a bad one, and I haven't been able to shake it.'

'This suspicion being?'

'That someone's screwing with us.' She closed her eyes, willing the flexy to finish uploading the data and prove her wrong. 'I started worrying about possible damage to the fuel tanks.'

'Reasonable, after what happened.'

'So I checked. I called up the numbers on my flexy when I was in the medical centre and looked for any anomalies in the pressure data around the time of the accident.'

'And you found—?'

'Nothing. Not even a blip. Nothing to indicate we'd even had an accident.'

'There must be some reason why the impact didn't show up,' Parry said.

The flexy pinged: it had finished uploading data from the sweatbox. Svetlana pulled out the fibre-optic line and allowed it to spool back into the wall. 'I thought of that,' she said heavily. 'Looked into it, too. And I saw no logical way that a pressure spike could have happened and not shown up in the data.'

'Did you talk to Bella about this?'

'Of course. She found it pretty odd as well, but she figured there had to be an explanation.'

'Which you haven't found yet.'

'Bella sent a message back home, outlining our concerns. A while ago we got the reply.'

'And?'

'Not to put too fine a point on it, it's a crock of shit.'

Parry looked confused. 'You mean they don't understand what happened either, but they're trying to gloss over it?'

'That's it exactly, and my nasty suspicion is that they're doing it because we can't be allowed to know the truth. Because if we did, this entire mission—' Svetlana took a moment to view the newly uploaded data on her flexy, superimposing the pressure–time curves over those she had already analysed. 'I was hoping this would prove me wrong,' she said heavily, 'but it doesn't.'

'What's going on?'

She breathed in deeply, feeling the cold air fill her lungs. This was it: the crux, the point at which she was about to reveal herself in all her paranoid glory. 'The data has been tampered with.' She held up the flexy, dragging a finger across the curves she had already annotated. 'All these numbers are made up.'

Parry did not ask her to repeat what she had just said, or accuse her of being mad. She was grateful for that. He just nodded slowly and worked a finger against his moustache, as he always did when he was puzzled.

'And you think the company's behind this?'

'It's the only explanation that makes sense.'

Now that she had said it out loud, now that her suspicions were in the open, she felt a thrilling sense of liberation.

'Okay. Explain it to me – start with how they'd change those numbers.'

'No big deal: there are plenty of ways of hacking into the ship. It's happening all the time: routine software uploads, bug fixes, patches, that kind of thing.'

'Could they sneak something like that past you?'

'I don't know,' she said. 'Maybe there's a dedicated back-door channel that bypasses the logging system. Or maybe they uploaded a piece of software that infiltrated the logging system itself, so that they could sneak a lot of other stuff in without our noticing.'

'I hope you have some watertight evidence for this,' Parry said.

'I have plenty of evidence,' she said, and passed him the flexy.

Parry lowered his eyes. 'This is supposed to mean something?'

'I've superimposed two sets of data that should be identical. They're not. The curves don't overlap.'

'One is real?'

She nodded firmly. 'The data I just uploaded from the sweatbox is what I expected to see. It shows the pressure data for the fuel tanks, including the glitch when the mass driver hit us.'

'And the other curve?'

'That's the data that shows up if you query ShipNet. It's what Bella sees. It's what Bella believes.'

Parry touched the curve that showed the mass-driver impact. 'How come this data didn't get changed as well?'

'It's buffered,' Svetlana said, 'stored in a short-term memory cache as a protection against a shipwide systems meltdown. Only way to get at it was to come down here. Whatever they used to overwrite the other copy couldn't get at this one. Or they didn't think about it.'

He handed her the flexy. She could tell by his expression that she had put a dent in his certainty, even if she still had some way to go before he was fully convinced.

'Why?' he asked. 'I don't get it – why change those numbers?'

Svetlana held up the flexy again. 'The curve of the real data is about fifteen per cent lower than the faked curve. That means there's less pressure. That means there's less fuel in the tanks.'

'Meaning what, exactly?'

'It was already tight,' Svetlana said. 'Based on the numbers we had before the accident, there was enough fuel to get to Janus, shadow it for a few days and then make it back to the inner system.'

'And now?'

'I'll have to re-run the calculations based on the real data, but I have a feeling I already know the answer.'

Silence stretched between them. She looked into Parry's wide, trusting face.

'Which is?' he asked.

'There won't be enough fuel to get home again. That's what they don't want us to know. They want us to reach Janus and make observations. The data we transmit home will still make DeepShaft's fortune.'

'And us?'

'If they have the data, we're expendable.'

Bella was with the taphead when the call came in. Thom Crabtree had a fawnlike quality about him: his eyes were large and trusting, but shy of hers; he could not look at her directly, but only over her shoulder, as if addressing someone else entirely.

'I don't think I'm making as much difference as I could,' Crabtree said.

'In what way?' Bella asked patiently.

'I'm not being allowed to be useful. I might as well not be on the ship at all.'

'I thought we went over this already,' Bella said.

'We did. But nothing changed.'

Bella glanced at an e-mail she had pulled up from her sent folder. 'I asked Saul to move forward the integration. It's important to me that we have you up to speed before we reach Janus. I'm convinced that you can play a crucial role in the investigation when we start deploying robots.'

'I hope so,' Crabtree said.

'So tell me how well the integration is going. Are you working with real machines yet?'

Crabtree shifted uncomfortably in his seat. 'Not exactly,' he said. 'We're still on virtuals.' He meant the simulated machines.

'There was a problem with the transition?'

'Yes – no. I mean, no *technical* problem. But Saul—' He squirmed, his eyes darting everywhere but her face. Bella felt just as uncomfortable: she took no pleasure in placing the delicate young man in such a conflicted state, but she had to have his side of the story.

'Saul halted the trials?'

'Yes,' he said uneasily. 'We've gone back to the virtuals again.'

She looked at his head, shaven close to the skull. There was no external sign that he was a taphead, no evidence of the surgery that had taken place back on Earth. The work was too good for that. DeepShaft had invested billions of dollars in Crabtree and his like. The intercranial microelectrode array implants formed an exquisitely delicate loom, wired into ten thousand cortical motor neurons. The IMA and its correlator neurochip allowed Crabtree to move machines with his mind. With proper training, he could control a robot with a fluency of motion that no teleoperator could approach: the robot would be fully assimilated into his own body image.

It was no wonder that so many of the crew feared Crabtree.

'Did Saul give a reason for halting the integration?' Bella asked.

'There was trouble,' the taphead told her. 'Threats.'

'Look, if it wasn't for Janus—'

'Janus?'

'These are extraordinary circumstances. Now we've had a couple of accidents . . . the crew are under a lot of pressure. If things were normal, I wouldn't hesitate to override opinion and place you in a position of real usefulness.'

'But at the moment you have to keep the rest of the crew happy.'

'Yes,' Bella said lamely.

'It's all right,' Crabtree said. 'I understand. It's natural that they resent my presence.'

'It's not right, though.'

Now, finally, he found the strength to look directly into her eyes. His own were as hard and cold as iron, and she felt her body temperature drop a degree.

'It is right. I'm the future. They *should* fear me.'

Her flexy chimed. Bella held up a hand. 'Just a second, Thom.' Seeing that the call was from Svetlana, she took it. 'Hi, Svieta. Can I get back to you in a few minutes?'

'I don't think so.' Svetlana leaned closer to the lens, her face looming large and distorted. 'It can't wait. Not this one. Not this time.'

Bella made her apologies to Thom Crabtree – he had come to her with a reasonable complaint, and she had done little to assuage his concerns – and showed him to the door. Watching him leave, Bella felt a familiar prickle of guilt knowing that she had ducked a problem, not solved it. Her choice of T-shirt slogan had not been the most apposite, either:

*I can only help one person a day.*
*Today is not your day.*
*Tomorrow doesn't look good either.*

She hoped he hadn't taken it personally. Then she put Thom Crabtree to one side in her mind, warmed herself some coffee and pressed the little nub near the hem that switched the T-shirt to a different slogan.

*I have one nerve left, and you're getting on it.*

*Not much better*, she thought, and hopped through the options. Just as she found the blank default, which was what she should have set it to all along, Svetlana arrived, accompanied by Parry Boyce, who filled the doorframe like a bodyguard. Bella blinked at the unexpected guest, but ushered him in all the same. They were both wearing suit inner layers, musty with sweat.

Bella looked at Parry, wondering what he had to do with all this. 'Could you use some coffee?'

'We're okay,' Svetlana said. 'I don't have much of a stomach for food or drink right now.'

Bella indicated that they should fold down seats and face her across her desk. 'That bad?'

'Much, much worse.'

Svetlana passed her a flexy. Bella only had to glance at the display to recognise the familiar curves of pressure data. 'Not this again,' she said, a little crossly. 'I thought we'd moved on.'

Svetlana told the story while Bella copied the data onto her own flexy. Parry filled in details, confirming that he'd been with her when she had gathered the evidence.

Bella poured herself some more coffee and drank half a cup before answering. She watched the electric flicker of her tetra fish, nosing inquisitively up to the glass.

'That's insane,' she said finally.

'I completely agree,' Svetlana said. 'It's still true.'

Bella pushed a finger to the bridge of her nose, digging the nail into the skin. 'But the report on the pressure spike—'

'They've been massaging that data ever since we got the call to go to Janus. But when the mass driver hit, they had to upload a new set of faked numbers to cover the fact that we turned off the engine after the accident. That was when they forgot to include the glitch due to the mass-driver impact.'

'But you didn't.'

'It's my job not to forget little details.' Svetlana glanced at Parry. 'I'm sorry about what happened to Mike, but if the driver hadn't broken off, we'd never have suspected anything was wrong with the data; that's what's saved us.'

'You say "saved us",' Bella said tactfully. 'I'm not completely sure I follow.'

Parry cleared his throat. 'We have to turn around. There's still enough fuel left to make it back now, but every hour that we push further from home gives us less and less of a margin for error.'

'Turn back?'

Svetlana picked up the flexy and allowed it to fall back onto the desk with a hollow thump. 'They're screwing with us, Bella. DeepShaft is lying to us, letting us think we have a hope in hell of getting back from this.'

'Let's not jump to melodramatic conclusions,' Bella said. 'There could be a million explanations. How can you be so sure, anyway?'

'Because these curves don't match. Because one is real and one is false.'

The coffee lent Bella's thoughts a treacherous clarity, like thin ice. 'How did you get hold of the real data, in that case?'

'There's a copy. Normally I'd have been able to retrieve it over ShipNet, but the damage to the spinal truss meant I had to dig it out of the sweatbox using a local hook-up.'

'Even I'd have had a hard time believing her if I hadn't seen those numbers with my own eyes,' Parry said.

'And now you believe her? You believe we're the victims of a corporate conspiracy?'

'I believe someone's altered those numbers. Svieta's explanation sounds as plausible as anything else.'

'You honestly think they'd do this to us?' Bella asked.

'Stakes don't get much higher than Janus.'

Bella picked up a pen and tapped it against her desk, hoping she looked and sounded like someone going along with a theory for the sake of argument and nothing more. 'Assuming there is a conspiracy, just how long do you think it could be kept hidden? If we truly are running low on fuel, what happens when we can't get back?'

'Maybe nothing will happen. They'll say it was all an innocent mistake.'

'The truth would get out eventually,' Bella said.

'Yes – if you wait long enough, to the point where no one alive cares what happened all that time ago. And even if heads do roll, they wouldn't necessarily be the right ones.'

'This is a lot to swallow,' Bella said.

'I wouldn't have come to you if I didn't think the evidence was watertight.'

'These numbers, you mean?'

'They're pretty incriminating. Enough to act on, at the very least.'

'By which you mean I should ask for clarification on the fuel situation?'

'No,' Svetlana said, with sudden urgency. 'We don't have time to sit and wait for them to come up with another pack of lies. We have to stop now, turn around and start our return journey.'

'And abandon Janus?'

'If I told you the ship was in imminent danger of break-up, you'd abort the mission immediately, wouldn't you?'

'You know the answer to that already.'

'Then accept that these numbers are just as damning. This is a one-way ticket to Janus, nothing more.'

'You've verified that we don't have enough fuel for a return trip?'

'I know that we have less fuel than they're telling us,' Svetlana said, confidence slipping from her face. 'I haven't had time to run a full flight-dynamics sim to see just how bad things are. But if the numbers were marginal to begin with—'

'Look,' Bella said, trying to be accommodating, 'I see that you have a concern here, but there has to be an honest explanation.'

Svetlana stood up angrily. 'What more do you want?'

Parry restrained her, standing up and putting a wide hand on her shoulder. 'Easy,' Bella heard him say under his breath.

'I can't act on this,' Bella said. 'I can't suddenly turn around and accuse the entire company of premeditated murder on the basis of a few discrepancies between two data files.'

'We're talking about more than a few discrepancies,' Svetlana said defensively.

'Hear me out,' Bella said, fighting her own instinct to shout down the other woman. 'I accept that there is something puzzling going on here. You've convinced me of that much. But I'll need to see more before I abort the mission.'

'You mean this isn't enough?'

'Not from where I'm sitting. I want a full flight-dynamics assessment, taking into account the mass we lost when the drivers detached. I want to see something in the telemetry logs that backs up your story.'

'I can't give you what isn't there.'

'Measure the remaining mass in the fuel tanks. Use our acceleration, Newton's first law. You can do that, can't you?'

'Not in any way that would convince you. *This* is the best you're going to get.'

'I refuse to believe they'd do this to us,' Bella said.

'Start getting used to it,' Parry said.

In all her years on the ship, there was one room Bella had never had cause to visit. She was in it now, with Ryan Axford. The two of them sat on fold-down seats. She'd had to put on a fleece jacket against the chill: even now her fingertips were turning numb.

'I keep wondering, Ryan: why four? Why not two, why not six?'

'Same thing occurred to me,' Axford, who seemed oblivious to the cold, said. He puffed lightly on the cigarette she had offered him. He smoked, he said, because he had seen too many non-smoking physicians explore other avenues of addiction. Besides, he argued, the health risks were down in the noise: months off a life, rather than entire decades. 'Some cost-benefit analyst must have decided four was the optimum number given our typical mission profile and the average time between shuttle visits. We're doing pretty well, aren't we?'

'One down, three to go,' Bella said.

The ends of four sliding mortuary trays occupied one wall of the narrow steel-grey room. There were even metal label holders on the ends of the trays. Three of them were empty, but now Axford had slid a medical card into the fourth, filled out in his customarily neat handwriting. Most of the people on the ship had laboured, childlike handwriting when they were forced to write; Axford, by contrast, had the most elegant and legible handwriting of any man Bella had ever met. It was calligraphic, rather beautiful.

The card said that the tray contained the frozen body of Mike Takahashi, who had died during an EVA accident. There was some allusion to the cryopreservation procedure, some mention of the chemicals utilised, but nothing overt. Axford did not need to state that he froze a man so that he might live again. When *Rockhopper* made it home, the right people would learn what had happened. To say anything more would be a mark of hopeless wishful thinking.

'You didn't come down here to chill out with the Frost Angel,' Axford said delicately. 'Something's bothering you.'

Bella had always been able to talk to Ryan Axford; she treated him as a kind of honorary second-in-command, her deputy in all but name, especially since Chisholm's health had deteriorated so badly. She supposed ship's surgeons had always enjoyed that unspoken privilege.

'Something's come up,' she said.

'The Chinese mess?'

'No – not that that isn't enough of a headache in its own right. But this is about us, about *Rockhopper*.' She waited for him to say something, but Axford just looked at her with the cigarette poised near his lips. *A good listener*, she thought. 'It's about Svetlana Barseghian. I guess you know her pretty well.'

'She's been in and out of medical a couple of times in the last month. First there was a muscle she pulled on her exercise bike, two, three weeks back. Then I had her in for treatment and observation after the mass-driver accident.'

'How'd she seem?'

'Patient confidentiality, Captain Lind.'

'Sorry.'

Axford smiled forgivingly. 'She seemed the way she always does: in good shape, mentally and physically, focused on her job. Not one of the problem cases, like . . . well, I'm sure you can fill in the blanks. But Svieta isn't one of *my* headaches. The crew like her. I like her. She's attractive, bright, a good team player.'

'Attractive, Ryan? I didn't think you'd notice.'

'Because I'm a gay man?' He gave Bella a stern look. 'I expected better of you, frankly.'

'I'm sorry. That was unspeakably crass.'

'I'll forgive you in return for another cigarette. That's absolutely my last for the day, though, so you're not allowed any more slip-ups.'

She let him take another cigarette, which he dropped into his shirt pocket for later. 'So what's the deal with Svieta? Why do you want to know what I think of her?'

'She's come to me with something, a technical matter that might impact on our chances of mission completion. On the face of it, it's pretty disturbing stuff.'

'You have faith in her abilities, don't you?'

Bella nodded firmly. 'Absolutely. She's never put a foot wrong.'

'So what's the problem? If she's flagged an issue, shouldn't you listen to her?'

'It's a bit more complicated than that. She's basically asking me to abort the mission. Turn *Rockhopper* around, forget about Janus.'

Axford blew out softly. 'Whew.'

'Under ordinary circumstances, I don't think I'd have hesitated for a second. But these aren't ordinary circumstances. Part of me's screaming to do what she says. I trust her abilities, I trust her as a friend, and I have no reason to think she might be exaggerating the dangers for her own reasons. But there's another part of me – call it my cold-hearted-bitch mode – that says *ignore her.*'

'On what grounds?'

'Svetlana raised a technical query – there was something in the numbers she didn't like. I thought she had a point, actually. I called headquarters and asked them to look into it. They came back with a technical explanation that ought to have resolved her concerns.'

'Except they didn't go away.'

'Svetlana thought it was a whitewash, so she went digging for more evidence and came up with something that looked even more compelling.'

'I can see how this would put you in something of a quandary.' Axford ran a hand over his salt-and-pepper crew-cut. 'Have you spoken to Craig Schrope about any of this?'

'Yes, of course. It would have been remiss of me not to mention her concerns to him when she first brought them to me.'

'So what was Craig's angle?'

'Like me, he thought she had a point. Like me, he thought DeepShaft had covered all the bases.'

'And the second thing – the other evidence she came up with?'

'I haven't mentioned it to Craig.'

'I see.'

'That's what I wanted to talk to you about. It's become delicate now. Svetlana could be digging a deep hole for herself. If she's right, then we're in trouble, but if she's wrong, it'll be the end of her career. They'll bury her alive. I don't want that to happen to my friend.'

'Which is why you've held back from telling Craig about the latest instalment.'

'You heard how he turned Shalbatana around. This is a man who doesn't give a shit about making enemies. It's what gets him through the day.'

Axford narrowed his eyes. 'What's your reading on Craig?'

'The crew don't like him. But they're not *paid* to like him. He's the right man in the right seat.'

'He is good at his job,' Axford allowed. 'Not everyone can be a Jim Chisholm, liked and respected at the same time.'

'Actually,' Bella ventured, 'Jim's the other reasson, I wanted to talk to you. This whole business—'

'You want to bounce it off Jim, see what he has to say.'

'I know he's ill, but I really need to talk to him.'

'Not going to happen,' Axford said, shaking his head slowly. 'I'm sorry, but he's under enough emotional strain as it is. I know you have your reasons – and I sympathise – but the last thing he needs is to be dragged back into the mire of command politics.'

'I understand,' Bella said. In truth, she had expected this. Axford had always been protective of his patients: she would have respected him less if he had given ground, even for this.

'But I don't mind you asking,' he went on. 'I really can appreciate the stress this puts you under, but I don't think for a moment that Jim would tell you anything you hadn't already figured out for yourself.'

'Which is?'

Axford took out and lit the second cigarette. 'Being captain is a bitch. But you knew that already.'

# CHAPTER 7

The face on Bella's wall was that of a young man, skin pulled tight to the bones by gravity. Padded restraints locked his head into immobility. What could be seen of his surroundings was red-lit and unfocused: perforated foamsteel bulkheads, a tangle of circulation pipes, screens burbling with text and schematics. Under his cross-buckled seat restraints, the young man wore a suit jacket over a white roll-neck sweater. Coloured ribbons and metal insignia offset the jacket's dark material. The young man had short black hair, neatly side-combed and gleaming as if he had washed and gelled it just before making this broadcast.

'Greetings to captain and crew of commercial vehicle *Rockhopper*,' said the face on Bella's wall. 'This is Commander Wang Zhanmin of exploratory space vessel *Shenzhou Five*, on behalf of the People's Democratic Republic of Greater China. It is my great honour to extend the hand of friendship on behalf of my nation. Please, honoured crew of commercial vehicle *Rockhopper*, accept offer of Chinese people to join in mutual exploration of Janus anomaly.'

Bella stopped the recording. 'It's the same as the last time – not exactly the same wording, but the sentiments haven't changed.'

'I like the way he emphasises the "commercial" bit,' Craig Schrope said. 'As if he didn't know this was a UEE mission with full diplomatic sanction.'

'The kid's just following a script, saying what Beijing told him to say,' Bella said. 'Look at it from their angle – why should they recognise our official status if we don't recognise theirs?'

'Because China is a rogue state, and we're a full member of the council. That's good enough for me.'

Bella wondered how much the strain was showing. She had still not spoken to Schrope about the second piece of evidence Svetlana had brought to her attention, and that omission was eating away at her. She worried about what would happen when she received a follow-up reply from home, as she had requested. She had hoped, guiltily, that the Chinese matter would resolve itself and leave her with only that one major problem to deal with.

Unfortunately, Beijing's beautiful creation, with its staggered, subtly pagoda-like lines, continued to function flawlessly. The fusion engine had been notched up to a fearful two gees, which would permit an even longer study window. Had the race been equal, with *Rockhopper* and the *Shenzhou Five* starting the run to Janus from the same position, there was no doubt that the Chinese would have been the clear victors. Already the *Shenzhou Five* had come within five light-minutes of *Rockhopper*: no distance at all out in the long, empty light-hours beyond the Kuiper Cliff. They would have to come closer, too, as both ships converged on the same target.

'You may as well hear the rest of it,' Bella said.

'I'll pass. Do we ever get to see anyone else, or is it always this one kid?'

'Just Wang,' Bella said. 'Maybe he's the only one Beijing trusts to talk to us. We still don't know exactly how many people they've got aboard that thing – the Chinese are talking as if there're dozens, but that might be an exaggeration.'

'Doesn't matter, anyway. We only need one of them to understand our response.'

'No one's discussed a response,' Bella said. 'It isn't for us to decide who gets to crawl over Janus.'

'That's the point – we don't *have* to decide. The UEE has decided for us. They've given us the mandate.'

'C'mon, Craig.' Bella looked at him reasonably, trying to crack the poker face of the man who had broken the Shalbatana bore. 'You know what that really means.'

'It means Wang the Man can take his ball home.'

'No, it means Powell pulled strings in Niagara Falls. He said as much himself. You know how tight he is with Inga de Jong.'

'DeepShaft has a seat on the Security Council,' Schrope said, with pedantic slowness. 'It's not exactly breaking news that Powell has some leverage in UEE affairs.'

'I think it goes a bit deeper than that,' Bella said. 'I think Powell knew how hot a commercial opportunity Janus was going to be. Maybe we're flying under a flag of convenience now, but do you think anyone's really going to care about that when we head back home with our cargo bay full of world-changing technologies?'

'So we get a bite at the big cherry.' Schrope shrugged in his best no-big-deal way. 'In case you've forgotten, it's a cherry that could very well kill us. We're taking a risk here. I suggest you point the greed finger somewhere else.'

'I'm not pointing the . . .' Bella trailed off, wary of losing it with Schrope. He was her subordinate, so she was entitled to cuff him down, but something always held her back. Schrope had strong political connections within the company that ran all the way to Powell Cagan. After his good work in Shalbatana, in spite of all the enemies he had made, Schrope was the new golden boy.

Bella had links to Cagan, too, but hers were of a different kind; perhaps they even worked against her. Before *Rockhopper*, even before Garrison, she had been Cagan's favourite. She had pushed hard on doors, but Cagan had made them open for her. He had helped her rise fast in the organisation, faster than could be accounted for by any measure of skill or ambition – neither of which Bella lacked – and she had believed that this was all there was to it, and that there would not be a price to be paid.

She knew now that there was always a price. Nothing that looked good was ever free, especially where men like Powell Cagan were involved.

He had wanted more than just a talented protégée. He had sucked Bella into a sexual relationship that she had been naive enough, even at the age of thirty, to believe was the real thing. Cagan was twenty-two years older than her, and an exceptionally wealthy man. For a year she had shared the luminous glamour of his world, with its private jets and private islands. Then Cagan's wandering eye had strayed to someone younger and Bella had found herself promoted off-Earth with no warning: one day the private jet took her to a launch complex instead of an island and that had been that.

Bella was in orbit before she realised what had happened. The promotion was a masterstroke: it was everything she had worked for up till then – and it was Cagan's way of getting her out of his life without having to feel a moment's guilt.

At the time she had been too numb to feel hatred or sorrow; instead she was ashamed and embarrassed that she had misread the rules of the game that were so childishly clear to everyone else. She never quite understood how she could have been the only one who hadn't known from the beginning that this was how it would – it *must* – end.

Other men might have had problems with the idea of a spurned lover remaining in the same company, but Cagan's capacity for remorse didn't stretch that far. When they spoke, he appeared completely untroubled by their past; he would even occasionally allude to their time together with a nostalgic twinkle in his eye, assuming perhaps that Bella looked back on their liaison with the same rosy glow of retrospection – as if their separation had been a matter of dignified mutual consent.

Losing Powell Cagan hadn't been the end of her life; Bella met Garrison not long after and their few years together had been good times – right up until that sour end. Garrison she kept in her heart; beyond a thin contempt, she felt nothing for Cagan. She had long ago vowed that her feelings would not impinge on their professional relationship: the CEO was an abstract figure who had nothing in common with the man who had so coldly disposed of her. For a long time that had worked: running *Rockhopper* gave her a certain independence from company control, but Janus was changing all that. The UEE business was already more than she needed.

Schrope had rotated aboard long before Janus hit the headlines, but Bella had had doubts about the real reason for his transfer from the start. Even if Cagan didn't particularly care about Bella one way or the other, he might want better things for his new protégé, and a captaincy wasn't out of the question. With his connections, Schrope could make life difficult for Bella if he chose. When she went out of her way to defend him, as she had done with Svetlana, it was as much to convince herself as anyone else.

With Schrope, she always felt as if he was trying to make her say something she would later regret – something that would count against her in the minutes of a professional-conduct tribunal. That was why she always bit her tongue when talking to him.

So many things had been better before Jim Chisholm had fallen ill. Now, whenever she was about to fly off the handle with Schrope, she tried to imagine Jim sitting with her in the room, a warning look on his face.

'All I'm saying,' she said, as nicely as she could manage, 'is why don't the Chinese deserve their own bite at the cherry?'

'It's our call,' Schrope said.

'But why does the UEE get to decide on Janus? Last time I checked, Janus was an alien artefact. Maybe I skipped a line of small print, but I don't think there's anything in the charter that says Inga and her pals automatically get first dibs.'

'If that was a problem for the Chinese, they shouldn't have got themselves kicked out of the club for messing around with stuff they didn't know how to handle.' He sounded stern. The Chinese had kept on experimenting with nanotech despite pressure from the other member economic entities, and eventually it had blown up in their faces. When twinkling grey mould ate half of Nanjing, China had been expelled from the UEE.

Even now there were lingering rumours of sabotage: that agents of those industrial concerns with a vested interest in preserving a world without nanotech had infiltrated the Nanjing facility and made the replicators go haywire. No one took *that* very seriously, but Bella could still not shake the feeling that the Chinese had been victimised in some subtle way. Although she did not necessarily approve of everything that they had done (and everything that they continued to do, outside UEE control) she could not bring herself to loathe them for wanting to take a look at Janus as well.

It seemed perfectly human to her.

'Look,' she said, 'if nothing goes wrong with their ship, they're going to get there whether we like it or not. Since that's going to happen anyway, maybe we should at least consider the possibility of cooperation.'

'They can cooperate by keeping the hell away from us,' Schrope said, 'or do I need to remind you about the exclusion zone?'

'It's one light-second wide,' Bella said, exasperated. 'It's a legalistic abstraction that no one actually takes seriously.'

'It's still a line in the sand. The moment they cross that—'

'What?' She had a sudden sinking feeling.

'We're entitled to a robust response. You know perfectly well that we're capable of giving one.'

On the fourteenth day, one week away from the Janus encounter, Powell Cagan's face reappeared on Bella's flexy. Wherever the CEO was calling from now was white with intense, heart-wrenching light, bleeding the colour from the day. He sat outside at a white table on a white-walled veranda. The tops of blue-grey trees poked above the wall and in the distance there were sun-parched treeless mountains, blank, like bleached paper cut-outs.

'Bella,' Cagan said, assuming an actorly calm, 'forgive the intrusion, but I thought this too important to leave to plaintext. If you are not alone, might I suggest that you excuse yourself: you should ensure that you and you alone are seeing this message.' He spread his hands then brought them back together, as if giving her time to pause the recording, but she was already in her quarters, secure and alone. 'I'll continue when you give voice authorisation.'

'Go on, Powell,' she whispered.

'What I have to impart is not entirely good news,' Cagan said. In the unflattering noonday light his skin had the same leathery quality as the surface of the flexy. Burnt a raw red, it was the only real colour in the image. 'But I'll start with the good news. One hundred and twenty hours at Janus is still practical, provided you ditch the remaining mass drivers on the return leg. You'll be moving a little too fast to make orbit around Earth or Mars, but that won't be a problem. We can get your crew off *Rockhopper* with shuttles, and then use tugs to refuel her tanks for a slow-down. Frankly, though, we'll happily scupper *Rockhopper*: the old boat will have more than earned her keep by the time she brings you home.'

A thought formed in her head: *Why are you telling me this, Powell? I already know this.*

'So you don't need to worry about any of that,' he said, with a flicker of a smile. Then his tone turned grave. 'But you do need to worry about Svetlana Barseghian.'

Bella narrowed her eyes as she mouthed the woman's name.

'I don't know how delicately I can put this,' Powell said, 'but this whole business with the pressure measurements has opened a rather distressing can of worms. Now, I know Barseghian has a good track record, but something disturbing is still happening here. We think she may be undergoing some kind of —' And here Cagan hesitated, as if searching for the right words, but Bella knew him better than that. There was nothing spontaneous or unscripted about Powell Cagan.

He found the words he had appeared to be searching for and continued, 'It's some kind of stress-related episode; a crisis brought on by the pressure of the Janus mission. This all started after the death of Mike Takahashi, didn't it? The death of a colleague—' He corrected himself. 'The *unpleasant* death of a colleague, a death that was unavoidably linked to the mission itself. We all handle that sort of thing in different ways, Bella. Most of us pick up the pieces and get on with our jobs, and we go on doing that day in, day out, year after year, through death after death. But for some of us there comes a day when it happens and suddenly we don't pick up the pieces. We become them. I'm afraid that's what appears to have happened to Svetlana Barseghian.'

'No,' Bella said, as if that negation might in some way influence the message Cagan had recorded many hours earlier.

'She's clearly been badly affected by that death,' he said. 'Her nerve has snapped, and she can't face going through with the rest of the mission. She can't back out either. Nor, for that matter, can she admit the true nature of her problem. But the mind is a resourceful thing. When a psychological need exists, it finds ways and means.'

Cagan leaned back from whatever flexy or cam was capturing his speech. For a moment Bella saw a stricken expression cloud his face, his features caught in a moment of disfiguring psychic stress.

'This isn't easy,' he said. 'I'm not for one minute suggesting that any of this was premeditated or consciously engineered, but the evidence at our end is beyond dispute. Barseghian's version of events is not the truth. The data she claimed was from the buffer memory was data that she had falsified.'

'No,' Bella said again.

'It was vital to her that she find a way to undermine your confidence in the mission,' Powell went on inexorably, 'but there was no way to do that without creating a lie. As I say, I doubt that she was even aware of that motivation. She's probably quite *sincere* in her delusion. But the simple fact remains that she can no longer be trusted to execute her duties. In seven days you will be at Janus, Bella. You will be operating not just under the aegis of DeepShaft, but also as an envoy of the United Economic Entities. You will be acting for all humankind. There can be no room for mistakes, no room for misjudgements. It is imperative that you reach your target with a crew in whom you can have absolute confidence. That means you have to act immediately. You can't wait until Barseghian makes another error. You have to remove her now, before things become worse. You must do so quickly and cleanly, so that you have time to restore operational structure – and morale, of course – before your arrival.'

Cagan shook his head regretfully. 'If there were some way that I could have avoided sending this message, I would have. For what it's worth, I've also spoken to Craig Schrope. He's fully in the loop. But I know it will be different for you. I know you are friendly with Barseghian, that you like and trust her. I can only hope this necessary action does not damage that friendship.'

Cagan's message ended, and for a moment the flexy was silent. Then the incoming-call icon popped up and Craig Schrope's face filled the display surface.

'Bella,' he said. 'I take it you've you heard from Powell?'

'Yes,' she said, still numbed.

'Then we need to talk.'

He came to her office. They sat looking at each other, waiting for the other to speak. The fish formed an anxious audience, crowding each other, darting around the tank with hyperactive attentiveness. Normally they would have been fed by now, but the strain of recent days had thrown Bella off her routine. She was neglecting the fish, neglecting herself. She felt a vortex of tension building and reaching out from her like a magnetic storm.

'I'm not going to do this,' Bella said flatly. 'I'm not going to screw Svetlana just because she's raised concerns that Powell doesn't happen to like.'

'No one's screwing anyone. We're just talking about the acquisition of facts. Facts first, then judgements. It's how I handled Shalbatana.'

'This isn't Shalbatana, Craig. This is my best friend we're talking about here.'

'Best friends run off the rails too.'

'Not Svieta. I've never known anyone less likely to lose it.'

'It doesn't matter. I've seen enough psych evaluations to know that these things hit you out of the blue. In high-pressure careers, people sometimes crash and burn.' He looked at her carefully. 'Happens to the best of us.'

Bella blushed. She'd had no idea that Schrope knew anything about her own burn-out episode. She imagined Jim Chisholm sitting across from her, willing her not to say something rash.

'I had problems, but no one accused me of faking data.'

'I know, I know. I'm just saying – nobody's immune.' He clicked the end of his pen, then tapped it against the table. 'Okay, got a plan. We need to look at those numbers ourselves, independently of Svetlana. That'll mean getting someone from her team to cooperate with us.'

'What?'

'Someone competent, but who doesn't have strong ties to Svetlana. I'm thinking someone who came on team during the last rotation.'

'Why? What are you planning?'

'I'm thinking Meredith Bagley. Young kid, right? She's a company player. She knows ShipNet. She can get us those numbers. Then we'll have the facts.'

Bella flustered. 'I want to talk to Svieta first.'

He looked at her sadly. 'Talking to Svieta now would be a serious mistake.

She's too clever, too resourceful. Talk to her if you absolutely must . . . but I'd advise strongly against it.'

'I'm not sure why I need to remind you of this, Craig, but I'm the one running this ship.'

'Absolutely.' He suddenly looked abashed. 'Look, I'm sorry – sometimes I catch myself sounding as if I'm trying to take over the show. It's insolent and inexcusable. It's just that on Mars I was given pretty much free rein to do what I wanted. The only person I answered to was Powell Cagan. It's a hard habit to break.'

'I understand,' Bella said, 'but I urge you to put some effort in that direction.'

'I will – and I'm genuinely sorry. I only want to do the best by DeepShaft.'

Bella managed a smile. 'Everyone knows you did a good job on Mars. That's why I was happy to have you as my second. But this is a woman I've known and trusted for years. I won't treat her like a common criminal, and I won't see her humiliated in public.'

'I'll make absolutely sure this entire matter is handled with maximum discretion.' He looked at her encouragingly. 'Do you mind if I use your flexy?'

Bella hesitated for a second, then slid the flexy across her desk. Schrope checked the duty roster, establishing that Meredith Bagley was awake. He placed the call, drumming his fingers against the desk while he waited for her to answer.

'Meredith,' she said brightly, as if she had been expecting someone else. 'What can I—?'

Bella leaned into the visual field of the flexy. 'Meredith, can you come to my office immediately?'

'And make sure you don't speak to anyone on the way,' Schrope added.

She arrived within two minutes, her demeanour visibly fearful, as if expecting a reprimand. Bagley was a young addition to Svetlana's flight-operations team: keen but nervous, still not fully meshed into the social matrix of the ship. She fiddled with her thick black hair, her eyes darting from Bella to Schrope and back again.

'It's all right,' Bella said, 'there's nothing to worry about, and you're not in any trouble. As a matter of fact I'm more than happy with your performance.'

'We need you to do a job for us,' Schrope said. 'It's simple, and it won't take long. The car-line's running today, isn't it?'

'We're still making some adjustments—' Bagley began.

'That's okay – we won't complain if the ride is a little rough.' Schrope leaned over and consulted the duty roster again. He glanced at Bella. 'She should be sleeping now. This is as good a time as we're going to get.'

Bagley looked at the two of them. She didn't ask who 'she' was, but she must have had some inkling.

They left Bella's office and worked their way to the nearest car-line access point. A car was already there, but Schrope took a moment to call up a schematic showing the positions of the other vehicles on the line.

'Someone's in the sweatbox,' he said. 'I was hoping we'd have the place to ourselves.' Using his flexy, he tried to get a picture from one of the sweatbox webcams, but the links were down.

'I'll call ahead and ask them to leave,' Bella said.

'Actually,' Schrope said, 'it might be better if we just showed up.' He paused and added, 'Just a suggestion.'

They filled the three-seat car and Schrope punched in their destination. The car took them down the spine at a slower-than-normal rate, easing to a crawl as it navigated the area where the worst damage had occurred. Then it picked up speed, passing the ruined mid-spine workshop and sinking between the four looming cylinders of the fuel tanks.

Bagley sat in the rear seat of the teardrop-shaped capsule. She said nothing during the entire journey.

As expected, another car was already on the line at the sweatbox end. Bella's car slowed to a walking pace and nudged the other car forward until her vehicle was aligned with the airlock and they were able to disembark onto the titanium flooring. They were a kilometre nearer *Rockhopper*'s stern than in Bella's office, with a good deal less shock-absorbing insulation between them and the engine. The floor rumbled, as if intense drilling work was taking place just a few metres below. Once more, Bella had that almost palpable feeling of the engine working ferociously.

Schrope opened the inner airlock door to find that the sweatbox was already lit and warm. Two figures turned around, surprised at the arrival of anyone else. Bella recognised them: Robert Ungless and Gabriela Ramos, long-serving crew members – in a crisis their loyalty would lie with Svetlana.

'Robert, Gabriela,' she said by way of greeting. 'I'm really sorry, but something's come up. We're going to have to ask you to leave the sweatbox for a few minutes.'

They looked at her with obvious affront. Their equipment spooled entrails of fibre-optic line into the walls. Their flexies, spread out on the floor and folding tables, showed mind-numbing three-dimensional fuel-flow diagrams: schematics that would have given Escher a headache.

'It'll only take a few minutes,' Bella insisted.

'You've been given an order,' Schrope said. 'Put aside whatever you're doing and leave. There's a car outside. You can wait in it until we call you back in.'

Ungless and Ramos knew better than to argue. They left their equipment where it was, still plugged in, and slid past Bella into the airlock. When the inner door had sealed itself, she said to Schrope, 'I don't think they'll wait. I think they'll ride back to the hab and wake up Svieta.'

'They'll be contravening an order.'

'They'll say they misunderstood. They'll say they didn't know you had authority to give orders.'

Schrope snapped his fingers at Bagley. 'I need a dump of the fuel-pressure data in the memory buffer. You can do that, can't you?'

'Yes,' Bagley said warily.

'Then get on it. Load the data into a clean partition on your flexy, then give the captain and me read-only privileges.'

'I'm on it,' Bagley said, fiddling with the flexy's data line. Bella was glad that the woman knew what she had to do. She wanted to get this whole tawdry business out of the way as quickly as possible.

She felt a momentary increase in the rumble through the floor, a shuddering reminder of the engine instabilities that occasionally shook the ship. 'What was that?'

'That was the car disengaging from the lock,' Schrope said. 'They're on their way up.'

Svetlana splashed water on her face, sponged herself into some state of cleanliness and slipped on her jogging pants. She fastened on her bra and reached for a fresh T-shirt. The one at the top of the pile was mud-brown, with a cheaply printed copy of the *Rockhopper* mascot on the front: that toothsome, grinning, drill-toting penguin that had now been censored from the hull of the ship. Her hand dithered, about to reach for another shirt. Then she said 'fuck it' and put on the penguin anyway. She pushed her hair into shape and exited her quarters, leaving Parry room to wash and dress.

Ungless was still waiting outside. 'Five minutes ago, you said?' she asked.

'More like six or seven by now,' he said.

'Did you ride the last car up the spine?'

'No,' Ungless said, 'there's another one down there.'

Svetlana jogged around the curve of the corridor until she reached a viewing window set into what was currently the floor. She slid back the glare shield, exposing a pane of scuffed and ablation-mottled glass. She looked down along the length of the ship. A car was ascending the spine.

Parry crouched next to her, his trademark cap already jammed into place. 'Are you ready to tell me what's happening?'

'What do you *think*?' she asked snidely. 'We took our fears to Bella. This is the response.'

'But you trust Bella.'

'I trust her. I don't trust Schrope. Schrope wins.'

She stood up and barefoot – she hadn't even had time to slip on her trainers – padded further along the corridor. Parry followed her, pushing his arms into the frayed sleeves of an old denim shirt.

'This could be anything,' he said.

'Behind my back? I don't think so.'

'Svieta, will you stop? You're acting as if this has already turned into a mutiny.'

'My judgement has been questioned. *Doubted.* That's good enough for me.'

The car was just arriving when they reached the line. No one else was waiting at the airlock. Svetlana stationed herself by the inner door, arms folded as if she were the one about to dispense summary justice. Behind the inner door's dark window, the car slid up through the floor. Figures bustled into the lock. With no pressure to be equalised, there was no delay between the closing of the outer door and the opening of the inner one.

'Svieta,' Bella said, as their eyes met. To her credit, she barely blinked.

'Bella. Nice to see you. Been anywhere I ought to know about?'

'You know where we've been,' Craig Schrope said. 'That's why you're here. I take it Ungless and Ramos tipped you off?'

'No one tipped anyone off. And if I find that you've even looked at Robert or Gabriela—'

'You'll what?' He looked amused. 'Come on, I want to hear it. What will you do?'

'Never mind,' Bella said, positioning herself between Svetlana and Schrope. 'Let's keep this civil, shall we?'

'Can I go now?' Meredith Bagley asked timidly.

'Yes,' Bella said. 'Thank you, Meredith.'

'Whatever it is, you shouldn't have dragged her into it,' Svetlana said. 'You shouldn't have *used* her against me.'

'I didn't drag her into anything. I asked her to do a job for me.' Bella glanced around. 'Look, we can't talk here. Let's take this to my office.'

'All of us?' Parry asked.

'No, not you,' Schrope said. 'This is between us and Svetlana.'

'Then it's between you and me.'

Schrope looked at him warningly. 'Don't clean out your options box, Boyce.'

'Or what?' Parry asked.

'Come on,' Bella said. 'My office. Parry, too – and let's all try to behave like professionals, shall we?

In Bella's room they faced each other across the desk: Bella and Schrope on one side, Parry and Svetlana on the other. Bella slipped her flexy from her zip-up jacket and flattened it on the table, turning it to face Parry and Svetlana.

'You know what this is about, I think, Svieta.'

'I have a pretty good idea.'

'You brought an issue to me,' Bella said. 'I listened to your argument and I consulted headquarters about it.'

'And they fed you a bullshit explanation.'

'So you said. That's why I decided I needed more help from home.'

'Oh, no,' Svetlana said, with a sudden sinking feeling in her gut, as if the engine had just skipped a beat. 'You didn't *send* it to them, did you? After everything I told you?'

'What else was I supposed to do?'

'You could have acted on it. You could have trusted me.'

'And scrubbed the most important mission in the entire history of spaceflight? A mission with UEE backing? A mission that the entire system is counting on to succeed? A mission that *cannot* be repeated? Give me a break, Svieta. This was never going to be an easy call.'

'I can't believe you *sent* it to them. Of all the things you shouldn't have done—'

Bella's tone turned strident. 'I took action on the basis of what you told me. I could have just dismissed it.'

'What did they say?' Parry asked, still maintaining a semblance of calm.

'They said . . .' But Bella trailed off, unable to continue.

Craig Schrope tapped his pen against the flexy. 'They said the data was faked.'

'That's what Svieta was telling you,' Parry said.

'No,' Schrope said. 'What they said was that Svetlana faked the evidence. There never was any smoking gun.'

'That can't be true,' Parry said, looking to Svetlana for confirmation. 'Can it?'

'It is now,' she said.

'You can see it here,' Schrope said, directing Parry's attention to the flexy. 'There's no difference between the two sets of pressure data. The information in the buffer matches the information on ShipNet.'

'But I saw it for myself,' Parry said.

'You saw . . . something,' Schrope said. 'It wasn't what you thought you were seeing.'

'Bella screwed up,' Svetlana said. She felt faint, drained, knowing that nothing she could say now would make any real difference. 'Bella screwed up by sending them the buffer data.'

'Don't be silly,' Schrope said firmly.

'It must have been difficult for them to doctor those numbers,' Svetlana said, 'but when I found the differences between the two data sets, they had no choice but to find a way. And *you* let them, Bella. You showed them the numbers. You drew their attention to the buffer.'

'You think DeepShaft tampered with the buffer data as well?' Bella asked.

'They'd have a found a way if it mattered enough.'

'She has a point,' Parry said. 'If it made enough of a difference—'

'I think this has gone far enough,' Schrope said, clicking his pen with judicial finality. 'For the record, Svetlana, DeepShaft has already recommended your removal from duties. We could have acted on that recommendation immediately, but we thought we'd at least give you the benefit of the doubt.'

'Thanks, guy.'

'We checked their story,' Schrope continued. 'We checked their story because our instinct was to believe you. But you betrayed that trust, Svetlana. You let *us* down.'

'Oh, please.'

'Can't you see she's been set up?' Parry said. 'She's done *nothing* wrong – Bella, you know Svieta better than this. You know she'd never betray you.'

Bella's discomfort was obvious. 'I'm sorry it has to come to this,' she said, 'but I have to take the evidence at face value.' She looked at Svetlana pleadingly. 'I have to remove you from duty, Svieta. If I do anything other than that I'll be in dereliction of my own duty as commander of this mission.'

'You don't have to justify your actions,' Schrope said.

'Craig,' Bella said, 'shut the fuck up. This is between me and Svieta.'

'Don't do this,' Svetlana said. 'Listen to me. Listen to me or *we will all die.*'

'I can't. I have no choice.'

'Then we're fucked. All of us.'

'When we get back home,' Bella said, 'you have my word that there'll be a thorough inquiry. No stone will be left unturned. If the company has done this, then we'll find that evidence. We'll find someone who'll talk, someone who'll vindicate you.'

'Don't you understand?' Svetlana said. 'If I'm right, we will *never* get back home.'

Bella closed her eyes. 'We'll get back home,' she said. 'Whatever happens, that's a promise.'

'Don't hate me for this,' Bella said, when they were alone. 'Do anything but that.'

Svetlana looked at her from across the table. What she saw in Svetlana's eyes was much closer to stunned incomprehension than the self-righteous fury she had been expecting. 'Then don't do this,' she said softly. 'If our friendship means anything, don't do it.'

'I have no choice,' Bella said unhappily. 'I can only go by the evidence. The evidence couldn't look much worse.' Bella stared hard into Svetlana's eyes, trying to make some final connection that would salvage their friendship. 'But I meant what I said – *when* we get home—'

'It won't happen.'

'I'm going to talk to Ryan Axford,' Bella said, brightening, suddenly seeing a solution. 'You had a bad accident out there. It's my understanding that you left Ryan's care before he authorised your discharge. Really, you should still be in the medical centre. The last few days shouldn't have happened. I don't think it'll be difficult for us to say that they never did.' She waited, hoping Svetlana would see the sense in her proposal.

But Svetlana just shook her head with stubborn defiance. 'My accident had nothing to do with this. You know that, so why pretend otherwise?'

'I'm only trying to help.'

With maddening calm, Svetlana said, 'If you remove me from duty, it still won't alter the fact that we don't have enough fuel to make it back home.'

'I don't doubt for a minute that you believe that. The problem is that I can't have you going around telling everyone else. I have a ship to run, Svieta. I have a mission to complete. I've got planet fucking Earth looking over my shoulder, waiting for me to screw up.'

'*This* is the screw-up.'

Bella bridled, but by an immense effort of will she kept her temper. 'If only it was that easy. I'm a fifty-five-year-old woman, Svieta. I'm the commander of fifty thousand metric tonnes of mining spacecraft. There are one hundred and forty-five people on this ship—'

'One hundred and forty-four,' Svetlana said icily, 'unless you think Mike Takahashi still counts.'

'One hundred and forty-four, then. Of whom a lot fewer than seventy-two are women. Things are better than they've ever been, Svieta, but we're still a minority. And as commander of this ship I cannot *for one second* be seen to show the slightest leniency with anyone: most especially not someone who happens to be another woman – let alone a close personal friend.'

'So you make an example of me, just to show that you can be as tough and stubborn as any man?'

'Spare me the piety, Svieta: in my shoes you'd do exactly the same.'

There was the tiniest flicker of agreement in Svetlana's face: an unguarded reaction that nonetheless said that, yes, in that regard Bella was right. But that did not make the thing itself right, the same look said.

'Please reconsider, Bella. Give me time to prove this is real. Let me drill a pressure tap into one of the fuel tanks, get a direct measurement . . . anything.'

'I wish I could. I wish I believed you, but right now I don't. I don't think you're lying, either. I think you're just—'

'Deluded.'

'I burnt out once, Svieta. I know how it happens. One minute you're just sailing along, the next you're in pieces. There's no shame in it. It doesn't make you a bad person.'

Bella dared to think, for a moment, that her words had hit home; that Svetlana had realised that she was taking no pleasure in this and that she felt a compassionate concern for her friend's wellbeing.

Then Svetlana said, 'This isn't about you and me, is it? It's about Powell Cagan.'

'I'm sorry?' Bella responded mildly.

'We all know what happened with you and Cagan, Bella. We all know you fucked him. We all know it's more than just business with the two of you.'

Bella's face stung. In all their years of friendship, she had never once spoken of the affair with Cagan. She had assumed, with absolute certainty, that Svetlana knew nothing of it. But she now realised it had been there all along, like a weapon waiting to be drawn and used.

'That was twenty-five years ago,' she said, on the edge of tears.

'But old habits die hard, right? You might not be fucking him now, but Powell still only has to say jump and you say how high—'

'Don't say another word. Please, don't say *one more word.*'

'After all this time, you just can't face it, can you?'

'Face what?'

'The possibility that Cagan might not be the man you looked up to back then.'

Bella moved to slap Svetlana across the cheek. But at the last moment she stayed her hand, even as Svetlana held up her own hand in defence.

'You shouldn't have said that,' Bella said. 'You really, really, shouldn't have said that.'

# CHAPTER 8

The great barrel of the mass driver swung slowly through space until it was brought to a halt by the free-fliers. Tiny pulses of micro-thrust finessed the aim.

Denise Nadis sat wearing a headset and wraparound mike combo, dreadlocks tied back, tapping a shiny purple fingernail against the mike as she talked to the AI of the newly deployed driver.

'We're okay?' Bella asked.

'She's all yours.'

Bella opened a channel to the *Shenzhou Five* using the reply protocols that the Chinese had already specified.

'This is Captain Bella Lind,' she said. 'I am commander of the UEE exploration vehicle *Rockhopper*. Thirty minutes ago our sensors detected the *Shenzhou Five*'s penetration into our exclusion volume. We are entitled – even obliged – to take defensive action against any possible threat.'

Bella halted and made a conscious effort to sound reasonable and conciliatory. 'We have the means to defend ourselves. We have deployed a steerable mass driver loaded with a free-flier robot equipped with a nuclear demolition device, the kind we use for comet reshaping. I can put that nuke close enough to hurt you; it may fry your electronics or stress your shielding. I am hoping I will not have to do that, and that this message will be enough of a warning for you to apply reverse thrust and start exiting my airspace. If you do not, I will put that shot across your bows. If that does not deter you there will be no second warning: I will just keep loading up the mass drivers until you get the message. The closer you get, the better my aim. I am asking you to turn around now. I will give you five minutes to signal your intentions by altering your thrust and vector.'

The message had been transmitted in real-time: even allowing for translating software delays, Wang Zhanmin should already have received her first communication. There would be no time for him to consult with Beijing for clarification on the best course of action. But Bella doubted that Wang would need such assistance. The appended video file, showing the deployment of the mass driver, should have been all the encouragement he needed. Everyone in space knew what a mass driver could do if you pointed it the wrong way.

But five minutes went by and there was no detectable change in the thrust signature or transponder Doppler of the Chinese ship. Bella gave Wang Zhanmin two extra minutes of grace, then ordered the driver to deliver its payload.

Telephoto cameras tracked the foreshortened gun-barrel shape of the driver. The iron cage that would normally have accelerated a lump of cometary material flicked to one end of the driver's long launch track in less than two-tenths of a second, faster than the eye could follow. Recoil shoved the driver in the opposite direction. By the time the payload emerged, it had gained fourteen kilometres per second of motion away from *Rockhopper*.

Nadis confirmed that the robot and its nuclear cargo had survived the launch: they were hardened like artillery shells. It would take five hours to cross space to the *Shenzhou Five*, but the robot's own thrusters would be able to make small course adjustments if the Chinese ship deviated from its predicted flight path.

Bella didn't expect much of that. What she knew of the Chinese indicated that if Wang Zhanmin had not backed down by now, he never would.

She called Nadis. 'Status on the driver, Denise.'

'Bruised and battered, but she can probably take another pulse.'

'Good. Load another robot into the can. I think Wang's going to need more than one bloodied nose before he sees sense.'

Bella took no satisfaction in being right: she would have liked nothing better than for the *Shenzhou Five* to turn away with its tail between its legs, but for the next six hours the ship remained perfectly on course, its fusion burn clean and even.

During the final phase of the intercept, the free-flier steered itself to within a hundred kilometres of the Chinese ship, close enough to make a point but not, Bella devoutly hoped, to do more than bruise it.

Slamming past, the FAD opened like a flower. The prick of hot blue light was visible across three hundred thousand kilometres: an evil little guest star that had no business in the sky. Then the nuclear flash died away, and the transponder signal from the *Shenzhou Five* was still there, ticking like a pulsar.

'The bastard didn't even blink,' Schrope said. They sat in her office and digested the news.

'He's brave, Craig. Anyone who comes this far out has my respect, no matter what flag they hang on their wall.'

'All the same, you made him a promise. I've reprogrammed the second free-flier for a closer intercept. One hundred klicks doesn't seem to have done the trick. How does fifty sound?'

'Be careful,' she said. 'We want to scare them off, that's all.'

'Fifty is still plenty of room. Wang the Man is probably bored out of his mind. Let's give him something to write home about.'

Bella waited another five minutes to see if the detonation had resulted in any belated change in the *Shenzhou Five*'s trajectory, but there was no alteration: it was as if their warning shot hadn't even registered. Part of her wanted to send another warning message – she couldn't help but see the amiable face of the young Chinese commander whenever she closed her eyes – but she had warned him that there would be no second chance.

She told Nadis to fire another shot.

'Kill margin set to fifty,' Nadis told her as the robot sped away.

'It isn't supposed to kill,' Bella said fiercely, 'it's just persuasion. Don't anyone forget that.'

Bella was off-duty. She knew she ought to be using the hours to catch up on sleep, but the idea seemed ludicrous. She worked on her static bicycle until she hit exhaustion like an iron wall, and then she worked through the exhaustion into the clean, clear limbo beyond it.

She was trying not to think about Svetlana, because that only made things worse, but even with the Chinese matter demanding her full attention, her thoughts kept wandering back to what she had done to Svieta. Her best friend.

With Ryan Axford's agreement, Bella had arranged for her to be detained in a separate annexe of the medical centre, in the room that was normally reserved for contagious cases. Axford had told his staff that Svetlana needed to be readmitted following complications – unspecified complications – after the mass-driver accident. Just a small white lie – and maybe not a lie at all, Bella thought; she was half-convinced that the incident *had* sent her friend over the edge. It was a way of saving both their faces. There was to be no mention of differences of opinion between Bella and her senior systems engineer; no one would have to know that Svetlana had been relieved of duty until *Rockhopper* was back home, at which point the matter could be handled with suitable discretion.

Bella could see how Svetlana – how *both* of them – felt wounded and wronged, but acknowledging that fact put neither of them closer to reconciliation. Right now she didn't want it either. Svetlana had put her in an intolerably difficult position, and Bella had tried to handle the issue with tact, despite the appalling pressure she had been under. But Svetlana hadn't been able to see that. All she had seen was her own damaged pride: *how dare Bella not take her warnings seriously?* She should have *known* that some part of Bella desperately wanted to listen to her friend.

If Svetlana had left it at that – if she'd been content to let Bella know how let down and undervalued she felt – then there might still have been some prospect for mending the damage. But Svetlana hadn't been able to stop there. The moment she mentioned Cagan, Bella knew that Svieta truly hated her. It was astonishing how quickly friendship could turn to enmity, she thought, like a compass needle swinging from one pole to the other.

They'd been excellent friends. They'd make excellent enemies as well.

When she finished cycling, the sweat was stinging her eyes and her legs felt as if the bone, marrow and muscle had been flensed out and replaced by fine, sharp slivers of shattered glass. She drank a litre of water, fed the fish and checked the acidity in the tank. Attracted by her presence, a group of bloodfins nosed through the upper layers.

The translucence of the bloodfins always startled her. She could see their spines: brush-thin, as if drawn in with lines of pale Indian ink. One was always bolder than the rest. Time after time it astounded her that something so simple, so toy-like, could be alive, and have the faintest glimmering of personality.

She considered fixing herself a meal. It was at least a day since she had eaten anything, but even if the exercise hadn't killed her appetite (which it nearly always did), she didn't think she would be able to keep anything down. Instead, she flicked through the uplinked newsfeeds, dismayed at how little airtime *Rockhopper* – and Janus, for that matter – now merited. The heavyweight channels carried some discussion about the prickly stand-off between the Chinese and the UEE, but it was buried a long way below the main items.

A plane carrying a young athletic troupe had crashed near the summit of Tirich Mir in the Hindu Kush. Planes didn't crash very often, and when they did they tended to make the news. The weather had cleared sufficiently for orbital and dirigible cams to obtain close-up imagery of the survivors: infrared blobs huddled around the broken crucifix of the wreck. Biometric recognition software dropped names onto the anonymous group, with tickertaping text along the bottom of the feed giving biographical data. Helicopters couldn't get to them, and although teleoperated robots of the Pakistani emergency services were trying to get through to them, it was a race against hypothermia, fluid loss and hypoxia.

Bella stared at the satellite imagery of the crash survivors with a vague resentment. Three of them had died since the last update: a teacher and two children. She watched the rest of them stomp around in the snow, trying to keep warm.

Her flexy chimed, filling with Craig Schrope's face.

'Bella,' she said, redundantly.

'I have some news,' Schrope said. He glanced away from the camera, as if concerned that she might see something in his face. 'It's the kind you might want to be sitting down for. We put another one across their bows.'

'That was the idea,' she said. 'Did it have any effect?'

'It did.'

There was a certain tone to his voice. 'Craig, what are you telling me?'

'We got too close,' Schrope said.

'Too close?'

'We took them out.'

He told her that the *Shenzhou Five* had fallen silent. There was neither transponder signal nor thrust signature. Confirmation that the ship had been destroyed would have to wait, but Bella knew that was merely a formality.

'We were supposed to be practising deterrence,' she said, forcing an icy calm into her voice. 'Please tell me what went wrong.'

'The kill margin was still dialled down to fifty,' Schrope said placidly. 'It shouldn't have hurt them.'

'Newsflash, Craig: *we blew them out of the goddamn sky!* I think that probably counts as "hurting them".'

'I'm aware of that,' he said.

'You want to take a stab at explaining how that came to happen?'

'They must have changed course. We were using a predictive model most of the way. If they deviated from that—' Schrope shrugged, as if nothing else needed to be said. 'That was their problem. Law was on our side.'

'Is that going to help you sleep tonight, knowing that some legal specialist in Niagara Falls says you were in the right?'

'Frankly, yes.'

All the rage bottled up since her encounter with Svetlana spilled over like a flood tide. 'You're a reptile, Craig. I've even bred cichlids with more humanity.' She slammed the flexy shut before she said worse.

Bella stepped into the green calm of the medical complex, grateful to find Jim awake, propped up in bed with a flexy spread across his lap. He peered at her over his half-moon reading glasses. 'If this is an attempt to cheer me up, I think you need to go out and come in again,' he said.

He obviously detected something in her expression, Bella thought. 'Sorry,' she said.

'Pull up a seat. You look like the world and his wife just paid you a visit, bringing all their troubles.' He looked at her shrewdly, eyes narrowed. 'Is it really that bad?'

'Oh, yes.' She folded down a seat and sat next to the bed, head lowered in contrition. 'It's bad. It's worse than bad. I've got Svetlana pinned down in isolation because she started undermining my authority.'

He blinked in surprise. 'What happened?'

'She's got it into her head that we're being conned, that we don't have enough fuel to make it home after the rendezvous.'

'Jesus. You didn't think to tell me about this?'

'Didn't want you to burden you, Jim.'

'But you're burdening me now.'

'Things got worse.'

'Oh, great. How could they get *worse* than imprisoning one of your senior crew?'

'Something really bad just happened – and to cap it all I just did something really, really stupid. You're up to speed on the *Shenzhou Five*?'

'Of course.' He dimmed the flexy and put it aside. 'The Chinese ship, the one that's been inviting us to join them in glorious mutual exploration of Janus.'

'We just destroyed it.'

He took off the half-moon glasses, folded them and placed them delicately on his bedside table. 'Tell me what happened.'

She told him about the UEE exclusion zone, the mass drivers and the payloads they had been firing back at the Chinese ship. She told him about her confrontation with Schrope.

'It was supposed to be a warning action,' she said. 'The idea was to scare them off, not to wipe them off the face of the galaxy.'

'Did you see any reaction from her captain after you put the first nuke across his bows?'

'None at all.'

'Meaning he was probably under orders not to back down.' Chisholm bit hard on his lip and shook his head. 'This was always going to be a tough call, but I don't think anyone did anything wrong here. The Chinese were yanking our chain. We had to take a stand. That's all we did.'

'I only wanted them to turn around—'

'We drew the line in the sand. No one made them cross it.'

'Commander Wang would have been under orders.'

'Don't feel too sorry for the guy, Bella. By tomorrow he'll be a national hero. They'll have named a square after him within the week and moved his widow into a nice mansion in Shanghai.'

'We killed him, him and all of his crew.'

'Beijing killed them.'

'They didn't even have time to send back for orders.'

'It was still Beijing, even if those orders were given weeks ago. Look, I'm sorry about what happened, but this *is* space exploration.'

'There's something else. I did – said – something inexcusable.'

'To Svetlana?'

'No, worse. Schrope.'

'So you finally lost it with the Shalbatana Terrier.'

'I came pretty close to accusing him of shooting them down deliberately.'

Chisholm mulled over the idea, as if he didn't find it totally preposterous. 'Could he have done that?'

'All he'd have to do is switch a few lines of code. It wouldn't have stretched his competence envelope.'

'I don't think he did it. He's a solid company stiff, but he isn't psychotic.' He sipped some water from the bedside dispenser. 'How did Terrier-boy take it, anyway?'

'Not great.'

Chisholm looked amused. 'Tell me.'

'By then I'd already accused him of being a reptile.'

'A reptile,' Chisholm said thoughtfully. 'But what type?'

'We didn't get into specifics.'

'Well, that's good. At least you left it open.'

'Trust you to find something positive to say.'

'Positivity is something I'm working on. Did Terrier-boy just lap this up?'

'He's asked for a written apology.'

Chisholm winced. 'He's got you there. It's not that you've offended him – this guy's skin is thicker than the Europan ice-crust. He wasn't *upset* that you called him a reptile. But you sure as hell gave him a pretext for pretending to be.'

'I know. That's what makes me so mad at myself: I just fell right into it.'

'You can bet the bastard had a flexy stuffed under his jacket, too, set to voice-record. If he doesn't see you eating some serious crow, he'll mail the whole thing home and let the psychs loose on it.'

'I know,' she said again.

'They'll raise questions about your command fitness, say the Janus thing is getting to you; that you've started to lash out at your senior staff. The Svetlana thing might not help.'

'Craig was the one pushing for her removal, Jim.'

'But you made the decision, right?'

'Yes,' she said, resignedly.

'That's the way he'd have known it would go down. He's angling for your suspension, Bella. He's itching to park his behind in your command chair.'

'So why wait for my apology?'

'Kid's building up ammunition. Even if he lets you ride this one out, he'll have a thick dossier to hand when we get back home. If it doesn't buy him *Rockhopper*, it'll still get him some kind of promotion.'

'The devious little shit.'

'Agreed. I think you ought to write that apology.'

'I thought that was what you'd say. Matter of fact, I've already written it.'

'Good for you. Bet it felt like pulling teeth.'

'If it keeps the ship together, I'll gladly pull my real ones.'

'Send Craig the grovel note, then send him to me. I'll have a word, see if I can smooth things out. I'll tell him you've been under a lot of pressure. And if he turns against you when we get home, you know he'll have me to deal with as well.'

'Thanks,' she said, doubtfully.

'I could talk to Svetlana, too. Ryan's got her in isolation?'

'It's just to keep her away from the rest of the crew. There's really nothing wrong with her. I feel lousy about it, Jim, but I didn't know what else to do.'

'She's pretty good, isn't she?'

'None better.'

'Then these doubts she has – you've looked into them?'

'I gave her the benefit. Evidence looked pretty compelling, too. But then I consulted with home – turns out her numbers didn't stack up.'

'Her maths was out?'

'Worse than that. Turns out the numbers she was showing me were faked, to bolster her case.'

'Woo.' He closed his eyes, as if the news caused him actual pain. 'That's pretty heavy stuff.'

'They say she's having some kind of episode. I wouldn't believe it, Jim – this is Svetlana Barseghian, not some green-behind-the-ears newbie on first rotation. She's been through every crisis scenario imaginable and I've never even seen her break sweat. But that's the way it was with me, too.'

'You think if it happened to you, it can happen to her.'

'You put anything through enough fatigue cycles, sooner or later it fails.'

'Including people.'

'We're just small parts in a big machine, Jim. None of us is invulnerable.'

He studied her with fierce intensity. 'I can see this puts you in a bind. Can't have been easy, I guess.'

'She didn't take it well. She said things.' Bella swallowed. 'I nearly hit her. I nearly *hit* my best friend.'

'Whatever you did, I'm sure you acted in the only professional way possible.'

'That's what I keep telling myself.'

'But it doesn't help.'

'No.'

He reached out and took her hand. In that moment of human contact Bella felt some tiny relief from her distress. She was glad, selfishly, that Jim Chisholm's illness had eased him from duty. It allowed them talk like this, unstifled by the protocols of command.

'Cut yourself some slack, Bella Lind,' he said. 'That's an order.'

She e-mailed the letter of apology to Schrope, then made the mistake of trying to sleep. When the alarm pulled her back into consciousness she felt worse than when she had gone under. Her dreams had been fitful and repetitive, replaying the day's events over and again, so that she saw the demise of the *Shenzhou Five* from different angles. Then the dream lurched narrative tracks, conflating the attack on the Chinese ship with the downing of the plane in the high mountains of the Hindu Kush, and she trudged knee-deep in snow, shining a searchlight into wintry darkness, looking for a survivor.

The dream kept ending just at the point when she found Wang Zhanmin, entombed in snow but still wearing his spacesuit. Somehow she always knew the exact spot to start digging. She would smear the snow from his visor and see that he was still alive behind the glass, his expression relieved and forgiving, simply glad to have been saved. Then she would wake, very briefly, and she would slip back into sleep, and the dreams would resume. As she crawled from her hammock, she felt a chemical burden in her body, a debt that had only been partly repaid.

If this, she wondered, was the price they were paying to catch up with Janus, what toll would it ask of them when they arrived?

Svetlana ripped away the adhesive monitoring patches Axford had pressed to her skin. Immediately the machines launched into a shrill, affronted chorus. She clattered them aside and climbed from the bed. Her clothes were still neatly folded on the bedside table: jogging pants, T-shirt, a plaid shirt that she wore unbuttoned. She felt light-headed, but that was to be expected after the length of time she had spent in bed. Opening the air-sealed door between isolation and the rest of the medical centre, she heard Jim Chisholm stir behind his partition curtain.

'Svetlana?' he asked in a pale croak of a voice. 'Are you all right?'

'I'm fine, Jim,' she said.

'What are you doing? You sound like . . . is something wrong?'

'It's better that you don't ask,' she said, 'much better.'

'I know why you're here,' Chisholm said. 'I know that you're here because you've had some falling out with Bella, and—'

She pulled the curtains far enough apart to see his face, half-swallowed by the pillow, with a damp grey patch next to his mouth. For the first time he looked properly ill to her, as if his condition had finally forced itself to the surface. What had looked like a sure thing three weeks ago – that Chisholm would survive the trip to Janus and the return journey to Earth – suddenly felt infinitely less certain.

'There *is* something wrong,' Svetlana said. 'Something that I've—' But now that she was on her feet for the first time in many hours, something stalled her thoughts. Something was different, but at first she attributed it to her light-headedness. 'The gravity,' she said, at last.

'You noticed, too,' Chisholm said, nodding as best he could: a vague adjustment in the angle of his head in its nest of a pillow. 'I thought it was just me.'

'We're not running at half a gee any more.'

'No. A bit less – two-fifths, perhaps? Maybe even less than that?' His eyes were uncomfortably wide as he sought confirmation.

'It's still only day twenty,' Svetlana said. 'We're a full day from the encounter.'

'There's got to be a reason for it.'

'There must be a problem with the engine: there's no other explanation.' And then a vile thought occurred to her: the engine had been throttled back because the fuel reserves had suddenly begun to run low. One of these minutes, one of these seconds, the engine was going to just snuff out and suddenly *Rockhopper* would be free-falling into the night, the terrible realisation setting in that there was no way to stop, no way to turn around.

But her immediate fears quickly faded: that couldn't be the answer. The engine would keep running at normal efficiency until the last gasp of pressure from the tanks. And even given Svetlana's assumptions about the real fuel load, they were still a long way from running dry. They had enough fuel to complete the Janus operations; it was the return trip that was problematic.

'When did this happen? Is there anything on ShipNet about it?'

'Nothing.'

'And neither Bella nor Craig has spoken to you about it?'

'In case you hadn't noticed,' Chisholm said, 'I'm not exactly in the command loop any more. They don't want to burden me with the pressures of command. They mean to be kind.'

He was drugged to the eyeballs, fading in and out of lucidity like a drowning man. *More than just kindness*, Svetlana thought. She hoped her face gave nothing away.

'I need to talk to someone about this,' she said. 'Maybe they don't even realise we have a problem.'

'Bella won't like you leaving medical.'

Svetlana smiled at the dying man. 'In the long run, I think she'll thank me for it.'

No one was on duty as she left the medical centre. Her footsteps fell with dreamy lightness on the catwalk panels. The more she mulled it over, the less likely a technical failure seemed to her. Either the engine worked or it didn't: there was no middle ground in which it would work at slightly reduced efficiency. And since the fuel could not be running out yet, that left only one possibility: Bella must have given the order to throttle back.

Bella was beginning to have doubts.

Svetlana made her way through the interior of the ship, glad that the lights had been dimmed to a gloomy red for the night shift. The only person she met on her way was Brenda Gammel, from Parry's EVA squad, but Gammel was deep in her own thoughts, giving Svetlana a polite but distracted nod as they passed. Good that it wasn't someone from her own team. Then there would have been too many awkward questions about where she had been and why she was now up and about.

As she walked, Svetlana became less certain about how to proceed. If Bella had already begun to come around to her point of view, then it might be best to let events take their course.

She reached Parry's quarters and tapped on the plastic door, quietly, until Parry slid it back. He blinked in surprise, then frowned, worried.

'Svieta,' he said, 'why are you—?'

She cut him off. 'Let me in, Parry. We need to talk.'

He slid back the door as wide as it would go to let Svetlana squeeze into his quarters. 'Could I get into trouble for this?'

'You're already in trouble. I don't think a little more will make any difference.'

'Did Bella give you permission to leave the medical centre?'

'Never mind that. What's up with the ship? Has Bella given an order to slow down?'

'Yes,' Parry said simply.

She allowed herself an instant of triumph. Bella's doubts would build like a landslide, from the tiniest of slippages.

'Has she said anything about it on ShipNet?'

'She'll make an announcement at the next shift change, if the situation stays the same,' Parry said.

'She knows the situation, Parry. It isn't going away. They can't *un*screw us.'

'Maybe we're not talking about the same situation. There's been a development. So far only the chiefs know about it.'

Her elation drained away to nothing. 'What kind of development?'

'It looks as if we may have enough fuel after all.'

'No,' she said forcefully, 'I know I'm right about this. Just because I can't prove it to Bella's satisfaction— Jesus, Parry: *you* know I'm right.'

'I believe you – but it may not matter now.'

'Of course it damn well matters,' she said, and then regretted it, because the one person she did not need to pick fights with was Parry Boyce. Moderating her tone, she added, 'Why? What's changed?'

'Janus,' Parry said.

'Oh, great. Tell me.'

'We've been shining a laser onto it for the last three days, a low-energy optical laser, nothing that could be mistaken for a hostile gesture.'

'I know about that,' she said, remembering that they had gone over the wisdom of this in Saul Regis's discussion group. 'Partly to map the surface details, partly to give us better distance information so we can refine our approach. What's happened?'

'Janus is . . . not exactly slowing, but reducing its acceleration. It's as if it's realised we're trying to catch up and is making it as easy as possible.'

She found the news intriguing and troubling in equal measure. 'Why would it run all this way and stop now? You can't tell me it's only just noticed us.'

'Maybe that's exactly what's happened.'

'I don't buy it,' she said. 'There's a catch. There's always a catch.'

'I don't see that there has to be one. Suppose it's committed to leaving the system, for one reason or another – it's received an order from Spica, or something like that. It can't stop running from us, but at least it can slow its departure enough to let us get a better look. A chance to say goodbye.'

Parry paused: it must have been obvious from her expression that she was not convinced by any of that. 'Look, if Janus stops accelerating, we can, too. Every gram of fuel we'd have burnt keeping up with it for the five days of the survey phase is a gram we'll still have for the journey home.'

'The bastards couldn't have known this was going to happen,' Svetlana said fiercely. 'And it'll *still* be marginal.'

'You may not have the satisfaction of proving you were right,' Parry said, 'at least, not until we get home. But don't let that cloud what a good thing this is. Janus hasn't attacked us, or fired a shot across our bows, or made any attempts to outrun us. It wants to meet us. Can't you see that?'

'I'm seeing something,' Svetlana said. 'Just not sure what it is yet.'

For a minute they said nothing, then Svetlana moved into the comfort of Parry's embrace and they held each other. They kissed, then someone knocked on the plastic partition: three authoritative raps, like the visit of a policeman.

A muffled voice came through the plastic. 'Parry. It's Bella. I'm guessing you know why I'm here.'

Svetlana slid back the panel. 'It's not Parry's fault I'm here. He wasn't sheltering me.'

'Why do you keep making this so difficult?' Bella asked. She was alone, looking tousled, as if she'd been roused from bed.

'Because you're killing us.'

Bella kept her voice low. 'Has Parry told you about the change in Janus?'

'You still need to turn this ship around.'

'No,' Bella said firmly, 'in a day we'll know whether Janus really is letting us take a closer look. If that's the case then we'll complete the mission as planned.'

'And if it begins accelerating again, so that we have to burn fuel simply to keep following it?'

Bella hesitated just a moment too long. Svetlana recognised a fissure in the surface of her surety: the crack of doubt she had opened and had prayed would widen. Whatever Janus had done, it was still there.

'We'll review things,' she said.

'You almost believe me, don't you? What's stopping you, Bella? Is it Craig Schrope?'

Clattering footsteps marked the approach of another figure. Svetlana pushed herself half-out of Parry's quarters, with her legs dangling into the corridor. The approaching man leaned forward, his hands whisking along the support rails. He wore a blue zip-up jumpsuit, padded around the joints.

'Hello, Craig,' Svetlana said icily.

'Problem here?' Schrope asked. He looked at Svetlana without surprise. 'Last thing I heard, you were supposed to be in medical. That was the arrangement, right?'

'She broke it,' Bella said sadly.

'What exactly is your problem, Svetlana?'

'Get out of my face, Craig. This is between me and the real commander of this ship, not some jumped-up company sock puppet.'

Somewhere along the corridor, another partition rasped open. Someone poked their head out, looked at them and then returned inside.

'Well, we've given reasonable a try,' Schrope said.

'What would you suggest next?' Parry said. 'Throwing her out of an airlock?'

'Don't be a jerk-off all your life,' Schrope said.

'Only following your example, Terrier-boy.'

'Parry,' Bella said, menacingly, 'I don't need this now. Please, just keep out of it.'

'You'll have to lock me up,' Svetlana said. 'If you don't, I'll try to take this ship from you. Just so you know where I stand.'

'Well, then,' Schrope said, 'that settles things, doesn't it? Thanks for the clarification, Svetlana. I've always admired transparency. It makes decisions like this so much easier.'

They locked her down with something close to regret, reminding her of parents banishing a child to her room for some infraction that the child barely comprehended but still had to learn was wrong. This was for her own good, not theirs. She was still allowed access to ShipNet, but only to the shallowest, least secure layers.

In an absurd twist, she had been assigned two 'guards' from Ryan Axford's medical section: Jagdeep Singh and Judy Sugimoto. Svetlana didn't care to speculate about what they had been told. All she knew was that when one or the other of them came to escort her to the washroom or the gymnasium, they did so with an exaggerated solicitousness that she had never known as a real patient. During these little expeditions there was never anyone else about, and she had the whole washroom to herself. It was the same in the gymnasium – some pretext had been used to remove everyone else. She could have refused to exercise, but part of her wanted to be strong and so she submitted to the regime they suggested. She jogged and used weights, and then showered away some of her pent-up frustration.

Parry was allowed to visit her, though only under the supervision of one of the nurses. He came once every six or eight hours, between his own duties with the EVA team.

'This is ridiculous,' she said. 'Bella's blocked everything. I barely know what day it is.'

'She isn't keeping you in the dark as much as you think,' Parry said. 'I'm not defending her – I think this is wrong – but I do think she genuinely hated having to do this to you.'

'She had a choice.'

'She didn't, not really. I know this is cutting Bella up really badly. She's not enjoying one second of it. She thinks she's destroyed a friendship, a really good one.'

'She's the one ignoring the evidence.'

'No,' Parry said, gently but firmly, 'she didn't ignore it at all. She looked at it, weighed it, took it seriously, but it just didn't convince her.' He sighed, kneading his red cap between his fingers in a strangely beseeching gesture, as if he had come to her in penitence. 'Look, it isn't all as bad as you think, anyway.'

'Looks pretty bad from where I'm sitting.'

'Bella hasn't shut you out of everything – at least, no more than she has the rest of us. That's what I meant when I said she wasn't keeping you in the dark as much as you think.'

'I can't see anything,' she said, 'not even the news from home. Is that what you mean by not keeping me in the dark?'

'That,' Parry said, 'is nothing to do with Bella at all. It's the uplink antenna – they're having problems picking up the signal.'

'What kinds of problem?'

'They don't know what's going on. It's just that there's nothing coming in on the uplink. Like the rest of the system's gone off the air.'

'But they must have a team looking into it,' Svetlana said. 'Haven't they figured it out yet?'

'Doesn't look like it.'

'If Bella would only let me back into ShipNet,' she said, 'then I might be able to look into it.'

'You'd do that?'

'I never asked to be removed from duty,' she said. 'I just said I'd do everything in my power to turn us around.'

'And now?'

'That's still true. But if Bella wants my input, she can have it.'

'I don't know,' Parry said. 'I'll mention it to her, but I think she'll probably wait and see what your team has to say first.'

'It can't be anything complicated. How long have they been working on it?'

'About twelve hours,' Parry said.

# CHAPTER 9

Day twenty turned into day twenty-one. News filtered through to Svetlana via Parry: Janus had continued its obliging deceleration; in response, Bella had throttled the engine back to one-tenth of a gee. *Rockhopper* was now making its final approach to their initial study position, ten thousand kilometres astern of Janus.

If the former moon's decelerating trend continued, it would soon be moving at constant velocity. The plan was to hold station at ten thousand kilometres for a day, then move in closer, to within a thousand kilometres of the surface. If Janus tolerated that, they would move closer still. By the third day of the five-day encounter, robots and unmanned autonomous vehicles would land on the artefact. If the robots and UAVs were permitted access, then people would follow. On day four they would limit themselves to passive surface investigations. If that went well, then on day five they would attempt to secure a physical sample of the machinery. They'd begin with microscopic scrapings and return each sample to *Rockhopper*, which by then would be standing off at a safe distance. If those small sample collections were successful, they would increase to larger specimens. On day six, *Rockhopper* would depart and Janus would fall away into the night, on its long ride to Spica.

There was still no news from home.

The technical team had been working on the problem for nineteen hours, but – so Svetlana's informant told her – nothing they had done had shed any light on the problem.

Parry passed her a flexy. 'Bella's beginning to stew. If she wasn't, she'd never have agreed to this.'

'She wants me to take a look at it?'

'She says that if you can find something, that would be good.'

As Svetlana's hands moved over the hide-like skin of the display, she tumbled through ShipNet layers without obstruction.

'How long is she giving me?'

'As long as it takes,' Parry said. 'There's a technical note in your inbox –

everything they've tried so far. It may give you a head start. There's no point trying to slow or stop the ship, Bella says – as soon as you go anywhere near critical systems, they'll lock you out.'

'Who led this repair team?'

'Belinda Pagis and Mengcheng Yang. They've been working around the clock.'

She nodded, for those were the names she would have pencilled in for the repair duty. 'Did anyone EVA?'

'No – too dangerous under thrust, given the location of the antenna. I wouldn't sign off one of *my* people to go outside, put it like that.'

She had expected as much. 'Robots?'

'We've already had Jens Fletterick look at it with one of the free-flier remotes – there's a video clip in the tech note. Doesn't seem to be any external damage to the antenna, no blown servos, but maybe you'll see something everyone's missed.'

'I'll look at it,' she said dubiously. 'Is Jens still on shift?'

Parry glanced at his big multi-dialled diver's watch. 'I don't think so. Should be catching up on some sleep now. Why?'

'I'd like to talk to Jens, or anyone in Saul's robotics team.'

'That'll have to go through Bella, I'm afraid. What are you thinking?'

'Something we should try,' she said.

Janus loomed as large in *Rockhopper*'s sky as a full moon seen from the Earth: a bright clenched fist peppered with tiny islands of ice amidst seas of dark, glinting mechanism.

*Rockhopper* was unspeakably close to it now: a mere twenty thousand kilometres from the object's machine-clotted surface. Soon they would halve that distance and come to a watchful halt relative to the moon. There had been no hint of a reaction from the alien thing; no warning to keep their distance. Equally, beyond the fact of the moon's slowing, there had been no invitation to come closer either.

Bella finished a cigarette as the nurse arrived with Svetlana. There was no physical contact between Svetlana and the nurse, but Judy Sugimoto never strayed more than a metre from her charge. Discreetly, but not so discreetly that Svetlana wouldn't have been aware of it, Sugimoto carried a sedative syringe, ready to be jabbed into the other woman's arm if she turned difficult.

'You didn't have to go to all this trouble,' Svetlana said. 'We could have met at my place.'

'If I could have kept this to just the two us, perhaps that might have worked,' Bella said. 'Obviously, that wasn't an option.'

Craig Schrope clicked his pen. He sat behind Bella's desk, leaning back in the seat. 'Parry said you might have an angle on the uplink issue.'

'I asked to see Saul Regis.'

'Saul's on his way. In the meantime, we'd like to know why you think he can help. We've already had a robot look the thing over, and there's no sign of damage. Diagnostic software hasn't flagged any mechanical issues.' He fingered his clean-shaven jaw. 'So what's the deal, Barseghian? Can a robot help us, or have you just cooked up some new scheme to sabotage the mission?'

He had said her surname with exaggerated care, as if everyone else in the world mispronounced it. Svetlana took an angry step closer to Schrope. 'I'm trying to help here, you sanctimonious prick.'

'Easy,' Schrope said, snapping his fingers at Judy Sugimoto. The nurse took gentle hold of Svetlana and pulled her back, bewildered but obedient.

'I appreciate that you offered to look into this,' Bella said, choosing her words diplomatically. 'I removed you from duty and placed you under arrest. At that point your obligations to me ended.'

'Where is this going?' Svetlana asked.

'I'm just saying: you've never disappointed me. No matter what happens to us, I'm still proud that we were friends. I'd like to think that one day we might be able to put—'

'Did you look at the video feed?' Schrope asked Svetlana, cutting across Bella.

'Yes.'

'Did you see anything wrong with the uplink system?'

'Nothing,' Svetlana said, speaking to Bella rather than Schrope. 'The system looks okay, inside and out. That's why I wanted to bring in Saul. I had another idea, something we should at least rule out.'

'Go on,' Craig Schrope said.

But Bella spoke before Svetlana had a chance. 'According to Parry, you wanted to talk to Saul about the feasibility of dropping a free-flier behind the ship, possibly to a distance where we'd run a risk of losing the flier. Is that the case?'

'It wouldn't have to be a robot, if we could instrument a package and send it back instead. But a robot would be quicker.'

'What are you worried about?'

'I'll tell you,' Svetlana said, 'but I want to negotiate first.'

Schrope nodded curtly at Sugimoto. 'Take her away. I've had enough.'

Sugimoto was moving apologetically towards Svetlana when Bella raised a hand. 'I can't let you go free. You know that much.'

'I know you won't turn this ship around, either: not until you've had a closer look at Janus. So I'll work with what's on the table. I'll help you with the uplink if you agree to something else.'

Bella waited. She made a little inviting gesture with her hand. 'I'm listening.'

'You cut down the time at Janus, from five days to one. We spend only twenty-four hours at the initial study point.'

'Completely unacceptable,' Schrope said.

'Hear me out,' Svetlana said. 'What I'm proposing will still give you solid science. Even if you don't put people down on Janus, you can still send robots. It doesn't matter if we abandon them there: we can keep teleoperating them until we reach an unworkable timelag, and even then we can still upload command sequences. They can carry on exploring Janus while we're on our way home.'

'That was always the plan,' Schrope said. 'You're not giving us anything that we didn't already have.'

'I'm giving you an uplink.'

'*If* you can fix it. From where I'm sitting, this looks like a bluff.'

'I can't do what you're asking,' Bella said, shaking her head. 'I can't come all this way, representing the entire human species, and then say that we decided to turn tail as soon as we arrived.'

'I'm talking about twenty-four hours, Bella – that's still a lot of time. Throw some of that caution away and I'm sure you can still achieve most of the objectives.'

'Look at the damned thing,' Bella said, gesturing to the image of Janus. 'Look at that and tell me it's going to take anything less than a century to do it justice.'

'Then five days won't be enough either,' Svetlana said reasonably. 'Given that, the difference between one and five doesn't seem so bad.'

Bella closed her eyes, wondering how things had ever come to this. She wanted to be able to walk out of her office, take a holiday and then return to this precise moment in the conversation, only this time sharpened like a new tool.

'I can give you something,' she said, 'but not everything you want. I'll concede to three days at Janus.'

'Still unacceptable,' Schrope said.

'For the first time in my life, I agree with Craig,' Svetlana said, with what sounded like genuine regret. 'Three days is too long.'

'That's my final offer,' Bella said.

There was a knock at the door. Saul Regis entered and studied the room's occupants with his usual reptilian equanimity, betraying neither surprise nor particular interest.

'You had a shot at redeeming yourself,' Schrope told Svetlana. 'You blew it. But it doesn't matter. I think I know what you have in mind.'

'Svetlana,' Bella said, 'please: I'm giving you one last chance. Help us. Help us and then maybe we can talk again.'

'Sorry,' she answered. 'Cast-iron guarantees up front. That's the only thing I'll settle for.'

Schrope clapped his hands together. 'Okay, looks like we're about done here. Saul: can you spare a free-flier? I'll bet money that Svetlana's idea was to drop a robot behind the ship, carrying a radio transmitter configured to match the output frequency and strength of the Earth uplink signal. Am I right?' He looked at her for a moment, then turned back to Regis. 'She thinks the uplink antenna might be working fine, but that there might be a problem with the signal.'

'What kind of problem?' Bella asked, instinctively directing the question to Svetlana.

Svetlana, to her surprise, answered. Perhaps she realised she had nothing to gain from silence. 'The uplink system is working normally,' she said, sounding defeated. 'The problem isn't at our end.'

'Earth has a problem?'

'That's the idea,' Schrope said, 'but we won't know for sure until we test it.'

Bella shook her head, unable to accept that this was the answer. 'Earth has gone off-air before,' she said, 'but only for minutes at a time, when they have a problem with the alignment. This has been going on for twenty-three hours now.'

Schrope shrugged. 'So it's more than a glitch.'

'Surely they'd have locked a back-up dish onto us by now.'

'*If* they know there's a problem. Maybe everything looks fine at their end. We're thirteen hours out now. We've been sending error signals back to Earth ever since we lost the feed, but even if they got those messages and acted on them immediately, we won't know about it for another three hours.'

Bella absorbed the information, mentally conjuring up a picture of the system's web of radio transmissions. Telecommunications around the Sun were pushed to the limit of data-crammed efficiency, which meant high-power signals squeezed into tight, pencil-thin beams between designated senders and receivers. Only one transmitter had been assigned to *Rockhopper*, and that beam carried every byte of information uploaded to the ship, from personal plaintext messages to the flood of data from the global news networks. *Rockhopper* was too far out to intercept any other communications unless they were deliberately aimed at the ship.

'There's nothing else we can tap into?' Bella asked. 'No omni-directional signals?'

'Too faint,' Schrope said. 'All the catalogued beacons are too far away for us to pick up at this range.'

'*All* of them? What about the beacon we left behind – the one we tagged on the mass driver we were going to use on the last comet—'

'It's a long way behind us now.'

'But closer than anything else. Did anyone remember to check the beacon?'

'I'll refer it to the technical team,' Schrope said.

'You still want my free-flier?' asked Saul Regis, his voice characteristically slow and somnambulant.

hardcopy of the earlier technical note. 'Not without something like the free-flier.'

'Agreed – but we've no reason to assume a problem with the sensitivity. And the uplink signal should be well above our noise limit.'

'Then there must be extra noise leaking in from somewhere.' Bella glared at the technical note: it swam in and out of focus like a fish under water. 'Have you looked at the cooling system on the pre-amplifier box?'

'Yes,' Pagis said with a heavy sigh. 'In fact, that was about the first thing we looked at.'

'Sorry – just trying to make helpful suggestions.'

'It *was* helpful,' Pagis said, with something like contrition, 'it's just that we've already gone through all the obvious stuff.'

'Keep trying,' Bella said. 'At least in half an hour we'll know if the sensitivity is the issue. That'll help, won't it?'

'I guess,' Pagis said, unenthusiastically.

Bella let her get on with her work. The next thirty minutes oozed past, the passage of time made slower by the regular notifications that probe and ship were still in contact, but with the signal becoming slowly fainter. The falling away of the signal strength was exactly as predicted, with no loss in detection efficiency due to some antenna fault.

Bella reminded herself that she still had a ship to run, and that Janus was still sitting there waiting to be examined. Her inbox contained a dozen messages from Nick Thale, each of which – as she skimmed them quickly – contained updating summaries of the latest remote-sensing operations. By contrast to the uplink, the equipment under Nick's guidance was all working normally. Thale's most recent message requested Bella's formal permission to launch a free-flier on a pseudo-orbit that would take it around the far side of Janus, observing the as yet unseen 'bow' face.

Bella authorised it without hesitation. The technical aspects of the mission had already been covered, and the flier would not be approaching any closer to Janus than *Rockhopper* had already come. There would be no additional risk.

With five minutes left until Fletterick's free-flier had reached its terminal velocity, Bella decided she could no longer stand the wait. She called Pagis again and asked her to meet her at the puppet booth. Jens Fletterick was still in the couch, barely moving. Every now and then he whispered some arcane command to his machine. Timelag was now appreciable.

'Here's something odd,' said Hinks, holding a Ziploc plastic bag in which she had gathered the free-flier's spare processor boards. 'That star-tracker glitch Jens tried to pin on me?'

Bella blinked back to an hour earlier. 'Yes,' she said, with an ominous sense of premonition.

'We've got a similar problem with the flier you just authorised Nick Thale to launch. I never went anywhere near the star-tracker boards on that machine.'

'Doesn't make any sense.'

Hinks nodded. 'Add it to the pile.'

'Wait,' Bella said. 'We have to clear this up. One star-tracker failure I can understand, but two, in completely isolated machines?'

Hinks looked at Bella with a dawning comprehension. 'You think the two things might be connected?'

'I don't know what I—' But Bella halted, looking at Jens Fletterick. He'd flipped up his visor.

'The free-flier has reached terminal velocity,' Fletterick said. 'All systems are functioning normally, including the uplink antenna.'

Bella looked to Pagis for confirmation. Pagis had a stiffened flexy across her forearm, hectic with sketchy, hand-annotated diagrams in primary colours. 'Still reading you,' she said. 'Signal's on the nose, too: it's exactly where it should be. Doppler's flattened out now that the machine isn't accelerating.'

'And this represents the strength of the uplink signal from Earth, *if* they were sending?' Bella asked.

'Within a few per cent of the modulated average.'

'Then our system *must* be good,' Bella said.

Pagis nodded meekly. 'We'll continue to collect data as the free-flier falls away from us at terminal velocity, but I don't think it's going to tell us much we don't already know.'

'Keep listening anyway.'

'Is it me,' Hinks said, 'or is this beginning to make no sense at all?'

'It's not you,' Bella said.

# CHAPTER 10

Jens Fletterick's hands moved in exaggerated arcs, like a shadow-boxer. Bella, Hinks and Pagis stared at him, mesmerised. He kept that up for another minute, his gestures gradually becoming slow and resigned, until he stopped moving completely. He lay still for another minute, breathing shallowly. At the end of that minute he flipped up the opaque mask of the immersion headset and unbuckled himself from the couch.

'It's gone,' he said.

'Gone?' Bella asked.

'The link is dead. I can't talk to the machine any more.'

'But you were nowhere near the limit of radio communications,' Hinks said. 'Was there a falling off of signal strength?'

'Nothing,' he said. 'It just disappeared. One moment I was there, looking back at *Rockhopper*. I could still see Janus. And then I just wasn't there any more.'

'As if someone cut the puppet strings,' Bella said.

'No,' he said, correcting her with gentle firmness. 'That's not quite how it felt. There was a moment . . . a transition.' For once, this usually precise man struggled for words. 'It was as if the strings became stretched, pulled, until they snapped. But not cut. Not cut at all.'

Hinks knelt down next to the couch. 'This looks funny,' she said, scratching a finger across one of her flexy read-outs. 'Look at the Doppler on your telemetry.'

Fletterick removed the heavy immersion gear. Still gloved, he took the flexy from her. 'It should have been flat,' he said.

'It was, after you stopped burning fuel. That is, right until the end. Then something funny happened.'

'Show me,' Bella said.

The free-flier had accelerated away from *Rockhopper*, firing its nuclear rocket until it had run out of fuel. The radio signals sent back by the free-flier had become red-shifted as its recessional velocity increased. That was entirely expected, as was the flattening of the red-shift curve from the moment that the fuel ran out and the free-flier coasted away at constant velocity. And it should have stayed like that all the way until loss of radio contact.

But it hadn't.

In the last six seconds before Fletterick lost contact with the free-flier, the Doppler curve had begun to rise again. The rise was sharp, as well, the slope of the curve steeper than it had been during the hour-long boost phase.

With a mere six seconds of data to go on, Bella could only estimate the surge in acceleration that the free-flier had experienced, but she judged that the slope was around five times steeper – which meant that the free-flier had experienced a boost in acceleration of five gees before radio contact was interrupted.

'That isn't possible,' she said, shaking her head in flat denial.' There has to be a mistake, a misreading.'

'It's all right there,' Hinks said.

'Then give me an explanation for it. Could there have been a re-ignition of the motor at five gees?'

Fletterick chose to answer. 'No. It was programmed to burn until the fuel was completely exhausted. And even if there'd been a small amount of fuel left in the system – which there wasn't – there's no reason why the motor would ramp up to five gees unless we specified that in the burn sequence. Which we didn't.'

'An explosion, then,' Bella said. 'Something uncontained. A detonation of fuel vapour violent enough to provide some impetus to the free-flier.'

'If there had been an explosion,' Fletterick said, 'I think we'd have seen some of the telemetry channels drop out. Unless it was a very selective explosion that managed not to damage any mission-critical systems, yet still hurl the free-flier away from us at five gees along exactly the same vector it was already following.'

Bella smiled at him. She loved sarcasm, especially from engineers.

'Oh, wait,' Hinks said, scowling at one of the flexy read-outs. 'This is really odd. This *really* makes no sense.'

'What now?' Bella asked.

'You see this telemetry channel?' Hinks indicated one of the boxed graphs containing a display of some system parameter against time. 'That's data from the free-flier's onboard accelerometer. It's like an inertial compass. But look how it starts: flat at one gee for one hour. Then it does a delta function to zero gees: that's the engine shutting down. All okay so far. Then it holds at zero for another twenty-five minutes, which is the time the free-flier spent in cruise phase.'

'And then it climbs to five gees,' Bella said.

'No – that's my point. It stays flat at zero, right until the last data packet.'

'That's . . . that's weird,' Bella said. 'Let me get this straight: the Doppler telemetry says the free-flier went shooting off at five gees during the last six seconds of transmission.'

'Correct,' Hinks said.

'While the on-board accelerometer says nothing happened.'

'Right.'

'Then one or both channels must be incorrect. So maybe my putative explosion really did happen, and knocked out the accelerometer.'

'Well, no,' Hinks said patiently, 'that's not what we'd see if that had happened. We'd get zero packets on that channel. Whereas the packets we received from the accelerometer were all well formed.'

'According to the accelerometer,' Fletterick said, 'the free-flier didn't feel that five-gee surge at all.'

'But it did accelerate,' Bella said.

'According to the telemetry.'

'So which is right?'

'They're both right,' Svetlana said. She had just appeared in the puppet booth. Bella had not given her permission to leave her quarters – indeed, her appearance here was a clear violation of the agreed terms of her confinement, which permitted her limited access to ShipNet if she agreed to treat her room as a locked and guarded prison cell. But at that moment Bella felt no inclination to punish her.

'You have an explanation?' she asked.

'I have one,' Svetlana said, 'but you're not going to like it.'

'Just tell me what you think is going on,' Bella said.

'I want Belinda to try something for me first. It shouldn't take her long.'

'I'm listening,' Pagis said.

'Point the uplink dish back in the direction of Earth, if you haven't already done so.'

'It's done,' Pagis said, shaking her head, 'and there still isn't a signal.'

'No, but I think I know where you can find one. You need to shift the bandpass well out of the frequency range you're searching.'

'We've allowed for the Doppler effect.'

'Just try it. Look on the low-frequency side, as if you'd underestimated the degree of red shift.'

'I don't see—' Pagis began.

Svetlana cut her off impatiently. 'Just do it, all right? Start at the nominal frequency and slide the bandpass into the red. Tell me when you hit a signal.'

It took less time than Bella had expected. Pagis entered commands into her flexy, talking directly to the uplink antenna. Within a few minutes Bella saw her frown and open her mouth in a silent, '*What?*'

'You've found your uplink signal, haven't you?' Svetlana said. 'Earth is still on the air. They always were: you were just looking off-frequency.'

'This isn't possible,' Pagis said. 'I've had to apply half as much red shift again.'

'That can't be right,' Bella said, but she could tell from Svetlana's expression – fearful and triumphant at the same time – that there had been no mistake.

'It's right,' she said.

'Svieta, what's happening?'

Svetlana coughed and looked at everyone in the little gathering. 'What's happening is that we're moving faster than we thought we were,' she said. 'That's why the Doppler shift was wrong. You weren't allowing for enough motion difference between us and Earth.'

'We know how fast we're moving,' Bella said.

'No, we don't. We think we do, but that's only because we've made a terrible mistake.' Svetlana paused; she had their absolute attention. 'It wasn't the free-flier that accelerated away at five gees. It was us. We're the thing that's accelerating.'

'At five gees? We're standing still, Svieta. We're not even moving as quickly as we expected to be.'

'No,' she said, with a resigned calm. 'We're moving much, much faster than we were.'

'All this since Fletterick lost his signal?'

'No. We've been accelerating for a lot longer than that, at least as far back as the time we first lost the Earth signal, and probably for several hours before that.'

'How can you know this?'

'Only thing that fits the data. You're also having problems with star-trackers. Fine – that's exactly what I'd expect if we'd suddenly picked up a lot of speed.'

'Explain,' Bella said. Her mouth felt dry.

'The trackers are set up to recognise bright stars in fixed constellations. They're programmed to ignore stars that don't fall at exactly the right angular separations from each other. The problem is that now the stars have moved relative to each other, so they can't find the matches they expect. It's called aberration: an apparent displacement in the positions due to speed.'

'I don't get it,' Hinks said. 'What has speed got to do with where the stars are?'

Bella was afraid that Svetlana was going to lash out at the robotics technician for not knowing basic astrogation theory, but instead she seemed drained of all fury.

'It's like this. You're driving at night, in snow. There's no wind, yet the snow seems to be falling horizontally, heading towards your windshield from the direction you're driving – even though you know it's really falling vertically. Well, the same thing's happening with starlight, only to a much smaller degree. Trouble is, it's still enough to throw the trackers.'

'And the trackers don't know that?' Hinks asked.

'No, they do know it, and they're programmed to correct their expected stellar positions to allow for aberration. But to do that properly they need to know how fast they're moving.'

'The free-fliers hitch a ride with *Rockhopper*,' Saul Regis said, speaking for the first time since Svetlana's arrival. 'They assume that *Rockhopper* knows how fast it's moving, so they query *Rockhopper* to keep their kinematic parameter file up to date.'

'In other words, they ask the ship how much of a correction to allow for, and the ship tells them,' Svetlana said. 'But this time the ship got it wrong.'

'We can check this as well,' Bella said. 'It won't be difficult. But it still doesn't answer my basic question: what *the hell* is happening?'

Bella called Svetlana and Craig Schrope to her office. Before Schrope could lodge an objection to Svetlana being there, Bella said, 'These are exceptional circumstances, which is why I'm turning a blind eye to Svetlana's presence. She's already solved the uplink problem, and I believe she has an explanation for the star-tracker errors as well.'

Schrope's pen glittered in his hand like a twirling six-shooter. 'Let's hear it.'

'It looks as if Janus is dragging us with it,' Svetlana said. 'We're caught in some kind of slipstream.'

Schrope pulled a face. 'It's moving through vacuum. You don't get slipstreams in vacuum.'

Svetlana kept her composure. 'There's a lot here we don't understand. Adding one more thing to the list doesn't strike me as the worst crime imaginable.'

Schrope responded with a noncommittal shrug.

'Explain what you think is happening,' Bella said, 'then what you think we should do about it.'

'I think we should reverse, and reverse *fast*. We should be doing it already, not sitting around discussing it.'

'I still need to hear your argument,' Bella said patiently. 'If I'm swayed by it, I promise I'll act with all due swiftness.'

Svetlana leaned forward. 'I'll tell you, but you have to act as soon as I'm done. Every second we spend—'

'Just tell us,' Schrope said.

'Janus never slowed its rate of acceleration. Our only point of reference was the laser we were shining on Janus, and suddenly we were closing the distance too quickly. So we throttled back our engine in response. By the time we reached the initial study position, we thought we were nearly in free fall. But we weren't. We were still accelerating.'

'Then why didn't we feel it?' Schrope asked.

'Because we're in an accelerated reference frame that just happens to feel inertial. I have no idea what this implies. Janus must be doing something weird to space-time, and we're caught up in that weirdness.'

Bella fingered her shark's-teeth necklace. 'So what happened with the free-flier?'

'My best guess is that we let it drop far enough behind us to fall out of the slipstream,' Svetlana said. 'It went from being caught in this accelerating field to not accelerating at all. We read that as the free-flier suddenly accelerating for no reason – but it was *us*, all along.'

'But five gees – that's ridiculous. Janus was never accelerating that hard.'

'Something's changed, in that case. When Janus left Saturn it was shedding ice, just as we'd expect if it were a physical object experiencing stresses due to its own acceleration. But at some point the ice-shedding stopped: we saw that in the images. We just didn't think about what it meant.'

'Which was?'

'Janus must have switched over to a different drive mechanism. Maybe it used one drive to leave the solar system, something relatively slow and primitive by Spican standards but which wouldn't do too much harm to the neighbourhood. But now it's a long way from the Sun. It's engaged something altogether more powerful: something capable of accelerating an entire *moon* at five gees.'

'And we're stuck in the wake,' Bella said.

Svetlana nodded. 'It's been at least a day. We'll have a better idea of how fast we're moving once we have precise numbers on the extra Doppler component. But I'll give you a good guess: we've been sustaining five gees ever since we lost contact with Earth, probably longer. We were moving at three per cent of the speed of light this time yesterday. Now you'd better make that four-and-a-half per cent, maybe even five.'

'What exactly does that mean?' Schrope said, in the voice of a man who had just seen his own ghost. 'In terms of the mission objectives, I mean.'

'I don't know about the mission objectives, Craig, but I'll tell you what it means to you personally if we don't get out of this fast. It means you're fucked. It means we're all fucked.'

Bella flinched, expecting Schrope to react. But nothing came. He just sat there in a slack-jawed stupor, as if he had been tranquillised.

'If this is confirmed,' Bella said tentatively, 'then . . . what should we do? Can we back out of the slipstream, or whatever it is?'

'We can try,' said Svetlana. 'The free-flier didn't appear to suffer any damage when it left the slipstream: we only lost contact with it because of the sudden shift in frequencies.'

'We'll need to know that for certain before we try anything. I'll have Pagis and Hinks see if they can widen the reception bandpass and pick up a signal.'

'We don't have time for this, Bella. We have to reverse out of this now, before it pulls us any faster than we're already travelling.'

'Not until we know that the free-flier survived the transition. It shouldn't take long.' She reached for her flexy, preparing to give the order. She already regretted not having Pagis and Hinks present in her office.

'Bella,' Svetlana said urgently, 'listen to me. Every minute you sit here thinking about this is an additional three kilometres per second of speed we have to lose if we ever want to get home. There isn't time to look into all the angles here. You have to move us *now*.'

Schrope suddenly came back to life. 'The free-flier . . . how long did it take it to clear the slipstream?'

Svetlana answered him with a flat absence of emotion. 'It was more than half a light-second out. If we push at half a gee now, we might reach the drop-out point in two or three hours, by which time we'll be moving even faster.'

Schrope looked at Bella. 'Perhaps we should consider a withdrawal—' He said it plaintively, like a child after sweets. Bella saw it plainly: the utter collapse of his neatly ordered corporate world. Until now Schrope had been in control. Now he was at the mercy of something frightening and powerful in equal measure.

Bella's flexy chimed with an incoming call from Belinda Pagis. She had a hard number on the aberration problem.

'This is . . . not good,' she said, as if Bella had imagined it could be anything else. 'To match the star positions as we see them, we need to allow for—' She lowered her eyes, reading data from another flexy. 'Four-point-nine-eight per cent of the speed of light.'

'Good work,' Bella said.

'We've picked up a faint signal from the free-flier,' Pagis said, almost apologetically. 'We allowed for the excess in our Doppler shift. It's . . . worryingly consistent.'

'Does the free-flier telemetry look healthy?'

'No sign of any damage. The accelerometer curve was—'

'Flat,' Bella finished for her.

'Um, yes.'

Bella turned to Svetlana. 'Then we could – theoretically – survive exiting the slipstream.'

'Start the process now,' Svetlana urged. 'Full burn at half a gee. We'll ditch the remaining mass drivers – anything we absolutely don't need.'

'We still have to turn the ship around,' Bella said. 'That'll take two hours, if we don't want to snap in two.'

Svetlana closed her eyes. 'Jesus, I forgot.'

*Rockhopper* didn't take kindly to torsional stresses, any more than a skyscraper took kindly to being tipped on its side. Slewing the ship – bringing the fusion motors around to reverse their thrust – was a delicate operation that could not be hurried.

Normally there was no need to hurry it.

'Belinda,' Bella said, 'drop whatever you're doing and prep for a one-hundred-and-eighty-degree turnaround. Emergency slew speed: I don't care if we blow the warranty on this one.'

'I'm on it,' Pagis said. 'Anything else?'

'Yes,' Bella said. 'While we're slewing I want a full flight-dynamics update. Do we still have enough fuel left to slow down? Do we have enough to make it home after that?'

'I'll get those numbers for you,' Pagis said. 'Permission to begin the slew as soon as we're stowed.'

'Granted – begin it immediately if you can.'

When the call was complete, Svetlana said quietly, 'We'll never make it in time.'

'We'll try. That's all we can do.'

A ship-wide siren alerted the crew of the impending slew, warning everyone to secure bodies, equipment and possessions against the impending kick from the steering thrusters. When it came, the jolt was no worse than a mild fender-bender, but it still felt ominous and wrong: a shove in a direction in which the ship rarely moved.

The water in Bella's fish tank sloshed to the lid and the fish looked agitated. The ship's frame creaked and groaned before settling down again.

'We're rotating at three minutes of arc per second,' Pagis told Bella, 'which is as fast as I can manage.'

Bella did the sums. 'It's not fast enough. It's still going to take us another hour to get the nose turned around at that rate.'

'The system won't allow a faster rotation,' Pagis said. 'Thruster control is under software override: I can slow the rotation, but not speed it up.'

'Pass me the flexy,' Svetlana said. Bella slid it to her and indicated that she should speak. 'Belinda, listen carefully. There's a file you need to update. I'll talk you through it, all right?'

'Go ahead,' Pagis said.

'Open a separate window and navigate to dynamics tasks. Make sure you do it under system privilege.'

Bella heard Pagis's fingers scratching against the hide of her flexy. After a few moments they heard her say, 'I'm there.'

'You should see two subdirectories. Go into "OMS" underscore "tasks" and look for a file called something like failsafe limits.'

'Not seeing it . . . not seeing it . . .' Pagis said. 'Oh, wait, there's something called "struct" underscore "lims".'

'That's probably the one. Open it and scroll down until you see a parameter called "slew" underscore "upper limits", or something similar. It'll be about twenty lines down.'

'Got it,' Pagis said quickly.

'The numeric field gives our maximum permitted slew rate in fractional degrees per second: it should say something like point-oh-five right now.'

'Yep, got it – you want me to change that?'

Svetlana glanced at Bella. 'That failsafe's there for a reason. It's to stop the ship tearing itself apart.'

'Increase it to point-oh-seven-five,' Bella said. 'I'll take responsibility if she snaps.'

'Do it,' Svetlana said to Pagis.

'I've made the change,' Pagis said.

'Close the file, go back to your navigation window and see if the ship accepts the new rate of slew.'

'I'm on it. Better brace, because if this goes through—'

Bella flinched, but nothing happened: no shove of motion; no creaking or groaning.

'Did you get a reaction from the rockets?' Svetlana asked.

'No dice. She still isn't accepting an increased rate of slew.'

Bella saw Svetlana screw her eyes shut in absolute concentration, her face taking on an expression that spoke as much of pain as it did of intense intellectual effort. Svetlana knew *Rockhopper*'s functional parameters better than anyone alive, but the ship was still too complex for any one person to know with an easy intimacy. 'Okay,' she said, her face slackening, 'I think I know what the problem is. The slew-management system won't pick up the changes to the file unless we zero the slew and start again.'

'Goddamn,' Bella muttered, 'who the hell designed this piece of crap?'

'Engineers,' Svetlana said tersely.

'All right, do it. Zero the slew and start over.'

After a few tense moments, the siren sounded again. The shove came from the opposite direction this time, halting the ship's inching rotation. There was another protestation from the structure, like an old building flexing in a squall.

'Zero,' Pagis said.

'Try it again,' Svetlana told her, 'and be ready to shut it down fast.'

Another siren warning sounded. The shove was half as powerful again this time, the difference perceptible. The water in the fish tank found its way through the gap between the top of the tank and the lid, sluicing onto Bella's carpet. The ship registered its disapproval, but so far it seemed to be holding together.

'How are we doing?' Bella asked Pagis.

'We're in one piece. No reports of pressure breaches or fatigue warnings.'

But the ship's nervous system was still in tatters after the mass-driver accident, Bella thought. Only vital command signals were being routed up and down the spine. She did not think it likely that damage reports would have been able to reach her anyway.

'Belinda, I need one of your team stationed at a viewing port. I want someone keeping an actual eye on the spine and engine assembly.'

'It's okay,' Pagis said. 'We're holding.'

'At the moment we are, but I'm going to zero the slew again. This still isn't fast enough.'

'We're already pushing the envelope here,' Svetlana warned.

'It can take some more pushing. Belinda: edit that file again and raise our slew rate to one-tenth of a degree per second.'

Svetlana shook her head in warning. 'You'll have exceeded the failsafe margin by a factor of two.'

'I thought you were the one keen to get out of here.'

'I am – but I know what this ship is built to take, and what it definitely *isn't* built to take.'

Timidly, Pagis said, 'I've updated the file. Shall I—'

'Zero the slew,' Bella said. 'Zero and restart.'

'I don't recommend that we do this,' Svetlana said.

'Duly noted. If the ship breaks up, you can have the satisfaction of telling me you were right.'

The thrusters killed the slew. More water sloshed from the fish tank, more noises signalled the ship's displeasure, but *Rockhopper* held together. Ten or fifteen seconds passed: then came the next warning siren. What, Bella wondered, did the rest of the crew think was going on? If she had been less preoccupied, she might have found time to speak to them. Then again, perhaps not speaking to them was the kinder thing: it was not necessarily good to know that the ship was being tested to its limits. *Please let me believe that this ship was designed to take more punishment than the design specifications*, Bella prayed. *Please let me believe that the engineers were in a generous mood.*

But the ship held. Bella's fish tank lost more water, but it would all be collected again by the humidity filters, even if it took months for the lost allocation to wind its way back to her cabin.

'We're in one piece,' Pagis said, her surprise unconcealed. 'Slewing at one degree every ten seconds. We'll be nose-around in about twenty-seven minutes.'

*Then we'll have to slow again*, Bella thought. But if the ship had withstood this latest jolt it would probably withstand that one as well. She would push it no further. They were inching around no faster than the minute hand of a clock, but it would be insane to push for more.

'I'm still going to need that flight-dynamics report,' Bella said. 'The sooner the better.'

Thirty minutes until they could fire the engine. Two hours more – at least – until they reached the point where the free-flier had appeared to accelerate away. And all the while Janus was pulling them ever faster, making their homeward journey increasingly difficult.

If flight dynamics said it could not be done, what then? She needed to have a plan in place for that eventuality, even if that plan consisted of nothing more than trying.

The best-case scenario was that they had enough fuel left in the tanks to not only slow down to the local solar rest frame, but also to make it back home in a reasonable amount of time. If that wasn't feasible, then Earth would have to meet them halfway with some kind of resupply operation. And if that wasn't possible, if all they could do was stop, then Earth would have to come all the way out here to rescue them.

Maybe they could endure that long. *Rockhopper's* closed-cycle life-support system could sustain them for a good long while. It wouldn't be comfortable – there would be no luxuries – but it could keep the crew alive. But it would still take power to make that life-support tick. And if they ran out of fuel, they would also lose their main source of power. There were back-up systems, but they were designed to keep the ship warm and habitable for a handful of weeks during reactor downtime; they were not designed for the months – or years – that it would take Earth to implement a rescue operation.

That was a pretty bad scenario.

But there was a worst-case option that she had to consider as well: what if they couldn't slow down? She was sure they would be able to decelerate a bit, but the amount necessary? If, when the fuel tanks gave their last splutter and ran out, the ship was still moving in the direction of Spica at one or two per cent of the speed of light . . .

Nothing might ever catch them.

Not for years, anyway. And by that time – would anyone even bother, just to recover a hundred and forty-five cold, dry corpses?

Not DeepShaft, at any rate.

Her flexy chimed. 'Yes, Belinda?' she asked, hoping that no one could pick up on the anxiety she felt.

'I have that flight-dynamics report. It still needs to be double-checked, but—'

Bella interrupted her. 'What's the verdict?'

'We can slow down, *if* we make it out of the slipstream within three hours.'

'And then?'

'We'll have a small margin, just enough fuel to put us on the return trajectory. We won't have enough to brake at the other end, but shuttles should still be able to reach us.'

'How long will it take?'

'Ten months,' Pagis said. 'That's the most optimistic estimate.'

Bella shot a glance at Svetlana. 'And that scenario – it was based on the assumption that our fuel-load reading is accurate?'

'Yes, of course,' Pagis said.

'Run it again,' Bella told her. 'Assume that the fuel-load reading is fifteen per cent lower than the systems are telling us.'

Schrope stirred. 'We've been over this already. There's no reason to take Barseghian seriously.'

'We won't make it,' Svetlana said, addressing Bella as if Schrope was not there. 'It's already marginal. Drop that fuel load by fifteen per cent and we'll never even slow down.'

'I'll wait for flight dynamics to get back to me,' Bella said. 'But if – for the sake of argument – you're right about this, is there anything we can do about it?'

'The time to do something,' Svetlana said, 'would have been two weeks ago.'

'But I didn't,' Bella said, 'and here we are, so let's deal with it. Assume the fuel load is marginal. Could we improve our situation by escaping the slipstream sooner?'

Svetlana's face glazed over as she thought about it. For all the tension between them, she could not ignore a technical query.

'Perhaps . . . but we're already basing our calculations on a half-gee burn.'

'I know that,' Bella said, 'but could you squeeze more thrust out of the engine? Would it give us a gee? Or more than a gee, if only for the time it takes us to clear the slipstream?'

'I— I don't know,' Svetlana said. 'I've never even considered it before. It's well outside the design limits.'

'What about the structural frame of the ship?'

'If we ditched the remaining mass drivers—'

'That's a given.'

'Then if it came to that she might hold. But the engine . . . I don't know. I'd need to look into it. We'd be burning fuel at twice our usual rate—'

'But presumably it's better to burn fuel now, while we're still inside the slipstream.'

'I understand.' Svetlana suddenly seemed distant, as if her body was a shell while her mind was elsewhere, roving the mental architecture of the ship, considering fearful new possibilities.

'Fifteen minutes to end of slew,' Pagis reported. 'Flight dynamics has those numbers. It doesn't look good for the fifteen-per-cent-less scenario. We'd still have a residual drift in the direction of Spica.'

'How fast?'

'Four thousand klicks per second. That's more than—'

'One per cent of the speed of light. Thank you, Belinda. Now do me one final favour. Re-run the simulation. Assume the same fuel deficit, but allow for a two-gee burn for the first thirty minutes, or until we've cleared the slipstream.' Bella spoke with exaggerated clarity, mindful that a single misunderstanding could cost them dearly. 'Oh, and Belinda?'

'Yes, Bella?'

'I need an answer on that pretty quickly.'

Bella sat down at her desk and breathed in deeply. Here it was, she thought: that cusp, that moment of maximum crisis she had always known would visit her at some point in her career. From time to time she had wondered what shape it would take, and, more importantly, how she would rise to meet it. She had always hoped her reaction would be adequate at the very least.

What she had *never* imagined was that when that moment came she would be sitting at her desk with her feet squishing soggy carpet.

But that was reality: always pissing on the epic moment.

The flexy shook a little: her hands were trembling. Flight dynamics said that a two-gee burn would compensate for most of the fuel deficit. It would not get them home, but it would bring them to a stop in the local rest frame – 'stop' in this case meaning that they would have a residual velocity relative to the Sun of no more than a few tens of kilometres per second. Planetary speed.

Manageable.

But they would still be horribly far from home. And that was assuming the ship survived the burn in the first place. She had read Svetlana's expression: there was nothing there that resembled optimism. It was a savage risk, and all it would achieve at best would be to strand them unspeakably far from home, with no fuel left to keep the ship running. They would be dead before any rescue or resupply effort ever reached them.

But what was the alternative?

Well, there was one.

She picked up her flexy and placed a call to her former second-in-command. Jim Chisholm was conscious, if not exactly alert: if he had been sleeping, the violent jolting of the slew would have been sure to wake him up, even in the green calm of the infirmary.

'Hello, Bella,' he said, favouring her with a weary smile. 'So what's up?'

'We're in a spot of bother.'

'That much I'd gathered.'

'I think I may have to make a very tough decision.' She tried to look him in the eye, as directly as the flexy's imaging system allowed. The blue-green cast of the dying iridophores made Chisholm's hold on life appear even more tenuous.

'The kind that affects me?' Chisholm asked, an amused wrinkle etching the corner of his right eye.

'The kind that affects us all,' Bella said, grimacing, 'but yes, you more than anyone.'

'Is it a matter of the crew's welfare?'

'As always.'

'Tell me what you think you have to do.'

She filled him in on everything they had learned in the last hour. Chisholm, as always, listened without interrupting; only the tiniest elevation of his eyebrows hinted at his instinctive scepticism. 'It's all true,' she whispered. 'We're caught in something and if we don't get out of it, it's going to carry us all the way to Spica.'

'But even if we do get out of it, that may not help us much,' Chisholm said. 'I could take the risk that we have enough fuel to make it home. I could take another risk that the engine will hold at two gees. But if I'm wrong about either of those two things, we'll find ourselves either stranded without power, or dead.'

'Either way, my chances of making it home in the next three weeks don't look brilliant, do they?'

'I'm sorry,' she said.

He shook his head, as if it was nothing she should trouble herself about. 'It was a calculated risk. I knew perfectly well that nothing was guaranteed.'

He sounded brave and accepting. It was a good act, Bella thought, but Jim had been given a shot at staying alive and he was now being denied that hope. She had just told him bluntly that he was going to die.

'You want my advice on which option to take?' he asked, with no detectable malice in his question.

'No,' she said, 'I know what I have to do. I still have a duty to my crew, Jim. I used to think it was my job to get them home in one piece—' She paused.

'And now?'

'Now I know it's my job to keep them alive. Getting home's a luxury, one I'll deliver if I can – but before I can deal with that I have to deal with the first problem.'

'You have something in mind?'

'Janus,' Bella said. She waited for Chisholm to say something, something incredulous or disdainful, but the slack mask of his face gave nothing away. Perhaps he had misheard her, or maybe he thought she'd finally gone mad. 'It's power we need,' she said, stumbling over her words in her eagerness to please him. 'Power matters more than fuel. *Rockhopper* is a closed-cycle system. With power we can last a long time.'

'But not for ever,' Chisholm cautioned.

'No, not for ever, I know that – but if we end up stranded on the edge of the system with empty tanks, we'll be lucky to last a month. Whereas if we stay where we are . . . well, we still have plenty of fuel in the tanks. It'll last a long time if all we need it for is to power the ship.'

'It'll still run out one day.'

'I know,' Bella said, 'but the fuel isn't all we have. We have Janus itself. We have machines and people. We have our wits. If we can't figure out a way to bleed some power from that thing – just enough to keep us alive – then do we really deserve to survive anyway?'

'Are you serious? Do you honestly think we'd have a better chance of surviving here than by running for home?'

'It would buy us an indefinite amount of time.'

'While we're being pulled further and further into interstellar space.'

'But we'd be alive. We can do it, Jim: I know we can. There's more than just power out here. Look at all the water ice still left on the rearward face. We can mine that to top up our reserves. We can sift it for organics . . . we can find ways to make this work.'

'You've given this some thought, haven't you?'

'About ten minutes' worth. But if you gave me a lifetime to think about this, I don't think it would make much difference.'

'No,' he said reflectively. 'You're probably right. That's always how it is with the tough ones.'

'It's my call, isn't it?'

'I think my situation disqualifies me from having an opinion,' he said, pausing to lick dry lips. 'But whatever you decide, you'll have my absolute support. You're right: bringing them home isn't your first duty.'

'Then you agree with me,' she said.

'I didn't quite say that.' His expression was reproving, but not without sympathy. 'I don't disagree with you, either. But like you said: it has to be your call.'

'I'm not sure how it will go down with the others.'

Chisholm was in the process of answering her when the siren drowned out his words. 'That's the end of the slew,' Bella said. 'We're facing the right way now. They'll be expecting me to authorise engine start-up.'

'You could still give them what they want,' Chisholm said.

'I could, but I think our chances of making it back home would be about one in four. I'm afraid those odds aren't good enough for me.'

The ship held together as the rockets fired to arrest the slew. More water spilled from her tank, but not as much as last time.

'Bella, would you do me a favour?' Chisholm asked, as if an idea had just occurred to him.

'Yes, of course,' she said, without thinking.

'Call Ryan. Ask him to disconnect me from this thing. I think my presence might help when you have to explain this to the crew.'

'No,' she said emphatically. 'You're staying in that bed.'

'I'm already dead,' Chisholm said. 'The least I can do is make myself useful.'

# CHAPTER 11

Bella floated in the gymnasium, weightless now that the ship was at rest. The assembled throng represented almost the entire crew. She could feel the unspoken force of their demand for action. There was only one thing that they wanted of her, and that was not in her power to give.

'We've turned the ship,' she said, making dutiful eye contact with her senior staff. 'I have it on good authority that the engine is ready to push us away from Janus.' She waited a beat. 'But we won't be moving.'

It took a while for the impact of her words to sink in; she watched as an almost palpable wave of affront passed through her crew – even those who would normally have supported any decision she took.

'The risk is too great,' Bella said, before anyone had a chance to shout her down. 'Our fuel situation is too precarious, even if we can trust the readings. If we can't – and I have good reason to doubt them – then the situation is beyond hopeless. With empty tanks we'll freeze to death within three or four weeks, long before any rescue mission could reach us. The best-case scenario allows us to limp home and just make it – but I can't allow myself to be tempted by false hopes. Your lives are too precious for that.'

Svetlana was the first to speak. 'Bella, we have to move now.'

Bella nodded understandingly. 'But you said it yourself, Svieta – there's no guarantee that the engine will get us out of here. What was the expression you used? You said it was a combustion regime you've never explored before? Sorry, but I'm just not prepared to put lives on the line like that.'

'You only listen to me when it suits you,' Svetlana said, hostile now.

'No,' Bella said, 'I've listened to every word you've ever said, every time, and I'm listening now. The risk of what you're suggesting is just too great.'

'Then we'll die out here.'

'No, we won't. At least, not for a long, long time. And that's my point, Svieta.'

There were more than a hundred and thirty people in the room, but those who disagreed with Bella appeared to be willing to let Svetlana speak for them. Bella had no idea whether they amounted to a majority, but their silence cut through her like an invisible wind.

'We can't survive,' Svetlana said.

'We'll survive longer here than we would waiting for rescue on the edge of the system. Here we have fusion power. When that runs out, we have Janus. There's an entire world only a few thousand kilometres away.'

'It's carrying us into interstellar space.' Svetlana sounded plaintive; there was an edge of hysteria in her voice. 'Bella, *listen to me*. Every second we're not running—'

'We're not running,' said someone else. 'We don't ever run.'

Collectively, the room tracked the voice: Jim Chisholm had dressed, but his painful thinness was emphasised by every hollow crease and sharp curve of his clothes. Bella wondered how he had made it down to the weightless volume of the gymnasium. She assumed that Ryan, or perhaps Jagdeep Singh, had carried him.

Chisholm coughed, and found some strength: his voice had a conviction Bella had not heard in months.

'Bella's right: running would kill us. I know this is hard, I know this is tough medicine . . . but what she's saying is true. Our only hope is with Janus. We should stay here and find a way to keep alive.'

Someone else started to speak now – not Svetlana – but Chisholm raised his voice again. 'Listen to me. I want to go home. I want to go home so badly it makes me weep. Most of you know that there's something in my head that's killing me, something that even Ryan can't cure, although he's done his damnedest; he's tried everything in his power.' He looked at Axford, stationed by the doorway, and Bella saw the doctor acknowledge this public thanks with a small, grave nod, as if, like an executioner, he took no pleasure in having done his best.

Chisholm turned back to his audience. 'When we were offered a shot at Janus, I took it gladly: it was my best hope of getting home before there was nothing of me left to cure. Things didn't work out the way I hoped . . . but if I were offered that chance again, I'd still take it, if only to see the things we've seen – the things we *will* see, in the weeks ahead, if we do the brave thing. Better to be here, now, than anywhere else in the universe. No one has ever been more privileged than us.'

He paused for a moment, and looked astonished. 'And some of you think we should *run*? With no guarantee of even making it back to the local stellar rest frame?' Chisholm shook his head wonderingly. 'It can't be true. Not aboard *Rockhopper*. We're miners. We push ice. They sent us out here to do a job, to mine Janus, only this time for knowledge. *It's still mining*. It's still what we do. I say we stay. I say we stay here and finish the job.'

It was a good speech, and it came from a member of the crew who was universally liked and respected. Bella dared to hope it might be enough to win the day. For some, perhaps, it was.

But not for everyone.

'I didn't come here to die,' said Christine Ofria, looking around for support. 'I came here to do a difficult job, yes. I wanted to look at Janus. But I have a life back home. I want to see it again.'

A chorus of voices added weight to her statement. Bella tried to judge numbers: who was with her, who was against. It was going to be a close call.

'No one's saying you won't see home again,' Bella said, raising her voice above the tide of dissent. 'What I'm saying is that if that's what you want, to get home, then Janus is your best – your *only* – hope.'

'She's right,' said Jim Chisholm again, his voice carving its own silence into the room. 'Janus is taking us away from home. Bella and I know that. But it's also a means to stay alive. If we can keep ourselves alive, anything is possible.'

'We may never find a way to slow Janus,' Bella said, 'but I'm damned if we won't try. And if that doesn't work, we'll still have options. If all we can do is stop Janus accelerating, that will still give us a chance of being rescued. Now that we've sent images home, the UEE will have a huge incentive to come and take a longer, more detailed look. They'll want to send out another ship – something fast enough to catch up with us.'

She swallowed a frog in her throat. 'Even if we can't make Janus slow down, we don't know that it will keep accelerating. There's still hope. And at the end of it all we'll still be *alive*.'

'Some of you probably want to take your chances on the return voyage,' Chisholm said. 'I understand, really I do. But it won't work. Luck would have to be on our side all the way home.' He looked confidingly at his audience. 'Take it from me: luck *isn't* on our side. And if we start counting on luck, we're finished. We're professionals. Luck doesn't come into the equation. Hard planning, guts and resourcefulness do.'

'We don't have to make it all the way home,' said Malcolm Fox, one of the mass-driver specialists, 'we just have to slow down. We can last in empty space, at least long enough until we're rescued.'

'We can last three or four weeks with no fuel in the tanks,' Bella said. 'No longer, unless you think metal burns.'

'Even if we had six weeks,' Chisholm said, 'that still wouldn't be enough time. The company wouldn't spare a rescue mission to take me home even when we were in comfortable shuttle range. They offered to freeze me. If we turn from Janus now, then we'll already have played our trump cards. We'll have nothing they really need from us, except the dollar value of this ship – and that can wait until someone sends out a recovery tug.' He paused, gathering his strength. No one interrupted him. 'But Janus gives us leverage. Right now, *we* own it, not DeepShaft, not the UEE. If they want a slice of it, they'll have to come out and negotiate with us. When they do, we'll be ready and waiting.'

Gregor Mair, one of Parry's mining team, broke the silence that followed. 'I'm not going to make any friends here,' said the sandy-haired Scotsman, 'but I think Bella and Jim are right: our best hope is to stay. That doesn't mean I have to like it. I think it's the lesser of two evils.'

'I agree,' said Saul Regis, tapping a finger against the braided strand of his beard. 'We stay, we live.'

'I'm with Bella,' said Reda Kirschner, one of the cometary scientists under Nick Thale. 'We're not finished with Janus. We didn't come all this way just to turn around.'

Bella was glad of the support, but she knew that those people who had publicly thrown in their lot with her had no strong ties to Earth, or to any of the space colonies. None of them were married; they had left neither lovers nor close family behind.

Unfortunately, that could not be said for everyone on the ship. No sooner had she framed that thought than Craig Schrope pushed himself away from his tether point at the wall and drifted into the middle of the auditorium. With expert timing, he brought himself to a halt three metres to Bella's right: close enough to command attention, but not so close that he looked like he was standing with her.

'This space vehicle is a DeepShaft commercial asset,' he said. 'We have an obligation to bring it back home. Bella and Jim can talk about professional duty all they like. We're miners – yes. But we're also custodians of this ship.' He looked pityingly at Chisholm, the way he might have looked at roadkill. 'I'm sorry, Jim, but you have no authority here any more.'

'Craig,' Bella said warningly, 'don't try to split the ship. It doesn't have to happen this way.'

'I'm not splitting anything,' Schrope said. 'I'm not the one talking about being abandoned by DeepShaft. I'm not the one talking as if the company has already forsaken us.'

'And don't try playing the company loyalty card, either,' Bella said. 'This is about human lives.'

'It is,' Schrope said, nodding emphatically. 'And I don't happen to think this is any place to spend the rest of my life.' An idea seemed to occur to him suddenly: a gloss of interested animation suffused his face. He looked at Svetlana. 'I will freely admit that you and I have had our differences in the last few days.'

'What about it, Craig?' Svetlana asked, with exaggerated civility.

'You never wanted this,' Schrope told her. 'Rightly or wrongly, you didn't buy into this. You were always ambivalent about Janus, and after the accident you had grave reservations about continuing the mission.' He waved a hand dismissively. 'It's true that we had a difference of opinion about the validity of your fears, I admit that. But if you'd had your way, we'd have never ended up in this mess.'

'Fuck you, Craig. You didn't listen. That's all that matters to me.' She was still furious with him.

'But I'm listening now,' he said. 'I'm listening, and I'm asking you to work with me: for the sake of *Rockhopper*, if not DeepShaft.'

She looked appalled. 'Work with *you*?'

'Bella can't operate this ship without you. You hold the reins, Svetlana; you are the one who gets to choose whether we stay here or make a run for home. It's in your hands.'

'Don't listen to him,' Bella said. 'We've been over this – it's suicide even to think of returning.'

'It won't be a question of taking the ship,' Schrope said, talking to everyone in the room. 'Bella has already abdicated authority here by giving up on us. That leaves me. I'm still in command. All anyone here has to do is keep doing their job.'

'If you listen to Craig, you will all die,' Bella said.

Schrope fixed his attention on Svetlana, as if Bella had not spoken. 'I need you to get us home,' he said. 'I need you to pull your team together and start the engine. We'll rig for two gees. It's all or nothing, Svieta: the engine will either get us home, or we'll go out in a blaze of glory. Both of those options are better than rotting out here.'

'Don't do this,' Bella said, but her voice died somewhere in her throat, reaching no one. They were no longer listening to her, or to any of the other senior staff. The gathering had erupted into heated debate, a ruction that at any instant threatened to boil over into violence. 'I've lost the ship,' she said, for the benefit of no one but herself, yet Jim Chisholm whispered, 'They'll come back to you. They'll always come back. Deep down, they know you're right.'

A voice boomed from the crowd, temporarily silencing them all. It was Saul Regis, his big form trembling with adrenalin. 'Fine,' he said. 'If it comes to this, so be it, but let's see how we all stand. Let's draw a line in the sand. Those with Bella, gather around me. Those who agree with Craig, gather around him.'

Bella watched her crew split into those two groupings, still a little stunned that it had actually come to this. At first it looked as if Schrope was going to win the day by a clear margin – but Bella had more loyalists than she realised. Saul Regis, supporting Bella, gathered most of his robotics team around him, with only Marcia Batista defecting to Schrope's party. Half of the science team came to Bella, and more than half of the medical team, and a handful of Svetlana's flight-systems party: mostly the younger, less experienced members, like Meredith Bagley and Mengcheng Yang. Bella counted heads: including Saul Regis and herself, she had around forty people. There were a lot fewer than forty people gathered around Craig Schrope. The rest of the crew formed an amorphous, jostling group between the two rival leaders. Most of Parry's mining team, as well as Parry himself, had yet to decide. Svetlana had not declared her allegiance either.

It couldn't have been easy for Svetlana, Bella thought: no matter how much she might have agreed with him, the idea of joining forces with Craig Schrope must have really stuck in her craw.

Bella caught her eye. Svetlana mouthed back something that might have been defiance, but might equally well have been an apology.

As if their friendship still counted.

She moved to Craig Schrope's side. A moment later, Bella observed Parry Boyce follow her. She could not blame Parry for that.

Where Parry followed, so did most of his EVA team. Gregor Mair was the only miner who stayed loyal to Bella.

So now it was done. There were no stragglers, no undecided votes, and there was no need to count the numbers: Svetlana's decision had been crucial. Craig Schrope could now count on more than half of the crew. His angry clique was visibly larger than Bella's motley assembly. The difference was fewer than twenty people, but the addition of the EVA party gave Schrope's group the cohesion of an army. With their expertise in ship systems, they had a clear technical edge over Bella's assortment of scientists, roboticists and medical staff.

Miraculously, a kind of calm fell upon the divided gathering. Schrope's party knew they had effective control of the ship. Bella's group knew there was nothing they could do about it. It had been a bloodless mutiny: her crew, even as it ripped itself apart, had not disgraced itself. Bella allowed herself a tiny, waning flicker of pride. They had behaved like adults, even as they spurned her.

'I have the ship,' Schrope said. He sounded relieved more than triumphant. 'We'll do as I said: prep for two gees. Immediate burn, as soon as we're ready. We'll drop the mass drivers.' He looked at Svetlana. 'Can you organise your team and get on this right away?'

Svetlana took a deep breath, crossing some mental Rubicon, and nodded. 'It's doable.'

Bella raised her hands. She had their instant, total attention. 'All right. You've done what you think is right. I can't blame any of you for that. You want to survive very badly. Believe it or not, so do I. To those of you who have joined Craig because you think that's the best way to keep serving the company, and that to follow me would be the disloyal act . . . well, I understand. I don't blame you for it. But you're still doing the wrong thing—'

'You've said enough, Bella,' Schrope cut her off. 'Now let me say my piece.'

'Be my guest,' she said.

'Bella is wrong about this,' he said, addressing the crowd again. 'Yes, we could eke out a living around Janus – maybe. But don't mistake optimism for certainty. We *know* we can slow down. That's not in dispute. That's physics.'

'Is this leading somewhere, Craig, or do you just want to rub my nose in it?' Bella asked.

He fixed her with a tolerant smile. 'You've said that you understand my people. Well, I understand yours. I'm extending the hand of reconciliation to all of you: Saul, Ryan . . . Jim – it isn't too late to throw your weight in with us.' He spread his arms magnanimously, as if welcoming them to the party. 'We're committed to the slowdown now. The ship is ours. But we can still behave like civilized human beings. Join us, accept that this course of action is going to take place, and we can all be friends.'

'Just like that?' Nick Thale asked. 'You're saying we just join you, and it's let bygones be bygones?'

'I don't see why not.'

'I do,' Thale said. 'You've stolen this ship from Bella Lind. The captain. I wouldn't piss on you if you were on fire.'

A line of tension creased Schrope's neck like a hawser. 'I have— I have secured this ship. That's all.'

'Why don't you go play in an airlock, Craig,' Thale snapped back.

'It's all right,' Bella said. 'I appreciate the support, Nick, I truly do, but let's keep this civil. Before very long we may all need each other again. I'd rather not stoop to personality attacks.' She turned from Thale and spoke up again. 'So, Craig: how do you want to play this? There are about forty of us against about a hundred of you. One of my people is terminally ill. It's obvious that we lack the numbers to retake the ship, but rest assured that my people will obstruct and impede your every move. We'll do all in our power to keep this ship from falling out of the slipstream.'

'I can't have that,' Schrope said.

'I didn't think you would. That means we have to discuss terms and conditions.'

'There isn't time for this,' Svetlana said. 'If we're going to do this, we have to start *now*.'

'Take whoever you need,' Schrope told her. 'Just make sure you give us five minutes' warning before you light the engine.'

Svetlana took Robert Ungless and Naohiro Uguru with her; she needed only two trusted members of her team. Together they would have no difficulty in bringing the engine back up to power. No one made any effort to stop them leaving. It was obvious that Schrope's party had a massive advantage, not just in numbers, but in strength, too: Parry's EVA miners were steroid-muscled and tough as nails, and they probably counted for double their actual number.

Once Svetlana and her engineers had left, Schrope stroked his jaw and studied Bella with curatorial interest, as if wondering where in his scrapbook to pin her. 'You're right about Jim,' he mused. 'The best place for him is the medical centre. You have Ryan, Jagdeep and Judy in any case.'

'I'm still the flight surgeon on this ship,' Axford said. 'You'll need my services if one of you slips and breaks something.'

'That's why I'm proposing that you occupy the part of the ship clustered around the medical centre. It'll be a squeeze, but I'm sure you'll manage. Like Bella said, we can't very well have you running around.'

'And you?' Bella asked.

'We'll need access to the critical flight systems, of course. Navigation and propulsion, life support. That means pretty much the rest of *Rockhopper*. But don't worry. We'll look after you.'

'You know,' Bella said, 'the more I think about it, the more I like Nick's suggestion about the airlock.'

'I thought you wanted to keep this civil,' Schrope said.

Five minutes later, Svetlana sent word that she was ready to start the engine. Schrope told her to start the burn at a quarter gee, and then to smoothly increase to half a gee over the ensuing five minutes. That would give everyone time to reach their berths for confinement during the immobilising lockdown of the two-gee burn. Then Svetlana could turn the engine up as far as she dared. Janus would fall away. In thirty or forty minutes, the ship would drop out of the slipstream – and Janus itself would look as if it was suddenly speeding away from them as its true acceleration became apparent.

By that time, Bella knew, they would already be lost.

Craig Schrope's intimate knowledge of *Rockhopper*'s layout had served him well. The medical centre and its surrounding cluster of rooms formed a near-perfect prison, isolated from any ship-critical systems. With only two air-locked passageways accessing the entire area, it was an easy matter to seal one lock and station an informal sentry point at the other.

Bella and her party were left to make their own provisions for comfort. Under two gees, walking would be nearly impossible, and even sitting would be unpleasant. While the ship was still at half a gee, Bella and Axford raided the medical centre for support cushions and pillows, and distributed these around. Jim Chisholm was helped back into bed, completely drained by the events in the gymnasium.

'I wish I could think of something we could do,' he said as Axford slipped nutrient lines back into his permanent cannulas. 'But Craig has us right where he wants us.'

'Just rest,' Axford told him gently.

Belinda Pagis held up the limp form of a flexy. 'We're locked out of anything useful. I've tried all the obvious tricks to get around the barriers, but they look pretty watertight.'

'Let me try,' Bella said. But the result was the same: the flexy would only allow her access to the most superficial layers of ShipNet. 'This is what I did to Svetlana,' she said.

'I'll keep trying to find a hole,' Pagis said. 'My guess is that Svetlana didn't set up these barriers – she'd have been too busy with the engine. More than likely it was Bob Ungless.'

'Ungless is good,' Bella said.

'I'm better.'

'It won't make much difference even if you do find a hole,' Carsten Fleig said. 'Even if you had unrestricted access, you'd only be able to stop the engine once. Then they'd come and take the flexies away from us.'

Fleig's calm pedantry often irritated Bella, but as usual he was absolutely correct. At best they could impede the escape effort, not block it for ever. 'If we could just inflict some damage on the engine,' she said, 'enough to put it out of action, but not destroy the ship . . .'

'Or damage the tokamak itself,' Pagis reminded her. 'If you win the day, we're still going to need that for power.'

'Whatever you might have in mind,' Mengcheng Yang said, 'it might be best not to talk about it.'

'Yang's right,' Bella said. 'If Craig's on the ball, he'll be listening to every word we say, and watching us on the cams.'

'And monitoring our flexy activity,' Pagis said. She gave Bella a pessimistic smile. 'But I'll keep trying.'

The speaker came to life. 'This is Schrope. Word is that Svetlana's ready to push to two gees. We'll increase smoothly through one gee, but I'd suggest you make yourselves comfortable. The ride may be a little rough until Svetlana fine-tunes the fusion parameters.'

Bella felt a tremor run through the ship as the engine pushed beyond half a gee. It was more power than they had ever generated before, operating well outside their textbook performance envelope. Bella felt her own weight increase. She tried to judge the moment when the acceleration passed through one gee. She sat on her haunches, pushing back against the padded side of a cabinet. Most of her people were in similar positions, dispersed through two rooms.

She thought about destroying the engine, and realised with bleak resignation that it was already far too late for that. *Rockhopper* had gained enough speed to escape the weak gravitational field of Janus. Even if the engine cut out now, the ship would continue on its drift to the edge of the slipstream.

She had lost. It was just a question of accepting it now.

Her weight increased until even sitting was unpleasant. Slowly, Bella stretched out until she was lying flat, with only a pillow under her head for support. It was easier that way: breathing still felt more difficult than normal, but at least now her weight was distributed more evenly across her whole body.

Pagis was still trying to crack the ShipNet lockout. 'I'm sorry,' she said. 'This is too difficult. And it doesn't look as if Ungless made any silly mistakes.' She put the flexy down, groaning with overworked muscles.

'No one's going to make any silly mistakes,' Bella said. 'We're too good a crew for that.'

Now and then the floor kicked up at them with renewed force as the thrust became momentarily unsteady, but the jolts gradually became less severe and less frequent as Svetlana adjusted the details of the fusion reaction.

'Bella,' Thom Crabtree said, his voice just loud enough to carry over the background noise, 'there's something you should know.'

Bella smiled reassuringly at the taphead. 'I'm glad you sided with me, Thom. It counts for a lot. You don't have to explain yourself.'

'I'm siding with the rightful authority on this ship,' Crabtree said, his nervous, feral eyes still not meeting hers. 'But that isn't what I wanted to talk to you about.'

'What, then?' she asked.

'I can do something. Something that might make them stop and take us back to Janus. But I'll need your permission first.'

She kept her expression fixed, her voice level. 'What do you think you can do, Thom?'

'I can destroy the ship. There's a robot – Nick's free-flier, the one he sent out to look at the forward face of Janus.'

He had her full attention now, but she could not show it. Microphones probably wouldn't pick up their conversation above the noise of the ship, but the webcams would reveal the slightest hint of conspiracy.

'You can control it?'

'Yes.'

'From *here*?'

'I'm in contact with it all the time.'

'But Saul Regis locked you out of control,' Bella said. 'That was why you came to see me – to complain about not having enough to do. All you had were the virtuals.'

'I did something about it,' Crabtree said, with an easy shrug. 'Saul wasn't really very thorough. I found a way around his blocks. I've been doing it for days now, looking through robots, making them move – not enough to be noticed, but enough to remember how it feels to do something.'

Bella looked around, but Regis was in the next room. 'But we're locked out of ShipNet.'

'I don't need ShipNet. The only way they can lock *me* out would be with a skull saw – or a hammer to the head.' Crabtree had the glazed and absent look that told her he was only partly present in the room. Much of his sensory world was already focused on a point of view beyond the hull.

'Are you keeping up with us?'

'Yes. I'm burning fuel pretty quickly, but I should be able to shadow *Rockhopper* for another ten minutes.'

'What can you do?'

'Nothing subtle,' Crabtree said, closing his eyes tightly.

Bella called Svetlana to medical.

Engine down. Full reverse thrust on steering rockets, followed by a slew that must nearly have snapped the ship's spine.

'Take us back to the initial study position,' Crabtree said. 'Take us back to Janus.'

By then they had no choice but to obey. At that point, the superior numbers of the other faction counted for nothing. They couldn't block Crabtree's link to the free-flier because it bypassed ShipNet completely. Given hours – or days – Bella was sure that they could have found a way to lock him out, even if it consisted of nothing cleverer than disabling the antenna that was talking to the free-flier, but they didn't have hours, or even minutes.

Crabtree had demonstrated his complete control of the free-flier by nearly ramming the ship, showing how easy it would have been to achieve a killing impact. He maintained a stand-off for as long as the free-flier's fuel situation allowed.

An hour passed, then another hour. By that time, even the most optimistic flight-dynamics scenarios said that they had no hope of ever making it back home.

Gradually, even the most determined of Schrope's faction realised that the battle was lost. They were still the stronger party, and many of them probably toyed with taking out their revenge on Bella's entire faction, but on some level they must have known that there would come a time when the other party's services would prove useful. They could have taken Bella – she was of no practical use to them, had no skills that she alone possessed – but she was the captain and something made them pass her by, as if to touch her would violate some unspoken taboo.

So they took Thom Crabtree instead.

They did it by stealth, when thoughts of revenge were beginning to recede. They waited for a moment when Crabtree was isolated, late in the ship's night, and grabbed him. It was done soundlessly, and no one was around to stop them.

They took him deeper into the ship, then secured themselves behind airlock bulkheads.

There were two men: Connor Herrick and John Chanticler, both members of Parry's EVA squad. They had always struck Bella as dependable crewmen, proficient at what they did. She had never imagined that they might be capable of murder.

They'd found an old spacesuit: an ancient Orlan fifteen, forty years old if it was a day, hopelessly beyond repair but kept aboard so that it could be cannibalised for spare parts. They inserted Thom Crabtree into it. They found a panel in the wall and wrenched it free. Behind the panel lay a gristle of coloured flexible pipes, one of which carried superheated steam.

Cams watched the proceedings. No matter where they were in the ship, everyone saw what was happening.

Herrick and Chanticler closed a valve and severed this pipe. They connected one end to the emergency air input on the old spacesuit, using geckoflex and duct tape to seal the bond. Crabtree, even then, could not quite grasp what they had in mind for him. Through the smeared faceplate of the old helmet, Bella thought she could see only puzzled curiosity on his face.

Then they turned on the steam.

Parry took some of his team to make a desperate attempt to stop the torture. No matter what else happened, that would always be to their credit. Eventually they broke through one of the sealed airlocks, but by then it was too late. Stoked up on adrenalin and steroids, the murderers came close to killing Parry as well.

When Crabtree was dead, when he had finally stopped thrashing in agony, they recovered the Orlan fifteen. They took his obscene roasted corpse to the nearest airlock and ejected him into space. But they kept back the suit. Now was not a time to start throwing things away.

# CHAPTER 12

Even for the victors, the next three days were not easy. By the end Bella was removed from whatever lingering hold on command she might have retained. She was taken to one of the standard crew sleeping pods and locked inside, without food, water or access to ShipNet. It was a day before anyone came to check that she was still alive, a day before she could ask any questions, but through the thin plastic sheet that served as a door, the ship's noisy convulsions provided a kind of news service of their own. She was close enough to the gymnasium for sounds to travel and she listened with a quiet mammalian attentiveness, like a shrew in a hole.

She heard Jim Chisholm, his voice strained with effort, desperately trying to forge some sort of reconciliation between the two shipboard factions. Because he was trusted, people were prepared to listen when he urged amity. What was done was done, Chisholm said. A life had been taken: wasn't that enough blood for one ship?

Let it end with Thom Crabtree. Let it end here and now.

She heard Ryan Axford making similar placatory noises. Axford said he would refuse to treat anyone he believed to have perpetrated violence against another crewmember. People liked and respected Axford, too, but he was a doctor, with a duty of care: they wondered if he really meant it.

Anyway, he wasn't the only medic on the ship.

There were still doubts about *Rockhopper*'s true situation. The big question – whether to run for home or ride Janus into the night – remained painfully unresolved. Some of Svetlana's faction were coming around to the idea that Janus was now their only hope of long-term survival, and that it would be suicide to leave the slipstream.

But there were others amongst her people who still thought it was better to try to get home, no matter how unlikely their chances of survival. They still thought Earth would find a way to rescue them, even as they fell away from the Sun like a stone down a well. As each hour passed, their argument became less sustainable, but that did not stop them fighting their corner – and fight they did, too. Bella heard the same frenzied arguments over and over again throughout the long hours of her confinement. They never quite boiled over, but there were times when people had to be restrained from clawing each other apart. And all the while Janus was accelerating, and pulling *Rockhopper* with it.

Then came Svetlana's speech.

She made it over the shipwide speaker, so that everyone would hear it. Pumps and generators were set to idle. People listened wordlessly, without even a cough of interruption.

'Crew of *Rockhopper*,' she began. 'We find ourselves in a situation. We didn't ask for it; we certainly didn't want it. That doesn't mean that some of us didn't anticipate it, that some of us didn't try to do something about it. I tried to persuade Bella to turn this ship around before we got to Janus, and I tried to turn it around when we got here.

'I failed on both occasions, and you must believe that no one is sorrier for that than me. I know there are some of you who feel we should make another attempt, that we should turn back around, leave the slipstream and lose as much speed as we can. Believe me, there's a part of me that feels the same way, that maybe we should just *try*, and see how far we get.

'But we can't do it.

'DeepShaft screwed us, people. They knew we didn't have enough fuel to make it to Janus and back, but Powell Cagan wasn't going to let that stop him. They hacked into us, altered our fuel data, made it look as if we could do this – but we never could. Powell Cagan knew from the word go that this was a suicide mission, and he signed off on it knowing full well what would happen to us. Not just Powell, either, but everyone at DeepShaft who was a part of it. He didn't put this together on his own.

'Ask yourselves this: do these sound like the kind of people likely to put time and money into a rescue operation? Not just any old rescue operation, but the most technically ambitious mission ever mounted in the system: one that will require a better, faster ship than anything currently sitting on anyone's drawing board – including the Chinese. And that ship would need to reach us before our last power supplies run dry.

'It isn't doable, people. No will in the world can save us now.

'But we're not going to die. Like I said, we didn't ask for this. But now we're in it, we might as well make the best of it. Bella dealt us a hand. It's a pretty shitty one. But we have to play it.

'We're staying with Janus. There'll be no further attempts to escape the slipstream. I've taken steps to ensure that the fusion engine can't run in cruise mode again. It'll keep giving us ship power, and we can use the fuel for *Avenger* and *Crusader* when we need 'em, but it'll never push *Rockhopper* again. That's the hand I'm dealing us. It says we have to stay here, no matter how difficult it gets, no matter how tempting the alternative might be. The alternatives *will* kill us.

'We're going to land on Janus. There's still a nice cap of water ice on the sternward face, and we should be safe there. No matter how fast Janus gets, we'll have two hundred kilometres of shielding between us and the bow. That should be enough.

'We can live. We'll have power from the engine in the short term, so keeping warm won't be an issue. We'll have light and amenities. In the long run, we'll find a way to use Janus for power instead, but that isn't a bridge we have to cross tomorrow.

'We have closed-cycle waste-recycling systems. We have aeroponics racks and zeolite beds. As long as that machinery keeps working, as long as the plants keep growing, we won't go hungry. We'll lose some water through the hull, but we can top up with Janus ice whenever we need to. We have enough medicine for the immediate future: not enough to work miracles, but enough to keep most of us alive. We have centrifuges for gravity. We have landers and tractors and surface domes. We have robots.

'We have fifty thousand tonnes of ship that DeepShaft ain't getting back in one piece.'

That got a muted cheer that echoed around the ship.

'We dock *Rockhopper* with Janus just the way we'd dock a mass driver: dig a deep pit and line it with sprayrock. Then we back the ship in, engine-first, nice and easy.

'Then we'd better start learning to like Janus, because we're going to be here for a while.'

Svetlana's speech did not work miracles, but Bella had to concede that there was a subtle shift in the tension levels throughout the ship in the hours that followed. Minor rumbles of dissension were swiftly quashed. Svetlana had indeed taken a spanner (or more likely a teleoperated fist) to some delicate part of the fusion engine, rendering it unstable for sustained thrust. Bella wondered how much pain that act of tactical sabotage must have caused her.

So Svieta had come round to Bella's point of view. In a perfect world, that would have been enough to let them see eye to eye again, but Bella knew better than that. It would take more than unity of purpose to heal the rift between them.

'I wasn't expecting *you*,' Bella said as Parry slid aside the compartment door.

Parry removed his red cap and scratched his scalp. He looked dog-tired, waxy and unshaven, stress oozing from his pores. 'Craig didn't want to talk to you,' Parry said, and she picked up something in his words beyond the surface content of the statement. Bella thought of everything she knew about Craig Schrope, everything she knew about the type of man he was, and nodded.

'Craig doesn't want to talk to anyone, does he?'

'Craig's having a tough time adjusting,' Parry said. 'Which isn't to say that it's exactly easy for the rest of us, but—'

'It'll be harder for Craig. Much, much harder. He's company to the marrow, Parry. But the company doesn't exist any more – not as far as we're concerned. It's just us and *Rockhopper*. Craig's little world is falling further away with every passing second.'

'We're working without him. Maybe he'll come round – maybe he won't.'

'You never liked him or his kind.'

'I'm just trying to find a way to run this ship. If Craig makes that easier, he'll become a part of it. If he doesn't, we'll manage without him.'

'And where does Svetlana fit into this? Or the other chiefs, for that matter?'

'You know who came with us and who didn't,' Parry said, with no apparent rancour. 'Right now, Svetlana and I are running operations. We have the support of two-thirds of the crew, more or less.'

'Two murderers amongst them.'

'They'll be dealt with.' The way he said that scared her more than anything else. 'You know I did everything in my power to prevent what happened.'

'If you'd sided with me, Thom Crabtree wouldn't have had to do what he did.'

'And if you'd listened to Svieta we'd never have ended up where we are today. Let's not play the blame game, shall we?'

'Fine with me,' Bella said. 'What game would you rather play?'

'The one where we pull this ship together. The people who sided with Craig can run things for the time being, but we'll need everyone's help if we're to start looking beyond the next few weeks. That's why I need to start healing wounds.'

'Beginning with me,' Bella said.

'I need something to appease the returners, bring them back into the fold.'

'My head on a plate?'

'No,' he said, but without the reflexive dismissal she had been expecting, as if her execution had at least been one possibility for discussion. 'What we need . . .' Parry stumbled, and was suddenly unable to meet her eyes. 'You're going to stay here until we're down. I'll make sure you're kept comfortable, in better conditions than you've been in for the last day.'

'I'm hearing a "but".'

'You won't be allowed contact with anyone. The only people you'll speak to will be me and someone from the medical section.'

'I need to talk to Svieta,' Bella said urgently.

'She doesn't want to talk to *you*. Ever again.'

'This ship needs me, Parry. I know I've burnt our friendship, but this is about more than that. I'll submit to Svieta's authority if that keeps her happy, but give me enough power to make a difference. Give me enough to help.'

'You've been deposed, Bella. The way Svieta sees it is you blew critical command decisions when there was still time to make things right. You took us deeper into the incident pit when we could still have climbed out. Deeper and deeper, until the sides were too steep.'

'I also saved this damned crew from a slow death in deep space. Doesn't *that* count for something?'

'That's . . . that's by the by.'

'I expected better of you, Parry.'

'This is the best you're going to get. I'm sorry, Bella. This isn't exactly a picnic for any of us. It's not as if we'll be partying it up while you're locked away. We'll be surviving. That's all. You'll have the easier time of it, frankly.'

'Look into my eyes and say that.'

He shook his head, not looking her way. 'When the ship's down, when we've established some kind of stable presence on Janus, you'll be taken away somewhere. Svetlana doesn't want you around any more.'

Svetlana sat in Bella's old office, wondering what she should do with the fish. For now she fed them as best she could, and ignored their dim, accusatory expressions, the way their constantly working mouths seemed to whisper conspiracies.

The ship was quieter now than it had been in weeks, and for the most part the crew had come round to her authority. They were even calling it the Interim Authority. It had nothing to do with DeepShaft, and everything to do with survival. Pushing forward, breath by breath, inch by inch, no matter what it took.

Saul Regis knocked on the open door. A Lind loyalist, Regis had never needed persuading that Janus was their only hope of survival. But the death of Crabtree had touched him on some emotional register Svetlana had barely recognised in him before.

'They're going to pay, Parry told me.'

'Yes,' she said. And it was true: the two men were in custody; no matter what else happened, they would never see Earth again.

Regis pushed a flexy across to her. 'Then it has to be done properly.'

'Properly, Saul?'

He scratched at his gut through the thin fabric of his sweatshirt. 'You can't just . . . do it to them. There have to be words. There has to be a ceremony.'

'We're miners, Saul. No one gave us the book on capital law.'

'Then we have to make our own book. No waiting for instructions from home. This has to be something *we* do. Communities make law. We need law, some kind of judicial apparatus.'

Something about his presence made Svetlana shiver, and she looked down at the flexy with dread. A static frame filled the image window: a group of figures crowded around a campfire in some weirdly lit desert landscape, with a cloud-streaked pink sky and too many moons. The figures wore body-hugging costumes and kinky boots, with lots of equipment and weapons hanging from their belts, sleekly moulded in matt silver. Their hairstyles and make-up were meant to look futuristic, but actually looked twenty or thirty years out of date. One man knelt by the campfire while another pointed a weapon at the side of his head. Next to the man with a gun, a tall, black-clad, clerical-looking alien read from a kind of scroll.

'Fuck, Saul,' she said, as recognition clicked in, 'this is—'

'*Cosmic Avenger*,' he said, before she had a chance to continue. 'Season four, episode five. *Avenger* drops through a plenum gash into the Unmapped Zone, out of range of Terrafleet communications. With the ship damaged, Lieutenant Theobald attempts to seize control from Captain Underhill—'

'Saul,' she said, softly, as if speaking to a sleepwalker, 'Saul . . . this is just a TV show. A bad TV show from my childhood, which no one even took seriously back then.' She handed back the flexy with a shudder of distaste. 'This is not some kind of . . . life manual. What are you actually suggesting – that we all start acting as if we believe that this is real?'

'The execution scene's an acknowledged classic,' Regis said. 'The writing in that fourth-season arc . . . Underhill's speech at the execution . . . I know a lot of people think *Star Crusader* was better, but it really wasn't. Of course, they'll never *understand* that.'

She kept waiting for Regis to blink, to show some indication that this was at best a sick joke at an inappropriate time. But there was no crack in that mask of sincerity.

She tried again. 'You really think this speech—'

'I'm not saying copy it word for word.' He shook his head, as if *that* was absurd. 'It's just that when Underhill said what she said – how things were looking for the crew, how Underhill knew what she had to do but regretted having to do it all the same . . . the template of it . . .' He trailed off, with the air of someone who thought they had made their point convincingly enough. 'We could do a lot worse.'

'I'm sure we could,' she said. 'Thank you for the input, Saul. Now please – get out of my office.'

He pressed the flexy to his chest, where it softened to bend itself around him. 'I just think it needs to be done right,' he said. 'For Thom Crabtree.'

She watched him leave, aghast at what had taken place but not entirely surprised by it either.

For some of her crew, the knowledge that they were now prisoners of Janus was already a kind of death. She knew, with an acute sense of precognition, that there would be suicides in the times that lay ahead. She thought she could predict with some accuracy who would choose that option, too.

But for a tiny minority, Janus would be a kind of liberation. The old world, with its bewildering emotional and political complexities, was receding.

What lay ahead would be simpler and more emblematic. Just as some people lived a kind of half-life until a war came along, at which point they flourished, so the austere simplicities of Janus might be attractive to a man like Saul Regis. A slate wiped brutally clean.

He had been gone a long time before Svetlana picked up her own flexy and navigated ShipNet, looking for the same ancient media files Regis must have already mined. She had no intention of copying the words of the execution – the very thought revolted her – but there could be no harm in simply looking at what had happened.

Could there?

Preparations for the mating of Janus and *Rockhopper* swallowed days. Svetlana dreamed multicoloured simulations and woke from fevered hours of stress analysis in which numbers and equations had battled like epic protagonists.

Once *Rockhopper* was down there would be no way of lifting it from Janus again. Gravity on Janus was a feeble three hundred and fifty times weaker than on Earth. A person weighed next to nothing. But a fifty-thousand-tonne space vehicle still needed one hundred and fifty tonnes of thrust to lift itself aloft, which was a lot more than the steering and station-keeping motors could supply. Even using the landers as tugs, *Rockhopper* would come in hard, punching down into the pit with all the force of a skyscraper-sized battering ram. The stress analysis said the ship would hold together, but the computations were mind-numbingly complex, and an error anywhere, however tiny, could mean doom.

As the car took her back to the hab, her flexy chimed unexpectedly. With her head swimming with engineering issues, she had asked not to be called unnecessarily.

She pulled the flexy from her jacket, shook it alive and found herself looking at Denise Nadis.

'You need to see this, I think,' Nadis said.

'What?' Svetlana asked.

'We were looking at Janus, at the icecap, mapping it with the high-res cameras, looking for alternative dig sites.'

'I thought we'd agreed on the site. Haven't we already got machines down there?'

Nadis blinked and swallowed. 'I just wanted to be sure we'd picked the best spot. Once we're down—'

'I know. No second chances. What is it, Denise?'

'We found . . . this.'

An image box swelled to cover most of Nadis's face. At first, Svetlana could make nothing of the mesh of false-colour hexels overlaid with numeric codes. 'You're going to have to help me, Denise.'

'I'm sorry – zoom's too far out. This is a section of the icecap, about fifty klicks south of where we're planning to dig. That's the limit of our search area – it was just luck that we happened to find it at all.'

'Find what?'

Nadis whispered a command to her own flexy. The image swelled and zoomed until Svetlana was clearly looking down at something blunt and metallic, mashed into the ice as if it had hit at high speed.

'It's a ship,' Nadis said. 'Part of one, anyway.'

A scale overlay dropped over the image. The crashed ship was only twenty metres across its longest axis.

'That's not right,' Svetlana said flatly. 'We already mapped the ice at enough res not to have missed—'

'We didn't miss shit.' Nadis interrupted her. She was on firm ground now. 'It wasn't there before. It must have come in since we completed the maps, slipped right past us somehow.'

'While we were otherwise engaged,' Svetlana said, understanding. The ship's form was familiar to her, albeit as part of a larger whole. She had seen the television pictures from Earth orbit. It was part of the *Shenzhou Five*.

'This isn't possible. We destroyed it. We shot it out of the fucking sky.'

'We're only looking at part of it,' Svetlana said. 'Like the smallest part of a multi-staged rocket. They must have planned on using one large fusion engine and fuel tank to get them out here, and then returning home using a smaller stage, with its own engine and fuel.'

'It's tiny.'

'I know. Maybe they weren't carrying as many people as they wanted us to believe.' Nadis still sounded spooked, as if the reappearance of the Chinese ship violated some fundamental principle of her personal universe. 'What the hell happened, though? Bella still shot it. Nothing changes that.'

'Maybe Bella just damaged it,' Svetlana said. 'Cooked their main stage with the FAD. Forced them to bail out into the second stage and make a run for it.'

'Run *here*?'

'Maybe they didn't have a hell of a lot of choice.'

'If that thing was built to take them home, why didn't they use it?'

'I'm guessing maybe because they had too much velocity in the wrong direction,' Svetlana said. 'They must have intended to use the main stage to slow down before they started their return journey.'

'Only Bella cancelled that option.'

'Looks like it. Wang must have known he had one shot at being rescued, and that was us.'

'Oh, Jesus. You mean he was trying to catch up with *Rockhopper*?'

'I think so.'

'After we shot the poor kid out of the sky.'

'Beggars can't be choosers, Denise. Trouble is, he didn't know about the slipstream either.'

'He must have used up all his fuel,' Nadis said. 'Never had enough to slow down.'

But even as Nadis voiced the thought, Svetlana knew she was wrong. If the *Shenzhou Five* had come in at uncontrolled speed, there would only be a crater where the ship now lay. For the ship to have survived at all, for the ship not to have smeared itself across the whole face of Janus . . . the crash must have been very close to a landing.

It must have been very close to survivable.

'There could be someone alive in that thing,' she said.

'There isn't,' Nadis said. 'No transponder, no SOS beacon. We've tried hailing on the Chinese frequency. Nothing.'

'Wang can't have died. You don't come all this way, make it this far, and just *die*.'

'They're dead, Svieta. I just thought you needed to know. Maybe there's some tech we can use—'

'Get me infrared,' she said.

'We've tried it – she's still hot – but if she'd come in from space in the last week or so, we'd expect her to be.'

'I still want infrared,' Svetlana said. 'And I don't want to have to ask a third time.'

Nadis made a huffing sound that she probably hoped Svetlana didn't catch. It was going to be tough for Nadis from now on, taking orders from someone who had been her equal in the old regime. But she was good. She would learn.

So they turned the cams on the *Shenzhou Five*, as they had turned cannons on it before, and this time they took a series of mid-infrared snapshots. When they scrolled onto Svetlana's flexy, they had the hyperreal clarity of images taken across a perfect and still vacuum. The ship was still hot, just as Nadis had told her it would be. Engine parts glowed in cherry-red false colour as they ticked and cooled down to Janus ambient. But there was a pattern to the radiating heat that made Svetlana's heart jump in her chest. The radiators sketched a neon grid across the exposed surface of the hull, but *only there*. The visible side panels were dark. So, judging by the lack of boil-off, were the underpanels.

'He's still alive,' she said excitedly. 'He's turned off the radiators in contact with the ice. If he didn't, he'd melt his way right down to the machinery. Machines wouldn't have done that. It must have taken human intervention, after the ship came to rest.'

'Why didn't he send us a message?' Nadis asked.

'He did,' Svetlana said. 'That was it.'

They went down in *Cosmic Avenger* and hovered near the smashed wreck of the *Shenzhou Five*, sending out robots to scout it from different angles. It looked bad at first, but that was only because every fragile part of the ship had been bent or broken off by the glancing impact. The airtight hull had weathered the crash with only a slight amount of buckling. Even in the optical, its heat radiators were visible as brick-red squiggles along its dorsal surface. There were no windows in the pale-green metal; no way to tell if the crew was alive or dead.

*Avenger* touched down nearby. Robots scouted again, poking and prodding the snowbound hull for a way in.

The Chinese used a simplified variant of the same rocket-age airlock door design as everyone else, but from the outside there was no way to tell whether a particular door really was an airlock, and not just a door leading straight into a pressurised cabin. They had to bring in an emergency outer airlock sheath from *Avenger* and glue it into place with dabs of fast-setting vacuum epoxy. They sealed it with a caulk of sprayrock, then pumped it full of trimix adjusted to their best guess for the Chinese taste in pressure and gas fraction.

Even the best airlock made settling sounds as pressure equalised on either side of it. With his helmet resting against the door, Parry heard these sounds like distant hammer taps. It told him there was probably air on the other side.

He knocked on the door. He waited and knocked again, knowing that a survivor might need time to complete final suiting-up procedures before working the lock. Even in a hurry, that might take five or six minutes. He knocked again, and waited: five minutes, then ten. He gave it fifteen to be on the safe side – there was no rush, given how long the Chinese had been down there already.

But still no one was coming.

Parry swung the door open using the manual release. They'd been right about the trimix, and although they'd also been right to be careful, there was an airlock chamber on the other side. Good omens. Maybe his knocks hadn't been audible through all those layers of metal and insulation.

He opened the inner door and stepped inside. It was crypt-dark: another Braille dive. But when he cuffed on his helmet light, he saw all that he needed to.

The ship was a wreck: a dislodged pile of equipment and furniture had been compacted into the nose under the force of the impact. Hull spars were sheared off like broken ribs. The Chinese were good at materials science, everyone knew that, but this ship had taken more of a kicking than even they built for.

Parry poked the torch into the rubble, wincing against what he expected to find: a brave crewman, pinned into his seat, mangled into something that would give him nightmares for the rest of his life.

But there was no one there.

He directed the light towards the back of the ship and saw a bulkhead door, framed on either side by Chinese symbols. He picked his way through the wreckage and knocked on the door. He waited, but again there was no answer. No telling if there was air on the other side, or just a vacuum pocket. If it was vacuum, the door would swing away from him as soon as he unlocked the catches. He braced himself against the possible outrush of air and worked the release. The door opened easily, without snatching away from his fingers.

He shone the light inside and the beam picked out a Chinese man wearing lightweight clothes. He lay on his back on a heavily padded couch, facing the rear of the ship. He was strapped in like a psychiatric patient, tied down with enormous cushioned restraints. One of his arms was bent at an odd, anatomically problematic angle. His eyes were closed, the lids blackened. He looked dead.

Parry moved towards the man and leaned in close, until his faceplate glass was only a finger's width from the man's mouth. A faint smear of exhaled breath misted the glass.

'Ryan,' Parry said, 'you'd better get over here. There's a survivor. He looks pretty beaten up.'

'What about the others?' Axford asked.

'There are no others. Just this one man. Just this one . . . this one *kid*.'

The man's eyes opened. They were red through the black slits of his lids. G-force haemorrhaging: the eyes bleeding from inside as they were squeezed out of shape. He must have heard Parry speaking through his helmet. The man started to move a limb, then aborted the motion. Pain creased his face.

'Easy, easy,' Parry said. He reached up and undid his helmet seal, unconcerned that he might be placing himself at risk. He lifted off the helmet and let it drift down to the floor. 'It's Wang, right?'

The man's lips moved. They were dry and very chapped. In a ghost of a voice he said, 'Commander Wang Zhanmin.'

'Parry Boyce,' he said. 'From the *Rockhopper*. Welcome to Janus.'

'I think I may have broken something in the crash,' Wang said weakly.

'There's a doctor coming over. We'll take care of you. You're going to be fine.'

'Where will you take me?'

'Back to *Rockhopper*,' Parry said.

'There's something you need to do first, before you leave the *Shenzhou Five* where it is, before she melts into the ice.' Wang lifted a finger, pointing to the back of the ship. 'In the rear compartment . . . I brought something for you.'

'You brought *us* something?'

Wang managed a nod. 'I thought it might come in useful. There was just time to transfer it before I had to undock. Consider it a gift from China.'

*

Parry landed *Avenger* on minimum thrust, kicking up only a tiny backwash of boiled ice. He emerged from the ship wearing a hardshell Orlan. Elias Feldman, Hank Dussen and Gillian Shimozu followed him, escorting two bound prisoners who were wearing softer spacesuits of older design. They progressed across the ice in gentle parabolas until they were about a hundred metres from the lander. They had arrived at a spot of ground roughly ten metres across, illuminated with a disc of projected laser-light from the distant form of *Rockhopper*. The circle was as sharply edged as if it had been marked with chalk. Their shadows were black and judicial, as dark as the interstellar night itself.

Parry brought the little party to a halt in the middle of the circle. The bound prisoners were made to kneel on the ice, shoulder to shoulder, while Feldman, Dussen and Shimozu stood behind. Parry stood before them, his legs slightly apart for balance. He peeled a flexy from the chest of his suit, where it had been drinking power. With a flick of his wrist the flexy stiffened itself until it had the rigidity of slate. He held the flexy to the level of his helmet, tilting it this way and that until he found the right angle. The words he had prepared were marked in bold black type.

His voice came from every wall and flexy on *Rockhopper*. At first his words were hesitant, but as he continued to speak he seemed to find some wellspring of authority within himself.

'John Chanticler and Connor Herrick, you have been brought here to face punishment for the death of Thomas Crabtree eight days ago. You were found guilty of this crime by a jury of your fellow crewmen.' Parry waited for the flexy to scroll to the next block of text: the hesitation seemed to lend the proceedings even more solemnity. 'The Judicial Apparatus of the Interim Authority has determined that murder must be punished by death. There were one hundred and forty-four of us before you killed Thom Crabtree. Now there will be one hundred and forty-one. Let your deaths mark an end to this. Let your deaths not go wasted. After this day, there will be no more killing.' He stopped again and looked up from the brightly lit tableau to the hovering ship most of them would see again. 'We will heal our differences or die together.'

Parry lowered the flexy. 'Let the sentence be enacted.'

Hank Dussen and Elias Feldman stationed themselves on either side of John Chanticler. Gillian Shimozu removed a cumbersome piece of mining equipment from her belt: a recoilless hammer-drill. A ribbed power line ran from the drill to her backpack. She held the drill two-handed and pressed its sharpened, glinting tip against the back of Chanticler's helmet.

With the thumb of her right hand she armed the drill's magnetic induction coils. Pink status lights flickered along the drill's barrel. The drill had been buffed to a high sheen.

Parry knelt down so that his helmet was level with the faceplate of John

Chanticler. No one else knew it, but the trimix of the condemned men had been adjusted before they stepped from the descent craft. They were drunk on oxygen: stoned and slightly euphoric. 'This will be quick and painless,' Parry said, while doubting that either of them heard him.

Then he looked over the crest of Chanticler's helmet and nodded to Gillian Shimozu.

She fired the hammer-drill. It flinched in her grip, but the counteracting weights held it steady even as the mass of the sharpened cutting tip rammed its way through the back of Chanticler's helmet on a ripple of magnetic induction. The helmet's self-sealing layer ensured that there was only a cough of air-loss before the helmet regained integrity. By then drill had done its work. Something vile coated the inner surface of Chanticler's faceplate.

Shimozu jerked the drill free. The tip was stained red. She knelt down and drove it into the ice until the friction worked it clean. Chanticler stayed in the kneeling position, held there by Hank Dussen. Feldman moved to Herrick and placed a hand on his right shoulder.

They repeated the process.

When Shimozu had removed the drill for the second time and cleaned the blade, she took a respectful step back from the two men she had just executed. Parry nodded and the men released their holds on Chanticler and Herrick.

With a horrid, almost comic synchrony, the two kneeling figures pitched forward in slow motion and buried their faceplates in the ice.

# PART TWO

# 2059+

# CHAPTER 13

Svetlana ignored the apprehensive knot in her stomach as best she could, her right hand clamped tightly around Parry's arm, fingers digging into the fabric of his sleeve. Typically, Parry had fallen asleep as soon as *Cosmic Avenger* was airborne.

They were still traversing ice – it was too dark to see much except in the weak backlight from the lander's engines – but the in-flight map told her they were over the very edge of the sternward cap, where it thinned out into a lacy and unstable shelf poised above dizzying spires and canyons of Spican machinery. The gravitational eddies from the machinery became more severe here, which was partly why the ice had failed in the first place. The lander pitched and rolled like an airliner in bad turbulence – the kind where they stop serving drinks.

It was possible that a smoother trajectory existed, but that it had been deemed too costly in terms of fuel expenditure. Fuel was still a problem, even now, and every gram that was burnt had to be accounted for with mandarin scrupulousness. Pilots were reprimanded if their journeys used even a fraction more fuel than the software had predicted.

Another lurch and they were no longer over ice. Svetlana looked back just in time to see the ragged, serrated blue-grey cliff receding behind the lander. Boulders as large as icebergs cluttered the base of the cliff, jostling amongst huge rectilinear formations. The lander now overflew a vista of dreamlike machines, vast as mountains, and the impression of speed diminished as the ground plummeted away into distant, indistinct complexity. For a moment it was almost as if they were hovering, unmoving.

It took Svetlana's breath away. It always did.

It was like a night-time flight over a major city, but with the scale increased a hundredfold. Yet there was a strange absence of vertigo. She'd felt the same thing swimming over empires of coral reef, or the time when she had swum out over the edge of a continental shelf.

The images of Janus taken soon after its departure from Saturn had suggested that the Spican machinery exuded a pale, twinkling luminescence. The truth was more complex. Up close, the machines appeared black across a wide spread of the electromagnetic spectrum, but many of their surfaces were in fact covered with light-emitting structures: coloured, glowing, window-like panels that merged seamlessly with the black background.

The current consensus held that the windows formed a kind of symbolic language. Early studies had revealed one hundred and fifty-five distinct window shapes, each of which was composed of five or six rectangular sub-elements arranged together like dominos. Most of these window shapes were repeated thousands of times across the visible surfaces, although a handful were, tantalisingly, much rarer. One shape – a simple structure resembling the letter 'T' – had been seen only once.

Jake Gomberg, *Rockhopper*'s language addict, had been assigned the task of making sense of the Spican markings. Amazingly, given their different temperaments, the garrulous Gomberg and the quiet, mouse-like Christine Ofria had become effective partners in this enterprise. They were a couple now, their marriage blessed by the Interim Authority. Their daughter Hannah had been the first child born on Janus, barely a year after the landing. She was one now, brimming with a fantastic precocity for language.

But in nearly two years of study her parents had made crushingly little progress. They still did not know what to make of the fact that some of the symbols occasionally changed hue, or sometimes switched off completely. Perhaps these changes were the crucial key to unlocking the mysteries of the Spican language, or perhaps they were as insignificant as the flickering of a dying neon tube.

Privately, Svetlana was glad that there had been no early breakthrough in the language study. She worried that the message, in the unlikely event that they ever succeeded in decoding it, might turn out to be dispiriting. The morale of her little community was already fragile enough without such a setback.

*Cosmic Avenger* dipped lower, following a flight path that took it below the tops of the highest structures. They crossed what appeared to be a sinuous river of molten lava, winding its way between enormous slabs of Spican machinery. Svetlana waited, knowing that sooner or later a transit would appear. Before long she spotted the swiftly moving node of the alien machine, gliding along the lava like a swelling in the flow.

Lava lines wrapped Janus from pole to pole. There were thousands of separate lines, tens or hundreds of kilometres long, joined together by complex cloverleaf intersections. The endpoints vanished into the sides of machines, terminating in blank walls that opened and closed a microsecond before and after the arrival of a transit.

Nick Thale and his team had invested much time studying the lava lines. Careful observation had shown that the transits emerged from five distinct 'factories' dotted around Janus, with neatly ordered pieces of material floating in their suspension fields. Transits running the other way tended to be ferrying a kind of slag, a rubble of misshapen pieces that might once have been intact components.

Once, in the early months of the first year, seismic monitors had detected a violent event deep inside Janus. The quake shook the newly grounded *Rockhopper* to its foundations, nearly toppling it. Observations from the free-fliers still in the slipstream showed that the moon's rate of acceleration dropped from five to three gees over the next week. During that same period, transit activity intensified, becoming much greater than at any time before or since. Huge amounts of rubble emerged from three closely spaced locations near a feature they had nicknamed Junction Box. The factories reciprocated by pumping out an enormous quantity of new components. There were 'traffic jams' as the endless flow of transits clogged up the lava-line system, allowing close study of the vehicles for the first time. Minor alterations to the lava-line system were observed.

At the end of the week, Janus resumed its former rate of acceleration as if nothing had happened. The implications, nonetheless, were clear: something had malfunctioned in the heart of the moon, perhaps catastrophically. The moon had throttled back, concentrated its repair resources and fixed itself.

It was good and bad.

It meant that while Janus was not infallible, that things could and did go wrong with it, it could repair itself. But by the same token, the ruthless speed with which the damage had been undone was in itself chilling. There had been talk of sabotaging the moon: throwing a human spanner into the heart of its alien drive system, like an FAD dialled to its maximum yield. Such hopes now seemed ludicrous in their naivety, like trying to stop a bulldozer with a feather.

The transit veered ahead of the lander and plunged into the sheer blank wall of a pyramidal structure. The lander followed a diverging lava line for another five or six kilometres, swerving to negotiate a region of high gravitational fluctuation. They passed under an illuminated bridge or conduit, and then made a hair-raising passage between the language-crammed walls of an incurving canyon.

There, dead ahead, lay the Maw.

Lava lines converged on the Maw from all directions, plunging over its curving lip into the glowing red heart of Janus. Although the 'floor' upon which the Spican machinery rested occasionally dipped down to twenty kilometres below its average level, the Maw was the only known opening into the deeper interior. Barely two hundred metres across and concealed from scrutiny by overhanging surface structures, the Maw had not been mapped until after *Rockhopper*'s arrival.

Robert Ungless brought *Cosmic Avenger* to a halt above the opening with a tap of reverse thrust.

Parry groaned, opened his eyes and pinched at their corners with his fingers. 'Are we there yet?'

'Patience,' Svetlana said. 'We're just arriving.'

The lander lowered itself into the Maw, surrounded by a throat-like tube veined with the fiery light of lava lines. When the lander had dropped another three hundred metres, the wall fell away in all directions, curving back towards the horizontal.

Svetlana had been expecting the vast cavern, but had not anticipated the claustrophobic feeling of entering a large, empty space through a narrow opening. As the lander put more distance between itself and the opening, the aperture began to appear treacherously small. The whole experience was too much like underwater caving for her liking. She could deal with swimming underwater at great depth, but not with having something between her and the surface.

'Fun, isn't it?' Parry said, grinning impishly at her.

She frowned at him. 'You're just saying that to wind me up. It's terrifying. Any sane human being would agree with me.'

The lander banked, bringing more of the near-spherical chamber into view. It was ten kilometres across at its widest point. Most of the chamber's machinery was confined to within a kilometre of the walls, with only a couple of needle-tipped spires jutting into the interior space. As on the surface, a scrawl of Spican symbols covered the machinery like neurotically precise tag graffiti. The illumination from these symbols gave the chamber its soft red glow: here, red symbols predominated over the other colours.

Across a stretch of floor unoccupied by machines or lava lines, flashing yellow strobes defined a landing apron. A cluster of pressurised tents lay to one side of the apron. A spacesuited figure tracked their approach, hand raised to visor to shield out the intermittent glare from the lander's main engine.

They came in fast – it saved fuel to use shock absorbers to cushion the landing instead of decelerating. *Cosmic Avenger* bounced a couple of times and then was still, its engine damped. Through the cockpit door Svetlana saw Ungless noting log details into a flexy.

'Thank you for using Vomit Airlines,' Parry said.

They fixed on helmets and gloves and squeezed into the airlock. Ungless stayed aboard, making no effort to hide his eagerness to leave. That was fine by Svetlana: she had no intention of making a long stay of it.

They stepped down from the lander onto the black floor of the Spican material. The surface resisted chemical or spectroscopic analysis, but was nonetheless grippy enough to walk on with geckoflex, and tolerated more permanent adhesive bonds. The hamlet of domes and equipment modules had been glued down to stop them drifting away during the mild gravity squalls that sometimes affected the chamber.

The waiting figure raised a hand in greeting. Svetlana's suit established a communications link and informed her via HUD that the other person was Gabriela Ramos.

'Glad to have you here,' Ramos said over the suit-to-suit. 'We were getting a bit desperate for company.'

'It'll be a flying visit, I'm afraid,' Svetlana said. She reached out and gave the other woman as much of a hug as the suits allowed. 'It seems ages since I last saw you. How long have you been down here?'

'On this rotation?' She tapped a finger speculatively against the chinplate of her helmet. 'This is my sixth . . . no, fifth week. I'm due back topside in another ten days. At least, that was the plan before *this* came up.'

Svetlana unclipped supply cases from the side of the lander. 'I wish we could cut down the shifts, but you know how tight things are with fuel right now.'

'I know, I know. We're not complaining. At least we get some work done. And maybe what we've found will help a bit.'

'That would be great,' Parry said.

'You don't sound convinced,' Ramos answered.

'I guess I'd sound a bit more enthusiastic if there hadn't been so many setbacks, but don't let my natural pessimism put you off.'

They carried the supply cases into a storage module and then spent ten minutes swapping recharged fuel cells for empty ones. When they were done, the spent cells loaded back aboard the lander, Ramos led them into the nearest tent. It was pressurised, so they passed through another airlock before removing helmets and gloves again. The tent's interior had been divided using fabric partitions into a commons, kitchen and three sleeping annexes. The occupants, past and present, had done their best to cosy-up the place a bit, but with only limited success. With her helmet off, Svetlana registered that it was uncomfortably cold. She wondered if Ramos ever removed her spacesuit.

'Axford says I'm to look at your bracelet,' she said.

Ramos fiddled with her suit cuff until the bracelet came loose. 'You know we're getting less exposure down here than you folks topside.'

'Just need to make sure – especially now that things have started happening.' Svetlana made a note of the dosage – it was comfortably within expectations – and handed back the bracelet.

'What about the others?' Ramos asked her.

'We'll assume you're all exposed to the same background. Can't check bone density until you're back topside, but I'll just have to trust that you're all doing your exercises.'

Ramos prepared coffee, rationing it out in precise spoonfuls. Svetlana sipped at hers with the knowledge of someone enjoying a fine and dwindling delicacy. Axford could prepare passable tea from the arboretum plants, but he'd drawn a blank on coffee. Maybe Wang could help them one day, but for now they were down to less than two hundred kilograms of coffee for the entire settlement.

Ramos pressed them mercilessly for topside gossip. Her mood seemed good. Svetlana liked Ramos: she always had, from the moment the young woman rotated onto *Rockhopper*, and she had adapted encouragingly well to Janus life. Reviewing her biographical notes, Svetlana had not been surprised. Ramos's life prior to DeepShaft had been one long climb out of the flooded *boca* shanty towns of Old Buenos Aires. She still had family back there, Svetlana knew, but after her transfer to the ship she had become a popular and well-integrated member of the crew. The mutiny must have been all the more traumatic for her, like a squalid divorce.

Lately, things had improved: there had been a kind of thawing in the strained relations between the two factions. Ramos had an on-off partner in Mike Sheng, one of those who had sided with the old regime. It would have been unthinkable even eighteen months ago – the wounds had still been that raw – but now such associations were becoming more commonplace. Ryan Axford's insistence on caring for everyone, irrespective of where their basic loyalties lay, had played no small part in fostering the spirit of reconciliation.

Of course, there were some differences that could not be glossed over so easily. And the general positive mood amongst the crew was partly due to the fact that most of them did not know how severe the fuel crisis really was. Svetlana did, and at times she found it very difficult to keep up a façade of breezy optimism.

When they were done with the coffee – the last she would have for a week – Svetlana helped Ramos with the washing-up. Then they all put their helmets and gloves back on and traipsed back into the airlock.

'I'm quite excited,' Parry said.

'I should warn you,' Ramos said, 'it's not actually that impressive.'

It was only when she stepped out of the tent that Svetlana had a real sense of the size of the chamber. She looked up, leaning back awkwardly, and made out the hole leading into the Maw, delineated less by its black epicentre than by the convergence of lava lines around it. It looked hopelessly far away: the eye of a needle in the sky they would have to thread to find their way back out.

'It's this way,' Ramos said. 'We'll be using geckoflex, so I hope you're all still in good shape.'

She led them away from the parked lander, out beyond the apron and along a trail marked with luminous paint. The route took them through narrow defiles between looming slabs of Spican machinery for two or three meandering kilometres. Gradually Svetlana noticed that they were climbing, ascending the curved side of the chamber. The effort involved was slight, and she had to keep forcing herself to maintain a level posture: it was all too easy to lean back until she was in danger of dreamily toppling over.

'The crazy thing is that we've been here so long without noticing this,' Ramos said.

'What tipped you off that there was movement?' Parry asked. Svetlana heard music coming over the voicelink, but she couldn't tell what Parry was playing. Probably not *Turandot,* she thought. He didn't play much Puccini these days.

'That was down to Jake and Chris,' Ramos said, referring to Gomberg and Ofria. 'If they hadn't been so keen to photograph and document all these symbols, we'd probably never have noticed.'

'I'll see word gets back to them. At least their study hasn't been a complete waste of time and flexy power.'

The going gradually became more difficult. Svetlana made increasing use of geckoflex, breathing more heavily and saying less. The curvature of the wall had steepened to forty-five degrees compared to their starting point, with the taller Spican structures looming at improbable, unsupported angles. Ramos pushed on eagerly, with a resilience that caused Svetlana to regret her earlier remark about the ground crew taking enough exercise.

They pushed cautiously through a thicket of black, bladelike formations – sharp enough to slice through suit material, Ramos warned – and there ahead was the object of their trek: the larger of the chamber's two main spires.

The spire was a drawn-out cone, pushing three kilometres out into the middle of the chamber. The base of the cone where it met the wall was a hundred metres across, or so Svetlana judged – huge, anyway, and ringed with the now-familiar ranks of Spican symbols. The symbols climbed the cone until they merged into a twinkling, crimson haze. At the very tip of the structure was a spindly cruciform thing like a wrought-iron weather vane.

Nearly lost around the curve of the base, two more spacesuited figures worked with equipment on tripods. They waved to the approaching group and then went back to their task.

Ramos led them to the base, slowing as her little party neared it. 'I told you it wasn't very impressive,' she said.

It wasn't – not by the scale of the surface structures, some of which were five or six times larger than this little spire. But there was something staggering, something crucially different about this feature: it was moving. Not quickly; the rotation of the spire was achingly slow, difficult to perceive with the naked eye even at its base. That was why it had taken so long for anyone to notice: it was only by paying close attention to the symbols that the rotation had become apparent. To all but the most vigilant eye, the spire looked the same every day.

Svetlana knelt down at the point where the base met the floor. Symbols ran all the way down to the join. She pushed a finger to the base of the nearest icon, and held it there.

'I can feel the motion,' she said.

'It's about half a centimetre per second at the circumference,' Ramos said. 'Obvious once you know it's happening – but dead easy to miss otherwise.'

Sure enough, the iron grind of the spire's rotation was just perceptible. But it wasn't obvious, no matter what Ramos said. The featureless floor offered no easy reference points against which to judge the motion.

'You think we can use this?' Parry asked.

'With the right mechanism, we can try,' Ramos said stoutly.

'This thing's rotating for a reason,' Svetlana said. 'Janus might not like it if we mess around with it.'

'My theory is that Janus won't even notice us. If it does . . . well, it's not as if we'll be skimming more than a tiny fraction of the power stored in this thing.' Ramos pointed to the other two spacesuited figures. 'They've glued metal plates to the base and used levers to measure the torque. Nothing we've done has made a measurable difference to the rotation rate. As far as we're concerned, the torque is infinite.'

'And the interface coupling – you think we can make that work?'

'Nothing here's ever a walk in the park, but we'll make it work in the end.'

'How long do you need?'

'Two years, give or take. It'll involve a lot of cargo flights, a lot of people down here.'

'Two years is too long,' Svetlana said. 'Any chance we could halve that?'

'Halve it?' Ramos said incredulously. 'Well, *that* might take some doing.'

'I want you to put together a plan for gearing this thing up within twelve months. I'll give you all the fuel you need, all the robots, and twelve people – that's the most we can possibly spare from topside.'

'Well . . .' Ramos hesitated, understandably fearful of committing to something she was not certain she could deliver. 'I'm not even sure we have enough superconducting cable to reach down here.'

'We'll have the forge vat online within six months. Priority one will be spinning out new cable.'

'Once you've dealt with all the other things on the list,' Ramos countered, unconvinced.

'We need this,' Svetlana said forcefully. 'Sooner rather than later.'

'But the fuel crisis – that's still a long way off, isn't it?'

'Yes,' Svetlana said quickly, trying to strike the right note of soothing reassurance, 'but all the same – better safe than sorry, right?'

'We'll do what we can,' Ramos said.

# CHAPTER 14

A sea of black ice flowed under the lander as it traversed the shelf. Parry dozed again, his head lolling against the window. Svetlana followed his lead and power-napped for ten dreamless minutes. When she came to, the lander was on final approach for Crabtree, Ungless making the same unforgiving economies with fuel. Svetlana thought about the easy promises she had given Ramos: all the fuel and machines she needed, and twelve strong workers. As if it was ever going to be that easy.

Lesson one on Janus: nothing was easy.

The lander made a descending curve around the central tower that had once been *Rockhopper*. Nine hundred metres of the ship projected above the foundation well Parry and his team had punched into the Janus ice. They had buried the ship stern-down, with the engine, reactor assembly and fuel tanks completely underground. Just like plugging a mass driver into a comet, Denise Nadis had said. All that was visible now was the spine and the top-heavy bulge of the habitat section. Tether lines splayed out from the hab in four directions, anchored to the ice with sprayrock-embedded pitons beyond the loose perimeter of the surface community.

The ship was never going anywhere again. No one even *thought* of it as a ship any more. *Rockhopper* was just the central tower of Crabtree: its administrative core and power station. It was a resource to be stripped and remade for the good of the community.

Of the hundred and forty-one people on Janus, most now chose to dwell outside *Rockhopper*. Thirty domes spread away from the base of the ship, linked by underground tunnels and pressurised surface corridors. Ice had been lathered up over the sides of the domes to provide additional insulation, lending them the look of half-melted igloos. Most of the domes were just large enough for a single family-sized unit: three or four people at most.

The domes closest to the ship had been put down first: Parry's EVA team had used them during the initial cometary operations. Those further out were improvised structures, lashed together using metals and composites scavenged from *Rockhopper*, with offcuts of parasol foil providing the basic pressure-containing envelope. Sprayrock was a quicker building medium, but like everything else it had to be used sparingly now. Between the domes lurked equipment modules, generators and storage shacks. A scattering of pale-yellow window lights hinted at human presence. Blackouts were enforced during long hours of each day. Svetlana would gladly have extended the duration of the power outages, but she was concerned about spreading panic.

The lander bumped to ground beyond the edge of Crabtree. They disembarked and boarded a wire-wheeled tractor that had been waiting at the edge of the apron. Ungless took the tractor's controls and drove it along a furrowed, slipshod road that cut between the tents and their snaking connections. Crabtree was still only a hamlet, but at times it felt as if it was poised to become something larger. If the deaths slowed and the births continued, then within ten years, by the time they arrived at Spica . . . But Svetlana closed the book on those thoughts.

She did not hold out any hope that Janus could be slowed, let alone reversed, but unless their current fortunes improved, they could not count on surviving until they reached Spica either.

She kept having to remind herself that it was not October 2059. It was . . . *some other date* that she did not want to think about. 2059 was just a lie they told themselves to stay sane, to comfort themselves that they had not already drifted too far upstream ever to return home.

It was the one piece of advice Svetlana had accepted from *her*, before the exile. Honour the old calendar: make a day count as a day, even as their increasing speed squeezed time until it bled.

Two months after *Rockhopper*'s entry into the Janus slipstream, the moon had reached a speed that was slower than light by only one-tenth of one per cent. Janus had stopped accelerating once it reached that speed, but it was still harrowingly fast. Relativity dictated that clocks ran twenty-two times slower on Janus than they did on Earth. Not just clocks, either, but every measurable physical and biological process. *Including time itself.*

In the hour that had passed since she had said goodbye to Ramos, nearly a full day had elapsed on Earth.

Janus had been at cruise speed for twenty-two months, as measured by *Rockhopper* time. On Earth, forty years had passed. It was somewhere near the closing years of the twenty-first century. If by some unlikely good fortune they were to succeed in turning around now, eighty years would have elapsed by the time they made it back home.

It would be nearly 2137.

Not everyone accepted this. With its antennae pointed back home, Crabtree was still intercepting radio signals originating from Earth. The messages were red-shifted towards ultra-long wavelengths, but information could still be gleaned from them. And according to the messages it was still only 2059. They heard news from families, loved ones, friends – but a little less with each week that passed.

The world they'd left behind spun on, half-familiar news stories still dominating the headlines. The same celebrities, the same scandals and tragedies. For a little while the plight of *Rockhopper* and its crew had even been one of those objects of global attention, until something quietly displaced it and they faded into the back pages. The messages were dangerous and comforting in equal measure. They told a lie, but only because they were bound to the same universal speed limit as Janus. Messages from 2097, or even 2137, would not catch up with Janus before it reached Spica. They would never learn the history of the world they had left behind.

Not until they turned for home – at which point they'd be flying headlong into that blizzard of information. The years would crash forward: eighty years of history crammed into the two years of their return flight even if they succeeded in turning around now. And if they did not begin their return journey until after Janus reached Spica, they would have to recapitulate five hundred and twenty years of history.

That was too much to take in, so they used the old calendar and pretended that every day that passed on Janus had the same measure as a day on Earth. It gave their lives some structure. They celebrated birthdays, holidays and festivals. They still talked of summer and winter, and made some effort to mark these seasonal changes in the way that the blackouts and brownouts were imposed on Crabtree's electrical supply. Svetlana had done all that she could to make the last summer a little better, a little more tolerable, than the grim winter that had preceded it.

But now it was winter again and the fuel tanks were running perilously low.

Above the settlement, a huddle of blood-red stars crowded the zenith directly over Crabtree's central tower. There were no stars at all anywhere else in the visible hemisphere of sky: they had been torn from their fixed positions by the iron hand of relativity. Most stars were red to begin with, so the Doppler effect only made them redder. On the bow side of Janus there was another, brighter huddle, where starlight had been shifted ferociously into the blue. It was as beautiful as it was lethal. Bracelet dosages went through the roof as blue-shifted cosmic rays sliced flesh and cell.

The electric tractor bumbled down an ice-walled ramp into one of the equipment bays dug out around the base of the downed ship. They disembarked, passed through another airlock and were helped out of their suits by a beaming Kunj Ramasesha. Like Ramos, Ramasesha had made the transition to Janus life with relatively little difficulty. The suit technicians – not just Ramasesha, but Ash Murray and Reka Bettendorf – were vital to the functioning of the new colony, and they revelled in their new sense of civic importance, guarding their expertise with the zealotry of a medieval guild.

Svetlana and Parry bade farewell to Ungless and rode a car up the spine to the hab. Although the Janus machinery gave off its own glow, none of it reached Crabtree. The ice around the little community was as dark as space, lent only the faintest midnight sheen by the cluster of red-shifted stars in the stern hemisphere. A few transponders winked out of the darkness like distant lighthouse beacons. As the car rose higher, Crabtree looked like the only human artefact in the universe.

Svetlana had timed her return well: she was only a minute late for the meeting with the other members of the Interim Authority. They had assembled in what had once been the captain's office and private quarters. The cramped old room was twice as large now: internal partitions had been torn down throughout *Rockhopper*, the material used elsewhere. The old carpet no longer met the walls, but it remained the focus of the room. Even the fish tank was still there, and there were even some fish in it. Some parts of the old ship were routinely spun to provide centrifugal gravity – Axford insisted on having such a facility since calcium loss was a real concern under the weak pull of Janus – but this was not one of them. The fish did not appear to mind too much.

Ryan Axford was present, along with Saul Regis, Nick Thale, Denise Nadis, Jake Gomberg and Christine Ofria. Like Axford, Regis and Thale had both been old-regime loyalists, but their expertise was too essential to ignore. Sometimes there was tension between the three of them and the rest of the Authority, but they were usually pragmatic enough to put such things aside if it helped Crabtree.

Svetlana and Parry took their places around the table, moving with the effortless glides that characterised locomotion on Janus. Svetlana lowered herself into her seat, folded her hands on the table before her and nodded briefly at the other members.

'I've just returned from the Maw,' she began, 'and for once it looks as if we might have discovered something that could almost be described as good news. To put that into the proper context, though, I must emphasize how truly shitty things really are. Parry: will you do the honours?'

Parry removed his cap and scratched a finger into his moustache. 'I won't even attempt to put a positive spin on any of this, and I'm sure it'll come as no surprise to any of you that fuel is our main problem. Before we landed on Janus, we had high expectations of tapping the moon's energy for our own uses. That was a nice idea, but it hasn't turned out to be so simple in practice. The Spican machinery is hellishly efficient: it doesn't give off a lot of waste energy for us to exploit. The only area where we've had much luck is with the thermoelectric generators – they exploit the heat difference between the Spican machinery and the icecap. But the heat difference isn't huge, and we don't have enough superconducting cable to run any more lines out to the edge of the icecap. If we were going back to square one now, we might choose a different landing site, closer to the shelf . . . but since we don't have a time machine—'

Nadis tapped a stylus against her flexy. 'How much power are we getting now?'

'From the thermocouples? Depending on fluctuations in the machinery, anything between three to five megawatts, which isn't enough to run Crabtree. We're fine at the moment because we can still run the fusion engine – we're easily extracting a hundred megawatts. But it isn't efficient: Lockheed-Krunichev built that engine to move *Rockhopper* around, not light up a village. We waste far more energy than we extract.'

'The fuel won't last more than fourteen months,' Svetlana said bluntly. 'Eighteen if we eke it out with even more power outages and shut down some of the outlying domes.'

'We might as well stop rationing the coffee, in that case,' Nadis said.

'There's no hope of squeezing more power from the thermocouples?' Thale asked.

'Even if we get the forge vat running and scrape together the raw materials and power to spin out more superconducting line, we'd only be looking at doubling our capacity from the thermocouples,' Svetlana said, 'which won't even get us through to next summer. We'd still be relying on the fusion engine.'

Parry cleared his throat. 'We've been looking at other options. Heat isn't the only thing Janus has to offer us. As most of you probably know, we've had a team looking into the possibility of extracting power from the lava lines – either directly, or by tapping the motion of the transits. So far we've had no success, but it *is* a possibility for the future. We just have to stick around long enough to get there.'

'Hence this meeting,' Svetlana said. 'Two weeks ago, we learned something significant about one of the structures in the Maw chamber: it's rotating. It's slow – almost too slow to notice – but it's regular and it appears to have immeasurably high torque. If we can tap that motion, there is every chance that we'll be able to turn off the fusion reactor and save the remaining fuel for the day when we really need it.'

Svetlana let the little party absorb that glimmer of good news. It was all they were going to get from her. 'Okay,' she said after a few moments, 'now for the hard part: actually doing it, and doing it before we all die anyway. It isn't going to be easy, but we think we have a roadmap.'

'There are two difficult parts to this operation,' Parry said. 'The first is tapping that rotational motion and converting it into electrical power. The second is getting that power out of the Maw and back to Crabtree. The first part is where most of the headaches are going to arise. Problem number one is that the spire – the rotating structure – is turning very, very slowly. But we think we can deal with that.'

Svetlana called up a diagram on her flexy and projected it onto the wall behind her. She leaned back in her seat, twisting her neck to take it all in. It was a crudely drawn sketch of the spire in the Maw chamber, with something approximating a set of gear teeth fixed around its base.

'We'll begin by attaching cogs all around the structure,' she said. 'They're basically just chunks of machined metal. We know glue works, and we know what kind of torques the adhesive bonds can tolerate before they fail. Ramos and the others say it can be done. That gives us a system for coupling a second, smaller wheel to the spire's rotation. That wheel will turn faster.'

'But still not fast enough,' Parry said. 'We're going to have to lash up loads of these things: a clockwork gear train like nothing you've seen since the sixteenth century. We're going to need a gear ratio up in the millions.' There were exasperated sounds, but Parry pushed on. 'We'll strip out one of *Rockhopper*'s main centrifuge rings and the associated drive system: that should give us the building blocks, or at least enough to make a start. Whatever we come up with, it'll have to work flawlessly. And at the end of it we'll need an output shaft turning at around one hundred hertz.'

'To which we can couple as many industrial-capacity dynamos as we can put our hands on,' Svetlana said.

'I expect there are some lying around here somewhere,' Nick Thale said, his voice dripping sarcasm.

'There are,' Parry said firmly. 'We used them every time we pushed ice.'

Thale's eyes narrowed. 'Mass drivers? I don't see how linear—'

'The parasol spinners,' said Nadis, nodding appreciatively. For the apparent benefit of Thale and Regis, she added, 'The electric motors we use to spin up the sunshade parasols, to shield the dayside of the comet during the infall cruise.'

'That's the idea,' Svetlana said, nodding approvingly. 'We reverse them, use them as dynamos instead of motors. We'll have to beef up some of the components, but I'm told it's workable. If we can solve the drive-shaft problem, we can tap fifteen to twenty megawatts. That'll free us from any further dependency on *Rockhopper*'s fuel – but only if we can convey that power to Crabtree. For that, we'll need about four times our current mileage of superconducting cable.'

'Then it's hopeless,' Nadis said, exasperated. 'We can't even fix the existing cables, let alone make more of them.'

'Not yet,' Svetlana said, 'but if we can get the forge vat running, we can spin out all the cable we'll ever need.'

'Have you spoken to Wang lately?'

Svetlana did not care for the tone of the other woman's voice. 'Not for a few weeks,' she said defensively. 'The last I heard, he was making good progress.'

'Maybe you should visit him one of these days,' Nadis said. 'I think you'll find it illuminating.'

'I will,' Svetlana said, annoyed with herself for not having kept a closer watch on Wang's stumbling progress. 'As soon as we're done here. Assuming we can get the vat up to speed, I take it everything I've proposed here has the committee's approval?'

'It's not as if we have much choice,' Parry said. 'If we don't tap Janus, we're finished within a year and a half.'

'I agree that it looks clear cut,' Thale said, 'but let's not underestimate the risks. So far we've barely scratched Janus. Sometimes I wonder if it's even *noticed* us yet. But if we start interfering in more obvious ways—'

'We have no choice,' Svetlana said.

'I'm just saying – there may be consequences.' Thale looked at the others, inviting support. 'We shouldn't kid ourselves that this is a risk-free strategy.'

'We all grasp the risks,' Svetlana said impatiently, 'but whatever we do in the Maw will be nowhere near as risky as sitting here hoping for something else to drop into our laps.'

Thale closed his eyes. 'I'm just saying—' he began again, before shaking his head. 'Never mind. You wouldn't go for it anyway.'

Svetlana sensed a trap, but spoke anyway. 'Go for what?'

'This is too big a decision to be left to a handful of people sitting around a table.'

'You mean we should poll the rest?'

'No . . . not that.' He spoke with infinite caution, as if every word might trigger the most devastating of reactions. 'I mean we should consider bringing other opinions into the debate. I'm talking about Wang, of course, and perhaps one or two others, but mainly I mean *her*.'

'No,' Svetlana said.

'You won't even consider it?'

'No,' she repeated. 'Not now, not ever.'

Thale shrugged, as if this was no more and no less than he had expected. He sank back into his seat. 'Fine, then.'

Svetlana felt a hot blush sear her cheeks. She was grateful when Parry filled the silence, sparing her the duty. 'We've been over this, Nick,' he said. 'We all know that some of us felt more loyalty to her than others. But that was then. Everything is different now: her opinions just don't have any further relevance.'

'You'd love to believe that,' Thale said. 'You'd love to believe that we can just put her in a box and forget about her, like an old toy we don't want to play with any more.'

'She had her chance to turn us around,' Parry said. 'Instead she dragged us into this mess.'

'She acted on the best information available to her,' Thale said.

'Nick's right,' Axford said. 'Nothing Bella did was motivated by greed or self-interest. She only ever did what she thought was best for her crew.'

'She couldn't face the idea that DeepShaft was screwing us,' Svetlana said. 'I gave her all the evidence she needed, and she blanked on it.' She thumped the table with her fist. 'Why the hell are we still talking about this? We've been over it a thousand times. She had her chance. She blew it. End of story.'

'Look,' Parry said, talking directly to Axford, 'I agree completely that Bella didn't act out of self-interest. No argument there.'

'Fine,' Axford said briskly.

'But she still made bad decisions. Maybe her heart was in the right place. So what? It was the decisions that mattered. That alone should disqualify her from having any further say in our affairs.'

'You just don't get it,' Thale said.

'No, Nick,' Svetlana answered, '*you* don't get it. We all know where your basic loyalties lie. You just can't let it go, can you? You just can't accept that things are different around here now.'

'Maybe it isn't me who has trouble letting go of the past,' Thale said.

'Meaning what, exactly?' Svetlana said, her voice low and dangerously sweet.

'When we grounded *Rockhopper*, you made a big speech about how we all had to pull together, how we had to heal old wounds and face the future with clear hearts, clear minds. I remember it well. It was a damned effective piece of sloganeering.'

'Careful, Nick,' she said.

He shrugged and continued speaking. 'I remember one other thing you said, about how we had to use every resource available to us, every possible means of staying alive. Well, some of us listened to you. Some of us thought you meant it.'

'I did,' she said, on the boiling edge of fury.

'Perhaps that's true, up to a point, but there's one resource you've never had the courage to tap. It's always easier to hate than to forgive, isn't it?'

'I think you've said enough,' Parry said. 'The decision regarding Bella's exile was unanimous—'

'That was two years ago,' Thale said. He stood up, flinging his flexy across the table. 'We need Bella, whether you like it or not. If we all die out here, it won't be Janus that kills us.'

Svetlana had regained some scant measure of calm by the time her wanderings took her to the buried laboratory where Wang Zhanmin spent his days and nights. She heard faint Chinese music as she neared the lab. It was on the outskirts of Crabtree, connected to the rest of the community by one ice-walled tunnel and a single superconducting power line as thick as her forearm. The line was glued to the inner surface of the ice tunnel with gobs of geckoflex. Placing her palm next to it, she swore she felt her hand tingle. One-tenth of all the power generated for Crabtree passed along the line.

She knocked politely and stooped into the icy cold of the kettle-shaped room. For all the energy at his disposal, Wang wasted none of it on his own comfort. The only concession was a speaker glued high up on one wall, out of which poured a constant tinny medley of twenty-year-old Chinese pop songs. Svetlana shivered and zipped her coat tighter. Her breath gusted before her in a white flourish. She could still feel the embarrassment on her face, reddened by the cold.

'I've brought you a present,' she said, raising her voice above a screeching girl group.

He turned from one of his desks, his face lost behind an improbable arrangement of magnifying lenses and improvised HUD read-outs, lashed together with solder and Day-Glo duct tape. He reached up with fur-gloved hands and tugged off the home-made apparatus. He wore a red woollen cap, like one of Parry's aquatics. His hair erupted in messy black coils from underneath it, tumbling over his ears and brow. A pale-green medical smock covered at least five layers of puffed insulation. His feet vanished into huge boots ripped from an irreparable spacesuit. He still looked too young and earnest for her. She had nothing against Wang, but it terrified her that so much depended upon him.

Wang turned down the music. 'A gift?' he echoed.

'Don't get too excited.' She held up the limp thing for his inspection. 'I heard your flexy died.'

'Yes,' he said, distractedly, as if he had not considered the matter for some while. 'Yes, it did die. Is that for me?'

'If anyone needs one, it's you.'

Coming closer, he took the flexy from her and held it in his gloved hands. 'They don't like the cold in here,' he said.

'Not much we can do about that. If you spared a bit of warmth for yourself—'

'I can't,' he said. 'The experiments run best when they're cold. If I heated the room, it would cost even more power to cool them down selectively. He stiffened the flexy, touched it with one finger so that it lit up with ShipNet options and then placed it gently on a clear spot on the nearest desk, amidst his equipment and notes. 'It's better this way.' He looked up at her. 'How many do we have left now?'

'Flexies? I don't remember. One hundred and sixty, something like that.'

'There were more than two hundred when we landed, weren't there? That means forty have died since our arrival.'

'They're not meant to last for ever,' Svetlana said.

'All the same. I am no computer specialist, but if more of them die . . . that will not be to our immediate advantage, will it?'

'Not exactly, no.'

ShipNet was a distributed system, spread amongst the processing nodes of the flexies. Already there had been a measurable degradation in the speed and accuracy of certain ShipNet queries. The remaining flexies were compensating for the loss of the other units by hoarding more and more data within each of them, but this was only possible because of a reallocation of bioware processor functions. Within six months, Saul Regis said, the degradation would become obvious even to casual users. Within a year, large parts of ShipNet simply wouldn't work at all.

'I'll do my best to look after this one,' Wang said, caressing the thing as if it had genuine sentience. 'Perhaps if I sleep with it . . . use it as my pillow—'

'Just use it,' Svetlana said. 'If it dies, we'll find you another one. If you can get the vat running, it will be worth the sacrifice.'

'I am sorry that I have not made better progress,' Wang said, turning to face the vat. 'I was overconfident. I shouldn't have promised so much.'

'You promised nothing, Wang. You just said you'd do your best to help us. That was all we could ever have asked of you. More than we had any right to ask.'

The forge vat sat in the middle of the room, resting on four welded legs. It was a fat red cylinder as large as a small lander, rising almost to the plasticized ice of the ceiling. Its lid had the concave curve of a pagoda. In one side was a small circular door, copiously hinged and armoured, surrounded by read-out ports, valves and input sockets. Ribbed power lines plunged up from the floor into the vat's flanged base. It drew power and control commands from the consoles arranged around it, most of which had been salvaged from the avionics of the *Shenzhou Five* before it melted its way into the icecap, lost for ever.

Unlike Wang, whose limbs had healed well enough under Axford's care, the vat retained evidence of the damage it had sustained during the *Shenzhou Five*'s crash. The red paint was bright and new on one side, where extensive patch repairs had been made.

They had all done their best, including Wang, but attempting to fix a forge vat using *Rockhopper*'s tools was like trying to repair a cuckoo clock with an axe.

They would keep trying, all the same.

'When we last spoke—' Svetlana began.

'I thought I might have something to show you. Well, I was right, I suppose.' He bent over the desk, picked up a pair of luminous plastic tweezers and fished around in a tray brimming with aquamarine fluid. The tweezers bit on something. With great care, Wang lifted them from the tray. Draped around their lower extremities was something that looked like milky seaweed or overcooked translucent noodles. 'I kept this because it was the most progress I had made to date.'

Svetlana looked at the fibrous white mass. 'What is . . . was it?'

'It was meant to be paper,' Wang said. 'Paper is a rather simple test subject for a forge vat. If you can't do paper . . .' He shook his head, not needing to say more.

'At least it's a kind of solid,' Svetlana offered.

'Yes, at least I made a kind of solid. And it is white. I suppose that has to count as progress.'

Svetlana looked back at the humming cylinder of the forge vat with an irrational resentment. All it did was drink power from Crabtree like a greedy baby and vomit out shapeless white pulp, when what they wanted was hard machinery, flexies, foodstuff, miles of superconductive cabling.

'It's progress,' she said, swallowing her frustration and disappointment. 'No doubt about it. I can't give you any more power, Wang, but if there's anything else you need – people, resources – you know I'll always see what can be done.'

He returned the white mass to its bath and then wiped the tweezers clean with a sterile rag. 'I have power enough for now. More hands would only get in the way.' He looked at her helplessly. 'I just need time, and patience.'

'Time and patience,' she echoed.

'Except there isn't any time, is there? That's what you came to tell me.'

'No, there's plenty of time,' she said, knowing that he was working as hard as anyone on the moon. 'I came to give you the flexy, and to see how you're holding up.'

He studied the gift again, as if some trick were involved. 'Someone must have been using this one until now. No one has died, have they?'

'No,' she said. 'No one has died. Nick Thale decided he could live without a flexy for now.'

'Oh,' Wang said, looking down.

'It was his choice,' Svetlana said.

'Yes, of course it was.' Wang pulled his cap straight and reached for his headset, adjusting one of the stalk-mounted lenses, and prepared to lower it down over his face again. 'If it is all right with you, I will continue trying to make paper.'

'You'll let me know as soon as you get anywhere?'

'You'll be the first person I call,' he said, scraping the headset down over his woollen cap.

'Wang,' Svetlana said.

'Yes?'

'No matter what happens in the future, I want to thank you for what you did.' She stopped: that was all she had intended to say, but now that the words were out, something more seemed to be needed. 'You didn't have to join us. You could have tried to make it back home.'

'I wouldn't have succeeded,' Wang said.

'You were a national hero,' she told him. 'They'd have found a way to bring you back.'

'Perhaps.'

'But you knew we needed you more. After all we'd done to you . . . you still put that aside and gave us this gift.'

'There was a degree of self-interest. If I was going to strand myself on Janus—'

'I don't want to hear it,' she said, holding up one hand. 'What you did was still a brave and selfless act. A beautiful thing.'

He said nothing, just returned to his experiments. She stooped out of the room and waited for the music to start again, but by the time she reached the end of the corridor all she could hear was the ruminative humming of the forge vat.

# CHAPTER 15

Late in the third year of the settlement, in the glow of the Maw, surrounded by the vast, dark clockwork of the power-generating machinery, Mike Sheng paused in his slow and solitary tour of inspection. He tabbed down through his helmet HUD options, bored with the Black Sabbath he'd been listening to. Against regs, some of the workers watched kung-fu movies or porn flicks, half their attention on the flickering images filling their faceplates and the other half on the real world beyond the glass. Sheng, who knew the limits of his own ability to multitask, had always been too conscientious for that. It was music or nothing, and when he needed to think really hard, even the music had to go.

But this work did not demand much of him. Twice during his duty shift, he followed an overly familiar path through the whirring machinery, ducking between enormous cogs and flywheels, pausing at designated intervals to check that some bearing or linkage was holding up well. His ballasted Orlan nineteen carried additional panniers filled with vacuum lubricant, and where necessary he used the jet nozzle clipped to his belt to add a dab to some hot or dry-running part. In an ideal world, they'd have instrumented the whole clockwork gear train with thermal sensors and monitoring cams, but this was Janus, and Janus – as the saying amongst the EVA crews went – was a long way from ideal.

Functioning cams and sensors were already spread pretty thinly monitoring other critical systems, and the magic vat still wasn't capable of brewing anything particularly complicated. If a job could be performed by a watchful human on a tour of inspection, that was how it was done. Sheng took the job seriously because he knew how much depended on the continued working of the clockwork contraption. All the same, it wasn't the most taxing of duties.

Scrolling through a small list of files, Sheng settled on some mid-period rock he'd copied over from Parry Boyce's much larger music library. Some of the other miners mocked Parry's tastes, but the way Sheng saw it, if you needed something to cut through the background drone of generators and pumps, there was not much out there to beat amped guitars, hammering drums and screaming vocals, no matter when it was recorded. It was driving music, for the ultimate drive.

'Tomorrow begat tomorrow . . .' Sheng sang along, music filling his helmet like a derailing freight train. With the long cylinder of the lubricator nozzle unclipped, he pulled some mean poses like the secret axe hero he'd always imagined he could have been. He knew he looked ridiculous making those moves in an ancient orange Orlan nineteen bulked out with panniers, but his only audience was ancient alien machinery. Sheng considered it a reasonably safe bet that the ancient alien machinery had no particular opinion on the matter.

Sheng was not quite correct in that assumption.

The machinery had no grasp of the significance of his gestures, but it *had* started to pay attention to him. It was happy to let the humans come and go, happy to let them prod and poke at it with their crude instruments, happy even to let them tap power with their primitive lash-up of clockwork gears and jury-rigged dynamos. On that level it ignored them completely, for their actions were of no consequence. But now the machinery took a more than casual interest in Sheng. Around him, unnoticed, the symbols flicked to warning configurations. It was not because of anything he had done, but rather the manner in which he had done them. The machinery was vigilant for patterns. In particular, it was designed to recognise repetitive actions.

Sheng was a creature of habit. He always took the same route.

He had been doing it for many turns of duty, and with each repetition the machinery's interest had been stimulated a notch higher. Had Sheng decided to take a different path through the clockwork, the machinery would have turned its attention away from him. He would have been safe, provided he didn't fall into the habit of repeating the new route. But now the machinery's highest threshold of alertness had been tripped. The warning symbols, unheeded by Sheng, urged him to break out of his stereotypical behaviour pattern.

Sheng continued on his customary way. Around him, the symbols turned dark.

He gradually became aware of the change, but could not immediately put his finger on what had happened. He stopped, stowed the applicator nozzle and turned the music down. Around him, the clockwork machinery continued its slow grind. It was the repetitious movement of individuals, not mechanisms, to which the Spican machinery was engineered to respond.

Sheng turned around slowly, conscious now of the darkness where before there had been a forest of interlocked symbols. He felt the first tickle of unease.

He turned on voice coms. 'Mike here. I'm up in the high clockwork, near train five. There's some weird shit going—'

That was as much as he managed.

The machinery moved with a merciful swiftness. A hole opened beneath his feet into a light-filled shaft plunging down through the abyssal kilometres of a vast engine-filled vault. A ferocious and highly localised gravitational field seized him and he fell like an express elevator into the heart of Janus, where he was dismantled and recycled in a matter of seconds. Where Sheng had been standing, the hole sealed itself. The symbols returned to their former configurations.

He was never seen again.

It took six months and another life to work out what had happened to him. Even as the clockwork continued running, Svetlana's investigators combed the scene of the disappearance. It fell to Parry to lead the inquiry – Sheng had been his friend and he did not want the death to go unexamined.

He considered the possibility of murder, even though no body had ever come to light. Although Sheng had been popular, he had also sided with the old authority during the crisis on *Rockhopper*. Ever since the landing, there had been rumours that some of the old-line loyalists – particularly those who had acted directly against Svetlana – would be targeted by vigilante elements within Crabtree.

But Sheng had never made any mention of threats being made against him, and the Maw was an unlikely choice of venue for an ambush. None of the other staff stationed there at the time struck Parry as plausible murderers. No one else could have made it into the Maw and out again without being noticed.

So it wasn't murder. Suicide didn't seem very likely either, given that Sheng had been trying to call something in when he went off-air. Gabriela Ramos, his on-off partner at the time of his death, was distraught. Nothing about Sheng's mood had indicated depression, and she was vehement that the explanation had to lie elsewhere.

Parry believed her, but he didn't know where else to look. Examination of the clockwork mechanism revealed no sign of misadventure. Dreadful accidents had happened when people got too close to the whirring machinery, but there was always gruesome evidence after the fact.

Finally, more out of desperation than any sense of rigorous procedure, Parry had one of the apparatus investigators retrace Sheng's footsteps, copying the route he was known to have taken. Perhaps Sheng had brushed against something, or had cause to grab hold of something, that might shed light on his disappearance.

The first time, nothing happened. The second time, Parry changed the investigator's route, realising that they had made a mistake with the first run-through due to a minor change in the layout of the clockwork since Sheng's death.

It was during the second reconstruction that the machinery roused itself.

It did not mistake the new man for Sheng, but it recognised the familiar trajectory he was following. Sheng's earlier behaviour had engraved a deep furrow in its memory. It was now conditioned to respond at a high level of alertness if the pattern was repeated, even though months had passed since the first death. Months or centuries, it didn't matter to Janus.

The machinery offered its usual generous warnings. The investigator observed the changes in the Spican symbols, changes that were also witnessed on flexies and cams by the other apparatus people.

'Hold still,' Parry said, awed that they'd finally provoked a recognisable response from the machinery, even though he didn't understand what they had done to provoke it. 'Must be the thing Mike was calling in about—'

The investigator took another step along the route, to place his feet on a more level surface.

It was enough: the threshold had been crossed. Janus took him with the same bewildering swiftness that had met Mike Sheng. This time, however, there were witnesses. They saw the ground open up and swallow the investigator. They made futile efforts to break through the sealed-over surface even though no tools had ever been able to mark the Spican material. But by then it was much too late, and on some level they all knew it.

Slowly, they came to an understanding of what had happened. It was Parry who bravely retraced the route one more time, up until the point where the symbols changed configuration. He backed off and observed the symbols flicker to their previous configuration. He took another step closer and saw them change again.

They still had no idea what it meant. If the investigators followed any other route through the machinery, nothing changed. It was another month before the idea began to form that Janus was configured to punish repetitious actions, and that it had taken Sheng because he always followed the same route.

Once the idea had formed, however, it was easy to test. Investigators mapped out routes through the machinery and followed them over many cycles, watchful for the slightest alteration in the symbols. When the symbols did change, they immediately deviated from the prior route. It was dangerous work and Parry saw that the volunteers who ran the maze were rewarded with a handsome allocation of extra rations and kilowatt-hours.

New directives were issued. Workers in the Maw, and wherever there was Spican machinery in close proximity, were to take pains never to repeat a particular route during any duty shift. They were instructed to memorise key symbol patterns and watch for any changes. Some of them cut dice from off-cuts of suit insulation and sealed the dice inside perspex boxes that could be chained to their suit belts. When they needed to plot a route, they rolled the dice to inject a degree of randomness into their movements, even if it doubled the distance they had to walk.

It appeared to work. No one was exactly sure whether the pattern-avoidance needed to be carried on inside the domes and shelters in and around the Maw – so far no harm had come to anyone inside them – but most of the workers preferred not to take unnecessary chances. They did not roll the dice when they were inside, or insist that every route had to be unique, but they developed a habit of moving furniture and partitions every few days, to disrupt any potentially fixed patterns.

Out on the icecap, in the tunnels and domes of Crabtree, life continued normally. Parry saw no need to impose additional pressures on people who were already coping with deprivation and anxiety about the future. If Janus had left them alone until now, it seemed likely that it would continue doing so in future. Besides, the machinery was kilometres below, unseen beneath that enormous tonnage of camouflaging ice.

Whenever Parry made the long, solitary drive away from Crabtree, however, those easy assurances lost their charm. He saw himself from the machinery's point of view: a lone *thing* far from companionship, following the arrow-straight line of the superconductor cable. And he imagined the machinery far below the tractor, focusing more and more of its attention on him, waiting for the moment when he exceeded some arcane condition of repetitiveness. He told himself that the machinery would not be able to touch him through all that ice, but another part of him reminded him that this was Janus, where nothing could be taken for granted.

Once he was clear of Crabtree, therefore, he steered the tractor away from the line and followed a random trajectory. The ride became rougher, since the route had only been graded along the line itself. When he could take no more of it, he steered back to the line, which he strove to keep in view. Sometimes he veered too far, and lost sight of it.

That had happened on this occasion. It seemed to take an inordinately long time for the line to come back into view, and when it did the angle was all wrong. He wondered if he had crossed over it by mistake somehow, and was now heading back to Crabtree. He had expected to catch sight of the dome by now.

He was about to turn around when his lights caught the crest of the dome, poking above a nearby horizon of scalloped ice. With his destination in sight, he gunned the tractor. The vehicle bounced across a ridge, losing all contact with the ground for one sickening moment. Pushed to its maximum speed, the tractor nudged one-seventh of the velocity needed to escape Janus's gravitational pull entirely. Driving on Janus was an art that Parry had no expectation of ever mastering, and now he pushed his modest skills to their limit, anxious to complete this errand as quickly as possible. He crossed the remaining distance and came to a skidding halt where the power line plunged into the doughy base of the dome. A couple of equipment pallets stood by the gently glowing dome, but there were no other vehicles in sight.

He stepped from the tractor and wiped a spray of frost from his faceplate.

In all directions there was only darkness, save for the little puddle of light cast by the dome and the tractor. Crabtree had vanished over the horizon hours ago. His HUD should have picked up navigational cues from transponders, but too many of them had failed lately. Without the directional arrow of the power line, Parry would have no idea how to get back. The notion of being lost out here, wandering the dark night of Janus until his suit ran down and he died of cold or asphyxiation, prowled the edge of his thoughts.

He wondered how long it had taken Bella to get used to this.

The dome was the standard kind used during cometary surface operations. They had secured it in place with sprayrock and added an additional layer of insulation, none of which was really necessary except as a purely psychological measure. Radiation levels on the rear face of Janus were lower than in normal interstellar space since most cosmic rays were moving too slowly to catch up with the former moon. Even the gamma rays were redshifted to 'mere' X-ray energies. And here on the sternward face there was no interstellar dust or gas to worry about. The vacuum Janus left in its wake was probably the most perfect in the galaxy.

Parry gathered a cargo crate from the rear deck of the tractor and walked to the airlock. He waited until his suit had swapped protocols with the lock and then opened a voice channel into the dome.

'Bella,' he said, 'this is Parry. Can I come in?'

He had a long wait before she answered him, in a dry croak of a voice that was both suspicious and hopeful. 'Parry?'

'Let me in, Bella. I have something for you.'

The red lights above the airlock flicked to green. He opened the outer door and squeezed inside. The atmosphere exchanger took a long time to pressurise the compartment, and when he cracked his helmet the air was musty and thin. The dome needed a full systems overhaul, he concluded, but that would mean pulling Bella out of it for a week.

Svetlana would never allow that.

The inner door opened, revealing one dimly lit partition. Paper walls fenced off different areas of the dome. Lighting nodes glowed a sullen gold, turned down so low that they were almost dead. What little power had been spared on Bella's prison was mainly used to keep her alive. The superconductor from Crabtree was an old one, too damaged to serve useful duty in the Maw, and it only carried a trickle of current. Parry had known this but it was still a shock to see how little there was to spare. It was even more of a shock when Bella emerged through the gloom of one ripped paper wall, like a paper phantom herself. She looked thin and old, as if decades had passed out here rather than the three years it had actually been.

'Bella,' he said, doing his best to smile.

'Why have you come?' she asked. 'I know she doesn't want anyone to have any contact with me. Especially not you.'

Parry put down the crate. 'Can I sit down?'

'Do what you like. You own the place.'

He parked himself on the crate and looked around, his eyes grudgingly accommodating the gloom. The partition was spartan, with no suggestion that Bella had tried to personalise it in any way. A crate loaded with silver-wrapped rations had been shoved against one wall. Most of them looked untouched. They brought food and water out to Bella, and once in a while Ryan Axford or one of his team drove out to examine her. Now and then someone came to fix a pump. That was all. There were no casual visits, not even from her old allies.

There had been two attempts to spring her from prison, but both had failed. Without Ash Murray's assistance, her would-be rescuers had been forced to purloin time-expired suits that were in need of overhaul. The first time, Thale and his collaborators had reached the halfway marker before suffering suit malfs that forced them back to Crabtree. Saul Regis had been lucky to survive, and Svetlana had refrained from punishing them too severely. The second time, not long after he'd been released from custody, Thale had succeeded in reaching Bella on his own. But he'd still returned empty handed, to a welcoming committee of Judicial Apparatus bailiffs.

No one knew what had gone on between Bella and Thale that had caused him to return alone, but everything Parry knew about Bella led him to suspect that she had refused to accompany him because she only wanted to be released from prison under official terms. She must have known that she did not have enough support to take Crabtree by democratic means or force, and she must also have known that the settlement could not withstand another violent crisis given everything else it had to deal with. So she had chosen to remain a prisoner, for the sake of the community.

Thale had been arrested and jailed.

Parry had pleaded with Svetlana to reward Bella with an easing of the terms of her imprisonment, but Svetlana had only tightened security. The frequency of visits to the prison had been reduced. Her power ration was cut back by thirty per cent, so that she had to spend long hours in darkness. Denied access to ShipNet, her knowledge of events in Crabtree was limited to what she could glean during those rare face-to-face encounters. Svetlana discouraged any conversation beyond the simple practicalities required to swap rations, fix the dome and check on her physical wellbeing.

Mostly, Parry believed, Svetlana got her way. With the exception of Axford and the other medics, the people who visited Bella were individuals who had turned against her during the crisis. Outright Lind loyalists were never allowed to make the journey.

Bella sat down on another crate, with her hands dangling in her lap. She wore three or four layers of clothes, but still looked thin. She had allowed her hair to grow longer than Parry remembered, and it had become greyer, retaining just a few salmony flecks of colour. Her hair was lank and uncombed, glued to her forehead in messy coils.

'What is this about?' she asked, fingering her shark's-teeth necklace, now yellowed with dirt.

Parry reached into his utility belt and brought out a small cardboard package. 'Someone found a box of these. We didn't think there were any left.'

He reached out to hand her the cigarettes. For a moment she hesitated, her eyes boring into him, quizzing him for a trap. Then she reached out one bony hand and snatched the packet from his grasp. She fumbled it open and stared at the neat white tubes neatly arrayed within.

'Does she know about you coming here?'

'Of course.'

'You didn't come all this way just to give me cigarettes, Parry.'

'There's more to it than just the cigs.' Then, remembering, he reached deeper into his belt and found a lighter. He passed that to Bella as well and watched in silence as she lit one of the cigarettes and sucked it to a stub.

'Something's wrong, isn't it? You wouldn't have driven out here unless something was wrong.' The thought seemed to delight her in some perverse fashion – though it couldn't have escaped her that she was completely dependent on Crabtree for her survival. 'What is it? Tell me.'

'It's nothing like that,' Parry said. 'Things aren't great, but they're not as bad as we thought they were going to be a year ago. The Maw project—' He caught himself, remembering that Bella was supposed to know nothing of the monstrous clockwork apparatus churning inside Janus. But what did it matter if she learned a few things now? 'We found a way to draw power from the moon,' he said. 'There are still some issues to be resolved, but no major show-stoppers.'

'I noticed the power outages. It gets cold and dark out here.' A little shiver passed through her. 'You wouldn't believe how cold and dark it gets out here.'

'No,' Parry said gently, 'I *would* believe it.'

'You're wasting tens of miles of superconducting line keeping me out here,' Bella said. 'You could always relocate me to Crabtree and use the line for something else.' She ground the dead stub of the cigarette against the top of the crate. 'Or just let me die.'

'It's neither here nor there, really,' Parry said, not unkindly. 'The line's near the end of its life. It wouldn't have been able to carry a useful load from the Maw.'

'You could still use it somewhere.'

'You can't come back to Crabtree, not right now, anyway. Maybe one day . . . when things get better.'

Bella laughed. It was brief, retching, doglike sound, as if a stone had lodged in her throat. 'Svieta'll never have me back.'

'I'm sorry it came to this,' Parry said sadly.
'Are you still with her?'
'Yes,' he said, guardedly.
'She'll hate you for even talking to me.'
'Perhaps. We'll get over it. She sanctioned this visit, so she can hardly blame me for talking.'
Bella narrowed her eyes to penetrating slits. 'Did Craig Schrope go along with it as well?'
Parry looked away. 'Schrope isn't really involved in such decisions.'
'That's what I heard. Some kind of withdrawal. Catatonic mutism, shell shock. DeepShaft was his life, and DeepShaft fucked him up the ass. That kind of thing can break a man, even a jarhead robot like Schrope. I'm right, aren't I?'
'You can discuss it with Ryan.'
'Is that what this is all about? A visit to the doctor?'
Parry patted the crate he had sat down on. 'There's a lightweight Orlan in here. If you agree to accompany me, you put the suit on and we leave now. I drive you to Crabtree for six hours, then I drive you back out here.'
'Six hours?'
'It's long enough. You'll have time to speak to him, and then Ryan can give you a check-up.'
Her eyes narrowed in the half-light. 'Talk to who?'
'Jim Chisholm,' Parry said.
She gave him a ghost of a nod, and he knew that she had forgotten none of it, not even the tiniest detail.
'I didn't think Jim would still be alive. I didn't think he would last . . . weeks, let alone years.' She looked into Parry's eyes, and for the first time since arriving he felt himself in the presence of the old Bella, however fleetingly. 'How is he, Parry?'
'Could be better,' he said.

Bella put on the suit and left her prison. Suit-to-suit communication was available, so Parry did his best to prepare Bella during the long drive back to Crabtree, even as he kept half his concentration on the business of steering the tractor, following the snaking path of the superconductor cable and willing the lights of the High Hab to crest the horizon.
Bella knew more and less than he had expected – clearly some of her visitors had done more than just swap rations and check her blood pressure, but there were still gaps in her knowledge. She knew about Wang Zhanmin and his heroic efforts to coax life into the forge vat. She knew something of the Ofria-Gomberg work on the Spican symbols. She knew nothing of the Maw project, or the study of the lava lines, or the fact that Jim Chisholm was still alive.

'Wang had Chinese medicine on his ship,' Parry said, 'some of it more advanced than anything Ryan had in his toolkit. It helped slow the spread of the tumour.'

'Slow but not stop.'

'No. That wasn't within his capabilities. Wang said it was just emergency field medicine – not even the best they had.'

'We were wrong about the Chinese,' she said. 'Badly wrong. We should have embraced them, welcomed their help.'

'Too late to kick ourselves about it now.'

'I think we might be wrong about the Spicans, too.'

Parry pressed her on that, but that was all she would say on the matter. The remark troubled him all the way back, until Crabtree began to emerge over the horizon. First the tower appeared, with the swollen cylinder of the High Hab perched at its top, then the outlying structures, then the squared-off trenches where water had been mined from the ice. They couldn't waste power illuminating the tower for its own sake, but its shape was defined by the light coming from its windows, and by the glow spilling from the spawn of domes surrounding it. Light raced along the guy lines, bluish as moonlit cobwebs.

'This is the first time I've seen this,' Bella said, something like awe in her voice.

'It's home.'

'It doesn't even look like a ship any more. If I didn't know—' She bit down on whatever she had started to say. 'How many are there now?'

'One hundred and forty-six – five more than we arrived with.'

'Children,' Bella breathed, as if the word was a kind of oath, or invocation: to be used sparingly, and with caution. 'How . . . how are they?'

Parry steered the tractor around one of the ice trenches. At the far end, a robot was carving out a block with a cutting beam. 'They seem okay. We take special care of them. We don't leave much to chance.'

'This is no place for children,' she said.

'We came here to live. Children are part of that.' He took one hand off the tractor's steering wheel to point to the hab. 'They spend a lot of time up there, in the centrifuge. Six hours a day, at one-point-five gees. Costs power, but we need to give them more gravity than Janus has to offer.'

'That works?'

'Ryan says bone development looks normal.'

'He isn't a paediatrician.'

'He's learning.' Parry returned his hand to the wheel in time to steer them down a tunnel ramp, into the labyrinth of corridors under Crabtree. 'That's all any of us are doing, from day to day: learning as best we can. What did you mean back there, by the way, about us being wrong about the Spicans?'

But Bella ignored his question, and silence stretched between them as they pulled into a parking cavern, the walls furred with whorls of hastily applied sprayrock. Robots and tractors huddled in vacuum, but there was no one living to greet them. Parry and Bella disembarked and made their way to a large airlock littered with machine parts.

'I'm glad you named this place after Thom,' Bella said as the lock cycled. 'It was bad, what we did to him.'

'What *they* did to him,' Parry corrected gently.

'No,' Bella insisted, 'what *we* did. All of us. Including you, including me.' She kicked one heel against the ground. 'This is our atonement.'

Ryan Axford still occupied his old medical complex in one of the two Hab centrifuges. He was alone when Parry dropped Bella off, and the lights in the medical complex were dimmed to their lowest settings. He stood up from a desk-mounted microscope with a glass slide in his hands, smeared with something yellow. He wore crumpled green scrubs and white gloves.

'Hello, Bella,' he said. 'It's good to have you back.'

Axford's aged appearance didn't alarm or surprise Bella: she had seen him many times during her exile, and could only guess at the burden of work he had been under since their arrival. He had been a young-looking forty-four before they chased Janus, but now he could have passed for a man in his late fifties, worn down by long decades of overwork. The salt-and-pepper crew cut she remembered was now nearly snow-white.

'I gather I won't have time to outstay my welcome,' Bella said.

'Six hours is better than nothing. We'll just have to make the most of it, won't we?'

She steadied herself against a cabinet. This wasn't even full gravity – the centrifuge had obviously been spun down for her visit – but it was still taxing after nearly three years in Janus's microgravity. She struggled to catch her breath before speaking. 'Parry told me you've been branching into paediatrics.'

'And obstetrics,' Axford added, with a gentle smile. 'Not just me, of course: there's Jagdeep, Thomas, Judy . . . Gayle.'

Thomas Shen and Gayle Simmons had taken Svetlana's side during the crisis. Bella wondered what it had cost Axford to keep his team together, despite that rift. Something in the lines of his face spoke of the toll that other kind of healing had taken.

'Parry said there are several children now.'

'Yes, and there's one more on the way,' Axford said. 'I shouldn't really tell you this, but it's common knowledge in Crabtree – Svetlana's pregnant.'

'Nice for her.'

'I don't suppose word reached you that she lost one child already? A daughter. I did what I could, but . . .' Axford faltered, as if something had caught in his throat.

'I'm sorry she lost the child,' Bella said, and for an instant she permitted it to be true.

'They named her Hope. Hope was stillborn. That says something, don't you think?'

'Mind if I sit down, Ryan?'

'I insist on it.' While she shuffled to a chair, he put down the slide, snapped off his gloves and reached for a flexy, glancing at it just long enough to review her case file. 'How've you been doing since the last check-up?'

Bella smiled bleakly. 'Better than Craig, from what I can gather.'

'Nothing to report, then?' He looked at her encouragingly. 'Nothing ailing you?'

Through her feet she felt the quiet rumble of the centrifuge, like a fair-ground ride. 'Oh, nothing worth mentioning. Sometimes I wake up screaming with terror because I think there are things outside, trying to get into the dome. Sometimes I catch myself standing naked in the airlock, halfway to the outside. Sometimes I find something sharp and think about killing myself.'

'We all have bad days.'

'Those are the good ones.'

He scratched a note onto the flexy. He held the stylus the way surgeons were trained to hold scalpels: four fingers on the shaft, like a violin bow. 'Something stops you, though. Something holds you back, when you could end it all.'

'Duty,' Bella said. 'Something that won't let me turn away from this mission, and my responsibility to it.'

'Your responsibility ended the moment Svetlana took over.'

'No,' she said quietly. 'It didn't. It just got harder. I went peacefully because I knew it was the one thing that would allow Svieta's people to forgive the others and work with them. It was the one thing that would bring the crew back together.'

'You had no choice. She made that decision, not you.'

'I went along with it.' She balled one fist and touched it to her heart. 'That doesn't mean I liked it.'

Axford placed the flexy back on his desk. Bella noticed that the display was discoloured, with many dead hexels blotching the iridophore array. 'You know you have many friends in Crabtree – almost half the population were on your side. A lot of the people who turned to Svetlana only did so because Parry led the way. And you know Parry doesn't have anything personal against you.'

She nodded, thinking of Parry's small kindness in bringing the cigarettes.

'For the last two years we've been pushing to make things easier for you,' Axford said. 'We haven't made much progress yet, but I'm confident that when the energy crisis is finally resolved—'

'I don't want things to be easier,' she said. 'I want them *harder*.'

'I think you'll get your wish – at least while Svetlana is running things. She can barely bring herself to mention your name.'

'So I've heard.'

'Don't take it to heart. That's often the way it goes when deep friendships turn bad. And there's no denying the fact that you were very good friends.'

'Whatever she feels about me . . . I don't hold it against her.' Bella looked down, feeling suddenly childlike and vulnerable. 'I knew Janus would come between us,' she said. 'I felt it coming, long before things turned really bad. I saw the lightning on the horizon.'

'Just . . . hang in there,' Axford said. 'For all your other friends. For all of us who still care.'

'Is it true what I heard about Craig Schrope?'

'I still hope Craig will come around,' he said, but something in his tone suggested that he never expected it to happen. 'Crabtree could always use an extra pair of hands. It already has to feed and water him, so why not make him work for his keep?'

'Has he tried killing himself?'

'Given what we allow him in that room, he'd need to be pretty creative. I don't think he was ever a particularly creative man.'

'No,' Bella said. 'I don't think so either. Is he up here?'

Axford nodded cautiously. 'It's better to have him close.'

'I'd like to see him.'

'Sorry. I can't possibly allow it.'

'Svetlana need never know. Who'd tell her?'

'Me.'

'You could choose not to. And Craig's not likely to go blabbing, is he?'

'Why, Bella? Why does it matter so much? Craig turned against you. He took the ship from you.'

'He thought it was the right thing to do. Even at the time, part of me wondered if he might be right about it. I just want to let him know . . .' She faltered, offering Axford her best pleading look, the one that had opened so many doors in the past. 'Just a moment with him. That's all.'

He cocked his head, his nostrils pinched. 'She'll have my hide if she ever finds out.'

'She won't.'

'Two minutes, Bella. That's all.'

'Thank you.'

He fished a key from his pocket and walked her to a door with a small circular window set at head height. Axford rose up on his tiptoes to peer inside. 'He's awake. That's good. I wouldn't want to wake him.'

Axford let her into the room. He remained by the door, watching Bella and his patient. Craig Schrope sat on the edge of his bed, wearing white pyjamas. He rocked gently back and forth, his hands tucked in his lap, fingers interlaced either in supplication or due to some intense, skin-crawling anxiety. His hair was shaved almost down to his scalp and he smelled strongly of disinfectant. His expression was blank, alarmingly neutral, with the waxy pallor of a shop-window mannequin. His lips moved but not much else. He was saying something, mouthing words at the very limit of audibility.

'Hello, Craig,' Bella said. 'It's me, Bella. I've come to see you. How are you doing?'

'He won't respond,' Axford warned in a low voice.

Bella lowered herself onto one knee to face Schrope on his level. He was staring at the floor, his eyes betraying no sign of having noticed her presence.

'Craig, listen to me. This is not how it has to be.'

'Bella,' Axford purred.

She reached out and touched Schrope's pyjama-covered knee. 'Something bad happened to us all,' she said. 'You were caught up in something you never wanted to be a part of. It's been hard for you ever since, Craig, probably harder than it's been for any of us. I can't begin to imagine what you're going through. But we still need you back.'

Axford stepped from the door and placed a hand on Bella's shoulder.

'I should run your medical, Bella.'

She ignored him, reaching up to place one hand under Schrope's clean-shaven chin. She tried to tilt his head so that she could look into his eyes. He was as stiff as a corpse.

'I said something bad to you once, Craig. You know what it was. I said sorry . . . but that wasn't enough. I want to say it again now. I want you to know that you're still a good man. You can still come back to us.'

His head moved the tiniest of degrees under the pressure of her hand. He did not look at her. She let go and stood up.

Axford worked efficiently: bloodwork, bone density, radiation dosimetry. Aside from the calcium depletion due to her permanent exposure to low gravity, Bella was healthy enough. She had an exercise cycle in the dome and she made a point of using it, even on the bad days. She might take her own life out there, but she was not going to let Janus do it for her.

She hated the moon and gave it no quarter.

When they were done, Axford sat her down in a quiet annexe and told her about Jim Chisholm.

'I give him a week, maybe two, of lucidity. The glioblastoma is interfering with normal brain function, squeezing some structures and infiltrating others. It's also competing with them for blood and nutrients. He has elevated arterial and venous hypoxia: his brain's literally being starved by the blastoma. Metabolic end-products are upsetting normal neurochemistry. For the last six months I've been seeing clear focal deficits.'

'Deficits in what?' she asked.

Axford ticked off fingers. 'Language, comprehension, spatial tasks – none of them are as good as they used to be. Seizures are getting worse – anticonvulsants can only do so much.' Axford pushed himself up in his seat and tried to look bright. 'Today's a good day, though. Jim knows it, I know it. That's why Parry came out for you.'

'So that I could say goodbye to Jim?'

'That's part of it, I guess.'

'I'm surprised Svieta allowed it.'

'Jim wanted to speak to you. That wasn't the kind of request she could turn down.'

'That must have stuck in her craw.'

'She always liked and respected Jim. She couldn't have lived with herself if she said no.'

'That's all there is to this? Jim just wanting to see me one last time?'

'That's between you and Jim,' Axford said.

Since *Rockhopper* had been grounded on Janus, Axford had expanded his medical complex, incorporating some of the surrounding rooms. Bella supposed he had more patients on his hands these days: not just the children and the pregnant women, but all the people who were falling ill with things that would otherwise have been fixed once they returned to Earth. He had set aside an entire room for Jim Chisholm, furnished with plants and pictures. The room was clean but careworn: there were chips missing from the green tiles on the walls and ceiling, smudges of ineradicable colour on the floor.

One wall was sewn with iridophores, dappled with dead patches like leaf mould. A ShipNet portal was open, flanked on either side by some kind of X-ray or PET image of a human skull in lateral section, with its bones and tissue and liquid secrets traced in pale-blue monochrome, overlaid with white text and digits. She made out the tumour, lurking in one side of his brain like a weather system in the Gulf of Mexico. It was a third bigger than the last time she had seen an image of it, and angrier, somehow.

As they entered, Gayle Simmons was leaning over the figure on the bed, adjusting a fawn-coloured medical cuff. It sat like an oversized bangle around Chisholm's stick-thin wrist.

'I'll give you as much time as you need,' Axford said, 'but don't tire him out. You don't have to leave Crabtree immediately – I can always invent some tests I need to run on you.'

'Thanks,' Bella said, and she squeezed his hand in gratitude.

Simmons stepped away from the bed as she approached. Bella noticed that she had something around her neck: a collection of plastic shapes in primary colours, threaded together on a nylon line. She whispered something to

Axford and then the two of them left the room, leaving Bella alone with their patient.

It looked at first as if Chisholm was comatose or absent, unaware of her presence. He stared dead ahead, his attention fixed on a spot on the ceiling. She moved to his side and was about to speak when he moved his head by the tiniest of degrees.

'Bella,' he said. 'Thank you for coming.'

'Least I could do.'

He fumbled for the half-moon glasses strung around his neck on an elastic cord. 'Have they been treating you well?'

She wondered how much he knew. She considered mentioning her visit to Schrope, but decided against it. It was not as if there had been any communication between them.

'I've only seen Parry and Ryan. They've never treated me with anything other than kindness.'

'That's good.' He nodded – an effort that must have been Herculean, given his situation. 'Parry and Ryan: good people. We need more like them.'

'I think we have a lot of good people,' Bella said. 'The fact that this place even exists, that they've managed to make it work—'

'It's an achievement,' Chisholm said. 'Did they tell you about the work in the Maw?'

'I'd have liked to have been a part of it,' Bella said. 'I'm as much of a burden on this colony as anyone else. She keeps me boxed away like an old pair of shoes she doesn't want to see again.'

'I've pointed out the value of bringing you back into the fold. You wouldn't need any formal position of power – just making you an advisor would be an improvement. But she won't listen.'

'We need union – now more than ever.'

'That's what I've told her. What's worse is that I think even she sees it. She may be proud, but she was never stupid.'

'No,' Bella agreed ruefully. 'Never that.'

Chisholm stared at the ceiling for a long time, as if lost in the mosaic of its chipped and discoloured tiles. 'I still believe you matter to us,' he said. 'That's why I wanted to see you. I guess Ryan told you that I don't have much time left. For a long while I only had headaches, a sense of pressure behind my eyes. Now I feel different . . . as if I'm moving into another room, another place. I have the oddest flashes of memory, the strangest dreams . . . sometimes when I'm wide awake. Everything feels vivid to me now. I can look at one of those tiles and see infinity in it. I've always loved Mingus, but now I hear things in that music I never dreamed of before. There was a sea there before, but now it's an ocean: deep, mysterious, wonderful. I could swim in Mingus for eternity.'

Bella looked at the brain images. 'Seeing that up there helps? Or was that for my benefit?'

'No, I wouldn't do that to you. I like to see it.' He must have observed something in her face, some twitch of unguarded revulsion. 'It's *my* dragon, Bella. I have a right to know its face.'

'Of course,' she said, chastened.

'It's going to kill me. Ryan says soon . . . weeks. They'll freeze me before that – I've already given my consent. I'll become a Frost Angel, just like Mike Takahashi. When the seizures become unmanageable, I'll let him put me under.'

Bella nodded. It was all she could do.

'You don't think it'll make any difference,' Chisholm said. 'You're probably right: dead is dead, whether they freeze you or turn you into ash.'

'Don't talk like that,' she said. 'If Ryan freezes you, then maybe we can fix you when we get back home.'

'Home doesn't even exist now. It's the future, Bella, no matter what our calendar tells us. We might be better off riding this thing to the end of the line.'

'And when we get there?'

Chisholm closed his eyes and spoke very softly. 'There's something I need to tell you, Bella – it's the reason I dragged you all this way.'

'What is it?' she asked, intrigued.

His lips formed a teasing smile. 'No one else will hear this from me – not even Ryan. Definitely not Svieta. I'm telling you because it will give you something she doesn't have.'

'Why?' Bella breathed.

'Because one day she'll have to come to you for it. One day you'll have something *she* needs, and that will give you leverage.'

'How will either of us know when that day comes?'

'You'll know,' Chisholm said, still with that smile. 'Trust me, you'll know.'

A tiny spark moved away from the puddle of light that was Crabtree into the great darkness that surrounded the township. From her vantage point in the highest level of the High Hab – above the centrifuge, so that the view from her window remained fixed – Svetlana watched the tractor bob into the distance, dwindling and dimming until it disappeared beyond the limit of visibility. Only then did she allow herself to feel anything resembling calm.

For the last six hours she had been in a state of wired tension, burning with the knowledge that *she* had entered her little empire again, and that she had no choice but to condone that return from exile, however temporary it might have been. She had sent Parry out to collect her because Parry was close to her and could be trusted not to talk. The involvement of Axford and the other medical staff could not be helped: she would just have to rely on their discretion. But no one else was to know that the exile had walked in Crabtree again, or that she had been granted an audience with the dying Chisholm.

'It's a kind of torture for her,' Axford said, standing behind Svetlana and a little to the right so that she saw his reflection in the window, flexy tucked under his scrub-sleeved arm. Behind Axford, dimmed so that it did not spoil the view, the wall showed a real-time feed from the Maw: the monstrous cogs and dynamos of the transmission system, threshing in the glare of multiple floodlights. Figures stood amidst a tangle of thigh-thick power lines, dwarfed by the clockwork mechanism. There was no shortage of energy down there, even if it was still difficult to convey it back to Crabtree.

'I asked you for an update on her medical fitness, not a commentary on her punishment.'

'It was meant to be exile, not punishment,' Axford said sharply. 'I know. I was there when we took the decision on how to deal with her.'

Svetlana turned angrily from the window and stood with her hands resting on either side of the swollen curve of her belly. Wang had grown her new clothes for the pregnancy, austere of cut. 'Are you saying she should live in luxury while we starve and shiver?'

'I'm saying you should understand what you are doing to her. If you want to torture her, there are cheaper ways to do it. We could ship her back to Crabtree unseen, just as we did today, find a nice little cell and lock her in it, with no access to the outside world. Frankly, that would make a lot more sense from where I'm standing.'

'Fuck you, Ryan.'

'If you're at all unhappy with my reading of the situation, you're welcome to dismiss me.'

He was the only man on Janus who could criticise her openly and not lose a wink of sleep over the consequences. She hated and prized him for that. He was her conscience.

'I gave her a flexy. I gave her books.'

'The flexy died a year ago.'

'We can't spare any more now.'

'Not now. A year ago . . . maybe we could have. But you turned my request down.'

'She's lucky we didn't execute her the way we executed Herrick and Chanticler. Do you really think what she did is any less of a crime?'

'In my darkest moments, no,' Axford conceded, 'but generally I don't allow myself to be ruled by my darkest moments.'

'It's easy for you. All you do is set bones and deliver babies. I have to hold this place together. She has to pay and be seen to pay.'

'She's paying,' Axford said quietly.

Svetlana looked back to the horizon, but there was no sign of the tractor now. She pulled the blinds, screening out the darkness. Sometimes it seemed to lap at her thoughts, probing them for points of weakness. She thought of Parry somewhere out there, and wanted him back.

'If there's something . . .' she said, falteringly, 'something that would keep her . . . intact.'

If Axford felt a moment of triumph, nothing showed. 'There are measures I could recommend. I'll make a note of them, submit them for your approval.'

Svetlana brooded over her answer for what felt like hours, even to her. Perhaps she imagined the kick in her belly, as the girl turned in her sleep. 'All right. But she's still an *exile*, Ryan. We never forget that.'

'No,' he said.

'One other thing – you escorted her to Jim. Did you hang around while she was there?'

'Absolutely not. I left them alone.'

'Then you have no idea what they talked about?'

'I'm a doctor,' Axford said, affronted, 'not a spy.'

# CHAPTER 16

The cliff soared far above, reaching over Svetlana in a dizzy overhang laced with ominous fissures. The calving of chunks of ice had slowed since the early days of Janus's departure, but large breakaways still happened occasionally. The odds against a calving event happening while they were under the overhang were comfortably low, but Svetlana still could not rid herself of a knot of disquiet.

She looked back, making sure that Parry and Nick were not too far behind her. They had trudged fifty metres north from the squatting form of the parked lander to the fiery ribbon of the lava line. It boiled orange, searing through the ice like a path of burning gasoline.

In one direction, the line curved away to the horizon. In the other, it vanished into a blocky, ice-covered chunk of Spican machinery the size of an office block. Where there was no ice build-up, the lava lines were observed to float just above the underlying machinery, unsupported except at the point where they entered or left the interior of Janus. Robots had been sent under the lines, but had detected no peculiar field effects.

Ahead, something was wrong with the line. Instead of following a customarily straight or gently curving trajectory, the line suddenly kinked, veering to one side at almost a right angle. After the kink, there was something subtly amiss with the line: the orange had taken on a pink tinge, and the diameter of the fiery tube was pinched. It looked stressed, like something about to snap.

Svetlana allowed Thale to step ahead of her and lead the way, traversing the path that the line would have followed were it not for the kink. *Don't straighten out now*, she thought.

'Nothing's come out to fix it,' he said. 'Maybe it's on a to-do list somewhere inside Janus, or maybe it just doesn't know or care about this one breakdown.'

'Ice did this?' Parry asked.

'Ice and rock,' Thale said. 'Sometime when Janus was parked around Saturn, a piece of chondrite rubble must have splatted onto the ice. When this part of the shelf collapsed, it took the boulder with it. The boulder smashed into the lava line just as a transit was passing.'

Parry and Thale had been doing most of the talking since their departure, filling awkward silences with a strained attempt at small-talk. Thale and Svetlana still didn't see eye to eye, despite his release from custody and the grudging changes Svetlana had made to the terms of Bella's exile.

Six years into the human settlement of Janus, the wounds were still raw. For months on end the colonists would muddle along as if the old grievances were history. For many of them – with their marriages and children – that was the case. But a few could not leave the past alone. Every now and then, something would happen to remind Svetlana that the crisis on *Rockhopper* had not been forgotten; would never be forgotten. Even if the troublemakers had no intention of changing the political situation in Crabtree, there were still scores to be settled.

Most of the time, their actions never went beyond threats and intimidation, but occasionally something more significant happened. Every apparently accidental death on Janus had to be examined in the light of past events. Meredith Bagley had been the latest unfortunate victim. She'd been working on routine centrifuge repair, squeezed deep inside the drive mechanism, when the centrifuge started up. The preliminary investigation revealed that certain safety interlocks had not been set, implying that she'd been in too much of a hurry to get the job finished.

Meredith Bagley had been known as a conscientious and thorough worker, but there was also the matter of what she had done on *Rockhopper*: when Bella had gone behind Svetlana's back to check the sweatbox numbers on the fuel tanks, she had done so with Bagley's visible assistance. Svetlana's allies had viewed it as a kind of treachery. Most of them had forgiven Bagley by now – she'd been young, newly rotated aboard the ship and consequently unlikely to refuse a direct order – and most were content simply to give her the cold shoulder. But that still left the possibility of a small core of loyalists who might feel that Bagley hadn't been adequately punished. Loyalists who thought they were obeying Svetlana's private wishes. Already there were rumours that she wasn't exactly displeased with the outcome.

More than likely the death was exactly what it looked like: an accident rather than murder. Even good workers cut corners when they were behind schedule with someone shouting at them to get the centrifuge up and spinning again. But even the slightest suggestion of murder could not be discounted. The Judicial Apparatus had to look into all the angles before it closed the book.

Bagley was just one case. Every accidental death was investigated with the same diligence. Likely suspects were brought to the High Hab and quizzed. No one liked it, and it certainly wasn't helping to erase the old divisions, but it wasn't the duty of the judiciary to bury the past.

Dealing with men like Thale didn't make it any easier, either. He'd nailed his colours to the mast pretty clearly when he tried to spring Bella from prison. No doubt where *his* loyalties lay, Svetlana thought acidly. But no one else on Janus had spent more time studying the lava lines than Nick Thale, and the knowledge he had accumulated was simply too valuable to lose by shutting him away.

Not for the first time, Svetlana was grateful to have Parry around – he was the one crew member no one had a problem with. The Lind loyalists knew that he'd been generous to Bella, so they forgave him his choice of wife. Even Nick Thale appeared relaxed in his presence: far more so than when he was forced to deal with Svetlana.

But in spite of her husband's comforting presence, Svetlana would still be glad when this particular expedition was concluded.

They could see the transit now, stalled a little further along the lava line from the kink. It was the first time she had seen one up close: normally they were moving too fast for the human eye to follow. Knocked off its course by the boulder, this transit had come to an abrupt halt, lodged against a chunk of protruding machinery. The transit's outward form was very simple: a pair of thick coin-shaped endplates, floating independently of each other, with the 'cargo' trapped inside a suspension field stretched between the inner faces of the endplates. But this transit was damaged, bent out of shape by the impact – the endplates were twisted at an angle to each other. The stressed, constricted lava line had broken up into fingerlike tubes, playing over the endplates like Saint Elmo's fire and etching a weird pattern of bronze-coloured erosion into their pewter-grey surface. Beyond the transit, the line kinked back onto something resembling its original path.

The broken transit had spilled its cargo. The suspension field was still active – a flickering, writhing cylinder between the endplates – but the freight had escaped from its confinement through some point of weakness on the nearside. Plates, coils and tubes of dull material lay scattered in a fan-shaped pattern on the ice, like an eruption of entrails through a hernia.

'You think we can just . . . take it?' Parry asked, when they had come to a halt, the toes of their boots only a few metres from the edge of the cargo.

'My guess is nothing will stop us,' Thale said. 'When the ice thins out, maybe this stuff will be reabsorbed into the normal machinery. Or maybe it'll just form a garbage layer on top, like dead skin.'

Parry fiddled with his helmet visor, snicking glare filters in and out. 'No other transits have come out on this line?'

'Not since the boulder came down. There was never much traffic on this one anyway – maybe one or two transits a week. If they've been re-routed onto other networks, we'd have a hard time spotting the difference.'

'Any idea what the stuff is made of?'

'Difficult call unless we take some of it back to Wang's lab.'

'It looks like metal,' Parry said. 'Lead, or something. My suit isn't picking up any rise in the background rads, so I guess it probably isn't radioactive.'

'Or the suit's faulty,' Svetlana said.

'Yeah, that too.' Parry managed a gallows laugh. 'You think we should try to take some back now?'

'I'd rather we sent in the robots first,' Thale said. 'If this is some kind of trap or set-up, or if the materials turn out to be toxic – better to let *them* take the risk.'

'I don't know if Saul can spare any robots for a few days,' Parry said.

'C'mon,' Thale said, his tone sceptical, 'is it really that bad? I thought that was just the party line, to keep us knuckled down.'

'It's worse,' Parry said.

In the last few months, breakdowns and accidents had thinned the robot pool to a dangerous low. Complex artefacts such as microprocessor boards needed equally complex blueprints, specified down to atomic scales. For most of their machines, no such blueprints existed. Wang was doing his best, combining the vat's built-in library files with a certain amount of reverse engineering, but so far he hadn't come up with much that actually worked.

'You must be able to pull some strings, though.' Thale pointed at the strewn cargo. 'This is raw material. It's what we've been waiting for.'

'I'll see what Saul can spare you.'

'We don't have to wait for Saul,' Svetlana said. 'There isn't time. We need to know if this stuff is any good, and if it is we need a strategy for stealing more of it.' And then she walked forward.

'Svieta—' Parry began.

But she was already on her knees, pushing her gloves into the ice under the nearest dark-grey slab. 'Feels okay,' she said. 'My fingers aren't tingling or anything weird. It just feels like a chunk of metal . . . really hard. It's moving, I think.' She whistled. 'Fuck, it's heavy – must be denser than anything we use.'

Parry and Thale stood either side of her, caught between fascination and alarm. She heaved at the slab until it lurched free from the ice in which it had buried itself. It came up easily then, although it still felt heavier in her hands than anything she had ever handled under Janus's gravity. 'Feels like a slab of concrete, or something. I don't want to even think about what this would weigh under a gee. We've got to be talking tonnes.'

'Be careful with it,' Thale said. 'It'll still have inertia. If you drop it on your foot, you *will* feel it.'

'Gather up some of this stuff,' she ordered. 'We'll load as much of it into *Crusader* as we can take. And keep an eye on your Sheng boxes.'

They were nervous at first, like children stealing apples from an orchard. But after three or four trips to the lander, following a different path each time to avoid tripping the route-repetition alarms retrofitted on their suits, it began to dawn on them that Janus simply did not care what they did with the spilled cargo. Only a certain disquiet about getting too close to the containment field prevented them from the removing the entire catch. That would have to be a job for the robots, when they could be spared.

Back in the lander, as it carried them aloft with tonnes of grey treasure in its hold, they couldn't suppress an elated feeling of breakthrough. Svetlana put in a call to the crèche and said hello to her daughter, who was busy finger-painting with Danny Mair. Danny and Emily were about the same age, and appeared to communicate on some channel incomprehensible to adults as they explored new parameters of messiness. Emily held her latest creation up to the cam: yellow and orange smudges that might have been flowers, a smear of blue along the top that might have been sky.

She had never seen sky or flowers.

Svetlana wanted to cry, but she kept it together. Then she called Denise Nadis and told her to prepare for their arrival.

'As soon as we're down I want Wang on the case,' she said. 'We have power now, and all the ice we can use. For once we may even have materials.'

'It's good,' Parry said, when she had finished the call, 'but let's not get carried away with this. We scored lucky this time – maybe. But we can't expect something like this to drop into our laps every week.'

'That's up to us,' she said. 'Janus has shown us a way. Now all we have to do is copy it. If nature can do that to a lava line, so can we.'

Thale opened his mouth a crack, but said nothing.

'What's up, Nick?' she asked, missing nothing. 'You don't think we should take what's there to be taken?'

'I'm not one of those idiotic cultists,' he said. 'I don't think there's anything sacred about this place. It's a fucking *machine*. On the other hand, I'm enough of a rationalist to believe we ought to be careful about provoking a reaction.'

'I didn't notice any reaction back there.'

'Maybe we weren't poking hard enough. Start dropping bombs on the lava lines and maybe you'll cross that threshold.'

She shook her head, disgusted by his timidity. 'Perhaps it's me, but I don't remember giving permission for Janus to pull us away from home. We've been pussyfooting around too long. It's time to start making this place work for us.'

'You always did think like an engineer, Svieta.'

She nodded. It was only hours later that she realised he had not necessarily meant it as a compliment.

One day, halfway into the seventh year, Ryan Axford called Svetlana to the medical centre. He had offered no explanation for the summons, but Axford would not have troubled her without excellent cause. Her contact with him had grown sporadic since Emily's birth, even more so since the passing of Jim Chisholm, but she still placed complete faith in his professionalism. The medical centre was a different place now that Chisholm was gone. Busier than ever – the influx of the children saw to that – but Svetlana could feel the absence where Chisholm had been. He had spent so much time in this place that he had left a kind of psychic imprint on the surroundings.

'What is it?' she asked when Axford had closed the door behind her.

'You asked to be told,' he said.

She looked at him blankly. 'Told what?'

'If there was any change.'

'Any change in *what*?' she snapped, a little exasperated now.

Axford's thin, timeworn face conveyed amusement. 'You barely remember, do you? He's been up here so long, never changing—'

Her jaw fell. 'Craig?'

For a moment, boyish enthusiasm stripped away the years and she glimpsed something of the younger Axford. 'He's coming out of it, Svieta. After all this time, I saw something human in there today. I think there's hope after all.'

'Is he talking?'

'The odd word, a sentence now and then. More than we ever expected – or hoped.'

Svetlana was surprised at how glad she felt. She had never seen eye to eye with Schrope on *Rockhopper*, and Schrope's strategic alignment with her cause had been so transparently self-motivated that it had done little to improve her respect for him. But what Schrope had become since then was so pitiable that she could not help but feel sympathy for him.

'What happened?' she asked.

'Time,' Axford said. 'The great healer. There's some truth in that, you know – and the one thing I can say with certainty is that he's had a lot of time.'

'Can I see him?'

'It's about time he saw a few new faces – it might help him along.' He raised a warning finger. 'But go easy. It's early days yet, and I don't want him pushed back into that shell.'

Axford led her to the room where they kept Schrope. Svetlana hesitated at the high, small-windowed door.

'Maybe this isn't such a good idea, Ryan. How much does he actually know?'

'Both much less and much more than you'd think.'

'I don't have much good news to offer him. If he thinks we're getting back to Earth any day soon—'

Axford answered softly, 'He doesn't – I've established that much. You don't need to soft-pedal the truth. Just . . . go easy. One step at a time.'

'I'll be careful.'

Schrope stood up as she came into the room. He'd been sitting in a chair next to a small bedside table. He put aside a book: not a flexy displaying text, but one of the very few actual printed books *Rockhopper* had been carrying, and which now formed a small and treasured library, like the valued collection of some medieval scholar. It was a dog-eared legal thriller entitled *The Firm*.

'Hello,' Schrope said.

'It's good to see you,' she replied, the words spilling out in an automatic utterance that sounded flatly unconvincing even to Svetlana. But what did she really feel? She had never liked Schrope during their days aboard *Rockhopper*, and she had despised him when (as she was now certain had happened) he had persuaded Bella that she needed to be removed from duty. But this was not really Schrope: this was some pitiful, fragile, damaged thing that had been shattered into a thousand psychological pieces and then glued back together in some haphazard approximation of its former shape. Hating Schrope now felt redundant, even spiteful. If she could hate a bullying child and yet feel empathy for the same child lying ill in bed, then she could feel empathy for the man who had once been Craig Schrope.

He looked better than she had expected. Now at least he was out of pyjamas and into normal clothes, even if they only ran to a drab grey T-shirt and a pair of white jogging pants. His hair was thicker, no longer shaved close to the scalp. There was an alertness in his eyes that she did not remember from her last visit.

'I'm sorry—' He paused, losing the thread of whatever he had meant to say.

'Easy, Craig,' she said gently.

'I'm sorry . . . for the trouble.' He looked abashed. 'All the trouble I caused.'

'It's all right,' she said.

'No.' He stood before her with his hands dangling at his sides. 'I should have . . .' He shook his head, exasperated with his own efforts. 'Difficult, sorry.'

'Take your time. No one's in a hurry.'

'I let you down. Should have pulled myself together.'

Svetlana felt a wave of magnanimity pass through her, all their enmities abruptly forgotten. 'You were never any trouble, Craig. It's just good to have you back with us.'

'I'm glad to be back,' he said earnestly. He lowered himself into his seat again and gestured towards the neatly made bed. 'Sit down. Please.'

Svetlana sat on the bed. 'You're doing fine, Craig – better even than Ryan led me to expect.'

'Ryan's been kind.'

'He never gave up on you.'

'Nor did you.'

She glanced away, hoping he didn't catch her guilty reaction. The truth was that she had given up on him long ago. She had not visited him in years and had come to pay little attention to Axford's less-than-optimistic medical reports. The last time she'd visited, it had been sufficient just to look through the window.

'I'm so glad you hung in there,' she said.

As they talked, he gained confidence. 'Your words meant a lot to me. I know you didn't think I heard much . . . but they did.'

'That's good,' she said. But she knew that in all her visits, she had never said anything to him. Axford had always warned her how pointless it would have been, and she had never had cause to doubt him.

'When you said that I was still a good man . . . that I should come back to you—'

'Yes?' Svetlana said, wondering what else his mind had conjured up during the long years of his exile from reality.

'It helped. It reached me. It gave me something to cling to, something to show me the way.'

'I'm glad,' she said.

'I'm still not ready for the world. You can probably tell that.'

She smiled quickly. 'Early days, Ryan said.'

'But I'll make it. I know I will. Now that I've come this far . . . I'm not going back.' There was an absolute assurance in his words that stunned her. 'I'll make it work this time. One day – not now, maybe not even this year – I want do something useful. I want to pay back my debt to Crabtree.'

'You owe us nothing,' she said.

'I know how hard it's been out there. I've heard about the deaths, the suicides. You could have let me die. That would have been easier, wouldn't it? One less mouth to feed. One less pair of lungs to fill. One less body to heat.'

'We're better than that, Craig.' His hands were trembling, she noticed.

'The company took away my life. My dignity. I invested *my whole fucking soul* in DeepShaft. They took that as well. I'll never get back everything they stole from me, but I can make a start, with your help.'

'What do you want?'

'To serve,' he said. 'To earn your forgiveness.'

When she had finished stitching the flexies together on the wall, Svetlana stood back and watched the children enjoy themselves. They were in a partition of the gymnasium, once the largest habitable space aboard the old ship. Coloured paper bunting hung in twisted arcs from one false wall to the other, pulled taut by the centrifugal gravity of the room's stately rotation. Party balloons floated in ripe bunches, bobbing where they had come to rest near the extractor vents. Some of them had been twisted into vague animal shapes; others had already burst, to the delight of some children and the perplexed anguish of others. Wang, who had made the ribbons and the balloons, had been persuaded to stay long enough to judge a painting contest, but he had gone now, back to his work with the vat. Svetlana hoped he would return, if only for the special treat she had prepared for the children later in the party. Wang was popular with the kids: somehow they sensed that he was the one adult on Janus totally unsullied by anything that had happened on the ship; the one adult everyone liked without reservation.

The party was in Emily's honour. She was five years old now, in this ninth year of human settlement. There were a dozen other children in the room, most of them younger than Emily. Hannah Ofria-Gomberg, the oldest child on Janus, was nearly eight now, and had taken to supervising the younger children with a precocious sense of duty. She was with Reka Bettendorf now, helping the older woman apply face paint (actually the harmless marker dye they'd once used to scrawl cutting points on ice) to a fractious group of three year olds, turning them into tigers, monkeys, bears and green-skinned space monsters. It kept the children entertained, although Svetlana wondered whether they would have been just as happy smearing the dye on themselves in abstract splodges. None of these children had ever seen a real cat, let alone a tiger.

'She's a beautiful little girl,' said Christine Ofria-Gomberg, nodding in Emily's direction. 'Your hair, your chin, Parry's eyes and nose. That expression she makes when she's not getting her way—'

'Pure me,' Svetlana agreed, smiling. 'Yes, I had noticed.'

'I can't believe it's been five years.'

'You should talk. Look at Hannah now – she's almost like one of the grown-ups around the other kids.'

'She'll be eleven when we reach Spica.' Christine lowered her voice as Hannah looked their way, conscious that she was being discussed. 'I remember being eleven, Svieta. It's as if we have two boxes for all the memories we acquire between the moment we're born and the moment we die: the child box and the grown-up box. You can still open the child box when you're an adult, sift through those memories, take them out for examination, but they never feel as if they happened to you. It's as though you see everything through thick glass, putting the world one notch out of focus. But by the time we're eleven, everything goes in the grown-up box. She'll always have grown-up memories of Spica.'

'Let's hope those are good memories,' Svetlana said, and then wished she had said something less pessimistic. Her dark sense of foreboding about the future did not belong at a birthday party any more than hilarity belonged at a funeral service.

She knew it was futile to dwell on what was going to happen to them when they reached the Spican structure: it was every bit as futile as dwelling on the inevitability of death. For years, indeed, Svetlana's immediate concerns had been so grave that she had not allowed herself the luxury of worrying about that remote event. So much else would have to go right for them before they could even dream of staying alive long enough to meet the aliens.

But now it was beginning to look as if things might go right after all. For the first time in years, Svetlana felt as if they were winning the struggle for survival and that they had a good chance of making it to journey's end. They had power from the Maw, and now they had the means to gather raw materials as well. It had taken time, but lately they had become very adept at harvesting the lava lines, stealing matter from Janus. Soon after that first discovery of the spilled cargo, Wang's analysis had revealed that it contained many elements and compounds that were either in extremely short supply or entirely lacking in Crabtree or the other settlements. Better still, the materials could be manipulated using routine chemical and nanotechnological methods that Wang already possessed. The Spican machinery might be invulnerable to analysis once it was in place, but the raw matter of which it was made was much more susceptible to human intervention. It could be cut, smelted, vaporized, ionised, even stripped down to its component atoms and segregated into isotopic fractions. It would not mean an end to certain forms of rationing, and the closed-cycle systems would have to be maintained as diligently as ever, but at long last Svetlana's people had the means to build, to keep building – even to toy with dreams.

Wang, too, had made progress. For years his efforts had been hindered because the forge vat was damaged and his understanding of its functions had only been superficial. Painstaking dedication had allowed him to fix the vat hardware and repair many of the damaged template files in its memory, but the basic shortage of raw materials had impeded his attempts to fully master its workings. Now he could experiment as much as he liked, and at last he was making useful components: basic medicines and machine parts that actually worked. He planned to achieve much more than that, however. A single vat was always going to be limited in its usefulness, and that limitation would become more acute as the population grew. He had plans to make another vat by growing its component parts in the first. Difficult, he said, but not impossible. He could then take some of the replicators from the first vat and use them to seed the second, so he wouldn't have to fabricate a fully functioning nanotech system from scratch. The second vat, if all went according to his plans, would be a mere duplicate of the first, but if he could make it work, he would have gained enough confidence to build something even larger. His third vat would have a cubic capacity eight times the size of the first, which would allow it to cast an entire lander engine in one go. Eventually, he said, he would be able to make a vat as large as the grandest industrial units back in China: a block-sized monster capable of forging an entire ship in a single pass, hatching it like a newborn chick. Svetlana wondered how far in the future he was thinking, and if anyone else had plans that reached that far ahead.

The face-painting done, the children had gathered around Parry who was dispensing chunks of chocolate: not the rubbery brown vat-grown approximation, but the real thing. A crate of Snickers bars had turned up during the clean-out of a cargo slot, and now the chocolate was kept under lock and key, strictly rationed and only to be dispensed during parties. The children only received two generous bites each, but such was their hyped-up expectation that they might as well have been portions of the finest caviar. Despite the minimal quantities of chocolate involved, it was gratifying how much mess some of the more enterprising kids were able to make. But the real chocolate stash was getting smaller with each birthday, and there were more birthdays to celebrate each year. Soon the kids would have to learn to like the vat-grown stuff.

'Come here,' Christine said, taking Svetlana's arm. 'There's something I want to show you while Parry's got them occupied.'

'And what would that be?'

'Did you see the pictures Wang came to judge?'

'A couple of them, but then I had to go and start stitching the flexies together.'

Christine led her to the table where the paintings had been spread out in all their wet, dripping glory. She peeled one from the table, yellow paint smearing her fingertips. 'Dawn Mair did this one,' she said, her tone confidential. 'I asked her what it was meant to be. She said it was the bad man.'

'What bad man?'

'The one she hears all the grown-ups talking about.'

Svetlana looked at the picture, applying mental filters to strip away the clumsy and smudged execution, trying to see what the child had intended. There was a yellow sky and a grey-green strip of indeterminate ground, and a stick-figure man standing on that ground, rendered in a murky shade of reddish black. The man had nasty scarecrow limbs, arms terminating in tree-like explosions of crooked black digits. The face – as far as she could make out – was vulpine and sleek and strangely menacing. In one skeletal hand the man held something that looked like a broken doll, more red than black.

'I've no idea who that's meant to be,' Svetlana said.

'Nor me, so I asked, and she just kept saying he was the "bad man". When I asked his name, she said something I didn't understand, at least not at first – something that sounded like "pull" or "pow". Then it clicked, and I knew exactly what she was saying, and I felt my blood temperature drop about thirty degrees.'

'What was the name?'

'Powell,' Ofria said, with a slow and delicious emphasis. 'Powell Cagan.'

'Holy shit.' Svetlana forced her startled voice lower. 'How could she—'

'Because people still talk about him, Svieta. Maybe not in public, but in the privacy of their own living quarters . . . he's the man who got us into this mess, after all. We all *know* that, it's just that most of us have . . . found a way to move on. We have enough to deal with here without projecting all our hate onto someone who probably died more than a century ago, hopefully in prison after serving a life sentence for corporate manslaughter, after receiving inadequate analgesics for his very painful terminal illness.'

'But not everyone has such an enlightened view.'

Christine shrugged. 'He's the new bogeyman, the demon some of the parents use to keep their kids under control. Be good or Powell will get you, and take you away to his wife.'

Svetlana looked at the doll-like figure in the man's fingers and realised that it was supposed to be a child he had stolen. 'His wife?'

'The wicked witch, the mad old woman who lives out on the ice.' Christine put down Dawn Mair's painting and picked up another from the table. 'Take a look at this. It's Richard Fleig's picture of Bella – or at least what he thinks she is.'

The seven-year-old son of Chieko Yamada and Carsten Fleig had drawn a creditably insane-looking old witch, squatting in a kind of fractured ice-blue igloo under an iron-black sky. Svetlana stared at it in cold horror: she had seen the picture earlier, but its significance had been lost on her. Just a witch, she had thought, never for one moment realizing it was meant to be Bella.

'I never put these thoughts in their heads,' she said, as if she needed to defend herself. 'The children aren't even meant to know about her.'

'Someone let it slip.'

'Who?'

'All of us, Svieta, in those unguarded moments when we forget that the kids are around. Can you honestly say you've never mentioned Bella, never even alluded to her, when Emily's been within earshot?'

'Alluded maybe, but—'

'That's all they need. Kids make their own mythologies, their own angels and demons. All we had to do was give them the tiniest helping hand, the tiniest nudge in the right direction. If they hate and fear Bella, it's only because they've latched onto the way we think about her.'

'They're too young for monsters.'

Christine returned the dripping painting to the table. The black line at the top of the picture had begun to bleed a tendril towards Bella's dome. 'Maybe not. In less than four years we'll meet the real ones. Perhaps it's time we all started thinking about monsters.'

By then the children were done with the chocolate and were swirling around the gymnasium again, laughing and screaming, bursting balloons and spilling drinks and food. Unable to suppress the disquiet that the paintings had provoked, Svetlana clapped for attention. When she spoke, her voice sounded troubled, evasive.

'Hi, kids – wanna see a movie?'

Damn right they did: they'd been hyped-up for it as thoroughly as for the chocolate, and their anticipation was no less intense. She waited until they were gathered before the flexy array, settled down and prepared for the long bout of concentration, silence and bladder control watching the movie would require.

'We found this movie in the archives,' Svetlana said, smiling brightly. 'It was lurking there for years, stored under the wrong file name. That means none of you will have ever seen it before. Isn't that *great*?'

Most of the children nodded their approval. Danny Mair started to cry.

'This is a film I saw when I was a little girl,' Svetlana said, soldiering on. 'Even then it was an old film: my mother remembered seeing it when she wasn't much older than any of you. I know you're going to like it, though. It's a film all about a little fish, a little orange fish with one fin bigger than the other one, who gets separated from his dad, and all sorts of magical adventures happen to both of them while they're trying to find each other again. They meet these really cool turtles and . . . well, I don't want to spoil it. Shall we just watch the film?'

There was a murmur of polite if not overwhelming enthusiasm. Some of the smaller kids were already looking distracted. Perhaps it would have been better to have said nothing, Svetlana thought. She used her own flexy to start the movie, and then took a place behind the kids to watch the show.

*Finding Nemo* wasn't a complete success. It went down well with a handful of the kids, but even then Svetlana couldn't be sure that they weren't just sitting still and looking engrossed because that was what was expected of them. The reactions of the others ranged from indifference to a kind of bewildered edge-of-tears dismay, as if she'd forced them to sit through an hour of algebra. They just didn't get it on any significant level. Few of them had seen Bella's old aquarium, so the things swimming around on the flexy screen were simply too unfamiliar to them, alien beings immersed in an utterly alien environment of which they had no experience. A few of the children were sufficiently amused by the bright shapes with human faces, but for others it was too much like watching an endless parade of abstract ink-blot forms. They had trouble following the narrative, trouble working out who they were meant to identify with. The sharks, meant to be funny, disturbed them profoundly. When the action shifted out of the water, they lost the thread completely. By the time the movie had finished, half the kids had drifted away to play with the balloons and make alterations to their demon-haunted paintings.

Svetlana felt dispirited. She had been in an excellent mood at the start of the party, but by the end of the film she was convinced that they were raising a generation of psychopaths: children utterly starved of the fundamentals necessary for adequate emotional development. How could they have responded so ungraciously to a movie in which she had expected them to take such untrammelled delight?

But then she saw the kids laughing again, having their face paint straightened out and de-smudged, and she forced her mood out of its rut. She had asked the kids to take instant pleasure in a movie that had been nearly sixty years old before *Rockhopper* met Janus. As a kid, there'd been things that her own parents had expected her to enjoy – films they'd liked when they were small – but which to her had seemed quaint and colourless and somehow melancholy, and even at this remove she could remember their quiet, brooding disappointment. They must have worried about her, for a moment. But she hadn't turned out to be a monster any more than these kids would.

She knelt down, picked up a balloon and punched it through the air towards Emily. While there were children there was hope, no matter how unamusing they found one deformed orange fish.

# CHAPTER 17

In the highest part of the High Hab, far above the sprawling lights of Crabtree, Svetlana sat in numbed silence. It was near the end of the twelfth year of settlement. The analysis team had just processed the latest data on the Doppler measurements, and the numbers were not remotely what she had been hoping for.

'This can't be right,' she said, shaking the aged flexy like a damp dishrag. 'We're fewer than eight weeks from Spica. We damn well should be seeing some slowdown by now.'

'Well, we're not,' Nick Thale said. He sat opposite her, his hands laced as if in prim contemplation. It was months since their last face-to-face meeting and Thale looked older than she remembered. He had allowed his hair to grow out around his bald crown, falling in snow-white waves that lent him the faintly simian look of an emeritus professor.

He was accompanied by Denise Nadis, her dreadlocks now shot through with grey, her dark skin age-spotted around the cheeks, the lines around her mouth deeper than Svetlana recalled. Unconsciously, Svetlana touched her own face and felt alien textures that had not been there a year or so ago.

They were all getting old, even in the time-dilated reference frame of Janus.

'Can I trust these numbers?' she asked.

'We're having trouble making measurements on the blue-shifted face,' Thale said. 'It's difficult enough getting our equipment to function against those fluxes. Symbolist sabotage isn't helping matters, either.'

'What sabotage?' Svetlana asked.

'Frida Wolinsky's extremists. Ever since Gregor died . . .' Thale shrugged, knowing that no more needed to be said.

'They don't like us making measurements into the blue,' Nadis said. 'Especially after what happened to Bob Ungless.'

Robert Ungless had left a suicide note and driven a tractor over the horizon from Crabtree, in the direction of the bow face. His last coherent transmissions had spoken of brightness, and the luminous, beckoning things he saw in that brightness even as the blue-shifted radiation chewed away his mind. After that he spoke only in riddles. The Symbolists claimed that Ungless had received divine information, that his every fevered utterance must be scrutinised for revelatory content.

'They think it's a kind of blasphemy,' Nadis went on. 'They send out robots from the Maw to cut our data lines and smash our instruments. They deny it, of course.'

'We should have locked them up years ago,' Svetlana said.

Parry grimaced. 'We've been over this. We need someone in the Maw to grease the clockwork, and it might as well be Symbolists. At least they're dedicated to their work.'

Svetlana gritted her teeth and moved on. 'Tell me about the data.'

Nadis shifted uncomfortably. 'The numbers are reliable. Within the stated margin of error, there's been no significant change in the frequency of the starlight. Either something freaky is happening to the space-time ahead of us, or we're not slowing down.'

At five gees of effective acceleration, Janus had taken two months to reach its present cruise velocity following its departure from Earth's solar system. Svetlana's best minds still had no idea how the moon had accelerated itself, but they had assumed that the same mechanism would operate in reverse during the anticipated slowdown phase. But they were already into that crucial two-month window, and there was no hint that the moon had begun its deceleration procedure. They were still shooting through space at a hair's breadth below the speed of light.

'If we're not slowing down,' Svetlana said, 'what the hell is going to happen to us when we reach Spica?'

'I guess that's up to Janus and the Spicans,' Thale said.

Parry coughed warningly. 'If you could err towards keeping your remarks constructive, Nick, that would be great.'

Thale looked nonplussed. 'Then I have nothing useful to add. You've seen the latest imagery: the Spican structure is still ahead of us, and it's turned its long axis around to align with our present vector. Whether we slow down or not, we're going to enter that tube.'

'And then what?' Svetlana said. 'Do we just shoot on through, like a rat through a pipe?'

'I've no idea. You might as well cast tea leaves.'

Nadis leaned forward, clicking her purple fingernails against the table. 'Maybe the slowdown mechanism is different.'

'Go on,' Svetlana said, with a strained smile of encouragement.

'Janus was alone in our solar system. It only had its own motive power to accelerate up to cruise speed. Up ahead, it might be different. Maybe the Spican structure is part of the deceleration system.'

Svetlana flashed her attention to Thale. 'Any thoughts on that, Nick?'

'It's as good a guess as any,' he said.

'What about the spikes?' Parry asked. 'Any idea where they fit into all this?'

'None whatsoever,' Thale said simply.

'It can't be coincidence, though,' Parry persisted. 'Two months from slowdown, and these things start pushing their way through the ice – there's got to be a connection, right?'

While she waited for Nick Thale to favour them all with a reply, Svetlana studied the latest map of the spire growth. Since the discovery of the first breakthrough point, nineteen similar features had been mapped around Janus, spaced more or less equidistantly. Enormous spire-like structures were pushing their way through the crust, ramming past machinery and ice, squeezing obstructions aside like erupting wisdom teeth. The spires glittered with symbols in new syntactical patterns that confounded the best theories of the linguists. They rose higher and higher, until they were a kilometre thick at the base and their needled tips were twenty kilometres from the surface of Janus.

Two of the spires were visible from Crabtree, thrusting up through the sternward icecap. Where there had been darkness, now there were tilted wedges of pastel light slanting from the horizon like frozen aurorae. Their sides were veined with lava lines, snaking in meandering trajectories to a point just below the spire, where they plunged inside. Around the clock, transits raced up the spires, laden with freight. Unguessable transformations must have been taking place inside them.

'Nick,' she pressed.

'You want guesswork, I'll give you guesswork, but don't blame me for it later.'

'I won't.'

'More than likely there *is* a connection. Janus seems to be preparing itself for something. It might be the slowdown we've all been expecting. Maybe these spikes are part of the mechanism, and they're going to bring us to a dead stop on a dime as soon as we hit the tube. Or maybe it's nothing like that at all.'

'I need *something*,' Svetlana said desperately.

'We'll know sooner or later,' Thale said, shrugging resignedly.

Svetlana thought about the skeletal tube they were approaching, with its struts and spars, its almost unimaginably expansive internal surface area – a million Earth-sized planetary surfaces, at the very least, each of which might easily contain several billion sentient creatures if the Spicans' idea of tolerable population density was anything like humanity's.

Then again, there might be no Spicans waiting at all, just their ancient and obedient machines. Perhaps it would be very difficult to tell the difference, from a human perspective.

She felt a bleak, premonitionary chill shiver through her. She thanked

Thale and Nadis and dismissed them. She moved to the window and hugged herself against the stellar cold that seemed to push infiltrating fingers through the glass. The distant spikes twinkled with ominous activity. Parry waited, saying nothing, leaving her with her thoughts.

'I'm scared,' she said at last, as if she had the room to herself. 'I'm scared and I worry that we might be terribly wrong about all this.'

She heard his footsteps, saw his dim reflection loom behind her in the glass. Parry wrapped his arms around and held her tight, and though she was glad of that, nothing he did could take away the chill and the fear.

'It's good of you to keep me informed,' Craig Schrope said, 'even if it isn't the best news.'

They were in the High Hab, in one of the administrative chambers of the Interim Authority. Schrope had an office to himself, lined with wangwood shelves brimming with hardcopy. He spent most of his days there, occupying himself with the legal processes of the Judicial Apparatus. It was solitary work, for the most part, but that suited Schrope. Despite years of rehabilitation, his emotional constitution was still fragile, and there were only a handful of people in whose company he felt truly at ease. Svetlana felt an elitist thrill at being counted amongst that number. They would probably never be close friends, but simply being on civil terms was an astonishing improvement on the old state of affairs.

'I wanted you to know that we aren't keeping anything from you,' Svetlana said. 'You'll hear rumours, I'm sure, but the truth is that we haven't got a clue what it is.'

'Do you have a name for it yet?'

'The Iron Sky,' she said tersely.

Shortly after attaining their final height of twenty kilometres, the spires had changed again. Their upper extremities – the last three kilometres – had thickened into budlike forms that had then split open along invisible seams, each of them forming six radial petals defined by faint tracings of lava. The petals reached out three kilometres from the central bud, oblivious to Janus's gravitational field. Then the petals had started growing, spreading and widening like oil slicks.

Over the next two months they had blocked off more and more of the sky until their edges met and fused, and then there was no sky except this oppressive black ceiling, suspended twenty kilometres above the ice. The lava lines had faded. Though the spires continued to be lit by Spican symbols, the ceiling was now as dark as the interstellar space it served to hide.

'Can you see through it?' Schrope asked, closing one of his legal binders. The paper was thick and vat-grown, the cover appropriated from an old Lockheed-Krunichev Fusion Systems spiral-bound technical manual entitled *Tokamak Start-up Procedures in A Nutshell.*

'Did you hear that we could?'

'Just rumours, Svieta.'

'No. We've seen nothing. Everything we shine at it gets absorbed. If there's something on the other side, we're not picking up the echo.'

'And the free-fliers?'

'Deadsville. If they're still out there, we're not hearing anything from them.'

'Does it trouble you?'

'Of course it troubles me. How did you expect it would make me feel?'

'It makes remarkably little difference to me,' Schrope said easily. 'Down here, entire days go by without me seeing a hint of the outside world. Legal work eats time like a machine, you know.'

He put the folder aside. Literally and metaphorically, he had been closing the file on Meredith Bagley. Every now and then, rumours had resurfaced that there had been more to her death than just a grisly accident during routine centrifuge maintenance. Svetlana's anger at the merest hint that she might have tacitly sanctioned it had spurred her to authorise the inquest Schrope had helmed. He was good with legal inquiry: it utilised the same forensic instinct that had worked so well for him in Shalbatana.

Terrier-boy's conclusion was that there had been nothing suspicious about the death. The rumours might continue, but there was nothing the Judicial Apparatus could do about that.

'Your work is important,' Svetlana said, 'but I have to take the wider view. What's the point of having a Judicial Apparatus if we don't have a world left to govern?'

'Things aren't that bad,' Schrope said soothingly. 'It's just a sky.'

'It won't let us touch it,' she said. 'We send free-fliers up to it and it repels them.'

'It probably has our best interests at heart.' One hand clicked the mechanism of a ballpoint pen, neurotically fast. 'Wouldn't you say?'

'I find it claustrophobic,' she said. 'I used to swim. I was a pretty good free-diver. Water never bothered me, no matter how deep and black and cold. But I always hated having anything above me but sea and clear blue sky.'

'It's no worse than what we had before – it's been a while since there were stars up there, Svetlana.'

'But we could always leave if we wanted to.'

He put the folder back onto one of the shelves, squeezing it into place between two other bulging documents. For a colony of under two hundred people, Crabtree and its peripheral suburbs generated a considerable amount of legal business. That wasn't too surprising, though. They'd had to build an entire economy from scratch just so that people could be paid for an honest day's work. After twelve years, the High Hab was still processing complaints from people who felt they had been short-changed in the initial allocation of credits. There was even a black-market economy of sorts. Officially, there was no coffee left anywhere on Janus, but if you knew the right people, it was still possible to obtain hitherto unallocated rations.

'It would have killed us to leave,' Schrope said, 'to drop out of the slipstream, out of the protective shadow of Janus. We'd have lasted about five minutes.'

'But it was an option. I'd always rather have the option, wouldn't you?'

'Judging by the business that comes through here, Svetlana, most people are just getting on with life.' Schrope indicated one of his shelves. 'That file on the end is a disputed paternity case. On Earth, we'd have settled it in a few minutes with a DNA profile. It wouldn't even have reached court. Out here, we don't have DNA sequencers. Axford's doing the best he can, but he's already a busy man, and I don't wish to take up more of his time than is absolutely necessary. That's just one file. We have divorce proceedings, personal-injury claims, accusations of libel . . . even the Symbolists are claiming religious discrimination.'

'They *invented* their religion from scratch,' Svetlana said indignantly. 'I've got every damned right to discriminate against them.'

'Yet by all accounts they do a reasonable job of running things in the Maw.'

She conceded his point with a pout of displeasure. 'Maybe. But how long can we rely on them? They're already saying I've been heavy-handed. I'm not even allowed in the Maw now. I have to send Parry.'

'All I'm saying is . . . life goes on. Perhaps the Iron Sky isn't as bad as you fear.'

'That's what people keep telling me – that Janus is still supplying us with power and materials, that the icecap is still there . . . that if we've survived for twelve years, we can survive a bit longer.'

Schrope stopped clicking the pen and put it down. 'You don't sound convinced.'

'I don't like it, Craig. I don't like not knowing what's out there. We should have arrived at the Spican structure by now.'

'Maybe we have,' he said soothingly, as if the matter was of only passing concern to him. 'The binary consists of blue stars, Svetlana, hot and very bright. Not a healthy environment for humans. Perhaps the whole point of the sky is to keep us safe from harm.'

'I hope so,' she said. 'I'm just scared of what we might see on the other side, if we ever get the chance to find out.'

He sighed and rocked back in his seat, fingers meshed behind his head. 'You've been good to me, Svetlana. You called me back from that place I was in and gave me a chance to make something of myself again.'

She nodded, but said nothing. Schrope still credited her with doing far more during his years of withdrawal than she knew to be true. Once, he had even told her how he had seen Bella, and how she had spoken to him. Svetlana knew for certain then that his memory of that time could not be trusted.

'I hope I've served Crabtree in some small way,' he continued, 'but I know I'm not indispensable. I know that there are a dozen people who could do this legal dogwork just as well as I can.'

'I don't know—' she began.

He shook his head and interrupted her. 'But one day I hope I can be indispensable. Not by shuffling papers, but by doing something concrete. Something no one else will do.'

'I don't follow,' she said.

'You're scared, and I don't blame you for that, but I've been to a place in my head worse than anything this universe has to offer. If they come, Svetlana, I'll go to meet them. You can send me first. I don't have anything to fear from the Spicans.'

'Craig—'

'I'm asking you to let me be your envoy. It's the least I can do.'

# CHAPTER 18

It came down without warning, nearly four hundred days after the sky had finally closed over Janus.

Seismic monitors, installed in concentric rings around Crabtree to detect signs of icecap break-up, registered a single massive spike. Time-of-arrival analysis revealed that the seismic disturbance had originated in a very small area of the icecap, about one hundred kilometres south of Crabtree. Once the initial reverberations had died down – the icecap flexing like a drum – the seismic activity returned to its usual quiet level. There were no after-shocks or hints of further movement after that first hammer blow.

Though she was unwilling to dismiss the incident, Svetlana was equally reluctant to send out a lander to scout the area. Fuel and spare-parts stocks were dwindling, and although Wang had lately become very good at coaxing miracles from the forge vats, complex spacecraft components were still a challenge. So Svetlana sent out a trio of tractors, which followed the line of a superconductor for twenty kilometres before turning south over hard, ungraded terrain. The tractors fanned out until they could just see each other's strobe lights, then made a series of awkward sweeps through the area of the seismic disturbance. But they found nothing, and the going was hard. When one of the machines damaged a mesh wheel, she ordered the trio to return home while they were still able to assist each other. She ordered a free-flier sent aloft, but the free-flier's cam was designed for inspecting hull damage at close quarters, not scanning a wide swathe of ice at high resolution. Nor did it have the power to generate effective ground illumination. It merely zigzagged ineffectively back and forth until it ran out of fuel.

A day passed while she brooded over the mystery. Should she risk committing a lander now, or send out another tractor sweep? All operations beyond Crabtree carried a measure of risk. Janus was quixotic, and the hammer blow might only indicate that something had happened deep in the machinery, even though the evidence, such as it was, suggested an event near the surface. There had been bangs and crashes in the night before, and people had soon learned not to let such things worry them. Not when there were a hundred other things more deserving of their anxiety.

Then – as so often happened – some other affair pushed itself to the forefront of her attention. In fact, it was a constellation of distractions. Trouble from Nick Thale and the other Lind loyalists, pushing for concessions. Symbolist agitation in the Maw. Yet another round of troubling rumours concerning the death of Meredith Bagley – had it really been accidental, or had someone made that centrifuge motor turn while she was deep inside its gears? A coldness between her and Parry that resurfaced occasionally, when she would catch Parry looking at her as if she was someone he barely knew, let alone liked. It would pass – it always did – but during these intermissions in their relationship she would glide into a neurotic spiral of self-examination. Parry was good. Parry was honest. If he had a problem with her, then there had to be a reason for it. Maybe she had taken too tough a stance on some things. But it was never Parry who had to make the difficult decisions. He thought he knew what she was going through, what it was costing her, but really he had no idea. He facilitated her decisions, but Svetlana made them. She never caught Parry awake at three in the morning, his mind overheating like a sixty-year-old reactor with jammed control rods.

So she put the hammer blow to the back of her mind.

Eight days later she had cause to remember it again.

There were reports of alien activity. This in itself wasn't anything unusual, and would not ordinarily have raised any flags. People had been seeing things on Janus for thirteen years. Out on the ice, on a lonely drive between outposts, it was east to understand why. The believers saw luminous entities, alien forms that could equally well have been angels or ghosts, who arrived with reassuring messages from loved ones left behind. The more spaced-out aquatics tended to see whales or dolphins in alien form. The *Cosmic Avenger* fans saw humanoid aliens that conformed to the show's stiflingly repetitive template for extraterrestrial intelligence. Now and then there was something weirder, but nothing that Svetlana considered evidence of a genuine external phenomenon. Granted, Janus could still surprise them – but nothing she had seen in thirteen years had convinced her that the former moon was anything other than an automated mechanism.

Indeed, the new reports were not of aliens per se, but of alien *things*. It was that difference that convinced her to look at them more seriously. All over Janus, from the Maw to Eddytown to the outskirts of Crabtree itself, normally reliable people were seeing things. Reports of sightings of swift, fleeting entities – machines, it appeared – with a fluid, glassy appearance. They came in fast, sniffed around something – a generator, battery or superconductor junction – and then left, vanishing into the night as quickly as they had come. So far, no active cam had captured more than a few smudges. Were it not for the number of witnesses, and the apparent reliability of their testimonies, Svetlana would have ignored the images. There was, of course, also the matter of the hammer blow. On more than one occasion, the visiting entities had appeared to originate from the same area.

Something *was* happening.

She sent out another party of tractors, six this time, but again they found nothing. Finally she sent out *Star Crusader*, hoping that the lander – with its engine glow, floods and elevated trajectory – might see something that the tractors and the earlier free-flier had missed.

It did.

The ice crater was wide but shallow, easy to miss amidst the ridged and wrinkled landscape. A trail showed where a tractor had passed within metres of its edge. At the base of the crater was a black disc, like a fat coin lying flat on one side. Its edge flung back reflected light, as if it had been polished to a high sheen.

*Crusader* landed. Parry and Naohiro Uguru went out in Orlan nineteen hardsuits. They picked their way over the crater wall, then down to the coin-shaped object. The closer they got to it, the more massive and foreboding it became. It had looked quite small from the lander, but distance and scale were always difficult to judge on Janus. Up close, it seemed impossibly huge. It was ten metres thick, perhaps sixty metres across. As they approached, warped versions of Parry and Naohiro loomed in the reflective edge, wide as monsters.

'This must be what made all that noise,' Parry said.

Uguru touched the mirrored edge with a gloved knuckle, the way firefighters were taught to test wires that might be carrying electricity. 'It's cold,' he said, as the glove's thermal read-out updated on his HUD, 'cold and slippery as ice. What do you think cut this edge so cleanly?'

'Good question, buddy.'

But Parry was already looking up, craning back as far as he could go. He crunched elementary trigonometry. If the disc was sixty metres wide and the Iron Sky twenty kilometres above his head, then he was looking for a hole about a third of the apparent diameter of the full moon seen from Earth . . . if he could remember what a full moon looked like.

But the Iron Sky was black, and there might well be total darkness on the other side of the hole. If the hot blue radiation of the Spica binary was shining through the hole, they would have detected it already: it would have lit up Janus like a welding torch in a dark room.

But unless the sky had healed itself, the hole had to be up there. It was just a question of finding it. They would worry about who had cut it later.

'This is good, isn't it?' Uguru said. 'It means someone's opened the tin. It means someone knows we're here.'

Parry looked at him, recalling a similar conversation with Mike Takahashi, thirteen years and two hundred and sixty light-years ago.

'Could go either way,' he said.

*

It was many years since events had moved so quickly on Janus. There was inertia at first, as if a once-great machine was now so encrusted with oil and filth that it could barely turn a cog. But once the movement began, it had no choice but to continue. Resources were reallocated and committed. Teams were broken up and reassembled in new formations. Crabtree hummed with expectation and rumour. Everywhere Svetlana went, everywhere her spies went, she heard the same thing: something *is* happening. Men, women and children alike were saying it, placing the emphasis on the second word, as if the events themselves needed encouragement, reassurance, to keep happening. The Iron Sky began to feel like a lifting depression. No one wanted the hole in the sky to close up again. It was like the first light of dawn after an appallingly long night.

Svetlana sent tractors out to drag the piece of sky back to Crabtree. She wanted to analyse it, cut it up, recycle it. There was more metal there (if indeed it was metal) than had ever been pilfered from the lava lines. Recovering it, however, turned out to be a more difficult task than she had anticipated: the harness kept slipping off the near-frictionless edges; the tractors couldn't get enough grip to dislodge the disc from the depression it had stamped in the ice when it fell; none of their tools were sharp or strong enough to cut it into more manageable chunks. Svetlana permitted one abortive attempt to haul the disc out of the crater using the lander, then conceded defeat. It would have to stay where it was, for now.

By then, they had established a small hamlet of domes and equipment shacks around the crater. Someone started calling it Underhole, and the name stuck. A superconducting line was reeled out from Crabtree and a smoothly graded tractor route carved into the ice.

Twenty kilometres above Underhole, there was also activity. The hole in the sky had been located: scans had revealed a spot where the near-total absorption efficiency of the sky became perfect, as radiation escaped to the outside world. But it was not completely dark outside. In the optical and near-infrared, the hole glowed slightly more brightly than the surrounding regions. With dark-adapted eyes, and knowing exactly where to look, it could be seen from Underhole as a tiny circle of not-quite-absolute darkness. Its dimensions had been measured and found to match the piece that had dropped to the ground. The sky did not appear to be healing itself.

Reports of alien sightings gradually died down. Nothing had been seen coming or going through the hole since its discovery. Perhaps the alien machines had already seen all that they needed to. After much consideration, Svetlana decided that it was safe to take a look at what was on the other side. Belinda Pagis stripped a spare free-flier to the chassis, then welded on as much high-res survey gear as the power and telemetry bus could run. She utilised the equipment *Rockhopper* would once have trained on comets for the benefit of Nick Thale and the other analysts – deep-penetration radar, terrain-mapping lidar, supercooled photon-counting cams with intrinsic energy-resolution – tools to unravel every secret light or matter could hold. She bolted on massive floodlights and then even more massive fuel tanks and reaction thrusters to handle the swollen payload.

'Okay,' she said, when her new creation was ready, parked like a bright-yellow wasp on a cradle thirty metres from Underhole. 'Let's kick the tyres and light the fires.'

Pagis programmed a vector into the free-flier, fired up the thrusters to haul it off the ground and then watched as it made its way up to the hole. Twenty klicks over Underhole, she took the joystick and slowed the free-flier to a hover. It nosed around the rim of the hole, recording the bright counterpart to the mirrored edge on the piece of sky lying below. Measurement of the diameter established that the hole had been cut through with something astonishingly fine, for there was no measurable difference in size between the hole and the piece that had dropped out of it. Perhaps the cutting tool had simply persuaded the inter-atomic bonds to unzip along a precise line.

Pagis tipped the free-flier on end so that its forward cam pointed out through the hole. Svetlana and Parry crowded around the meagre little array of flexies that was the best they could assemble. Scratches and hexel dropouts blotted the image as the ailing gelware struggled to process the incoming telemetry. There wasn't much to see: just a blank absence stained orange by the false-colour display, like the sodium-light sky over a big city. Graphics boxes framed the image portion, updating with line plots and columns of numbers. Once, they would have meant something to Svetlana, but now all she felt was a faint prickle of recollection. Fluency with mathematics – in the context of any kind of engineering discipline or physical science – was a use-it-or-lose-it skill.

In thirteen years, she had lost it badly. Now all she could do was brazen her way through and hope the likes of Pagis wouldn't spot the mile-wide dropouts in her understanding.

'Radar?' Svetlana asked. 'Seeing anything?'

'Not sure,' Pagis said, chewing on the tip of some strands of hair she had tugged into her mouth. 'Something's bouncing back at me, but I'm not sure if I believe what I'm seeing.'

'Could be backscatter off the edge of the hole,' Parry commented. 'Used to get a lot of—'

'Ain't backscatter,' Pagis said. 'Too far out for that. Too damn faint, as well. Could be a logic ghost, something bouncing around in the overflow buffer . . . don't think so, though.'

'How far out?' Svetlana asked.

'Eighty thousand kilometres – just over a quarter of a light-second.'

Once Svetlana would have laughed at such a small distance. It was nothing compared to the operational sphere of *Rockhopper*, carved up into entire light-hours. But for thirteen years her world had been two hundred kilometres across, and her mind had become accustomed to handling things on that scale. Now it struggled to make the mental adjustment back to the larger universe beyond the Iron Sky.

'We need to see what it is,' Svetlana said. 'Take us through. Maybe we'll have a better view on the other side.'

Pagis looked over her shoulder. 'You sure about this?'

'Take us through.'

Pagis nudged the joystick and powered the free-flier up through the hole. The silver edge reflected back the free-flier's lights, and then suddenly it was out, rising from the hole.

'Hold at one hundred metres,' Svetlana said.

Pagis nodded and brought the machine to a halt again, suspended on a breath of thrust.

'Pan around. Let's take a look at the hole from the outside.'

Other than the glimpse they'd obtained from the upper surface of the fallen disc, this was their first view of the other side of the Iron Sky. At first glance, there was nothing very surprising about it. The outer side was as smooth and dark as the inside surface, at least as far out as the free-flier's floodlights were capable of reaching. It raced away in all directions, black and flat as an oil slick, but with its own dull lustre.

'It's a tiny bit more reflective than the inner surface,' Pagis announced, 'but that's about the only difference. I think I can already see the curvature in the backscatter. We can map it, if you like: there's enough fuel in the free-flier for a couple of loops.'

'We'll lose contact with it once it drops over the horizon, won't we?' Parry said.

'Most likely, but the autopilot should bring it back, provided the inertial compass keeps working.'

'I want to find out where the hell we are first,' Svetlana said. 'Are you still seeing that eighty-thousand-klick echo?'

'Still there,' Pagis confirmed, 'although that's only part of it. Now that we're clear of the hole I'm seeing a spread of return times. There are reflective surfaces a lot further out than eighty thousand klicks – although the bounces are weaker.'

'How far are we talking?'

'Hundreds of thousands of kilometres. Entire light-seconds.'

'Pan the cam around, see if you can pick up anything else now you have a wider field of view.'

'I'm on it,' Pagis said, with a hint of irritation, as if she didn't need to be told these things. Svetlana buttoned her lip – she was obviously trying too hard.

'Hey,' Parry said, 'that looks like . . . something.'

'Yup. Looks like,' Pagis agreed.

Something was creeping into view as the free-flier changed its angle of study. The featureless orange background was still there, but now there was a kind of wavy line showing up along one side, like a glowing human hair trapped in the optics.

'Can you zoom in on that?' Svetlana asked.

'Sorry, no – didn't have time to install a zoom platform.'

Svetlana nodded – she understood the pressure Pagis had been under to put the free-flier together. It was a miracle that they had any pictures at all. 'Can you pull back, broaden the field of view?'

'Also a no-no, but we can raster scan the whole area – build up a picture in stripes and then stitch them together in flexy memory. It'll take a little while, though. And we'll be burning fuel like a bitch.'

'Do it – even if we don't have enough left to make an orbit. We can always do that later. Right now I'd really like to know where we are.'

Lately on Janus, things had a habit of taking longer than anyone expected, even when this trend was taken into account. The simple business of making the raster scan and gluing the elements together to produce a single mosaic ought to have been child's play. But the remaining flexies did not have enough combined memory to handle the image manipulation without some tricky algorithmic sleight of hand, which taxed Pagis's ingenuity to its limits.

Svetlana knew better than to pressure her, and to avoid the temptation to breathe down her neck, she took a tractor back to Crabtree on the new road, enjoying the mindless pleasure of just driving, hypnotised by the endless flow of the superconducting line. Emily was just out of school that afternoon, so she took her daughter out to visit Wang Zhanmin, who (Emily remembered from the last visit) had promised her a rocking horse. Svetlana half-expected him to have forgotten, but he had it ready when they arrived, gleaming with vivid scarlet paint. Learning to make wood – or at least a close analogue of it – had been one of Wang's recent breakthroughs, and he was intensely pleased with himself. In recent months the forge vats had been churning out the parts for wooden furniture, ornaments and toys faster than Crabtree could use them. The lab was bursting with these new creations.

'I made you this,' Emily said, offering Wang a cardboard tube.

Wang popped the end on the tube and slid out a roll of paper. Svetlana looked over his shoulder. It was a painting of fish, swimming through rocks and fronds. The picture had been rendered with a childlike delight in the application of bright, clashing colours, but also a certain adult fastidiousness in the way the colours were never allowed to merge or blot. The sea was a joyous, saturated turquoise and the striped and mottled fish seemed to float an inch or two closer to the viewer, as if they had been etched on a sheet of glass resting on the background.

'Thank you,' Wang said, holding the picture to the light so that the paper shone like stained glass. 'Anything to brighten this place up.' He looked at Svetlana and said, under his breath, 'Thank God for the kids.'

'You hear that a lot these days,' she replied quietly.

'I thought it would make you happy,' Emily said.

'It does.' He looked down at the picture again, stretching it between his hands like a scroll. 'It's lovely. Lovely and a little sad, but in a good way. Do you like your rocking horse?'

'Yes, thank you.'

'I'll make you another one when you're bigger, but this fellow should do you for now.'

'It's very kind of you, Uncle Wang,' Svetlana said.

'I'm glad I can make something,' he said, shrugging.

She smiled quickly and looked away, not wanting to acknowledge the unspoken truth that hung between them. Stools and rocking horses were all very well, but no amount of colourful wangwood knickknacks was ever going to make up for the failing flexies.

Svetlana ate a meal with Emily, and then they spoke to Parry on the link to Underhole. Parry asked Emily what she had been doing in school today, and promised he would see her soon. He put on a brave face, but Svetlana could see something there that he did not want his daughter to pick up on.

When Emily was asleep, Svetlana dosed herself up with black-market coffee, signed out an Orlan and drove back to Underhole, gunning the tractor at fifty kilometres per hour. Everyone was still awake when she cycled through the lock. They had been waiting for her.

'I think we know where we are,' Parry said, an edge of unease clouding his voice.

Pagis had finished stitching together the raster data. She had also begun to get a handle on the data from the deep-penetration radar.

'So tell me,' Svetlana said, as she struggled out of the bulky suit.

'We're inside a tube-shaped structure,' Pagis said, directing Svetlana's attention to the mosaic image spread across the flexy array. 'The walls are dark, but there are filaments in them – wavy glowing tracks, a bit like the lava lines. They're peaking at about five thousand five hundred angstroms, which is why everything looks yellow-orange out there. We haven't seen any transits moving on them, but it does look like a similar technology.'

'If the Spicans have brought us here, then maybe we shouldn't be too surprised by that,' Svetlana said.

'That's what we figured.'

The raster image looked like the view down a drainpipe, with perspective traced by the converging density of the wavy, intertangled lava lines.

'The first echo I got was off the nearside wall,' Pagis said. 'The tube's about one hundred and sixty thousand klicks across, so we're floating pretty near the middle. We're getting optical data about two hundred thousand klicks down the shaft – we'd see further if we had a better cam.'

'And the radar?'

'The radar bounces are coming back from much further down. We're reaching two and half light-seconds into the tube before the echo peters out. It isn't a smooth spectrum of return times – there must be irregularities in the cladding acting as discrete reflecting surfaces.'

'And beyond the last echo?'

'Anyone's guess. One thing we can be pretty sure of, though: the tube reaches further than we can see.'

'And in the other direction?'

'Our view's not as good since Janus is in the way, but there's nothing to suggest we wouldn't see a similar picture.'

Svetlana looked at Parry. 'You said you knew where we are. Are you going to let me in on the secret?'

'It's not a secret. We're exactly where we expected to be after two hundred and sixty light-years. We've achieved slowdown. We're at Spica.'

'And the Spican structure?'

He smiled gently. 'We're in it, babe.'

'I don't—'

'Remember the scale of that thing? We always did have a hard time getting our heads around it. It looked skeletal, but remember what Bella said?'

She bridled at the name. 'What?'

'Just one of those longitudinal spars would have the internal surface area of fifty thousand Earths. A million Earths' worth in the entire structure. Well, I think we're in one of those spars now. Or maybe one of the cross-connectors. The numbers fit. If it's a longitudinal spar, the tube could be three light-minutes long. If we're seeing two and half light-seconds into it, there's still a hell of a lot more tube down here.'

'We have to know for sure,' she said. 'We've been inside one cage for four hundred days. I don't like the idea of punching through and finding another set of walls out there.'

'I agree absolutely,' Parry said vehemently.

'And what kind of fucking welcome committee is this anyway?' Irrational, directionless anger rose in her like bile. 'We've come all this way – been *dragged* all this way – and all that happens is they drill a hole in the sky and then *fuck off.*'

'There's no sign of alien presence out there,' Pagis said timidly. 'We did get a weird transient echo off something for a while, but it didn't show up again.'

Svetlana rubbed tired eyes. She was close to tears, close to some kind of breaking point she did not want any of them to see. 'What kind of echo?'

'Something small, something local.'

'Maybe one of their probes, leaving?' Parry said.

'Don't think so,' Pagis said. 'If the probes showed up on radar, we'd have already seen them. This was a big fat bounce, with a hint of rotation. Then it was gone.'

Parry looked keen. 'So maybe there is something out there.'

'Or was,' Svetlana said.

The opening of the sky had offered them hope. That was why they had all been so keen for it to stay open, for that glint of dawn to hold steady and true. But beyond the Iron Sky was just another kind of Iron Sky: more distant, more enormous, more inhuman, more oppressive.

Svetlana felt crushed. She knew that everyone else was feeling it as well but was desperately trying not to show it, as if by an act of collective denial they could pretend that this was somehow good news.

'Wait,' Svetlana said, pressing fingers to her eyelids. 'I know what it was you saw. It must have been a piece of our junk: the free-fliers that were still in the slipstream when the sky sealed up. They must have been out there all this time.'

'Maybe you're right,' Pagis said glumly. 'I was hoping it might be something more . . . exciting.'

'Maybe this is as good as it's going to get.'

'It's still early days,' Parry said, forcing strained optimism into his voice. 'Someone drilled through the sky, and they must have done it for a reason. Just because we don't see them immediately, it doesn't mean they won't be back.'

'We can go out and look for them,' Pagis said suddenly. 'Fuel up *Crusader* or *Avenger*, see what's really out there. At the very least we need to see deeper into the tube.'

'At least that way we'd be doing something,' Parry agreed, 'instead of just sitting down here, waiting for them to make the next move.'

'What if there is no next move?' Svetlana asked. 'What if they've let us out of one cage into another, and that's *it* – end of story?'

'I can't believe that,' Parry said. 'We were brought here for a reason, not just to be locked away in a pipe for the rest of eternity.'

She looked at him sullenly. 'Maybe that *was* the reason.'

'Even godlike aliens have to act rationally – don't they?'

'I wouldn't know,' she said. 'I can't recall ever meeting any.'

They sat in a brooding silence for half a minute. Svetlana looked at the flexy array again, with its intimations of further mysteries. Parry and Pagis were right, of course: they had waited thirteen years for something to study beyond Janus itself – some key to the deeper purpose behind the deceitful moon. It had brought them here, and it had kept them alive during the flight. Maybe all that had been accidental, and they'd simply hitched a ride in the slipstream of something that neither knew of nor cared about their existence.

But maybe it hadn't.

'All right,' she said, trying to shrug aside her own sense of fatalistic hopelessness. 'We take a look down the tube. We'll send a free-flier first and see what we turn up.'

It wasn't good news.

The probe encountered the end of the tube two light-minutes downstream from Janus. First its radar began to detect bounces from a solid structure blocking the tube; closer, lidar and the optical cam recorded a circular plate one hundred and sixty thousand kilometres across, snugly filling the tube.

By then, the free-flier had consumed most of its fuel and was speeding towards the end wall at its terminal velocity. The final images, transmitted back to Crabtree just before impact, revealed the presence of radial spokes running from the rim to a smaller wheel-shaped structure at the plate's centre, a mere thousand kilometres across. The grainy pictures suggested that the wheel-shaped structure was etched with inwardly curving lines, like the diaphragm in an old camera.

'It's a door,' Svetlana said.

No one saw any reason to argue with her.

But the door was closed. It looked immeasurably ancient and heavy, like something that hadn't moved in a million years. The free-flier dashed itself against the structure like a gnat against a dam. If it left a smear, there was no trace of it when a second free-flier sent back another set of images.

A third free-flier had also been dispatched in the opposite direction. One light-minute up the tube, it encountered a blank endcap with no trace of any doorlike mechanisms.

It died as well.

Svetlana had deemed that a trio of free-fliers could be sacrificed in the interests of speedy data acquisition, but that was as many machines as Crabtree could afford to lose. Further investigations would need to be made using recoverable craft, slowly, with the minimal expenditure of fuel and logistics. At least now they knew that the tube was finite, and that there was nothing immediately threatening inside it. That, she supposed, could be construed as a kind of good news. But it was also bad, since there was still no sign of an alien welcoming committee. And the door and endcap both had the brutal look of something impenetrably thick, so thick that even their demolition nukes would be lucky to leave a scratch on them. They had established the parameters of their new prison and the situation was not encouraging.

That left the other piece of news.

They had found something tumbling end-over-end in orbit around Janus. It was the object Pagis had already picked up on the free-flier radar, but Svetlana's original guess had been wrong. It was not one of the old free-fliers that had been monitoring the slipstream when the Iron Sky had appeared. Of those, there was no longer any trace. This was something else, and it was not remotely what anyone had been expecting.

In a way it was good news, because it was a concrete sign that their arrival had been noticed and – unlike the opening of the sky – it appeared to be a message addressed specifically to them.

The bad news was that it was odd, unsettling and devoid of useful content, and ever so slightly threatening.

It was a solid cube *exactly* two metres along each side, and very black, although not so black that it hadn't thrown back a radar bounce. A manipulator-equipped free-flier was able to approach the object, touch it and stabilise its tumble. It massed *precisely* two hundred metric tonnes, but appeared otherwise quite inert and unresponsive. Svetlana weighed the risks and decided to permit the object to be brought back to Underhole for further study. A dome was thrown around the cube, initially unpressurized. Once a battery of tests had established that the cube probably wouldn't be harmed by the presence of air – it appeared to be chemically inert – the dome was flooded with a normal atmospheric trimix. Denise Nadis, Josef Protsenko and Christine Ofria-Gomberg were running tests on the cube when Svetlana came to visit them a day after the dome had been pressurised.

In the harsh floods rigged around it, the cube was dismayingly black. Its surface albedo was exactly 0.999999, to the limits of measurement. As it rotated on the electric turntable installed under it, the cube became a chunk of abstract form, almost appearing to ooze from one shape to another as it turned from face to face. It was surrounded by monitoring devices mounted on spindly tripods, trailing tangles of optical data cables and thick, frayed, heavy-duty power lines.

The cube was smooth on all but one of its six faces. X-ray and acoustic probing revealed no hints of interior structure. Surface analysis, using atomic-force microscopes, drew blank on the matter of the object's composition. For an artefact that had presumably spent some time in space, even in the hermetic environment inside the tube, it was astonishingly free of imperfections. The cube's edges were still absurdly sharp.

Must be self-renewing, the science team informed Svetlana: stuffed full of sleek alien nanotech, correcting any fault or imperfection before it had a chance to register. No chemical analysis was possible because the surface was itself in a state of constant overhaul and flux. If they had better tools, they said ruefully, they might have been able to glimpse these processes in action.

Except – as they all knew – the nanotech might not be alien at all. The cube's dimensions and mass suggested prior knowledge of human measurement systems.

But that was not all.

The sixth face contained an engraving.

It was turning towards her now. By some trick of surface effects, the finger-thick lines of the engraving had a higher albedo than the surrounding face. It was da Vinci's drawing of a man standing in a box, one of the most familiar and iconic diagrams imaginable. It had been stylised, reduced to the essentials, but it was still recognisable. It seemed unlikely that any alien mind had created this cube.

The technical team wore masks, gloves and surgical scrubs, but that was just a token precaution: nothing they'd measured had suggested that the cube was in any way harmful. It just sat there, revolving slowly on the turntable, presenting five blank faces and then the da Vinci design.

'You can touch it if you like,' Denise Nadis said, handing her a pair of recyclable surgical gloves inlaid with a matrix of haptic sensors. 'We've all done it. It's almost like a ritual. You don't really believe it's *there* until you've pressed a hand against it.'

Svetlana snapped on one of the gloves. 'What would happen if I touched it with my bare skin?'

'You'd leave a nasty set of fingerprints – one of us already tried.'

'They faded with time,' Christine Ofria-Gomberg said. 'No harm was done. I just had to know what that material felt like under my skin.'

'The haptics weren't good enough?'

'I had to know. What if there was a difference that the gloves weren't picking up?'

'And was there?' Protsenko asked.

'No,' she said, sullenly. 'It felt exactly the same.'

Svetlana's fingertips registered the tingle as the haptics engaged their microscopic contact cilia against her skin. She brushed her hand over the rough texture of her trousers and felt the bias of the fabric as if the gloves were not there at all.

She moved to the cube and touched one of the slowly turning blank faces. It was cold, solid, mute. It felt old: shockingly so, as if it had been waiting an eternity for this instant of human contact. Her fingers skirted the sharp edge as the next face revolved into view. She wondered – as they were surely all wondering – who had put this thing into orbit around Janus. What was its message? What were they meant to make of it?

The next face hove into view. She had only put on one of the gloves. She glanced back and saw that Nadis, Protsenko and Ofria-Gomberg were preoccupied with a flexy read-out. They were all looking down, not at her. Shielding her movements with her body, she reached out to touch the engraved face with her bare hand.

'Svetlana,' Nadis called, 'I think you need to see this.'

She turned from the cube, snapping off the haptic glove before anyone noticed she had only been wearing the one.

'Denise?' she asked innocently. 'What is it?'

'It's the door,' she said. 'It's closing.'

She realised that she meant the door at the end of the shaft, two light-minutes down the tube. 'I didn't even know it was open.'

'Nor did we,' Nadis said. 'It must have happened after we lost the second free-flier, before we got the hovering cam into place.'

'I don't like it,' she said.

'Then you're going to like this even less: something came through.'

# CHAPTER 19

Underhole was a smear of ruby light twenty kilometres under their feet. With the helmet binocs cranked up to full zoom, Svetlana could just make out the figures, tractors and temporary support domes of the little outpost. They were really no safer down there, not if one took the long view, but in that moment she would have given everything not to be up here, standing on the wrong side of the Iron Sky.

She wondered how her partner felt. It was Schrope who would be taking the long stroll into the alien ship, not her. *Let me be your envoy*, he had said. He'd shown no sign of it, but she wondered if he was regretting those words now.

Parry's voice buzzed in her helmet. 'Talk to us, boys and girls. We get nervous when we don't hear anything.'

'We're still here,' Svetlana said.

'No ill effects?'

She looked at Schrope, who shook his head briefly. 'We're both doing okay. It's no different up here than down here.' She risked a glance up towards the distant structure of the new sky: the inside of the huge shaft in which Janus had come to rest. 'Just a lot more . . . exposed. I don't think any of us realised how claustrophobic it was getting down there.'

'Ryan says you're both looking good. If you could breathe a bit slower, that would be great.'

'Just getting over the flexwalk,' Svetlana said. 'Seriously out of practice here.'

'We'll forgive you. Could you do us a favour and pan around?'

She unclipped the cam from the side of her helmet and offered Parry a three-sixty sweep, without dwelling on the Spican ship. Part of her still hoped it would go away, like a psychotic aberration they could all just agree never to mention again.

'How's that?'

'We're dropping packets now and then, but other than that the images look pretty good.'

'Maybe we should have brought that booster up with us after all.'

'Nah. Not a good idea to have anything up there that they might not recognise as being one of us or belonging to us.'

Svetlana nodded – they had been over that, of course, and she saw the logic in keeping the contact situation as clean as possible. But just having a relay box by the lip would have made her feel one degree less disconnected from the people below.

Almost as soon as the ship had landed, it had extended what could only be interpreted as a boarding ramp. They had hoped to send robots into the ship before they sent a human volunteer, but every time they sent a free-flier or a legged robot anywhere near the alien ship, it pulled up the drawbridge.

They were as close now as any of the machines had reached and the ramp was still down. Presumably the ship recognised that they were armoured organisms, not robot envoys.

'Craig,' Parry said, 'we're getting some fuzz from your cam. Could you give it a clout, see if that clears things?'

'Just a sec.' Svetlana watched Schrope knuckle the side of his orange-painted helmet. Sometimes a well-delivered jolt could separate bonded layers in the gelware of the Belousov-Zhabotinsky sandwich, allowing reaction fronts to propagate more freely. Wang had achieved great things, but the BZ tech was still too subtle for his forge vats.

'Any better?' Schrope asked.

'We'll manage. Audio is good, at least. You still cool about going through with this, Craig?'

'Well, cool isn't *quite* the word I'd have chosen.'

'It's not too late to back out,' Svetlana said.

She caught his sceptical look through the faceplate. 'One of us has to do this, Svetlana. It might as well be me.'

'You don't owe us anything,' she said.

'No,' he said, almost too quietly to be picked up by his helmet com, 'but I do owe myself something.'

Svetlana nodded once, briskly. 'We're about to start walking,' she told Parry. 'Ship looks about a klick away, give or take, should be there in under twenty minutes.'

'Let's take things nice and slow,' Parry said. 'Every twenty paces I want you to stop and hold your cams on the ship. We'll review the situation before proceeding closer. Any changes we don't like the look of, we scrub. Clear on that?'

'Clear.'

'No arguments, no heroics,' Parry said firmly.

'No problem,' Svetlana answered. 'This is a heroics-free zone.'

They started walking. After twenty geckoflex paces they halted and allowed Parry and the contact team time to get a good look at the squatting ship.

It sat on the outer surface of the Iron Sky like a chandelier that had fallen from a ceiling and somehow avoided shattering. It rested on a dozen or more curved arms that angled down to make contact with the ground before rising again to form tapered, nearly horizontal tips. The boarding arm differed from the others by resting flat on the ground all the way to its extremity, which pointed directly at the hole. The arm was flat in profile, except for two wall-like flanges running along its entire length. Svetlana might have had her doubts before, but from this perspective it looked more like a ramp than ever: a clear invitation to step inside.

The boarding arm led into a bulbous, onion-shaped core that consisted of many concentric layers of glassy material. Long chains of Spican symbols floated on the outer layer, as if drawn in neon. Darker structures were dimly visible within, faint as the suggestions of organs in glassfish. Dozens of much thinner arms emerged from the central structure without contacting the ground. Some of them bulged into node-like structures that might have been sensors, or engines, or living quarters, or weapons. Soft light gleamed from the curves and joints, partly refracted from the ambient light of the chamber, but partly emanating from the ship itself.

It was very, very large. The central core alone could have swallowed Crabtree from ground to hab.

They stopped, advanced, stopped again.

'No visible change,' Parry said, 'but they haven't pulled up the drawbridge either.'

'Any word on those symbols yet?' Svetlana asked.

'Jake and Christine are still working on the correlations. You'll hear the moment they come up with something.'

'But don't hold my breath.'

'You've got the idea.'

Svetlana managed a gallows laugh. 'Maybe we should bring in the Symbolists, see what they have to say.'

'We're not that desperate,' Parry bounced back.

They walked, stopped, walked again. After ten or twelve minutes, Svetlana judged that they had crossed half the distance to the squatting ship. She glanced back and the hole in the sky looked foreshortened, difficult to make out against the dark pewter-grey of the surrounding undamaged surface. She wondered why the Spicans had been forced to cut the hole, rather than ordering the smart matter of the Iron Sky to open up like a door. So many questions. So few answers.

A few more stops and starts and the ship loomed much larger, beginning to tower over them, its glassy intricacy all the more striking the closer they came. Rather than surrendering its secrets as they neared, the ship only became more bewilderingly complicated to look at.

'Ease up, airhogs,' Parry said.

Svetlana nodded, realising that she had been breathing too heavily again. The slow death march across the other side of the sky was getting to her. 'Coms still okay?' she asked, just to be saying something.

'Thready, but we can live with it. How are you feeling?'

'As if I'm about to feed the fishes, but otherwise . . . I'm holding it together, more or less.'

'How's Craig doing?'

Schrope cut in. 'Verging on the apprehensive, but I'm holding it together as well.'

'That's good. Must be a hell of a view out there – I mean, with just a centimetre of helmet glass between you and *it*.'

'You're right,' Schrope said, and suddenly there was a tone in his voice that lifted the hairs on the back of Svetlana's neck. 'We shouldn't forget how privileged we are. This is . . . *it*. What we've been waiting for all these years. Not just for the thirteen years we've been stuck on Janus, but all the thousands of years that have passed, the tens of thousands of years, even, ever since one of us looked up into the sky – into all that darkness – and wondered *what* was out there. Not *if* there was anything there, but what. We've always known they were out here somewhere, and that it was only a matter of time before we met. Well, this is that time. It's here and now, and out of all the billions of people who have ever lived, it's happening to us.'

'Amen to that, buddy,' Parry said slowly, 'but let's not lose focus on the fact that this is just another job. It's no more or less dangerous than planting a mass driver, or firing up a cold tokamak.'

After another ten minutes they had arrived within twenty metres of the tip of the boarding ramp. They panned cams around and waited for word from below.

'Are we still go?' Svetlana asked.

A crackle, then Parry's voice. 'If Craig is still happy, we see no reason not to proceed.'

'I'm ready,' Schrope said.

'Ash says you're good to go on suit systems. Your call, buddy.'

'I'll start the walk. Suggest Svetlana retreats to a midpoint between here and the hole. Shouldn't make much difference to coms.'

'I'm staying right here at the foot of the ramp,' Svetlana said.

'I appreciate the offer,' Schrope said, 'but at the slightest sign of anything happening, I want you to clear out. Remember what Parry said: no heroics.'

She nodded. 'How long are you planning on staying inside?'

'I'm zeroing my suit timer and setting the clock for thirty minutes. When the alarm pings, I'll finish my drink and ask for my coat.'

Svetlana set her own timer for the same duration. 'Sounds good. If you're not out after thirty minutes—'

'You forget about me. Do you honestly think there'd be any point sending in the cavalry?'

'Not really,' she said, on a falling note. 'Good luck, Craig. I know you and I haven't always seen eye to eye—'

'Forget about it. That's a lot of water under a lot of bridges.' Schrope reached out and took one of her gloved hands. 'Pushing ice, right?'

She closed her hand around his. 'Pushing ice. All the way home.'

Schrope let go and turned to walk the remaining distance to the end of the ramp. Svetlana stood her ground, training her cam on his flexwalking form. At the base of the ramp, he paused and looked back, and then placed one foot onto the nearly horizontal surface.

'Keep talking, Craig,' Svetlana said.

'Traction is good. Bond seems to be about normal. No trouble removing or repositioning. I'm about to place my other foot on the ramp.'

'Easy does it.'

'It's done. I'm still standing. I'm on the ship.'

'Describe the stuff you're standing on,' Parry said.

'It's like glass, tinted a kind of purple-grey. I can just see the ground through it. Feels solid under me: there's no give, no resilience, no vibration.' He unclipped the cam and waved it across the floor. 'Getting this?'

'Check your focus, buddy.'

Schrope knocked the cam against his kneepad. 'Better?'

'Better. Hold it there for a second. Good. Now pan left, then right.' Svetlana heard Parry break off to discuss something with one of the other watchers. 'Okay, you can stow the cam again.'

Schrope fiddled the cam back onto its mounting. 'I think I'm ready to take another step.'

'In your own time,' Parry said.

Svetlana watched him walk another pace along the ramp. 'Still looking good here,' Schrope said. 'I'm going to continue: I don't want that alarm going off before I'm inside.'

'Steady as she goes,' Parry said. 'We're not in a race here.'

Schrope continued: five paces, then ten, then twenty. By now the ramp under him had begun to curve upwards, away from the floor. 'Traction's still good,' he said.

'Take it nice and slowly all the way to the top,' Parry said.

Schrope stopped after another dozen or so paces. Svetlana heard his breathing: it was harsher and faster than she would have liked, but that was entirely understandable given the circumstances.

'I'm finding it difficult to judge my angle to the floor,' he said. 'Horizon line looks tilted. I think there might be a field effect here, like at Eddytown.'

'Copy,' Svetlana said. 'It looks to me as if you're tilting backwards: I can see more of your helmet crown than I ought to be able to.'

'I don't feel it.'

'You wouldn't. We already know the Spicans have complete control of gravity on local scales. Be odd if they didn't make the ramp easy to climb.'

'I'm continuing.'

She watched him complete his ascent to the top of the ramp, until his suit was just a smudge of orange against the smoked-glass intricacy of the ship's central core. He was leaning at about twenty degrees to Svetlana's local vertical. She saw the tiny movement of his arm as he unclipped the cam again and panned it around, taking in the ship and the wider view. A window on her HUD showed the same feed. Transmission was good most of the time, but now and then packet loss would shatter the image into blocks of static hexels.

'Show us the door,' Parry said.

Schrope angled the cam around to take in the large aperture where the ramp terminated. 'I'm not sure how much sense you're making of the pictures,' he said, 'so I'll try to talk you through it. The ramp levels out here and feeds into the ship for about ten metres, passing through a corridor – at least, that's what I'm going to call it. There's a floor, two walls and a ceiling. Everything's slightly curved. No single source of illumination, although the whole thing seems to be glowing gently. Can't see much detail in the walls. Again, they're translucent, and there's a hint of more stuff behind them, but even with my naked eye, that's the best I can do.'

'What's at the end of the ramp?' Parry asked.

'I can't tell. It bends down into the ship at a pretty steep angle. I guess I'll have to go inside to take a look.'

'Take it nice and slowly to the end of the flat section,' Parry said. 'Keep filming all the time.'

Svetlana's HUD view lurched forward with Schrope's every pace. The glass threw back dull, blurred reflections, as if from a scuffed mirror. Schrope reached up and turned down his helmet light, relying on the ambient illumination.

'You still reading me?'

'We're getting it all,' she said. 'Packets are a bit erratic, but we should be good for a little while. Could be the ship's blocking some of the signal.'

'I've reached the end of the flat section. Looking down now and . . . okay.'

The picture dropped away, then reassembled hexel by hexel. Schrope had the cam pointed down into the next sloping section of the corridor. Without him in the view, there was no obvious way to tell up from down. It looked as if the corridor curved down and then swung left around a sharp hairpin.

'We're still reading you,' Parry said.

'I'm stepping onto the sloping section. One foot at the time . . . testing for traction.' He paused, his breath grating in Svetlana's ears. 'Feels secure. About to place second foot.' Another pause. 'I'm transitioning to a new local vertical.

Standing up again.' He gave a small chuckle. 'Christ, this feels *weird.*'

'You're doing a fantastic job,' Svetlana said, trying to sound reassuring. 'We're right behind you, Craig.'

'I'm going further inside. Pretty straightforward so far.'

'Coming up on ten minutes on the clock,' Svetlana said. 'You've got twenty left.'

'Copy. Sounds like more than enough.'

'Keep up the voiceover,' Parry said. 'We're still getting pictures, but the quality's beginning to deteriorate significantly. We should be good on voice for a while yet.'

'I've descended – guessing here – five or six metres from the flat section. Floor's curving back to the horizontal again. Looking at a left-hand bend ahead of me.'

'Any change in texture, illumination?' Svetlana asked.

'Nothing obvious. Maybe a little bit more glow . . . could be my imagination, though.'

Another voice cut in on the com. 'Craig, this is Ash Murray.'

'Go ahead, Ash.'

'I'm seeing some drift in your trimix.'

'Anything to worry about?'

'No, just the usual regulator problem with the softs. Up $O_2$ by two per cent, please.'

Through the HUD window, Svetlana saw Craig's thick-fingered hand tap the revised air mix into his suit sleeve. It was years since he had worn a suit, but he did it with a creditable lack of fuss.

'Copy. Feels better already, Ash.'

'Okay, but keep an eye on those trimix levels and self-regulate accordingly. You should see a small histogram in your lower-right faceplate HUD. Don't let the red line drop under the white marker.'

'The day we get back,' Svetlana said caustically, 'I'm putting in a letter of complaint to the dickhead who designed these suits.'

'The dickhead who designed these suits died about two hundred years ago,' Ash Murray said, 'but I take your point.'

'I'm approaching the corner,' Schrope said. 'Angling the cam around the bend . . . let's see.'

'Craig?'

'Still here.' But his voice had a fractured quality to it. The visual feed had become a series of static images, updating every two or three seconds. 'I'm moving along another straight section of corridor. Traction still good. Hard to tell, but—'

'Keep talking,' Svetlana said.

'Things widen up ahead. There's some kind of spherical opening. I'm going to call it a room.'

The visual link improved momentarily, permitting Svetlana a glimpse of the end of the corridor, feeding into a wider space bathed in the same sourceless spectral light. Then the image crashed back to static frames.

'Keep an eye on those trimix levels,' Ash Murray said.

'Roger that. Everything feels okay in here. Wish I'd taken a leak before we left Underhole.'

'Ash didn't plumb you in?' Svetlana asked.

'Told him not to. I'm not planning on spending the rest of my week in this thing.'

'Visuals are getting scrappy down here,' Parry said. 'Keep up that commentary, buddy.'

'I've reached the opening into the room. The corridor comes out into the side of the spherical chamber. There's no level floor, just one continuous curved surface.' He jogged the cam around. 'No sign of any other way out, either – although it's tricky to tell with all this glass-on-glass.'

'You mean it's a dead end?' Parry asked.

'Looks that way. I'm going to take a closer look inside, provided I can still grip.' He grunted as he lowered himself over the edge, legs dangling into the spherical space. 'Glove traction feels okay. Should be able to climb out if I have to.'

'Keep the cam steady for several seconds at a time,' Parry said quietly. 'We're down to still frames here.'

'I'm lowering myself. Hold on a sec.' There was a grunt and a wheeze as he completed the movement. 'Okay. I'm down and standing. The floor material is the same stuff we've seen all the way in. No problem with grip. I'm going to give you a panoramic view of the chamber now.' Making an obvious effort to hold the cam as steadily as he could, Schrope pointed it in six different directions before holding it at arm's length, aimed at his own faceplate. He managed a nervous grin. 'Hope this one makes the cover of *Newsweek*,' he said.

'Craig,' Parry said, 'do me a favour and pan back to the entrance hole.'

'Like this?' The HUD box greyed into motion blur, then stabilised. 'Oh, wait.'

Svetlana saw it, too. Unless there was some strange trick of the light caused by the chamber's optics, the hole in the wall had narrowed – it was, in fact, narrowing even further as they watched.

'Okay, we have a situation here,' Parry said, with a calmness that was just a bit too insistent to be convincing. 'Craig, I want you to keep cool and get out of there. You still have time.'

Schrope said nothing. He clipped the cam back onto his suit and headed quickly back the way he had come in. The cam picked up his hands reaching ahead, palming down against the wall for geckoflex traction.

'No good,' Svetlana said, under her breath. 'Hole's already too small for him to squeeze through.'

Schrope had seen it as well. He pushed back, his hands shaking. 'Too narrow,' he said. The cam lingered on the closing entrance as the glass sphinctered down to a gap smaller than fifty centimetres across and kept on closing. 'There's no way I can get through.'

'Stay where you are,' Svetlana said, not caring how much it sounded like an order. 'This is . . . not necessarily a problem.'

'It's a problem to me.'

Now the refresh rate was even slower, with more and more of the image being filled in by software guesswork based on the previous frames.

'You must be in an airlock,' she said. 'We should've expected something like this. It's good – it means they want to meet us.'

'There's no way out now,' Schrope said. His voice had gone metallic, stripped of harmonics. The imagery had stalled on the last full frame, refusing to update. The bit rate was barely enough to carry audio now.

'Craig,' Svetlana said, 'if you can hear this – stay calm.'

'Losing suit packets,' Ash Murray said.

'No visuals at our end,' Parry reported.

'Craig,' Svetlana said, 'talk to me. Tell me what's happening.'

His voice came through in short, breathless shards. 'I think the chamber's pressurising. Pressure's counteracting my suit inflation. Gas is . . . colourless. Maybe it's my imagination, but—'

'Talk to me.'

'Getting heavier in here. Suit's weighing me down. Can't stand up much longer.' She heard another grunt and wheeze of effort. 'Kneeling down. Still getting heavier.' He broke off and sucked in a deep, laboured breath. 'Breathing's getting tricky.'

Parry cut in. 'Craig, it looks like you're in a lock for gravity as well as atmosphere.'

'I figured.'

'You need to lie as flat as possible, to ease the blood supply to your head.'

'I'm trying. Can't get flat . . . fucking backpack's in the way.'

'Oh, no,' Svetlana said, remembering all the arguments they had gone over as to whether he should use a soft- or hardsuit. The softsuit had been considered less threatening, more obviously anthropomorphic, but the hardsuit would have allowed him to lean back much more easily, and it would have maintained normal suit pressure no matter what the external conditions.

Bad call. Bad, bad call.

'Still getting heavier. Pressure's pushed my suit all the way in. Seeing a lot of red lights on the chin board.'

'Just . . . hold on in there,' Parry said. 'Sooner or later—'

But Svetlana heard the hopelessness in his voice. It was already too heavy in there for someone burdened with a suit. If the gravity and pressure increased much more, Schrope would soon slip into unconsciousness as the blood left his brain. Shortly afterwards his heart would stop.

'Wait—' she heard, suddenly. 'Something happening. Glass is clearing . . . I can see through. I can see the other side.' He made a wretched gurgling sound, every breath a universe of pain. 'It's them. They're here. Oh, God. They're *here*. They're outside. They're coming nearer.' A fevered urgency entered his voice. 'I gotta get the cam. *Gotta get the cam.*'

'Craig, never mind the damned cam,' Svetlana snapped.

'You need to see this. You need to see this. You need to see this.'

'He's losing it,' Ash Murray whispered.

'Keep that shit together, Craig,' Parry said.

'I can see them,' he said. 'They're . . . *funny*. Big. Bigger than I expected. They're like—' Audio broke up into static, reassembled in some scratchy, parodic approximation of human speech. 'Mountains.'

Then there was silence.

'We screwed up with the suit,' Svetlana said, over and over again. 'We screwed up with the suit.'

Murray helped her out of her own gear. 'Don't cut yourself up about it. For all we know it hit a hundred atmospheres in there.'

'Speculation, Ash.'

'It was getting worse all the way until the end. Irrelevant, anyway: the grav would have got him no matter what kind of suit he was wearing.'

'We shouldn't have let him into that chamber without securing the entrance point.'

Parry grabbed her roughly by the elbow. 'Secure it with what, Svieta?' he said angrily, frustrated by his inability to comfort her. 'Do you honestly think anything we could have put there would have made a damned bit of difference once that door decided to close?'

'Maybe it wouldn't have closed on him. Maybe it would have detected the obstruction and—'

'Too many maybes.' He took her chin and gently steered her face to look at him, eye to eye. 'Craig knew this was going to be a tough one. He went in there knowing the risks, knowing this was his one shot at redeeming himself. Well, he got what he wanted. And he got what *we* needed: hard data on the inside of that thing we'd never have had otherwise. We owe him thanks. He came back and did something for us.'

'He saw them,' she said.

Ryan Axford, who was sitting down at the Underhole meeting table with a bulb of water before him, shook his head with tight-lipped regret. 'I don't think he saw all that much, Svieta.'

'I'm sorry?'

'We already know he was having problems with trimix control. Coupled with the respiratory and circulatory stresses he'd have been experiencing . . .' He rotated the bulb between his birdlike surgeon's fingers. 'Hallucinatory imagery wouldn't have been unexpected.'

'No,' Svetlana said sharply. 'He saw something. He was clear about that. Beyond the glass, he said. Coming closer.'

'I really wish I could believe that, Svieta,' Axford said kindly, 'but all he saw was his brain being starved of blood.'

'He saw mountains, Ryan. Since when do *mountains* have anything to do with seeing Jesus at the end of the tunnel?'

Axford looked at her placidly. 'Since when do mountains have anything to do with aliens?'

'Craig saw *something*,' she insisted. 'He saw something and sent us a message. He saw *them*. And he wasn't frightened. He sounded more . . . mesmerised.'

'Or intoxicated.' Axford shook his head again. 'I'm sorry. I'm not trying to take anything away from what he did for us – it was a brave thing to go inside. But unless we recover that suit, we'll never know what he really saw.'

Suddenly deflated, unable to stand up even in the weak gravity of Underhole, Svetlana sank into the seat opposite Axford. 'He was trying to get a cam onto it.'

'Hallucination doesn't preclude a rational response to that same hallucination.'

Parry eased into the seat next to Svetlana and held her hand, massaging her fingers. They were always stiff after an EVA. 'Ryan's got a point,' he said softly. 'We both heard that little sermon Craig made before he went up the ramp. He was already on the edge before things turned bad.'

'He saw something,' she said, but now it sounded mechanical, her own defiance thin and unconvincing. Denise Nadis pushed a drink and a foil-wrapped lunch in front of her, but Svetlana shook her head. There was an acrid taste in her mouth and she had no appetite, no thirst.

'We need to consider our next response,' Parry said, when the silence between them had grown uncomfortable. 'If we took a hardsuit, beefed up the coms—'

'Gravity would still get you,' Murray said, examining Svetlana's helmet with a jeweller's squinting attentiveness.

'Not if we pumped out the air and replaced it with an oxygenated solution—'

Svetlana banged her unopened drinking bulb against the table. 'Stop treating this like a fucking engineering problem, all right? A man just died in there. No one else is going back inside.'

'We can't just leave him there,' Parry said, incredulous.

'That's exactly what we're going to do. I don't give a fuck about any macho code of conduct horseshit.' She closed her eyes, lowered her voice to something like a normal speaking tone. 'I'm not adding to the death toll just to retrieve a corpse.'

'We need his suit, Svieta,' Parry said gently. 'His cam was logging to memory the whole while. If he did see anything – and you seem to think he did – it'll be stored in the suit. Get that back and we'll have our slideshow.'

'We have no reason to believe his suit is still where he died. That ship's much bigger than the tiny part Craig saw. They could have taken him anywhere inside it by now.'

Now it was Nadis's turn to speak. 'But to do nothing . . . they *killed* one of us, Svieta.'

'We screwed up,' she said. 'Maybe they screwed up as well. Maybe they didn't realise we were so fucking *easy* to kill.'

'That still doesn't mean we have to let them get away with it.'

'So what are you proposing? That we smack them with an FAD, just to make a point?'

'We have to do something. We can't just sit here in a state of stalemate, like it never happened.'

'It took us thirteen years to reach this point,' Svetlana said, fighting to hold down her fury. 'Do you honestly think a few days are going to make any difference?'

'They're getting restless in Crabtree. They want a response.'

'I'll give them a fucking response. How does martial law sound?' She grimaced, livid with herself. But it was out there now. She had said it.

'You sound like Bella sometimes,' Nadis said, turning away.

On her way back down to the surface of Janus, Svetlana had glued a webcam to the edge of the hole with a dab of geckoflex, using her HUD window to point the cam at the alien ship. They had been concerned before not to invade the aliens' space with anything that might have been construed as intrusive or threatening technology. Now, given what had happened to Schrope, such considerations seemed less important.

For several hours nothing had happened. Then the software detected changes above its noise threshold and sent a flag to Svetlana's flexy. She enlarged the cam window so that they could all crowd around and examine it. The symbols on the ship, fixed until now, were undergoing rapid cycles of change.

'It wasn't doing this before,' Svetlana said. The Ofria-Gombergs still had not come up with any correlations against their database of Janus symbol patterns, but the one thing they had confirmed was that the ship's symbols had been static ever since its arrival.

Not now.

'It's as if it's agitated,' Denise Nadis said, 'as if it's upset about what just happened. As if the Spicans know they did something wrong, and they want us to know how sorry they are.'

'Or they're angry,' Parry said. 'Pissed off at us for sending Craig inside in the first place.'

'Either way, it's a reaction,' Svetlana said. 'That's more than we've had so far.'

'You can't consider this progress,' Parry said.

'I'm clutching at any straws I can find. At least now we know they noticed what just happened. At least we know it's provoked some kind of reaction.'

'I was hoping we'd get through this without using the word "provoked",' Parry said.

Nobody said anything after that. They just looked at the cam window, hypnotised by the storm of alien language, daring to dream that it indicated remorse rather than rage.

Parry leaned against the doorframe. 'How're you feeling, babe?'

'Not quite as bad as I look. Have you spoken to Emily?' Svetlana had been too tired, too frayed at the edges, to call their daughter before her excursion to the alien ship. She had been afraid Emily would pick up on some of that.

'She's fine,' Parry said.

'No one's told her about what's going on here, I hope.'

'I think some of it filtered through, but not enough to worry her. It's all just big adult stuff going on over her head. Great being a kid, isn't it? Here we are screwing up first contact and she's worried about the doll Wang promised her.'

'We were all like that once. I wonder what happened to us?'

'You should get some more sleep.' Parry's own face was puffy with strain and fatigue. 'There's nothing happening here we can't deal with without you.'

'That does great things for my pride.' Wide awake now, she picked at a loose eyelash gummed to her eye. 'Sorry. I know you're trying to help. Did anything happen while I was out?'

'Nothing worth mentioning. No sign of any activity from the ship. Shall I fix you some breakfast, or are you going to try to catch a few more winks?'

'So what happened that isn't worth mentioning?' After so many years together, Svetlana was familiar with all Parry's various distraction techniques.

'You won't like it,' Parry said warily.

'I never like it. What happened?'

'We heard from Bella. Word got out to her somehow.'

Svetlana growled her annoyance. 'She wasn't supposed to know about any of this.'

'Crabtree already has the full story. It was only a matter of time before Bella got wind of it.'

'What did she want, anyway? To rub our noses in the mess we just created?'

'That's not the impression I got.'

'There you go, always ready to jump in and defend her,' Svetlana said with a spitefulness she knew Parry did not deserve.

'I take it that's a "no" on the breakfast front?'

Svetlana pulled herself out of bed. She was still wearing the clothes she had gone to sleep in, now as wrinkled and musty as week-old laundry.

'Give me a break, Parry. I'm doing my best here. And you do have a habit of defending her.'

'Maybe because she's not always wrong.' It was said too placidly to have been intended as a goad. Svetlana gave him a poisonous look as she pushed her hair into shape, making the best of the sleep-matted mess. 'Bella heard about Craig,' Parry went on, immune to the look. 'She wanted to talk to you about your next move.'

'Like I need her advice now.'

'She says it's very important that you talk to her.'

She pulled a fresh T-shirt from her overnight bag, one of her old ones, not one of the new garments from the forge vats. It was red with a masked mermaid and the words *'Dive Chick'* in faded silver glitter. Animated fish that had once swum around the mermaid no longer did anything.

'She would say that.'

'She also said it concerns Jim Chisholm.'

Svetlana paused with the T-shirt half-on. 'Say again?'

# CHAPTER 20

Parry crossed the open ground from the lander and waited politely for Bella to let him inside. In the hardsuit, it would have been impossible for her to tell whether it was Parry or Svetlana waiting in her airlock, but when the inner door opened he saw no surprise on her face.

'Sit down,' she said, taking the helmet from his hands and racking it. 'I know you were hoping to speak to Svetlana.'

'Hoping. Not expecting. There's a world of difference.'

She had brewed him tea from her rations. He sipped at it from a vat-forged china cup with a hinged lid designed to keep the tea from wandering. Wang had printed it with the willow pattern, drawn from memory but with great accuracy and delicacy of line. The tea was weak, the colour of muddy rain-water, just the way he liked it. He wondered if Bella had remembered that from his last visit. 'You're looking well,' he ventured.

'For a sixty-eight-year-old woman, you mean.'

'Not every compliment has to be swatted down.' He peered at her over the rim of his cup. 'Not that Svieta's any better at accepting them.'

'Would it have killed her to come in person?'

Perhaps she caught his glance towards the window. Svetlana had forbidden him to mention that she was aboard *Crusader*. 'It's not been easy for her lately,' he said. 'Since Bob Ungless died . . . since the Iron Sky went up . . . since *this*. How much did you hear about what happened to Craig?'

'Enough.'

'She blames herself for ever letting him inside that thing.'

'Did she point a gun at his head and frogmarch him to the door?'

'Of course not.'

'Then she doesn't need to feel like a martyr.' Bella shrugged. 'Unless she gets a kick out of it.'

'Craig died badly. We were listening in. We heard everything.'

'I heard he saw mountains.'

Parry nodded, amazed at how much information had seeped out to Bella.

'He says he saw the Spicans. Axford isn't so sure – he thinks it was just Craig's neurochemistry shutting down.'

'I'm sure he saw something.'

'This is going to sound harsh,' Parry said, 'but in a way I'm glad it happened to Craig. We'd already lost him once. Losing him again . . . it's bad, but it's bound to hurt less than losing someone else.'

'That does sound harsh,' Bella said. She poured herself a little more tea, using a strainer improvised from a suit dust filter. Under Janus gravity, the liquid did not so much flow as meander into the cup. 'But I know what you mean.'

'Will you tell me about Jim Chisholm?'

'I said I'd speak to Svetlana.'

'I've done all I can. She's still not ready to deal with you.'

Bella raised an eyebrow speculatively. 'Why is that, do you think? Could it possibly be that she doesn't want to acknowledge my existence? Because that would force her to confront what a mistake it was putting me here in the first place?'

'You'd have made no material difference, Bella. We'd still have been on this ride, unable to get off.'

'I heard about the trouble with the Symbolists. I'd have handled them better.'

'Easy to say from here.'

'Easy for you to dismiss. But I'd have had my ways. Svetlana's mistake was treating the Symbolists as an aberration, something that could be diagnosed and cured like a pathology. I'd have accepted their inevitability and made them work for me. More tea?'

'No thanks.'

'She tried to keep them from the Maw because it offended her puritanical sensibilities to think that a bunch of cultists might actually be capable of running something. So she antagonised and marginalised them, sent spies and agitators in to try to break them up. Which, of course, only made things worse.'

'Whereas you would have . . . ?'

Her eyes widened. 'I'd have embraced them, encouraged them. Zealots are exactly the sort of people you want running delicate machinery. The clockwork mechanism would have been in safe hands for evermore.'

'It wouldn't have worked.'

'Svetlana's methods were hardly a raging success, Parry.' Bella sniffed. 'Still, if she won't talk to me . . . no sense arguing with a sulking child, is there?'

'Then you'll talk to me?' Parry asked.

'If that's what it takes. The difference is I care about Crabtree, not my pride.'

Parry leaned forward and softened his voice, trying to connect with the woman under whom he had once served. 'Then tell me what this is all about. Tell me what Jim Chisholm has to do with what just happened to Craig Schrope.'

'Everything,' Bella said. She put down her teacup and studied Parry with an intensity he found disquieting, as if his very soul were being scrutinised for flaws.

'It's about what Jim said to you, isn't it? The day you came back to Crabtree to visit him.'

'Of course.'

'But that was . . . what? Nine or ten years ago, easily. Jim knew nothing about the Spicans.'

'But he knew we'd meet them one day, and that when we did it might be—' Bella paused and hunted for the right word. 'Difficult.'

'But his knowing that – it doesn't *help* us.'

'I think it does,' Bella said. 'You see, the thing is . . . This is difficult as well. I only have one thing still of value to me, Parry.' She looked down at age-spotted fingers laced in indecision. 'It was a gift from Jim. He could have told you, could have told Svieta, or Ryan, or anyone else . . . but he didn't. He told *me*, because it was the only way he could give me something useful. And I've kept his secret all these years, knowing it might one day help us, knowing it might one day help *me* . . . but at the same time hoping, praying, that the time would never come when I needed to reveal it.' She looked into his eyes with a sudden fierce gaze. 'But now I think that time has come.'

'Tell me,' Parry whispered.

'I'd always hoped that I might use this to bargain with you. That's why I wanted to talk to Svieta.'

'I'll relay any requests to her.'

'I'm not asking for the world. Just let me come back to Crabtree. Allow me to play some kind of role in our affairs.'

'Pass me my helmet,' Parry said.

Bella obliged. He locked the helmet back into place and returned to the airlock. With the door closed behind him and the helmet tightly sealed, he was sure Bella would not be able to hear him talking to Svetlana on the *Crusader*.

'Well?' she asked.

'Bella's ready to talk. Jim told her something that might help us. She'll reveal it if we make concessions.'

'I'm not negotiating. Get it out of her.'

'Svieta—'

'We're halfway through screwing up the most historic event in human history, Parry. I am not in the mood to bargain. Tell her that if she doesn't talk we'll start taking stuff away.'

'She'll clam up. You know Bella.'

There was a resentful silence at the other end of the line. Svetlana must have known he was right. The two women were too alike in temperament. 'What's she asking for?' Svetlana asked after a few moments.

'A return to Crabtree.'

'No fucking way.'

'Listen to me,' Parry said. 'Give her one of the outlying domes. It doesn't have to be in the hab. She'll still be a prisoner.'

Again there was silence. It stretched for twenty or thirty seconds, while Parry imagined Svetlana's anguished thought processes.

'Just Crabtree, she said? No other requests?'

'She'd like to play more of a role in Crabtree affairs.'

'No.'

Parry thought of Bella waiting on the other side of the lock, wondering what was going on. 'There's a way,' he said. 'We already have a private channel for anonymous policy suggestions.'

She sounded surprised. 'Do we?'

'Yes. Just because you never look at it.'

'But you do.'

'I skim the suggestions now and then. Sometimes there's good stuff in them. When there is, I occasionally let it influence my thinking. Bella's locked out of that channel now, but it wouldn't cost us much to let her have her say. Anonymously, of course. She'd just be one voice amongst many.'

'Does this run on ShipNet?'

'It used to. Lately we've had to go back to paper notes dropped into sealed boxes, but it still works.'

'I know her handwriting.'

'It doesn't matter – you never read the damned things anyway. I don't know her handwriting, so what difference will it make?'

'All right,' Svetlana said, with a world-weary sigh. 'Offer her this much: an outlying dome at Crabtree – surface access via airlock only. No one visits her without a suit. And she doesn't get one.'

'I'll see if that flies. And the other thing?'

'She can use the suggestion box. She'll be allowed a limited ration of paper. I don't want her flooding the fucking thing.'

'Generosity's a lovely thing.'

He opened the inner door of the airlock and returned inside, unlatching his helmet at the same time.

Bella shot him a knowing look. 'I can tell that went smoothly.'

Parry sat down opposite her. 'You've got your deal. You'll be moved to Crabtree, into one of the perimeter domes. No tunnel access. No suit.'

'Continue,' Bella said, giving nothing away.

'You get to submit policy suggestions through an anonymous channel. I'll read and screen them, not Svieta. Anything I think has wheels, she gets to hear. None of us will ever know who originated the suggestion.'

'Very democratic of you.'

'You'll be part of Crabtree life again. You can build on that.'

'Perhaps,' she said doubtfully. 'Everything that you've just offered me . . . I can trust you to deliver, can't I?'

'Of course,' Parry said.

'It's always been good to be able to talk to you,' Bella said. 'It was a relief knowing not everyone hated me. There was always Axford, but you had every reason to turn against me. You didn't. I've appreciated that more than you'll ever know.'

'You've always had my respect. Nothing's ever changed that.'

'Then perhaps we had better talk about Jim Chisholm.'

Svetlana watched Parry cross the ground to *Star Crusader*, observed by another figure looking out of the dome. Parry passed out of view into the lander's airlock, and for a moment Svetlana felt as if Bella was looking at her, and she looking at Bella, even though they were too far away to see each other's eyes. Somehow that didn't matter, though. The human mind was so attuned to the importance of gaze that it could just *tell*.

There was a moment of electric connection, like an emotional short circuit, before Svetlana flinched and looked away.

Parry cycled through the airlock. She met him on the other side and helped him out of the suit, fingers urgent against the catches. Her fingertips felt raw, the nails chewed to the quick.

'Did she bite?'

'She bit. Took some persuading, but she went for it in the end. I don't think she was all that excited about being transferred to another isolated dome. Being able to post suggestions, though – that mattered a lot to her.'

'Whatever she needed to hear,' Svetlana said.

'It wasn't about what she needed to hear,' Parry replied. 'It was about what we were comfortable offering.'

Parry followed her into the lander's passenger lounge, with its scuffed decor and worn seats. Svetlana called Denise and told her they could return to Underhole. When *Crusader* was aloft, she said, 'Now tell me what this is all about.'

Parry took off his red cap and rubbed a hand through his greying hair. 'It's about what Jim told her in Crabtree. About his plans for what would happen when they came.'

'They,' she echoed flatly.

'The aliens he always guessed we'd meet. He figured that when we got to Spica, something like this was bound to happen. He knew he'd be dead by then, too.' Parry paused, making sure he had her attention. Of course he did. 'Dead but frozen.'

'One of Ryan's Frost Angels.'

He nodded solemnly. 'Jim knew he was going to die, and he didn't think we had much hope of ever making it back to Earth. But aliens? He thought we had every chance of meeting them. After all, Janus was taking us somewhere. Pretty good bet there would be aliens at the end of the line.'

'He was right,' Svetlana said, thinking back to Schrope's cryptic final words in the alien ship. 'What does that have to do with our current predicament?'

'Jim reckoned aliens would have a better chance of bringing him back than people ever did. He told Bella that when they came, if things didn't work out so well at first, we should send him to them.'

'Send a dead man,' she said.

'Dead men don't have a lot to lose.'

'That's insane.'

'Maybe. But is it any more insane than sending someone else inside that thing and waiting for them to die the same way Craig did?'

'You don't send a dead man in as your negotiator,' Svetlana said.

'Maybe I missed something, but I don't remember ever being shown the rulebook for this situation.'

'We've given them one corpse already.'

'No,' Parry said firmly. He was doing that maddening thing of staying calm, rationally arguing his case, never raising his voice or showing the least sign of irritation when she did not immediately see his position. 'We gave them a living man and they killed him. Probably not intentionally, but it still happened. But they didn't get a clean corpse at the end of it. They got a man who'd been crushed alive by gravity and pressure, a man who died in his spacesuit. He was still warm after his heart stopped, after the blood stopped flowing, but by the time they got to him, his brain must have looked like the Antarctic shelf. The damage was already done.'

'Jim's just as dead.'

'Jim's a Frost Angel. That makes all the difference. He's been frozen solid by a controlled medical process. He was euthanized before the cancer took away too much of his brain. There's still material there for them to work with.'

She emitted a small, humourless laugh. 'You're saying . . . they might be able to bring him back?'

'To them he's like a broken clock. If we take him in like that – how can they not see that we want him mended?'

Ash Murray was there to meet them when *Crusader* docked at Underhole.

'Parry, Svieta – there's something you really need to see.'

They followed him back into the conference area. The dinners had been cleared away and the table laid with a loose mosaic of semi-functioning flexies. Everyone was looking expectantly at Svetlana, as if she was the long-awaited guest of honour finally showing up at a party.

She swallowed to clear a mouth suddenly flooded with saliva. 'What?'

'We got more than we thought,' Murray said, picking at the corner of one eye with a finger. 'Near the end, when Craig was in the airlock chamber – or whatever we're calling it – we got a momentary improvement in signal throughput.'

She stood by the table, looking down at the ragged mosaic with its mismatched colour boundaries. 'I don't get it. What are you saying?'

'Craig came through – he got us the imagery. He pointed the cam and . . . we got a frame. It came through in low-end bits, riding the audio. That's an emergency protocol that kicks in automatically when the system decides that audio needs priority – it's why we missed it initially.'

'A single frame.'

'It's way better than no frame.'

She looked at the distorted composite image created by the flexies, but at first she could make no sense of it. It was blurred like a picture taken out of the window of a speeding car: vague shapes, streaked hyphens of bleeding colour. Under the force of all that gravity, his breathing impaired by the rising pressure, it must have taken superhuman effort for Schrope to point the cam in even roughly the right direction, let alone hold it steady.

But he had done his best. And he had got them *something*.

'I take back what I said about hallucinations,' Axford said quietly.

Parry pointed at one of the blurred forms. 'There's definitely something here.' He moved his finger. 'And here. And maybe here as well.'

'Spicans?' Svetlana said.

'Craig said there were several of them. He said they were big. He said they looked like—'

'Mountains,' Nadis said.

'Except they don't.' Svetlana narrowed her eyes, trying to mentally unscramble the effects of cam blur and the distortion due to the intervening glass. The aliens were large, upright forms of marine colour – blue, green and turquoise. They looked like barnacles, rising from a flared circular base, but that basic tapering shape was all they had in common with mountains. Their sides curved over to form a flattened top surface, not a peak. They had no obvious front or back, no recognisable limbs or sensory apparatus, no clear means of locomotion. They looked as if they had been baked in a cake mould.

'But he saw them,' Parry said, 'got the cam onto them. He said they were moving, coming closer.'

'If the optical properties of the glass changed, he might have mistaken that for motion,' Axford said. 'What we're seeing here might not be living – we might just be looking at mechanical structures.'

'No,' Svetlana said firmly, 'Craig knew what he was looking at. Let's give him the benefit of the doubt, shall we?'

'They're not what I was expecting,' Parry said.

'I'm not exactly sure what any of us were expecting,' Svetlana said, smiling at Parry.

'If these are the Spicans,' Nadis said, 'do we keep on calling them that, or should we stick with the name Craig gave them?'

'Craig got us this picture,' Parry said. 'That's enough to remember him by.'

'I'm wondering,' Svetlana said slowly, tilting her head, 'whether he might not have said "mountains" after all.'

Axford left for Crabtree on *Crusader*. When he returned four hours later, he had one of the Frost Angels with him. The body was in a grey metal medical cabinet, still in a state of cryogenic suspension.

Svetlana had confirmation by then that Bella had told the truth about Jim Chisholm's wishes. Bella had given Parry a code phrase – *multitudinous seas incarnadine* – that unlocked a private partition in Jim Chisholm's old data partition; his flexy had died years ago, but the entries he'd made on it had been distributed throughout the surviving network, and they remained intact. The codeword conjured up a short video clip Chisholm had made from his deathbed, holding the cam in one hand while he spoke.

Svetlana shivered to hear him speak again.

'If you're hearing this,' he said, 'then you either talked to Bella or you got damned good at decryption. Don't take this the wrong way, but I'm guessing the former.' A ghost of a smile touched his wasted features. 'I hope things are okay for you all. If it's come to this, then at least some of you made it all the way to Spica, and there is someone or something waiting for you now you're there.

'If Bella has relayed my wishes, please be assured that she's told you the truth. As difficult as it may be for you to grasp, this is what I want you to do. We all remember those discussions about the theoretical nature of alien intelligence – I reviewed the summaries even though I couldn't sit in on them in person – the long conversations about how if we ever do meet anyone, they'll most likely be tens of millions of years ahead of us in every respect. Makes sense to me: if there's anything we've learned from our own history, it's that intelligence is a precious thing: rare and vulnerable. If the Spicans are still out there, then they've probably been starfaring for an awfully long time. I'm sure putting Humpty Dumpty together again won't be too much of a stretch for them.

'So bring me to them, and see what they make of me. At the very least they might learn something about us just by taking me apart and seeing what makes me tick. Maybe it won't work out, but if it doesn't, I'll have lost nothing.'

Jim Chisholm smiled a dead man' smile. 'And if I *do* come back, I'll do my best not to scare the living daylights out of you.'

*

Svetlana returned to the hole in the sky. She carried the Frost Angel with her on an improvised sled, dragged it all the way to the Spican ship, which was still running its symbol dance. But when she neared the ramp the flicker of symbols slowed and stilled, as if the ship recognised her presence and wished to show it. Its watchful attention lifted the hairs on the back of her neck.

She walked up the ramp and followed Schrope's trail into the glass interior. She found the spherical chamber where he had come to grief. She pushed the sled over the lip and watched it slide all the way down until it skidded to rest, the frozen body lashed to it like an offering.

The glass airlock sphinctered shut between her and the chamber. Nothing happened to the space where she stood; she could still see the sled and its cargo through the glass.

Presently, they came.

At first they were vague shapes approaching from beyond the far wall of the chamber. They were huge, just as Craig Schrope had said, three metres tall and at least as wide across at the base. They moved in an odd way, unlike any form of animal locomotion she had ever witnessed. They were blue, mainly, a pure chromatic blue shot through with twinkling filaments of green and turquoise and sometimes a flash of bright ruby.

They crowded the glass to see what she had brought them, flattening themselves against the surface like children pressing their faces against a window. Slowly, so as not to alarm them, she unclipped her cam and shot some footage. If the aliens were aware of her, they gave no sign.

She could see them better now. Cylindrical in horizontal cross-section, they had no obvious front or back. What had looked like a solid form in the single frame Schrope had sent them was revealed to be a curtain of very fine fronds erupting from a central point and spraying down in all directions to brush against the floor. Not like mountains at all, but *fountains*. That was what Craig Schrope had said.

His description captured their essence in a single word: they looked like ornamental fountains spraying coloured water. They were constantly moving even when they stood still, the fronds rippling, flexing and interlacing like a nest of glittering snakes. They moved by flicking the fronds against the floor in a propulsive wave. Whenever a curtain of fronds parted, all she saw within were further layers of frondlike structure.

These, then, were the aliens – they were clearly not part of the ship. They were definitely not robots, not even alien robots: something about the way they moved, the way they squeezed against the glass, suggested living individuals rather than directed units.

A door opened in the chamber's far side and one of the blue things oozed through the gap – the door looked far too narrow at first, but Svetlana had seen octopuses pull off similar tricks – and flowed down to the sled. Another alien followed it. She kept the cam trained on the pair as they flowed around the sled and then engulfed it completely. For a moment the two shapes were as one, as if conferring over the prize, then one of them disengaged, flowed back to the door and squeezed through. After some hesitation the other followed it. The sled and the Frost Angel had vanished.

'Take good care of him,' Svetlana whispered. She turned around and began to make her way back to Underhole.

# CHAPTER 21

Parry had the impression Bella had been waiting for him. The inside of the dome looked barer than before. Her meagre belongings had been neatly packed in storage crates, waiting to be moved through the airlock. Parry pretended not to notice. She prepared him tea, as usual.

'I've heard nothing from Crabtree,' she said, while the water was boiling.

'Svetlana's tightened the blackout. Craig's disappearance was one thing, but using Jim in this way, regardless of his wishes, is something else entirely. It was difficult enough for Axford to get the body out of the morgue without too many awkward questions from the medical staff.'

'I imagine he was discreet about it. But Svieta can't keep up the blackout for ever – sooner or later they'll have to know.' She spooned tea into the improvised strainer. 'How long has it been now?'

'Three days, give or take.'

'And no change at all from the ship?'

'The symbols have quietened down again, fewer than there have ever been. It's as if the penny's finally dropped that we just don't understand them. Although why they ever expected we *would*—'

'They didn't expect,' Bella said. 'They assumed. I've seen the pictures of that ship, and it doesn't look particularly Spican to me. It's sleek, glassy, curved. The Janus machinery is huge, monolithic and mainly black.'

'I don't follow – how can it not be Spican? You've seen the symbols. Jake and Christine might not have found a precise match with any of the patterns we've mapped on Janus, but it's clearly the same language.'

She poured him his tea. 'The same language, I agree, but what other language would they show us? Not English or Chinese – they don't know us that well, at least not yet. But suppose they do know a little about us: enough to guess that we've had time to crawl around Janus and study the Spican machinery. Suppose they've come into contact with Spican artefacts as well. Suppose they actually found the language easy to crack – so easy that they naturally assume we'll have had no trouble with it either.'

'But we did have trouble. Lots of trouble.'

'I think they may have realised that by now,' Bella said ruefully.

'In which case – if they aren't the Spicans—'

'I don't know. And it could be that I'm totally wrong about all this. But I do have ideas. I've always had ideas.' Bella paused. 'A long time ago, I told you that I thought we might be wrong about the Spicans.'

'I remember,' Parry said. 'It was when I was taking you back to visit Jim for the last time.'

'Being out here on my own, with nothing to distract me . . . I've had a lot of time to think about things – Janus, mainly, and what it says about the creatures that made it.' She cocked her head, as if an idea had suddenly occurred to her. 'We were very lucky, weren't we?'

He'd lost her train of thought. 'Lucky?'

'We found ourselves caught in the slipstream, bound to this thing like Ahab to his whale . . . "Beneath this smiling sky, above this unsounded sea".'

'Bella,' he said, with a forgiving smile.

'Janus took us away from home, but it also kept us alive. We thought we were being so clever, the way we took power and materials from it for our own purposes.' She fixed him with that familiar intense gaze that had lost none of its power during her long years of exile. 'But what if that was always the point? What if the Spicans expected us to make use of Janus? And to be amused by it, too. I think that was the point of it all, Parry. I think Janus was a puzzle designed to keep us alive and sane, like a cage at the zoo. You feed and water the animals, give them toys to play with and challenges to keep them alert.'

'We ended up on this thing by mistake,' he said. 'The incident pit, remember?'

'The Charlie Foxtrot,' she said, nodding. 'And yes, we did make mistakes. But an animal makes a mistake when it walks into a trap. Janus was our trap and our cage. It was designed to entice close study. It was designed to snatch us away, and then keep us alive for the journey.'

Parry's voice came out paper-thin. 'The journey to where, Bella?'

'Where else?' She flipped back the lid of her cup to take a sip of tea. 'The zoo, of course.'

They had finished the tea, and the matter of the packed belongings could no longer be avoided. Bella pottered with a cheerfulness he hadn't seen in her in thirteen years, washing the cups and tea-making equipment.

'It's true what I told you,' she said over her shoulder, while Parry examined his helmet as if it were the most fascinating artefact in the world, entranced by every micrometeorite crater, every cosmic-ray scratch. 'I've had a lot of time to think out here. Now at least I'll be able to have some influence on policy, even if it's only through the anonymous channel. I didn't like the sound of that at first, but now that I've had time to sleep on it, I actually think it might be rather a good arrangement. Very democratic, very egalitarian. Difficult as it might be for you to believe, I actually have some sympathy with the Interim Authority. Svieta could have handled the Symbolists better, but that was never going to be an easy nut to crack.'

'She lied.'

Bella kept on pottering. 'It'll be good to be close to Crabtree, as well. I know I'll still be living in an isolated dome, and that I won't be able to make any unscheduled visits outside, but at least it won't be so difficult for other people to come and visit me, even if it's only more visits from Axford. But Ryan's been kind to me over the years. Good man, Ryan – we could have done a lot worse than him.'

'She lied,' Parry said again.

Bella looked around. 'I'm sorry?'

'She lied to you,' he said in a dead, deflated voice, still not looking up from his helmet. 'Svetlana lied. You're not getting what you thought you were promised.'

'No,' Bella said, with a kind of half-smile.

'Everything I said to you, I said in good faith. I meant every word.'

The smile was gone now, the truth hitting home. 'No. She can't do this.'

'She has. You had one thing she needed. Now she has it. You are of no further use to her.'

Bella's voice dropped to a croak. 'You can't let her get away with this.'

'I've tried. She won't listen.'

Bella sat down on one of the packed crates, all her sprightly enthusiasm gone. 'It was stupid of me,' she said at last, as if chiding herself. 'I took the risk of trusting her.'

'You didn't do anything wrong,' Parry said. He wanted to comfort her, but knew that nothing he could say would ease the pain of this betrayal.

'I trusted her.'

'You did the decent thing. You told us the thing that mattered.'

'I bargained, Parry. I thought I was getting something in return.'

'But you'd have told us anyway, in the end, even if I'd promised you nothing, because above all else you care about Crabtree. Crabtree and doing the right thing by Jim.'

'Parry,' she said quietly, 'would you leave now? It was kind of you to come here in person – I know it can't have been easy – but I would very much like to be on my own now.'

He followed the power line back to Crabtree and made his way to Svetlana's office still wearing most of his suit. He had to pass through the centrifuge section, spun up for a gee, but had dropped most of his depleted-uranium ballast weights in the tractor before taking the elevator.

He used his key to open the office. It was dark: Svetlana was still in Underhole, as he had expected. He brought the lights up to their dimmest setting and moved to the familiar rectangle of the fish tank, bubbling quietly in the gloom. The fish had adapted easily to near-weightlessness, which was just as well given where he intended to take them now.

With the tank unplugged from power and water, Parry made sure the lid was dogged down against spillage. He set his helmet on top of the lid, for easy access when he reached the tractor. The tank was wide, but he could just about brace his gloved hands on either side without too much strain. With an involuntary grunt of effort, he tried lifting the thing.

On Earth, it would have weighed a tonne: there was easily a cubic metre of water in there, not to mention all the gravel and rocks on the base. On Janus, its effective weight should only have been a few kilograms, yet it didn't budge when he tried to lift it. He tried again, unsuccessfully, then realised – stupidly – that the tank was fixed to its table with four dabs of geckoflex. He levered it loose one corner at a time and then suddenly it was free. It still had fearful inertia, but he was used to manhandling massive objects on Janus. Keeping it level, he walked awkwardly to the door.

That was when he saw Svetlana, watching him from the corridor in dim silhouette.

'I thought you were still in Underhole,' he said uneasily.

'So I see.' One hand rested on her suited hip, the other dangled her helmet. 'What are you doing?'

He stopped, still holding the fish tank. 'I'm doing the one thing that might let me get through this day with a shred of dignity. How about you?'

She pushed her helmet against a ribbon of geckoflex on the ceiling. 'Put the tank back.'

'I'm taking it to Bella. We screwed her over the deal with Jim. The least we can do is give her something in return.'

'Put the tank back,' she repeated.

He took a step nearer the door. 'No.'

'Put it down.'

'Get out of my way, Svieta.'

She closed on him and got her own gloved hands on the tank. Geckoflex adhered tightly to glass. She was stronger than he had been expecting – Svetlana had always taken the time to keep in shape, even during the hardships of the Iron Sky. But Parry was stronger – he had kept in shape as well, and he had better leverage on the tank than she did. They wrestled with it, neither able to gain any ground on the other. Parry's helmet slid off the top and settled to the ground with featherlike slowness. Even though he had tightened the lid, water still found its way through the seal. It emerged in a silvery sheet, breaking up into pearly blobs as it drifted to the floor.

'Put it back,' Svetlana said, breathing heavily now. 'She isn't getting this.'

Between grunts of effort, Parry said, 'It's been thirteen fucking years. Hasn't she paid enough, without being lied to, without being cheated?'

'Put . . . the tank . . . back.'

His grip slipped where the geckoflex patch on his right glove had been wearing thin. Svetlana took advantage, heaving the tank her way, trying to twist it from his grip. Parry scrabbled for another purchase with his free hand but ended up overcompensating for Svetlana's twisting motion. The tank skidded from his hands. For a moment Svetlana had it, but while she could manage the tank's weight easily enough, it still had a tonne of inertia. In that one fumbling instant it had picked up dangerous speed. It was like trying to catch a falling engine block.

The tank slipped from her grip. She tried to catch it, but it was already on its way to the ground, picking up momentum with every second it fell. The stiff articulation of the suits made it impossible for them to dive down and catch it. All they could do was watch as the tank rammed the floor like a rudder-locked supertanker. The glass held – it was space qualified, after all – but the lid popped free, allowing the remaining water to slurp out in a slow, sickly tidal wave, freighted with fish.

'Oh, fuck,' Svetlana said.

The water oozed in all directions, surface tension pulling it into an amoeba-like shape that appeared to spread out with a vague sense of will. The startled fish flopped around in the shallows with uncomprehending goggle eyes, flapping their tails and gaping their mouths in existential crisis.

Parry and Svetlana looked down in horror. Some awful span of time passed before they suddenly moved as one, kneeling stiffly, trying to scoop up water and fish in huge silvery handfuls. By the time they had got most of the fish back into the tank, much of the water had soaked into Bella's old carpet. What remained in the tank looked scummy and stagnant. The fish hung in it at limp, stunned angles. Their fragile sense of up and down had been destroyed.

Wordlessly, Parry and Svetlana manoeuvred the tank up onto the table and plumbed it back into the water supply.

'They're not going to like this,' Parry said, when the tank was half-full. 'I think you're only ever meant to change a little water at a time, so that the ecosystem doesn't suffer too much of a jolt.'

'I'm sorry,' Svetlana said, shaking.

Parry looked at her. 'Are you talking to me or the fish?'

'Take the tank to Bella. Maybe she can . . . fix things.'

'What do you want me to tell her?'

'Nothing,' she said. 'Just take the tank.'

At that moment they both noticed the quietly insistent chime coming from their helmets. Parry knelt down and collected his from the floor as Svetlana reached up to the ceiling for hers. The chime was coming from the HUD alert, so Parry settled the helmet over his head without engaging the neck ring. The HUD visuals lit up.

'I think you need to put your helmet on,' he told Svetlana.

# CHAPTER 22

The spacesuited figure stood at the top of the ramp leading down from the chandelier-shaped ship. At full zoom the cam traced details of the suit's design, but no face was visible behind the reflective surface of the helmet's visor.

The suit did not resemble any aboard *Rockhopper*, but on some level that Svetlana could not quite identify, it carried the unmistakable signature of human thinking. Its pale-grey exterior flexed in some places and looked as rigid as armour in others. There were no seams or articulation points. The helmet, gloves and chestpack were part of the whole, as if the entire suit had been moulded in one piece. There was no sharp division between the face-plate and the rest of the helmet, merely a soft transition.

The figure started walking. At first its movements were stiff and uncoordinated, as if it were a doll being propelled by an invisible hand. Once or twice it hesitated, or appeared to be on the point of stumbling, but with each pace the figure gained a measure of confidence and fluidity. By the time it was halfway down the ramp, it had settled into a purposeful stride. The fingers worked constantly, clenching and unclenching.

The figure reached the bottom of the ramp and stepped onto the Iron Sky. It paused for a moment, twisting its upper body to look back at the ship from which it had just emerged. Then it continued walking in the direction of the hole, halting at the very lip. It moved to the cam that had been watching it, then reached down and detached the device from its geckoflex mounting. It held the cam at arm's length, pointed at its head, but there was still nothing to be seen except the glossy mirror of the helmet visor.

The figure returned the cam to its geckoflex and moved out of sight. The HUD window inside Svetlana's helmet switched to a different cam, one of those stationed under the Sky, angled up through the hole. The figure had lowered itself over the edge and was now descending the sheer face where the sky had been drilled through, attached only by fingertips and the toes of its boots. It moved confidently, but with no apparent sense of haste. Soon it reached the inner side of the Sky, and for a minute it hung upside down, as motionless as when it had first stepped from the ship. Then it dropped.

It gathered speed with the usual lazy reluctance of all falling objects on Janus. Once it had reached a rate of fall of twenty or thirty metres per second, it stopped accelerating. Slowly, the suit revolved through one hundred and eighty degrees and fell the remainder of the twenty vertical kilometres to Underhole feet first. It decelerated somehow just before contacting the ice, landing daintily.

It walked up to the main dome in Underhole and knocked on the outer airlock door. No one heard the knocks, but by that point there wasn't a HUD or flexy that wasn't tracking the grey-suited figure.

The figure waited, then raised its hand and knocked again.

'What do we do?' Denise Nadis asked, an edge of hysteria in her voice. '*It wants to come in.*'

'So let it in,' Svetlana said, over the com from Crabtree. 'Let it in, then tell it to wait. I'm on my way.'

Nadis met Svetlana, Parry and Axford in the airlock as they were undoing their helmets. They had lost the com feed to *Crusader* during the journey back from Crabtree, so Svetlana had no idea what had happened since the last update.

'We're still sitting tight,' Nadis said, looking as if she was running on willpower alone. 'All it's done since we let it in is sit at the table.'

'It's made no attempt to communicate?'

Nick Thale stood behind Nadis, stirring a fork through the remains of a meal. He had just been rotated out to Underhole after a week back in Crabtree. 'Not from its side. We haven't tried much, either. Thought we'd best wait until you arrived.'

'I think if it meant us harm, we'd have known about it by now,' Parry said.

'Thing freaks me out,' Nadis said under her breath. 'That's all *I* need to know.'

The grey-suited figure had seated itself at the head of the conference table with its arms resting on the wangwood, fingertips just touching. It still had the helmet on. The suit made a faint, rhythmic wheezing sound, despite there being no visible vents or grilles.

'There's clearly something alive in there,' Axford said, brushing aside the remains of foil-wrapped meals to make space on the table for his medical kit.

'No visible suit diagnostics, though,' Thale said.

Svetlana had expected the suit to reveal more of its secrets up close, but it was as seamless and inscrutable as it had been in the cam view. She hesitantly touched the seated figure's forearm: the pale-grey material had something of the same neoprene slickness as wet dolphin skin. When she pushed her finger against it, it resisted a little and then absorbed the pressure, dimpling inwards. She scratched a fingernail against it, but left no mark.

She sat down at the opposite end of the table from the figure. Parry stood behind her, with a reassuring hand on her shoulder. Axford had opened his medical kit, but so far had removed none of his equipment.

'It's Jim, isn't it?' she said, staring at her own reflection in the black mirrored faceplate. 'I'm guessing you can hear me, so . . . welcome back, Jim. It's good to have you with us.'

The figure spoke in an amplified voice that approximated Jim Chisholm's. 'Hello, Bella.'

Something caught in Svetlana's throat. 'It's not—' she began, but Parry's hand tightened on her shoulder, clearly warning her not to contradict the figure. 'Hello,' she said.

The figure reached up with both hands and removed the helmet. It separated from the collar along an invisibly fine seam, like a piece of clay being torn in two. The edge was as clean and deliberate as if it had been cut with a sword. The figure placed the helmet on the table.

Svetlana stared at what had been Jim Chisholm. It was his face, but it took an effort of concentration to convince herself of that fact. The features were different than she remembered, even near the end. It was thinner, the skin drawn so tightly against the bone that she could see the shape of the skull underneath. No hair, just a fine layer of stubble. No expression, either, beyond a kind of stunned incomprehension.

'It's good to have you back,' she said again.

He looked at her, his eyes painfully wide. 'I was away somewhere . . . away for a long time.'

'But now you're back,' she said, reaching out to touch one of his gloved hands. 'Safe with us again.'

'I was somewhere cold.'

Svetlana nodded encouragingly. So there was memory there; not just the memory of faces (it was understandable that he had mistaken her for Bella, after so many years) but the memory of what had happened to him near the end, under Axford's care.

'You were a Frost Angel,' she said gently, 'but now you're back. You're home again, where you belong.'

'I'm glad,' Chisholm said.

Parry leaned down, resting his chin on her shoulder. 'Hi, Jim. Do you remember me?'

'Yes,' he said. 'I remember. Parry.' Then he blinked, as if clearing his vision. 'Older now. What happened to you?'

'The same thing that happened to all of us,' Parry said. 'Except you, Jim. You were the lucky one. You got to sleep.'

'Sleep with angels,' Chisholm said.

'Hi, Jim,' Axford said. 'Do you remember me? I was your doctor. Your friend, too. We used to spend a lot of time together, talking stuff over, listening to music. You taught me to hear things in Mingus . . . things I'd never have noticed without you. I'm still grateful.'

'Ryan,' Chisholm said, his eyes widening. 'I remember it, too . . . Mingus. An ocean of Mingus. *Bird calls*. Oceanic. But all that was—' He averted his eyes, as if he had seen something shameful. 'All that was *such* a long time ago. How can you remember it now?'

Axford had removed an ophthalmoscope from his medical kit. 'Jim, do you mind if I look into your eyes?'

'No . . . please,' he said, with a childlike willingness.

Axford moved close to Chisholm and gently touched the fingers of his right hand to the skin around Chisholm's left eye. With the other hand he shone the light of the ophthalmoscope into the eye. The eye blinked at first and then held steady. Axford moved to the other eye, then switched off the ophthalmoscope and looked back to Svetlana.

'Strictly preliminary,' he said, 'but before we lost Jim, the glioblastoma was elevating intracranial pressure. Elevated ICP has a number of external symptoms, beyond the headaches and vomiting Jim was experiencing. Papilloedema's one of them – outward bulging of the retina. But I'm not seeing anything like that now. I'm reading normal pulsation of the retinal vessels, no blurring of the optic disc margin. Maybe some old retinal haemorrhages, but nothing recent – nothing that he'd notice.'

'What are you saying?' she asked.

'I'll need to run proper tests in Crabtree – scans, bloodwork – but it very much looks if they've debulked, or maybe even completely removed, the blastoma.' He touched a hand against Chisholm's forehead. 'He's running one hell of a temperature, though. I'm keen to get him out of that suit and back to Crabtree as soon as possible.'

'Jim,' Svetlana said, 'do you remember this place? This world we're on?'

He cocked his head, as if searching for the answer. 'Janus,' he said, after a moment.

'Yes,' she said, brimming with relief. So Chisholm remembered: maybe not in sharp detail yet, but he had at least retained a basic skeleton of the facts. A skeleton that they could build on, flesh out with texture and colour, if his own memory was unable to supply the rest.

'How long now?' he asked.

'We've been here for thirteen years,' she said. 'It's been nine years since you left us.'

For the first time he showed some wider interest in his surroundings. He looked around stiffly, to the walls and ceiling. The effort of moving his neck seemed to tax him. 'Is this Crabtree?'

'No. We're in Underhole now – it's just a monitoring outpost. You fell from the Iron Sky, remember?'

'Yes,' he said, smiling, as if the memory amused him. 'The Sky. I walked on it.'

'And then you fell through the hole, the hole the aliens drilled through to us.'

'I remember falling.' He lifted one of his hands from the table and spread the fingers. 'This is a good suit. Better than the ones we had before.' Then he looked back sharply to Svetlana. 'I don't remember the Sky.'

'It wasn't there before,' she said. 'The Spicans put it around us just before we started slowing down. We figured it was some kind of shield, to protect us during the deceleration phase.'

'How long since they made the sky?'

'It's been over a year, Jim. It's served its purpose, though. We've arrived in the Spica Structure. Safe and sound, like you.'

'The Spica Structure,' he said, with a widening smile.

'You remember it?' She smiled back. 'That's great.'

Chisholm's smile slipped. His voice became flat and emotionless again. 'I remember the Spica Structure, yes.'

'We're there now. Two hundred and sixty light-years from home . . . but we're still here, still alive. We made it. Now all we have to do is make it back.'

His voice slowed. 'I remember . . . yes.'

'Easy,' Parry breathed.

'I . . . remember—' Then a kind of shadow crossed Chisholm's face, his expression reverting to the absolute blankness he had shown when he first removed the helmet: less a face than a death mask, emotions sucked back into whatever tiny core of personality remained. 'I'm sorry.'

Svetlana reached across the table and grasped his hand. 'Jim, it's okay. I know this is going to be tough for you, but . . . everything's going to be all right. You're with friends now. We'll take care of you.'

'Sorry.' His throat made a wet clicking sound, as if an invisible garrotte were tightening around his neck. 'So sorry.'

'Jim—' she said.

'Sorry.'

Chisholm started making rhythmic moaning sounds, like a person deep in the coils of nightmare, his breathing becoming heavier, the mask of his face pulling into something tortured. The moans became a howl of distress like nothing Svetlana had heard before, like nothing she would ever care to hear again. Distress transmuted to terror, as if moaning was the only human response to the paralysing burden of knowledge now unpacking itself inside his head.

He stopped. The silence was worse than the moaning. Panting, his face slick with sweat, his eyes wide and unblinking, he looked around at his audience.

Then he closed his eyes and pitched forward, his head lolling against the neck ring of the suit.

# CHAPTER 23

They laid out Jim Chisholm on the floor of *Crusader* as it returned to Crabtree. He was still alive, still breathing regularly, but there was nothing they could do for him until he was out of the suit.

'We could try cutting it open,' Nadis said quietly, as if wary of letting Chisholm hear her. 'If we did it slowly . . . it's not as if we have to worry about pressure loss.'

'Last resort only,' Axford said. 'If he arrests, then we cut. Until then I'm the only person going anywhere near him with a knife. He's stable for now, and I could probably get an airline into him if I have to.' He had been monitoring Chisholm's carotid pulse.

'I agree with Ryan,' Parry said. 'There has to be an easier way to get him out of that thing – we don't want to damage the suit if we can help it.'

He knelt by the comatose man and ran a hand across the flattened bulge of the suit's chestpack. There were no display windows, input sockets or keypads, but there *was* a kind of mosaic of shaped panels set into the slope of the top surface, where it blended with the upper chest. The panels might have been nothing more than some form of baroque ornamentation, but why there and nowhere else on the suit? The top of the chestpack was the logical place to put controls: smack in the middle of the golden triangle where a suited figure could reach things easily. He brushed his hand against the leftmost panel, which was shaped like an equilateral triangle.

'Careful,' Svetlana whispered. 'One of those things might be a self-destruct.'

Parry looked up at his wife. 'And that information is going to help me how, exactly?' He turned back to the suit and pressed his thumb against the triangular panel. The helmet said something: a few quiet phrases in a language he didn't recognise. It was a woman's voice, calmly authoritative.

'Anyone get that?' Parry asked.

'Nuh huh,' Nadis said, but she held the helmet over her head, so that her ears were closer to the source of the sound.

'Try it again,' Svetlana said.

He pressed the panel. The helmet spoke again: what sounded like the same voice saying the same phrase, but in a more strident tone. Parry waited a moment, then pressed again. The voice sounded even more firm, as if this was absolutely the last time it wanted to have to say whatever it was saying.

'Wrong thing to press,' Parry said. 'That's what she's telling us. The tone of her voice, it was like, *I've told you three times now . . .*'

'Why put a command button there if you're not meant to press it?' Svetlana asked.

'I'm thinking . . .' Nadis said, her purple fingernails clicking against the grey globe of the helmet. 'Maybe it only makes sense to press that thing when the helmet's locked down.'

'She could be right,' Parry said.

Svetlana knelt down next to him. 'Let me see that thing. You were pressing the triangle, right?'

'Yep. Could mean anything.'

'Or something very specific and obvious.' She looked around at the little party. 'Triangles, people. Three sides.'

'Nope,' Parry said. 'Still not getting it.'

'Three gases: $O_2$, $CO_2$, $N_2$. Sure as hell wouldn't make much sense to adjust the trimix without putting on the helmet. Maybe that's what she's saying: *Put the helmet on, dummy, then I can actually do something for you.*'

Parry laughed. 'Maybe you're right.'

'What's the next symbol along?'

'Three horizontal bars, on top of each other.'

'Press it.'

The voice came out of the helmet again: calmer this time, and with what sounded like a different set of phrases.

'Anyone recognise any of that?' Svetlana asked.

'Not me,' Parry said, 'except that it almost sounded like . . . well, Japanese, or something. But not Japanese.'

'Maybe Chinese,' Nadis said. 'Perhaps we should get Wang to listen in—'

Svetlana shook her head. 'I don't think it was Chinese, but we're in the right ballpark. It's something Oriental or Asian, a language we've all heard, stuff that's seeped into our brains on vacation, at a subliminal level. We recognise the music, the structure, but not the content.'

'Why did you say vacation?' Parry asked.

'Because I keep thinking about a diving trip I was on years ago, about the way one of the dive instructors spoke to her boyfriend. I was just a kid – no certification, nothing. Cattleboat stuff, off . . . fuck, where was it? Phuket, maybe.'

'Phuket,' Nadis said. 'As in Phuket, Thailand?'

Parry stroked the barred symbol again, making the helmet utter the same sequence of phrases. Nothing strident or chiding about the tone now. 'It's Thai,' he said. 'The spacesuit is speaking Thai.'

'Why, in God's name . . .' Svetlana said, and then trailed off. 'That symbol you keep pressing – I'm guessing here, but maybe those bars are meant to represent radiator grilles, or . . . something.'

'You've lost me, babe.'

'If the first one's trimix control, maybe the second one's thermal regulation. Would make a kind of sense, right? If you're going to put controls on a suit, those would be near the top of the list.'

'The third symbol is a kind of . . . sunburst motif.'

'Coms, maybe? Okay, big guess, I admit. So sue me. Next?'

'Something similar . . . kind of like an eight-pointed star, or a compass.'

'Directional control, maybe? We know the suit has built-in thrust, enough for hovering under Janus gravity.'

'No,' Parry said. 'Too complex. This is just a single symbol. You can't input enough information into a single control button to specify direction.'

'It doesn't have to work like that. We've no idea what happens when the helmet's locked down. Maybe those symbols just call up HUD menus, or open voice-command channels, or maybe even thought control.'

'Okay, maybe.' Parry's finger dithered over the chestpack. 'There's one last symbol: just a square. You want me to go ahead and press it?'

Nadis looked nervously at the helmet. 'Go ahead.'

Parry pressed it. The helmet said something – a shorter sequence of phrases this time – but nothing obvious happened. He pressed it again; got the same verbal message.

'This doesn't make any sense,' Svetlana said. 'Why Thai? As far as I know, Jim didn't speak Thai any more than we do. They can't have dug the language out of his head.'

'I agree it's weird,' Parry said, 'but then so is the fact that he strolled out of that ship in the first place. We're in weird territory here. This suit is just part of it.'

'The suit bothers me,' Svetlana said.

'Bothers me, too. It's not like any of our suits – certainly not like the one Craig was wearing, which was the only suit of ours the aliens got a look at.' Parry stroked the square symbol again, just in case something might have changed. He heard the same message in Thai. 'It's beyond anything we've got; beyond anything the Chinese had, or that Wang is capable of making for us. But it isn't like anything we saw on that ship, either. It's modern-looking – but not so modern that I'm terrified just being in the same room as it.'

'So maybe it isn't alien,' Nadis said. 'Maybe this is just . . . a suit. Made by people. Maybe even made by Thai people. But not from our time. From after we left.'

'A suit from the future, you mean?' Parry asked.

'Sorry to break it to you,' Nadis said, still holding the helmet close to her head, 'but we're *in* the damned future. Two hundred and sixty years into it, to be precise. Maybe we shouldn't be too surprised if we run into pieces of it now and then. We might kid ourselves that it's still only 2070, but we all know that's just a big white lie to keep us all from doing the same thing Bob Ungless did.'

'Please confirm that English is your preferred language option,' the helmet said in its usual voice.

Nadis almost let go of it. 'Whoah,' she said, grinning in delight and surprise.

'Please confirm that English is your preferred language option,' the suit said again, more firmly this time.

'Maybe you should answer the thing,' Svetlana said.

'Yes,' Nadis said, speaking into the open circle at the base of the helmet. 'English is my . . . preferred option. *Holy shit.*'

'Switching language preference from Thai to English. To switch back, or select another language, please access menu modes or provide statistical speech baseline.'

'It was listening,' Parry said, 'waiting for us to say something in Thai. When we didn't, it figured out what we wanted to hear from Denise's speech.'

'Why'd it take so long?' Nadis said, still looking at the helmet with a silly grin on her face.

'Must have needed a big chunk of language to get to work on. That's probably what it meant by "statistical sample".'

'So it knows English,' Axford said. 'That I can handle. But Thai? Why would anyone programme Thai into a spacesuit?'

'Wait,' Svetlana said, with a wicked look. 'Pass me the helmet.'

Nadis pushed it across the room in a slow, shallow arc. Svetlana caught it easily and started speaking into the base of the helmet. Something guttural and Eastern European, hesitantly at first, but then with increasing fluency.

Nadis looked at Parry. 'What the hell language is that?'

'Armenian,' Parry said. 'At least, I think that's what it is.'

The helmet started speaking to Svetlana. She looked up, wide-eyed. 'It's answering. It sounds weird, like some dialect I've never heard before, but it still makes sense. It's better at it than me.' She shook her head in amazement. 'The damned thing speaks *Armenian*. How many languages does this thing hold?'

'I don't know,' Parry said. 'Why don't you ask it?'

They forced it to switch back to English. Svetlana stood with the helmet under her chin, like a soup bowl. 'Er . . . can I ask you something? You're a spacesuit, right?'

'I am a general-purpose spacesuit, yes.'

Svetlana's questions tumbled out in a rush. 'Who made you? Where were you made? When were you put together?'

The helmet answered her after only the briefest of pauses. 'I am a general-purpose spacesuit of the Chakri five series. I was quickened in the Kanchanaburi Corporation manufacturing complex, New Far Bangkok, Triton. Quickening commenced at 15:12:34 GMT, July 27, 2134. Quickening finished at 04:22:11 GMT, August 9, 2134.'

'You mean 2134 as in . . . the year 2134?' Svetlana said.

The suit did not answer.

Svetlana sounded less sure of herself. 'What happened after you were quickened? Who owned you? How did you get here?'

'After two months of adaptive training with human subjects, I was certified spaceworthy. I became the corporate property of Surin Industries on October 15, 2134. On February 3, 2135, I was delivered to Surin Industries space vehicle *Spirit House* as part of a batch of thirty suits of the Chakri five series. I remain the property of Surin Industries, but since I contain no user-serviceable parts, I must be returned to the Kanchanaburi complex for repair and upgrade.' The suit paused momentarily. 'Since I cannot establish my present location, either by navgrid reference beacon, inertial vector trace-back or event memory stack, I cannot say how I got here. Wherever here might be.'

'So you're lost,' Svetlana said.

'Please assist me to update my location file. I do not require high precision at this point. Kindly specify coordinates in any of the following recognised positioning formats—'

'That can wait,' Svetlana said. 'We need you to do something for us now – are you still understanding me?'

'Yes,' the suit said, with the merest hint of irritation.

'Then you need to open up so that we can get at the man wearing you.'

'Are you asking me to release you?'

Svetlana glanced at the others. Parry nodded. The helmet appeared to have no sense that the person talking to it was not the person inside the suit's lower section.

'Yes,' Svetlana said. 'Go ahead and release me.'

'My sensors indicate that the helmet has been disengaged and that the ambient environment is safe. However, there is a small but finite chance that these observations are in error. You may suffer injury or death when I release you. Are you prepared to accept this risk?'

'Yes. Open. Let me out.'

'Would you like me to ask you that question again should similar circumstances arise?'

'Just open.'

'Please wait a moment. In the event that you wish to abort the opening procedure, any sudden vocal utterance will be interpreted as a command to reverse the process. If you do not wish to reverse the procedure, please refrain from making any sharp vocal utterances for the next ten seconds. I am now opening.'

Parry stepped back from the suit. It opened in an odd way – not at all how he had been expecting. A crack appeared in the front of the neck ring, widening and elongating until it reached the top of the chestpack. The crack then veered sideways to run down the left side of the chestpack, under it, and then down to the suit's crotch. The two upper halves of the suit sagged aside easily, with the right side retaining the asymmetric extension of the chestpack. Chisholm was naked under the suit – there was no inner layer, no biomonitor patches. Parry and Nadis worked his arms free of the sleeves and then hauled him from the lower part of the suit. His legs slipped free easily despite the apparent tightness of the suit design. His body was pale and completely hairless, even in the genital area, with none of the scars or blemishes that inevitably came with a career in space. All lean tissue, with so little fat that his ribs were painfully obvious. Jim Chisholm had been fifty-two when he died, but this could have been the body of a man in his twenties.

'They did a pretty good job,' Axford said appreciatively as the others lifted Chisholm onto one of the lander's passenger couches.

'Is he going to be okay?' Svetlana asked.

'He was *dead*, Svieta,' Axford said patiently. 'Anything else has to count as an improvement.'

'But he was with us and . . . now he's gone again.'

'We'll just have to keep our fingers crossed that he comes back,' Axford said.

'Fingers crossed – that's the best you can offer?'

'I'll do everything I can, but if you want miracles, you've come to the wrong doctor.'

Three times a day, at the end of every eight-hour monitoring shift, Svetlana received an e-mail summary on her flexy either from Axford himself or one of the duty nurses. Axford's preliminary assessment had been that Chisholm was in a deep coma, but there were no indications of grave damage to his central nervous system. Axford had placed him on a nutrient drip, but more aggressive intervention seemed unwise. The fever was abating, although his temperature was still a cause for concern. Scans were inconclusive: there was no sign of the glioblastoma, but his brain was awash with chemical and electrical activity, all of which clouded Axford's view of the real damage.

So they watched, and waited, and hoped.

Days passed, then a week. The fever vanished. Axford ran more scans and found the fog clearing: familiar brain structures began to emerge from the chaos. The blastoma was gone. It was as if it had never been there: perfect symmetry had been restored across the commissure. Axford compared the new scans with the old printouts in his medical records. The new scans looked like images of a younger brain, before the disease had taken hold. No surgeon would ever have been able to guess at the distortion Chisholm's brain had suffered in the final months before he had become a Frost Angel.

Axford refrained from hypothesizing, refusing to speculate about how the aliens had repaired the damage: for all he knew, they'd simply filled in the missing brain tissue, like builders bricking up a gap in a wall; or perhaps they had regrown Chisholm's entire body using the template provided by the frozen corpse Svetlana had carried into the ship.

Whatever the aliens had done, Svetlana was sure of one thing: they had returned Jim Chisholm to them. But the face she had looked into across the table had been more like that of the younger brother of the man she had known, not the man himself. And she did not know that younger brother at all.

# CHAPTER 24

Jim Chisholm came out of the coma on the ninth day. He opened his eyes and asked the duty nurse – Judy Sugimoto that shift – if he might have a glass of water.

Sugimoto roused Axford. Axford was still rubbing sleep out of his eyes when Svetlana arrived, with Parry in tow.

'How do you feel, Jim?' Axford asked, while Sugimoto helped him sit up in bed and swabbed his lips.

'I feel fine. Much better than before.' He looked around at the wary faces of the welcoming party. Nine days on, Axford's nutrient line had filled out some of the contours around Chisholm's face and skull. His scalp was shadowed with regrowing stubble, although Axford had taken care to shave his beard, the way Chisholm had always done. Chisholm smiled apologetically. 'I'm sorry if I alarmed anyone.'

'We weren't alarmed, just concerned,' Svetlana said. 'Do you remember much of what happened in Underhole?'

He blew out. 'Oh, yes. As if it happened yesterday. Which it didn't, of course. How long ago was that, exactly?'

'About nine days,' Svetlana said.

'It doesn't feel like it. I remember falling from the sky, sitting at the table, mistaking you for Bella—' He pursed his lips and shook abashed. 'I'm sorry about that. It's just that you all look a little older than I remember. And you always *did* look a little like Bella, Svetlana.'

'It's okay, Jim,' Svetlana said, smiling to let him know that she had taken no offence. It was so strange to be talking to him – so strange that, even as it was happening, she could not honestly say that it was pleasurable. This was uncharted emotional territory, and the further she went into it the more adrift she felt. Nothing in her life had prepared her for this. Hoping it sounded sincere, she said, 'It's just good to have you back with us.'

Chisholm nodded in reply. 'Not half as good as it is actually to *be* back,' he said. 'And to feel well again . . . I never thought this would happen.' He paused with the glass of water halfway to his mouth, studying the fine, hairless skin of his hand, with its utter absence of wrinkles and veins. For an instant, Svetlana thought she saw a shudder of horror pass through him.

'They fixed you,' she said.

'I know. They told me – or at least allowed me knowledge somehow – of what they were doing, but it's only just sinking in. I'd like someone to bring me a mirror, in a while. They changed my face, didn't they?'

'They put the clock back,' Svetlana said, 'that's all. You still look like Jim Chisholm.'

He stroked his clean-shaven jaw the way one might feel an object in the dark, and then his stubbled scalp. 'I'm not so sure about the mirror now.'

'You look fine, buddy,' Parry said. 'You're thickening out by the day. You always were a handsome bastard. Pity they haven't done anything about that.'

'Just . . . leaner and meaner, right?' Chisholm said, smiling ruefully. 'Well, I can live with that – I suppose I can live with anything, given the alternative. I don't want to sound ungrateful for what's happened to me.'

'Wasn't anything we did,' Parry said.

'Someone had the guts to carry me into that ship. That must have taken some nerve. Who drew the short straw?'

'I took you in,' Svetlana said. 'And there were no straws. There isn't a person on Janus who wouldn't have done it in my place.'

'You still did it, Svieta.'

How much, she wondered, did he know about what had happened to Craig Schrope? Had any knowledge of that filtered through to him while he was under the aliens' care?

'You deserved it,' she said. 'It was a privilege . . . an honour. And I wasn't scared. Not of the ship, anyway. I was scared about what would happen if we didn't do something.'

'Well, you did the right thing. Again, I'm sorry about what happened in Underhole. I didn't mean to cause any alarm. I don't think I was fully awake then: I mean, I remember it all . . . but it doesn't feel as if it was me speaking to you back then.'

'And now?' Svetlana asked.

'I feel clearer. A lot clearer. Like the way the air feels after a storm. It's passed now.'

'You're not out of the woods just yet,' Axford said firmly. 'By any objective measure you've been through an extremely stressful series of events, even if you don't remember all of it on a conscious level.'

'To be honest, I wish I remembered more of it. But it was only when the aliens put me back together that there was much of me capable of remembering anything.'

Svetlana sighed inwardly, relieved that Chisholm had brought up the matter of the aliens. Now at least she did not have to worry about broaching the subject, and possibly tipping him into another shock-induced coma.

'Do you remember them?' she asked.

'Absolutely. They made themselves known to me before letting me out of the ship. And to save you asking the one thing I'm sure you want to know above all else – they're friendly. They mean us no harm. We have nothing to fear from them, and a great deal to learn.'

He sounded as if he meant it, Svetlana thought, but as the aliens had wired his head back together, that was hardly surprising. They could have programmed him to say anything, with any amount of conviction.

'I'm all for learning from them,' she said doubtfully, 'but I can't see what they'd hope to gain from us in return.'

'Not much from us per se,' Chisholm said, 'but we do have one thing they have a use for: Janus. They don't want to invade, or subjugate us, or anything banal like that, but there are things in Janus that they can exploit for their own ends: power and materials, basically, just like we've been doing, but in a more sophisticated way.'

Svetlana frowned: there were a lot of questions she wanted to ask, and she wasn't quite sure how to prioritise them. 'Where would that leave us?'

'No worse off than we are now. So far, we've only extracted a tiny fraction of what Janus has to offer. The aliens want to tap Janus at a deeper level, one that won't impact on our energy-skimming at all. We can keep on doing what we've been doing since we arrived here – I've got some catching up to do, I know, but I would guess that things haven't changed particularly drastically in the last nine years.'

'No point pretending otherwise,' Parry said.

'In that case we lose nothing. We grant them access rights to the interior, and in return they'll give us more than we can dream of.'

'Okay,' Parry said, 'but if they want Janus that badly – and right now I can't quite see why they need it in the first place, they're so advanced – why don't they just take it from us? To them we must be like . . . I don't know, a little kid with a big lollipop.'

Chisholm shook his head. 'That isn't the way they do things. They've found in their travels that it's always better to arrive at a negotiated agreement.'

'But what if we say no?'

'They'll respect that decision.' Chisholm smiled. 'Look, I know you'll find this difficult to grasp, but overwhelming us with force wouldn't be a sensible strategy for them for two reasons. Firstly, although we're less technologically advanced than them, like any other spacefaring culture they're likely to meet we do have a rudimentary understanding of controlled fusion. Even if we don't have nuclear weapons with us, we'll have the means to make them. And nuclear weapons are already enough to rule out takeover by force. Not because we'd be able to use the weapons against them very effectively –

although we might try – but because we could very easily destroy the one thing they want. Nukes are the ultimate trump card, you see. It's like paper, scissors, stone. Nukes beat matter, every time, hands down.'

'They're afraid we'd blow up Janus to stop them getting at it?' Parry said.

'That's about it. Similar spoiling actions have been documented enough times in their past that they won't risk a forceful takeover unless they really have run out of options.'

'You said there were two reasons,' Axford said.

'Secondly, we may look like a pushover, but they – or possibly alien entities known to them – have occasionally run into advanced cultures pretending to be at a lower level of development. They won't attempt the big-stick approach in case we've got an even bigger stick hidden away somewhere.'

'But again, if we say no, they'll just walk away?'

'No, I said they'll respect that decision, but that won't stop them exploring other avenues for negotiation. They have a lot of time to play with, you see. They'll need Janus eventually – but not right now. They're just taking the long view, before the resource gets snatched up by someone else.'

'Someone else,' Svetlana echoed, with a prickle of disquiet. 'So there are other aliens out there?'

'The one thing I've learned,' Chisholm said, 'is that it's a big, wide universe, and not everything in it is as friendly as these guys.' He leaned forward in the bed. 'Which is why we really should listen to them. They put me back together. We already owe them something.'

Chisholm was still Axford's patient, and Axford was not going to let him be worn out by endless rounds of questions. Svetlana bowed to his wisdom, but made sure she arranged her own sleeping and working patterns to coincide with Chisholm's visiting hours. He looked a little healthier, a little less wraithlike, each time she entered the room. He always smiled encouragingly when he recognised her, made all the right moves, did all the things that ought to have put her at ease. He made small talk and dropped jokes and self-deprecating observations into the conversation. But every now and then he still came out with something that brought an alien chill into the room.

'The suit you came back in,' Svetlana said, when it was time to push him further. 'It spoke Thai. It claimed to have been manufactured on Triton in 2134. Do you know anything about that?'

'If the suit told me it'd been manufactured on Triton, I'd be inclined to believe it.'

'The suit bothers us, Jim.'

He'd been making notes on a sheet of vat-grown paper with a ballpoint pen. Now he put the sheet aside. 'It shouldn't,' he said. 'It's just a spacesuit. It can't harm you.'

'That's not the point. What bothers us is how did the suit get to Spica?'

'The aliens found it. They're not the Spicans, incidentally – but you've probably worked that out already.'

Parry had already told her of Bella's suspicions. As much as it galled her, she had to concede that Bella had a point. 'We're calling them Fountainheads for now. If they turn out to be the Spicans after all, we'll rethink the name.'

'Fountainheads.' He cocked his head, then nodded agreeably. 'I like it. They'll like it, too, I think.'

'Craig Schrope coined it,' she said. 'He saw them first.'

He'd been told what had happened to Craig Schrope, but although he had absorbed the information, he did not seem to connect with Schrope's death on an emotional level. 'Good for Craig,' he said.

'What bothers us,' Svetlana said, 'is how the aliens ever came into contact with the people who made that spacesuit.'

'They're starfaring,' Chisholm said. 'It's what they do.'

'So at some point they encountered a human ship, one that happened to be carrying a spacesuit manufactured in 2134?'

'Pretty reasonable assumption.'

'Except it doesn't cut it. We left the solar system in 2057. We've come two hundred and sixty-odd light-years since then, mostly at a speed only slightly slower than light. The latest information that could possibly have reached us out here would be from only one or two years after our departure. Even if the Fountainheads made contact with humanity in 2059, they'd only just have had time to race out here in time for our arrival – assuming they have the ability to travel slightly closer to the speed of light than us. But that suit's from nearly eighty years after we left! Information about 2134 is on its way to us, but it won't get here until somewhere around *our* version of 2134.'

'Nonetheless, the suit exists.'

'It doesn't make any sense, Jim, not unless we throw out the light-speed limit. Are we ready to do that? Even Janus didn't travel faster than light.'

'But it was the Fountainheads that brought you the suit. Their technology's clearly of a different order than the machinery inside Janus. Perhaps they did exceed the speed of light to get here in time.'

'What did the aliens say, Jim? Did they tell you where they got hold of that suit?'

'No,' he said. 'They didn't tell me that.'

'You didn't think to ask?'

For the first time, he sounded needled. 'I didn't care about the suit, Svieta. They fixed me up, let me get to know them a bit, then wound me up and set me walking back to you like a clockwork clown. You saw what I was like then. Do you think I gave the suit more than a glance?'

'Still bothers me, Jim.'

'Well, don't let it. They're benign, like I said. They want something that it'll cost us nothing to give, and in return they'll give us the world.'

'Alien technology?'

He gave her a short, derisive smile. 'No, but they can give us more things like the suit – data and technology from our own future history. Think of that, Svieta. We're not just talking about useful hardware like a suit. We're talking about medical advances, computing advances . . . nanotechnology that'll make Wang's forge vats look like blast furnaces. You've done well to keep the colony alive all these years, but I've been awake long enough to know how tough things must have been. Thirteen years alone didn't put all those lines on Axford's face.'

'It's been tough,' she acknowledged, shrugging.

'But now it can get better. Let the Fountainheads give us what's already our due. Negotiate with them. Send me back in as your spokesman. They know me inside out. They trust me.'

'I'll think about it,' she said.

'Good. But don't think about it for too long.'

'I won't,' she said. She rose to leave. 'I ought to let you get some rest now. Is there anything you need, anything I can do to make things better in here?'

He tapped the ballpoint against his lip. 'No. Axford and the rest of his team have been treating me like a king.'

'If there's anything, you only have to say the word.'

'I will,' he said. Then, just as she reached the door, he called out, 'Svetlana . . . there is one thing, but I find it a bit awkward to talk about.'

She returned to his bedside. 'Say it, Jim.'

'People have been kind to me since I got back. I know you've all been trying to put me at my ease, making it as easy as possible for me to adjust to the time that I've lost. But really, it's all right. I can deal with things.'

'That's good.'

'So you can tell me.'

'Tell you what?' she asked.

'Look, I know you're all trying to be kind, but I can deal with the truth.'

'The truth?' she said, nonplussed.

'Bella's dead, isn't she? That's why no one ever mentions her, and why you all look away whenever I mention her name. You're worried about how I'll deal with it. Well, I *am* dealing with it. Hour by hour, day by day . . . I'm handling it. I just need to know – did she come to you with my wishes, or did you crack the encryption on my message?'

'She came to us,' Svetlana said, reluctantly forcing out the words.

'How long ago was that? Was she ill? Did she know she was going to die?'

'She isn't dead.'

Chisholm's lip twitched. 'I'm sorry?'

'She isn't dead,' Svetlana repeated. 'She's alive, alive and in pretty good shape. Axford can tell you better, but . . . she's okay.'

She watched expressions play across his face: relief that Bella was alive, then confusion, then something like disappointment. 'I would have thought—' he began.

'That she'd have come to see you?'

'It wouldn't have been asking much.'

'She couldn't. She can't come and see you because she's still in exile.'

'In exile? Where?'

'The some place. The dome.'

He stared at her in revulsion. 'You've had her in that place for *thirteen fucking years*? I always knew you were tough, Svieta. So was Bella. I guess it came with the territory. But I never had you down as heartless.'

'This isn't about me and Bella,' she said.

Chisholm shook his head slowly. 'It is now. I want to speak to Bella in person, in private. Just the two of us, just like old times.'

In that instant she could already feel the first ominous slippage, the beginning of a fatal loss of control. It had been a beautiful and humane thing, to bring Chisholm back from the dead. It had given her a line to the Fountainheads. It had also been the gravest political error of her thirteen years in command. She should have found another way . . . sent someone else in. Takahashi, perhaps, or one of the other victims. Bagley, maybe, or Fletterick, Mair, Ungless. There were always dead. There would always *be* dead, as long as people tried to live on Janus. Why had it never occurred to her that sending in Bella's closest confidant and friend might not be the shrewdest of actions?

'You're too weak to go out to her,' Svetlana said, grasping for an excuse.

'Then bring her here. Bring her back to Crabtree.' His eyes sparkled with schemes and dreams. 'It's time she was rehabilitated. Time things changed around here.'

Then he clicked the ballpoint pen, three times, slowly.

# PART THREE

# 2090+

# CHAPTER 25

The Underhole Express gathered speed with its usual smooth surge of acceleration. As it threaded between Crabtree's outlying precincts and domes, Bella buckled into her seat and made sure all her belongings were secured to the fold-down table.

'Before you fall asleep,' Liz Shen said, passing Bella a live flexy, 'I need your okay on this.'

Bella glared at the document. It was the go-ahead for the Tier-Two feasibility study, which would see human expansion erupt onto the outer surface of the Iron Sky. She signed it with her customary flourish, despite the arthritis that was making it increasingly awkward for her to write. It was largely formality: the Tier-Two project had strong advocates in Crabtree and the more influential eddytowns, and it would take more than Bella's obstructiveness to hold it back now.

'Any other business?' she asked guardedly.

'There's the matter Avery Fox wants to discuss with you – I can brief you, if you like.'

'I'm sure he'll tell me all about it when we get to Underhole, but I suppose it wouldn't hurt to know the basics.'

'Basically, they found something when they were sinking some new foundation piles last week. No one quite knows what to make of it, but we're pretty sure it hasn't been down there for ever. It looks as if Svetlana buried it there just before she had to clear out of Underhole.'

Bella thought back to those events, compressed paper-thin by the weight of intervening years. 'Why would she bury something? I gave her more than enough time to get out of there. Couldn't be a bomb, could it?'

'Avery says not. Whatever it is just sits there – doesn't do anything. It's heavy, though, even under Janus gravity. Maybe that's why she left it behind.'

'All right – Avery can fill me in on the details. Probably isn't anything significant. Is there anything I *do* need to worry about?'

The smart young woman dimmed the flexy and slipped it under her floral-patterned jacket. 'You're keen. I have a paper copy of the latest draft report on the Bagley affair, if you want to review it.'

Bella rolled her eyes. 'I've reviewed umpteen versions already. Show it to me when they have something that'll hold up in court. Then I'll think about reopening the inquiry.'

'There'll be a lot of people hoping it never makes it that far,' Liz Shen said. 'Of course, if you'd rather they didn't have anything to worry about—'

'Oh, just give it to me,' Bella said grumpily, knowing Shen was right.

As the train whisked towards Underhole at a comfortable one hundred and eight kilometres per hour – just below orbital speed – Bella skimmed the latest draft report on the Bagley murder. The paper smelled faintly of peppermint. It was twenty-eight years since Meredith Bagley had been found dead, crushed by the movement of a centrifuge during scheduled maintenance. Five years ago, however, Hank Dussen – one of Parry's old EVA men – had confessed to being one of three participants in her murder. Dussen had been on his deathbed at the time of his confession, riddled with radiation carcinomas from a lifetime of spacewalking. An affiliate of one of the more obscure Symbolist sects, he refused to entrust himself to the rejuvenative medicine of the Fountainheads. He saw his confession as a necessary step to absolution, but he had not named his co-conspirators.

The case had simmered on since then, unable to progress due to a lack of further information. Then, unexpectedly, Ash Murray had uncovered a paper log containing fault reports for the three suits that had been signed out for that shift. The log contained no names, but the three sets of faults had all been written in different handwriting. One set matched known documents linked to Hank Dussen, while the other two were good matches against samples from the suspected co-conspirators. After a lifetime of working in suits, filling in the fault documentation had been second nature to them.

Bella put down the document with a sigh. 'Do you really think I should pull back this scab, Liz, just when we're all beginning to live together in peace again . . . just when things are starting to settle down?'

'Has to be done,' Liz Shen said.

'I know, I know. It's just . . .' Bella sighed heavily. 'This is going to raise hell. It may not stop at just two names. God knows how many people have been involved keeping this covered up over the years.'

'Has to be done,' Shen repeated firmly. As ever, she appeared wise beyond her years, like the older sister Bella had never had. 'And we'll pull through it, too,' she added. 'Maybe we actually need this, to finally move on from all that.'

There were many like Liz Shen now: children of Janus, pushing inexorably into adulthood, many with children of their own. Earth meant nothing to them. It was like some distant, exotic, vaguely perplexing foreign country – the way Japan or China had been to Bella when she was a girl. They were happy to take what they could from it – its fashions, music, clothes and consumer goods – but they had no gripping desire actually to visit the place. If Shen and her generation were nostalgic about anything, it was the version of Janus they remembered from their youth, with its deceptive simplicities and easily forgotten hardships.

Things had improved during the twenty years since the Fountainheads drilled through the Sky. After months of uneasy negotiation, the aliens had been allowed to sink energy-sucking taproots into the luminous vaults under Janus. In return, the Fountainheads had given the humans access to technologies, artefacts and data the aliens had acquired during their earlier episodes of human contact. None of these items dated from later than 2135 – the 'Cutoff', as it was now known – but that was still nearly eighty years of human progress to catch up on. Careful not to overwhelm the humans, the Fountainheads had drip-fed these marvels one dose at a time, in return for increasing access to the interior of Janus.

Liz Shen was an object lesson in how well these lessons had been integrated into the normal flow of Janus life. The flexy she carried with her was for Bella's benefit, not hers. She regarded flexies with the eldritch horror Bella might have reserved for a steam-driven typewriter. Liz Shen's computational needs were handled by her clothes and the kernels of Borderline Intelligence packed into her minimalist jewellery. The clothes and jewellery drew their tiny power requirements from her movements. The computational textiles exchanged data with the environment via rapid subliminal alterations to their colour patterning, too brief to be picked up by the human eye. The apparently serene environment, in turn, flickered beneath the level of perception with a frenzy of encoded data patterns.

The clothes had become so adept at reading Shen's muscular intentions (they were sewn with superconductors, to pick up the myoelectric field pulses of her nervous system) that she rarely needed to complete the gesture itself. When she was busy, Shen's muscles pulsated with a kind of low-level palsy, like a person receiving mild electroconvulsive therapy. She had the hard muscle tone of a ballerina. It might have looked odd, but there were people like Shen everywhere nowadays. Bella and the other old-timers were the oddities, with their quaint attachment to flexies.

Bella had tried to keep up, but she had been sixty-eight when the Fountainheads came, already set in her ways. Now she was twenty years older. There were many like her, too: mired in the past, dressing like ghosts from a vanished era, blinking in bewildered surprise at the rush of events.

Shen pulled down her sunglasses and went into a brief data-tremor. 'We're approaching Underhole,' she said. 'We had a security scare a few hours ago, but everything's normal now.'

Bella handed her back the papers on the Bagley case. 'You'd better keep hold of these for now. If they can tighten section three, I think we're there.'

'You're going to have to subpoena Ash Murray,' Shen said. 'I can start the paperwork on that, if you want. He's not going to like it, though.'

'Of course he's not going to like it. I have a feeling he expected to stay dead for rather longer than four years.'

'Serves him right for joining the Skippers.' Shen tore off a chunk of the Bagley report and pushed it into her mouth, talking as she chewed. 'They called it "exporting expertise to the future". Social cowardice, if you ask me.'

'Don't be too hard on them,' Bella said. 'We all lived through some pretty bad times. People like Ash . . . they'd just had enough.'

'I'm still glad you closed that loophole. Why should we carry their dead weight across the decades?' Shen tore off another corner from the report and offered it to Bella. 'You haven't eaten since this morning. Would you like some?'

'No thanks,' Bella said, touching a hand to her belly. 'Paperwork always disagrees with me.'

Liz Shen handed Bella a plastic filter mask as they disembarked from the train into the unfinished transit plaza at Underhole. Dust hung in the air in languid, drifting sheets, never settling to the ground. The few human workers present guided their construction machines with slow full-body gestures, like t'ai chi masters. Avery Fox came bustling over to see them, snatching down a dust mask and apologising for his lateness. He was twenty-six, born in the seventh year of the human occupation of Janus. He was the only child of Reda Kirschner and Malcolm Fox, a marriage across the lines of allegiance dividing Bella and Svetlana.

'They tell me you've found something,' Bella said.

'I thought you might like to see it sooner rather than later. We've booked a heavy tractor to haul it back to Crabtree, but it probably won't get there for another week.'

'I've kept the Fountainheads waiting long enough. I'm sure a few more minutes won't make any difference.'

'It's true, then?' Avery asked. 'You're really going through with it?'

'Even old women are allowed to change their minds.' She softened her expression: in recent years she had become dimly aware of how sternly disapproving she could appear. 'The years have caught up with me, Avery. Look at these useless old hands of mine.'

'I hope it all goes well,' he said.

'It will. They ought to be getting good at it by now.'

He led them into the bowels of the Underhole transit complex, through dust screens and airlocks. Soon they arrived in an excavated space with a pit in the floor, where drilling had been suspended. A makeshift walkway had been geckoflexed to the ice. Bella tightened one of her useless old hands on the railing and looked down.

'That's it?' she asked, dismayed.

It was nothing to look at: just a black cube about the same size as a transport crate.

'It's heavier than it looks,' Fox said, slipping into the peculiar lilting accent she often heard amongst the young. 'Two hundred tonnes of mass, easily – it weighs more than five hundred kilos even on Janus. If they only had a few pairs of hands, they'd have had a hard time loading it onto a tractor. Easier to dig a hole and bury it.'

'If Svetlana didn't want me to see this thing, why didn't she just destroy it?' Bella asked, not really expecting an answer.

Liz Shen said, 'What is it, anyway?'

'No one knows,' Fox replied. There's a design cut into one of the faces – some naked guy in a square.'

'Not ringing any bells here,' Bella said, but something bristled the hairs on the back of her neck. 'How closely have you examined it?'

'We've poked and prodded it enough to be certain it isn't a bomb. Looks solid all the way through.'

'Composition?'

'Funny thing is,' Avery said, 'we haven't had much luck shaving anything off for analysis. Tough as old boots, whatever it is. Maybe that's why Svetlana didn't destroy it – she couldn't have even if she'd wanted to.'

'And it's been down here for twenty years?'

'Unless someone tells us otherwise. If you want the facts, I guess Svetlana's the person to ask. Do you still want us to ship it back to Crabtree?'

'We'll take the risk if it means we'll have a better chance of studying it. But keep this under wraps – I don't want this all over town by the time it gets there.'

'I'm sure we can handle it with the necessary discretion,' Shen said, with the conceited glow of someone who knew they were extremely good at their job. 'But what about Svetlana? Do you want someone to bring her in from Eddytown for questioning?'

'No,' Bella said, 'just dig out the names of everyone who might have been at Underhole just before the takeover. That's where we'll start.'

'You really want to get into this on top of the Bagley investigation? Isn't one hornet's nest enough for you?'

'Actually,' Bella said, 'that's a very good point. When you pick them up – whoever they turn out to be – drop hints that it's all part of a peripheral inquiry related to the Bagley case. Don't be afraid to take the train to Eddytown, if that's where your investigations lead, but never let Svetlana suspect that this has anything to do with the cube.' Then she found herself looking back down at the ominous black object, as if it were exerting a magnetic tug on her thoughts, forcing her attention upon itself. 'That . . . thing,' she said uneasily. 'Has anyone actually *touched* it?'

'I did,' Fox said, looking down shamefacedly. 'It was stupid – I should have waited until we'd run tests. But no harm came from it.'

'What did it feel like?'

'Very cold,' he said. 'Cold and very, very old. A lot older than twenty years.'

Bella shivered: she swore she could feel that antiquity without even touching it. But that was absurd.

# CHAPTER 26

Bella and Shen walked up the steep temporary ramp to the waiting elevator car, where a small security retinue waited. It was easy going now, even for Bella's ageing muscles and knee joints. The gravity was currently Janus ambient, but when construction was completed the underlying machinery would be tweaked to induce a hotspot of point-five Earth gravities. It was a simple trick that the Fountainheads had taught the humans: one of the few gifts that had not involved the transfer of prior human knowledge.

They'd already upped the gravity at Crabtree: the last centrifuge had been spun down and dismantled three years earlier. People had moaned and grumbled, but the medical benefits of permanent high gravity were too significant to ignore, and with the birth rate shooting up, the centrifuges could not have coped for much longer.

Bella and Shen entered the elevator car with one of the security men and took seats. Soon they were rising, to the accompaniment of a tinkly rendition of 'The Girl from Ipanema'. The car passed through an airlock into open space and Bella looked down at the sprawl of Underhole, imagining the deep foundations plunging through kilometres of ice to the Spican bedrock. If the Tier-Two advocates had their way, Underhole would form a throbbing arterial bridge between the interior and the new territories scheduled to spill out across the other side of the Sky.

The upper works were much less impressive. A crane had winched the elevator across the twenty-kilometre gap, and now it swung its boom to one side and deposited the little compartment next to a cluster of domes barely larger than the original Underhole settlement. Bella and Shen passed through an airlock into a reception area. Furniture oozed into readiness, anticipating their arrival. A chair nudged Bella's ankles with puppy-dog eagerness. She kicked it aside irritably.

Nick Thale was waiting for them, as white-haired and patriarchal as a wizard. He was in his mid-fifties, but had turned down all offers of rejuvenation:

he wanted to wait another twenty years, he said, just in case there were any unexpected complications.

'It's been a long time, Bella,' he said. 'You should come and see us more often.'

'You should see how difficult it is to drag her out of her office, let alone Crabtree,' Shen said.

Bella shot the other woman a sidelong glance: was that an attempt at humour, or just a bald statement of the facts? Perhaps she needed to revise her opinion of Shen.

'There's enough to keep me busy, Nick. I trust you to keep a handle on things this side of the Sky.'

'We do our best. How is Crabtree, anyway?'

'You should pop down one of these days, take a stroll in one of the new biomes. We've got trees now – real, honest-to-god trees. Junipers . . . oaks. I never thought I'd see a tree again in my lifetime.'

'Gene-edited from the aeroponics plant stocks?'

'No,' Bella said. 'That never worked. Turned out the plants we brought with us had already been hacked about to protect DeepShaft patents. Major chromosomal deletions, genetically impoverished: not enough material to work with.'

'So the trees . . .?'

'Cultured straight from Fountainhead data. It was buried in the last batch of stuff they sent us, almost as an afterthought, as if they didn't think we'd find it all that interesting.'

'I'd like to touch a tree again,' Thale said wistfully.

'Then come down to Crabtree. I'll show you around. Things are buzzing now – it feels like a city.'

Thale grimaced. 'A city on Sunday, perhaps, when everyone's left – even the ice-cream vendors.'

'It's filling out more and more every year. The kids make a difference. The grandchildren. Blink and there'll be great-grandchildren, kids for whom even the Year of the Iron Sky is ancient history. Earth'll be like . . . I don't know, Sparta, or Mesopotamia, a thing they look at in picture books before smiling and turning the page to something more exciting.'

'You frighten me sometimes, Bella.'

'I felt this way before I ever set foot on *Rockhopper*, as if the world was slipping away from me. It's just got worse, that's all.'

Thale led her along the glass connecting walkway that led to the Fountainhead embassy, while Liz Shen stayed behind in the reception dome. Bella hoped her nervousness was not too apparent, but with every step closer to the aliens she found her resolve crumbling. She had delayed this visit long enough, and would have continued putting it off had Jim Chisholm not requested her immediate presence. Chisholm was still technically her subordinate, but she had long ago learned that sometimes it paid to obey him.

The embassy occupied the former landing site of the original Fountainhead ship. In some regards it was still the original ship, but due to the dream-like malleability of Fountainhead technology it was difficult (and perhaps futile) to say for sure. The embassy was much larger, at any rate: its perimeter had encroached across half the distance between the original location of the ship and the hole, and it was much taller. But it had something of the same layered glassy architectural style, with many chandelier-like arms curving upward to tapering spires, forming a thicket of refractive structures around a gherkin-shaped central core. Now and then sub-units would arrive and depart, some of which were nearly as large as the original ship. Their mode of propulsion, like everything else associated with the Fountainheads, spoke of technologies far beyond human science at the time of the Cutoff.

The glass tube led into a domed vault in the base of the embassy. Layers of transparent structure surrounded them, aglow with a soft and calming violet light. As they walked across the floor, two cylindrical kiosks rose seamlessly from its surface. Thale and Bella stepped through doorlike apertures in the sides of the kiosks, taking one each. Bella held still and waited for the kiosk to seal itself around her. After a moment the cylindrical form contracted until the inner surface of the enclosure was only centimetres from her body. Seen through the optically perfect glass, Thale's kiosk had also shrunk down to something resembling a fat bottle.

They started walking and Bella's enclosure reshaped itself, bulging to accommodate the throw of her legs and the swing of her arms. It all happened so swiftly that Bella was never able to touch the glass. Thale led the way out of the vault and up a shallow helical ramp that led to a higher part of the embassy. As they walked, Bella knew, the external atmosphere was being swapped for the dense and poisonous broth of atmospheric chemicals necessary to sustain the Fountainheads. Gravity was also ramping up, but she felt none of that inside the suit's protective envelope.

The helix carried them into what Bella had always thought of as the diplomatic reception area. It was a cavernous space that must have taken up a third of the interior volume of the embassy's central core: a room as large as a gutted skyscraper. Luminous pastel motifs ringed the space, suggesting – to Bella, at least – vast stained-glass windows of intricate abstract design. Angular structures plunged down from a distant ceiling, spiked and barbed and threaded with lines of soft illumination. It paid not to think about the gravitational forces struggling to rip them down. No Fountainheads were here yet, but – just as she had anticipated – Jim Chisholm was waiting to meet them.

He still looked human, but she wondered how deep that resemblance actually went. Chisholm did not require any visible protective armour in the presence of the Fountainheads. On the increasingly rare occasions when he returned to Crabtree, Axford sometimes managed to run medical tests on him. He never found anything anomalous, nothing to suggest that the man in his care was anything but human on a cellular level (and Axford's tools were much more sophisticated now); but that was Chisholm in Crabtree, and this was Chisholm in the Fountainhead embassy, and the two apparitions were not necessarily the same being.

He smiled, spreading his hands in greeting and urging them further into the reception area. 'I'm glad we finally talked you into this, Bella,' he said, his voice sounding as clear and normal as if they were talking across a coffee table, rather than through toxic metres of alien atmosphere.

'You've always had great powers of persuasion,' Bella said.

'There's nothing to fear,' he said, 'nothing in the world. They've got better at it since my day. It took them three days back then – can you imagine that?'

'I imagine practice has helped.'

'I suppose it has.' He wore loose, billowing garments in fawn and beige that – to Bella at least – were faintly suggestive of some minor theocratic order. His hair was longer than it had ever been on *Rockhopper*, combed back from his brow in thick waves. In twenty years, he'd shown little visible evidence of ageing: a few lines around the mouth, one or two creases in the forehead, but that was all. Such was the case with all the rejuvenations generally: even when there were signs of ageing, they appeared at a much slower rate than before. The half-moon glasses he still wore had to be an affectation. 'Bella,' he said, 'when all this is done . . . when they've made you young again—'

She knew from his tone where he was headed. 'Jim—'

'It's not forbidden to move on, you know.'

'I know you mean well.'

He spoke as if Nick Thale were not there. 'No one expected you to change overnight after thirteen years of exile, but how long has it been now since I came back?' He held up his hands, smiling. 'Rhetorical question.'

'Clearly.'

'There's no law that says you have to spend the rest of your existence alone.'

'No one ever said there was.'

'You sometimes act as if there was.'

They'd had this conversation enough times for Bella to know that Jim Chisholm was not talking about the two of them having any kind of relationship. He meant that she should find another man amongst all that were available to her. As if it was that easy. As if pulling out that knife in her stomach was a matter of childish simplicity. A knife buried so deep that it felt familiar and even, at times, comforting.

He'd returned from the aliens gifted with strange wisdom, knowledge of things he barely dared speak of. Yet there were times when he appeared to know less about human affairs than he had before he died.

He must have seen something in her face. 'Forgive me. I didn't mean to pry.'

'I am what I am, Jim. I was like this long before we ever got to Janus. Nothing that's happened here has changed that.'

'I'm sorry.'

'Don't be. Perhaps some other time . . . further down the line.'

'None of us knows how far the line goes,' he said. 'Things change. Things that we thought would last for ever suddenly aren't as immune to time as we'd imagined. It's just that there are times – like now – when we should all seize the moment. It was inexcusable of me to lecture you about your private life, Bella, but I hope you understand why I'm so concerned.'

'Something's happened, then? Something that makes you wish I'd make the most of what I have now?'

'Something's on the horizon.'

'Good or bad?' Nick Thale asked.

'Not good,' Chisholm said, glancing at Thale and then looking back at Bella, 'but nothing that need alarm us immediately.'

Bella could have wished for better news, but she was glad not to have to talk about her arid love life any more. Anything was an improvement over that topic of conversation. 'Somehow that's not as wonderfully reassuring as I think you meant it to be,' she said.

'What is it?' Thale asked.

'Something's got them rattled. I don't know what, exactly. All I've been able to gather so far is that it's something they've found deep in the tube. Something that wasn't there the last time they looked.'

'What kind of something?' Thale asked.

'I'd better let them tell you in person,' Chisholm said. 'They're on their way down.'

One of the ceiling structures pushed its way to the ground. Three Fountainheads emerged from a bulb-shaped aperture in the tip and moved across the floor. As they approached, gliding like ghosts, their many fronds made a whispering sound.

They were three metres tall, slightly wider at the base. Under normal conditions, all that was visible was the outer curtain of blue 'tractor' fronds that sprayed out from a central core, then curved down to contact the ground. These fronds – which were relatively thick and prehensile – supported most of a Fountainhead's weight, enabling locomotion and the manipulation of its surroundings. The fronds' constant swishing motion, even when a Fountainhead was stationary, was believed to be linked to thermal regulation, respiration and the transport of microscopic detritus from the inner layers.

The next layer consisted of finer fronds, each only a millimetre across, with the partial translucence of fibre-optic lines, and was only glimpsed intermittently. Flashes of red and green were believed to relate to emotional states. These finer fronds also functioned as more delicate manipulators for work requiring greater precision than that offered by the tractor fronds. The fine fronds evidenced a high degree of functional specialisation. Some were furred with cilia of varying lengths that presumably permitted the Fountainheads to detect sounds and discriminate between frequencies. Some were tipped with tactile pads that were thought to be attuned to a wide range of chemical flavours. Other fronds were seamed with a dark lateral line that was believed to be the functional equivalent of an eye. Although the single line offered only a one-dimensional slice of its surroundings, the constant overlapping motion of many eye-fronds presumably allowed the Fountainhead to synthesize a rich visual landscape, akin to the ground-mapping radar of an orbiting spacecraft. Now and then they were capable of focusing their attention on a particular object of interest and a number of visual fronds would be deftly interlaced to form a kind of basket-weave mesh about thirty centimetres across, perhaps enabling a 'high-resolution' mode, as Bella's analysts had dubbed it.

Within the curtain of sensory fronds was a second, smaller set of tractor fronds, rarely glimpsed, that might also have played some role in the exchange of reproductive material. Finally, at the heart of the creature there was a turnip-shaped central mass to which all the fronds were anchored, and which was itself supported ten or fifteen centimetres above the ground by the fronds. This central trunk contained, it was assumed, the aliens' central nervous system. A fringed mouth at its base served to anchor the creature to the mound-like pedestals that were the Fountainhead equivalent of stools, and which allowed the tractor fronds to be elevated and rested. It was also speculated that the mouth permitted the ingestion of foodstuffs (assuming they were not absorbed directly through specialised frond structures), the excretion of waste and – perhaps – the birthing of infants or the laying of eggs.

Most of it was complete guesswork, though. Bella's analysts didn't even know the chemical make-up of the Fountainhead atmosphere, let alone the biological adaptations that allowed the creatures to survive in it. No data existed on the physical conditions or whereabouts of the Fountainhead homeworld, or how much time had passed since they had left it. Every attempt to interrogate the aliens on these matters had met with either polite silence or playfully cryptic answers.

Perhaps even the Fountainheads didn't know.

One of them moved ahead of the other two. By its confident glide and the slight excess of ruby patterning in the sensory layer, Bella recognised it as McKinley – a name it had taken for itself. The other two were almost certainly Kānchenjunga and Dhāulagiri, although she could not yet tell them apart. She wasn't at all sure what to make of the fact that the aliens had chosen the names of terrestrial mountains. Was it a mocking echo of Craig Schrope's misheard 'fountains', or something completely innocent? No one knew.

McKinley's tractor fronds parted like a stage curtain. The inner layer of sensor fronds interlaced to form a high-resolution array, which it held towards Bella for a moment before directing it at Thale.

'Hello, Bella,' the alien said. 'It's good of you to come. We always enjoy your visits. You too, Nick.'

The Fountainheads created human phonemes by rubbing fronds against each other and opening and closing temporary acoustic chambers within the frond mass. It was an audacious performance that nonetheless conveyed the ghostly impression of wind whispering through trees.

Bella could never forget the abyss of profoundly alien cognition lurking behind the attempt at a human mask.

'Thank you, McKinley,' she said. 'If Jim wasn't such a safe pair of hands I'd be up here all the time, checking up on him.'

McKinley unravelled the high-resolution array and withdrew its sensor fronds back behind the outer curtain of tractor fronds. 'You'll hear no complaints from us: we're very happy to have Jim up here. Still, it's high time you paid us a visit. You don't want to become *too* much of a challenge for us, do you?'

'Not at all,' Bella said, 'although I don't doubt your abilities for a moment.'

'Make a good job of it,' said Thale. 'It took her friends so damned long to talk her into this that most of us haven't got the energy to face it again.'

'We'll do our best.' The alien made an oddly familiar gesture: elongating two tractor fronds and clasping them together, like a person rubbing their hands before getting down to business. 'Anyway, the procedure itself is nothing you need worry about.'

'That's a relief,' she said, not quite telling the truth.

'But there *is* something we need to discuss – I believe Jim's already alerted you regarding our concerns.' McKinley rotated its entire body, giving the impression that it was turning to face Chisholm. 'Right, Jim?'

'I told Bella what you told me. I mean no disrespect, but the information was rather short on hard facts. I told her you'd found something—'

'Yes, we have. Several things, as it happens.'

Thale shot a glance at Bella and asked, 'Where, exactly?'

'In one of the adjoining tubes,' McKinley said. 'Not more than four light-minutes from here.'

'That's twice as far as we've ever been,' Bella said, wondering whether the Fountainhead caught the mild note of resentment in her voice. The aliens had been careful to dissuade the humans from venturing too far into the

Spica Structure, with vague warnings of the hazards that lay in wait for the unwary.

'There are sound reasons for the caution we advise,' McKinley replied, with a hint of admonition. 'You have done very well in the last twenty years, but your technologies are still limited in comparison to most of the entities you might encounter in the deep Structure. Doors open and close without warning. We inhabit a relatively stable region, but other zones are subject to disputes that occasionally overspill into nearby volumes. You would not wish to become embroiled in something like that.'

'But it's fine for you.'

'Even we must act with caution. Of course, you are free to do what you want – we've never attempted to prevent your explorations.'

To be fair, Bella thought, that was true, but the aliens were masters of dissuasion, and that had been effective enough. Except for one or two isolated incidents – quickly punished by her own administration – no human envoys from Crabtree had ever contravened the Fountainhead guidelines.

'So what have you found?' she asked.

'Items of technical detritus,' McKinley said, 'paraphernalia associated with another culture known to inhabit the Structure.' It flicked its tractor fronds, as if shooing away a fly. 'They're messy. Wherever they go, they leave a trail of discarded junk.'

'Who are they?'

'The closest human equivalent would be "Musk Dogs".'

'Are they dangerous?'

'Musk Dogs are not in themselves belligerent or aggressive, nor are they exceptionally advanced by Structure standards. They are just . . . trouble. In their dealings with lesser cultures, they are indiscriminate and clumsy. They have caused great damage, great harm. Some cultures have proven robust enough to withstand contact with Musk Dogs, but most have been left wounded, or even extinct.'

'Do you think Musk Dogs are on their way here?'

'The discovery of their detritus is certainly worrying – it indicates that they have sent scouting missions into this part of the Structure. It may be that they have been routed . . . banished from other regions. Now that the Uncontained are loose again, the balance of power is shifting across large volumes of the Structure.'

He had never mentioned the Uncontained before. 'Now you're scaring me, McKinley.'

'And me,' Thale said. 'When, exactly, can we expect them to show up?'

The alien's fronds stirred languidly. 'Impossible to say, unfortunately. Relevant doors are closed now, but there is no telling when they will reopen. The Whisperers – another culture – have passkeys which permit some doors to be opened at their discretion. If the Musk Dogs talk to the Whisperers, or if they simply wait long enough, until certain doors choose to open . . . It could happen tomorrow. It could happen in fifty years. But when the doors open, the Musk Dogs will arrive. You must be ready for them.'

'How?'

'You should evolve a societal stance that precludes contact. Ignore their temptations. Historical data suggests that there is no safe level of exposure to Musk Dogs.'

Thale looked aghast. 'What if they come anyway? What if they force themselves upon us?'

'They won't, unless you respond to their overtures.'

'What's to stop them?' Bella asked.

'Us,' McKinley said. 'We'll protect you if the Musk Dogs are foolish enough to force contact upon you. But that is not how it will happen. They are shrewder than that, slyer. They know their limitations. They will attempt to insinuate themselves into your trust. They will cast aspersions on us. They will sully our motives, cause you to doubt our intentions.'

'You hate them,' she said, marvelling.

'We hate what they have done. It is not the same thing. They are simply runaway creatures that have somehow managed to acquire interstellar capability. Confined to their own niche, they would not be problematic.'

'I believe we should take McKinley's concerns seriously,' Chisholm said, his arms folded into his voluminous beige sleeves. 'We've had twenty years to adapt to the idea that the Fountainheads aren't out to eat us, or turn us into slaves. I told you they were benign the day I stepped out of their ship, and nothing that's happened since has given any of us cause to doubt that.'

'I know,' Bella said, nodding to all three aliens. 'And I'll reiterate: we're all extraordinarily grateful to you. More than likely we'd be dead by now if you hadn't come along. And I thank you for warning us about the Musk Dogs. But please – see how things look from our side, as well.'

'I'm always striving to do just that,' McKinley said, with a sway of his tractor fronds that could have been taken for a huff.

'It's just . . . you've given us so much, but you've told us next to nothing.' Inside the cocoon, Bella felt a nervous prickle of sweat on her forehead. 'I appreciate that you have your reasons for withholding certain forms of knowledge. You know our history – you've seen the kinds of screw-up we're capable of making.'

'Since you mention it—' McKinley said.

'But we put our history behind us the day we left our own system. The old rules don't have to apply. We managed to survive for thirteen years on Janus before you arrived without wiping ourselves out of existence. We've learned to live with each other.'

'To a degree,' the Fountainhead allowed. 'You are, however, still prone to an alarming amount of factional squabbling. You do your best to conceal it from us, but we still see it. The Musk Dogs will also see it, and make it work for them. It's what they're good at – they're factional animals, as well.'

The 'as well' chilled Bella to the marrow, but she forced herself not to falter. 'I agree there's room for improvement, but that doesn't mean we have to be kept in the dark about everything. For all you know, more knowledge may help us achieve greater wisdom.'

'Or it may rip you apart.'

'Please give us something more,' Bella said. 'You've pushed further into the Structure than we have. You've encountered other cultures. That much you've already told us.'

'We have,' McKinley said.

'Then tell us why we're here. Tell us why Janus dragged us across two hundred and sixty light-years to this place. Tell us what it means to you. You must have *some* idea.'

'We have data . . . theory. But you're not ready.'

'When will we be ready?'

'In time. At the moment you are still absorbing the lessons of your own lost history. New knowledge – the kind you're asking for – could be catastrophically destabilising.'

'How much time are we talking about, McKinley?' Thale enquired.

'Several decades. Fifty years. Perhaps longer.'

'And if the Musk Dogs come sooner than that, how would that change things?' Bella asked.

McKinley shivered: a powerful ripple of his tractor fronds that exposed the ruby-streaked shimmer of the sensor fronds within. It was the only innately alien gesture Bella had learned to recognise: all the others, she felt certain, were a conscious mimicry of human action and revealed nothing about the aliens' true emotional states. But the shiver indicated a profound agitation.

'They will offer you the world,' McKinley said. 'If you take it, you will lose everything.'

They made her young again. Or at least younger: she had not requested a full rejuvenation, simply the resetting of her clock to the approximate physiological age she had been when *Rockhopper* first encountered Janus. Her decision might have been considered eccentric by some, given that the complete restoration of youth was also on offer. But Bella had enjoyed being middle-aged a lot more than she had enjoyed being young. She had felt good at fifty-five, and it felt good to be fifty-five again, even though she still carried the burden of a further thirty-three years of memory, pressing against the limits of her skull like a migraine.

She remembered little of the experience itself. Nobody ever did. She had said goodbye to Nick Thale and Jim Chisholm, and the Fountainheads had escorted her into the base of one of the spikes that lowered itself from the ceiling. The spike retracted, transporting her deeper into the embassy. Presently the aliens brought her to a kind of garden, enclosed by glass: a place of running water, rock pools, wind chimes and simple plants with a delicate blue-green lustre. The Fountainheads remained behind the glass, pressing their ever-moving fronds delicately against it. Unaccountably, she was reminded of something she hadn't seen for forty or fifty years: the whirling brushes of a car wash sliding against a windshield.

The cocoon opened, allowing her to step out. The air was breathable and pleasantly scented, somehow encouraging deep inhalations. The burble of water and the tinkling of the chimes induced an overwhelming sense of ease and well-being – she supposed that the aliens had dredged the human psyche and extracted the parameters for a maximally relaxing environment. Knowing that it was engineered, the product of conscious and quite possibly ruthlessly pragmatic design principles, did not lessen its soothing effects.

Some chemical influence in the surroundings eased her into a state of serene acceptance, blasting away the last residues of trepidation. The aliens instructed her to disrobe and lie down in one of the larger rock pools. The rock was soap-smooth beneath her skin and the water lapped and burbled gently against her shoulders. It was cool enough to feel invigorating, drawing the blood to her skin, but not so cool that she could not have imagined spending all day in the pool. But she soon felt a pleasant, seductive drowsiness. She had no will to move, no desire to think. She was aware, without any sense of alarm, as the water rose to cover her completely, and when they brought her back she retained some murky recollection of drowning. But there was nothing in that memory that felt like fear or anxiety, only a serene acceptance, a childlike sense that she was in wise hands.

She did, however, remember a dream.

It was a dream of an all-surrounding darkness, and of a child lost in that darkness. A girl lost in the snow, in the thin air and cruel cold of a night somewhere in the Hindu Kush, hoping and praying for the lights of rescue to pierce the darkness. Eventually a light swelled to the brightness of day, and Bella was back, lying in the shallow burbling water. She held a hand up towards the false sky and saw that the aliens had done all that she had asked of them. But she had smuggled something of that cold back from the dream, and when they asked her to stand she could still feel the chill in her strong new bones.

'It's time to go home now, Bella,' McKinley said, and for a moment she thought the alien meant Earth, rather than Crabtree.

# CHAPTER 27

Sooner or later, Bella thought, she was going to have to move to a bigger office: it was either that or scale back her plans for the fish. The old glass tank was still there – she had brought it back to Crabtree when she returned to power – but now it formed only one part of a much larger series of linked environments. The huge tanks swallowed three walls and most of the ceiling of her office, throwing a constant trembling light across her paper-strewn desk. There was a window somewhere behind one of the tanks, but it was twenty years since anyone had looked through it. Even at night, when she darkened their tanks, Bella preferred the shadow-world of the fish to any view on Janus.

Genetic manipulation had taken her original stocks and radiated them into a hundred brilliant forms. When her paperwork grew distracting, Bella could easily lose herself in the chrome-yellow flash of a foxface, or the azure dazzle of a blue devil or damselfish. The Fountainheads did not have the genetic templates for many fish, but they knew how to sculpt convincing simulacra that produced accurate copies of themselves.

It was late, the tanks were dimmed and she was paging distractedly through paragraphs of pre-Cutoff history. She made handwritten notes on creamy sheets of vat-grown paper, annotating those historical passages that could be safely released to the populace, highlighting those that would need to be withheld or doctored.

The business of censoring history gave her no pleasure, but it was as necessary as it was gruelling. The truth would come out eventually, she was sure of that, but it had to be administered in controlled doses, like a potent drug. She had background files on every surviving member of the original *Rockhopper* crew manifest: names, nationalities, birthplaces, teasing hints of biographical data. Take Gabriela Ramos, for instance. She was still alive – a recent grandmother, as it happened. She was happy, well balanced, a solid member of the community. Though she had sided with Svetlana in the mutiny, Bella had never found cause to dislike her. But Gabriela Ramos was from Old Buenos Aires, and that was where she had left most of her family when the ship went out to Janus.

Ramos had adapted, as they had all been forced to adapt, to the fact that she would never see her family again. That had been wrenching and cruel, but to one degree or another most of the crew had found a way through it. Part of the healing process involved accepting that life would inevitably go on back home, and that friends and loved ones would also find a way to continue with the business of existence. If one could achieve a state of mind whereby one believed that the people back home were happy, or at least not living their lives in a state of permanent sadness, then it was possible to feel a little happier on Janus as well. It didn't mean that anyone had been forgotten, or that the pain of separation was any less acute, just that – as if by a kind of unspoken consent between the sundered parties – life had to go on.

But in Old Buenos Aires, life had not gone on.

In 2063, only six years after *Rockhopper*'s departure, hackers had gained control of a satellite power station and steered its space-to-ground beam onto Old Buenos Aires. Two point eight million people had died in the flash fires that consumed the city, mostly in the wooden slums of the *boca* shantytowns. Gabriela Ramos's family would almost certainly have been amongst the dead.

Bella could not stand to see Ramos tortured by this news. She knew it would destroy her and cause terrible harm to those close to her. The waves of grief would touch everyone on Janus. No one needed that, most especially not Gabriela Ramos.

So Bella sat up late, evening after evening, scanning the latest batches of data released by the Fountainheads, making sure that the automated editing systems hadn't missed anything. Now and then something did slip through: an oblique reference to the event that might not even mention Old Buenos Aires, but which could be enough to set the curious on a dangerous hunt for further data. She blue-pencilled anything that had the slightest connection with the atrocity.

That wasn't enough, though.

After she was done, there was a glaring hole in the world where Old Buenos Aires used to be. Ramos was curious, naturally, about the future history of the city where she had been born. So Bella had to concoct just enough of an invented history to be convincing: seeding the real news with little white lies just to keep Ramos from guessing the truth. Nothing about her family, of course, but enough information to allow her the comforting fantasy that they had all gone on to lead normal, happy lives, instead of dying in raging hellfire.

It didn't stop with Gabriela Ramos, though.

Hers was the most extreme case, requiring the most brutal historical intervention, but there were other people who deserved to be spared the truth about those they had left behind. When Mike Pasqualucci – one of Parry's miners – rotated onto *Rockhopper*, he had left a son behind on Earth. Losing his boy had nearly destroyed him, but somehow he had found a way to keep on living, throwing himself into the numbing routine of duty. He was out of that darkness now, with a new wife and a new son, but Bella knew he had never stopped thinking of the boy he had left behind.

The trouble was, the boy back home had grown up bad: a string of serial murders and rapes across three continents, followed by arrest in Stockholm and – as was the custom of the European Union in the twenty-seventies – sentencing for 'accelerated neural reprofiling'. Mike Pasqualucci didn't need to know all that, Bella thought. He deserved to keep the precious memory of the little boy he had left behind, untainted by the grown-up monster the boy had become.

So she had doctored that strand of history as well, removing all references to the crime spree and fabricating a happy-ever-after story where Pasqualucci's son ended up running a profitable lobster-boat business off New Bedford. She made nothing overt of that, but it was buried in the data if Pasqualucci cared to look: a fabricated write-up in the gourmet section of the *New Yorker*. And via search-history traceback, Bella knew he had done just that on many occasions, as if he needed to keep reassuring himself that things really had worked out well for his son.

Such tinkering had been deceptively easy at first, but as the trickle of news became a torrent, so the complexity of her task rapidly became overwhelming. Sooner or later, she knew, she was bound to make a mistake – even with the aid of the Borderline Intelligences guiding her hand. A lie that exposed another lie, a paradox that would cleave open her doctored history like a crack in an iceberg. All she hoped was that she could keep postponing that moment of exposure, so that when it came – years or decades down the line – those it hurt would be psychologically buffered against feeling too much pain by the years they had already lived on Janus. They would hate her for it, she knew, but she also hoped that they would understand why she had done it: out of love, and a sense of dutiful obligation to her children.

Her flexy chimed. Bella pushed aside the latest set of edits and took the call from Liz Shen.

'I knew you'd still be up,' the young woman said reprovingly.

'Did you call me just to check whether I was still awake?'

'Actually, no. I thought you'd like to hear about the Underhole investigation.' Tactfully, she reminded Bella, 'The cube, the thing Svetlana left behind.'

Reminding Bella of things was a habit Shen would take some time to lose. Before the rejuvenation, Bella's memory had been increasingly slow and unreliable. Now it growled like a supercharged engine.

Oddly, Bella realised that she had hardly thought about the cube since returning from the Fountainheads. She remembered Avery Fox showing it to her, and she remembered tasking Liz Shen to track down the individuals who might have been at Underhole when Svetlana had evacuated. But since then the matter had barely merited a second thought.

Something about that neglect troubled her now.

'The cube, of course,' she said hastily. 'What have you got for me?'

'Names,' Shen said. 'It wasn't easy, digging back twenty years. I had to call in favours and twist arms. But I've found out who was on the team.'

'Tell me,' Bella said.

'Denise Nadis, Josef Protsenko and Christine Ofria-Gomberg.'

'Staunch Barseghian loyalists,' she said, disappointed. 'They'll be tough nuts to crack.'

'Can't have been accidental,' Shen agreed. 'Svetlana knew she was dealing with something sensitive. She wouldn't have wanted to bring Thale or Regis into the loop if she could help it.'

'I need to talk to them.' Suddenly she was unsure of herself. 'They are all still alive, aren't they?'

'Yes, but Nadis and Protsenko will be difficult to bring in without causing a fuss: they're in small eddytowns where word travels fast.'

'Do you think Christine might be less problematic?'

'She's in Crabtree right now. Of the three, she's the one you're most likely to get sense out of.'

Bella watched her fish absent-mindedly: dark shapes cruising the twilight gloom of the dimmed tanks. 'She's still on good terms with Nick Thale, isn't she?'

'As far as I know.'

'Then talk to Nick, see if he can get anything out of her without making this official.'

'I'll do my best, but don't expect anything to happen before tomorrow.'

'I won't.'

'One other thing,' Shen said. 'You really should get some sleep. If you're not careful you'll work yourself into an early grave. Again.'

Days passed. Bella busied herself with the routine chores of Crabtree administration: Tier-Two review committees, presentations of the latest data from the deep-shaft probes, grumbles and complaints from the outlying communities, mass-energy budgets that needed balancing. She settled her mind by wandering the arboreta, recalling how she had always found solace in the aeroponics lab aboard the old ship. The latest saplings were growing with the eagerness of self-assembling skyscrapers, flinging themselves towards the sky.

Word returned that Nick Thale had spoken to Christine Ofria-Gomberg. At first, she had been reluctant to discuss anything that had happened during the last few days of the Barseghian regime, but Bella knew she would be open to persuasion with the right manipulation. Christine and her husband Jake were still deeply involved in their studies of the Spican language. The arrival of the Fountainheads hadn't dented that particular enthusiasm at all, especially since the essential mystery remained intact. The Fountainheads might well have cracked the language themselves, but they were sharing none of that wisdom with the humans.

For twenty years, the Ofria-Gombergs had continued their private study, subjecting their data to increasingly sophisticated statistical tests in the hope of teasing out at least the existence of meaning. When a heavy nugget of lexical data was being subjected to a complex piece of analysis, the drag on the distributed system was visible. People's clothes stalled and crashed under the processing load, and the normally seamless environment flickered with eye-wrenching patterns. There had been at least one instance of someone suffering an epileptic fit during a particularly protracted piece of number-crunching, and there was a nasty whiff of lawsuit in the wangwood-lined halls of the High Hab Court.

They could call it blackmail if they wanted, but all Bella was saying was that the Ofria-Gombergs' continued utilisation of the system might be contingent upon their cooperation with the cube inquiry.

'I don't know what you expect me to tell you,' Christine said, as they followed a meandering gravel path through the arboreta. It was twilight – the topside lights had been dimmed – and they had the place to themselves. Bella's security had made sure of that.

'We found the cube,' Bella said. 'It was buried beneath Underhole. It was only a matter of time, what with all the digging they've been doing there.'

Christine had never visited the Fountainheads, yet she seemed young beyond her years. Her hair was grey now, but she carried herself with the poised elegance of a much younger woman. *A good spine*, Bella thought idly.

Christine's expressive face shifted from playful amusement to lofty disdain. 'Where is it now?'

'Here in Crabtree,' Bella said. 'I've got a team working on it. So far they haven't come up with anything we didn't know a month ago, but it's still early days, I suppose.'

'What have they tried?'

'It's you I want answers from, Christine.'

'I'm sure I won't remember anything useful.'

'Tell me what you do remember, and I'll be the judge of what's useful.'

'It was just a cube.'

'Where did it come from? How did it end up in Underhole?' Bella waited a while, as they walked around half the perimeter of a little rock pool. She was prepared to be patient, but only up to a point. 'Start giving me something, Christine, or I'll have to seriously reconsider your allocation of algorithmic cycles in the next assessment round.'

'That's your problem,' she said. 'You only ever offer the stick.'

Bella's shoes crunched pleasantly on the gravel. It was nice to walk under half a gee, the loading painless on her bones and joints. 'All right, then,' she said slowly, as if it had only just occurred to her. 'I'll hold up a big orange carrot: tell me about the cube and I'll offer you a place on the analysis team. I'm sure you have *something* to contribute.'

They had walked to the end of another line of caged and bound saplings by the time Christine spoke again. 'It came from space. After the hole opened in the Sky, we sent probes out to examine our surroundings.'

'Free-fliers, yes,' Bella said, pleased that she was making progress. 'That was when we had our first glimpse of the shaft surrounding us.'

'There was something else,' the other woman continued. 'We got a radar echo off something very near. It vanished, then showed up again. It turned out to be something orbiting Janus. Svieta sent out another free-flier to snare it, pull it through the hole, down to Underhole.'

Bella thought about that for a few paces. 'How long do you think it had been up there?'

'How should I know?'

'I was asking for your opinion, that's all.'

Christine's defensiveness cracked. She let out a quiet sigh, as if she had finally decided to stop being obstructive and there was a kind of relief in that. 'All we had was guesswork. We know now that the Fountainheads drilled the hole, and that it was the Fountainheads that sent down the probes that people had started seeing.'

Bella nodded, remembering the spate of alien sightings that had led up to the discovery of the hole in the Sky. She had heard about that even in her place of exile. 'So you think the Fountainheads put the cube into orbit around Janus?'

'That's one possibility,' Christine said.

'But not the only one.'

'If you've seen that cube, you know it doesn't look like anything else we've encountered. It isn't Spican. It isn't Fountainhead.'

Bella thought about the Musk Dogs. Since her return to Crabtree she had mentioned McKinley's warning to no one. 'Could another species have dropped it off?'

'I suppose so. We know that the endcap door opens now and again. The Year of the Iron Sky lasted for four hundred days. For all we know we completed our slowdown in one day and spent the next three hundred and ninety-nine days sitting inside the shaft, waiting for someone to let us out.'

'Are you suggesting that the Fountainheads might not have been the first aliens to reach us?'

'I think that's a possibility we should consider.' She paused, one foot lingering in the air. 'Anyway, there's another problem. If you've seen the cube, you'll know what I'm talking about.'

Bella stopped, too. 'The da Vinci engraving, you mean.'

'It's a human message, Bella. It was meant for us.'

'Which rules out the Fountainheads,' Bella said. 'If they'd recognised us as human from the outset, they'd have cut to the chase and used a language we spoke from the get-go. They didn't start talking to us until after we sent Craig and Jim inside. *Then* the penny dropped, but not before.'

'Maybe there's someone else out there.'

'The Fountainheads have never pretended that there aren't other aliens in the Structure,' Bella said.

'Some of those aliens could be human. That's definitely a human symbol, Bella. How else did it get here, if humans didn't bring it?'

'The Fountainheads brought human data with them,' Bella pointed out. 'That means they made contact with another branch of humanity. If it happened once, there's no reason why another alien culture couldn't have met another branch.'

'It's a pretty cryptic calling card, though.'

'That's why I'd like to know more about it.' Bella walked on a little further, considering her options. Above, an owl swooped under the ghostly supports spars of the arboretum.

'I've told you all I know.'

'What about the others?'

'I don't think you'll get anything more out of them – including Svieta. We answered to her, that's all. She wasn't running her own independent investigations.'

'I believe you,' Bella said, 'and I'd like to offer you that position on the analysis team. Are you interested? It'll take time away from your language studies, but I'm sure your husband can take up the slack.'

'Especially if you let us have that computer time we need,' Christine said quickly, before Bella changed her mind.

'Of course. That was the deal.'

After a moment, the other woman said, 'Aren't you worried that I'll report back to Svetlana, tell her that you've found the cube?'

'She already knows it exists, and given that she's well aware of the Underhole project, she must have known that there'd be a good chance of us uncovering it one of these days.'

'I suppose so.' Christine sounded less sure of herself.

'Then it doesn't matter. Tell her, or don't tell her. I don't care.' Bella looked at the other woman, wishing there was some way to convince her of her sincerity. 'It's up to you.'

'You trust me?'

'I'm not interested in keeping secrets from Svieta. It's been twenty years, Christine. It's time to move on. I don't hate her for what she did – she had her reasons, I suppose. To be honest, I barely think of her at all these days.' She paused. 'And yes, I do trust you. The question is: do you trust me?'

'Sometimes.'

Bella smiled. 'That's exactly the right attitude: trust your leaders, but be careful not to trust them *too* much.'

They walked out of the woods, saying nothing, moving in silence except for the honest crunch of gravel under their shoes.

# CHAPTER 28

Bella was not ungrateful for the rejuvenation that the Fountainheads had bestowed upon her, but even alien science had its limits. The days tore by as quickly as they ever had. Faster, perhaps, now that the metronomic tick of sleep had returned to her world, its nagging beat a constant reminder that there was always more to be done; never enough hours in the day; never enough days in the year. No one could honestly say that they felt immortal. No one had returned to the Fountainheads for a second rejuvenation, and while Bella had little doubt that the aliens would oblige if asked, it was unclear whether the process could be repeated indefinitely.

And sudden, violent death was still as much of a problem as it had ever been. What might once have felt like an acceptable risk to an eighty-eight-year-old woman now struck her as the utmost foolishness, when so much was at stake. She dreaded any business that required her to fly, even though there had only been one fatal lander accident in the last thirty-three years. In the new climate of forgiveness and reconciliation, there had never been less risk of assassination from Barseghian loyalists or other rogue elements. Yet still she spent hours tightening her security arrangements, as if every crowd concealed a knifeman, sniper or toxicologist.

Months passed, and her new body began to feel comfortably familiar again, to the point where it required an effort of will to remind herself of its novelty. She buried herself in her work, pushed the limits of endurance. But despite early progress in several areas, soon all avenues of investigation came to dead ends.

The black cube remained stubbornly enigmatic. Even the gleaming new tools of pre-Cutoff science could only scratch the surface of its mystery, and they'd learned depressingly little more than had been gleaned by Svetlana's first fumbling probings. The best working hypothesis was still that it was some kind of massively advanced replicating technology, endlessly self-repairing, running on a substrate far finer than the atomic granularity of the Chinese nanotech in the forge vats. Nuclear-scale femtotech, perhaps, or even some kind of replicating machinery cobbled together from the basic structural units of space-time. Working with such materials would, Nick Thale had told her, be akin to trying to build a functioning lathe out of wet spaghetti.

Such difficulties clearly hadn't daunted the cube's creators.

She still had no better idea who they had been. Nothing in the pre-Cutoff history files hinted at any human faction with the means to make something like the cube, and even if that had been possible, there was still the awkward question of how they had placed it into orbit around Janus.

Never mind what they had intended by that.

Now and then Bella went along to the research lab where Ofria-Gomberg and the others were studying the cube. It was a white room, sunk deep in a bunker. Caged between sensors, the cube stood out like an offcut of sculpted granite in an upmarket gallery.

Something about the cube still touched an ominous chord in her, as if it was trying to pull her in, whispering something to her hindbrain. She could only compare the feeling to the dark allure of dockside water, that seductive force that compelled people to fall in.

She did not want to fall into the black cube. She was afraid of what it would show her.

The ongoing inquiry into the death of Meredith Bagley had also ground to a halt after a promising start. Bella was still convinced that she had identified the three perpetrators, but had lost faith that the suit-repair log was enough of a smoking gun to convince a tribunal of their involvement. Hank Dussen was out of reach, but she still intended to bring the two surviving men to justice. Morbidly it occurred to her that if either of the two suspects showed any sign of dying before the investigation had run its course, she would have to pull strings to get them bounced up the queue for rejuvenation.

But the case still demanded more evidence. The repair log alone wouldn't clinch it; the only thing that would really persuade a sceptical tribunal would be the missing EVA log files showing who had really been on duty during that fatal shift. It was generally accepted that the logs had been lost accidentally, corrupted or deleted in the flexy die-off. But perhaps that was just too convenient. What if the logs had been deleted to protect the killers? Any one of the three men would have had reason to do that, but Bella could not be sure that any of them would have had the means. But someone had been in charge of managing those log files. Perhaps Parry could help her: he'd at least know whether it was feasible for an involved party to have tampered with the logs.

She made a mental note to contact him. She brightened at the prospect, wondering why it had taken her so long to think of him again. It had always been good to talk to Parry. He had been kind to her during her years of exile, often at the cost of his relationship with Svetlana. Things had obviously changed during the last twenty years, but in their rare meetings, Bella had never sensed any enmity or coolness on Parry's side. He appeared to recognise that it was not Bella that had deposed Svetlana, but the return of Jim Chisholm. And, of course, Bella had been lenient with Svetlana and her allies. None of *them* had ended up in exile at the end of a superconducting line with only ice and silence for company. She might have marginalised them, stripped them of real power, but she had not treated them unfairly. Even her worst critics could never accuse her of indulging in tit-for-tat, and Parry had never been her worst critic.

But something happened the next day – a lander malfunction, of all things – and she forgot to call Parry. More days slipped by, then weeks, and a succession of minor crises pushed their way onto her agenda. The Bagley case remained on the backburner, and it would be many years before it once again returned to the forefront of Bella's attention.

By then, someone else had come back from the dead.

Mike Takahashi awoke to the sound of burbling water and tinkling wind chimes.

'Hello,' Bella said, with what she hoped was the right tone of soft reassurance. 'It's me, Mike – Bella. Everything's okay.'

She remembered how it had been for her: a moment's disorientation, and then everything had clicked cleanly into place. No grogginess, no sense of fumbling around for her own sense of identity, no difficulty with coherent thought or language or even seeing things clearly. It was not like waking up at all, but more like opening her eyes after a few moments of intense meditation. Except that those few moments of meditation had contained infinities of time and space, and mysteries she had not even begun to unpack.

Takahashi moved to sit up. Bella offered him a blanket to preserve his modesty.

'Where am I?' he asked, looking around. He sounded mildly perturbed, that was all. 'I don't remember this place.'

'I'm not sure what you do remember,' Bella said, 'but let's start at the beginning. Do you remember *Rockhopper*?'

'Yes,' he said immediately. 'Of course I do.'

'And Janus?'

A moment of hesitation there, but it didn't last long. 'Yes,' he said. 'I do.'

'We were chasing after it – powering out of the system. Do you remember that?'

He looked at her and said, so quietly that she had to strain to hear him over the water, 'Something went wrong. I remember something going wrong.'

'Yes,' she said, gladdened, because it was all going to be so much easier now. 'There was a problem with one of the mass drivers – it snapped off the spine and took another one with it on the way down. The ship held together, but there was a lot of superficial damage to the fuel tanks. We had to patch things up before we could continue to Janus at full thrust. You were part of the repair team, Mike.'

'Something happened,' he said. 'Something bad.'

'Do you remember?'

She caught a flash of concern, as if he had, for a moment, remembered everything. But then he shook his head. 'No. What happened? Why am I here?' He glanced down at himself. 'I'm all right, aren't I?'

'You're more than all right,' Bella said, smiling.

The Fountainheads had put him back together, but they had not rejuvenated him to any significant degree. There had been no need: he had been a young and healthy man when the sprayrock took him.

'I still don't remember what happened,' he said forlornly.

'You fell into sprayrock. You were trapped, your suit overheating. We couldn't get you out of it. Parry did everything he could, but nothing worked. And time was running out.'

'Parry,' he said. 'Is Parry okay?'

'Parry's fine. You'll see him soon.'

'What happened to me?'

Bella reached for his hand, closing her own around it. She had never had a son, but this, she thought, must be very much how it would feel to comfort a son during an emotional crisis. 'We had to do something to you. There was a procedure that we could use to save you. It was called Frost Angel. Do you remember that?'

'No,' he said, but she caught the dilation of his eyes that told her that he did, on some level, remember all the salient details. They had never been sure how much of the experience of the accident would have had time to transfer to his long-term memory.

'Ryan Axford froze you. He had no choice. It was the right thing to do.'

'No,' Takahashi said, Bella feeling his distress welling up as the memories slotted back into place. 'No. I didn't want to die.'

'There was no choice,' she said. 'We had to do it.'

Takahashi convulsed, the truth hitting them like a drug. 'No! I didn't die! This didn't happen!'

'You died, Mike,' she said, as firmly as she thought he could handle. 'But we brought you back. It's all okay now.'

'No,' he said again, but he was slightly calmer now.

'You're fine. Everything's all right now.'

He shivered beneath the blanket. 'Where am I?'

'In a ship,' Bella said.

He looked around, but there was nothing overtly alien about the revival area. Bella had even asked the aliens to tint the glass, and not to present themselves behind it. There was only so much Takahashi could take in at one time.

She wanted to make it as easy as she could. She'd always liked him, from the moment he rotated aboard *Rockhopper*. He was a solid EVA man, as dependable as any of them, but there was more to Mike Takahashi than his professional competence. There was a quiet modesty about him that she found attractive, a quality that she'd also cherished in Garrison. The two of them had the same way of laughing.

'After Janus,' he said, warily, 'did we make it back okay?'

Bella smiled tightly. This part was never going to be easy. She nodded towards a small pile of clothes folded neatly on a dry rock like a miniature kiln. Most of Takahashi's belongings had long since been recycled – there simply hadn't been any choice in the dark days of the early occupation. But they had always kept a few things back, as a kind of assurance that he would one day return to them. The clothes were very old now, but they had been well cared for and their age was not obvious.

'Get dressed,' she said, 'then I'll tell you everything you need to know.'

Takahashi tightened the blanket around himself. 'What happened to Janus?'

'We did,' Bella said, and then she helped him stand.

She told him what had happened, ladling out the truth in kind little measures, as she had always done for the people of Crabtree. At every opportunity she reassured him that he had nothing to fear, that everything was all right and that he had many, many friends who would be overjoyed to see him again. Takahashi said very little. Now and then he would repeat something that she had said, or ask her for some mild clarification on this matter or that, but in general he appeared emotionally disconnected from it all.

'Just like the Swiss Family Robinson,' she said, after she'd finished telling him about their arrival on Janus, and the early hardships they had overcome.

Takahashi didn't laugh.

They were riding the express elevator to Underhole, racing down a glass tube lined with chrome-bright maglev induction rails. They had the entire compartment to themselves, save for the eternally vigilant security systems haunting every cubic millimetre of the car's decor.

'But that all happened a long time ago,' Bella said. 'We rode Janus all the way to Spica. Thirteen years, that took us. For most of that time, we were moving very close to the speed of light. Two hundred and sixty years passed in the outside world.'

Bella had dimmed the cabin lights so that they could see the view beyond the car. It was always dark under the Iron Sky. Underhole sprawled beneath them, a jewelled octopus of light, each of its arms tracing a different maglev line from somewhere else on Janus. Although the trains still arrived and departed from the same transit plaza, new developments continued to spill out along the tracks. The lines themselves curved out to the horizon in eight directions, glowing with blue filaments of embedded neon. At one time, the wastage of so much power would have appalled Bella. It was years since anyone had worried about a few lost kilowatts, though.

'You didn't do all this in thirteen years,' Takahashi said.

'No,' Bella conceded, 'it took a bit longer than that.'

'How long?'

'After thirteen years the aliens came.'

He nodded. He had needed to be told about the Fountainheads before anything else, although he hadn't seen them yet. 'How long ago was that?'

'Thirty-five years,' Bella said, 'which makes this the forty-eighth year of the human occupation. We've been on Janus for almost half a century. There are nearly five hundred of us now.'

He looked at her wonderingly. 'How old would that make you, Bella?'

'Too old to answer that question,' she said, not quite able to meet his gaze. 'Actually, it would make me more than a hundred years old. Which is sometimes how old I feel.' She paused, anticipating his next question. 'When I was eighty-eight – which was fifteen years ago – I went to the Fountainheads. They made me young again: set my body clock back to about the same age I was when we met Janus.'

'You don't look much older now than you did then.'

Takahashi wasn't the type to dole out insincere flattery. Plus she had mirrors. She knew how she looked. 'I should look seventy, I suppose, but clearly I don't. I look a little older than when I walked out of the Fountainheads' ship fifteen years ago, but not by that much.' She held up her hand. 'For the first time I can feel the arthritis coming back. If it hadn't happened to me already, I doubt I'd recognise the signs.'

He studied her with unconcealed fascination. 'My memory isn't all there yet, Bella, but I remember that you were alone on the ship.'

'Yes,' she said simply.

'I'm guessing that's changed after all these years, right?'

She answered sharply. 'I'm still alone.'

'But it's been . . .' He shook his head in amazement. 'Wasn't there anyone, Bella?'

She could have lied to him, and to herself, but Takahashi deserved better than that. 'I tried to make it work with someone, once. He was a good man, one of the best in Crabtree. For a few months . . .'

He must have mistaken something in her voice. 'What happened to him?'

'Nothing – he's still around. We just couldn't make it work.'

'I'm sorry.'

'Don't be. It's my fault. I drag too much of the past around with me.'

After a long silence, as the elevator slowed into the transit plaza in Underhole, with its concourse ramps and rows of boutiques and restaurants, Takahashi said, 'Will they make you young again?'

'They had better,' Bella said. 'There's still work to do.'

*

Takahashi's good progress continued. In the sixth week, Bella decided that it was safe to introduce him back into the colony. She chose to arrange a party in his honour.

It took place in Crabtree's largest arboretum. It was evening. The ceiling lights had been turned down from their daytime glare and false stars sprinkled the strutted canopy. The largest trees had been strung with lines of paper lanterns in reds and golds and greens. Choral music floated from concealed speakers: Bella had chosen Arvo Pärt from the files because she had discovered one of the Estonian composer's recordings amongst Takahashi's personal belongings.

She had considered it vital not to exclude anyone from the party, and consequently almost every adult citizen who could make it was there. They circled and talked in the still, scented air of a midsummer night. Hovering lanterns followed little groups, offering them light until they were shooed away good-naturedly. BI robots maintained a discreet presence, only emerging from the darkness between the trees to offer drinks, sweetmeats and the occasional helping hand.

Bella was too nervous to fully enjoy the party herself, but as the evening wore on it gradually began to dawn on her that it was not going to be the abject failure she had feared. Takahashi was easy with the sudden flood of attention, moving comfortably from one group to the next, telling the same stories over and over again, laughing patiently at the same well-intentioned jokes. Now and then he would retire to a convenient tree stump for a few moments to himself, but whenever Bella talked to him he assured her that he was going to be fine, and that he was rather enjoying the whole affair. He was enchanted with the variety of costumes on parade: eighty years of fashion history that he had never lived through. Despite the collision of styles, the evening ambience and the soft light from the lanterns lent everything a subtle unity.

'How do you like the music?' Bella asked, as they sat together with only a hovering lantern between them. 'We found your old helmet, looked through the access statistics in the file memory. You used to listen to this a lot.'

'It's great. The main thing is that it isn't Puccini.'

'Puccini?'

'I died while listening to *Turandot*. How many people can say that?'

Bella put a hand on his knee. 'I know this isn't all going to be easy for you, Mike, but you'll get there in the end. You're a miner.'

'Pushing ice,' he said, a touch too confidently to be convincing.

She noticed that he had been watching a young woman standing at the edge of a nearby group. Her luminous, neon-patterned gown scooped low on her back, revealing more than it hid. The lantern light played softly over her shoulders and the incurve of her spine. Bella tried to remember the woman's name, but nothing came.

'You didn't have to go to all this trouble just for me,' Takahashi said.

'I think we did.'

'Not that I don't appreciate it, but . . . does everyone get this attention when they come back?'

'You were different,' Bella said, gently chiding. 'We never expected to get you back. That made it worth celebrating.'

'You've all been through such hard times. I almost feel like a fraud . . . as if I've missed out on all the hard work.'

'You shouldn't feel that way. In fact, I'll make a point of being cross with you if I even suspect that's how you feel.'

Takahashi accepted a BI's offer to refill his wine glass. The glasses had been spun in the forge vats: miracles of crystalline delicacy, the stems braided from dozens of filaments of whisker-thin glass like the vapour trail of a corkscrewing fighter jet.

'When you brought me down from the ship,' he said, meaning the Fountainhead embassy, 'you told me there had been a difference of opinion on *Rockhopper*, that it hadn't been a unanimous decision to come here.'

'That was all a long time ago. No sense in going over old ground.'

'I heard you brought *Rockhopper* here – that it was your decision not to try to return home.'

'What do you think you would have done?'

Takahashi looked through his glass at the attractive woman. 'At the time, I doubt that I'd have gone along with it, but in retrospect I think you did the right thing. You'd never have made it back. DeepShaft and the UEE would never have put together a rescue plan.'

'Hindsight is a wonderful thing. It's just a pity not everyone saw it that way at the time.'

'Svetlana put you in prison. She punished you for saving us.'

Bella felt a tightness in her throat. She hardly ever talked about her exile now, or the spite that had caused it. 'Svieta had her reasons,' she said, savouring the pious little thrill that came with magnanimity. 'Had I listened to her, we would probably never have made it into the slipstream in the first place.'

'You had equally compelling reasons not to do as she asked.'

'Yes,' Bella said, 'but it was still a mistake. I hope I redeemed myself later, but . . .' She trailed off: to say anything more in her defence would have been distasteful.

'It cost you your friendship with Svieta,' Takahashi said.

'We used to see things similarly. I considered her a good friend.' She paused, watching the orbiting groups of partygoers. 'But friendships are always difficult to maintain across lines of rank, even in a civilian organisation. It was a wonder ours lasted as long as it did.' She shrugged, trying to make out that it was no great thing to her any more.

'How long has it been since you last spoke to her?'

Bella smiled: it was not a difficult question. 'We haven't exchanged a word since *Rockhopper* landed on Janus.'

He shook his head in appalled fascination. 'That's as long as I've been dead.'

'Yes,' she said, 'I suppose it is.'

'It isn't right, Bella.'

She felt, then, the first hint of irritation with him. What business did he have coming back from the dead and lecturing her? But she fought to keep it from her voice. 'Mike, it was not because I didn't try. I wasn't asking for our friendship back. I wasn't even asking for her to talk to me, or send a letter. I just wanted her to offer me one tiny shred of human dignity: the smallest acknowledgement that I could be something other than the force for evil she obviously considered me. But nothing came.'

'Do you think she hates you?'

'All I know is that when an intense friendship ends, this is often what happens.'

Takahashi swirled his wine. 'I don't think men have those kinds of friendships – I mean, not unless they're lovers. I've never had such an intense friendship with another man. One guy, I crewed with him for eight years – helped him suit-up, ran EVA shifts with him, got drunk with him – and yet all that time went by before I even found out he was married.' He laughed, shaking his head. 'Knowing that stuff about each other wasn't even on our interpersonal radar. And yet we were as good a pair of EVA buddies as I've ever known.'

'What was his name?'

'Can't remember.'

They sat in silence for several minutes, alone with their thoughts. Bella smoked a cigarette – it was the first she'd allowed herself in weeks. Groups of partygoers mingled in the lantern light, faces aglow with the pleasant intoxication of good drink on a glamorous evening. Just a glimpse of this evening would have sustained her through the darkest days of her exile.

Takahashi pointed to a sandy-haired boy standing with a party of adults. 'Who's the kid?'

'Axford.'

Takahashi frowned. 'Axford had a kid?'

'No,' Bella said patiently, 'the kid *is* Axford. He had the full reset the last time he went up.'

'You trust a kid to look after you now?'

'The kid still has Axford's memories and adult experience. He thinks like a man, just happens to look like a little boy. Axford told me he'd put off going Skyside for so long that he didn't want to have to go back for many, many years.' Mischievously, Bella added, 'Besides, he says his hands can slip into surgical openings they could never fit through before.'

'Did they . . . you know, fix him?'

Bella feigned puzzlement. 'Fix him, Mike? In what way?'

'Axford was gay.'

'Axford is still gay, as far as I know. I don't think he saw it as something that particularly needed fixing.'

'Okay,' Takahashi said, shrugging.

'He's still Axford, Mike. He's just more efficiently packaged. You'll get used to it in the end. When I look at him now I hardly remember what the old Axford used to look like.'

One group dispersed, and in the sudden opening of a sight line she saw Svetlana, standing twenty or thirty paces away, her back to Bella, talking to Parry Boyce and a young couple she couldn't name.

She experienced no shock at seeing Svetlana – she had been invited (or, rather, had not been deliberately excluded) and there had always been an excellent chance that she would attend. Takahashi's return was as much part of her world as Bella's, after all.

But Bella still felt uncomfortable to see her. This was the closest they had been in nearly fifty years. They were in the same room at last, even if it was the huge enclosure of the arboretum. Had they wished, they could have called out to each other.

'You saw her as well,' Takahashi said in a low, conspiratorial voice.

'I'm not surprised. I never exiled her. I never forbade her from setting foot in Crabtree.'

'Are the two of you going to say anything to each other?'

'I think we've said all that needs to be said.'

Svetlana started to look back over her shoulder, as if she had become aware of Bella's guarded scrutiny. In profile she looked older than Bella remembered, even allowing for the flattering effect of the lantern light, but not fifty years older. Svetlana had visited the Fountainheads at least once, as had Parry. Like Bella, the clothes she wore were of antique cut – loose denim jeans, cowboy boots, a T-shirt and a brown leather jacket slung over one shoulder. Her red hair was cut spikily short, catching the lantern light.

There was a moment when they might have been close to making eye contact, when another group of celebrants blocked her view. A tumbling acrobat – Bella couldn't tell if it was a person or a BI android – flung itself head over heels, its wrists and ankles spitting golden fire. When the tumbler had passed, Svetlana's party had moved on.

Takahashi looked up as something huge rumbled towards them along a wide tree-lined avenue. 'Hey, is that—'

'Yes,' Bella said, glad that the awkward moment had passed. 'It's McKinley. I hoped he'd accept the invitation.'

The Fountainhead had arrived in a four-metre-wide transparent sphere containing no visible instruments or life-support systems. Muscular waves of his tractor fronds propelled it forward. Bella shuddered to think of the pressure and gravitational forces trapped behind that glass.

McKinley must have seen her. He – she had come to think of him as male – rolled to a halt before her, before forming a high-resolution cross-weave.

'Hi,' she said, aware of how ludicrously banal the greeting was given the circumstances.

McKinley tipped himself forward in the Fountainhead approximation of a nod. 'Hi yourself. And hello to Mike, as well.' The voice was louder and more human in texture than she remembered, but perhaps that had something to do with the acoustic amplification of the mobility sphere.

'Hi,' Takahashi said, raising a hand.

The alien turned the cross-weave towards him. 'It's good to see you up and about.'

'It's good to *be* up and about,' Takahashi said. 'Don't let anyone tell you differently – being dead is no party.'

'No walk in the woods,' McKinley said, unravelling the cross-weave.

Takahashi smiled. 'Nor that.'

'Everyone looks very happy to have you back,' the alien said. 'You must have been very popular in your time.'

'I'll try not to blow it this time around.' Takahashi stood up decisively from the stump, glass in hand. 'I'm going to mingle for a while. You two stay and chat, and I'll hook up with you later, okay?'

'Okey-dokey,' McKinley said.

Takahashi patted the glass sphere. 'And no talking about me behind my back.'

Bella watched him stroll into the night until he was absorbed into a gaggle of well-wishers. As much as she enjoyed his presence, she was quietly glad that Takahashi had decided to leave her alone with McKinley.

'They're happy for Mike,' the alien observed. 'He was lucky to have someone like you in charge.'

'We owed it to him.'

'You'd be surprised how many species don't take such a charitable view of their weaker members,' McKinley said, with an idle flick of his tractor fronds.

'I knew you were buttering me up for something,' she said. 'That was, incidentally, a very nice segue to the main topic – which I take it has something to do with another species?'

'You're a shrewd woman, Bella Lind.' McKinley made a weird twisting motion that she had not observed amongst his usual repertoire of gestures. It was almost, Bella thought, as if he was checking over his shoulder for eavesdroppers. He lowered his voice until she had to lean forward to hear him above the choral music. 'That matter we discussed a little while ago . . . prior to your rejuvenation?'

'A little while? That was fifteen years ago, McKinley.'

The human perception of different units of time was still problematic for the Fountainheads. Through their conversations, Bella had come to suspect that the Fountainheads measured time in terms of the density of events, rather than the number of elapsed units of some specific interval. To Fountainheads, a hundred years in which nothing much happened was less time than an event-filled minute.

'But you know what I'm talking about,' McKinley said.

A BI stalked over, anxious to charge her glass. Bella waved the robot away. 'The Musk Dogs, I imagine.'

'I am glad that you remember. They've been showing renewed interest in this region of the Structure. We think their arrival is now imminent.'

'The last time we talked about this, you defined "imminent" as anything ranging from years to decades. I don't suppose there's any chance of narrowing it down a bit?'

'Now I would be inclined to talk in months. You should be ready for them.'

'Perhaps we are. You said it would be bad if we were in a state of social fragmentation, remember? Well, maybe we were then, but we've never been more unified than we are now. Just take a look at this party. There's a representative of every faction on Janus here tonight, and so far I haven't seen any fights breaking out.'

'It's certainly encouraging.'

'You don't sound convinced.'

'When they come, they will find the tiniest rift and open it wide. They will make blood enemies of cool rivals; rivals of the best of friends.'

Bella shook her head, exasperated. 'Being factional is part of what we are.'

'Perhaps you're right,' the alien said, with a gloomy note she couldn't miss. 'Things are better now, at least. Perhaps that will make enough of a difference.'

'If the Musk Dogs are so bad, why don't you just make them go away?'

'We can dissuade them, but only if you ask it of us.'

'What does "dissuade" mean?'

'It means we would emphasize the exclusive nature of the beneficial trading relationship we've established with your people. If Musk Dogs see no potential for undermining that mutually productive state of affairs, they will probably leave.' The Fountainhead paused, and added darkly, 'Sooner or later another vulnerable species will arrive. They always do, even if the intervals grow longer.'

'So we're just another vulnerable species?' she asked.

'You have your weaknesses, but like most newcomers, you also have something immensely valuable to those of us already here.'

'The world we rode in on.'

'You're making quite a home of it.'

'We're making *do*, McKinley. That doesn't mean we plan to spend the rest of eternity here.'

His fronds swished thoughtfully. 'It's good to have plans.'

Just as he said that, Bella became aware of a presence behind her. She glanced around and saw Mike Takahashi, wine glass in hand. Next to Takahashi, standing a little further back, was Svetlana.

'Mike—' Bella started, ready to protest at his interference.

Takahashi blocked her with his palm. 'If a recently dead man is to be allowed one concession, let it be this. I'm sorry about the feud, or the falling out, or the political schism, or whatever you want to call it. I'm even sorrier that two former friends can't even say "hello" to each other when they're in the same room. Well, it's time to do something about that, before it puts too much of a dampener on the evening.'

'This was a bad idea,' Svetlana said, not looking at Bella.

'I agree,' Bella said. She was blushing intensely, even though she had drunk little all evening. 'Mike, I know you mean well but this isn't just some playground spat you can put right with a sprinkling of fairy dust and some good intentions.'

Takahashi sipped from his glass. 'Fine. But just out of interest, how long were you two planning on holding this grudge? Another fifty years? A century? Or will you just be getting started then?'

'There is no grudge,' Bella said. She was uncomfortably aware of McKinley taking all this in.

Takahashi turned to Svetlana. 'I spoke to Bella earlier this evening. She admitted that you had your reasons for taking over the ship. She made a mistake, a bad one, in not listening to you. She doesn't deny that.'

'A mistake is still a mistake,' Svetlana said, her lips barely moving.

'Which she freely acknowledges. But given that she made that mistake – given the situation *Rockhopper* was then in – can you honestly deny that she did the right thing by forcing the ship back to Janus?'

'That doesn't make amends,' Svetlana said.

Takahashi held up his hand again. 'There's more you need to hear, Svieta. When I spoke to Bella earlier she was . . . how shall I put this? Not without praise for the way you ran Crabtree?'

He looked to Bella for confirmation. She blushed again, for this – as Takahashi surely knew – was an outright lie. And yet, in private, in the most grudging of tones, she might have admitted as much.

'We all did our best,' Svetlana said, looking at Bella properly for the first time.

Bella reached deep into herself, groping around for something nice to say. 'It can't have been easy. Especially during those first few years, before the Maw came on-stream.'

'We got through it,' Svetlana said tersely.

'It took leadership.'

Svetlana looked at Bella, held her gaze and nodded just so. The acknowledgement was as frostily diplomatic as they came, but it was more than Bella had expected. 'Thank you,' Svetlana mouthed.

Takahashi's eyes gleamed in the lantern light. 'Svetlana, for her part, admits that you've handled things very capably since you returned to Crabtree. Your management of the Symbolists was an exercise in tact and restraint.' He glanced at Svetlana. 'Wasn't it?'

'You did okay,' she said, after a moment's pause.

'Svetlana also had a degree of praise for the way you refrained from exiling your former adversaries. Rather than indulging in petty recrimination, you put the needs of the colony first.'

'Bella still marginalised us,' Svetlana said.

'That was her prerogative. But I can't help noticing that she did invite you along tonight.'

'I suppose so.'

Bella ventured, 'I thought you'd like to see Mike again. Now I'm beginning to wonder why I invited *him*.'

'Yes,' Svetlana said, directing an acid glance at Takahashi. 'It would have saved us both some embarrassment if you hadn't.'

Takahashi nodded, smiling ruefully. 'Yes – without my intervention, you two could still be playing your avoidance games, whereas now you've been standing next to each other for five minutes already, without a single drop of blood being spilled. Sorry, but where I come from that *has* to be considered an improvement.'

'Not where I come from,' Bella said, just as Svetlana said exactly the same thing.

They looked at each other and both let out a single, cautious, self-conscious laugh. Then there was nothing to say. The silence was the most exquisitely awkward part of the encounter so far. They could turn away now, Bella thought – having had this brief, bloodless, dignified encounter – and return to their own groupings, and for a while it might seem as if something had changed for the better. But soon things would be exactly the way they had been before.

It was now or never, to make a change that might stand a chance of lasting. Bella's throat was furnace dry. She opened her mouth, willed words to emerge. 'You must be proud of Emily,' she said. 'I see her in Crabtree nearly every day. She's very talented, very beautiful. I don't know anyone who doesn't speak highly of her.'

'Thank you,' Svetlana said, and this time she spoke the words rather than just grimacing them. Another awkward silence descended, and then Svetlana added, 'It was kind of you to arrange that line of work for her.'

Bella glanced at McKinley. 'Oh, don't worry about him. He's fully aware that we have a study group dedicated solely to discovering the secrets of the Fountainheads. If they will insist on dropping little hints every now and then, what do they expect?'

Bella had observed real analytic skill in Emily Barseghian, and had seen to it that she was rewarded with a position in the coveted Fountainhead intelligence section. There had been disappointingly few breakthroughs, but none of that failure could be placed at Emily's door.

'She enjoys it,' Svetlana said.

'I knew she would. I see a lot of you in her.' Bella offered a half-smile. 'Maybe a little of me, too.'

'I could never do what she does,' Svetlana said. 'I'm still just an engineer at heart.'

Recklessly, Bella said, 'Crabtree always needs good engineers.'

'I'm still keeping busy.'

Yes, Bella thought: dead-end spanner work, a long way from anything interesting. 'But maybe I could have made better use of you. I must admit I didn't go out of my way to involve you in the most exciting projects. You've been to Underhole recently, I take it? You've seen the Tier-Two development?'

'I haven't been on the other side of the Sky in thirty-five years,' Svetlana said. 'This is only the third time I've been back to Crabtree in all that time.'

'I'm sorry,' Bella said, as the magnitude of that span of time hit her with physical force.

'You don't need to apologise. At least you didn't lock me away for thirteen years. For what it's worth . . . I made a mistake, okay? But right now that's the closest you're going to get to an apology.'

'I'll take whatever's going.'

'And I screwed you over the Chisholm affair. If it's any consolation, that's one of the things I'm least proud of.' Something changed in her expression, a closing up, as if she realised that she had said too much, too quickly. 'Look,' she went on, 'I really should be getting back. I'm glad we talked, Bella. If you'd have asked me this morning . . . well, I'd never have believed we could be talking like this. But it's time to go now.'

'No,' Bella said firmly. 'Stay. I still want to talk to you. I'm not done yet, Svieta.'

'*You're* not done?'

'No. And neither are you.' Bella looked around. 'Look, let's find somewhere quiet to sit down. Just the two of us – no Takahashi, no McKinley.'

'All right,' Svetlana said uneasily, as if she still did not quite trust Bella's motives.

Svetlana had nothing in her hand. 'Do you want a drink?' Bella asked. 'I'd offer you a cigarette, but as far as I remember you don't smoke.'

'I'll take a drink, yes,' Svetlana said.

Bella snapped her fingers at the nearest BI. 'Over here,' she called.

# CHAPTER 29

The music was muted and the lanterns dimmed. They sat together in the gathering quiet as the party wound down to its natural conclusion. McKinley and Takahashi had wandered off into the woods, leaving Bella and Svetlana alone. The remaining handful of revellers watched them guardedly, while pretending not to notice. Everyone must have been aware of the significance of this meeting.

They had gradually become easier in each other's presence. It was not exactly a relaxed state of affairs – Bella was acutely conscious of monitoring every nuance of every word she and Svetlana uttered – but they were at least able to have something that, to a casual witness, might have approximated a normal conversation.

'Now and then I hear things from Emily,' Svetlana said. 'I know she probably isn't meant to talk about her work, but I can be very persuasive.'

'I'm not surprised,' Bella said. She corrected herself quickly. 'That you'd be interested, I mean. Sometimes I think I should release all their findings and speculation at once, and damn the consequences. But another part of me worries about how we'd all deal with that.'

'You're probably right,' Svetlana said.

'Things are pretty stable and well adjusted now, even if I say so myself. But we still don't know much more about the aliens, or the Spica Structure, or what our long-term situation is. I worry that if we learn something unpleasant, we might not hold together.'

'Do you ever think—' Svetlana stopped and looked at her hands.

'What?' Bella asked gently.

'Does it ever occur to you that maybe we're going to be stuck inside this thing for ever? It's been thirty-five years now, and we're still no closer to finding a way out.'

'It sounds like a long time.'

'It is, Bella, by any measure.'

'Not compared to the two hundred and sixty years it took us to get here, though. From the standpoint of whoever made this thing, we might just be in some kind of quarantine period now.'

'And the Fountainheads?' Svetlana asked dubiously. 'Are they in quarantine as well?'

'I don't know,' Bella said.

'Well, where exactly do they fit in? And all the other species you have intelligence data on?'

'The data's sparse. We really don't know as much as you might think.'

'But you know that we aren't the only species inside this thing. That's why the Fountainheads are so keen not to have us go poking our noses beyond the endcap door.'

Glumly, Bella remembered McKinley's recent warning about the Musk Dogs. 'I think they have our best interests at heart,' she said.

Svetlana nodded knowingly. 'They certainly have someone's best interests at heart.'

'Nothing we've learned in all these years has made us doubt that we can trust the Fountainheads.'

'They've been good to us,' Svetlana allowed. 'Rejuvenations, little gifts of technology and culture. But the technology and the culture were already *ours* – we had every right to them. They've given us nothing of themselves beyond a few hints and tips about how to get more out of Janus.'

'They know best, I think.'

Svetlana's expression was troubled. 'I've been thinking about the Cutoff a lot lately. Doesn't that strike you as odd?'

'In what way?'

'That they know so much about us up to a specific date, and then nothing.'

'They only made contact with us on that one occasion,' Bella said, reciting the standard line. 'They acquired human cultural data up to the time of the contact, but beyond that, they have no information.'

'We already know they must have superluminal signalling, Bella – maybe even superluminal travel. How else did that knowledge overtake us?'

Bella shifted uncomfortably on the tree stump. 'I'm not sure what you're getting at.'

'If they had that signalling capacity, doesn't it strike you as odd that the Fountainheads only ever encountered one single ship from Earth? We already know that the Thai expansion was a concerted effort to establish extrasolar colonies around more than one star. They must have sent out lots of ships, in all directions, across many decades.'

'Only one of which encountered the Fountainheads,' Bella pointed out.

'But the Fountainheads are a starfaring culture with a technology far beyond our own. I remember those discussions aboard *Rockhopper*, Bella. Once you get one advanced starfaring culture, you expect it to encompass a huge swathe of the galaxy – tens of thousands of solar systems, at the very least – in very little time.'

'Which is very little time by galactic standards,' Bella said, detesting the pedantic tone she heard in her own voice.

'Okay – we might still be talking hundreds of thousands of years, but that's still nothing in cosmic terms. It's just an eye-blink. The Fountainheads should have been *out there*, massively established in all directions.'

'Maybe they were.'

'And yet when the Thai expansion fired ships into the night, only one of them ran into the Fountainheads? That just doesn't stack up, Bella. There should have been multiple contacts, and not all happening simultaneously, either. Some of the ships would have further to travel before they hit the Fountainheads, and some of them would have left later. They'd all have been carrying different sets of historical and cultural data – some of them updated later than others. And unless those ships were moving very close to the speed of light, they'd have had no trouble receiving newer data from Earth.' Svetlana smiled and shook her head. 'Listen to me – like I thought all this up for myself. I didn't. I just listened to the right people.'

'I do the same thing,' Bella said.

'All the same, it still bothers me. The Fountainheads should have collected data from dozens, maybe even hundreds, of different contact episodes. And with superluminal signalling, they should have had no difficulty in merging those data sets.'

'There'd still have been a cutoff,' Bella said. 'No matter how many individual contacts took place, there'd still have been one ship that was carrying the most up-to-the-minute cultural data.'

'I know, but by then the Thai expansion should have been under way for many years. It should already have been part of the history records aboard the ship – even if they were based on updates beamed aboard after launch. But that isn't how it's presented to us, is it?'

'The Fountainheads haven't presented much to us at all,' Bella said. 'They've allowed us to draw our own inferences.'

'Based on the data they allow us to see.'

'I still don't see what you're driving at.'

'I'm saying it doesn't add up. I'm saying there's something wrong here, something that doesn't make sense. If we believe the story that the Fountainheads apparently want us to believe, then we have to accept that they've only ever made contact with us once – despite our expectation that it would either never happen, or happen many separate times. We also have to accept that – for reasons of their own – they choose not to act in any of the ways we'd expect a starfaring culture to behave. There is, of course, an alternative.'

'Which is?' Bella asked.

'That they're lying to us,' Svetlana said.

*

Bella woke early the next morning, glad that she had refrained from drinking much at Takahashi's party. Her mind was gin-clear now, yet it rang with the world-changing implications of her renewed communication with Svetlana.

It would be too much to expect them ever to be close friends again – Bella was too much of a realist for that. But simply to be on cordial terms would be a wonderful improvement on the way things had been since the crisis on *Rockhopper*. And while friendship might be ruled out, perhaps they could become allies again, of a kind.

The transformation ought to have enlivened her, and filled her with a renewed sense of purpose. It did, for a little while. She busied herself with administrative affairs and renewed promises to herself to close a number of issues that had been left pending for far too long, including the Bagley inquiry. With a reinvigorated sense of optimism, she rubberstamped funds for a slew of projects she had been dithering over for weeks. New perpetual-motion wheels, new maglev routes, new massively serial computer mainframes to handle the most taxing analysis tasks required by the Ofria-Gomberg Institute. An offer from the Fountainheads to drill two new skyholes, to ease congestion at Underhole. Go-ahead for a Phase-A feasibility study for the Crabtree dome, which would encompass the entire community as far out as the Mairville and Shengtown suburbs, and reach twice as high as the High Hab itself. An even longer-term scheme for pumping atmosphere into the entire volume between Janus and the Iron Sky, so that they could dispense with domes altogether.

Such matters would normally have consumed every iota of Bella's attention, but now she could not stop thinking about her conversation with Svetlana. Try as she might, she could not dismiss the doubts Svetlana had raised concerning the truthfulness of the Fountainheads.

By lunchtime, she had completed more than her usual quota of business for a day. As arranged, she met Parry Boyce in one of the arboreta and treated him to lunch while she told him about her progress on the Bagley case.

'I thought I was getting somewhere fifteen years ago,' she said, while they ate out of picnic bags, 'but I let it drop. I was too worried about stirring up old ghosts back then. Now's the time, though.'

Parry asked her what she wanted of him. Bella explained that she needed information concerning the EVA log files: how easy it would have been to delete or alter them, using the flexy die-off as a cover.

'Easy enough for someone on the inside,' Parry told her. He had been Skyside for rejuvenation thirty years ago, and now had a physiological age somewhere in the early sixties. His moustache was grey, his hair peeking out in sparse grey curls from beneath the ancient and faded red cap that bore the evidence of numerous repairs. He was still stocky, with the unforced musculature of someone who spent a lot of time in the high-gee zones.

'Would there have been a back-up somewhere?'

Parry grimaced. 'You're going back a long way now.'

Bella flicked crumbs at a loitering squirrel, one of the gene-constructed mammals populating the arboreta. 'Forty-three years really isn't that long any more.'

'You'll kick up a storm.'

'Better now than later. I can't let it slip for another fifteen years, Parry. We need to open one last wound, heal it and move on.'

'I guess you're right.'

'You know I'm right. Back when they killed Thom Crabtree, you moved quickly to punish the men responsible. It was fast, brutal, effective. I've never said this before, but I agreed with the way you handled it.'

She saw flinching pain in his eyes, as if she was forcing him to review memories he would much sooner have kept locked away. Memories of the quick, percussive impact of hammerdrills against the thin armour of helmets, memories of blood spattering ice, memories of two kneeling corpses pitching forward as if in supplication.

'I'm not proud of what we did to Chanticler and Herrick. It was wrong to kill them.'

'We don't kill any more. We incarcerate.'

'Only because we've got the aliens looking down on us.'

Bella scrunched up her picnic bag. 'It's a matter of practicality, that's all. People in prison can still fulfil useful functions for Crabtree.'

'Would you still kill them if they weren't useful?'

'I don't know,' Bella said. 'Would it make any difference if I said yes?'

Parry stood up. 'I'll see what I can dig up for you. I just want you to understand that there'll be consequences.'

'There always are,' Bella said.

When she had finished with Parry, she made her way to the secure laboratory that housed the black cube. It lay under one of the outlying suburbs, screened within nested layers of sprayrock, acoustic-dampening material and multiple Faraday cages.

The cube was never left unattended. Today it was Hannah Ofria-Gomberg's turn to mother it, while robot sensors clicked and hummed through some methodical analysis sequence. It was deeply boring work and Hannah looked both delighted to have any company at all and startled that it was Bella paying her a visit.

She was sitting in a padded seat, booted feet up on the desk, when Bella arrived. Hannah snatched tortoiseshell glasses from her face. They were deliberately hefty: late-twenty-first-century retro-chic. Opera music buzzed from the earpieces. Opera was the new thing now, Bella had noticed. All the kids were into it.

'It's all right,' Bella said, 'I didn't come to check up on you. I just dropped by to see how things are coming along.'

'Nothing new down here,' Hannah said, bending her long legs under the desk. 'We're still running the same old same old. Did you see the last report we put together?'

'Oh, yes,' Bella said, rolling her eyes. 'The usual thrilling document. You all deserve some kind of medal for bashing your heads against that thing for so long.'

'Maybe if it wasn't just our heads we bashed, we might get somewhere.'

Bella nodded gravely. 'I'm sure we'd learn a thing or two about the cube if we sliced through it with a fusion flame. But then we wouldn't have much of a cube any more.'

'We could snip off a corner.'

'One day, maybe. Until then, you'll just have to be patient.' Bella walked closer to the rotating cube, careful not to cross the red line on the floor that marked the limit for human observers. Closer than that and her own bio-electric fields would ruin the scans.

'Is there something—' Hannah began.

'Not particularly,' Bella said. 'I just like to come down here now and then and take a good look at it. It's like a puzzle I'm hoping will one day solve itself before my eyes, like one of those psychology problems.'

'It does that to people,' Hannah said. 'They come down here, take a look at the thing . . . and then they keep coming back to stare at it, transfixed. It's as if they've seen something in that blackness, some hint of a message.'

'Do you experience that?'

'I just see a black cube. One I'd really like to cut open one of these days.'

'I'm glad the job isn't getting to you.'

Bella had studied the reports endlessly, even when they threatened to send her to sleep, but nothing in those summaries offered any hint of the cube's real purpose. It was a human artefact, but it did not appear to have originated within the timeline leading up to the Cutoff. If it dated from after the Cutoff, what secrets did it hold? More than that: how had it reached Janus?

The Fountainheads had never spoken of it. If they knew of its existence now – if they had picked up that knowledge from their human contacts – then they must have chosen not to mention it.

Why?

A thought tickled the back of Bella's mind, nastily. Were the Fountainheads neglecting to mention the cube because they did not want to draw attention to its significance?

She thought again of her conversation with Svetlana, and of the poisonous doubts Svetlana had insinuated into her mind. Bella had visited the Fountainheads for the first time just after she had been shown the cube. The knowledge of its existence would still have been in her short-term memory, gleaming like a jewel.

They must know about it.

So – again – why had they never mentioned it?

The cube continued its slow, hypnotic revolution, squirming between one abstraction of blackness and the next. The da Vinci face turned into view – the stylised man, spread-eagled as if for dissection. The analysis machines tracked and scanned. Bella held herself back from the red line, at the same time imagining reaching out to touch the cube. She had touched it once, wearing haptic gloves: had stroked the Euclidean hardness of its surfaces, like something carved from the very bedrock of reality itself. She had felt something of its antiquity creep through the data channels. But she had never had the courage to remove the gloves and press skin against matter.

Suddenly it was vitally, crushingly necessary that she do *just that.* The compulsion came over her with the force of a seizure. The cube urged her to reach out and touch it.

It wanted human contact.

Bella gasped and stepped back from the red line before she did real harm. Her heart was racing. The anticipation had been almost sexual, like the rising moments before climax.

'Bella?' Hannah asked. 'Are you—'

Bella found her breath and took another cautious step away from the cube. She could still feel that compulsion: it was weaker now, but still there, still exerting some measure of control. The da Vinci figure came into view again: the details of the man's face had been simplified to little more than a motif, but that calm expression appeared to hold back some vast, lacerating knowledge – a burden it was almost too much to bear.

'What do you want with me?' Bella whispered.

It was almost certainly her imagination, but in that moment she felt a silent answer flood her brain like a hot summer tide: not a word, not even the memory of a word, but just a single, devastating truth.

*You.*

# CHAPTER 30

When Parry showed up in the High Hab three days later, she had almost forgotten why he had come. It took several free-falling moments of mental stall before she remembered the Bagley case.

'Maybe you're right,' she said dolefully. 'Maybe we are better off letting this one sleep.'

Parry looked disappointed. 'That doesn't sound like the Bella I spoke to three days ago.'

He was right: it didn't. It was a measure of how thoroughly the cube had upset her ordered view of things. 'I'm sorry,' she said, offering Parry a seat amidst the shifting green radiance of her fish tanks. 'I'm the last person who should be talking like that.'

Parry removed the red cap and scratched at his wiry tangle of thin grey hairs. He looked at her with one eye narrowed. 'Are you all right, Bella?'

'I'm fine,' she said, a touch over-emphatically. 'It's just been a funny few days. A funny few weeks, come to think of it. Mike coming back . . . what happened at the party—'

'I'm glad you talked to Svieta. Did you put Mike up to that?'

'Absolutely not,' Bella said, alarmed that Parry had even considered the possibility. 'I went into the arboretum determined I wasn't even going to make eye contact with Svetlana. I was doing pretty well, too.'

'I think she felt the same way.'

'I could have killed Mike,' Bella said. 'Which is saying a lot given how long we'd all waited to have him back.'

'If it's any consolation, Svieta wasn't exactly thrilled either. He told her he'd arranged a one-on-one with McKinley. He never mentioned that you'd be sitting there as well.'

'How is she now?'

'Deeply, deeply relieved. I'll be truthful: I think you both had your reasons for not wanting to see each other again.'

'I can't disagree with that.'

'But by the same token I don't think either of you really wanted it to continue for ever. You know, even in the darkest days, when Svetlana couldn't even stand hearing your name mentioned in her presence—' Parry stalled and looked at her, seeking permission to continue.

'Go on,' she said, warily.

'Well, she still wouldn't tolerate anyone criticising you. I mean, it was all right for *her* – she could accuse you of anything under the sun. But if anyone else had the temerity to do it – woe betide them. She was the only one who had the God-given right to criticise Bella Lind. No one else had earned it.'

Bella smiled slightly. 'I can believe that. Maybe I felt the same way at times.'

'If it's any consolation, I know how much it meant to Svieta that you two were able to talk. I know she could have ended the silence years ago—'

'So could I,' Bella interjected.

'But you didn't, and neither did Svieta. Maybe you both wanted the other to make the first move, or maybe you were both afraid of what would happen if you did speak . . . that the sky would fall, or something like that. Well, I'm here to tell you it didn't. And I think the world is a better place now than it was a week ago.'

'I think so, too,' Bella said, but she heard something in Parry's voice that unsettled her. 'What is it?' she asked uneasily.

'It's about Meredith Bagley,' he said. 'About the murder investigation.'

'I know. That's why I asked you to come here.'

They sat and stared at each other. On several occasions Parry seemed about to speak, but then pulled back from whatever he had in mind. Bella remained silent, forcing herself not to prompt him. Parry looked down and closed his eyes, as if seeking some higher strength. Finally he looked up at her and said, very softly, 'You have the right names.'

'I know. I've always known. It was just a question of putting together enough evidence.'

'I can help you.'

'Only if you can prove that the logs were tampered with.'

'I can do better than that. I concealed the evidence. I doctored the files, to protect those three men.'

She heard the words, but she did not want to believe them. 'No,' she said. 'I called you here because you might have known how someone else got away with it. Not because you did it.'

'You struck lucky, Bella, that's all.'

'No,' she said again. 'You can't have done it. You would never do this.'

'But I did.'

Slowly, the possibility that he might be telling the truth began to sink in. 'They murdered her horribly. You would never have wanted any part of that.'

'I didn't.' Again, Parry paused to collect his thoughts. 'I'd always known there was bad blood against Meredith, ever since you asked her to help you, forced her to act against Svetlana—'

'Wasn't Thom Crabtree enough for them?'

'They killed Crabtree in blind rage. This was always going to be more premeditated. It was five years after our arrival on Janus. They wanted to show that they had long memories.'

'Did you know it was coming?'

'I thought her life might be in danger and I tried to warn her – advised her to get work in another section, away from Svetlana's loyalists. She didn't listen: she thought I was the one threatening her. But I had no idea when they were going to strike, or who was going to do it.'

Bella allowed herself a moment's relief. 'So you had no part in the killing itself.'

'Death is death. I only ever wanted an end to it.'

She stared at him with appalled incomprehension. 'But if you didn't approve of the Bagley murder, why did you doctor the EVA logs? Those men could have been brought to justice forty-three years ago.'

'I didn't want them brought to justice.'

'I don't understand.'

'You remember what it was like in those days. Every pair of hands mattered. We were barely holding on.'

He was right. It was a long time ago, but she could still remember what it had been like in that hard first decade.

'But justice,' she said plaintively. 'Justice should have been done. They shouldn't have been allowed to get away with it.'

'They've spent every day since worrying that they'd be discovered. I told them I'd concealed the evidence of who was in that EVA party, but I always made it clear that the evidence could be retrieved again, if I deemed it necessary.'

Bella's mind ran through the implications. 'Didn't it occur to them to kill you?'

'Wouldn't have helped. For all they knew, I'd told Svetlana, or someone else I trusted.'

'So they've lived out their lives in a state of constant worry,' Bella said. 'Haven't we all?'

'It's lasted a lot longer for those men. It's still going on.' He scratched at his moustache. 'For fifteen years it's been common knowledge that the Bagley case was open again. I doubt that the two survivors have gone a day since then without wondering when they'll hear that knock on the door.'

'Why now, Parry?'

He offered her a consoling smile. 'You'd have got there in the end, even if you didn't necessarily like where it took you. Then you'd have been arresting me.' Parry opened his hands in surrender. 'Whereas I've come to you freely.'

'You deleted a log file, Parry. You didn't kill Meredith Bagley.'

'I concealed a crime.'

'You did it to help Crabtree – so we wouldn't lose another three lives.'

'That's what I'll tell the tribunal. Whether or not they believe it . . .' He shrugged. 'It doesn't matter now. Let the tribunal decide.'

'I can't do this,' Bella said.

'Do you want justice or not?'

'Of *course* I want justice, just not . . . this way. You've been good to me, Parry, good to us all. It can't end like this.'

'It has to. I've come to you, not the other way around. The choice isn't yours, it's mine.'

Bella felt sick. 'What about Svetlana?' she asked. 'What does she think about all this?'

'She doesn't know.'

'Oh, no.' Bella closed her eyes, willing someone to come in and take over from her, tell her that she had nothing to fear, that everything was going to work out all right in the end. 'I can't do this,' she said, so quietly that she doubted Parry had heard her at all. But he had.

'Be brave,' he said. 'Do the right thing.'

'You're telling *me* to be brave?' she asked, incredulously.

In some already resigned part of her mind, Bella knew that she had no choice. She allowed Parry to return to Svetlana for forty-eight hours. As he left the High Hab she gave him her assurance that she would have him called before the tribunal. But two days was long enough for doubts to circle. The case had already lain dormant for long periods since it had been reopened. If Bella were to tell the others that she had drawn another blank and needed time to explore other leads – time that might easily stretch to months or years – no one would have thought it suspicious.

Each time the doubts arose she crushed them and forced resolve upon herself, knowing that she must finish what she had started. And for a little while that was enough. And then the doubts began circling again.

After a day she heard from Svetlana. From her tone of voice, Bella knew instantly that Parry had spoken to her.

'I have to see you,' Svetlana said.

Bella should have refused to take the call, and having taken it she should have refused to meet with Svetlana. But when she reached for the strength of mind to do that, there was nothing there.

'Where?' she asked.

'You tell me, Bella.'

'I have to be at Underhole in four hours – I'm due Skyside. I can meet you in Sugimoto's, in the plaza.'

Bella was there on time, travelling alone except for a haunt. The haunt was a BI robot stealthed for maximum discretion, a paper-thin thing like a full-sized origami figure. It trod silently beside her, semi-transparent as a ghost image in the corner of her eye, folded into knife-edged invisibility when she was still. Haunts were technology from the last days before the Cutoff, troublesome to manufacture even with the latest forge-vat protocols.

Sugimoto's was all wangwood screens, ornamental fans, miniature rock gardens and delicate watercolours. Judy Sugimoto had opened the Japanese restaurant in the early years of the transit plaza, content to do quiet business until the population curve ramped through the roof. Which it would, soon.

The place was in its usual state of near emptiness. Bella spotted Svetlana in a corner booth, finishing off a dish of thick-lipped, thuggish *fugu* – pufferfish.

Bella ordered a glass of sake for herself. She had no appetite.

'I know what this is about,' she said, as she settled into the booth. Through its curved window they had a dizzying view of the transit plaza, with its intersecting geometries of maglev tubes and Skyside-bound elevator shafts.

After a long pause, Svetlana said, 'I don't condone what happened to Meredith Bagley.'

'I'd have been surprised if you did.'

Svetlana cast an uneasy eye at the haunt as it folded and changed colour to blend into the seat. 'Those men deserve to be punished for what they did to her. But Parry didn't do what he did to protect those men. He did it to protect all of us.'

Bella sipped at the sake. 'At least you accept that Parry was involved.'

'He told me he was. Did you expect him to lie?'

The haunt stiffened at the aggression in the other woman's voice.

'I only meant that it might be a lot for you to take in,' Bella said.

'I never said it wasn't.'

'Svetlana, I came to see you voluntarily. Please don't take that tone with me.'

Svetlana pushed a chopstick into the remains of the pufferfish and shook her head, disappointed as much – it appeared to Bella – with her own actions as with Bella's.

'I want you to reconsider,' she said at length.

'Reconsider justice?'

'There are other kinds of justice. You know the names now – Parry's given you that much.'

'Yes,' Bella said carefully.

'Then isn't that enough? You have one line of evidence from Ash Murray that points to these three men.'

'Ash Murray is dead.'

Svetlana dismissed her objection with a stab of her chopstick. 'No dice, Bella. You can bring him back with one signature on the right form.'

'It still wouldn't be enough for a conviction.'

'You have another witness now. Parry will testify that he saw that log, that he knew the three men were on that shift.'

'And the fact that he wiped that selfsame log?'

'It doesn't have to come out.'

'The tribunal would get to the bottom of it sooner or later,' Bella said. 'They'd want to know more – how he saw the names, why he didn't mention it sooner. And even if the tribunal doesn't figure it out, there's still the problem of the other two men. They know what Parry did. Do you honestly think they'll go down silently?'

'They still look up to Parry.'

'If they looked up to him that much, they wouldn't have killed Meredith.'

'They won't betray him.'

'Svetlana, he's already betrayed them by coming to see me. As far as I'm concerned, all bets are off.'

'You'd have found Parry sooner or later.'

The sake nibbled the edge off her thoughts. 'Let's get one thing straight: I have, and continue to have, nothing but respect and admiration for Parry Boyce. In all the years of my exile—'

'Here we go,' Svetlana said, rolling her eyes.

'Hear me out – this isn't about *you*, Svieta, or even about me. It's about Parry, and that one lifeline of sanity he offered me. Other people were kind to me – Axford, Nick . . . Jim, of course – but it was Parry who drove out there. It was Parry who brought me the fish tank. It was Parry who left me with one microscopic shred of self-respect.'

'He trusted you,' Svetlana said. 'He came to you voluntarily, so that you would know the truth, believing that you would have the good sense to bury it.'

'From where I was sitting, it looked very much like a confession, as if Parry expected me to arrest him.'

'That wasn't how he meant it.'

'I can't go second-guessing hidden intentions. I'm running an investigation. I was hoping to find the man who deleted those files, and to punish him. I can't stop just because it turns out that he's a friend, or because he had noble motives.'

'You could if you wanted to.'

'Thirteen years in power really taught you very little,' Bella said, closing a shutter on the little window of friendship that had opened up between them. She turned to the haunt. 'We're done here.'

The robot emerged from its camouflage, peeling itself from the chair.

'Bella, please,' Svetlana pleaded.

Bella did not look back. She left the restaurant and took the first outbound elevator.

*

'This is a nice surprise,' McKinley said, expressing enthusiasm with an exuberant swish of tractor fronds. The other two aliens present – Kānchenjunga and Dhāulagiri – kept their usual discreet vigil at the rear. 'I wasn't expecting to see you up here again quite so soon after Mike's revival.'

Jim Chisholm looked at her concernedly. 'Everything's all right, isn't it?'

'There's no problem with Mike,' Bella said. 'He's settling in very well, as far as I can tell.'

'The party was an excellent idea.' Chisholm kept his arms folded into the capacious sleeves of his gown. His hair was a little longer and whiter than Bella remembered from the last time she'd seen him, his beard a little fuller and shot through with white at the corners of his mouth, but as always time seemed to pass much more slowly in the embassy than it did in Crabtree. 'I'm sorry I couldn't make it down, but I didn't want anyone to think I might be trying to hog the limelight.'

'That's all right. I'd have liked to have seen you – there's a lot we could have talked about – but I appreciate that you had your reasons.'

'I'm sure Mike will do fine, in any case. And I hear that the party was successful in other ways.'

'If you mean Svetlana and me—'

He nodded sagely. 'I was encouraged by the news. Let's hope some small good comes of it.'

'Yes, let's,' Bella said tartly. It was over, she knew. It would only be a matter of time before the news reached the embassy. A deceitful moment of thaw between two endless winters.

'Perhaps you'd like to discuss the scheduling of another rejuvenation?' McKinley asked.

'Ask me again in ten years.'

The alien formed a half-hearted high-res grid with its optic fronds, lashing them together in the sloppy manner of a poorly made basket. It was McKinley's signal that she had his attention. 'What is it, Bella? Would you like some time alone to talk to Jim in private?'

'That's kind,' she said, 'and an hour ago I might have said yes. But there's no reason for you not to hear this as well. It would get back to you in the end, after all.'

'Does this concern us, then?'

'Yes,' she said, and felt a wash of dizziness pass over her, the feeling that she was horribly out of her depth, far from home and way off the script. 'Forgive me, McKinley. This might be considered indelicate, but there are a few things I've been meaning to ask.'

Chisholm cleared his throat. 'Bella, let's not forget that the Fountainheads have never pretended that we're ready for all the answers. There are certain truths that, in themselves, are as dangerous as any advanced technology.'

'I know that, Jim. I've been hearing the same story for years. Maybe I believe it, too. But now and then there are things you absolutely have to know.'

'It would be a mistake to assume that we have all the answers,' McKinley told her.

'But you must have some. Let's talk about the Cutoff, shall we?'

McKinley's fronds invited her to continue. 'By all means. There's nothing taboo about it.'

'You've never actually spelled this out, but in every exchange we've ever had, you've consistently alluded to the fact that you made contact with a human ship launched from Triton, somewhere around the time of the Cutoff.'

'That's what the data tells you.'

'I'm not talking about the data,' Bella said, fighting to hold her temper and nerve in check. 'I'm talking about what *you* know. The Fountainheads are a starfaring culture. You've been out here a lot longer than we have, even by the standards of the Thai expansion.'

'We have starfaring capability,' McKinley said, as if that ought to settle her doubts.

'Then answer me this: how extensive was your empire, or realm, or whatever you want to call it, when you bumped into the Thai ship? Did any of your kind ever meet any other representatives from the expansion? What about ships that were sent out after the Cutoff? What happened to them?'

His fronds brushed each other in obvious agitation, like the arms of an anemone stirred by some sudden marine tide. 'These are problematic questions.'

'That's why I'm asking them.'

'Our territory is large. It encompasses a volume of space containing many solar systems.'

'Put some numbers on that for me, McKinley. Are we talking hundreds, thousands, millions, or what?'

The three aliens squirmed. Flashes of ruby red and emerald green from their deeper frond layers signalled some frantic exchange of visual signals. 'I have always striven to be straight with you, Bella,' McKinley said at length.

'So why can't you just tell me?'

'Our realm encompasses hundreds of thousands of systems.' His tone became probing. 'Why is this of such immediate and pressing interest, Bella?'

'Because it's odd to me,' she said, 'that you only ever chanced upon one ship from the Thai expansion.'

'Would it make much difference if we had encountered more?'

'Possibly.' She shrugged noncommittally. 'Then tell me about the Musk Dogs. Do they have a realm as well?' Bella did not wait for McKinley's answer, for she was certain now that she would hear nothing resembling the truth. 'And the other species, the ones you've as good as admitted are stashed away elsewhere in the Structure – what about them? What kind of empires do they have? Hundreds of thousands of star systems, like you? Where are all these starfaring species, McKinley? Why didn't we see any sign of these jostling empires when we looked out into the sky from Earth? Why did it all look so damned empty out there?'

'You saw the Spica Structure,' the Fountainhead pointed out.

'Yes. One alien artefact around one star system, in one direction of the sky, two hundred and sixty light-years away. Made, incidentally, by beings we've still not seen. Where are they, McKinley? Where are the Spicans, after all this time?'

Jim Chisholm clapped his hands. 'Okay, maybe we should wrap things up here.'

'I'm not done,' Bella said.

'Yes you are, Bella,' Chisholm said, with a sudden and uncharacteristic firmness. 'You've said your piece. You've expressed reasonable concerns. McKinley, in turn, has made clear his reservations about revealing everything you'd like to know. You must respect that, as well. Would an adult answer every question a child asked? Of course not. It would be damaging.'

'Maybe I should have started with you,' she said sourly, 'as you obviously see things from such a lofty perspective.'

'You'd have learned nothing from me you haven't already learned from McKinley.'

'The difference is I can always tell when a man is lying. Even *you*, Jim.'

He looked at her with something like pity, shot through with love and compassion. 'If I did lie to you, Bella, do you honestly imagine I wouldn't have your best interests at heart?'

'I have a right to know the truth.'

'So do the citizens of Crabtree and greater Janus,' he countered. 'Have you told Gabriela Ramos what happened to Old Buenos Aires? Have you told Mike Pasqualucci about the monster his son became?'

'That's not the same thing,' Bella said, brimming with her own wounded self-righteousness. 'You can't say that's the same thing!'

'It's all the same,' Jim Chisholm said. He moved to turn his back on her, like a teacher let down by a promising pupil. 'Call me when you've calmed down, Bella. Then perhaps we can make some progress.'

# CHAPTER 31

Bella stormed into the bunker, cycling through the many layers of security. Martin Hinks was on duty, supervising the scanning run. The cube turned within a loom of analysis instruments. Hinks – who had been born ten years into the Fountainhead era – jolted awake at Bella's entry and tried to plaster on some vague simulacrum of alertness.

'Go back to sleep, Martin,' Bella said reassuringly. 'It's all right.'

'Madam—' he began.

But Bella had already crossed the red line on the floor. An alarm sounded, warning her that she was in danger of impairing the scanning run. Bella shoved aside the robotic scanners, toppling one of them on its spindly tripod. The fragile equipment crunched to the floor. Hinks redoubled his protests. Bella ignored him.

She reached out and touched one bare hand against the smooth black side of the cube. If asked, she could not have said exactly why she was doing this. All she knew was that the compulsion to touch the cube was now overwhelmingly strong, as if her entire life had been a vector aimed at this one moment. As if she had been born to touch the cube, and the cube had been born to embrace her touch.

The moving surface was iron cold. Nothing happened. Her fingers tingled, but that was all.

Bella pulled back, confused. Nothing had happened.

She flexed her fingers: the old stiffness was creeping back in with each year, like an invisible glove that was beginning to harden in place.

The alarm still blared. She looked back at Martin Hinks, expecting him to be angry that she had ruined the experiment, but instead he just looked embarrassed.

'I'm sorry,' Bella said. 'I shouldn't have . . . I just wanted to know what it felt like.'

'It's all right, madam.'

'I'm sorry,' she said again.

Hinks left his desk and moved to the fallen machine, gently tipping it back into place. The white casing was badly dented where it had hit the floor and Bella wondered idly whether it would ever work again. If they had not turned up the gravity in Crabtree, all would have been well.

'It's okay,' Hinks said. 'I've touched it. We've all touched it. It's just something you have to do.'

'Did I mess things up?'

She caught the hesitation in his voice before he answered. Yes, she had. 'No, no. We'd only just started this run. It won't take long to restart it.'

'I've damaged the equipment.'

'It's fixable. It'll still work fine.'

The cube revolved again and she saw the icy smudge where her fingertips had transferred a micro-layer of grease and dead skin to the artefact's perfect black surface. She felt ashamed. 'I'm sorry, Martin. I've ruined things. That was indefensible.'

Hinks helped her to a vacant stool, pushed back from one of the science consoles. 'Can I bring you something to drink, perhaps, Madam Lind?'

'I'm fine,' she said, but even as she said it she realised that she did not quite feel fine. She flexed her hand again – the fingertips were still tingling, as if the blood was just returning to them. She looked at the cube again. It was still turning, still oozing from one form to another, but the compulsion to touch it had disappeared. Her mind felt as clear as the dawn sky.

Too clear, in fact. Like a blackboard that had just been scrubbed.

'Martin,' she said calmly, 'you need to do something for me. Call Ryan Axford, or whoever's still on duty in the Hab, and tell them they need to come and fetch me. Tell them I think the cube has injected something into me. And tell them to hurry.'

She slept, woke, slept again. Axford was always there, frowning over a hard-copy read-out, tapping keypad instructions into some reassuringly antique item of medical hardware, whispering quietly to one of the other medics. Visitors came and went, through the quiet hours of the early morning and into the day shift. Bella watched the wall clock lurch forward in spasms, then appear to stall for subjective hours. In fever, she knew, the processes of the mind ran at an accelerated rate, distorting the perception of time. Something like that was happening to her now, as the cube's machines spun havoc through her skull.

It was clear now that the cube had pushed something into her: its mass had decreased by half a gram since she touched it.

The day lulled into afternoon. Shifts changed, but Axford was always present. Once, when she came around and saw him looking askance at some display, she saw a weary old man packed into the shape of a boy.

Afternoon bled into evening. Nurses came and gave her something to drink – it might have been to slake her thirst, or to provide some isotopic tracer for the scans. They never offered her food, but she wasn't hungry. Now and then they fiddled with the lacy imaging coronet Axford had positioned over her hair, or nipped blood from her thumb, or ran some other inscrutable test whose function she couldn't guess.

Later, in the small hours, she had another visitor.

She felt more than usually alert. Normally she heard the hissing of the medical centre's security doors, the exchange of words between visitor and duty staff, hushed confidences about her state of mind. There had been none of that this time.

The visitor was simply there, standing by her bed.

She was a woman, dressed in white. Bella saw only her face and hands. The rest of the woman's head was concealed under a kind of flat-topped wimple of the same electric-white fabric as the rest of her gown. Her hands emerged from subtle folds, joined as if in prayer. Her skin was dark, her racial background otherwise indeterminate: Nordic bone structure, perhaps, or even Inuit? She was beautiful and severe, but there was a kindness and a wisdom in her face that touched Bella on some basal level of total trust.

'Hello, Bella,' the woman said. 'You can see me now, can't you?'

Bella found the energy to call out, 'Ryan. Please.'

She had not even been sure that Axford was still there, but he came, bustling over with a concern that cut through any fatigue he must have been feeling.

'What is it?'

'I'm hallucinating,' Bella said calmly. 'I'm hallucinating a woman dressed in white, standing immediately to your right.'

Axford looked guardedly to his side. 'I'm not seeing anything, Bella.'

'She's there. Solid as daylight. Looking at me.'

'Bella,' the woman said, with a searing empathy, 'there's no cause for alarm.'

Axford adjusted the imaging coronet. He snapped glasses from his pocket and placed them on his nose. They were ridiculously oversized for a child. 'There's a lot of activity in your occipitoparietal area, and in the auditory cortex,' he said, tapping a finger into midair to enlarge some detail of the scan.

'I think the machines must be there. I think they're making me hallucinate.'

'Describe the woman,' Axford said.

'She's tall. Black. Dressed all in white. Like a nun—' Bella scowled at her own imprecision. 'But she's *not* a nun. This isn't some stock religious imagery my mind's conjuring up during a moment of crisis.'

The woman looked on sympathetically, head tilted to one side, waiting for Bella to finish.

'Do you recognise her?'

'I can't see much of her, just her face. I'm not experiencing any heavy jolts of déjà vu.'

'Bella, listen to me,' the woman said, with infinite patience, infinite serenity. 'You don't know me. You've never met me. It would have been difficult:

I lived and died a long time after you left us.'

'She's talking to me, Ryan.'

Axford pulled the ungainly glasses from his nub of a nose. 'Perhaps you'd best listen, in that case.'

'Bella, the short form of my name is Chromis Pasqueflower Bowerbird, but you can call me Chromis – the whole thing *is* a bit of a mouthful.'

'Hello, Chromis,' Bella said, feeling awkward as Axford looked on, yet compelled to acknowledge the woman's presence. 'You can understand me . . . right?'

'Completely,' Chromis said, with a smile.

'Do you mind if I ask who you are, and what you're doing in my head?'

'Not at all – it would be rude of me not to explain myself, after all. Well, to begin with . . . let's just say that I'm a politician of quite some seniority – what you might call a senator, or a member of parliament. The political body I serve is – or was at the last census, at least – a grouping of worlds encompassing fifteen thousand settled solar systems, spread across a volume of space more than four thousand light-years in diameter.' Chromis extended a hand, showing Bella a ring she wore on her right index finger. It was embossed with an interlocking geometric design that squirmed and shifted somehow before Bella's eyes, teasing her with hints of dizzying complexity. 'This is the seal of the Congress of the Lindblad Ring. That's the name of the political administration I serve.'

'You're a message from after the Cutoff,' Bella said.

'I'm not sure what you mean by "the Cutoff", but I can tell you this much. You left Earth's system in 2057, by your calendar. The exact date at which I'm recording this image is unimportant, suffice it to say that it's more than eighteen thousand years since your departure.'

Bella shook her head. 'No. We've only come two hundred and sixty light-years. A lot of time has passed, but . . . it's only hundreds, not thousands of years.'

Chromis looked at her with that searing clemency. 'There's no mistake, Bella. We know what happened to you at Spica. We know what happened during your passage through the Spica Structure.'

'We didn't pass through anything,' Bella said, all the while knowing that it was pointless and infantile to argue with the woman's godlike wisdom. 'We reached the Structure and now we're in it.'

'You are somewhere,' Chromis said, 'but it is definitely not within the Spica Structure.'

'How can you be so sure?'

'Because we destroyed it.' The woman looked rueful: it was the first glimpse of human fallibility Bella had seen in that gravely imperious face. 'It was not intentional. We were studying it, trying to understand the principles underlying its function.'

'When?' Bella asked. 'When did you destroy it?'

'Seventeen thousand years ago, by my calendar – around the early thirty-third century, by yours. And when I say "we" destroyed it, I don't mean any extant powers affiliated to the Congress of the Lindblad Ring. I'm simply referring to envoys of the human species – people from much nearer your own time.'

Bella's mind reeled, but she didn't have the slightest doubt that Chromis was speaking the truth. 'This is a lot to take in.'

'I know, and I'm sorry.'

'When you say we passed through—'

'For two hundred and sixty years, you were under way to the Spica binary at ninety-nine point nine per cent of the speed of light. You experienced a time dilation factor of twenty-two, which compressed that two hundred and sixty years of flight into twelve years of subjective time, as measured by your clocks.'

'It was thirteen years,' Bella said.

'No. If thirteen years did indeed pass before your arrival here, it was because it took you twelve years to reach Spica, plus another year to reach somewhere else.'

'I still don't—'

Chromis interrupted her gently. 'The Spica Structure was a booster, Bella. Its purpose was to accelerate you even closer to the speed of light. A time-dilation factor of twenty-two, while high, was still insufficient for the long journey you eventually had to make.' Chromis's serene face showed strain, as if imparting this information caused her genuine discomfort. 'To adapt an analogy from your own era, Bella, the first two hundred and sixty light-years of your flight – that first twelve years of subjective time – was simply the process of taxiing to the runway. The Spica Structure was the runway. Your journey had not really *begun* until then.'

Bella wanted to deny it, but the woman's conviction left no room for doubt. Chromis was telling the truth. 'So where did we go?' she asked.

Chromis looked abashed. 'We can't be sure, even now. By the time you passed through the Structure, the nearest follow-on probes were still a hundred light-years behind you. Their observations were made from a great distance. They detected faint signals from your free-flier probes: enough to measure the change in your velocity as you completed your transit through the Structure. But by the time you emerged, those signals had been lost.'

'You couldn't see us any more.'

'No. The envelope was too dark, too absorbent.'

Bella supposed that she meant the Iron Sky. 'But you must have had some idea where we were headed.'

'We had a rough idea. We extrapolated and located a counterpart to the Spica Structure two thousand light-years beyond Spica. Another booster, we presumed, or a course-adjustment element. We knew you'd probably reach it in two thousand years, but beyond that we had no means of tracking you, or estimating your subsequent time-dilation factor. You were too dark, too fast. We lost you.'

'But you found us again,' Bella said.

'We never forgot about you,' Chromis said. 'The Janus anomaly changed history. The existence theorem says that it is always much easier to find a solution when you can be confident that one exists. Within a hundred years of your departure, there had been cataclysmic breakthroughs in fundamental physics. Janus taught us to look for loopholes in theories that had looked watertight for decades. Eventually, we had our own frameshift drive. It wasn't as efficient as the Janus motor, and probably didn't employ anything like the same principles, but it sufficed. Eighteen thousand years of expansion, Bella, at velocities very close to light speed. Frameshift made us a glorious human empire. The Congress of the Lindblad Ring is just one of the larger political entities in the great dominion of human space. I represent a small cluster of likeminded systems – about a hundred and thirty worlds – bound together by long-established trade routes and a common democratic framework – what you might call a state, or constituency, within the Congress. There are hundreds of such constituencies, some of them very alien in their modes of society. Anyway, as I said – you were never really forgotten. We found your self-sacrifice inspirational.'

'Our self-sacrifice?'

'Even when it became clear that you could not escape Janus, you kept sending data back home. But then you always promised as much.'

'I did?'

'The interview, Bella.' Chromis said it with a peculiar reverence. 'You must remember.'

'I'm not sure I do.'

Chromis's voice shifted, mimicking Bella's own. 'I'm Bella Lind, and you're watching CNN.'

Bella blinked. 'CNN. You just said CNN.'

'The interview was repeated many times during the years after you left, Bella. It became a touchstone for a kind of bravery, the noblest kind of selflessness. Children were taught to learn it, like a prayer or declaration of patriotic intent.'

'I'm having trouble dealing with this.'

'The Janus data changed history. It accelerated a hundred different scientific disciplines, revealed connections no one had ever suspected before. Our knowledge of mass-energy, mass and inertia became logically complete. It gave us the stars, and for that we're enormously grateful. But at the same time it was always taken for granted that your ultimate destination – your ultimate *destiny* – must remain unknown. The boosters were shuttling you into the future, out of our reach.' Chromis smiled primly. 'Then we had a modest idea. It was approaching the ten thousandth year since the first settlement of the first world in the Congress of the Lindblad Ring. There were many competing ideas for the best way to commemorate this anniversary. My people sent me to table a proposal to the delegates on New Far Florence, and after a degree of persuasion it was accepted. We would commemorate the founding by sending a message to the Benefactor.'

'The Benefactor being me, I suppose?'

'Now perhaps you begin to see the importance you assumed to us. It would be a message of thanks, of course, but also a message that might be useful to the Benefactor and her people, wherever they might find themselves. I am, self-evidently, that message. As the instigator of the project, my personality was encoded into the memorial cube you must have found.'

'How did it reach us?' Bella asked. 'How far did it travel to get here?'

'I can't tell. We made vast numbers of cubes. Short of being dropped into a star, there isn't much that can harm them. We were thinking long term, extreme deep time.' Chromis anticipated Bella's next question. 'We scattered them to the four winds. Dispersed them throughout the galaxy via automated probes. Dropped them into orbit around a hundred million dead worlds. Cast them into intergalactic space, on trajectories that would eventually bring them into the gravitational influence of every major galaxy, satellite galaxy or globular cluster in the local group. We launched some of them far beyond the local group, towards the great galactic superclusters, halfway to the edge of the visible universe. They'll take a while to get there, of course. We even fired some of them into naked black holes, in the hope that their information would be encoded and released in the immeasurably distant future, when the black holes surrender their parcels of entropy back to the universe. We continued making them for four thousand years. Of course, we never *really* expected success – it was just a gesture, the decent thing to do.'

'But you succeeded,' Bella said. 'One of them found me.'

'Yes, it did, but there's no telling where or when. All I know is that this cube – the copy that this personality was dropped into – was one of the last to be launched. By then, the memorial project had already been under way for nearly four thousand years, and in all that time, no contact had ever been claimed.' Chromis meshed her fingers nervously. 'We can presume that you travelled a great distance, or we would have heard from you before the last cube was launched.'

'But you can't tell me how far I've come.'

'The cube only knows its subjective history. It has no record of how much objective time passed before you touched it. It may have been picked up and discarded a hundred times, like a lucky coin. Even so, it *was* a long journey.'

'Tell me everything up to that point,' Bella said.

'In time,' Chromis answered. 'All in good time.'

# CHAPTER 32

Chromis disappeared, but Bella knew she had not seen the last of her. Afterwards, feeling a restfulness that she had not experienced since touching the memorial cube, she told Axford all that she remembered of the conversation – Axford interrupting here and there to probe for more details, which Bella was sometimes able to supply and sometimes not.

'I believed her,' Bella said. 'Absolutely, implicitly. I've never been more sure of anything in my life.'

'She might have been manipulating you to achieve that effect.'

'What does it matter? She's gone and I still believe it now. It has the ring of truth, Ryan. It explains a lot. The Iron Sky, for instance: it must have been a shield to protect us against the effects of super-relativistic velocity. Janus put it up as we were approaching the booster.'

'I don't like it. It's one thing to accept that you've fallen a few hundred years down the rabbit hole. How are people going to adjust to the fact that we've actually come eighteen thousand years?'

'More than that,' Bella reminded him. 'That's only the length of time that had passed when Chromis made her recording. There's no telling how many more years passed before we picked up the cube.'

'You might want to consider sugaring the medicine here, Bella.'

'I thought you didn't approve of that.'

'I don't, as a rule.'

'But this would be one of the exceptions.'

'Perhaps. While we're at it, incidentally, for every answer Chromis gave you, she threw up at least as many questions. If we're not in the Spica Structure, where are we? We've already established that we're inside something that matches the size of one of the spars.'

'I didn't get an answer on that,' Bella said, with a creeping feeling of inadequacy.

'Here's another thing: Chromis told you about a human civilisation spanning hundreds and thousands of worlds, spread across thousands of light-years – right?'

'Yes,' Bella said.

'And she dropped hints that they'd looked deep in the galaxy, right?'

'Yes.'

'Well,' Axford said, 'remind me: when exactly did she mention the Fountainheads?'

The ordinary business of the High Hab rolled on with its own oblivious momentum.

Parry returned to Crabtree and surrendered himself to Bella and the Judicial Apparatus. He was detained in a secure room close to the court, with an excellent view over Crabtree. The room was clean and comfortable, but still had the air of a place of detention or psychiatric internment. The soft-surfaced walls had the profoundly dead look that told Bella they were not flickering with subliminal data patterns. There was a bed and a bedside table and a tray containing a half-eaten meal. Parry sat on the bed, seemingly unfazed by whatever might happen to him.

'Hello,' he said, standing up to meet her.

She motioned him to remain seated. 'Are you all right?'

'They're treating me very well.'

Bella didn't doubt it. Parry had friends everywhere, and hardly any enemies. 'I've some news for you,' she said. 'The preliminary hearing's set for tomorrow. You'll be required to be there, but other than that you won't have to do or say much.'

'Mm.' He scratched under his cap. 'Other than state my guilt.'

'Yes,' Bella said. 'If you still want to do that, of course. There's nothing to stop you pleading not guilty.'

'Except I've never claimed that I didn't do it. It's the extenuating circumstances I'm interested in.'

'As I said, I'm sure a solid case can be made for that.'

'But not a watertight one.'

Bella remembered something she had been meaning to ask. 'Parry, you're a bright man. You have a lot of contacts, a lot of friends with good skills. When you knew I was closing in on whoever tampered with the log files, didn't it ever occur to you to hide your trail? I'm sure you could have concealed the concealment, especially now, after all these years. I doubt it would have taxed you.'

'You're probably right,' he said, 'and maybe it did occur to me – for about five minutes.'

'So why didn't you do it?'

'A couple of reasons, Bella. Firstly, it would have involved dragging more people into this shit, and I didn't want to do that. This is my mess, no one else's. Secondly, when I did what I did, I always knew it might come back and bite me one day. And I always promised myself that I'd stand up and take the punishment when that happened.'

'That's what I thought,' she said. 'And I'm glad I was right about it. I want you to know that whatever happens here, whatever the tribunal decides, I've never doubted your intentions, not for a second. And I never will.'

'Thank you,' Parry said.

During one visitation, Bella asked Chromis for a demonstration of her physical capabilities.

Chromis smiled patiently. 'I have no physical capabilities, Bella. I'm just a ghost in your head. I can't move a feather. I can't even make you move a feather for me.'

'You know I mean the cube.'

'Ah,' Chromis said, as if the cube had been the last thing on her mind. 'That.'

Bella walked on through the ice-lined tunnel under Crabtree. She had been on her way to the nursery, to talk to a class of babbling five year olds. 'You told me that the cube is more than just a message. You said it might be useful to me.'

'It could also be very lethal. Now that I've learned a little more about the state of affairs here on Janus, I'm inclined to take the cautious line.'

'I'll tell you what we think we know,' Bella said. 'The cube is two hundred tonnes of replicating material squeezed into eight cubic metres. It's not nanotech, since we can analyse that, but something as far beyond nanotech as nanotech is beyond clockwork.'

'Continue,' Chromis said, as if this was all just a mildly diverting parlour game they'd elected to play on a rainy afternoon.

'Some of that stuff must provide something to run on, and some of it presumably enables the cube to keep repairing itself, but I doubt it needs all two hundred tonnes just for that.'

'That would be excessive.'

'So what does the rest of it do?'

Chromis hesitated before answering. 'Many things.'

'No shit. Really.'

'There isn't much it can't do, truth be told.'

'I suspected as much. Why are you quite so reluctant to discuss this, Chromis?'

'You would be, in my shoes.'

'If you meant for me to find the cube, why is there such a problem with telling me what it does?'

'Mm. The problem is—' Chromis made a frustrated face. 'The problem is, we sent out the cubes with the best of intentions, but we were not hugely confident that any of them would find you.'

'So you said.'

'But we assumed that if by some great good fortune one of the cubes did find you, then it would more than likely be after a considerable period of time had elapsed.'

'A lot of time *has* passed,' Bella said impatiently.

'But not by your reckoning. How many years has it been, Bella, since you encountered Janus? A few decades, that's all. That's nothing compared to the eighteen thousand years between your time and mine.'

'It still feels like a long time to us.'

From their conversations, Bella had pieced together a coherent picture of Chromis's world and history, and how it connected to her own. Somewhere around 2136, various lines of development had collided. What had once been servile Borderline Intelligences had jumped the tracks into genuine sentience. The luminously clever engines of Trangressive Intelligence had been much too clever, much too willing to oblige.

In an instant, humanity had found itself in possession of tools powerful enough to remake entire worlds, but equally capable of shattering them to dust. There was no war *as such*, but there were dreadful accidents, regrettable misunderstandings and hugely disproportionate retaliations. Around the edge of the system, those powers not embroiled in the transformation had looked on with something between horror and awe. The Thai expansion was less an attempt to establish a human presence beyond the solar system than a desperate effort to outrace that whirlwind of change.

The people of Chromis's era looked back on that period with a feeling of collective disquiet, a kind of shuddering disbelief that they had made it through.

It had nearly ended everything.

'I don't doubt that it feels like a long time to you, but it isn't really, is it? You've done well to survive here at all, but it's not clear to me that you're ready to accept the cube's gifts. Perhaps in a hundred, two hundred years—'

'Don't give me that!' Bella snapped. 'You started it by appearing to me, Chromis!'

'I did, yes,' she said ruefully, 'and that might have been a mistake. Not because I don't like and admire you – I'm hardly capable of anything else – but because it's begun to dawn on me how damaging it might be to open the cube now, rather than later.'

'So you'd withhold the opening of the cube, is that it?'

'Not exactly. I *am* your servant, and I won't refuse a direct command, but I'll do my level best to talk you out of it.'

'Because the technology in the cube is so dangerous?'

'In unwise hands, yes.'

Bella considered this as they walked on. 'What if you judged that we were in danger anyway? How would that change things?'

'Like I said, I wouldn't refuse a direct command.'

'But would you intervene to help me anyway, even if I didn't command it? Does your impulse to protect me go that deep?'

'I'd do almost anything to protect you,' Chromis said.

'Then I think it likely that at some point you will have to intervene. I already have intelligence on at least one approaching threat. There may be others.'

A frown creased Chromis's delicate features. 'I'm not sure I follow.'

'Since it's as good as guaranteed that I'll need to see the cube do its stuff sooner or later, there's no harm in me seeing a demonstration now.' Bella glared at her ghostly companion. 'Is there?'

'Since you put it like that . . .'

Bella looked at her watch. 'I'm already late for this nursery thing. When I'm done – which'll be in an hour or so – I want you to pop back into my head. Then we'll take a little walk to the laboratory and you can show me something of the cube's abilities. It doesn't have to be much – I just want some basic idea of what I'm dealing with.'

'I can give you a basic idea now,' Chromis said.

'We're not at the cube.'

'We don't have to be.' Again, Bella sensed the other woman's profound unease. 'Are you certain you want this, Bella?'

'Yes.'

'Absolutely certain?'

'I can keep saying yes all day, Chromis.'

'Very well. Since you *insist.*'

Bella felt the air move around her, as if a flock of *things* – things that were very big and completely invisible – had just swooped past her by a hair's width. A little further ahead along the ice-lined tunnel, a clot of darkness formed in midair, then enlarged into a hovering cube about the size of a hat-box. The air stilled.

Bella stepped back reflexively.

'It's all right,' Chromis said. 'You did ask for a demonstration.'

'Is it real?'

'Reach out and touch it.'

Bella extended and hand and brushed her fingers against the black surface of the hovering form. It was as cold and hard as the memorial cube, and felt as if it were fixed solidly in place, anchored in position somehow.

'How . . . how did this get here?'

'It . . . arrived.'

'Don't get clever, Chromis.'

'The cube donated a few hundred kilograms of itself, at my command.'

'We're a long way from the cube.'

'The machinery travels quickly, especially through air. It disassembles itself into countless individual entities that move independently and then reassemble at their destination. Doors and barriers won't stop it – at least not the kind you're capable of making. It finds ways to ooze through. If it can't ooze, it drills. You'd never even notice the invisibly small channels it makes for itself.'

'You were right to be worried about my reaction.'

'There's more.'

The black cube enlarged, as if being inflated from within, and the sharp edges became curved. The cube elongated into a mummy-like form, and then sharpened its details. Colours and textures bled across the black surface.

Bella stared at a perfect image of herself. 'Okay, I'm officially impressed.'

The image spoke in perfect harmony, with no detectable lag in its responses.

'Then you're satisfied with the demonstration?'

Bella swallowed and nodded. 'Yes.'

'Good, but I'm not quite done yet. In for a penny, in for a pound, as they used to say.'

'Chomis—'

The image darkened and shrunk back down into the cube form.

'You were on your way to the nursery, were you not?'

'Yes . . .' Bella faltered.

'And you are running late.'

'Yes.'

'Then we'd best do something about that, hadn't we?'

'Chromis—' she said again.

'Quiet now, Bella. Quiet now and listen. The machinery is going to assemble itself around you. We call it a travel caul – it's how we move around where I come from. The caul is going to take you the nursery. It will happen very quickly, and you will feel nothing. The caul will infiltrate your body to gird you against the acceleration and deceleration during your journey.'

'Infiltrate my body? I don't like the sound of that.'

'Unfortunately, it isn't practical to generate a frameshift field on this scale, so there's no option but to construct a temporary intracellular scaffold. But don't worry – you'll feel nothing, and there'll be no evidence after the fact.'

'You're scaring me now.'

'And taking rather a childish delight in doing so. You will forgive me, won't you?'

'I can still make it on time if I run.'

'Running?' Chromis looked appalled. 'How utterly undignified. We wouldn't want you showing up in front of the children all sweaty and out of breath, now, would we?'

Bella started to say something, but the cube was already changing shape, flattening and flowing towards her. She took a reflexive gulp of air before the black surface wrapped around her. There was a moment when she felt its iron coldness seeping into her skin, and then the surface was pulling itself away again, as if something had gone wrong . . .

But nothing had gone wrong. She was somewhere else.

Bella was standing in the plastic-walled corridor outside the nursery complex. By her estimation she had moved three or four hundred metres in the blink of an eye.

'So now you've had your demonstration,' Chromis said.

The caul had disappeared. There was no sign of the miniature black cube. Bella opened her mouth and tried to speak. 'I . . .'

'It's all right. You're fine. Your first time was bound to be a little disorientating.'

Through the thin plastic door Bella heard a clamour of infant voices, raised in expectation of her arrival.

'I can't just . . . go in there. Not after *that*.'

'The whole point was to make up lost time.'

'I need to sit down. I need to get my head together.'

Chromis cocked her head at the door. 'The children, Bella – they're beginning to sound fractious.'

Bella felt as if her entire existence had slipped a gear. 'Did anyone see me arrive?'

Chromis tutted. 'Oddly enough, it did occur to me to check that no one was around first.'

'I'm sorry. I'm just a bit . . . taken aback.'

'I won't do it again. Not unless you ask.'

'There's a door,' Bella said, 'a heavy-duty airlock between here and where we were standing. It would have been closed. I have an access key to open it – how in hell did we get through?'

'One piece at a time,' Chromis said. 'Or is that too much information?'

There was something new in the embassy: an enormous circular table formed from a thick black material. It had a low rim, and the surface was marked with hundreds of luminous blue squiggles in concentric rings, none of which appeared to correspond to the Spican alphabet. A reflective silver ball the size of an orange rested in the precise middle of the table.

'You didn't call me here to deliver good news, did you?' Bella said.

Chisholm smiled apologetically, as if this was all somehow his fault. 'Musk Dogs have reached the endcap door. They're on the other side, waiting to get through.'

'When will the door open?'

'Soon.' He looked back at the huge round table. 'McKinley mentioned the Whisperers to you before, I think?'

'Yes, when he first spoke of the Musk Dogs – and the Uncontained.'

'There's a Whisperer envoy here now.'

'In the embassy?'

'In this room.'

Bella measured the glassy environment of the embassy chamber against her memories. The table was the only thing different since her last visit. If there was another alien in the room, either it *was* the table, or it had blended expertly with its surroundings.

'I don't see anything,' she said.

'They're . . . elusive.'

McKinley bustled closer, vivid parks of ruby and green flashing through the curtain of his tractor fronds. 'In the past, the Whisperers have tended to confine their activities to a single chamber of the Structure. Lately, disturbances have forced them to do business with other cultures, across the matter gap.'

'The door hasn't opened in a while. How'd it get here?'

'The doors don't trouble Whisperers – they can usually slip through them. If a door's too heavily shielded for them to slip through, they have passkeys that talk to the locking mechanisms.'

'If they can get through the doors, what's to stop them leaving the Structure?'

'The walls are much stronger, laced with fields that even the Whisperers can't cross. Whoever made this place must have anticipated that it might have to contain something like the Whisperers.'

Bella's skin tingled. 'How do you know there's one here now?'

'We're detecting it,' McKinley said. 'Whisperers reveal themselves by their gravitational influence, and by inducing subtle, statistically weak asymmetries in quantum chromodynamic interactions.'

'Why has it come here?'

'To warn us,' McKinley said. 'It says that other Whisperers have done a deal with the Musk Dogs.'

The silver ball started moving, rolling away from the middle of the table. Something about the way it rolled conveyed an impression of tremendous, unstoppable mass. It rumbled around the table, then slowed above one of the symbols before moving on. The symbol shone red. The ball moved to another symbol, which also changed from blue to red. Three more symbols followed, before the ball returned to the middle of the table.

McKinley translated. 'The Whisperer says it has been banished by the others of its kind because it opposed the deal with the Musk Dogs. It says it fears the consequences of the deal.'

The red symbols faded slowly back to blue.

'What is that thing? Is the Whisperer inside that ball?'

'The ball is just a ball,' McKinley told her. 'The Whisperer has a counterpart to the table on its side of the matter gap. When it wishes to talk to us, it moves a gravitational point mass from symbol to symbol. The ball senses the gravitational field across the gap and moves accordingly.'

The ball rolled again, highlighting a different sequence of symbols.

'The Whisperer says that the Musk Dogs are not the main problem, although they shouldn't be underestimated. The real problem is the Uncontained.'

'So tell me about them – sounds like I'm going to find out about them sooner or later no matter what happens.'

'Regrettably, that may be the case. The Uncontained are made of normal matter, like you and me. In Structure terms, they arrived very recently and immediately set about implementing a policy of aggressive hegemonization of the entire habitable volume. Their activities wiped out one culture and pushed another to the brink of extinction. After that, a coalition of like-minded entities – the Shaft-Five Nexus – succeeded in confining the Uncontained to a single volume. Unfortunately, a small contingent of Uncontained recently escaped from this volume back into the larger Structure. They are now at large again, which is leading to new difficulties.'

The ball moved again, highlighting a different symbol chain.

'The Whisperer warns that the Musk Dogs cannot be trusted to use passkeys responsibly.'

'Hold on,' Bella said. 'Let's back up a minute, while you're willing to answer questions. How many cultures are there inside this thing?'

'After the last extinction? We know of thirty-five. Present company included, of course.'

'Any particular reason why you couldn't have told me this sooner?'

'It's been our experience that knowledge of the true extent of the Structure, and the number of entities contained within it, can have a dispiriting effect on certain cultures.' McKinley paused delicately. 'Most especially those cultures deemed to be at high risk for self-destruction.'

'Like us, I presume. So why the big change of heart?

'The arrival of the Musk Dogs precipitates a certain shifting in our affairs.'

'You think they'll bring the Whisperers with them?'

'The Whisperers aren't the main problem. Many cultures find their presence unsettling, but they are not amongst the worst hostiles, and we have done useful business with them on a number of occasions. In any case, the Whisperers don't need the Musk Dogs to open doors for them. The problem is that if the doors *are* open, we won't just be dealing with the Musk Dogs and the Whisperers.'

The ball moved again, trundling around the table. When it had spelled out its message, McKinley said, 'The Whisperer speculates that there may have been contact between the Musk Dogs and the Uncontained. If so, that is a *most* worrying development.'

'Why would the Musk Dogs talk to the Uncontained? What do they want or need from each other?'

'The Whisperer isn't sure. Nor are we. The Whisperer is trying to obtain more data on the negotiations.'

'What will happen if the Uncontained reach us? Will we die?'

'If only a small contingent of Uncontained have broken loose, the Shaft-Five Nexus may be able to slow or repel an incursion. As affiliates of the Nexus, we will press for early intervention.'

'Nice to know you care.'

'We do care, and not just because of the energy you let us draw from Janus, although we value that. We also prize your company. We may be exotic to you, Bella, but there are entities in the Structure that even we find disturbingly strange.'

Despite McKinley's generous words, a spiteful impulse seized her. 'That's all very well, but I know this isn't the Structure. It's *a* structure, but not the one we always thought it was. We're nowhere near Spica. We've come a hell of a long way further than that.'

'We've never lied to you,' McKinley said.

'No,' Bella said, 'but you've done a damned good job of not correcting any of my assumptions.'

# CHAPTER 33

A few days later, Bella was awoken in the early hours of the morning by Liz Shen. She had been dreaming of the tribunal, watching Parry being taken out onto the ice to be drilled through the back of his helmet, watching the spray of blood and gore fan out across the ice, as if that was still the way they did things. The horror of it stayed with her into consciousness. When she answered Shen, she still assumed that the call must have something to do with the Bagley investigation.

It didn't.

'I'm sorry, Bella,' Shen said, 'but you asked to be called the moment something happened.'

Bella forced her mouth to work. 'The moment wash . . . the moment *what* happened?'

'It's the endcap door,' Shen said. 'It's open. Something's coming through, and it isn't like anything we've ever seen before.'

'Put it through to me.'

Bella dressed and crossed from her sleeping quarters to her office, grabbing a cigarette along the way.

Cams stationed at intervals between Janus and the endcap door captured views of the emerging ship, or whatever it was, across a multitude of angles and spectral bandpasses. The cams blurted their data back to Janus through light-seconds of empty space and into waiting dish aerials, and then it passed through fibre-optic lines strung from the Iron Sky, through the Underhole pinchpoint and along kilometres of maglev track to Crabtree. In the city, BI minds sucked in the data and forced it through the shrieking turbine blades of intense computation. Within fractions of a nanosecond, the intelligences had already assembled an astonishingly complete composite model of the alien entity.

One of Bella's walls – the only part of her office not lost behind fish tanks – showed a mosaic of the best views overlaid with a tumbling wireframe graphic of the Musk Dog vehicle, with tick marks delineating scale in units of a tenth of a kilometre.

Bella lit the cigarette and studied the graphic.

Liz Shen's initial assessment had been correct – the Musk Dog ship did not resemble anything they had seen so far. It did not look like Spican machinery, or Fountainhead machinery, or any product of the long-vanished Congress of the Lindblad Ring.

It looked, in fact, like something coughed up by a very large cat.

The ship was long but crooked-looking, as if at some point it had snapped and then been allowed to heal, like a poorly set broken leg. At one end it flared into a kind of porous, rock-seamed ball, like the upper part of a thighbone in the final stages of osteoporosis. There was a smaller clump or knot at the other end, flared like a hoof. Along the broken thing, at irregular intervals, were fatty nodes and wart-like calcifications. Sinewy strands, like the remains of veins or nervous tissue, wrapped the ship in an interrupted, straggly circulatory system, bulging here and there with a kind of sclerosis. Irregularly shaped objects dangled from the main body, attached by the flimsiest of connections. Smaller gobbets of material accompanied it, despite the absence of any physical linkages back to the main vessel. The entire ensemble looked obscene, half-digested, like nothing designed by a sane intelligence. Gristle, Bella thought: that was what it was. A ship made of gristle.

A gristleship.

It was big, too: three kilometres from end to end and several hundred metres across. And it was moving fast: it was rapidly eating up the hundred and fifty light-seconds between the endcap and Janus. According to the BI analysis, it would reach them within ten hours.

She called Jim Chisholm.

'In case you had any doubts,' he said, 'it's them.'

'What do I do now?'

'Exactly what McKinley's said every time he's ever warned you about the Musk Dogs: sit tight and ignore them, no matter what they say. Don't even *listen* to their transmissions, let alone respond. It may take a while, but they will, eventually, desist.'

Behind the gristleship, the endcap door remained partly open, the gap just wide enough to admit the gristleship. The sensors had detected nothing else crossing the gap, but now that Bella knew of the existence of such elusive entities as the Whisperers, that was scant consolation.

'It's just the Musk Dogs,' Chisholm said, obviously picking up on her concern. She hoped she could believe him.

Bella stubbed out the cigarette. She knew that the wise thing would be to catch another few hours of sleep, but her mind was already buzzing. No one, she suspected, would be getting much sleep in the next twenty-four hours.

She called Liz Shen to her office and together they looked at the steadily improving images.

'Not exactly the prettiest thing in the world,' Bella said, 'but I've been reassured that they won't cause us any trouble. Provided, that is, that we ignore them completely.'

'And if we don't?'

'Then they might be problematic. In the meantime, I'm hoping it won't come to that.' She tapped a finger against her flexy. 'I've recorded a statement: a calming message to the people, telling them that we have things under control and that they don't need to worry about the Musk Dogs.'

'Musk Dogs,' Shen said, with a shiver of distaste. 'Is that what they actually call themselves?'

'I suspect not.'

'Why Musk? What does that mean?'

'I hope we never have to find out.' Bella slid the flexy across her desk to Shen. 'You're welcome to review my message and suggest any edits, but make it quick. I want it out there and repeating on all ShipNet feeds before Crabtree wakes up to the fact that that *thing* is headed our way. I'll make a live statement in four hours.'

Shen regarded the gristleship with the revolted air of a vegetarian offered a half-eaten chicken drumstick. 'It looks pretty vile. Almost *too* vile. Do you think they're really so bad?'

'Just look at it, Liz. Does that strike you as the product of the kind of intelligence you really want to do business with?'

'I don't know. We shouldn't judge by appearances, after all.'

'This time,' Bella said, 'judging by appearances is exactly the right course of action.'

Four hours later Bella made her statement, urging calm and forbidding anyone from attempting to make contact with the newcomers. She did not tell her people all that she knew, but she told them everything she felt they needed to know about the new aliens, without once mentioning Chromis or her doubts about the nature of the Structure. They would find all that out in good time, when Bella had decided which version of the truth she was inclined to believe: that of the Fountainheads, or that of the politician from the ancient past.

Six hours later, the gristleship moved into position above the Fountainhead embassy. It came to a jarring halt at a deceleration that would have pulped a human vehicle, but the gristleship showed no sign of having been affected. Even its satellites – the unconnected gobbets and shards that moved with it – achieved standstill in the same perfectly choreographed instant. Once it had stopped, the gristleship remained still except for a slow longitudinal rotation, like a piece of meat on a spit.

The cams had their best view now and details that had been blurred before were now anatomically clear and precise. It was evident that many of the nodes and thickenings in the structure of the gristleship owed their existence to artefacts of distinctly different origin – hard-edged and metallic in some cases; jewelled, faceted and glittering in others – that appeared to have been incorporated into the basic mass of the Musk Dog vessel. Already there was speculation that these artefacts might be alien mechanisms of foreign provenance, providing propulsion and inertial control. More and more the ship appeared to be a haphazard collection of disparate parts loosely united by a common chassis of meat and bone, slime and sinew.

Then it waited, saying nothing, doing nothing, as if the simple fact of its arrival ought to have been sufficient to draw human attention.

Again, Bella urged calm.

In Crabtree, in Underhole, in the Maw and the eddytowns, in the construction dormitories of the Tier-Two expansion, it was not exactly business as usual. No one could block out the knowledge of that alien thing poised above Janus, or refrain from wondering what it might do to them. But Bella's reassurances carried some weight. Amongst the citizenry it was known that Bella enjoyed the confidence of the Fountainheads, and that when she spoke of alien matters, it was their knowledge that she was revealing. If the Fountainheads said that the Musk Dogs were safe provided they were ignored, then many people were happy to believe that. The Fountainheads had, after all, given many of them the gift of rejuvenation.

So people tried to get on with the ordinary routine of living, and some of them came close to succeeding. But not many managed that. Most people could do little more than shuffle through the motions, waiting anxiously for each new announcement from the High Hab. For the older adults – those who remembered the old crises aboard *Rockhopper*, the difficult years of the early settlement, the predations of the Year of the Iron Sky – this was just one more uncertainty to be looked square in the eye and stared down. It was much harder on the young, who had never known anything but the stability and comfort of the Fountainhead years. Bella pitied them, and she pitied the children most of all. They were frightened, and they wanted to be told that there were no monsters out there. Bella hoped she was right, but there was nothing more she could do to comfort them.

A further day passed, and then the transmissions began.

No one was quite sure how the Musk Dogs had done it – nothing had been observed coming or going from the gristleship – but somehow they had succeeded in tapping into ShipNet at its most secure, supposedly inviolable level of security. ShipNet continued to function normally, but suddenly there were extra channels and extra data frames interlaced into the existing streams.

The content of the extra channels and the additional frames – when they were strung together in time order and played as a video feed – was disarmingly simple. It was a senior CNN anchordoll: a simulation of an attractive woman in her forties with styled auburn hair, wearing a crisp maroon blouse with a starburst brooch, backdropped by the jostling screens, clocks and global maps of a busy television newsroom somewhere in the middle of the last century.

She spoke with the measured and emphatic tones of a Shakespearean actor. 'Hello, and welcome. Permit me to introduce myself. I have the pleasure of being the spokesperson for the entities you already know as the Musk Dogs.' The anchordoll smiled, showing good teeth, and rearranged a sheaf of papers laid on the desk. 'Please – we urge you – do not be afraid to keep using that name. Given our cultural differences, it's as accurate a translation as we're likely to agree on. Which is to say, not very accurate at all, but an infinite improvement on the alternatives.'

Bella told herself to stop viewing the clip, remembering McKinley's warning that there was no safe level of exposure to Musk Dogs. But what was to be gained by not viewing it? It was already out there now, available to everyone on Janus. She would be derelict in her duty if she did not study its content.

'I'm speaking to you from inside the ship – the gristleship, as you call it,' the anchordoll went on. 'It's a fine name, and pleasingly close to the one we favour. Again – please do not feel in any way inhibited in using it. As you'll discover – as we fervently *hope* you'll discover – we're very, very difficult to offend. We have had a great deal of experience in contact situations during our time in the Structure, including most beneficial interactions with many cultures. During that time we have learned that a thick skin is a prodigious asset.' She touched a hidden earpiece, as if receiving studio instructions, and nodded to an unseen director. 'Which brings me to the point at hand: it would please us greatly to establish a dialogue with the people of Janus. It is our understanding that you have already enjoyed a degree of reciprocal trade with the entities you call the Fountainheads, and we are sure that you have enjoyed *some* benefits from that arrangement. It is clear that the Fountainheads have shared some of their knowledge with you, and that this has facilitated a modest improvement in your standards of comfort and security. But now we must reveal a state of affairs that you may find vexing. It is our most regrettable duty to inform you that the Fountainheads are not all that they claim to be.'

She looked intently at the camera, then composed her expression into one of grave solemnity, the way all anchordolls did before they delivered bad news: a plane crash, a political assassination, the death of an actor or pop star.

'Their history of dealings with other cultures is characterised by an unfortunate tendency towards parasitism. They prey on cultures like your own, offering meagre titbits in exchange for things the true value of which *you* hardly understand. Time and again their true intentions are exposed, causing them to move elsewhere in the Structure to seek new victims. You simply have the singular misfortune of being the latest culture to fall under the malign influence of the Fountainheads.' The anchordoll looked convincingly sympathetic. 'We appreciate that this will be a difficult truth to accept after what may have appeared to be many years of beneficial trade. Nonetheless, and with due regret, it *is* the truth. Doubtless the Fountainheads will have sought to protect their position by disseminating misinformation concerning those other cultures with whom they would sooner wish you had no contact. We expect this. We know their methods, and we are accustomed to them.'

She could turn off ShipNet, Bella knew. It was unprecedented – ShipNet had not been interrupted since the flexy die-off – but it was within her administrative powers to order a blackout. But that would not stop the Musk Dog poison spreading further via word of mouth and the countless unregulated networks over which she had no control.

She could issue a counterstatement, but all she would be doing was restating what she had said before: that the Musk Dogs were not to be trusted, that they would go away if they were ignored, that spreading doubt and suspicion was precisely how they operated. It would be unlikely to make much difference now that the poison was out.

She would do it anyway.

The anchordoll was wrapping up her transmission. 'We know that the Fountainheads will have advised that you should not engage in any form of contact with us. That is to be expected – how else are they to maintain their parasitic relationship, unless they obstruct competitors? But please listen to what we have to offer. What the Fountainheads have given you in exchange for access to Janus is what we would have given you freely, as a sign of our good intentions. In thirty-five years, they have bestowed upon you a few crumbs of prior human knowledge. We would never have *sold* you what was already yours. We would have given it gladly, as a courtesy. And then we would have invited you to enter into trade for items of genuine value.' The anchordoll paused and gathered her papers, tapping them together into a neat stack. 'But it isn't too late to change all that. The Fountainheads probably told you that we wouldn't force ourselves upon you. That's true – absolutely. And if you so wish, we will leave. But in the meantime, you have only to contact us. One word is all that it would take. Then we can start doing business.' The anchordoll smiled. 'We look forward to hearing from you. We are sure that we can enter into arrangements of great mutual benefit.'

# CHAPTER 34

Bella took the maglev to Eddytown. There were many eddytowns on Janus now, but this was the original one, and by far the largest. One hundred and twenty people lived there, a number not much smaller than *Rockhopper*'s original manifest. It was a sprawl of varying sized domes and micro-arboreta glued to the side of Junction Box, like a mass of barnacles on the sheer metal hull of a tramp steamer. In recent years the Fountainheads had shown the humans how to increase the gravitational field under Crabtree, Underhole and the other icecap settlements, but by then the eddytowns were already well established.

The maglev rollercoasted through ninety vertical degrees, passing a vast farm of perpetual-motion wheels, turning slow and stately as the huge grey wind turbines Bella recalled from her childhood. Their ballasted rims were tilted partway into a region of high field strength, imparting a torque on the wheel that could be converted to electrical power.

The maglev slowed into a glass concourse. Bella disembarked from the train, followed by Liz Shen and the stealthy wisp of the haunt. To Bella's left, the rest of Janus was a wall that reached a dizzying distance above her head, until its scrawl of bright details – symbols and weaving lava lines – were reduced to a foreshortened smear. The side of Junction Box felt like a flat-topped ledge jutting out from that wall. To the right, two or three hundred metres away, the ledge ended abruptly. Beyond lay only the sucking, abject darkness of the Iron Sky. The effect was exactly as upsetting as Bella had feared: a disorientation calculated to put her at a disadvantage. No wonder Svetlana had declined her invitation to come to Crabtree.

Inside Eddytown, local agents escorted Bella, Shen and the haunt to a secure chamber where Svetlana was already waiting. The lavish room was panelled with deeply stained wangwood, enclosing lifelike holographic vistas from pre-Cutoff Mars. Save for the fact that the views represented locales from all over the planet, the room could easily have been a windowed belvedere situated high on a Martian promontory. The horizon lines and local lighting conditions had been carefully adjusted to assist the illusion of a seamless panorama. As Bella settled into her seat, dust devils lashed against the weather shields of some nameless surface colony, whose high turreted walls enclosed armoured minarets and mosques, glinting bronze and gold in the late afternoon of a Martian autumn.

Svetlana and Bella had both dressed formally, by their own standards: Bella in a black jacket over a plain black T-shirt and narrow black jeans, Svetlana in a high-collared navy-blue dress suit with black gloves. She had arrived with her own advisors and security: not a haunt, but a chrome BI that hung from the ceiling like an ugly light fitting, dangling a mass of bladed and beweaponed arms. The rumours that Svetlana had at least one working forge vat were obviously true. The table was set with glassware and a carafe of water.

'Thank you for agreeing to see me,' Bella said.

Svetlana opened her hands, then closed them again. 'I don't know quite what you're expecting to hear from me.'

'Reassurance,' Bella said, 'nothing more.'

'You've an odd sense of timing, in that case.' Svetlana tapped the flexy before her. Like Bella, she had a lingering attachment to the old ways. 'I just saw the news from the Judicial Apparatus. They've set the terms. Parry's going down for fifty years, following administrative rejuvenation.'

Bella fought to keep her reactions under control. The tribunal had not gone as well as she had hoped, but she had never expected that the punishment would be so severe. The sentence must have been announced while she was on the train. She glanced at Liz Shen, who returned her enquiring glance with a microscopic nod.

'I'm sorry,' Bella said. 'That's far longer than I was expecting. I did recommend clemency—'

'It's more than you used to get for murder.' Svetlana stroked a gloved finger across the flexy. 'They say sentencing policy's been reviewed in light of the increased lifespan we all enjoy. Now that we live longer, murder means more. But he didn't *murder* anyone, Bella.'

'I know. Again, I'm sorry.' She was flustered, disorientated. The news could not have come at a worse time. 'I'll put pressure on the Apparatus—'

'It'll do no good. They've made up their minds to make an example of him. The last of the great crimes.'

'We all know he meant well,' Bella said. 'Can't that be some consolation?'

'I don't know how you have the nerve to talk about consolation. He's my husband, Bella. They're taking him away from me for fifty years. We haven't even *been* here that long.'

'They'll review sentencing. They always do. Maybe not this year, but when the next set of appointments come through—'

'So they reduce it to forty years, thirty if he's lucky. Do you honestly imagine that will make it any better? At one point you told me his punishment might not even be custodial!'

'I couldn't be sure.'

'But you must have had a shrewd idea of how unlikely that was. You've enough contacts in the judiciary. I doubt you were entirely in the dark.'

Bella bit her lip and fought to speak calmly. 'Do not accuse me of anything improper, Svetlana. The Judicial Apparatus was your invention, not mine.'

'I thought I'd left it in safer hands.'

'You left it in excellent hands. It's a machine for dispensing justice, and that's exactly what it does.'

Svetlana raised her voice. The ceiling-hanging robot stirred its vicious arms in response. 'You call fifty years justice?'

'I call it fifty years. It's a long time – I don't deny that, but Parry won't be any older at the end of it than he is now. That's the point of administrative rejuvenation. If those years mean so much to you, you could always skip over them.' On a cruel impulse that she would later regret, Bella added, 'I'd gladly fast-track the paperwork, Svieta.'

'That would suit you very well, wouldn't it? Me out of your hair for half a century.'

'Now that you put it like that . . .' Next to her, the haunt flexed one of its paper-flat limbs. The ceiling robot crept forward. Bella shuddered to think what would happen if one of the security systems made an unanticipated move. The haunt would win, she thought, but not quickly enough to spare blood.

'I'm not going anywhere,' Svetlana said. 'Not while I suspect it might be of the slightest convenience to you.' She rubbed her gloved fingers together, then looked up sharply. 'Remind me: what was it you wanted to talk about?'

'Oh, I'm sure you know. Despite all that's happened between us, I'm still going to make a personal plea. I know you have certain . . . qualities, Svetlana. I've told you as much. I don't even particularly blame you for hating me now. If Parry were my husband, I probably wouldn't be any more inclined to forgiveness than you are.'

'Where is this going, Bella?'

'I'd still see sense. I'd still know a dangerous and foolhardy gesture when it came along. Doubtless you've seen the transmissions from the Musk Dog vehicle.'

'They're difficult to miss.'

'Yes, and they're seductive. A long time ago, McKinley warned me that the Musk Dogs would do everything in their power to undermine our faith in the Fountainheads. Now we've both seen the evidence. McKinley was right.'

'Perhaps, but does that necessarily mean the Musk Dogs aren't to be trusted?'

'McKinley told me how damaging they are.'

'But if what the Musk Dogs are telling us is true, wouldn't he go out of his way to discredit them?'

Bella shook her head. 'We have to trust someone here, Svieta. After thirty-five years, I've no reason not to place absolute faith in McKinley.'

'No reason at all, Bella?'

'No reason that matters.'

'Tell me, then: what is the function of the Structure? Who brought us here? Why are there other cultures here as well? What brought them here? What do the Fountainheads know that they aren't telling us?'

'There are answers to all those questions,' Bella said, 'and McKinley will reveal them in due course, when he judges that we're ready to hear them.'

'Perhaps the Musk Dogs were right, in that case, and the Fountainheads are just a bunch of parasites, feeding on lesser cultures. No wonder McKinley's so unwilling to open our minds.'

'They've given us wonderful gifts,' Bella said.

'The stream has been somewhat dry of late.'

'Look,' Bella said defensively, 'even if you don't trust McKinley, at least trust Jim Chisholm. You *do* trust him, don't you?'

Through the nearest window, a wall of dust roared down a canyon like a piston, swallowing a lacy suspension bridge thrown from wall to wall.

'I trusted Jim,' Svetlana said. 'I'm just not convinced we ever got all of him back.'

Chromis found Bella troubled, during her apparitions. Lately Bella had discovered that the dead politician was the only counsel whose advice she had no compelling reason to distrust.

Days and weeks had passed. The Musk Dogs had become cleverer, more inventive. Their messages continued to infiltrate ShipNet, but the tone had become more insidiously persuasive, the promises more concrete. In return for access to Janus, the Musk Dogs would gift humans with the door-opening passkey that they had acquired from the Whisperers. They would give humans the frameshift technology to which Chromis had already alluded.

'Fountainheads and now Musk Dogs,' Chromis mused. 'And Whisperers and the Uncontained, while we're at it. Doubtless there are many others.'

Bella had decided to tell Chromis everything she had gleaned concerning the other cultures in the Structure. 'Thirty-five, McKinley said, including us.'

They were in the civic aquarium after closing time, following a winding, balustraded route around huge looming tanks. When the larger fish – geneconstructed skates, rays and sharks – had outgrown the tanks in Bella's office, she had gladly dedicated this public amenity to the people of Crabtree. It was built into the old tokamak chamber, under the remains of *Rockhopper*. The fish cruised through the disused magnets and mirrors of the plasma-confinement system, now as rusty and coral-bound as the timbers and cannon of some ancient wreck.

'You arrived on Janus,' Chromis said, 'pulled here across space and time. It's not inconceivable that the other cultures were lured here in a similar fashion.'

'Aboard their own versions of Janus?' Bella asked.

Chromis paused to study the luminous text under one of the tanks as an iridescent blue eel oozed through a crack in one of the magnet housings. 'Why not? An icy moon, suddenly moving under its own motive power? That would be enough to attract the attention of most cultures, don't you think?'

'Why, though?'

Chromis moved on. 'I can think of several reasons, none of them especially reassuring. Let's consider the simplest, and therefore the one most likely to be correct. Imagine that the Spicans – we'll keep calling them that, for the sake of argument – were a very early galactic culture, one of the first to arise. I'm talking a very long time before humanity, obviously – more than just a few million years.'

'Someone had to be first, I suppose,' Bella said.

'If they weren't the first, they were certainly amongst the very earliest. And they'd have done just what we did – looked out into the night sky and wondered where everyone else was. The Congress of the Lindblad Ring – and the other polities surrounding us – sent probes into the galaxy, but they'd only reached ten or eleven thousand light-years by the time I was encoded. Within that ever-expanding boundary, all our searches had failed to identify any other extant intelligences. And when we looked deeper – trained our instruments on stars beyond the Hard Data Frontier – we saw no signs of living intelligence. As far as we were concerned, we were expanding into an empty, dead galaxy.'

'You think it was the same for the Spicans.'

'If there had been other cultures out there, they hadn't lasted long enough to survive into their era. The Spicans might have concluded that intelligence was both rare and unlikely to endure across cosmic timescales. Contact between intelligent cultures was therefore highly improbable. If it ever *did* happen – if by some chance two starfaring cultures happened to occupy the galaxy at the same time – they were unlikely to meet on equal terms. One of those cultures would have been around a lot longer than the other. There'd have been such a technological and intellectual disparity that dialogue – let alone something as banal as mutually beneficial trade – would have been unthinkable. What could a monkey offer you, Bella, that you don't already have? Or a shrew, for that matter? That's the kind of gap we're talking about.'

Bella nodded. They'd been over this line of reasoning so many times that it had the ingrained familiarity of a mantra. 'They couldn't experience anything resembling meaningful communication.'

'No – that would have been out of the question. But the Spicans wanted more than that. They wanted contact so badly that they were prepared to tamper with the rules.'

'Hence the Structure,' Bella said.

Chromis nodded her approval. 'Constructed at the end of time – or at the very least deep into time, long after their own era: a gathering point for samples of other intelligent cultures *yet to come*. The Spicans seeded the galaxy with lures – Janus-type devices – and waited. Apart from the envoys they must have sent into the distant future to assemble the Structure, the Spicans themselves vanished from the galaxy. Perhaps they became extinct, or perhaps they went somewhere else. Yet after they had vanished, other cultures inevitably developed. The intervals between the emergences of these cultures may have been many millions of years, Bella, but that is nothing compared to the age of the galaxy.'

'Eighteen thousand years makes me dizzy, Chromis. Much beyond that and my brain just can't cope.'

'I know how you feel. But if I'm right – and this *is* only speculation – the point of the Structure was to reduce those intervals of time to nothing, and to bring those cultures together at the same time, as if they had always co-existed. A zoo compresses space and brings together creatures that could never have coexisted in the same location. The Structure does the same for cultures, by compressing time.'

'Using the lures to bring them here,' Bella said.

'They were the key. Sooner or later, representatives of those cultures were guaranteed to stumble on their equivalents of Janus. With us, we'd barely left Earth. With other cultures, it may have been thousands or even hundreds of thousands of years before they found the lures.' Chromis offered Bella a sympathetic smile. 'With something like frameshift, hundreds of thousands of years is enough time to cross the entire galaxy. It's enough time to forge an empire of a hundred billion worlds, something so glorious that you cannot comprehend that it will not last for ever. But even a hundred thousand years is a sliver, a moment, compared to the kind of deep galactic time we're talking about here. In terms of contact between two cultures, it's barely of consequence.'

'The Fountainheads are a long way beyond us.'

'They'd obviously been starfaring a long time before they rode their lure to the Structure, if that's how they got here. It may even have been millions of years since they left their home world. But it wasn't so much through time that they became incomprehensibly advanced. Their psychology is evidently alien, but they still have material needs. You have something *they* can use. That's what matters.'

'And the Musk Dogs?'

'Another galactic culture snatched here from some different point in time.

The same goes for all the others. Those that emerged later may have some dim knowledge of their predecessors, just as the Fountainheads appear to have learned of us by our ruins.' Darkly, Chromis added, 'There may be entities in the Structure who know the Fountainheads by theirs.'

'Why do this, though?' Bella asked. 'If the Spicans are so interested in first contact . . . where are they?'

'Perhaps they're less interested in contact so much as the diligent study of how it proceeds. When the endcap doors are open, cultures are permitted to interact with each other. It can't always go well. But then, if there are already thirty-five alien races in this thing, there are a lot of permutations.'

'I thought they were zookeepers,' Bella said, 'but you make them sound more like game-players.'

'Perhaps that's what they are.'

'Then what happens if we want out of the game?'

Chromis pursed her lips tactfully. 'You may have less choice than you think. If the Structure is capable of holding the Fountainheads prisoner, not to mention the thirty-three *other* alien cultures, some of which are not even made of baryonic matter, then leaving may not be an entirely trivial exercise.'

'That shouldn't prevent us from trying,' Bella said.

'No, it shouldn't, but keep one thing in mind: you still no have idea how much better off you might be by staying inside this thing.'

'I made a promise to get my people home.'

'Some promises are best broken. Trust me on this: I'm a politician.'

Bella jumped at the sound of approaching footsteps. The haunt, which had been with her all the while, folded out of the shadows and then resumed its low-threat posture.

'Hello, Liz,' Bella said.

'Is Chromis still with you?'

Bella shook her head. She had disappeared the moment Liz Shen had arrived. 'Is something the matter?'

'Yes,' Shen said. 'Something's very much the matter. It's Svetlana. She's on her way to the Musk Dogs.'

# CHAPTER 35

Svetlana climbed towards the broken bone of the gristleship, the Skyside terminal gradually shrinking to a knot of light next to the larger citadel of the Fountainhead embassy. The construction domes and supply lines of the Tier-Two settlement project barely dented the great blackness of the Iron Sky's outer surface. Humans might spill out into that darkness, but it would be centuries before the population density approached that of the most crowded cities on Earth. And when that was done – when the Iron Sky itself had been wrapped from pole to pole in a hot, twinkling sprawl of human habitation, they could keep expanding outwards.

The HUD blinked: an incoming contact.

'Is that you, Svetlana?' asked the anchordoll, in her well-mannered, nearly accentless voice.

'It's me.'

'We're sending out a shuttle to bring you into the ship. Do nothing, and all will be well.'

Svetlana killed the suit's thrust and let it drift. She observed a small, cyst-like node detach itself from the gristleship, stretching fatty tendrils until they snapped. The node approached her with deceptive acceleration. Like the mother ship, it consisted of sinewy strands bound around a handful of hard, foreign-looking mechanisms. A pair of fleshy doors opened like a ribcage that had been cracked and spread for heart surgery. The suit coasted into the soft red interior and came to rest. The ribbed doors closed, locking Svetlana inside. Through the faceplate she made out a vague pink-red glow, and a suggestion of throbbing surfaces. The status read-outs on the HUD remained placid. The Chakri five had detected nothing that caused it concern.

The journey to the gristleship must only have taken a few seconds. Svetlana felt no acceleration or deceleration before the doors cleaved open, revealing a much larger enclosure bathed in the same pink-red glow. It was a cavernous space with no obvious distinction between floor, ceiling or walls. The decor, such as it was, consisted of a complex layered accretion of waxy blobs and hardened, stringy residues. Here and there were smears and daubs of distinct colour – yellows, browns and nasty mucosal greens. Blank spheres set into wrinkled, eyelike whorls provided the illumination.

For the first time since leaving Eddytown, she had weight again. She stepped out of the shuttle onto a scalloped, sloping path that ambled down to the lowest part of the chamber. The gravity felt close to a standard gee, though inside the suit it was difficult to tell. She panned around, taking in the whole grotto. She felt an obligation to observe, knowing that the suit would be storing the data for future playback.

Another pair of rib-like doors swung open in the far wall. The sudden movement startled her, but she kept her cool. Then a Musk Dog came through the wall.

She got it badly wrong at first. She thought there were several of them, not just one individual. The alien looked like two or three scabby street dogs fighting over a scrap of meat: an unruly mass of mismatched limbs, fur the colour of sun-baked mud, too many tightly packed eyes above a toothsome black muzzle. It was difficult to make out its basic body shape, for the thing kept scratching and scrabbling and pissing, arcs of steaming urine jetting from too many places as it made its scratching, scrabbling, sniffling way through the chamber. It only came as high as her waist.

When it spoke, Svetlana heard a rapid, strangulated retching and gargling. Overlaid on that, produced by some mechanism she couldn't see, was the cool, synthetic voice of the CNN anchordoll.

'Svetlana Barseghian, welcome aboard the gristleship. We trust your stay here will be pleasant. Feel free to leave at any time, but we hope you will stay awhile.'

'Thank you,' she said, the suit transmitting her voice to the outside world.

'It is safe to breathe our atmosphere. There are no toxins, viruses or micro-organisms that might cause you harm or discomfort.'

She glanced at the HUD read-out. It confirmed that the external atmosphere was safe to breathe, while warning her that its readings might be in error and that she should therefore proceed with due caution.

'I'm okay in here, thanks.'

The Musk Dog snuffled around her suit. It brushed against her, lingering with its hindquarters. 'Please consider breathing our air. It would please us very much.'

She shook her head, hoping that the creature recognised the gesture. Their use of the anchordoll suggested that they already had a thorough grasp of human body language. 'If it's okay with you, I'll keep the suit on for the moment. It's not that I don't trust you – just that I feel safer inside.'

The Musk Dog paused in its inspection of her. 'That's fine. We understand. Perhaps next time, when you have grown more accustomed to our ship?'

'Perhaps,' Svetlana allowed.

'I must introduce myself. I am The One That Greets.'

'Hello, One That Greets. Thank you for having me aboard.'

The Musk Dog paused to squirt urine against part of the chamber. Where the urine impacted, Svetlana noticed, the chamber walls gained a temporary, fading discoloration.

'It is our pleasure. Now, will you please follow me? I am tasked to take you to The One That Negotiates.'

'Lead on,' Svetlana said.

She followed the flailing mass of red-brown limbs, pausing every now and again as the creature halted and urinated against the wall. The Musk Dog brought her to a sweaty chamber deep within the gristleship. The walls were covered with the same fused secretions, years upon years' worth of them, layered in a crusted impasto that she guessed was metres thick. On some level, Svetlana judged, the ship was the product of those secretions and daubings.

'I will leave you with this one,' the Musk Dog said, retreating the way they had come.

The other Musk Dog was crouched down in front of a kind of display wall: a mosaic of randomly shaped facets pressed into a claylike matrix at odd, arbitrary angles. Each of the facets was displaying a different ShipNet channel. The creature's attention hopped from screen to screen with manic inattention. Svetlana heard a babble of human voices, and over that a synthetic rendition of the Musk Dog language.

The second Musk Dog waited until The One That Greets had left before acknowledging Svetlana's presence. It turned from the display wall, raised its muzzle and examined her, sniffing vigorously.

'The other one touched you,' it said, walking around her. Limbs thrashed and tangled against each other, as if there was something fundamentally wrong with the alien's motor coordination.

'It brushed against my suit,' Svetlana said.

The creature cocked its head, as if weighing the significance of what she had just told it. After a moment it said, 'I am The One That Negotiates. I am most gratified that you have come aboard the gristleship. There is much that we can offer in trade. With the Whisperer passkey, you will have access to closed regions of the Structure. With femtomachinery and frameshift technology, you will enjoy a negotiating advantage over several less advanced cultures. Now that the Uncontained are loose again, such things may make the difference between extinction and survival. You should not rely on the Shaft-Five Nexus for protection against the Uncontained. The Stiltwalkers did, and look what happened to *them*. Yet these are only the first of many things that we will offer you. There will be much more to follow, if negotiations proceed harmoniously.'

Very little of what the alien had just told her meant anything to Svetlana, not being privileged to the information Bella had gleaned from McKinley.

'What do you want from us?' she asked.

'The same commodity as the Fountainheads: we seek access to the deep mechanisms of your world.'

'You want to draw power from Janus.'

'The very thing,' the Musk Dog said, after a moment's consideration.

'What would you need from me for that to happen?'

'Simply your permission, as a delegated negotiator for your culture.' Again, the Musk Dog cocked its head. 'The method of your approach was eccentric. Was there some technical problem that required you to drill your way out of the transparent structure?'

'Yes,' Svetlana said. In order to reach open space, she'd had to use a suit-mounted cutting torch to drill her way through the elevator shaft blocking the skyhole, ascend the shaft until she was on the far side of the Iron Sky and then cut her way out again. The shaft would repair itself easily enough, but news of the damage – and the fact that she had attempted to visit the Musk Dogs – would be sure to have reached Bella by now.

'Very well,' the Musk Dog said shrewdly. 'No further questions are required, then?'

'None at all.'

'That's good. It's always most satisfying to us when we can be sure that we are dealing with a delegated negotiator rather than an adventurous free agent. You can imagine the great vexation that has caused us in the past.'

'You need have no fears in that respect,' Svetlana said.

The Musk Dog knew she was lying, Svetlana was certain. It knew she was lying and it didn't care.

'Then we may begin. As a token of our goodwill, you will already find forge-vat construction files uploaded into your suit memory. These concern technologies postdating the emergence of the Transgressive Intelligences. You will find tools, weapons and protective devices, together with protocols for more efficient forge-vat designs. All these gifts must be used with due scrupulousness.'

'I understand.'

'We trust that these gifts will enable you to consolidate your position as designated negotiator, Svetlana Barseghian.'

'I'll do my best.' Svetlana called up a HUD read-out. The suit's memory inventory contained many new files, in the format used for forge-vat blueprints. Even after the technological convulsions of the last thirty-five years, the Musk Dog's names for the gifts conveyed a shuddering implication of profound futurity. 'How did you do that?' she asked.

The Musk Dog glanced at the wall of screens. 'We have already subjected your data protocols to exhaustive study. Your suit is less secure than you imagine.' It looked back at her, opening its muzzle in a drooling smile. 'But don't be alarmed. We would never seek to disadvantage a valued trading partner.'

Svetlana glanced at the wall screens: business as usual in Crabtree, judging by the ShipNet content. Bella had yet to make an alarmist statement denouncing Svetlana's actions. 'So how do we proceed from here?'

'We discuss terms of access. We will begin with a single energy tap. It will have no detrimental effect on your own energy-gathering activities. In return for this, we will offer you the blueprint files to build a Whisperer passkey.'

'And that will get us through the endcap door?'

'It will function on four occasions, and then it will cease to operate. You would need to negotiate with us again if you wished to open more doors. We would then sell you another limited-use passkey.'

'I'm not quite sure how this will work,' she said.

'What, exactly?' the Musk Dog asked.

'There's only one route into our world – through the skyhole at the Fountainhead embassy.'

'So we noticed. The Fountainheads placed energy taps inside Janus, didn't they?'

She answered with the automatic authority of a leader. 'Yes.'

'Are there physical power linkages between the interior and the embassy?'

'No,' she said, masking her hesitation.

'Our technology requires linkages. They will need to be routed back to the gristleship through skyholes.'

'Can you drill skyholes?'

'Very easily, with your permission. We'll begin with a single skyhole, a single discreet tap. We can cut the skyhole immediately.' The Musk Dog studied her with a peculiar attentiveness. 'That will make your return journey less problematic, we hope.'

'That sounds reasonable.'

'Does that mean we have your permission?'

'I suppose so.'

'Then the passkey blueprint will shortly appear in your suit memory.'

'Can we make it in one of our vats?'

'Yes, but with caution. The passkey must be assembled using femtotech machinery, but that machinery need only constitute a temporary kernel, quickened within a shell of normal nanomachinery. When the passkey is complete, the femtotech layer will self-disassemble.'

'It sounds complex.'

'The blueprint will take care of the details. Later, we can negotiate for the transfer of a permanent femtotech kernel, which will enable you to make a frameshift engine.'

'Let's just start with one hole, one tap.'

The Musk Dog nodded. 'There is one other matter we must resolve before this arrangement can be said to be satisfactorily settled. It is a small thing, and will cost you nothing. When the matter is concluded, the passkey file will be transferred.'

Something in its tone alerted her. 'What?'

'It concerns the other Musk Dog, The One That Greets.'

'Yes,' she said uneasily.

'It will arrive here shortly, intending to escort you back to the arrival chamber. That is its duty: to escort visitors on and off the ship. That is why it is called The One That Greets.'

'I understand that, but—'

'When it arrives, you must refuse to accompany it. The One That Greets will be offended and alarmed, and will plead with you, but you must hold firm. You must inform it that you found it offensive, and that you do not wish to spend any further time in its company.'

'I didn't have any problem with it.'

'Nonetheless, you must lie, otherwise these negotiations cannot reach a settlement.'

'I don't get it. Why do I have to lie to it?'

'I did not expect you to understand.' The Musk Dog emitted an audible yawn, very much like a human sigh. 'We are a factional species. The operation of the gristleship is divided amongst many groupings . . . packs of Musk Dogs. At any one time, one or more of these packs may attempt to assert dominance over another.'

'I see.'

'Currently, there is a factional dispute between the department of the ship under my responsibility – the handling of affairs of trade – and the department of the ship served by The One That Greets. It is necessary that I assert my authority. If the other one is not shamed, my own position will become untenable. If that were to happen, so would yours. We would have no option but to discontinue negotiations.'

'It still didn't do anything wrong.'

'When the first one brushed against you,' the Musk Dog said, 'it was attempting to assert ownership over you. It left a chemical tracer on your spacesuit, specific to The One That Greets. It was claiming you as its own. I cannot tolerate this.'

'It claimed ownership of me?'

'We have never pretended to be anything other than a highly territorial species.'

The suit conveyed a scrabbling, scuffing sound to her ears. The first Musk Dog had returned, almost tumbling over itself in the hectic flail of its multiple sets of limbs. Seen together, there was no way she could distinguish between the two aliens.

'If negotiations are concluded, I am ready to take you back to the travel pod,' The One That Greets informed her.

'Negotiations have proceeded very well,' The One That Negotiates said, unctuously. 'Very, very well indeed. Haven't they, Svetlana Barseghian?'

When it was done, when she had locked the helmet back into place and purged her lungs of the fetid, vile-smelling air of the gristleship (although it was, as the Musk Dog had promised, quite breathable) she said, 'What will happen to the other one now?'

'The other one?'

It was scent-marking her spacesuit now, overwriting the earlier traces left by the first Musk Dog. It smeared weeping glands against the suit, leaving rapidly hardening secretions. It cocked legs and urinated. It moved around the suit, pausing here and there, watering her with the fastidious care of an elderly gardener.

'The one you just asked me to humiliate,' she said.

'Oh, *that* one. It will return to its faction. They will learn that it did not earn your approval, that you spurned it, that you have entered into negotiations with my pack.'

'And then?'

'They will reprimand it.'

She had to know. 'And what form will that reprimand take?'

'It will be dismembered,' the Musk Dog said, disinterestedly. 'Dismembered and then eaten.'

# CHAPTER 36

Bella was making plans to pay an unscheduled visit to the Fountainheads when she learned that Jim Chisholm was already on his way down. She caught the maglev and met him in Underhole, in a secure part of the plaza. The area had been cordoned off by an impromptu wall of flickering haunts, joined hand in hand like a chain of paper men.

Beyond the cordon, the usual thin straggle of passers-by watched the proceedings uneasily, unpleasantly aware of how dire things must have been to merit a visit from Chisholm. Bella could feel it, too: her old friend no longer belonged amongst his own people. Of all of them, of all the dead who had been revivified, he was the only one who had never really returned from the grave. Svetlana had been right all along, she thought peevishly. They got back *someone*, but it was not the man they had known on *Rockhopper*. It wasn't just the fact that some parts of his mind had been filled in using structures salvaged from Craig Schrope, although those instances when the Schrope patterns broke through were unsettling enough. There was also an alien aura around him, like a haze of static electricity. She did not fear him for a moment, or doubt that he meant well. There was still goodness in him. But it was the shrewd and analytic goodness of the paternally wise, which could sometimes feel very much like coldness.

His eyes were serious behind the old half-moon glasses he still wore. 'It's bad, Bella.'

'Your news or mine?'

'Both, I suspect. The Musk Dogs are playing true to form. Sooner or later they were bound to tempt one of you into making contact. Short of imposing martial law, there's not a lot you could have done about that. McKinley's very agitated, as you can imagine. I just hope the situation isn't irremediable.'

'McKinley said there was no safe level of exposure to Musk Dogs.'

'McKinley was right, but if you act now, you may be able to salvage something.'

'I don't know how much damage she's already done.'

'You'll find out sooner or later.' Chisholm removed his half-moon glasses and wiped them on the beige sleeve of his gown. 'You've played things very well up until now: not issuing a public statement was exactly the right thing to do. Let the Musk Dogs think this is all officially sanctioned.'

'What next?' she asked.

'Reason with Svetlana, if you can. Persuade her to back out of further negotiations. If the Musk Dogs get the message that there's nothing more to be gained here, they may cut their losses and leave.'

'I'll do what I can. Maybe I should send Ryan – she's more likely to listen to him than me.'

'That sounds wise. I'd offer to talk to her myself, but if she's bought the Musk Dog line, my protestations won't count for much.' He tucked the glasses back onto his nose. 'Besides, there's another matter currently pressing on my attention.'

'Your bad news,' Bella said.

'The Musk Dogs have allowed the Uncontained to penetrate an adjoining volume. Doors are open clear through to five light-minutes. They're on their way.'

'This can't get much worse, can it?'

'It's about to. The exiled Whisperer returned to the embassy. It's even more certain that there's been some kind of deal between the Musk Dogs and the Uncontained. There may have been nothing accidental about their leaving those doors open.'

'And they still have no idea what that deal's about?'

Chisholm was grim-faced. 'The Whisperer had obtained some new intelligence – it's beginning to look as if the deal might have something to do with access to Janus.'

'Tell me what you know.'

'Janus was a machine designed to bring us here and keep us alive during the journey. It contained enough energy to move itself across interstellar space at relativistic speed, with a little bit set aside for emergencies. Now that we've arrived in the Structure, its job is done. We may not have noticed it, but the energy reserves in Janus are finite and dwindling.'

'It's dying,' Bella surmised.

'Running down. We could keep tapping power for decades, but sooner or later there won't be anything left. That's what happens to all the moons that arrive in the Structure, in the end: they run dry like old batteries. But in Structure terms, we've only just arrived. Our moon still has a pretty hefty charge inside it.'

'Enough to do what?'

'If the Whisperer's intelligence is good, the Musk Dogs may be trying to tap all that remaining energy in one hit.'

'I don't get it. Why—'

'To blow a hole in the Structure,' Chisholm said quietly. 'To blast a way out to the external universe.'

Bella shivered at the implications. 'Can it really be done?'

'It's *been* done, according to Structure lore, but only once. And nothing was ever heard from the culture that escaped.'

'At least they tried. At least they didn't accept being penned up in this thing for the rest of time.'

'It may not be that simple. None of the cultures has any firm data on conditions beyond the Structure. Until you get out there, you won't know what you're going to find. A cage can also be form of protection.'

'Those who want to stay would always have that option,' Bella said.

'Remember what I said: nothing was ever heard from the escapees again.'

'I don't get it. If someone already blew a hole in the wall, why can't the Musk Dogs use that one?'

'The walls heal,' Chisholm said. 'After a week or two, they're as good as new.'

Conflicting emotions wracked Bella. She liked the idea of finding a way out of the Structure, even if it cost them Janus, but not the fact that she had no control over whether or not this happened. 'What would it take for the Musk Dogs to achieve this?'

'They'd have to reach deep into Janus, access the right machine layers. The Musk Dogs aren't clever enough to figure out what to do on their own, but they'll have had help from the Uncontained.'

'How long do we have?'

'No guessing. Could be hours, days, or even longer.'

'And then Janus goes nova.'

'Something like that. Needless to say, the Musk Dogs won't want to be inside this chamber when that happens. They'll use their passkey to seal themselves into the next chamber.'

'We, on the other hand, will die.'

'If we're still here when it happens, I wouldn't put much on our chances.'

'Okay, I've heard enough. We need to stop this before it starts.'

'Not quite as easy as it sounds,' Chisolm said.

'Why not? The Fountainheads can take out the Musk Dogs, can't they?'

'They could, but they'll need something more solid than the Whisperer evidence before they move, or they'll risk censure from the rest of the Shaft-Five Nexus. Whisperers haven't been the most trustworthy of cultures in the past, and there's always the possibility that this might be a ploy to provoke action against the Musk Dogs.'

'But you said the Musk Dogs had bought passkeys from the Whisperers.'

'It's all only intelligence, Bella. There isn't a single piece of information that isn't questionable on some level.'

'So you're just going to sit tight and let us die?'

'I didn't say that. I said we'd need something more solid than what we have so far. Don't assume that McKinley and the others don't care – they're already doing everything they can to protect you from the Uncontained.'

'I'm scared,' Bella said.

'So am I. More scared than I've been in a long, long time.' He touched her hand, tenderly. 'I need to be with the Fountainheads now. They've become very good friends and I can't let them stare into that abyss alone. When the Uncontained come, I want to be with them. Whatever happens.'

'What should I do about the Musk Dogs? Can't you give me something?'

'I wish I could, but I've seen our history – I know what would happen.'

'I understand,' she said resignedly. 'I know what happened after the Cut-off, Jim. I know what that knowledge almost did to us.' For the first time in years, she knew she had the advantage of him. She felt cruel and delighted and sad at the same time.

'You can't possibly know,' he said.

'I do. Someone told me.'

'Who.'

'A friend called Chromis Pasqueflower Bowerbird.'

He closed his eyes. She sensed the racking of ancient, inhumanly vast memories. 'The politician? The Congress of the Lindblad Ring?'

'She found me. I know everything, Jim.'

He looked at her, amazed and rueful. 'I had my suspicions when you said that you knew this wasn't the Spica Structure – how could you know that unless someone else had told you how far we'd come?'

'I think I trust her to help, if things turn bad.'

'She was considered wise, in her time. But you don't know Chromis, Bella. You know a thin shadow of her, like a death mask. It may *mean* well, but—'

'She may be all we have.'

Bella stood before the memorial cube, in its armoured laboratory under Crabtree. It felt as if many months had passed since she first touched it. After Chromis had entered her head, she'd had no further cause to visit the lab. She had ordered a halt to all studies into the cube, dispersing the scientific team onto other projects. The analysis instruments had been cleared away; the cube was no longer rotating on the inspection platform. There was no allure to it now, no sense that it sought her touch. It looked no more alive, no more purposeful, than a cut and polished mother lode of coal.

'I always wondered,' Bella said, as she stood with Chromis and Axford before the embossed face with its da Vinci motif, 'what would have happened had I been dead. If the cube was programmed only to react to my DNA, and no one else's—'

'Oh, that was no great matter,' Chromis said dismissively. 'Frankly, we thought the chances of *you* finding the cube were effectively zero. We always assumed it would be one of your distant descendants who made the lucky find.'

'But who's to say my DNA would have been passed on? What good would the cube be to them if they didn't have the means to open it?'

'We didn't think it would prove an obstacle for them. We assumed they'd keep your blood – or at least the relevant DNA sequence – as a kind of heirloom. It wouldn't have cost them much to preserve a fragment of you, in case it was ever needed again.'

'Would that have fooled the cube?'

'It wouldn't be a question of fooling it,' Chromis said, 'simply of letting the cube decide whether or not it had arrived in safe hands. If it detected something that corresponded to your DNA, that would be deemed good enough.'

Bella pondered the matter. 'What if they hadn't kept my DNA?'

Axford looked on, amused and intrigued by the one-sided exchange.

'They'd still have been your descendants. With the right methods, they could have worked their way back to your sequence.'

'I still haven't had children.'

'There's time,' Chromis said. 'But even if you don't, your people care for you, Bella. They'd keep something of you, trust me. Look at us! We managed to find a sample, after all.'

'I've been wondering about that—'

'It was tricky,' Chromis admitted. 'Your DNA sequence would have been stored in many places at the time of your departure: medical databases, insurance databases, and so on – but by the time the Congress of the Lindblad Ring agreed upon the memorial project, those sources were long gone. So we had to be more . . . inventive.'

'How, exactly?'

'We excavated the Sinai Planum on Mars. Where your husband died.'

'Garrison?' she asked, astonished. 'But they never found the wreckage.'

Chromis could not help but look slightly pleased with herself. 'We did. It was buried deeper than anyone looked, that's all, and spread out over a rather larger area than they anticipated. When we found Garrison's remains, they'd been under Martian soil for two complete cycles of attempted terraforming. But there was still enough to work with.'

'But I'm not Garrison,' she said.

'No, but you *did* give him a lock of your hair. It was still there, Bella. He'd carried it in his suit. It was in his hand, safe inside the glove. It survived across all those years, all that history, waiting for us.'

'My God.'

'He'd taken good care of that lock of hair, Bella. He must have loved you very much.'

*

Later, she watched the Fountainhead embassy break apart into a hundred glassy shards. It called to mind the sudden, explosive scattering of a school of brilliant fish at the first glimpse of a predator. The shards rearranged themselves into loose, shimmering associations and raced away from the Iron Sky in the direction of the endcap. In less than an hour they would reach the door leading into the adjacent chamber, ready to make a stand against the Uncontained.

Bella thought about Jim Chisholm, or whatever he had become, and imagined him journeying towards that point of engagement, out of a sense of honour and obligation to his alien friends. It was brave, and it moved her. But at the same time she wondered how far from humanity he had come that he could feel such compassion – maybe even love – for the Fountainheads. Bella was grateful for the gifts they had bestowed upon her people, and reassured to a point by the knowledge that they were a known and trustworthy quantity, but her feelings were an ocean away from compassion. She felt too small, too fragile, too finite ever to imagine *loving* the Fountainheads.

It awed her to think that Jim Chisholm had closed some of that distance. It also took him further away from her, into a territory of the heart for which she had no maps, no compass, no desire to venture. She wished all of them well, but she could not say for sure how sad she would be if Chisholm did not come home. She knew that she had already said goodbye to him, and that the farewell had happened a long time ago.

Instead of sadness, she felt something utterly strange: an emotion lost to her for so long that it tasted exotic, like an unfamiliar spice. But it was not completely unknown. It was something she had known once, long ago.

It was peace of mind, and it had nothing to do with Jim or the aliens.

Across all those years, all those decades, she could finally think about Garrison without feeling a hitch in her thoughts. The knife in her stomach was gone. They had argued over the Earth–Mars link before he left on his final mission, but she knew now that he had forgiven her. Even as he went down, with his ship frying around him in the fires of re-entry, he must have had time to think about her, about how she would feel when she heard of his death, and he had clasped that lock of hair in his hand as a sign that it was all right, that the argument was forgotten, that he still loved her. He could not send her a voice message, but he had sent her something tangible, hoping that it would be found. And for eighteen thousand years it had lain under Martian soil, as the rains came and went, as seas and forests swept across the plains and then retreated, as the skies turned to a cloud-flecked blue and then back to a wind-torn, cloudless Martian ochre, as that cycle repeated, as empires rose and fell and humanity pushed out into the stars and became something strange and wonderful, of which Chromis was a part. And then the message that Chromis herself carried – this single redeeming fact – had itself crossed an incomprehensibly vaster span of time and space, a gulf against which eighteen thousand years was no more than a moment.

It had found Bella. The message had been delivered, the loop closed. The ironic thing was that for all the future wisdom Chromis carried with her, it was this single instance of human contact that mattered most to Bella. She felt as if she had been stalled all this time, blocked from moving on. All those relationships that had never worked out, all those men she had never allowed close to her because she felt the twisting of that knife.

The lock of hair said it was okay. She didn't have to forget Garrison, but at least she could let go, and know that when they'd really parted – when the universe had taken him from her – they'd still been friends.

The calm she experienced was like the easing of seismic stress after an earthquake. It was delicious, and she would have liked nothing more than to take the time to enjoy it, to feel the possibilities opening before her. But the easing came just as her world was about to unravel. She would be doing very well if she was still alive by the end of the day.

That was the universe: you could beat it once, you could float a message in a bottle across half of eternity, but the universe would always find a way to have the last laugh.

Chisholm called her on the embassy channel. 'We'll be at the endcap in thirty minutes, Bella. Nexus sensors place the Uncontained in the next-but-one chamber. They're moving quickly, and it looks as if they're tooled up for a fight.'

'Will you win?'

'We'll give them a bloody nose they won't forget in a hurry. But if we don't make it, if the other Nexus elements don't get here in time . . .' Chisholm trailed off, but somehow found the strength to continue. 'I can't promise you much. We've left a small emplacement behind on the Iron Sky.'

'I know.' Bella had seen it.

'There's room in it for five hundred people. If you can get them inside, we can at least move them to safety.'

She started thinking about what it would take to empty Crabtree and every other settlement on Janus. 'You mean into the chamber that's soon going to be crawling with Uncontained? Since when does *that* count as safe, Jim?'

'If Janus goes up, you'll still be better off in a battle zone than inside the present chamber. At least the Shaft-Five Nexus will be able to shelter you.'

'If they show.'

'They will: the Nexus take their responsibilities very seriously. As soon as the engagement starts turning our way – as soon as it becomes clear that the Nexus has the upper hand – I'll return to Janus and do what I can to help.' He narrowed his eyes at her. 'Are you all right, Bella?'

She nearly laughed. 'The world's going to hell in a handcart. Why shouldn't I be all right?'

'It's just that you look different.'

'In a bad way?'

'No,' he said. 'Not in a bad way at all. You look like something good just happened to you.'

'It did,' Bella said. 'Something beautiful. Now let's hope some of my good luck rubs off on the rest of us, shall we?'

The new skyhole was perfectly circular, drilled to the same dimensions as its counterpart over Underhole. A chunk of Musk Dog machinery – a lander-sized thing like an offcut of meat wrapped around a carburettor – followed Svetlana all the way in, trailing a whipping, wire-thin tendril that reached all the way back to the gristleship. It was still with her as she neared Junction Box, at which point it swerved aside and vanished through a hitherto undiscovered aperture in the Spican machinery, something that all the patient years of human scrutiny had failed to illuminate.

In Eddytown, Svetlana expected to find that all hell had broken loose, but a review of the ShipNet feeds showed nothing out of the ordinary. She unsuited and asked Denise Nadis to supervise the transfer of the production files into her secret forge vat. Within an hour, something miraculous and strange was assuming existence within its red belly.

The maglev arrived from Crabtree. Svetlana half-expected Bella to step out of the train, but the figure that emerged was the boylike form of Ryan Axford, alone save for a protective haunt. Svetlana had him brought to the negotiating room, with its panorama of Martian landscapes.

'You can leave the haunt outside,' Svetlana said. 'I won't hurt you – we've always seen eye to eye.'

'What happened to you?' Axford asked.

Svetlana rubbed a latex-gloved finger against the mark of ownership the Musk Dog had secreted across her forehead. It felt ridged and leathery, like scar tissue or a hardening scab. Beneath it her skin itched terribly. She wanted to rip the chemical marker away, rid herself of any lingering trace of alien contamination.

'Nothing much,' she said.

'Does it hurt?'

'It itches, that's all. The Musk Dog assured me no harm would come of it. Can you smell it?'

'No,' Axford said.

Svetlana smiled equivocally. 'Some people can, I think. It must depend on something very subtle in the human olfactory system. To the Musk Dogs the smell's like a neon sign. It tells them all they need to know.'

'Can it be removed?'

'I could tear it away now, if I wished. There'd be some damage to the underlying tissue, but nothing that wouldn't heal in time.'

Axford couldn't take his eyes off it. 'Then why don't you?'

'Because if I did, that would be the end of my dealings with The One That Negotiates.'

'One of the Musk Dogs?' Axford guessed.

'It owns me now, while we trade. If I return to the ship without this mark of ownership – or if the Musk Dogs obtain evidence that I've had the mark surgically removed – that would be very damaging for the pack status of my Musk Dog.'

'What would happen?'

Svetlana smiled slightly. 'He'd be reprimanded. I wouldn't want that.'

'You shouldn't have done it.'

'I took an initiative. From where I'm standing, it looks as if I did the right thing. They've given me more in one day than we've got from the Fountainheads in the last ten years.'

'Maybe there's a reason for that. Maybe the Fountainheads don't care to see us wipe ourselves out with technologies we barely understand. Maybe they have a sense of responsibility.'

'That would be Bella's line, of course.'

'That doesn't necessarily make it wrong.'

'There's another, equally valid view,' Svetlana said. 'The Fountainheads have nothing else to offer: certainly nothing that we can use. Yet they still need Janus. So they keep us here, denying us access to the rest of the Structure.'

'They've warned us of the dangers lying beyond the endcap. That isn't quite the same thing.'

'Have they given us a passkey?'

'You don't give razor blades to a baby.'

'Then it's time we stopped acting like babies. That's why I went up there today, Ryan. It wasn't to spite Bella, or to punish her for what she did to Parry. It was to move us forward. To do *something*.'

'Well, you certainly did that.'

The woman and the boylike man studied each other as curtains of dust flung themselves across the arid, salmon-red landscape of Mars. A golden dirigible, emblazoned with a crescent and star, made a perilous docking with one of the high minarets of the walled city.

Svetlana said, 'I was expecting more of a reaction from Bella.'

'Such as?'

'I don't know. A police action against Eddytown, perhaps. Arrest and detention of known Barseghian loyalists.'

Axford looked disappointed. 'Bella's shrewder than that. I thought you'd have realised that by now.'

'She sent you for a reason, I suppose.'

Axford studied her coldly. 'A long time ago, Bella was warned about the Musk Dogs. The Fountainheads told her to expect their arrival one day. They also told her that the Musk Dogs would exploit the slightest visible rift in our society. That's why Bella worked so hard, and for so long, not to alienate you. She did everything in her power to bring you back into the fold, Svetlana. There was no exile for you. She even had you invited to Takahashi's party.'

'All that just in case the Musk Dogs showed up?'

'Basic human decency had something to do with it, as well.'

Svetlana scoffed. 'There was nothing decent about what she did to Parry.'

'You'd love to think that was purely personal, wouldn't you?'

'Wasn't it?'

'I think Bella came very close to letting Parry go. I'm certain that would have been her preferred option. She likes and admires Parry.' Axford's attention continued to drift to the mark on her forehead. He had, Svetlana thought, a child's inability not to stare. 'The whole episode hurt her more than you'll ever know, Svetlana.'

'Lecture over, Ryan? Or was *that* the reason you came?'

'I mentioned the need for visible unity,' Axford said, unriled. 'Bella still feels it's important not to show the least sign of discord to the Musk Dogs. That's why she's made no announcement denouncing your action, or the imposition of a police state, or mass arrests.'

'I don't follow.'

He appraised her. 'Bella has a proposal. She will disregard what you have done. She will pursue the matter no further, and make no effort to clamp down on your sympathisers. You will not be punished, and you may continue your activities such as they were before this day. On, needless to say, one condition.'

'Let's hear it.'

'You report back to the Musk Dogs – by radio or in person, Bella doesn't care. Presumably you told them you were entitled to negotiate on behalf of the entire colony?'

Svetlana shrugged off the question.

'You maintain whatever lie you told them,' Axford continued. 'The Musk Dogs will go on thinking we sent you. And you will tell them that you wish to curtail all dealings with them. Whatever deals you've made – whatever you've given them, or received from them – all that becomes void. If that means giving things back to the Musk Dogs, we'll pay that price. Just as long as they leave us alone.'

'It's too late,' Svetlana said. 'They've already cut through the Sky. Or didn't you notice?'

'We noticed. We noticed the thing that followed you in, as well. The Fountainheads are taking a great interest in it. According to Bella it may not be the simple energy tap the Musk Dogs told you it was.'

'And Bella would know, would she?'

'The Fountainheads have intelligence. The intelligence says that the Musk Dogs may be trying to destroy Janus.'

'As if that made any sense.'

'It'd make a lot of sense if you were interested in blowing a way out of here.'

She laughed at him. 'Very good, Ryan. Handy how this intelligence arrives now, just when Bella needs something on me.'

'So you don't believe it.'

'Bella's entitled to believe what she likes. I know a spoiling action when I see one.'

'I don't think the Fountainheads would lie about this.'

Svetlana felt a sudden, overwhelming need to connect with him, make him see her side of the argument. 'Ryan – listen to me. I was up there. I've seen what the Musk Dogs are like. They're unpleasant.' She fingered the scent mark. 'I didn't *like* them, in case you were wondering, but I sensed that all they cared about was business.'

'Business can kill if you're on the wrong end of it. I thought we learned that lesson on *Rockhopper*.'

'This was a price worth paying. They're going to give us real power here. We'll be players, finally. I want to get out there, Ryan. I want to see what the rest of the Structure looks like. I want to meet the Spicans and ask them some hard questions.'

He looked at her with bruising unfamiliarity, as if they had never known each other. 'I'm glad you gave the matter that much thought, at least.'

She stood up sharply. 'We're done here. My answer – pretty obviously – is no. All that remains is to find out what Bella plans to do about it.'

Axford stood up as well – he had to lower himself down from one of the high chairs around the conference table. Despite his stature, Svetlana still found that he had the physical presence of an adult man, combined with a gaze that penetrated through to her hidden frailties, laying them open for slow, measured, clinical inspection.

'It's not too late,' he said.

'For what?'

'To step back from the brink. Bella's forgiving. She always has been.'

'Give her my regards,' Svetlana said.

They talked, via ShipNet. Svetlana stared at Bella with a defiance that cut across fifty years, back to the darkest hours aboard *Rockhopper*.

'Let's keep this brief,' Svetlana said.

'I thought you'd listen to Ryan,' Bella said. 'We both owe him so much, after all this time. He's been kind to both of us.'

'This wasn't about me and Ryan. And I did listen.'

'Ryan told you what the Musk Dogs really want with Janus.'

'He told me a story – and he believed it, I'm sure. *You* may even believe it. That doesn't make it any more convincing.'

'The thing they sent back with you is going to destroy Janus.'

'So you say.'

'Jim Chisholm believes it, too.'

'Chisholm's part of the problem. Who knows how much of Terrier-boy they put into his head?'

'I heard you patched things up with Schrope before you sent him into the Fountainhead ship.'

Svetlana shook her head. 'He volunteered for that mission. It was one good deed after a lifetime of being a creep.'

'Think whatever you want about Jim, but I know he isn't lying. I'm so sure of it that I'm already putting together an evacuation plan.'

That news, for a moment, broke through Svetlana's glaze of indifference. 'You're evacuating Crabtree?'

'I'm evacuating Janus. There's no official word of it since I don't want mass panic, but when the time comes I'll have things in place to get all of us Skyside in a matter of hours. Maglev to Underhole, Underhole to what's left of the Fountainhead embassy. The Fountainheads will take care of us until we get back on our feet again. There are only five hundred of us, so it's still doable.'

'Send me a postcard.'

'Listen to me, you self-centred bitch. I'm evacuating the whole place. That includes Eddytown. That means your people. That means you have an obligation to help.'

Svetlana looked as if she had just been slapped hard across the face. 'Help you?'

'Help us all. You need to get your people to Crabtree so that we can shuttle them to Underhole and the embassy. We can't afford to wait until I begin the mass evacuation. We have to start now, which means you need to invent a pretext to get your people here.'

'I get it. I clear Eddytown, then you send in the Apparatus bailiffs and take it from me.'

'You still think this is just about me and you, don't you?'

'I outflanked you with the Musk Dogs. You can't deal with that, so you're trying to spoil things with some fear-mongering shit about them blowing up Janus.'

'You want to talk about fear? I'm scared, Svieta. So is Jim. So are the Fountainheads. You're messing with stuff you don't understand, and it's about to blow up in all our faces. Damn right we're fearful.'

'Then I guess you only have yourself to blame. All those times when you could have shared the big picture with me—'

'You want a piece of the picture? Okay, here's one: the Musk Dogs left doors open behind them. They've allowed the Uncontained to leak through.' Bella watched her old friend's face, alert for the slightest tic of recognition. 'Or didn't they mention the Uncontained?'

Svetlana lied badly. 'I don't remember.'

'Let me fill you in, then. They're a hostile intelligence, worse than the Musk Dogs. They've already wiped out another culture that was *at least* as advanced and clever as us. And they're on their way. When the Musk Dogs blow a hole in the wall, the Uncontained will use it to escape as well. There's no telling what kind of damage they'll do before they leave, just to make sure no one follows them.'

Something of that got through. Bella saw it: the slightest crack of doubt in Svetlana's armour.

'What's done is done,' Svetlana said. 'If the Musk Dogs left doors open, the damage was done long before I spoke to them.'

'But you can do something about it now,' Bella urged. 'I'm pushing ahead with the evacuation, but there's still a chance we won't need to leave. Go back to the Musk Dogs. Tell them the deal is off. Tell them to take their fucking machine out of Janus and leave us alone. Tell them to leave, and to shut the door on the way out.'

Across the ShipNet link, Svetlana eyed Bella with a guile that froze her blood. 'They wouldn't need to,' she said. 'I have the means to make a passkey.'

Bella remembered the Whisperer technology. 'Something the Musk Dogs gave you?'

'Something we negotiated for,' Svetlana corrected. 'I have the forge-vat construction file.'

'Are you making it?'

'No, not yet. Other things to attend to first.'

'You can't trust the file. The Musk Dogs aren't expecting to do repeat business with you. It could be anything.'

'I'll take that chance.'

'Even if the file is valid, you're attempting to make something alien in one of our forge vats. Doesn't that give you the slightest pause for thought?'

'So you don't want the passkey.'

'Of course I want it,' Bella said urgently, 'but I want to make damn sure it isn't a trick.'

'How would you know?'

'Wang's good. He's done nothing but eat and dream forge-vat files for forty-eight years.'

'So I hand it over, just like that?'

'Please, Svetlana, let me have the passkey file.'

'Without talking to the Musk Dogs, you won't have the faintest idea what to do with it.'

'Jim can show me. He'll know. In the meantime, all you have to do is tell the Musk Dogs that negotiations are suspended.'

'And then what?'

'Then we'll talk.'

'Not good enough. I'd want guarantees up front, starting with your resignation and Parry's immediate release.'

'You won't let that go, will you?'

'I dealt you a strong hand when I brought Jim back from the dead, Bella. It cost me Crabtree. I don't blame him for that . . . I don't even blame *you* for it. But I'm not letting this one slip. If the passkey means so much, you'll do what it takes.'

Bella nodded, accepting that this was how it must happen. She could already feel thirty-five years of rule slipping through her fingers, and she knew that not one instant of that could be measured against the preservation of her people.

'They're coming, Svieta. Whatever you want to do with me, decide quickly. We need to start making that passkey. At the very least it'll let us get out of the chamber before Janus blows.'

'Will you resign?'

'Whatever you want. Just hand over the file.'

Svetlana must have considered her options before the meeting, for she answered quickly, with an assurance that left no room for negotiation. 'I'll ride the maglev into Crabtree. I'll be wearing a suit, and I'll have the file with me. You won't do anything to threaten me. If you do, you'll lose the passkey.'

'I understand,' Bella said. 'When can I expect you?'

Svetlana glanced at a watch. 'It's ten now. I'll need a little over an hour to prepare, then I'll can catch the train. We can be at Crabtree thirty minutes after departure. How does noon sound?'

'Noon sounds fine,' Bella said.

Something emerged from one of the blank faces of the memorial cube. It broke the smooth surface as if stepping through a curtain of thick black rain and then stopped. It was humanoid, only a little larger than a man. The glossy, sharp-edged surfaces of its midnight-black carapace suggested some close-fitting martial armour. It had no head, only a kind of evil-looking hatchet, too flattened ever to have contained a human skull. In place of hands it had perforated edged foils, thinned to a devastating sharpness.

Bella barely dared speak. 'What is it?'

'An instrument of local government,' Chromis said. 'We call it a reeve. It enforces the policy decisions of the Congress when they need enforcing. Which isn't very often, thankfully.'

'It's a machine.'

Chromis nodded. 'Little more than a hollow shell of femtotech, with all its intelligence crammed into a few millimetres of skin.'

'What can it do?'

'Anything. A reeve can shape itself into any enforcement device, for any legally sanctioned purpose.'

'What could do it against Eddytown, if I sent it in?' Bella had already informed Chromis of the worsening situation.

'After a certain amount of time,' Chromis said, 'there would be no Eddytown. But one reeve can only do so much. It cannot replicate: it's forbidden to transmute local matter except to facilitate self-repair. But the cube can make many reeves. This unit only masses fifty kilograms. The cube could produce a regiment of a thousand reeves before its own mass was depleted by one quarter. They would already outnumber the entire human population of Janus. If that were deemed insufficient, I could issue an emergency directive and instruct the cube to convert its entire mass into reeves. There would be four thousand of them.'

Bella looked at the cube. 'What would happen to you, Chromis?'

'I would continue to run on the reeves until they returned to the cube. I wouldn't notice any difference, provided a significant number of reeves did not come to harm.'

'How can one of *those* ever come to harm?'

'It probably won't, not here, provided we move quickly, before the Musk Dogs give Svetlana weapons that might trouble the reeve.' Chromis paused. 'But you needn't worry about me. I am more resilient than you can imagine. I had to be, to last all this time.'

'I'm glad you found me, Chromis, no matter how long it took.'

'I'm glad as well,' the politician said. 'I just wish there was a means to send a message back to those obstinate fools who nearly blocked the memorial project. Not enough funds, they said. A pointless gesture, doomed never to succeed. Belts need tightening. Perhaps in *another* ten thousand years. Build a monument instead, or a civic amenity. A nice ornamental fountain.' Chromis snorted her derision. 'As if that was ever going to stop me.'

'You were right to push.'

'I was, wasn't I?'

Axford coughed a little boy's cough. 'Are you going to tell me what that thing is, Bella, or do I have twenty guesses?'

'It's a tool,' Bella said. 'A robot. Chromis says it will be enough to pacify Eddytown, to seize control. There'd be a good chance of obtaining the passkey by force if Svetlana has already copied the file into the forge vat.'

'Just that one robot?'

'Chromis can always make more of them.'

'How many more?'

'Lots.'

'Good. Then let's send this one in before things get any worse. We know she has a forge vat, and we can be pretty sure she's brewing something unpleasant in it.'

Bella looked back at Chromis. 'How long would it take for this thing to reach Eddytown? She'll be leaving on the maglev in under the hour.'

A breeze touched Bella's cheek. The reeve had flicked to the other side of the room with no hint of intervening motion.

'Reeves usually need the element of surprise to enable effective pacification,' Chromis explained. 'It reshapes itself to move from point to point, like water being poured from one glass to another. In vacuum, it's even faster. It could be inside Eddytown within five minutes, if you wished.'

The horror of what she was on the verge of doing was enough to make Bella feel sick. 'How would it . . . operate?'

'It can stun or incapacitate,' Chromis said. 'If it does not encounter significant opposition, there need be no casualties.'

'But it will encounter opposition. They'll already be expecting a police action. They won't have weapons – yet – but they'll have drills, cutting torches, mining armour—'

'Then there may be casualties. Reeves know that when they encounter significant resistance, it is better to accept a small number of deaths before stray fire causes many more deaths and injuries. But they never kill needlessly.'

Bella turned to Axford. 'It can take care of Eddytown, but there'll almost certainly be deaths.'

'There'll be deaths if Svetlana moves against Crabtree,' Axford said. 'Even if you give her what she wants, even if you hand over the High Hab in exchange for the passkey, there'll still be people who won't go easily. You've earned their loyalty, Bella. They won't go without a fight, no matter what Svetlana might think.'

'I'll surrender rather than see more blood spilled.'

Chromis interrupted gently. 'Your primary concern, Bella, is not political control of Crabtree, but intercession to gain the passkey file. Then you must erase all the other Musk Dog construction blueprints before they do any damage.'

'I know. I just—' She shook her head, incensed and saddened. 'How did things go from being so good to being so wrong? It only seems like yesterday that Svetlana and I were sitting together in the arboretum, putting the past behind us. Now I'm wondering how many of her people I can get away with *killing*.'

'You didn't ask for this situation,' Chromis said. 'She went to the Musk Dogs, not you.'

'You can't tell me what to do, can you? For all your wisdom, all the thousands of years you have on me, you can't and won't do that.'

'I'm sorry,' Chromis said. 'I hope I've been a friend to you, albeit for such a brief span of time. But I cannot be your master. You are the captain, Bella Lind. This has to be your call.'

Bella returned to her office, seeking a few minutes of calm alone with her fish before she had to meet Svetlana. In the office, with the door closed, she could pretend to herself that there was no crisis, and for a moment she allowed herself that solace.

Then Nick Thale knocked on the door and let himself in.

'This had better not take long,' she said, knowing that the train was already on its way from Eddytown, knowing also that Thale would forgive her the discourtesy.

He passed her a flexy, letting Bella read the display before he said a word. She studied the data and then looked into his old man's face.

'I don't get it. Why are you showing me lava lines?'

'I'm showing you patterns of traffic,' Thale said, with the slightest hint of reproach. 'Notice how the activity's hotted up during the last three hours? The lines are busier than they've been since the Sky went up.'

Bella was about to say something when Thale jabbed a finger at the display and made it change. 'Here's seismic data,' he said. 'And here's a plot of grav-field variations at the main eddy points. Every parameter we can measure is spiking at five or six sigma outside normal variations.' He paused, then said solemnly, 'If Janus was a brain, and we had it in a scanner, I'd say we were looking at an epileptic seizure.'

As one of her inner sanctum, tasked with preparing the evacuation, Thale knew all the salient details about the Musk Dogs and their intentions regarding Janus. 'You think this is it?' Bella asked, warily.

'Something's happening. You either believe in coincidences, or you conclude it has something to with that thing that came back with Svieta.'

Bella closed her eyes, willing the world away. But the world had no intention of leaving.

She opened her eyes again to face a stubbornly present reality. 'The Musk Dogs have started the countdown. It's time to say goodbye to Janus, Nick.'

# CHAPTER 37

Before she left her office, Bella received disquieting news from the far end of the shaft: the engagement had commenced. Two and half light-minutes down from Janus, the Fountainheads, and perhaps their allies in the Shaft-Five Nexus, had encountered the Uncontained. Through the still-open door in the endcap, evidence of the battle leaked through in stuttering flashes: blue-white light shading through ultraviolet into hard X- and gamma-rays, and God knew what else. The radiation took two hundred seconds to crawl its way to Janus, where it was detected by monitoring cams stationed on the surface of the Iron Sky. Cams situated near the endcap door had already expired, fried by stray fire from the battle.

Bella tried to call Jim Chisholm on the embassy channel, but after allowing five minutes for timelag, she concluded that the link had gone down. She did not immediately assume that Chisholm had been killed, although the lack of a reply hardly reassured her. Clearly someone was still fighting someone else, so the Uncontained could not have won yet. Perhaps the Nexus was just cleaning up the last of the resistance. They had already dealt with the Uncontained on an earlier occasion, according to the Fountainheads. They must have learned something of their enemy's vulnerabilities in that earlier encounter, some data that had tactical value in the present engagement.

But the flashes continued. Now and then there'd be a pause, and Bella would hope (or fear) that the battle had reached a conclusion. Then the flashes would resume, sometimes with renewed ferocity, drenching the still-active sensors with radiation fluxes that would have been lethal even to a suited human. Occasionally, the embassy channel crackled with static, as if something or someone was trying to get a message through but was being jammed.

Even this far from the source of the flashes, Bella felt the ferocity of the engagement. It was bad enough witnessing it from a distance, worse knowing that – if Jim Chisholm was to be believed – Bella and her people would shortly be better off there than here.

Bella had often contemplated the shape and texture of her life and wondered how it might one day come to an end. She'd always imagined soft light and hospital drapes, fake smiles and plastic flowers, sad visits from well-wishers. Somehow – even given what had happened to Garrison – she had never imagined dying in space, *because* of space. And it had certainly never occurred to her that she might become collateral damage in a strategic conflict between warring alien cultures, so far into the future that her own species was little more than an archaeological data point.

Perhaps she was being ungrateful, but this development did not necessarily strike her as a positive one.

She wondered how Svetlana felt about it.

The train arrived on time. Doors aligned precisely with luminous docking apertures etched into the side of the tube. Glass barriers whisked open, accompanied by warning chimes.

No one on the platform moved or spoke. There were eight of them: Bella, Ryan Axford, Liz Shen, Mike Takahashi and another four of Bella's closest allies. She had asked Takahashi to come along because he'd been one of Parry's old EVA miners and was liked by everyone, and she hoped that his presence would defuse some of the tension. Parry was also present: the Judicial Apparatus of the High Hab had just handed him over. He stood a little back from Bella's party, detained by a hatstand-shaped robot bailiff. No one was wearing spacesuits, as per Bella's orders. They wore normal clothes, markedly bare of ornament or ostentation, so that the absence of weapons or instruments of mass disorientation might be obvious.

Three figures stepped from the train wearing suits of the Chakri five series – white and smooth-limbed as soapstone figurines. The suits carried no external equipment that might have been mistaken for weapons. Bella had examined Jim Chisholm's original Chakri five and she knew that while the suit was capable of protecting its occupant against all manner of hostile environments, it was not in itself capable of inflicting serious harm on others.

The three figures stepped away from the glass partition and the train doors chimed and closed behind them. They formed a triangle, one figure ahead of the other two, and walked slowly towards the committee, stopping when they had covered half the distance. By the manner of her walk, Bella knew that the person in the lead suit was Svetlana.

Bella spoke first. Her throat felt dry, but she forced out the words. 'Thank you for coming. As you can see, we're all unarmed and unprotected. You have nothing to fear from us.'

Svetlana's amplified voice boomed from the first suit. 'You've brought Parry. That's good.'

'We had a deal,' Bella said. 'I've every intention of sticking to my side of it.'

'Then you're ready to hand yourself over?'

'Just as soon as you hand over the passkey. We need it more urgently than ever now. I don't know whether you've noticed, but Janus is showing worrying signs of instability.'

'Not that story again.'

'It's the truth. The first evacuees are already on their way to Underhole. When you assume command, I want you to continue with the evacuation plan. Leave Nick in charge: he'll see it through.'

'You presume to tell me what to do when I take over?'

'I have a duty to Janus until the last second of my command.'

'Fine. It's coming up fast.' Svetlana's tone became businesslike. 'I have the data in my suit: standard constructor format. If you try anything, I'll erase the file. You won't be able to recover it.'

'I'm not going to try anything. All I want is that passkey. Nothing else matters to me except evacuating this colony and getting us behind that end-cap door.'

'She's telling the truth,' Mike Takahashi said.

Svetlana reached up slowly and released her helmet. She lifted it free and touched it against the hip of her suit, where it formed a temporary adhesive bond. She glanced back at her companions, who reached up and removed their helmets. Denise Nadis shook free her dreads, letting them spill out over the suit's neck ring. Josef Protsenko was the third member of the party. He nodded at Bella with no visible animosity, as if this was all simply some mildly unpleasant bureaucratic necessity, like a bankruptcy hearing.

'I'll give you the passkey,' Svetlana said, 'but not in one go. I've split the document into two. Neither half is any use without the other.'

Bella shrugged. 'However you want to play it.'

'Send Parry over to me. I get him back, you get one half of the file.'

Bella motioned to the bailiff robot. The machine escorted Parry across the platform to a point just in front of Svetlana.

'Release him,' Bella said. The Judicial Apparatus had already given her verbal authority over its bailiff. The robot released Parry's restraints and stepped back on its spindly black hatstand legs. Freed, Parry stretched his arms and examined his wrists where the bonds had been applied.

'Did she hurt you?' Svetlana asked.

Parry shook his head. 'I'm okay, babe. Bella treated me good.' He tried to kiss her, but the bulk of her suit got in the way. Abandoning the attempt, Parry looked back at Bella. 'I came to you willingly with that evidence,' he said. 'I never resented what you did.'

'I know,' she said. 'You don't have to feel bad about this. It isn't your battle.'

Svetlana pulled her helmet from its grip point. 'I'm going to put this back on now, Bella. I need to be wearing the helmet to tell the suit to send the file. You trust me, right?'

'Do whatever you have to do.'

Svetlana dropped the helmet back into place. After twenty or thirty seconds, she reached up and pulled it off again. 'Transfer should be in progress: it's a big file, even split in two. I've e-mailed it to the address you specified.'

'I need to confirm that it's gone through,' Bella said, unzipping her jacket. 'I'm going to pull out a flexy and make a call to Wang. You cool with that?'

'Go ahead.'

Bella removed the flexy, stiffening it with a flick of her wrist – a movement so familiar now that it felt burnt into her muscles. The flexy came alive with ShipNet options. According to the high-level menu, normal services had been suspended due to the state of emergency. Bella, however, did not need normal services.

After a few moments Wang was on the line: white-haired and wizardly, ancient as the hills, utterly unrecognisable as the eager young man who had dropped into her world half a century ago. Until he smiled, that was, and then the years fell away. He was a brave man, willing to remain behind in his lab while the rest of the colony raced to the hills.

'I have the data, Bella. Half of a construction file.'

'That's great – you'll get the other half shortly. Does it look valid to you?'

'I'd need days just to skim the surface operations. There's really only one way to be sure that a construction file is valid, and that's to see what happens when you feed it into a vat.'

'I understand. Just keep in mind this is something a little out of the ordinary.'

She ended the call, folded up the flexy and stuffed it back into her jacket to warm itself. 'We'll discuss the other half now.'

'That means you,' Svetlana said.

Bella spread her arms magnanimously. 'I'm all yours. How would you like to proceed?'

The pace of events and Bella's pliant willingness clearly unsettled Svetlana. 'You can begin by announcing your resignation.'

Bella barely blinked. 'I resign. What else?'

'Announce that you are handing over authority to me.'

'I'd love to.' Bella touched a finger to her lips. 'Problem is, I just resigned. I have no more authority than you do. Or do you want me to unresign, for the sake of procedure?'

Svetlana growled her displeasure. 'Walk to the train. There's an open door at the back.'

'Just me?'

'Just you, Bella.' Svetlana looked pointedly at Liz Shen and the other Lind loyalists on the platform. 'This isn't about recrimination. Everyone will be treated fairly, including you.'

Bella did as she was told, then paused when she was almost at the door. 'I'm going to get inside now. I take it the train will return me to Eddytown, to some state of incarceration?'

'Janus isn't big enough for both of us,' Svetlana said. 'The only way we can share it is if one of us is locked away.'

'Just get your people out of there. I don't care if you leave me behind, but evacuate that town.'

'We've been over this. No one's going anywhere.'

'Is Emily there?'

'You know she is.'

'Then you're sentencing your own daughter to death. If you care about her – if you care about anyone – get them on the train.'

'Pretty low, Bella, emotional blackmail like that.'

'I know you care about Emily. You still have a chance to save her.'

'Get on the train.'

Bella paused again just as she was about to step through the luminous aperture into the waiting maglev. 'As soon as I know Wang has the second file.'

'He'll have it the moment you step onto the train.'

'Just a second. Before I step inside, I want to show you something.'

'You played yourself, Bella.'

'Maybe I did, but I didn't play Chromis.'

'Chromis?' Svetlana asked, the name meaning nothing to her.

Bella looked at the memorial cube. So, following her gaze, did Svetlana. The cube had been there all along, quietly waiting in the shadows at the back of the concourse.

There was just enough time for Svetlana to register recognition and then surprise.

Then the air moved. A storm of black shapes erupted from the visible face of the memorial cube. They were awesomely fast, cutting through the air like the shadows of fast-moving clouds on a summer day. The reeves poured forth, orbiting the two parties in a vicious black gyre, creating a savage draught that chivvied their clothes and forced them to lean into its pressure. Still they poured forth from the cube: an endless gush of black that defied the common-sense laws of what could possibly be contained in such a small volume. In a flash, the gyre of motion halted and the reeves were suddenly on the ground – many dozens of them, poised motionless on the platform: black, sleek, knife-handed, hatchet-faced terrors from the depths of history.

The wind dropped, the concourse suddenly silent.

'Do nothing, say nothing, think nothing,' Bella said, still poised at the side of the maglev carriage. 'These things are very, very dangerous.'

Svetlana had the nerve to speak. 'What are they?'

'Reeves,' Bella said. 'Instruments of government. They're pure femtotech. There must be a hundred of them here now, but the cube could make thousands of them if I ordered it.'

Svetlana frowned at the cube. 'I knew you'd found it. I also heard you'd had no more luck than I had in figuring out what it did.'

'That was true at first,' Bella said. 'The difference is I touched it.'

'You *touched* it?'

'It was a message for me, sent eighteen thousand years after our departure. A token of goodwill, and a kind of toolkit.'

'Eighteen thousand years,' Svetlana said, with an automatic headshake of disbelief.

'That's just the start of it,' Bella said. 'I'm sorry, but we've come a lot, lot further into the future than eighteen thousand years. How far, I don't quite know – but it has to be tens of millions of years, probably more.'

'And you just know all this somehow.'

'I know that the human species is extinct, and we're all that's left. The cube told me a lot, Svetlana, but it wasn't just that. You had your doubts as well. You came to believe that the Fountainheads were lying.'

With a trace of unease, she said, 'Yes.'

'Well, you were right. But they were lying out of kindness. We simply weren't ready for the truth.'

'What now, Bella?' Svetlana looked around at the massed regiment of reeves. 'You appear to have the upper hand.'

'Nothing's changed,' Bella said. 'This was a demonstration, that's all. In a moment, the reeves will return to the cube and everything will continue as planned. I'll get on the train, you'll send the file to Wang, Wang will make the passkey, you'll get yourself and everyone else off Janus.'

'Then *why* show me all this?'

'Because I could. Because I wanted you to know that I could have ended all this hours ago. I could have taken Eddytown, Svieta. In minutes. There'd have been casualties, but the reeves would have prevailed.'

Still Svetlana didn't understand. 'So why didn't you?'

'I'm tired, Svieta,' Bella said. 'I felt the same way Parry did when he concealed those murderers. I didn't want any more killing. If the only way to achieve that was to surrender to you, to give you everything you wanted, then fine, I was ready to do that. But I wanted you to know that it could have ended differently.' Bella paused, about to stop speaking, when she felt the need to add something else. 'You'll win now, Svieta. You'll get the High Hab, and Parry. But when I board that train, I'll ride it to Eddytown knowing I did the right thing. If you want to think of all this as a demonstration of my moral superiority, I won't stop you. It's not going to be much consolation to me when Janus goes up.' She moved to board the train.

'Wait,' Svetlana said. She lifted up her helmet, frowning at something on the internal HUD.

'Send Wang the second half of the file,' Bella said.

'Wait, damn it. Something's happening. I don't understand, but—'

'What?' Bella asked.

'The suit's not happy about something. I need to put the helmet on. Tell your . . . *reeves* not to pounce.'

'Do it slowly,' Bella warned.

Svetlana lowered the helmet back into place. She took longer than before. When she lifted it again and let it glue itself back to her hip, Bella could not gauge the expression on her face. It was somewhere between affront and abject dread.

'What?' she asked again.

'I don't know,' Svetlana said, her eyes wide with incomprehension. 'All I know is . . . I'm not seeing Eddytown.'

'What do you mean, not seeing it?'

'It isn't there. It's dropped off the net.'

Something convinced Bella that this was no ruse. She retrieved her flexy, stiffened it and examined ShipNet.

It was exactly as Svetlana had said: Eddytown was out of contact.

'Something's happened,' Bella said.

'I know. I *know* something's happened.'

'It's specific to Eddytown. It can't be anything to do with what the Musk Dogs have done to Janus.'

'This was a trap,' Denise Nadis said. 'This whole set-up – these . . . *things* – it was all to keep our eyes off the plot. She's done something to Eddytown.'

'I haven't,' Bella said firmly. 'Believe me, this is none of my doing. Maybe I'm wrong and Janus is going to blow up in a few minutes. Maybe the Uncontained have slipped through already—'

'It isn't Janus, and it isn't the Uncontained,' said Chromis Pasqueflower Bowerbird, stepping fully formed from the embossed face of the memorial cube. 'But it is, possibly, a question of containment.'

They were all looking at her, not just Bella. They could all see Chromis.

Chromis stopped and looked apologetic. 'I'm sorry – I wish there was more time for introductions. Bella can vouch for me, I think. My name is Chromis Pasqueflower Bowerbird and I've been dead a very long while. But don't hold that against me.'

'You're solid,' Bella said, almost dumbfounded.

'There is little further point in subterfuge now that the reeves have made their appearance.' Chromis touched the electric-white fabric of her gown. 'I must emphasize to all concerned that I'm not human: merely a plausible simulation of a long-dead personality. This body is simply another shell of femtotech machinery, like the body of a reeve.' She looked momentarily sad. 'Although it does feel very convincing to me, if my memories of life are to be trusted.'

'What's happening, Chromis?' Bella asked.

'Something very unfortunate has occurred in Eddytown.' Chromis looked sternly at Svetlana. 'You have a forge vat there. You were attempting to create the passkey.'

'Yes,' Svetlana said, with a renewed flash of defiance, 'but there was no deception in that. I agreed to hand the construction file to Wang. I never said I wouldn't make one myself. I thought that *might* be the wise thing to do.'

'I'm afraid you've run into certain . . . difficulties,' Chromis said.

'I don't understand,' Svetlana said fiercely. 'Tell me what's happening to Eddytown. My daughter's there. I want to know that's she's okay.'

'She may not be,' Chromis said simply.

'Talk to me!' Svetlana demanded.

'The passkey required femtotech machinery. The Musk Dogs may have warned you about this.'

'They did,' Svetlana said. 'They also said I could get around it using a normal vat.'

'I don't doubt that they did.' Chromis looked furious. 'They probably mentioned something about a temporary kernel, or some such? *Hellishly* dangerous. There's only one safe way to create femtotech, and that's with a metastable kernel.'

'What's gone wrong?' Bella asked.

'The kernel has ruptured,' Chromis said. 'Replicating femtotech has escaped. It will have consumed the forge vat within a few seconds, the room within a few dozen more, major areas of Eddytown within a minute. Imagine a nuclear explosion, Bella – slowed down, black and boiling. That'll give you some idea of what it looked like.'

Svetlana and Bella both spoke at the same time. 'How do you know all this?'

Chromis looked at both of them crossly. 'Because I'm already there. How else do you think?'

'You're standing right here, Chromis,' Bella said.

'Part of me is here,' she said patiently, 'but several hundred kilograms of me are now in Eddytown, and I'm reallocating more of myself there by the second. Do you need these reeves any more?'

'No,' Bella said.

The air screamed. The reeves were gone.

'They're on their way,' Chromis said. 'When they arrive, they'll fuse with the material I've already dispatched.'

Bella glanced at Svetlana, wondering how much of this she was understanding. 'To do what?'

The question tested Chromis's usually saintlike patience. 'To do something constructive about the runaway event, of course. What else?'

'I'm sorry,' Bella said.

'Can it be stopped?' Svetlana asked.

'I don't know. Possibly.'

'My daughter . . . the other people – you've got to do something for them.'

'Many of them are already dead,' Chromis informed her.

Svetlana paled. 'Emily. Tell me Emily's okay.'

'What can you do?' Bella said. 'She's right – whatever's happened, the survivors need to be saved.'

'Early indications are that the replicating elements are malformed, which may be in our favour. If my femtotech elements can form a containment envelope around the bad matter, I may be able to hack in and persuade the replicators to self-disassemble, as they were always intended to do.' Chromis tightened one fist, as if the effort were already costing her something. 'Nothing is certain, though. Femtotech is not child's play.'

Bella suddenly noticed something: although the reeves had departed, there was still a mild breeze stirring the air. Then a faint, nearly subliminal flicker of motion caught her eye.

A line of black emerged from one blank face of the memorial cube. She followed it as it flowed through the air, out through the concourse, snaking through the space above her until it reached and pierced the concourse roof, tunnelling a path through to the clear vacuum beyond, and then pushing itself across eighty kilometres to Eddytown.

A hosing line of black femtotech, bleeding out of the cube.

'How much of you will it take?' Bella asked.

'More than I'd hoped.' Chromis's jaw was stiff with determination. In that instant, Bella saw the political steel that had brought the memorial project into existence. Chromis Pasqueflower Bowerbird would not have been a woman to be crossed.

'How much of the cube have you sent so far?' Svetlana asked.

'I've pushed a hundred tonnes over already. It's formed a shell, but it isn't strong enough. It's being assimilated as fast I can deploy it. It'll need more of me.'

'How much more?' Svetlana asked.

'I don't know. I'm doing everything I can.'

'How many have died? How many are still alive?'

Chromis didn't reply.

Bella noticed, with consternation, that the cube was not as large as she remembered it. It was visibly shrinking as it gave up more and more of itself to the battle at Eddytown.

'Chromis . . .' she said, hopelessly.

'This must be done, Bella.'

'You're dying.'

'I was sent to be useful.' Then she looked at Bella with a stern but conciliatory expression. 'You still need that passkey.'

'You're absolutely right,' Bella said, suddenly remembering that Svetlana still had not sent Wang the second half of the file. 'Svieta – we need the rest of the data right now.'

'Send it all to me,' Chromis said, her tone commanding attention. 'Both files, Svetlana. While I still have time, I will attempt to remove the worst bugs. Then there will at least be a remote chance that you may achieve success in a larger forge vat.'

Svetlana looked helpless. 'How do I *send* it to you, Chromis?'

'You're right. There isn't time. Step forward.' Svetlana obeyed, almost without thinking. 'Now, do you trust me?'

Svetlana looked at Bella. There was something in that look Bella had thought she would never see again. It was not friendship, or even affection – it was much too late for such things – but it was something very close to respect, and that in itself was something Bella had not seen in a long while.

Svetlana was asking Bella what she thought.

'Trust her,' Bella said.

Svetlana let Chromis touch her. The white woman immediately lost form and enveloped Svetlana, flowing over her like a wave of spilled milk. The white membrane trembled, held steady and then poured away to reshape itself into the form of a standing woman.

Svetlana was still there, her mouth open, breathing heavily.

'I have the data,' Chromis said. 'This will take a few moments, so bear with me.'

Bella shuddered to think at the agonies of frantic computation Chromis was putting herself through. The politician must have known that she was dying, or would at least be left wounded and weakened by the battle she was fighting at Eddytown. The memorial cube was down to half its original size, still visibly shrinking with each passing second as the flow of matter intensified.

'It isn't working, is it?' Bella asked disconsolately.

'Yes,' Chromis said, with savage emphasis. 'It *is* working, finally. I said it was badly formed and I was right. It just took a little more time and effort than I anticipated—'

'Then you're winning.'

'Yes.' But the cube was still shrinking. Bella wondered how much of it Chromis could afford to lose before the distributed simulation of her personality began to lose coherence.

'I'm afraid,' she said.

'You should be. A word of advice: when you start the next vat run, take the vat into space first. At least it won't be able to gorge itself on surrounding matter if you get another rupture. The file is ready, by the way. It's still far from safe, though I've endeavoured to remove the more egregious instances of sloppy assembly programming—'

'Can you send it to Wang?' Bella asked.

'It's done. He already has it.'

'Thank you,' Bella said.

'I wish you the very best of luck with it, Bella. Unfortunately, I won't be around to see the results.'

The cube had shrunk down to the size of a footstool and was continuing to shrink, like a chunk of abstract black receding into the distance.

'Chromis . . . no! You said you were winning.'

'I *am* winning. Don't doubt that for a second. Unfortunately, the task is using up more of me than I can spare for computation.'

'But when the containment's dealt with – can't you reassemble?'

Chromis shook her head regretfully, as if it was Bella's misfortune they were discussing rather than her own imminent destruction. 'There won't be much femtotech left, either from me or the runaway kernel.' Chromis sighed and fingered the fabric of her gown again. 'I can't spare this mass any longer, I'm afraid. I'll have to throw it into the fray. It's a shame. It was rather *nice* to have a body again after so much time in the cube.'

She vanished.

Bella stared, numb with loss, at the space where she had been. An instant later, Chromis reappeared.

'It's all right,' she said, 'only you can see or hear me now, Bella. I can't stay around long in this form, either – I'm running very low on processing capacity now. I just want you to know that I enjoyed being found.' Bella started to say something, but Chromis cut her off with gentle insistence. 'No – please let me finish, before I go. I'm not the only one, Bella. I told you we sent out a great many memorial cubes. If this one survived, others might have, too. Somewhere out there, there could be others like me. You only have to find one.'

'But it wouldn't be you.'

'But it *would* be Chromis,' she corrected kindly. 'And every Chromis deserves to find her Bella one day. You have made me very happy. Now do the same kind deed for another one. Promise me that, will you?'

'I'll do my best,' Bella said.

'That will have to do.' Chromis smiled, held up a hand in farewell and vanished. It was for good this time. Bella knew this on a neural level: suddenly there was an echoing emptiness in her head, like a house grown too large after the departure of a guest. She had liked Chromis, and she knew she would come to miss her quiet wisdom in the times ahead.

She looked for the cube, but there was nothing left of it.

For a long time no one dared speak. Even those who had never known Chromis were moved by her sacrifice, and there was a collective unwillingness to disturb the reverential silence that followed.

It was Bella, finally, who spoke. She nodded at the bailiff. 'Detain Parry Boyce, please.'

Parry made no effort to avoid the robot as it stalked over to him and reapplied the bonds. Everything Bella thought she knew about him had told her that he would not resist, but she still allowed herself an upwelling of relief that he had not disappointed her.

'Now summon other bailiffs,' she said, then turned to the three representatives from Eddytown.

'What now?' Svetlana asked.

'I'm resuming control,' Bella said, forcing any hint of triumph from her voice. It was not difficult. All she felt was a dejected sense of obligation. Someone had to pick up the reins again.

'Then what?' Svetlana said.

'We continue with the evacuation. Nothing's changed there: we're still sitting on a ticking bomb. In the meantime I'm going to organise a rescue party to Eddytown.' She looked at Axford. 'Ryan – you'd better warn your people to expect casualties. All we have to do is keep them alive until we reach the embassy. Nothing else matters.' Then to Shen, 'Liz – I want you to get on to Nick and see what he can spare from his end. Assume anything up to a hundred and twenty people are going to make it out.'

Shen nodded. 'I'll speak to Wang as well. He can start brewing emergency rations and clothing.'

'By all means, but remind him that we still need the passkey. If he can't give us anything without delaying work on the key, we make do with what we already have.'

'Okay,' Shen said, on a falling note.

'We need that passkey,' Bella insisted. 'Nothing else will matter if we can't get that door closed.'

'I'm on it,' Shen said, heavily.

Svetlana said, 'You haven't mentioned landers. A lander could reach Eddytown in a few minutes.'

'There are no landers on this side of the Sky,' Bella snapped back, annoyed at having to remind her of this fact. 'And forget about drilling through the plug at Underhole: it'd take too long.'

'The Musk Dogs drilled a new hole – that's how I came back through.'

Bella had completely forgotten about the new hole. She wondered if she would have remembered it if Svetlana hadn't reminded her. 'Is it big enough to squeeze a lander through?'

'One of the old ones should fit easily enough – *Crusader* or *Avenger*.'

Bella glanced at Shen. 'Get on it, Liz. It'll take time to fuel and prep them, so we'll still need the maglevs and tractors. You'll need to designate a landing area near Crabtree, preferably within reach of a docking umbilical from one of the outlying domes.'

'I'm on that, too,' Shen said.

Bella turned to Svetlana. 'You were right. I shouldn't have forgotten about the landers.'

'Let's just hope it works, okay?'

'Let's.'

'What's going to happen to us?'

'Protsenko and Nadis are free to go. They can report to Nick Thale and offer assistance at Underhole after they've handed over their suits.'

'What do you want with their suits?'

'I want them for the rescue operation. I'll need two volunteers to wear them, preferably people who've had at least some experience of Chakri fives.'

'I'm in,' Parry said automatically, before Protsenko or Nadis had a chance to say anything. 'I've used a five, and I know Eddytown as well as anyone here.'

'Count me in as well,' Takahashi said, stepping out of Bella's group.

Bella shook her head flatly. 'No way, Mike. We didn't bring you back to lose you again.'

'Parry goes, I go.'

'You don't know Eddytown. You've probably only logged an hour of suit time since you came back from the embassy.'

'Parry can show me the ropes on the train. Don't argue, Bella. This is a miner thing.'

She glared at him for a moment, then sighed. 'All right,' she said, knowing this was one battle she could never win.

Protsenko and Nadis started removing their suits, ready to hand them over to the two miners.

'I'm in as well,' Svetlana said. 'My daughter's there. I'm not letting anyone else go after her in my place.'

Bella stared hard into her eyes. 'You know I'm still going to have to arrest you when we get back from Eddytown. You disobeyed a direct ruling not to talk to the Musk Dogs. In addition, you owned and operated an illegal forge vat and ran an unauthorised construction file. Your actions may cost us Janus. You've already cost us Eddytown. I'm hoping there are survivors, Svieta, but I'm damned sure there are going to be casualties.'

'Done with the lecture?'

'Pretty much. For now.'

Svetlana's eyes narrowed suspiciously. 'What you just said – about "us" getting back from Eddytown – that was a slip, right?'

'No – I'm still coming with you.'

'But you think Janus is going to blow.'

'Yes.'

'And you're still willing to go back there, even though you could go with everyone else to the embassy?'

'Yes.'

Something behind Svetlana's eyes gave in. 'You don't have to do this,' she said softly.

'Oh, I think I do. Like Mike said: it's a miner thing. Once upon a time we were all miners, all in it together. Pushing ice.'

'That was a long time ago.'

'Still appears to be about the only thing we're good at, if this mess is anything to go by.'

Takahashi and Boyce were already inside the Chakri fives Nadis and Protsenko had vacated, the conformal suits adjusting their dimensions to match the differing builds of the two men, elongating here, tightening there. 'You'll need a suit, too,' Takahashi told Bella. 'Have one of the bailiffs bring you down a five, then we can move out.'

'I haven't trained in them,' Bella said. 'As a matter of fact, it's about thirty years since I last wore any kind of suit, even an Orlan.'

'You need something, Bella,' Takahashi insisted.

'There'll be emergency suits on the train. As long as it holds air, I'm not fussy.'

# CHAPTER 38

The train came to a vicious stop on the vertical face of Junction Box, the line ahead of it buckled and broken. They had just crossed the boundary where the lines of perpetual-motion wheels were still turning, gyring like crazed windmills. They were spinning faster than Bella remembered from her last visit, as if the brakes had failed.

She dimmed the cabin illumination and stared through the windows at the place where there had recently been a community of more than a hundred people. It would have been easier if there had been no trace of it: then at least she could have closed her mind to the remote possibility of any survivors. But something of Eddytown was still there, picked out in the harsh clarity of the train's forward headlights: a fringe of structures bordering a bowl-shaped absence. Many of the structures had been torn in half, or pancaked down as if they'd been stepped on with bullying force. Only those furthest away from the depression were in anything approaching one piece, but there was no sign of power or lighting in any of them.

'I'm sorry,' Bella said, aware that Svetlana was looking over her shoulder at the same grisly scene. 'It doesn't look very good. That depression must be where the femtotech accident happened—'

'The vat was in the middle,' Svetlana said numbly.

Bella imagined the boiling black explosion Chromis had described, its epicentre the illegal machine in which Svetlana had tried to brew the passkey. There was no sign of any part of the memorial cube machinery now, save a fine black dust that layered every visible surface. Bella tried to extract some thin measure of comfort from the fact that Chromis had succeeded.

But Janus was still going to die.

Before they left the train, Bella called Wang. He answered immediately, pushing white, sweat-matted hair out of his eyes. 'Yes, Bella?'

'Any progress?'

'We're still here. Something's taking shape in the vat, but don't ask me how it works or what kind of range it needs. It'll be completely useless if we can't work out how to turn it on.'

'That's where I'm praying Jim will be able to help us,' Bella said, hoping Wang didn't pick up on the strain in her voice. 'He told me he'd return to Janus as soon as it looked as if things were going according to plan at their end.'

'*Return* to Janus?'

'Just long enough for us to rendezvous with him and get as far away from here as possible. If we can have the passkey installed in a lander, ready to be carried through the skyhole, we'll at least have a shot at closing the endcap door.'

'Once we're all safely on the other side of it, I hope.'

'We may not have that luxury. The door takes a long time to close: if we wait until we've made it into the next chamber before activating it, it may not close in time to protect us when Janus goes up.'

'So we'll have to start closing it before we arrive. For some reason that doesn't fill me with overwhelming enthusiasm.' He smiled tightly.

'If we time it right, we'll be able to slip through the gap before the door closes completely.'

'And if Janus goes up before then?'

'No one will ever be able to accuse us of not trying.'

'I suppose that will be some consolation,' Wang said, philosophically. He glanced distractedly aside. 'I'd best get back to the vat: it's shaking around like an old washing machine.'

'Be ready for us,' Bella said.

She left Wang to his work and put another call through to Nick Thale while Svetlana and the others were cycling through the maglev's single-person airlock. It took a moment for the call to find its way to him. When it did, she recognised the plaza at Underhole, where at least a hundred people were being marshalled into a Skyside-bound elevator.

'Give me the good news, Nick.'

'The good news is that we don't have to worry about the Musk Dogs any more. Their ship left an hour ago – it's on its way to the endcap door.'

'Oh.'

'It looks as though they're in a hurry to get through.'

A weight descended on Bella's heart like a stone. 'They know there isn't much time, then. They've lit the fuse. They'll use their own passkey to close the door, then sit tight in the adjacent chamber until we blow a hole through the wall. Then they'll reopen the door and come back inside, along with their Uncontained friends.'

'I think you're right.'

Bella looked at the airlock. It would soon be her turn to go through, onto the Spican machinery outside. 'I was hoping you weren't going to say that. I was hoping you were going to shoot my theory down in flames.'

'It gets worse, Bella. Those indications I showed you earlier? They're through the roof now. Janus is shaking itself to bits, and I don't think the accident in Eddytown helped matters – it may have stressed an already overloaded system.'

'Any idea how long we have?'

'If I could get the data to the Fountainheads, they might be able to give us a hint, but I think it's pretty safe to say they're otherwise engaged.'

'The battle's still going on?'

'If anything, it's heated up in the last thirty minutes. The door's still open, at least. We'd be in even more trouble if it was closed.'

'Wang's making progress with the vat,' Bella said. 'I told him we'll need to get the passkey spaceborne as soon as it's brewed.'

'Let's hope it comes with a user manual,' Thale said.

Bella signed off and cycled through the airlock. The others were waiting for her further up the line, near the point where it met the edge of the depression. Normally, the scene would have been bathed in the pastel light of the Spican symbols on the surrounding machinery, in addition to the lights of Eddytown itself. Many of the Spican structures were completely black now, except for the occasional flickering symbol. The hard floor that was the sheer face of Junction Box trembled under Bella's feet, like metal decking over an engine room. The visible lava lines flashed with hectic activity as materials were shuttled at emergency speed from one part of Janus to another. The moon was performing emergency surgery on itself.

It wasn't going to work.

There was no further need for Nick Thale's parameter readings. The fact that the moon was convulsing itself to death was obvious in every footstep, every glance.

Bella caught up with the others, finding the going harder than she had expected. 'This feels like more than one gee,' she said, catching her breath.

Svetlana turned the sleek form of her Chakri five to face Bella. Her voice rasped over the common channel. 'It's heavier than when we left. My HUD says one point five and rising. Something's wrong with the eddy effect – that's why the wheels are turning so damned fast.'

They had built Eddytown here to exploit this focus of enhanced gravitational field, but now that focus was intensifying, dragging matter against the side of Junction Box. Bella suspected it wouldn't be the last good idea they'd have cause to regret by the end of the day.

'I just talked to Nick – he says things are getting worse all over Janus. I don't think we have much time, Svieta.' Bella looked at the huddle of ruined and deformed structures on the fringe of the crater, their outlines furred with the black ash from the dead femtomachines. The heightened gravity had pulled it down like a blanket. 'We'll scout the nearest buildings,' she said, trying to sound more optimistic than she felt. 'That should give us a clearer idea of survivors. Once we know what kind of numbers we're looking at—'

'You don't think we'll find anyone,' Svetlana said bluntly.

'If anyone survived, we'll find them. Including Emily.'

'She could have been at the epicentre.'

'Or she might have made it out. We know it didn't happen instantly, Svieta. Chromis held it back for a while before it swallowed the whole town. There's still hope.'

But a small, private voice said: *there's hope, and there's desperation.*

They walked to the very edge of the depression and looked down. It was a polished black bowl, with no trace of former human habitation. Even the maglev line ended sharply at the rim.

Bella knelt down and scooped up a handful of the black dust in her gloved palm. It seeped between her fingers like water. She had just held part of what had once been Chromis. She wondered, with a little pang of unease, if some ghostly echo of Chromis was still running in the ashes covering Eddytown.

'Grav's higher again here,' Svetlana said. 'One point six, nudging seven. Our suits have power-assist, so we can manage. You're going to find it tougher, Bella.'

Bella felt the extra weight in her hip joints: a discomfort that would very soon turn into pain. For now she blotted it out. 'Good job I kept up with Axford's exercise programme, then.'

'There's nothing on this side of the bowl,' Parry said, as they edged past some ruins that were only just recognisable as having once been domes and connecting tubes. 'We'll skirt the crater and check out the admin core and the public annexe. That whole complex still looks pretty stable.'

*But dead,* Bella thought. Dead and cold and airless, as if it had been abandoned for a hundred years.

Beneath them, the ground tremored with a renewed fury. Frantic patterns of Spican symbology flashed across distant regions of the surrounding machinery, changing colour and shape so quickly that they looked like neon advertisements in speeded-up movie footage of some long-vanished, long-forgotten city.

They worked around the edge of the depression until they were close to the buildings Parry had identified. Bella found the going even harder, feeling with each step as if her bones were going to shatter under the load.

'How heavy now?' she gasped.

'One point eight,' Svetlana said.

'One nine,' Takahashi said, breathing heavily despite his power-assisted suit. 'Nudging two.'

'I'm reading one point six,' Parry, who was walking to the left of his wife, said. 'Field's like a patchwork quilt. I suggest you follow my line, Bella – between us we should be able to plot the optimum path.'

'Copy.'

'It's shifting around us,' Parry said. 'Could be the average is getting stronger.'

He glanced back at the perpetual-motion array. 'Wheels look to be turning even faster than when we arrived.'

'Then we've even less time than we thought,' Bella said, between gasps, as she did her best to follow Parry's path.

They approached an armoured airlock set into the side of the nearest dome-shaped building, the door bordered with luminous wasp-coloured stripes. The frame was buckled, sagging to one side as if a fierce gravity squall had swept over it. Svetlana reached it first, quickening her pace with the servo-assist suit.

'Looks pretty skewed,' Parry warned.

The building and its airlock dated back to the very earliest days of the settlement, cobbled together from pieces of *Rockhopper*. Svetlana brushed black dust from an instrument panel and thumbed the thick, multi-coloured control buttons. After an agonising interval, amber strobe lights signalled the opening of the door. It slid into its frame with a laboured, jerky motion, encountering obvious resistance from the buckled structure.

At least it was open. The airlock chamber was large enough to take two people in bulky suits. Bella let Parry and Svetlana through first, waiting outside with Takahashi. The outer door closed to allow air to cycle into the lock, assuming that the dome still contained any pressure. It felt like an eternity before the outer door shuffled open again. Bella wondered how many cycles the ancient mechanism would stand before it burnt out completely, freezing the door in place.

When Bella and Takahashi reached the interior, it was as dark as she had feared it would be, but at least her suit was telling her that there was air pressure.

'Dome held,' Parry said. 'That's good. There might be some survivors, after all.'

Helmet flashlights activated automatically on the Chakri five suits. Bella had to make do with a ghostly green HUD overlay as her emergency suit – which had no light of its own – sensed its surroundings via radar and ambient light. Parry had described this building as the admin core, and now that Bella looked around she saw evidence of businesslike partitions and spartan office furniture. Chairs had been upended, plants and ornaments tipped over and strewn across the floor, coffee cups spilled on the dark carpeting.

'Must have been a blow-out somewhere in the dome,' Takahashi said, 'enough to whip up a gale in here before pressure normalised. The people working here must have had time to reach safety.'

'Not of all of them,' Parry said quietly.

They followed the shaft of his helmet light until it fell on a pair of legs jutting out through the open doorframe leading into the next major room of the admin core. *Maybe a survivor*, Bella thought – the person could easily have been knocked unconscious by flying debris during the blow-out and abandoned here after everyone else reached safety. But when they rounded the corner and saw the rest of the body, she scrubbed any possibility of survival.

'It's Malcolm Fox,' Parry said, kneeling down as best as his suit allowed.

Something invisible had crushed Fox's upper body. He looked as if he'd fallen onto concrete from a skyscraper. Both his arms were broken and twisted, glued to the carpet in unnatural positions. His head had lolled to one side and although his face was still recognisable, the side pushed into the carpet had been squashed flat with brutal force. Blood had oozed out around the crushed skull, dark and thick as tar.

'Poor Malcolm,' Takahashi said. 'Maybe we—'

'He's gone,' Bella said sadly. 'There's nothing we can do for him. Even the Fountainheads wouldn't be able to bring him back now.'

'Bella's right,' Parry said. 'We have to leave Malcolm now.'

It was only then that any of them paid any real attention to the rest of the room in which Fox had died. It was another section of the admin core: an open-plan area with seats, desks and display media. Their lights probed darkness, falling on chaotic details. A gale had ripped through this room as well, but that was not the worst thing that had happened. Across from the dead body of Malcolm Fox, another worker remained in his seat. The strong alloy and composite chair had barely buckled, but the worker had been pressed into it with savage force. His head had rolled back, its weight twisting his neck unnaturally through ninety degrees. Bella stared in numb horror at the corpse, grateful that she did not recognise the dead man. Another victim, a woman this time, lay sprawled across a dividing barrier separating one part of the room from another. It had almost cut right through her.

'The squall must have come through this room,' Parry said. 'A bad one, tens of gees . . . maybe even hundreds. Would've been fast.'

'Not fast enough,' Svetlana said, pointing to another pair of bodies sprawled in broken-doll formation across the carpet. 'They were trying to get out.'

Bella asked, 'Did Emily work anywhere near this section?'

'No, not usually, but if there'd been an emergency—'

'Let's not assume the worst. There's still pressure, and we know these squalls can be very localised.'

Takahashi moved ahead of them through the room, placing each footstep like a man navigating a minefield. Bella understood: there could easily be a sharp gravity gradient still present in the room. Step into a pillar of a hundred gees and it might as well be a landmine. Without the suit, he might have felt the currents caused by the flow of air across the pressure discontinuity. Inside the suit, all he had was the HUD warning for comfort, and the HUD would only report the gradient when he was halfway through it.

He looked back, having plotted a path to the exit. 'I think it's safe if you follow me. Peaks at around two for a metre or so back there, but if you push through it fast . . .'

They followed him into the next room. By the time Bella crossed the threshold, she felt as if she'd walked up and down a mountain. Every muscle screamed with the effort of holding her upright against nearly twice her normal weight.

Takahashi made a slow orbit of the room. 'Feels okay,' he said. 'One point six, on average.'

Bella recognised the wide table and picture windows of the conference room where she had pleaded with Svetlana not to talk to the Musk Dogs. Some of the fittings had been ripped from the walls: the depressurisation must have been most violent here, Bella judged. One person lay on the floor at the far end of the room, crushed by a closing emergency airlock door. The door had jammed hard against the body and failed to seal, leaving a fifteen-centimetre gap between the door and the frame.

'Richard Fleig,' Parry said. 'Carsten's son. Jesus, he didn't need this, not after losing Chieko.'

It was difficult to tell whether he'd just fallen and been pinned in place by the closing door, or whether the gravity squall had held him down first as it moved through the conference room. He'd prevented one door from closing, but the doors were always set in pairs for dual redundancy and the second one had closed fully just beyond the heels of his shoes.

'Let's see if we can get it open,' Parry said.

The floor shook under Bella's feet as she walked towards the jammed airlock door, the tremors now strong enough to overcome the damping field installed under the dome. Somewhere in the room they'd just left, she heard the crash of something collapsing.

'We're running out of time,' she said urgently.

'I'm in touch with Nick,' Takahashi said. 'He says we can expect *Star Crusader* in ten minutes. They're using *Avenger* to evac the other outlying communities.'

The floor shook again. Suddenly, ten minutes sounded like eternity. Bella worked the manual control, but the door didn't move. 'Stuck tight,' she said, with what she hoped was the right note of regretful finality.

Parry eased her aside gently and took hold of the door with one hand, bracing himself against the frame with the other. He applied the maximum amplified force of the Chakri five.

'Nothing,' he said, panting at the effort.

'It moved a little,' Svetlana said. 'Let me try as well. Maybe with the two of us . . .'

Bella stepped aside to let the two of them tackle the door. It looked futile, but just as they were about to give up, the door suddenly sprang open, doubling the width of the gap. Svetlana immediately tried to squeeze through, but even the sleek design of her suit was too bulky.

'Almost. If we try again, squeeze another few inches out of the bastard . . .'

They tried, but this time there was no hint of further movement. The door had locked solid, jammed tight against some broken or burnt-out internal mechanism or the stress-buckled frame.

'It's no good,' Parry said, his chest heaving with the effort. 'That's as far as she's going to go.'

'Then we have to double back,' Svetlana said, 'leave by the lock we came in by, walk around to the rear of the public annexe and come in via the freight lock.'

'Two-fifty, three hundred metres, babe, assuming we don't have to detour around eddy points. By the time we've cycled through locks, you're looking at ten, fifteen minutes before we're even inside. Then we'll probably need to clear the internal lock into dome two—'

'We still do it.'

The floor shuddered again. Parry steadied himself against the door frame. 'It's not going to happen, babe. We came to look for survivors, but we always knew there might not be any.'

'Don't talk as if she's already dead.'

'I'm not . . .' Parry faltered. Bella heard the strain in his voice, the effort it was taking to keep it together. 'I'm just saying . . . things are worse than we expected.'

'Traffic,' Takahashi said, cutting across Parry. He held a hand to his helmet, a pointless but automatic gesture of concentration. 'I'm hearing com traffic. Weak as hell—'

'You're hearing spillage from Crabtree,' Bella said, resignedly.

'Then why didn't I hear it until we came inside?'

'Someone's still alive. I knew it,' Svetlana said.

'Maybe,' Bella allowed.

'We have to get through that door,' Svetlana insisted.

'It's as wide as it's going to go,' Parry said. 'We can't squeeze through, babe, no matter how much we want to.'

'Then we take the long way round. At least now we know there's a reason to do it.'

Takahashi still had his hand pressed against his helmet. 'They can't hear me,' he said, 'but I think I heard someone mention Batista. Sounds as if there's more than one survivor.'

'Batista's here, not at Crabtree,' Svetlana said. She sounded too drained for elation, but Bella could imagine her hoping and praying that Emily would be amongst the survivors.

Bella looked at Takahashi. 'How do they sound, Mike?'

'Not great. Kind of panicked, if the voices are anything to go by. But they're alive. Dead people can't panic.'

'Chances are they're in the holding bay by the freight lock,' Svetlana said. 'There were good links to the other domes from that bay – they'd have been able to get there fast.'

'That puts them one chamber away, on the other side of the next admin section,' Parry said.

'Then we'd better find a way through this thing,' Svetlana said. 'Maybe we can use something from the other room as a lever, some furniture, maybe—'

'There's no need,' Bella said. 'You can't get through in a Chakri five, but I'm not wearing one. I should be able to squeeze through the gap pretty easily now.'

Parry touched her shoulder. 'It's good of you to suggest it, Bella, but that emergency suit's like a soap bubble. You so much as scrape it against something sharp and you're going to be sucking vacuum when that second door opens onto the freight lock.'

'Then I'd better make sure I don't, hadn't I?'

The floor jogged violently. Bella felt the force of gravity notch higher, and then steady at that heightened level.

'Even if you find survivors, we still have a problem,' Parry said. 'If they'd been able to get into suits, they'd be outside by now.'

'Then we'd better make sure they *have* suits, hadn't we?' Bella glared at him. 'Give me a break, Boyce. Do you honestly imagine I'd let a little detail like that slip my mind?'

'So what's your plan?' Svetlana asked.

'My plan is for you to form a supply chain. One of you – make it Mike – goes back to the train and starts unloading emergency suits from under the seats. There must be thirty or forty of them, at least. They're small, so you can easily carry several at a time. Just make damned sure you don't pull the activation tabs.'

'We'll need to bring them through the other airlock – that's going to take a lot of time if we have to cycle through it more than once,' Mike said.

'We know there's no one alive in this room, and there's definitely vacuum in the next room along,' Bella said. 'That means no one's getting out of here without a suit on. I'm going to have to open this door anyway, so we'll lose nothing by opening the other lock.'

'Makes sense,' Takahashi said. Like all EVA people, he had a deep-rooted aversion to any kind of depressurisation procedure, treating vacuum as a necessary evil that had to be endured but definitely not encouraged.

'You'd better find something to hang onto,' Bella said. 'It's going to get a little draughty in here.'

Bella squeezed gingerly through the gap and appraised her options for a safe bracing position. In the tight confines of the interior cell, she judged that she would be able to hold herself steady against the outrushing air until it vented into the adjoining admin section and either settled down or continued on into empty space. It would all depend on the nature of the blow-out, which in turn would depend on the age and design of the dome.

'I'll wait on this side of the door,' Svetlana said. 'Parry can relay the suits to me from the lock, if Mike relays them from the train.'

'Copy. Watch those gradients, people. Mike: you're going to be making repeated movements between the annexe and the train, so keep at least one eye on your Sheng box.'

'Oh, Jesus. You don't seriously think I need to worry about that as well, do you?'

'I doubt it, but let's not take chances, okay?'

'I'll do the Sheng shuffle one more time, then.'

Bella gave them all a minute to find handholds, then started the door-release procedure. It was designed to be quick enough to use in an emergency, but not so simple or fast that there was any danger of anyone tripping it accidentally, or before they could be stopped. Four heavy, childproof levers had to be pulled down in sequence, with five-second intervals before the next one could be moved. Alarms blared and strobe lights flashed. A synthesized voice cautioned that the door was about to open onto vacuum.

'Hold tight,' Bella said.

The door slid open, smoothly this time, and the gale of outrushing air seized Bella with shocking force. She'd trained for emergency decompression scenarios during the early days of her career, but somewhere along the line she had forgotten how bestial air could be, like an enraged animal clawing its way out of confinement.

The pressure ramped all the way down to zero, her paper-thin suit puffing out again as the air inside it was allowed to expand. It was either vacuum outside or close enough not to matter.

'Still with us, Bella?' Parry asked.

'Still here, still frosty. Gravity doesn't feel higher than in the rest of the admin core, although I'm taking things slowly.'

'This is Mike,' Takahashi said. 'Parry and I are at the main lock. We're cycling it open now.'

'Good. Watch out for the lander – it should be here any minute now. Make sure they know to keep away from the eddy zones. Best if they don't come any closer than the train.'

'Copy,' Takahashi said.

'You still hearing voices, Mike?'

'Fainter now, but then I'm nearly outside.'

'I'm getting something, too,' Svetlana said. 'Like Mike says – it's weak.'

'If they're on reserve batteries, they're doing well to be sending any signal at all,' Parry said.

Bella's suit was picking up none of the traffic Takahashi and Svetlana had tuned into, but that didn't discourage her. The emergency suit was not designed to sense a wide spread of com frequencies.

She peered through her faceplate, measuring the gloomy dimensions of the new room in the green light of her HUD. No bodies, at least: if anyone had been trapped in here when the blow-out started, they'd presumably been sucked out with the air. She felt sorry for them, but she'd come to find survivors, not to trip over corpses.

At the other side of the freight lock, her HUD traced the outline of another airlock door, sealed shut. She scanned around, but while there were a few open doors leading into darkness, this was the only visible lock. It had to lead into the holding bay Parry and Svetlana had talked about. Bella wished she had paid more attention to the layout of Eddytown, but there was no point blaming herself now.

Taking each step as if her bones were made of glass, she made it to the second airlock. She flipped up the indicator cover, then strained to read the feeble display. The HUD overlay made it difficult without an extra source of light from one of the other suits. There was no way to tell whether the door was holding back air or more vacuum.

'This is Bella,' she said, catching each breath as if it were her last. 'At the door. It's sealed tight, but I'm going to try to open it from outside.'

'Better hope they have the inner door sealed,' Parry said.

'If they haven't, there isn't a lot we can do for them.' Bella's hands worked the controls, her mind blotting out any possibility save the one that allowed those people to stay alive. She pushed the four heavy levers down, each one more difficult to move than the last, each five-second delay stretching to a minor eternity. It all happened in deathly silence this time: no alarm, no synthesized voice.

Then the door opened.

At the last minute, Bella remembered to brace against outrushing air . . . but there was none. The inner door was sealed, and the airlock had held only vacuum.

'I'm halfway through,' she said. 'How are you doing with those emergency suits, Mike?'

His voice was thready. 'I'm at the train, cycling aboard. *Crusader*'s not down yet, but Nick says they're on final approach. The large-scale eddies around Junction Box have become treacherous in the last few minutes—'

'What's the story on the Uncontained?'

'We're still getting a nice fireworks display from the endcap. I guess that means the good guys still have some mopping up to do.'

Or that the good guys were getting the kicking of their lives, Bella thought. 'And Wang?'

'No news, I'm afraid. Didn't want to push Nick – they're not having an easy time of it, by the sound of things.'

'Okay.' She realised, with chagrin, that she had overlooked how difficult it might be to land the ship. It was years since anyone had flown anything that large to Junction Box, an approach that would have been tricky even if the gravity fields were not lashing around like a nest of vipers. 'Are you still hearing those voices?' she asked, hardly daring to frame the question.

'Now and then. They've been a bit subdued for the last few minutes.'

'See if this makes any difference.' She hammered on the door.

'Nothing,' Takahashi said.

Bella hammered again, as hard and regularly as she could manage. In vacuum, she heard nothing of her efforts. It was like hitting a mattress. 'How about now?'

'Do it again.'

Bella hammered until she feared that the glove would rip apart from the force. 'Talk to me, Mike.'

'Someone heard you, Bella – I can hear voices again!'

She hammered until her fist felt bloody. 'Now?'

'They're hearing it, all right. Must mean they're on the other side!'

'I'm going to try cycling through. Coms might get patchy when the other door closes on me.'

'We'll be waiting for you.'

'Good, but don't wait too long. We may be wrong about the location of these people – they could be somewhere else in Eddytown, somewhere we can't reach, or it might just be coms spillage from Crabtree after all.'

'They heard you, Bella.'

'They heard something. In any case, I don't want that lander hanging around a minute longer than necessary.'

Bella started the door sequence. When the outer door had sealed itself, air gushed in through floor vents. She tried raising Takahashi, but all she got was the hiss of static. He might have heard her, but she wasn't picking up his reply. Not that it mattered much now, she told herself. Bella rested her weight against the airlock wall until the pressure climbed up to normal. Normally the inner door would have opened automatically once equalisation had been achieved, but the lock was running on a power-conserving mode. The lights had not come on, and she had to use manual controls to open the inner seal. She worked through the thick levers, the muscles in her arms aching from the effort of carrying extra weight.

The door began to open, then jammed halfway.

Lights stabbed into her eyes. People were crowded into a dimly lit room, some of them holding flashlights. She raised one hand, then tried to speak, hoping that they'd hear her through the helmet. 'Who's there?'

'Who the hell are you?' someone said, on a falling note.

'The person who's come to rescue you. You could at least *try* sounding jubilant.'

A face loomed from the darkness as one of them lowered a light from her face. She recognised something in the face, if not the face itself.

'Oh, hell. I'm sorry. I'm Andrew Dussen.'

'Hank Dussen's son,' Bella said.

'We're completely frazzled here. When we heard knocking . . . *shit*, it's you, isn't it?' Dussen turned to the other people huddled into the room. 'It's Bella! Bella Lind!'

'What the hell is Bella Lind doing here?' someone else asked. 'Not that we aren't grateful to be rescued—'

'But you were expecting someone taller?' Bella looked from face to face, recognising some but not others. None of them were wearing suits, and most of them looked cold and scared. 'We know something bad happened here – we probably have more information than you do. I need to ask something: did Emily Barseghian make it out?'

'I'm Emily,' said a voice from the back.

'Your mother and father are here. They're going to be pleased to hear you made it.'

'They're *here*?'

'Just outside,' Bella said. 'And we're going to get all of you outside as soon as we can. There's a complication, though. None of you have suits, and we can't get a lander close enough to rig up a temporary docking tube.'

'We're all going to die,' someone said, voice thready with panic.

'No, you're not,' Bella said quickly. 'We're fetching you suits, same as the one I'm wearing. They'll be good enough to get you to the ship. I have to go back into the lock to collect them.'

'How many suits?' Emily asked.

Bella looked into the face of Svetlana's daughter, seeing a world of similarity and a world of difference. Svetlana's red hair, but Parry's eyes and nose, and something in the set of her mouth, the curve of her chin, that belonged to no one but Emily herself.

'How many of you are there?'

'Twenty-seven,' Emily said. They would already have counted heads to work out how much air and power they had to ration.

'Is there anyone anywhere else?'

'Just us. We all made our way here from different parts of Eddytown. None of us saw any other survivors on the way over.'

Bella nodded sadly. 'Then the suits won't be a problem.'

She resealed the inner door, cycled through the airlock and crossed quickly to the other dual lock, where Svetlana was waiting on the other side of the jammed door with the first batch of flat orange rectangles. She had eight of them, stacked in her hands like a pile of library books. 'Parry's on his way with eight more,' she said, handing them over carefully.

Bella could only manage four of the suits at a time – they were dense with Thai nanotech, heavy as paving slabs in the local field. She put the others down at her feet, to collect on the next trip.

'Tell Parry we're already more than halfway there – there are only twenty-seven survivors.'

'You reached them?'

'All of them – including Emily. She's going to be okay, Svieta.'

Svetlana studied Bella for a long moment and then let out a gasp of pleasure and relief as the weight of all that worry was removed from her. Bella remembered how she had felt when she learned about the lock of hair in Garrison's hand. For the first time in more years than she cared to think about, she felt an empathic connection with Svetlana.

'Thank you,' Svetlana said eventually.

'I'm glad she made it. Glad all of them did, but especially Emily. She's a good kid.'

'She's older than I was when we were aboard *Rockhopper*, Bella.'

'We were all still kids back then. Even me.'

The ground shook with a force that nearly upended her. 'Mike says the lander's here,' Svetlana said. 'I guess we'd better speed this up.'

'Send the word to Nick that we've found survivors and we're bringing them out in suits.'

'I will.'

'Then tell him to send word to Wang that we're on our way back to Crabtree. If he doesn't have the passkey ready, we'll evacuate him anyway, along with the last few stragglers.'

'And if he does have it?'

'I hope Jim's going to be able to show us how it works.'

Bella turned to go. Through the gap, Svetlana reached out and touched the arm of her suit. 'Bella—'

'I should be going.'

'Everything that's happened between us—'

'Now isn't the best time, Svieta.'

'I need to say it. I just need to say that . . . it isn't as if I think things could ever have been any different.'

Bella thought about that, then nodded solemnly. 'Given everything I know about me, and everything I know about you . . . I think you're right.'

'But that doesn't mean I have to like what happened. I liked having you as my friend a lot more than having you as my enemy.'

Bella stepped away from the lock, watching her footing. 'I know how you feel,' she said.

Svetlana started to say something else. 'Do you think—'

'Fetch the other suits, Svieta. We've got lives to save.'

Svetlana nodded and backed away to meet Parry, who had arrived with the next batch of suits. Bella steadied herself, the load weighing heavy on her arms, and set off back to the survivors.

When she reached the lock, she carried the suits inside and waited for the pressurisation cycle to run again. Emily Barseghian reached in and took the first four suits as soon as the door opened.

'Okay, listen carefully,' Bella said. 'There are another twenty-three suits on their way. They're all identical, all good enough to keep you alive until you reach the lander. Here's how you activate them.' She pulled the tab on one suit, engaging the Thai nanotech, letting it unpack from the dense orange rectangle into a suit like the one she was wearing. She showed them how to put it on, how to control its rudimentary systems. 'You've got more than enough air and power in one of these things, so don't worry about that. Just watch out for obstructions on the way out. We experienced pretty sharp gravity eddies getting here, so watch your step.'

'Guess we'd better start deciding who goes first,' Emily said.

'No,' Bella said firmly. 'That's not how it's going to happen. Get four people prepped, by all means, but if we cycle you through the lock in ones and twos, it's going to take way too much time. It makes more sense to wait until I've shipped over all twenty-seven suits, get everyone inside a suit, then blow the pressure here. You can all leave in one go.'

'What about the other locks?' Emily asked.

'There aren't any. You've got a clear run through vacuum all the way to the ship.' She paused. 'It *is* a bit of a squeeze at one point, but you should all cope fine.'

'Thanks, Bella,' Emily said. She didn't sound keen, but at least she understood why they had to wait.

'Start getting suited,' Bella said. 'I'll be back with the next batch as quickly as I can. I won't be hanging around once I've left the last batch in the lock, so don't expect to see me again after that until we're all aboard the ship.'

'Where are you taking us?' Emily asked.

'Crabtree,' Bella said. 'But we won't be getting out to stretch our legs.'

# CHAPTER 39

Svetlana hugged her daughter as soon as she was clear of the airlock in *Star Crusader*. They were still on the ground, but the pilot kept the thrusters running all the while, ready to shift them fast if the local field showed any signs of climbing higher. If it exceeded three gees, the ship would be pinned down, unable to pull away from the side of Junction Box.

Inside, the ship reeked of fear and exhaustion. Nick Thale was counting heads, making sure all twenty-seven of the Eddytown survivors were through the lock and secured for takeoff. The ancient lander had never been designed to take more than a dozen bulkily-suited people, but in the years since her last cometfall, Star Crusader had been stripped and refurbished as a passenger-carrying transport. That had been when there was still hope that the Fountainheads would permit – or at least not actively discourage – human exploration beyond the confines of the present shaft. Where once a large fraction of her internal volume had been occupied by DeepShaft equipment: drills, stowed robots, suit ballast, sprayrock applicators, decompressed and folded tents, and the occasional handy ex-MIRV nuclear device, the lander was now outfitted with additional seats, berths and extra life-support systems. Not that it wouldn't be a squeeze by the time they'd picked up Wang and the other survivors – but Svetlana wasn't hearing any complaints.

'I thought you were dead,' she said to Emily. 'When it happened, we didn't think anyone could have survived. I know I should feel sorry for the people who didn't make it, but right now the fact that you got out is all that matters to me.'

'We didn't know about what was happening to the rest of Janus,' Emily said, tearing her way out of the emergency suit. 'We knew there was something going on under Eddytown, but we assumed it was because of the accident.'

'Some of it probably was. Not all of it, though.' Svetlana felt a bracing sense of freedom as she spoke the truth. 'I made a mistake when I talked to the Musk Dogs. They lied to me, Emily. They've put something inside Janus:

not to tap energy like the Fountainheads, but to make it blow up.'

Emily appeared to accept this unquestioningly. 'Why would they do that?'

'They're trying to blow a hole in the Structure. Janus is their one best shot at escape, until the next moon rolls in. Which might be a long, long time from now.'

'And they didn't think to mention this to us?'

'I guess they knew what we'd say.'

'It's still going to happen, right?'

'Looks like it. Bella's been advised to evacuate everyone. Everything we've made, everything we've built, every place that we've tried to make feel like home – it's ending today.'

'I can't deal with this. It's too sudden.'

Svetlana kissed the side of Emily's forehead and ran a hand through her tousled hair, straightening it. 'We're all going to have to deal with it sooner or later.'

'Where will we live? How will we find enough energy and power to stay alive?'

'We'll just have to figure something out, the way the Fountainheads did.'

'We'll be poorer, though, by losing the one thing we have that makes us worth talking to.'

'In which case we're about to find out who our friends really are, I suppose.'

'How long before we're all off Janus?'

'Bella was talking in terms of hours. The sooner the better, I think.'

'And you still came back for us?'

'I was hardly going to abandon you, was I?'

'Not you,' Emily said. 'But Bella – why did she come back, when she could have left with the others?'

'Ask her yourself,' Svetlana said, looking over the heads of the evacuees, trying to locate the small woman she knew had to be somewhere inside. She drew a blank, then looked harder.

Bella wasn't on the ship.

'Where is she?' Svetlana asked. 'She should have been with you, after she handed over the last set of suits.'

'She said she wouldn't be sticking around while we got into the suits,' Emily said. 'I assumed she'd have come aboard ship before any of us arrived.'

'But she didn't. Didn't you notice?'

Emily pulled away from her mother. 'She could have been anywhere aboard.'

'She isn't on the flight deck. Where else could she be?'

Emily looked affronted. 'Don't give me a hard time – I had twenty-six other people to think about.'

'But Bella somehow escaped your attention.'

Parry pushed through to them, steadying himself via an overhead handrail. 'We're about ready to dust off, unless there's a problem I don't know about.'

'Bella isn't aboard,' Svetlana said.

He looked around, his expression hardening. 'You double-checked?'

'She isn't here. She told Emily she'd be back on the ship before any of the evacuees.'

'Who was the first through?'

'Elias Feldman's son. Bella definitely wasn't with him.'

'Fuck.' He looked stunned, as if the universe could not possibly be doing this to them, after everything they had already been through on this day. 'Something must have happened to her between the two airlocks.'

'It was dark,' Emily said. 'If she'd fallen, stumbled away from the track we were following . . . we were moving quickly, not paying much attention to what was on either side of us. Jesus, don't look at me like that! No one told us she was going to fall!'

'Easy,' Parry said. 'No one's blaming you.'

'*She* damned well is,' Emily said, looking pointedly at Svetlana.

Parry reached for a helmet stowed on one of the equipment racks. 'I'll go back for her. Tell the pilot to keep the lander down until the last possible moment. If he has to leave, I'll carry Bella beyond the wheels.'

'You'll never get through that half-open door,' Svetlana said. 'I'll go out in one of the emergency suits, same as Bella was wearing. Mike brought some extras aboard the lander, right? It's the only way.'

'Not going to happen, babe. Don't want you falling the same way she did.'

'We don't know what happened yet, which is why one of us has to go back to look. Could be she's just trapped, or disorientated. She didn't know Eddytown the way we did.'

Parry held his resolve for a moment longer before giving in. 'I'll sweet-talk the pilot into keeping us grounded for another six minutes. If you haven't found Bella in three, you turn around and head back. That's not negotiable.'

Svetlana started removing her Chakri five, ready to slip into an emergency suit as soon as it had assembled itself. She did not care who she elbowed in the process, or even hear the disgruntled noises they made. Barely two minutes later, she was back on the surface, looking for Bella. Retracing the course they had followed before, groaning with the effort of walking through the high-gee zones, heedless of whether or not she was repeating herself enough to provoke the machinery, she found her way back into the admin core, to the jammed door that she had not been able to squeeze through before. Now it was easy.

It did not take long to find her. As Emily had guessed, Bella had fallen not far from the route that the evacuees would have taken from their place of shelter through the admin core to the lander. In the darkness, with all their concentration focused on getting to safety, it did not surprise Svetlana that none of them had noticed the fallen woman, lying amidst the debris and clutter of the depressurised building. As Svetlana put her hand into the space above Bella's fallen form, she understood instantly what had happened: the field strength was much higher there – three or four gees, easily. One errant footfall into that region of influence and Bella would have been ripped from her feet. She would have hit the ground with calamitous force. The emergency suit was not designed to protect her from that kind of harm.

Nor had it.

With great effort, Svetlana dragged Bella's body back onto the path, without exposing herself to the field gradient. But even then Bella was almost too heavy to carry unassisted. By the time she got her through the jammed lock, Svetlana had passed through every state of exhaustion she had ever experienced and into some strange new landscape of fatigue. Afterwards, she remembered very little of the journey. It was only much later that she learned that Parry had been waiting for her in a Chakri five, ready to carry the two of them back to *Star Crusader.*

Bella was dead. The impact of the fall had driven a piece of debris into her skull like a piton.

But what, Svetlana wondered, did it mean to die on Janus?

Aboard the lander, Svetlana insisted that they must do what they could, no matter how futile it might prove. Bella had died instantly, but even though her suit had been punctured, even though all the breathable air had flashed into vacuum, the trace oxygen in her body would have continued to trigger a damaging cascade of cellular processes. Those processes were continuing even now, still working their harm.

Those last traces of oxygen had to be flushed out; the cellular receptor sites blocked. Moving more by reflex than conscious direction, Svetlana pushed her way to the nearest medical kit and ripped it from the wall. She fumbled it open and tugged out the Frost Angel kit, with its childishly lucid instruction sheet. They'd had better methods of immersion for decades, but the equipment on the lander had barely been touched since the settlement.

Parry took her arm, squeezing it gently. 'It's too late, babe. She's been under for too long.'

'We can do this.'

He spoke with a calm insistence. 'This isn't the way it's meant to happen. Frost Angel is for preserving structure before it collapses. In this case the collapse has already happened.'

'Then we don't allow it to get any worse.'

'I know you want to do all that you can. But we've lost this one. Bella would have seen that.'

'Parry,' she said, her temper snapping, 'either let go of me or start doing something useful.'

'Babe . . .'

She shouted now, loud enough that it silenced all other talk in the ship, even against the background of roaring machines. 'Parry – listen to me. Fucking *listen*. Bella Lind isn't dying on my watch. Either accept that or get the fuck out of my way.'

He opened his mouth as if to answer her, but at first nothing came. Then, quietly enough that only she could have heard him, he said, 'What do you want me to do?'

She lowered her voice. 'Get her out of that suit, quickly. Get her into a hardshell so we can flood it with $H_2S$. And do it *fast*.'

'Okay,' he said, and started moving.

They had her in the suit, flooded with hydrogen sulphide, by the time *Star Crusader* touched down at Crabtree and took aboard the handful of people who hadn't already left for Underhole via the maglev. The people – as well as the BI robots that had accompanied them to the lander – were all carry-ing as much as they could salvage from Crabtree's great arboreta and aquaria. It was pathetic how little they'd be saving – a few twigs from a forest, a few fish if they were lucky – but everyone who had left the city had taken something, often at the expense of their own belongings. Perhaps it was a pointless gesture – perhaps the settlement could never be remade the way it had been until today – but sometimes a gesture was better than nothing, no matter how hopelessly futile it might have been. It was the human thing to do, as Bella had said. The twigs and fish were a promise that whatever happened here, whatever the next few days or weeks had in store, there was still a future. Somewhere else in the Structure, they'd find a way to make Crabtree again, or die trying.

First, though, they had to make it through the next day.

By the time they landed, Wang Zhanmin was ready with the passkey, still hot from the subnuclear fires of its creation. They got their first good look at it as the robots carried it with reverent care aboard the waiting lander. It resembled an insanely complicated piece of abstract sculpture in delicate blown glass: a cylindrical thing the size of a jet turbine, ripe with intertwined pipes and flanges twinkling with chromatic flashes of refracted light, and yet conveying the sense that it was not *quite* all there: clefts and gaps in its elusive shape hinted at missing structures, like a three-dimensional jigsaw with some of the pieces missing. It was only later that Svetlana realised that the Whisperer artefact was made of materials from both sides of the matter gap, and that the missing pieces were in fact fully present, integrated into the whole by gravitomagnetic coupling fields and trans-gap energy ducts, sharing some but not all of the same spatial volume as the visible parts. On any level of analysis, the passkey was at least twice as complex as it appeared. The Whisperers, had any of them been present, would have seen the other half of the machine, and wondered about the ghostly parts intruding into the universe on the human side of the gap.

'I was expecting to deal with Bella,' Wang said, with no apparent rancour, when Svetlana quizzed him about the passkey.

'Bella's dead,' she told him, the words themselves tasting sordid in her mouth, like something she needed to spit out.

'Can she be saved?'

'I don't know,' she said, and for the first time she began to wonder if Parry hadn't been right after all. 'We froze her . . . did all that Axford would have done. Maybe it's better than nothing.'

'There were times when you must have wished her dead,' Wang said, and all she could do was nod, for the truth of it was unavoidable. Then he added, 'But this isn't one of those times.'

'No,' she said, softly. 'It isn't.'

They left Crabtree, pulling away from the landing pad, thrusting slowly so as not to damage the delicate-looking passkey before it could be properly cushioned and stowed. Through one of the lander's armoured portholes, Svetlana watched the settlement fall away and below. From the High Hab to the outlying suburban domes, the lights of Crabtree were still burning, as if there were still people down there. It would have been pointless and time-consuming to power-down the community now, given its likely fate. But to Svetlana there was something wrong, something almost disrespectful, about abandoning Crabtree in this way. After all the years that it had sheltered them, it was as if they had all simply tired of it and decided to leave on a whim, before it noticed their absence. Life-support systems were still running, oblivious to the fact that the city's human burden was now zero. There should have been some ceremony of closure, with all of the colonists turning back for one last solemn nod of thanks before they fled Janus completely.

Even after all this time, it occurred to Svetlana, Crabtree had only begun to feel like home at the moment of its abandonment.

From Crabtree they flew directly to the hole that the Musk Dogs had made and passed through to the other side of the Iron Sky. They traversed an ocean of curving black Spican material until the remains of the Fountainhead embassy came into view, twenty kilometres over Underhole. Every now and then, the black surface lightened perceptibly. From overhead, in the direction of the endcap, stray emissions were still reaching Janus from the next chamber.

They landed at the embassy, using the sole remaining docking connection into the Fountainhead structure. The pillars buttressing the Iron Sky must have been absorbing some of the quakes from within Janus, but it was still trembling under the ship.

'It's not getting any quieter down there,' Nick Thale said, after he'd checked the latest read-outs on his old flexy. 'If we were still in Junction Box, we'd be pinned down by now. We left just in time.'

But they hadn't left, not really. They were no safer here than they had been underneath the Iron Sky. Sanctuary was still two and half light-minutes away, in the direction of battle.

'Any news on the other evacuees?' Svetlana asked.

'Three hundred and fifty of them are on their way to the endcap, according to Jim, some of them inside Fountainhead vehicles, the rest squeezed into *Avenger*. We should follow them.'

'We'll wait for Jim,' Svetlana said.

'I've been in touch with him. He said to expect him aboard shortly, and to make room for a guest.'

Svetlana went down to the lander's cargo airlock. Jim Chisholm was arriving as she got there, removing his glasses to rub condensation from the lenses. He wore no suit, only his usual loose-fitting outfit of nondescript pre-Cutoff origin.

'I hear we have a passkey,' he said, like a man who wanted to get down to business.

'I'll show you. First, though—' But Svetlana could hardly force out the words. 'Something happened, Jim. I'm so sorry.'

He seemed to look through her, as if her soul had become a stained-glass window. 'Bella,' he said simply.

'She didn't make it. She died helping the survivors get out of Eddytown.'

'Nick Thale told me she'd gone inside to help them.'

'She died saving people. She got my daughter out of that place. Even after everything that happened between us, she still did that.'

'Nick told me something else.' He pushed the glasses to the bridge of his nose and looked down at her, over them. 'That you went back in to find her.'

'You'd have done the same.'

'The difference is I've already died once. You, as far as I'm aware, haven't yet had the pleasure. That took courage as well, Svetlana.'

'I couldn't leave her there.'

'Of course you couldn't. You of all people wouldn't have been able to do that.'

'Because I hated her?'

'In all the years of enmity, I doubt that you ever stopped feeling some bond of friendship, whether or not either of you would have admitted such a thing.'

Svetlana looked sceptical. 'I don't think so.'

'Then why else did you insist on going back into that building, knowing you might not make it out either?'

Svetlana looked aside sullenly. 'It didn't matter. We've frozen her, run the Frost Angel process . . . but we all know it's too late. She was hurt really badly, Jim, and she was dead for a long time before we ran the process.'

'They made me good again. Maybe they can do something for her as well.'

At that moment Svetlana felt a spiteful urge to remind him that the aliens had not remade the former Jim Chisholm, but had instead created a chimera of two dead men, of which Chisholm only formed the larger part. The glioblastoma had taken so much of his brain that the aliens had no option but to fill in the missing pieces of his memory and personality with what they could salvage from Craig Schrope. Bella, when she fell, had lost as least as much.

'We should be leaving,' Svetlana said.

He looked out through the window of the cargo lock. 'Didn't Nick mention the other guest?'

Through the window she saw the rolling approach of a Fountainhead travel sphere, with one of the blue-fronded aliens propelling it from within.

'Is that McKinley?' she asked, remembering the alien that had come down for Mike Takahashi's homecoming party.

'One and the same.'

'I didn't expect him to come back with you.'

'The Shaft-Five Nexus arrived while you were engaged in Eddytown,' Chisholm said. 'They began to turn the tables on the Uncontained.'

'The battle's still going on.'

'It's not over yet, but it now looks unlikely that the Uncontained will prevail. Luckily it wasn't a large contingent, and they'd suffered some attrition during their journey here. McKinley felt it was safe to return here, for now.'

'Are the other Fountainheads okay?'

'Yes, although that can't be said for all the elements of the Nexus.'

'But it's safe to cross into the next chamber?'

'Let's just say it's safer and leave it at that, shall we?'

They let McKinley aboard, squeezing the travel sphere into the last available space in the lander's already overcrowded cargo bay. Then they pulled away from the embassy, accelerating hard away from the Iron Sky until it became nothing more than a black circle falling away beneath them, backdropped by the distant orange light of the shaft.

'You must have come here in a Fountainhead ship,' Svetlana said, as she showed Chisholm to the passkey. 'Why aren't we leaving in one? Wouldn't it be faster?'

'McKinley thought about that and suggested it might be better if the Musk Dogs continued to believe that this was a purely human evacuation vehicle, with no Fountainhead presence.'

'Apart from McKinley, it is.'

'Not quite. When you landed, McKinley attached something to the lander's hull. It's small enough that the Musk Dogs won't see it until much too late, if at all, but it'll make quite a difference to our ability to overtake them.'

'What did he do?'

'Loosely speaking, he bolted a small frameshift drive onto *Star Crusader*. It's a human invention, so don't feel bad about that. Chromis would have given the technology to Bella sooner or later, I'm sure of it.'

'A frameshift drive.' She remembered that the Musk Dogs had promised her something like that, in return for further negotiations. More teasing lies, she now realised.

'Like I said, it's only a small one: not enough to go gallivanting around the galaxy, but certainly enough to make a difference to the acceleration this lander can sustain, with its engines cranked to maximum.'

She thought of the Musk Dogs, still somewhere between Janus and the endcap door. 'Why do we need to overtake them?'

'Because they'll be hoping we don't make it through the door ahead of them.'

'They've already lost, if you've got the Uncontained under control.'

Chisholm looked pained. 'I didn't say we had them under control, just that things were going more our way than theirs. The arrival of the Musk Dogs – let's assume that we can regard them as strategic allies of the Uncontained, at least until Janus blows up – would be a complication we could really live without.'

'So what's your plan?'

'My plan is punishment,' Chisholm said.

They reached the passkey. Chisholm ran his hand over the glass intricacy of the Whisperer instrument, as if luxuriating in the erotic contact between skin and sleekly transparent machinery. Once, his fingers strayed into one of the absences where it appeared more machinery should have been crammed and he withdrew them sharply, as if he had touched live wires or hot water. But the passkey was cool now – cool enough to chill flesh, as if in some arcane way it was self-refrigerating. It had survived transportation from the forge vat to the lander (so far as Svetlana could tell) and was now mounted on a rigid framework of perforated spars, hastily adapted from the kind of cradle that would have held a FAD warhead.

'I can tell you one thing,' Chisholm said, looking back at Svetlana. 'It looks real. If it isn't a functioning key, it's a damn good imitation.'

'Now tell me it works.'

'We really won't know whether it works until we see a measurable result at the endcap.'

'How do we operate the thing?'

'Point and click, really. Just like a garage-door opener, only the garage is more than two light-minutes away and the door's wide enough to drive Madagascar through in one piece. Otherwise . . . piece of cake.'

'If it works.'

'Yes,' he said, as if the remote possibility of failure had only just occurred to him. 'There is that.'

'The Musk Dogs must have their own passkey, right? How else would they hope to close the door after them?'

'The Musk Dogs or the Uncontained.'

'So why haven't they used it yet? Bella said we'd need to start closing the door before we got there. Doesn't the same thing apply to the Musk Dogs?'

'They aren't close enough yet. If they started the closure now, the door would be shut tight before they got there. Not clever, even by their standards.'

'So why not just wait until they're safe and sound on the other side?'

'That would involve taking too much of a risk of Janus blowing first. They'll be aiming to time it very tightly indeed.'

'And us?'

'We'll just have to do better.'

Chisholm took hold of one heavy end of the machinery and applied a firm twist to it. Along lines of separation Svetlana had not even noticed, one part of the passkey rotated against another. Like some cunningly assembled puzzle, the shape of the thing altered out of all proportion to the change in orientation of the two pieces. A lemon-yellow glow spread through the glass whiskers and intestinal coils, edged in blue wherever it met the abrupt disjunctions between different matter phases. The passkey trembled, as if it sought to break free from its cradle.

'It's working now?' Svetlana asked, astonished.

Chisholm touched a finger to his lips and whispered, 'Almost. One more twist and it'll be active, transmitting the closure command. We'll have to point the lander in the right direction: it's putting out a very narrow beam and if it doesn't touch the endcap receptors, nothing will happen.'

'A very narrow beam of *what*?'

'I'd love to explain,' Chisholm said, with no hint of condescension, 'but unfortunately we don't have all day.'

Svetlana let him get on with it.

There was nothing elegant or subtle about his intentions for the Musk Dogs. His plan depended solely on guile and misdirection: the hope that the Musk Dogs would pay insufficient attention to an apparently human vehicle making a feeble attempt to reach the next chamber before Janus went up. The only other thing in his favour was the expectation that the Musk Dogs would do nothing overtly hostile, even at this late stage in developments. If they had been pressed on the matter by the other agencies in the Shaft-Five Nexus, the Musk Dogs would have expressed bemused and plausible ignorance about the transformation of Janus into an instrument of escape. Given all that he had learned of the Musk Dogs through McKinley and the other aliens, he knew the parameters of their slyness. They would claim that they had only ever been trying to tap Janus for energy, in accordance with the agreement they had negotiated with the human population. They would claim that they had been as surprised as anyone when their innocent tinkerings appeared to set the moon on a course for violent self-destruction. Of course they were trying to reach safety – what else were they to do? If it had been within their means to help the poor, beleaguered humans . . .

It was all lies, but the Musk Dogs had scraped through on lies before: it was one of the reasons they were so tricky to deal with. But if they were to keep up the pretence of innocence, they could not afford to take hostile action against *Star Crusader* while the rest of the Shaft-Five Nexus was watching events.

Which was why *Star Crusader* was able to slip past the gristleship before the Musk Dogs paid due attention to its unusual rate of acceleration. But by then it was too late.

Jim Chisholm made the final alteration to the passkey. The passkey shone a rich brassy gold and shook so violently that it looked about to shatter into a billion twinkling shards. Somehow, it didn't. Since there was no means of pointing the delicate instrument within the lander, Chisholm directed *Star Crusader* to shut down its engines just long enough for the whole lander to be used to aim the passkey's beam towards the distant target of the endcap receptors.

There was a minute of gnawing anxiety before word came back from the Fountainheads that the door had begun to close. After that, it was just a question of making it through the narrowing gap in time. Svetlana could not find the self-discipline to sit around waiting for that to happen. Instead, she joined McKinley by the suited, frozen form of her old friend and former adversary.

'I did what I could,' she said plaintively. 'Perhaps you can undo some of the damage . . .'

Even though he remained within his travel sphere, McKinley must have had some means of peering inside the suit, into Bella's damaged, pierced skull. His tone, when he answered Svetlana, offered little consolation. 'You did the right thing. It's always better to try and fail than not to try. But the damage to the orbito-frontal cortex is grave.'

'Too grave for you to fix?'

'You can't put together a mind with guesswork. You may resurrect someone, but it won't be the person you used to know.'

'We've lost too many people today, McKinley. I don't want to lose another.'

'You risked yourself to bring her back. Whatever debt you owed her, whatever debt she owed you . . . I'd hazard that the slate may now be considered clean.'

She peered through the glass shell at the mass of swishing blue-green tendrils inside. 'You're good at this, McKinley.'

'Good at what?'

'Sounding human, making all the right noises. You've been learning ever since you met us, and you've got better at it with every passing day. But sometimes I don't think you understand what makes us tick at all.'

'I understand that you value existence over non-existence,' McKinley said.

'We have that much in common, at the very least. Take it from me: it can't be said for all the cultures you'll meet in the Structure.'

'If that's meant to be reassuring—'

'It isn't.'

She closed her eyes and drew in a deep, weary breath. 'I didn't mean to sound ungrateful. It's just . . . she used to be my friend. A lot happened between us, but not so much that I don't want her back in the world.'

'I'm sorry,' McKinley said, soothingly. 'I wish there was something we could do. But organised structure is the most precious thing in the universe. When it is lost, it is truly lost.'

A little later, Svetlana left Bella and the alien and climbed through the innards of the lander until she reached an inspection porthole, far enough from the other people to allow her a measure of solitude. She stared back along the route they had already flown, trying to make out the distant, dark speck of Janus against the dull orange lining of the shaft. They had overtaken the Musk Dogs now, gunning the pocket frameshift drive to the limit of its capabilities. The Musk Dog ship was just visible several thousand kilometres to stern: a tangle of gristle backlit by the glow of its own arcane propulsion system. The Musk Dogs, too, were pushing their ship to the limit: so much so that entire chunks of the gristleship were falling off, leaving a radar-trackable trail of fatty gobbets and meat-wrapped shards of broken machinery.

That same radar also revealed that the Musk Dogs were losing the race to reach the endcap. The door ahead of *Star Crusader* was closing with perilous speed, swiftly enough that Svetlana had cause to doubt the accuracy of Chisholm's timing.

She needn't have worried.

Just after *Star Crusader* passed through the narrowing endcap, Jim Chisholm asked her permission to send a message back to the gristleship.

'Why?' she asked, frowning.

'It's a matter of form,' he explained. 'Doing things by the book is terribly important to the Nexus.'

It was simple to arrange and she had no objections. She had the transmission piped through to everyone on the ship, so that they could all hear what Chisholm had to say to the Musk Dogs. Once again a silence fell across the evacuees.

It was not something she would soon forget.

'This is James Henry Chisholm, human representative of the Shaft-Five Nexus, speaking to The One That Negotiates. In a very short while, you and the other Musk Dogs on your vessel will die. If you are not killed by the detonation of Janus, you will die when you are intercepted by the surviving elements of the Nexus, in punishment for crimes against a client species of that same Nexus, and for negligent actions that permitted the recent incursion by hostile elements of the Uncontained. This decision has been reached unanimously by Nexus tribunal, and is not open to appeal. However, since the Nexus is not without compassion, it has been agreed that you may transmit a final message into our safekeeping. This message will be archived until such time as we encounter any other Musk Dog parties, or specified alien third parties that you may designate as the intended recipient. No restriction will be placed on the message content, and we will continue recording until the moment of loss of contact.' Chisholm inserted a judicial pause before ending his statement. 'We will be listening. If we do not detect a return transmission on this frequency within five Nexus standard time units, as measured by our clocks, we will assume that no message will be forthcoming.'

When he was done, Svetlana asked him how long five Nexus standard time units was.

'Just under three minutes,' he said.

Three minutes passed with no word from the Musk Dogs, then four, then five. During the sixth minute, the radar witnessed something catastrophic happen to the gristleship. Stressed beyond the limits of its own structural integrity, it broke into two huge tumbling pieces.

It stopped accelerating. Only in the seventh minute, as the endcap door was almost sphinctering shut, was a fragment of signal detected on the return frequency. Svetlana had it played over the same shipwide speaker. It was a horrible wet, phlegmatic sound, like something being strangled and drowned at the same time. Then Janus went up.

Cams on the inner wall of the Structure caught much of the show and sent images up the shaft towards the lander until the blast scoured them out of existence. For an instant, the detonation shone through the skyholes in two lancing beams of cruel white energy. Then the Iron Sky gave way, shattering into a thousand black shards as it could no longer dam the upwelling energy of the moon's end.

The endcap door had narrowed to within a few hundred metres of closure when the blast hit. A sharp needle of cruel intensity pushed through the tightening circle in the middle of the irising door, the pure white radiance stained with the trace elements of the dying gristleship.

Then the door snapped shut.

# CHAPTER 40

A little while later, after a day that had felt longer than some years, when she had finally made up her mind about what she would do next, Svetlana arranged a private meeting with McKinley.

'I'm sorry about your losses,' she said. 'I know not everything that happened here was my fault. The Uncontained were coming no matter what happened on Janus.'

'This is true.'

She steeled herself. 'But I accept responsibility for some of it. You warned us, I chose to ignore that warning and it cost us dearly.'

The alien stirred its curtain of powerful tractor fronds. 'Bella always gave you the benefit of the doubt. She believed you thought you were doing the best for the colony.'

'I was. But I also wanted to damage her.'

The Fountainhead had formed a high-resolution array and was holding up the meshed pattern of fronds like a shield. 'To admit that is already the beginning of reconciliation, Svetlana.'

'It's a little late for that, I suspect.'

'You said you had a proposal,' the alien said, with the faintest suggestion of impatience.

'I've considered my options. Janus doesn't exist any more, but the Judicial Apparatus survived. Parry was already being punished, and now I've done something that also deserves punishment. My actions were far worse than Parry's well-intention little crime. I cost us more than a hundred lives, McKinley. If we still had the death sentence . . .' Though it would mean nothing to the alien, she mimed the blow to the back of the head that signified death by drill, in the old manner. 'Bella may be dead, but her authority isn't. Nick Thale, Axford . . . they have every right to put me behind bars. But that isn't going to happen.'

At last, the alien unfurled the array. It had seen enough of her. 'It isn't?'

'I've proposed a different form of punishment to the judiciary. It's come back with tacit approval, although there's been no official statement yet. That'll have to wait until I get something from you.'

'I'm not sure I understand.'

'I'm leaving,' she said, 'taking a ship out through the hole the Musk Dogs made for us.'

'Fleeing justice?'

'Far from it. According to you, the last lot that tried to leave were never heard from again.'

The mere suggestion of leaving brought shimmers of ruby and green agitation to McKinley's fronds. 'It would be foolish to understate the dangers. We – and many other sensible species – prefer to remain within the Structure, where the risks are quantifiable.'

'That's your prerogative. Ours is the right to leave, if we choose to do so.'

'With official blessing?'

'The judiciary will grant Parry and me full pardons in return for volunteering our services to explore the space beyond the Structure. No one's pretending that this isn't pretty damned close to a suicide mission, but we'll run as hard and as fast as we can, and we'll take lots of pictures on our way. We're not setting out to die.'

'Just the two of you?'

'You'd be surprised at who's agreed to come with us, if we can put this together. There are plenty of people who'd rather run than stay inside a prison.'

'Pity the poor fools.' He waved a frond encouragingly. 'But continue.'

'We'll need to equip one of the landers for interstellar flight, and we'll need to do it pronto, before the wall fixes itself. No time to tick all the boxes on this one, McKinley.'

'A tall order.'

'I'm sure you'll rise to the occasion. At the very least we'll need another frameshift drive, a forge vat with a lot of files and maybe even some weapons, just in case we run into anything we don't like the look of.'

'You've obviously thought this through.'

'It's the only way this can work, McKinley. Janus is always going to be Bella's show. Even if we finished our sentences . . . I'd always be chafing against that.'

'But Bella is gone. Bella is dead. It could all be yours.'

'I've made up my mind,' she said. 'We're leaving, subject to your assistance.'

'If the matter has tribunal blessing, then I have little choice. The fact that these technologies you desire may kill you will hardly be an issue outside the Structure. They will be all that might keep you alive, as well.'

'Good.' Svetlana turned to go, somewhat theatrically, but stopped herself and looked back at the Fountainhead. 'There's one other thing, McKinley. It concerns Bella.'

'I am sorry that we could not do more for her.'

'I know – we've been over that. We froze her too late, and in any case the damage was too extensive.'

'You must recognise that even Fountainhead medicine has its limitations.'

'But you rejuvenated her once already. You took her apart and put her back together again.'

'Yes, but—'

'Surely you learned something during that process. Surely you remember *something* about the parts she lost.'

'It would always be imprecise, a sketch where a blueprint was required.'

'But better than nothing. This is death we're talking about here, McKinley.'

'A damaged mind is not necessarily an improvement on no mind at all,' the alien said sternly.

'Then you'd better find another way to fill in the gaps.'

'Again, I'm not—'

She interrupted him. 'The tribunal's authorised administrative rejuvenation for Parry and me. If we're going outside, we'll never have another chance to reset the clock. The idea is they make us younger now, so we'll at least have some hope of staying alive long enough to find something useful out there.'

Some flicker of understanding ran through him. 'I see.'

'It means you're going to be taking me apart again, McKinley. It means you're going to look into my head, strip it down like an old motor. All I'm saying is, while you're in there . . .'

'Yes?'

'Take whatever patterns you need. Then make her well again.'

They walked across the crystal translucence of the viewing deck, Svetlana feeling the smooth skin of Parry's hand in her own. It was a young man's hand, carrying no memory of the scars and blemishes of a working life. There were still moments when she underwent a shock of non-recognition, seeing a stranger out of the corner of her eye and then realising with a delicious jolt that it was Parry, her husband, and that she must look as fleetingly unfamiliar to him as he did to her. At the discretion of the tribunal – Svetlana had no knowledge of the debate that must have taken place – their biological clocks had been reset to early adulthood. Allowing for the beneficial effects of the rejuvenation process on the normal mechanisms of ageing, Parry and Svetlana could expect seventy or eighty years of life ahead of them. That, Svetlana supposed, should be time enough for anyone. But she had already lived through more than eighty years and she knew the heft of those years; how swiftly and cruelly they would slip through her fingers again. At the end of it, there would be no Fountainheads to reset the clock one more time.

But, she reminded herself, this option was as much punishment as reward. It was not meant to be the easy way out.

'Well?' McKinley asked. 'How do you like it?'

She turned to face his travel sphere. 'It feels fine. Everything's just the way it should be. I feel wonderful.'

'Actually, I meant the ship.'

'The ship's beautiful,' Parry said. 'That goes without saying.'

'You like it?'

Parry was still holding her hand. 'Absolutely. You've done a grand job. It's more than we ever expected, especially given how little time you've had.'

'Needs must, when the devil comes calling,' McKinley said.

The ship – visible through the armoured window of the viewing deck – was indeed beautiful. It floated within a great bay in the heart of the reassembled Fountainhead embassy, a vacuum-filled opening whose walls were studded with haphazard cones and helices of unknown function, jammed tight like the sound-absorbing baffles in some mighty anechoic chamber. A cradle of curved, tentacle-like arms wrapped the newborn ship in a armature of light, as if it was being embraced or devoured by some luminous seamonster. Had it not been for its surroundings, the vessel would have struck Svetlana as awesomely strange and alien. Instead, she recognised it for the essentially human artefact that it was.

In truth, it wasn't completely newborn. The aliens had taken the fundamentals of Cosmic Avenger and remade it into something else . . . as if that earlier version of the ship had only been a pupal stage for this. But the bones of the old ship showed through the skin of the new. The hull had been resheathed in an armoured plaque as sleek and clean as melting ice, but that was post-Cutoff human technology, rather than anything intrinsically alien. The same went for the new drive systems, the new sensors, the new weapons: they were either gifts from the distant future, or the distant past, but all of it carried the unmistakeable grain of human thinking.

'Is she ready?' Svetlana asked.

'A couple of hours, then we'll hand her over. I take it you're ready to depart as soon as the paint's dry?'

'More or less,' Parry said. 'We're just chewing over the last few candidates. The Apparatus gave us power of veto over any applicants, but we won't want to turn anyone away unless we have excellent reason. It's just a pity there isn't more time to think things through.'

'Believe me,' the alien said, 'if I could shave five minutes from the remaining build-time, I would. There won't be time to learn all the ropes before you depart, unfortunately. You'll just have to let the ship handle itself until you have time to study her systems.'

'Don't worry. It won't be the first time we've had to learn on the fly.'

'We're not sure about Saul Regis,' Svetlana said, tightening her hold on Parry's hand. 'He wants to come with us, but . . .' They'd talked long and hard about Saul Regis, unable to decide whether or not he would fit in with the exploration crew as it now stood. Time and again Svetlana found herself thinking back to that awkward conversation in Bella's office, when Regis had mentioned the execution scene in the old TV series that had given the ship its name. She had sensed his craving then, longing for a world more like that cartoon-bright show and less like the one he inhabited, and she had sensed it again when Regis came to petition for a place on the new ship.

'Would you care for my opinion?' McKinley asked.

The two of them looked at each other and shrugged. 'It can't hurt.'

'Take Regis. Take anyone who really wants to come, until you've allocated all the seats. They know the risks involved.'

'You think so?' Svetlana asked.

McKinley rolled past them, halting at the limit of the viewing platform. 'We didn't soup up the specification on those weapons for nothing, Svetlana. Or put in triple thickness hull-armour. There's something out there that doesn't welcome the curious. You're going to meet it.'

She nodded, and for the briefest of moments considered the alternative: abandoning this scheme, submitting to the original punishment plan, the one that had been on the table before she had ever suggested this to the Apparatus. But the moment did not last. She would be going.

Parry, as if sensing her flicker of doubt, renewed his grip on her hand. Whatever happened out there, his grip told her, they would face it together, and they would face it as lovers, unafraid.

'We're doing this, McKinley. No second thoughts now.'

'Okey dokey,' the alien said cheerily.

'About Bella . . .' Svetlana began. 'How's it going . . .'

'It's not going to be as quick and easy as we imagined,' McKinley said, before spinning around to roll past them.

# CHAPTER 41

Bella woke, after a long and unhurried climb out of the most oceanic state of unconsciousness: something so close to death, so close to nonexistence, that there was little distinction. She did not know where she was, except that it was either somewhere she had already been, very long ago, or a place so like it that it induced precisely the same combination of calm and enchantment. Serene acceptance filled her, a childlike sense that she was in infinitely wise, infinitely knowing hands. She had come to wakefulness in a pool of shallow water, burbling like the distant laughter of happy children. She held a hand up to the false sky and felt a thousand resonant echoes of déjà vu.

'Bella,' a kindly voice said, 'you're back.'

She gradually became aware that she was not alone, that someone had been watching and waiting for her to show signs of life. A man squatted on his haunches, hands on his knees. He avoided looking at her, directing his attention instead slightly to one side, as if a bird or butterfly of some rarity had alighted on a nearby stone.

'I'm cold,' she said.

'I brought you a gown. If you sit up . . .' He turned away for a moment and she found the strength within herself to rise from the cool water. The strength was elusive: when she found it, it came with startling force, but it had been so long that she barely remembered how to command it. A gown wrapped itself around her, drying and warming her as it pressed itself to her skin.

'You obviously understand me,' the man said, 'but how much do you remember?'

His face resolved slowly into focus, colour bleeding into it as the blood returned to her eyes. 'I think I know you,' she said.

'I used to look younger.' He pushed himself upright. 'I'm Ryan, Bella.'

'Ryan,' she said.

'You do remember, don't you?'

'Axford,' she said, as if the word might unlock the most sacred mysteries of creation.

He nodded approvingly. 'That's good.'

'You used to be a little boy.'

'I got older again. It's been a while, Bella, since you were last with us.'

She remembered almost nothing. All she could be certain of was the single fact of her former existence, and that she had known someone named Ryan Axford, a man who had been kind to her on more than one occasion, and that he had once looked passingly like the man who had come to help her.

Forlornly, she asked, 'What happened to me?'

'You died. You died and then they brought you back to us.'

'They?'

'The Fountainheads.'

There was something there: some thread of memory she could almost grab hold of. 'Aliens.'

'You're doing well, Bella. It's all going to come back in time.'

She stepped out of the pool. There had been something wrong with her hands, something that made them useless and painful – but that was gone now. They were smooth and lithe, like the expressive hands of a Balinese dancer. Nowhere in her body was there anything but the memory of pain or stiffness or infirmity.

'Where am I?'

'In the embassy – the new one, that is.'

She almost remembered the old embassy, the memory of it entangled with the intimation of some larger, vaguely felt catastrophe, like the faint unease that chased a nightmare into daytime.

Something terrible had happened.

'Janus,' she said.

'Do you remember how it ended?' Axford asked her. His face was familiar to her, but there were lines and age spots on it that belonged to an older man.

'I made a mistake,' she said.

'It wasn't your mistake, Bella.'

Without quite knowing what it meant, she said, 'I went to the Musk Dogs. They tricked me. Everything went wrong.'

He studied her, saying nothing for a while. 'It's true that mistakes were made. What matters now is moving forward, not dwelling on old errors of judgement.'

She remembered the smell of the Musk Dogs even before the memory of them had sharpened. Smell plumbed the ancient basement of her mind, short-circuiting slower, more rational processes.

The recollection of the Musk Dogs stirred something else. 'Svetlana,' she said, in the panicked tone of someone who had just recalled something urgent. 'What about—'

'Svetlana's gone, Bella. It's just you now.' He held out an inviting hand. 'Let me show you.'

Axford led her from the waking garden. They stepped through opaque glass doors into a kind of gallery, walled on one side by a long, high window of midnight black. He kept hold of her hand, enfolding her smooth fingers in his leathery old man's grip.

'You do remember Svetlana, then.'

'She was my friend.'

'But not always.'

'No,' Bella said, as more connections slipped home. 'Not always. Especially not near the end.'

'Do you remember what happened to Janus, after the Musk Dogs—' He smiled tightly. 'After they tricked you?'

'We had to leave. Evacuate.'

'Because?'

'Janus was going to explode. Something that they did—' Simply thinking about events that close to the end made her uncomfortable. All the blissful calm she had felt in the pool was gone now, scoured away by a rising surf of bitter apprehension. Perhaps sensing this, Axford tightened his hand around hers. 'What happened?' she asked at length, with a child's fearfulness.

'Janus did blow up. Most of us survived, though. We had time to evacuate Crabtree and the other settlements, and the passkey allowed us to sit out the explosion in the next chamber.'

'Svetlana,' she said again. 'She died, didn't she? I went back for her . . . found her body. Too late.'

Again Axford felt that tightening of her grip. 'She made it, Bella. But after Janus had blown up, she had a decision to make, and not an easy one.' He sighed, as if burdened by the effort of revealing what had taken place. 'The Musk Dogs detonated Janus in order to blow a hole in the Structure. You remember the Structure?'

'Yes,' she said, after a brief moment of uncertainty.

'Well, it worked. Janus punched a thousand-kilometre-wide gap in the outer wall, through matter and fields. But like Jim had already said, it wasn't going to stay that way for ever. Self-repair was already cutting in. The Structure was healing itself, patching the damage. In a matter of days it was going to be sealed up again. Svetlana knew this was going to be our only chance of getting outside for a long, long time.'

A memory spoke to her. 'She went.'

'She knew it would be a risk. Jim told her only one culture had ever made it outside in the recorded history of the Structure, and nothing more had ever been heard from them. But she still wanted to do it. There wasn't much time, so she had the Fountainheads give her what they could – technologies they'd held back before, but which – given everything that had happened with Chromis and the Musk Dogs – it no longer seemed so vital to withhold. They took *Cosmic Avenger*, outfitted it with a large frameshift drive, a forge vat and enough construction files to keep improving things once they were under way.'

'*Cosmic Avenger*,' she said, with a half-smile. The name had always been a bad joke, not something to be bestowed on an actual starship.

'They got through,' Axford said. 'It was close: the containment fields were already re-meshing. Another day and they'd have been trapped inside with the rest of us.'

'How many did *I* . . . did *she* take with her?'

'Thirty,' he said. Something crossed his face: some hint of concern, quickly quelled. 'Svetlana, Parry, Nadis and the rest – all the people who'd always been behind her, plus a dozen or so who hadn't even been born back then but who couldn't face spending another minute in the Structure.'

'What about everyone else?'

'They didn't have to turn many people down. By the time they were putting together the crew, word was already circulating about that other culture, the one that no one ever heard from again. The surviving majority were quite happy with the idea of remaining inside the Structure, at least for the time being.'

The obvious question pushed itself into her head. 'What happened to the ones who left?'

'We don't know. We hope they're still alive, that they found enough out there to make life possible. They were hoping to reach a solar system, somewhere with a warm, wet world. But we don't know.'

'Why not?' Knowing what had happened to Svetlana suddenly felt like the most vital thing imaginable.

'They kept transmitting data back to us once they'd passed through the wall, but within a day it became difficult to pick up their signals through the healing surface. Within two, we couldn't detect them at all.'

More memories clicked into place, like tumblers in a lock. 'But they saw the Structure from the outside,' she said, wonderingly. 'Didn't they?'

Axford swept his arm towards the black window, bringing it to life. There was panache to his gesture, a conjuror's quiet pride in the excellence of his timing. 'This is a picture taken one hour after departure,' he said. 'They were on frameshift drive by then, so there was some image distortion due to the drive wake, but we've fixed most of that with software.'

It was the outside of the shaft: a long, gently glowing cylinder with a ragged hole punched in one side. Numerics and annotations bracketed the image: it had clearly been worked over by a furiously keen science team, intent on gleaning a mother lode of wisdom from every image hexel.

'Exit plus two hours,' Axford said.

The image jumped scale, leaping back so that the cylinder became a thin branch, the hole so small as to be barely visible. 'You're seeing most of the distance between the two endcaps we first mapped,' he said. 'The structure's self-illuminated. Why it glows, we have no idea, but that made life a lot easier for us, so Nick says: they'd never have had time to sit and wait for radar returns.'

It was like a filament of human hair, Bella thought, traced with the luminous false colour of a highly magnified image.

'Exit plus six,' Axford said.

Now she could not make out the hole at all, even with an arrowed overlay pointing to the position of the wound in the wall. The shaft was whisker-thin, thousands of times longer than it was wide. It was not the only one in view, either. Two other branches cut across the image at oblique angles, one slightly smaller and dimmer than the other.

'Exit plus twelve,' Axford said. 'Image corrected for both wake distortion and relativistic effects. After twelve hours, *Avenger* was moving at fifty per cent of the speed of light.'

Not just three branches of the Structure now, but an entire intertwined mass of them, dozens of them. There was no geometric order that Bella could discern: it looked as if they'd been tossed into space in random configurations, like a magnification of one microscopic part of a child's demented scribble.

'Exit plus twenty-four,' Axford said, 'one day out. By this point the signal was very difficult to intercept. Useful frame rate was down.'

Bella shuddered at the jump in scale. A twig had turned into an entire forest. Individual filaments of the Structure were less obvious now than the gross organisation of those filaments on a much larger scale. It had looked random at twelve hours, but now she could see that the filaments were indeed ordered, bunched and braided into macroscopic, ropelike groupings that must have been entire light-hours across, wider than the orbits of some planets.

'Exit plus thirty-nine hours, the last useful image. *Avenger* was at ninety per cent of the speed of light and holding, prior to final acceleration boost.'

The window filled with something twinkling and vast, something engineered – so it seemed to Bella – for the sole purpose of crushing the human spirit. She wanted Axford to hold her, so that she did not fall into that paralysing, deadening immensity. The Structure was far, far larger than she had ever imagined: as complex in its knotted, neural topology as a mind, as wide across as an entire planetary system. It was a torus of light, tilted at an angle of forty-five degrees so that its shape was suddenly revealed. It was only at thirty-nine hours that *Avenger* had managed to grab an image that encompassed most of the Structure.

'Look at the middle,' Axford said.

Bella complied. Many spokes of light – each of which was a thick braid formed from hundreds of individual strands – pushed inward from the inner face of the torus, as if they were meant to connect with each other, or form a bridge to some other knot of strands in the middle of the torus.

But there was nothing there. The braids splayed apart, ragged as the branches of a lightning-struck tree.

'Something's missing,' Bella said. 'It looks as if it isn't finished.'

'Or it was finished but something was destroyed. Perhaps that's the answer to the question, Bella.'

'The question?'

'About where the Spicans went. Perhaps the animals revolted, and stormed the zoo.'

Fragments of ancient conversations came to her in rainlike drabs: the memory of a friend now gone, a woman of wise counsel.

'Then the Spicans are dead.'

'Or they've gone into hiding. Either way – it changes the picture, wouldn't you say?'

For a moment, the dizzying shifts of scale overwhelmed her. 'It's all too big. What is it? *Where* is it?'

'We don't know – there aren't enough background stars, not enough recognisable background galaxies, to give us a handle. *Avenger* was still moving through outlying structures when we stopped reading her. Maybe if we'd had another day's worth of data . . .'

Bella stared numbly at the image. 'At least they got us this.'

'Svetlana thought it might come in useful. We've made a map of the local connections, out to several light-hours of shaft travel. Nick's people are still squeezing more data out of the frames, improving the map all the time.'

'It's still just a map.'

'It's better than nothing, Bella. According to the aliens, it's exactly the kind of data some cultures will be prepared to trade for.'

'In other words, we have something to sell.'

He swept a hand towards the window and the last image faded back into perfect blackness. 'Now that we don't have Janus, we have to make the most of what we salvaged.'

'That was always the way we did things,' she said. Then something that had been nagging at her, pushing uncomfortably to the front of her mind, could no longer be resisted. 'You were young, Ryan, the last time I saw you.'

His face was sad. 'You want to know how long it's been, I suppose.'

'That would help.'

Again, she heard that troubled sigh. 'You were a hard case, Bella. The aliens didn't want to bring you back too soon, not until they'd made the best job they felt they were capable of. And we didn't want to have you back until we were . . . well, back on our feet.'

'How long has it been, Ryan? How long since those images came in?'

'Sixty-one years,' he said, and made another gesture towards the window.

The darkness cleared. They were inside a shaft – maybe not the old one, but a similar region of the Structure. Bella recognised the suffocating orange light from the distant glow of hundreds of snaking, intersecting lava lines. But they were not on Janus, not standing in the High Hab in Crabtree or on the other side of Iron Sky. They were some way above the wall – far enough that she could not be sure whether they were standing in the uppermost levels of a very tall building, or in a hovering spacecraft.

Axford directed her gaze to a particular part of the wall where the glow of the lava lines was eclipsed by a smear of light, organised into a grid plan.

'That's New Crabtree,' he said. 'Most of us live there now, on the wall.'

The smear – which Bella judged to be tens of kilometres across – threw out pale-blue tentacles of light that linked it to smaller communities many hundreds or thousands of kilometres away up and down the shaft.

'You made it,' she said. 'Found somewhere new to live.'

'It wasn't easy. Of course, we had the Fountainheads to give us some guidance, but the transition was still difficult. You remember how hard it was during the Year of the Iron Sky.'

She nodded meekly.

'No one talks about the Year of the Iron Sky now. It's ancient history, forgotten except in children's playground rhymes. We got through something tougher.'

'You let me sleep through it,' she said, with an odd sense of resentment.

'We knew things would improve. There was no other way for them to go.'

'And now?'

'We want you back. Crabtree's waiting, Bella. There are a lot of people who'll want to welcome you home.'

'I've been gone so long. What possible use—'

'That's for you to decide,' he said, before she had a chance to say another word. 'Mike Takahashi runs the place. He'll be more than willing to surrender some of that responsibility, if you give him half a chance.'

At the mention of Takahashi's name, she recalled how she had been there when he came back from the dead, back from the glacial cold of the Frost Angels. She had helped him adjust to a future he had never expected to see, and now Axford was helping Bella in the same fashion. It was a comfort to know that, however difficult this journey might be, someone else had already made it.

But thinking about Takahashi brought her back to the end of Janus, and the people who had not made it out alive. She remembered trying to rescue someone, yet the more she tried to pin down the memory, the more it squirmed from her attention.

All she felt was a vast sadness.

'But if it wasn't Svetlana I went back for . . .' Bella trailed off, and looked into Axford's grave and kindly face. 'Who was it?'

'We'll come to that,' he said gently, and turned her away from the window.

# EPILOGUE

They asked Chromis to step outside while the vote was cast. Evening had begun to fall since she had made her case inside the Congress building, and although the sun was still catching the summit of the building, tinting the icecap a hard brassy gold, lights were coming on in the shadow-locked footslopes and inlets far below. The warm breeze on the balcony was a carefully maintained fiction. It felt as if it was blowing up from the tropical landscape twenty-two kilometres below, carrying a delicate freight of spices from the fishing villages around the nearest shore of the great lake. But the balcony was in fact shielded from the ambient atmospheric conditions by an invisible shell of femtomachinery, which also happened to provide protection against almost all conceivable modes of assassination. Admittedly there hadn't been a documented assassination inside the Congress of the Lindblad Ring for three and a half thousand years, but there were still dissident elements out there. Just ask the good citizens of Hemlock, after the reeves had been sent in to restore public order.

Chromis wondered how the vote was going inside the meeting room. She felt, on balance, that her speech had been received about as well as she had dared to hope. She had not deviated from her script; she had not stumbled or lost her rhythm. Rudd had come in on cue with perfect timing, and had played his role with conviction. No one had tried to trump her with some other equally lavish proposal, and none of her habitual enemies had voiced any criticism while she was in the room. Doubtless a certain reverence had held them back: in criticising Chromis they would have been implying that they did not consider the Benefactor's deeds worthy of commemoration. She had counted on that, but was nonetheless relieved.

Still, she hadn't received an ovation either. Even as she stepped out of the room, she had still found the delegates' collective mood inscrutable. Their lack of questions, their lack of antagonism, might even have suggested bored indifference. She hoped not: Chromis had allowed for many things, but it had never occurred to her that her proposal might crash on the rocks of moderate apathy.

Not for the first time since starting her journey to New Far Florence, she felt the Benefactor's quiet presence, as if Bella Lind stood silently next to her on the balcony, as keen to know the outcome as Chromis. It was, she supposed, impossible to spend so long thinking about a single person without them assuming a degree of reality. And she doubted that anyone had thought as long and hard about Bella Lind as she had, during all the centuries of preparation. Once, the Benefactor had been a distant, schematic historical figure; now she was a tactile person whom Chromis felt as if she had met on many occasions. The more strongly this sense of solidity took hold, the more she vowed not to fail the ghost that her imagination had conjured into being.

Overhead, the brightest stars were coming out. The glare from the sunlit icecap washed out any hope of seeing the Milky Way, but Chromis knew roughly where to look. Somewhere out there, she thought, Bella was waiting.

Doors opened behind her. She turned to see Rudd walking towards her, carrying news from the delegates. She studied the hard set of his expression and felt her imaginary companion slip away politely, leaving them alone.

'It's not good news, is it?'

'I'm sorry. It nearly went your way, but . . .' He offered the palms of his hands.

'Tell me.'

'Forty-three ayes, forty-nine nays, seven abstentions.'

'Damn.'

'You came close, Chromis. It wasn't an overwhelming defeat, not by any means. There'll be another chance.'

'I know, but . . . damn.' Disappointment hit her in slow, soft waves rather than a single, crushing onslaught.

'You've planted the seed now. All you have to do is hope that it takes root in half a dozen delegates.'

'I was hoping to win them over on this round, Rudd. I never expected it would be so close. I always thought in terms of majestic defeat or total, storming victory. Either way I'd have been able to walk out of there with my work done: heading back home either with my tail between my legs, the tragically vanquished hero, or as champion. Instead I'm faced with this messy compromise.'

'That's reality for you,' Rudd said. 'Always pissing on the epic moment.'

'How am I going to win them over?'

'With iron will and stubborn determination.' He looked at her with horrified incomprehension. 'You didn't come all this way to give up, did you?'

'I suppose not.'

'The Benefactor wouldn't have given up.'

'I know.'

He joined her by the balcony rail and gave her a brief consolatory hug. 'I think we need to work on the guilt angle. It's all very well pointing out to them how noble and civic this scheme of yours will make us all feel, but that'll only work on some of them. To win the rest of them over, I think you need to emphasise how the future will view us if we fail. Remind them that – if history's any guide – one day there won't *be* a Congress of the Lindblad Ring, just records of our deeds.'

Perhaps it was some brief fluctuation in the femtotech bubble shielding the balcony, but she could have sworn that she felt a breath of the evening's true chill touch her flesh.

'That's pretty close to heresy, Rudd – especially when we're supposed to be gearing up to celebrate our very permanence.'

'Ten thousand years is just a pebble tossed into eternity's canyon, Chromis.'

'All right, all right, I'll work on the guilt angle.'

'Good girl. And you might want to think about approaching someone else to act as your tame devil's advocate next time. I'd be happy to oblige, but I don't think they'll tolerate our little parlour game twice.'

'You're probably right.'

'Chin up. You've done very well, considering.'

'You think so?'

'Absolutely. I'm pretty sure you've already knocked some of the competition out of the running. That's the last we'll hear about fountains.'

'That's something, anyway.'

'The blood thing worked well.'

'I've been thinking,' Chromis said, as an idea began to form in her mind. 'That point I had you make about a copy of the message falling into the wrong hands?'

'What of it?'

'There's something more to that. Keying the message to the Benefactor's DNA is a good precaution, and I didn't go all the way to Mars for nothing. But we could probably use an additional safeguard.'

'Go on,' Rudd encouraged.

'I think each copy of the message – in whatever form it takes – ought to be able to decide for itself whether or not to divulge its contents. That'll demand a degree of intelligence – enough to grasp the ins and outs of human behaviour, so that the copy can base its decisions on what it sees.'

'In other words, it'll need to be human as well.'

'It's within our means, Rudd. Looking at it this way, it would be almost negligent not to equip the message copies with full sentience.'

Rudd pondered this for long moments, while Chromis watched the shadows below turn a deep, mysterious purple. More and more communities were lit up against evening now, and small boats were plying across the lake, bright and colourful as paper lanterns.

'I think I agree,' he said, 'but there's an obvious stumbling block: who would ever consent to having their personality copied into a billion green bottles, like some cheap, mass-produced commodity?'

'I'm sure a volunteer could be identified.'

He nodded knowingly. 'And I bet you have just the candidate in mind.'

'I'll cross that bridge when I win.'

'Remember: play on their guilt. Works every time. Should have reminded you of that before, really.'

'Might have helped, Rudd. Then at least we could have gone out celebrating tonight.'

'Oh, that won't stop us. We can always celebrate the fact that we weren't defeated by an overwhelming margin.'

She smiled, something of her former good mood returning. 'Any old excuse.'

He looked in the direction of one of the lakeshore communities. 'In fact, I know this really great place – we can caul there now, if you like.'

'Shouldn't I go back inside and face the music?'

'I think a dignified silence might work better. Let that guilt start eating away at them.'

'If you say so.'

'I know so. Years of experience at this sort of thing.' Rudd closed his eyes for the moment it took to summon a pair of cauls. Shortly, the local femto-tech would allocate a small fraction of itself for the safe conveyance of the two friends.

While they waited, Chromis asked, 'Do you really mean it, about the Congress not lasting for ever?'

'Like I said, ten thousand years really isn't all that long. I'm sure the Spicans expected to last for ever, too. But one day the same thing will happen to us – we'll be gone, and there'll be something else in our place.'

'Something human?'

'Not necessarily.'

The cauls arrived, orbiting them like a squadron of black moths before meshing into their final travel configuration. Sensing that a conversation was in progress, the cauls waited for a decent pause before snatching the two people from the balcony.

'Then all this,' Chromis said, gesturing at the vista before them, 'everything we've lived for and made, everything we've dreamed into existence – you firmly believe it won't always be here?'

'It'd be egocentric to think otherwise. Almost every sentient being who ever lived belonged to a society that doesn't exist any more. Why should we be any different?'

'But our deeds will remain.'

'If we're lucky. There's every chance they won't survive either.'

'That's so bleak, Rudd.'

'Bracing, I prefer to think.'

'But if nothing we do here has any guarantee of lasting, if even the best gestures have only a slim chance of outliving us – is there any reason not to just give up?'

'Every reason in the world,' Rudd said. 'We're here and we're alive. It's a beautiful evening, on the last perfect day of summer.' He turned and nodded at the waiting cauls. 'Now let's go down there and make the most of it, while it lasts.'

## ACKNOWLEDGEMENTS

Deep gratitude to George Berger, Hannu Blomilla, Peter Hollo, Rick Kleffel, Paul Kloosterman, Kotska Wallace and (last but not least) Josette Sanchez, all of whom were kind enough to read and comment on various parts of this book. And thanks as ever for hard work, patience and a necessary dose of good humour to Jo Fletcher and Lisa Rogers.

Some of the science in this book is real, and some of it is made up. One of the real bits, perhaps surprisingly, is the biomedical argument underlying the Frost Angel process. Interested readers are pointed to the article 'Buying Time in Suspended Animation' by Mark B. Roth and Todd Nystul, which appeared in *Scientific American* in June 2005. Suspended animation has suddenly gone from looking like one of science fiction's least likely prophecies to one of its canniest.

AR